WILD

Belinda Alexandra is the daughter of a Russian mother and an Australian father. She has lived in New York, California, Sydney and Melbourne. She has an MA in Creative Writing from the University of Technology, Sydney and a BA in Asian Studies from the University of California. She is currently studying French and jazz ballet while working on her next novel. Belinda lives in Sydney.

For automatic updates on Belinda Alexandra, go to www.harpercollins.co.uk and register for AuthorTracker.

Wild Lavender

BELINDA ALEXANDRA

HarperCollins*Publishers*

HarperCollins*Publishers*
77–85 Fulham Palace Road,
Hammersmith, London W6 8JB

www.harpercollins.co.uk

A Paperback Original 2006

1

A catalogue record for this book
is available from the British Library

ISBN-13 978 0 00 720280 5
ISBN-10 0 00 720280 6

Set in Sabon

Printed and bound in Great Britain by
Clays Limited, St Ives plc

For my beautiful mother, Deanna

You were my greatest supporter and truest friend

Contents

Part One

ONE

'Simone, the lavender is waiting for you!'
Honk! Honk!
'Simone! Simone!'

I don't know which woke me first: the horn on Bernard's new car or my father calling me from the kitchen. I lifted my head from the pillow and frowned. The room was full of the smell of scorched cotton. The morning sun streaming through the open shutters was white with heat.

'Simone, the lavender is waiting for you!'

There was mirth in my father's voice. It sounded like there was mirth in Bernard's car horn too. Sitting up, I saw the maroon touring car through the window, its top down, rolling along the road past the pine trees. Bernard was beaming at the wheel. The spokes on the tyres matched the brilliant white of his suit and panama hat. I wondered if Bernard chose his outfits to coordinate with his automobiles. The previous year, when British cars had been fashionable to drive, he had arrived in a black suit and bowler hat. He brought the car to a stop in the yard near the wisteria and looked over his shoulder. Further down the road a wagon trundled along. The driver was a swarthy-faced man and the passengers on board were as dark as aubergines.

I rolled out of bed and scurried around the room searching for my work dress. None of my clothes were hanging in the armoire; they were

3

scattered under the bed or overflowing from the drawers of my dresser. I brushed my hair and tried to remember where I had left my dress.

'Simone!' my father called out again. 'It would be nice to see you while it is still 1922.'

'Coming, Papa!'

'Oh! Did I disturb our Sleeping Beauty?'

I smiled. In my mind's eye he was sitting at the kitchen table, a mug of coffee in one hand and a piece of sausage perched on the end of a fork in the other. His walking cane was propped against his leg and his good eye was staring patiently at the landing for a sign of life.

I spotted my dress hanging on the back of the door and remembered that I had put it there the night before. I slipped it on over my arms and managed to fasten it without catching my long hair in the hooks.

Bernard's car horn blasted again. I thought it strange that no one had invited him inside and looked out the window to see what was going on. But it wasn't Bernard blowing the horn; it was a boy standing on the running board. His eyes were as round as plums. A woman with her hair tied under a scarf pulled him off and scolded him. But her displeasure was only for show. The boy smiled and his mother covered his forehead with kisses. The three male passengers unloaded trunks and sacks from the wagon. I watched the tallest one take down a guitar, cradling the neck and body as gently as a mother holds a child.

Uncle Gerome, his work hat pulled over his grey hair, spoke to the driver. From the way Uncle Gerome's moustache turned down at the corners, I knew they were talking about money. He pointed towards the forest and the driver shrugged. The gesticulating went on for some minutes before the driver nodded. Uncle Gerome reached into his pocket and produced a pouch, counting each coin he placed in the other man's palm. Satisfied, the driver shook hands with Uncle Gerome and waved farewell to the others before climbing back on the wagon and setting out on his way. Uncle Gerome plucked a notebook from his pocket and a pencil from behind his ear and scribbled the amount he had paid in his record book — the same book that kept account of the debts my father had to repay.

I kissed the crucifix near the door and rushed out. I was halfway down the hall before I remembered my good luck charm. I ran back to my room, picked up the sachet of lavender from the dresser and secreted it in my pocket.

My father was exactly where I'd expected, coffee and sausage in hand. Bernard sat next to him, nursing a glass of wine. Bernard had fought with my father in the trenches during the war. They were two men who would never have met if it had not been for those circumstances, and who had become the most loyal of friends. My father welcomed Bernard into our family, because he knew his friend had been rejected by his own. Bernard's blond hair seemed even paler than it had the last time I saw him. He sniffed the wine before drinking it, as he smelled everything in life before trying it. The first time Bernard came to visit, I found him standing in the yard and testing the air with his nose like a dog. 'Tell me, Simone, down that hill and near those juniper trees, is there a stream?' He was right, only you couldn't see the juniper trees from where we were standing and the stream was no more than a trickle.

My mother and Aunt Yvette darted about the kitchen, cleaning up the remains of breakfast: sausage, goat's cheese, boiled eggs and bread soaked in oil. Aunt Yvette felt in her apron pocket for her glasses and slipped them on so she could see if there was anything worth saving among the clutter on the table.

'What about me?' I cried, grabbing some bread off a plate before my mother snatched it away. She smiled at me. Her black hair was pinned in a roll on top of her head. My father called her his *señorita* because of her colouring, which I had inherited. My mother's skin was lighter than the complexions of the workers outside but dark compared to the Fleuriers, who, apart from me, had always been fair-haired and blue-eyed. Aunt Yvette's white eyebrows and pigmentless skin put her at the other extreme of colouring; she was salt and my mother was pepper.

My father held out his arms and feigned a hurt expression. 'Ah, thinking about food before the men in your life,' he said. I kissed him on each cheek and then again on the scar where his left eye had been. Then I leaned over and kissed Bernard too.

'Careful of Bernard's suit,' Aunt Yvette warned.

'Nothing to be careful about,' answered Bernard. He turned to me and said, 'You've grown even taller, Simone! How old are you now?'

'I turn fourteen next month.' I sat down next to my father and flicked my hair over my shoulders. My mother and aunt exchanged a smile. My father pushed his plate over to me.

'I took two portions this morning,' he said. 'One for myself and one for you.'

I kissed him again.

There was a bowl of dried rosemary on the table and I sprinkled some on the bread. 'Why didn't you wake me up earlier?'

Aunt Yvette ran her fingers over my shoulders. 'We thought sleep might be more important to you.' Her wrist smelt of roses and I knew she had tried some of the perfume that Bernard always brought with him from Grasse. Aunt Yvette and Bernard were the civilising influences in our lives; although Uncle Gerome was the richest farmer in our region, we wouldn't have known what a *bidet* or a *croissant* was without them.

My mother poured a glass of wine for my father and refilled Bernard's half-full one. On her way back to the cupboard she cast a glance at my espadrilles. 'Bernard is right,' she said to me. 'You are growing so fast! When the shoe pedlar comes by next month we must get you proper boots. You'll lose your toes if you continue to wear those.'

We shared a smile. I didn't have my mother's gift for reading people's thoughts, but when I looked at her face — calm, reserved, proud — I always sensed her love for me, her only child.

'By next year she will have more pairs of shoes than she knows what to do with,' declared my father. He and Bernard clinked glasses.

Uncle Gerome caught my father's words as he came through the door. 'Not if we don't get to work on the lavender now,' he said.

'Ah, yes,' said Bernard, standing. 'I'd better be off. I have to visit two more farms before the morning is over.'

'Shall I take the gypsies some food?' I asked. 'They might be hungry after the journey.'

My father ruffled my hair, even though I had just brushed it. 'They're not gypsies, Simone. They're Spanish. And, unlike you, they're early risers. They've eaten already.'

I turned to my mother who nodded. I slipped a piece of bread into my pocket anyway. She had told me that the gypsies did that for good luck.

Outside, the workers waited with their sickles and rakes. Aunt Yvette tied on her bonnet, pulled down her sleeves and slipped on her gloves against the sun. Chocolat, her cocker spaniel, picked his

way through the grass, followed by my tabby, Olly, only his ginger
ears and tail visible above the tall stalks.

'Come here, boys!' I called.

The two balls of fur scampered towards me. Olly rubbed himself
against my legs. I had rescued him from a bird snare when he was a
kitten. Uncle Gerome said I could keep him if he caught mice and we
didn't feed him. But my parents, my aunt and myself, we all fed him,
slipping cheese and meat under the table whenever he brushed past
our feet. As a consequence, Olly was as big as a melon and not much
good for catching mice.

'I'll be back tomorrow for the distilling, Pierre,' Bernard said to
my father. He kissed my mother, aunt and me. 'All the best for the
harvest,' he said, stepping into his car. He gave a farewell wave to my
uncle although Uncle Gerome had little time for our lavender-broker.
No sooner had Bernard and his car disappeared beyond the almond
trees than Uncle Gerome began an imitation of Bernard's mincing
walk. Everyone ignored him. It was Bernard who had run through
the gunfire and mud to the military hospital with my father on his
back. A shell had exploded in their trench, killing their commanding
officer and everyone else within ten metres. And now, without
Bernard's devotion to my father, and no thanks to Uncle Gerome,
our side of the family would be without a sou.

We crossed the narrow stream. The lavender fields were oceans of
purple before us. The plant never looked more arresting nor smelt
sweeter than when it was about to be harvested. The summer heat
brought out the rich essence and the colour was at its deepest, having
changed from the mauve spikes of spring into sprays of violet florets.
I was sad knowing that in a few days the fields would be reduced to
clumps of butchered shrubs.

My father leaned on his walking stick and assigned each of the
workers a section while Uncle Gerome brought the cart and mule
down to the field. The workers took a truss each from my father,
knotting it at the corners and turning it into a belt bag in which they
could gather the cut stalks.

The boy went to sit under a tree. I picked up Olly and called over
Chocolat. 'Would you like to pat them?' I asked him, placing Olly by
his side.

He reached out and stroked their heads. Chocolat licked the boy's
fingers and Olly put his chin on his lap. The boy giggled and smiled

at me. I pointed to my chest and said, 'Simone', but he either didn't understand what I was saying or was too shy to tell me his name. I looked at his large eyes and decided to call him Goya, because I thought he seemed sensitive, like an artist.

I sat down next to him and we watched the workers spread out in the fields. I didn't know how to speak Spanish to ask Goya the workers' real names, so I made some up for them from the few Spanish names I knew. The lanky Spaniard I called Rafael. He was the youngest and had a strong chin, straight eyebrows and good teeth. He was handsome and strutted about as if he knew all about lavender cutting, but every so often he would turn to look at Rosa — the name I had given to the woman — to see what she was doing. The stocky man I called Fernandez. He could have been Uncle Gerome's twin. Both men lunged at the shrubs the way a bull charges a matador. The other Spaniard was the father of Goya, a gentle giant who followed his own path and approached the harvest without fuss. He was the one who had so lovingly held the guitar. I called him José.

Aunt Yvette stepped back through the lavender and towards us. 'We'd better get started on the food,' she said.

I stood up and brushed the grass off my dress. 'Do you think he would like to come?' I asked, pointing to Goya. Chocolat was nestled against the boy's shoulder and Olly was asleep in his lap. Goya stared at the wisps of platinum hair sticking out from under my aunt's hat. I was so used to her appearance that I forgot people were surprised the first time they saw an albino.

'He thinks you're a fairy,' I told her.

Aunt Yvette smiled at Goya and patted his head. 'He looks happy where he is, and I think it pleases his mother to be able to see him.'

⌘

In the evening, we ate dinner in the yard that separated our two farmhouses, and stayed there after darkness fell. The air was thick with the essence of lavender. I swallowed and tasted it at the back of my throat.

My mother was stitching one of my father's shirts, her handiwork illuminated by a hurricane lamp. For some reason known only to herself, she always made repairs to clothes with red thread, as if the snags and tears were wounds in the fabric. My mother's hands were laced with cuts, but harvesters never bothered about minor wounds. The essential oil was a natural disinfectant and cuts healed within days.

Aunt Yvette read *Les Misérables* with me. The village school had closed two years earlier, when the railway was extended and many people moved to the towns, and without her interest in my education I might have ended up as illiterate as the rest of my family. Uncle Gerome could read ledger books and fertiliser instructions but my mother couldn't read at all, although her knowledge of herbs and plants was as extensive as a pharmacist's. Only my father could read the newspaper. It was because of what he'd read in it in 1914 that he went to fight in the Great War.

'The revellers continued to sing their songs,' I read out loud, 'and the child, under the table, also sang hers —'

'*Bof!*' scoffed Uncle Gerome, picking at his teeth with a knife blade. 'All right for some to read useless books, especially when they don't break their backs in a field all day.'

My mother's hands stopped moving and our eyes met. The muscles in her neck tensed. My aunt and I leaned closer to her, picking up the end of the cloth and pretending to study it. Although none of us could confront Uncle Gerome, we always came to each other's aid when one of us was mocked. Aunt Yvette couldn't work in the fields because of her skin condition. An hour in the southern sun and she would have had third-degree burns. She was from the town of Sault, and the superstition surrounding albinos was the only reason I could see why a bright, attractive woman would have been married off to Uncle Gerome. He was shrewd enough to know that what she didn't contribute as a farm worker she more than made up for as a cook and a housekeeper, but I had never heard him acknowledge her merits. As for me, I was simply unsuited to harvesting. They called me 'the flamingo' because my skinny legs were twice as long as my body, and even my father, with his one eye and lame leg, could clear a field faster than I could.

Laughter burst from the barn. I wondered where the Spaniards found the energy for joviality after a day in the fields. The sound of a guitar floated across the yard. I imagined José strumming the instrument, his eyes full of passion. The others kept the beat, clapping their hands and keening in flamenco style.

Aunt Yvette glanced up then turned back to the novel. Uncle Gerome reached for a blanket and tucked it around his head, play-acting his dislike of the music. My father stared at the sky, lost in his own thoughts. My mother kept her eyes focused on her handiwork, as if she were deaf to the sounds of celebration. Her posture from the waist up was so erect that she resembled a statue. My eyes drifted to under the table. She had slipped her feet out of her shoes and one foot was tapping out a sensual rhythm, rising and falling in a dance of its own. Her deception reminded me that my mother was a woman full of secrets.

While photographs of Grand-père and Grand-mère Fleurier were displayed on our mantelpiece, there were no pictures of my maternal grandparents anywhere in the house. When I was a child, my mother showed me the hut where they had lived at the base of a hill. It was a simple stone and wood structure that had lasted until a forest fire and a violent mistral swept through the gorge in the same year. Florette, the postmistress from the village, told me that my grandmother was so famous for her remedies that even the mayor's wife and the old *curé* used to turn to her when conventional medicine or prayer failed. She said that one day my grandparents, who were then middle-aged, appeared in the village with my mother. The enchanting girl, who they named Marguerite, was already three years old the first time the villagers saw her. Although the couple swore that the child was theirs, there were many who believed my mother was the abandoned child of gypsies.

The mystery surrounding her origins and the rumours of her own healing ability did not endear my mother to the strict Catholic household of the Fleuriers, who had opposed the marriage of their favourite son. Yet no one could deny that it was my mother who had nursed my father back to health when all the army doctors had given him up for dead.

The Spaniards continued their singing long after Uncle Gerome and Aunt Yvette had returned to their house and my parents and I had retired to our beds. I lay awake, staring at the ceiling beams and feeling the sweat run down the hollows of my ribs. The moonlight through the cypress trees created wave-like shadows on my wall. I imagined the shapes were dancers moving to the sensual music.

I must have fallen asleep because I sat up with a start some time later and realised that the music had stopped. I heard Chocolat bark.

I slid out of bed and looked out the window into the yard. A breeze had cooled the air and the silvery light splashed over the roof tiles and buildings. I glanced towards the wall at the end of the garden and blinked. A ring of people danced there. They moved silently, without music or singing, their arms sweeping over their heads and their feet stamping to an unheard rhythm. I peered into the night and recognised José dancing with Goya on his shoulders, the boy's white-toothed smile a gash in his dark face. My own heels lifted from the floor. I had the urge to run downstairs and join them. I gripped the window frame, not sure if the dancers were really the Spaniards or evil spirits disguising themselves to trick me to my death. The old women in the village spoke of such things.

My heart skipped a beat.

Apart from Goya, there were five dancers: three men and two women. My mouth fell open when I glimpsed the long dark hair and fine limbs of the second woman. Fire smouldered under her skin and sparks flew from her feet where they touched the ground. Her dress flowed around her like a stream. My mother. I opened my mouth to call to her but found myself stumbling back towards my bed, overcome by sleep again.

When I opened my eyes, the first light of day was breaking. My throat was dry. I squeezed my palms over my face, unsure if what I had seen had been real or a dream.

I pulled on my dress and tiptoed down the stairs and past my parents' room. My mother and father were asleep. I may not have inherited my mother's powers but I did have her curiosity. I crept to the edge of the yard, near the wall where the almond trees grew. The grass was tall with summer and undisturbed. I glanced over the trees and plants for evidence of intrusion, but found none. There were no tied twigs, no fragments of bone, no sacred stones. No signs of magic at all. I shrugged and turned to go, but as I did something flashed in the corner of my eye. I reached out and touched the lower branch of a tree. Caught over one of the leaves was a single red thread.

❦

My aunt's pale skin and my long legs did not spare us the work involved in distilling. My father and Uncle Gerome, their faces twisted with exertion, winched a steaming tube of compacted lavender stalks out of the still. My mother and I rushed forward to poke the mound with our pitchforks. We spread the stalks out on mats before dragging them into the sunshine to dry.

'There's no time to lose,' my father told us. 'With the new still we can use those stalks for fuel when they are dry.'

My mother and I turned the cut lavender to prevent it from fermenting, while Aunt Yvette helped the men pack the next load into the still. When it was full my father told me to jump on top of it to compress the stalks and 'bring us good luck!'

'She's too skinny to make a difference,' Uncle Gerome scoffed, but reached out his arms to help me into the still anyway. 'Mind the sides,' he warned, 'they are burning hot.'

They say lavender is a mood enhancer; I wondered if the delicious scent wafting through the air had managed to improve even Uncle Gerome's disposition.

I stomped down the lavender, not minding the scratches on my legs or the heat. If my father and Bernard's plan to harvest and distil lavender commercially worked out, my father would be able to reclaim his part of the farm. With each stamp of my foot, I imagined that I was helping him take a step closer to his dream.

After Uncle Gerome had helped me out of the still and sealed the lid, my father pulled himself down the ladder to the lower floor. I heard him stoke up the fire. 'I can tell from the first load that the oil is good,' he beamed when he returned.

Uncle Gerome rubbed his moustache. 'Good or not, we'll see if it sells.'

At midday, after the fourth load, my father called a break. We dropped onto the damp straw or sank to our haunches. My mother soaked pieces of cloth in water and we pressed them against our burning faces and palms.

A motorcar sounded outside and we went into the yard to greet Bernard. In the passenger seat was Monsieur Poulet, the village mayor and manager of the local café. In the rear sat Monsieur Poulet's sister, Odile, with her husband, Jules Fournier.

'*Bonjour! Bonjour!*' Monsieur Poulet called, stepping out of the car and wiping his face with a handkerchief. He was wearing the black suit he kept for official occasions. It was a size too small and pinched his shoulders, making him look like a shirt pegged on a line.

Odile and Jules stepped out of the car and everyone moved inside the distillery. Monsieur Poulet and the Fourniers studied the still which was much larger than the ones that had been used in the region for years. Although they were not farmers, they had an interest in the success of our venture. With so many people leaving Pays de Sault for the towns, they hoped that the lavender would bring back business to our village.

'I'll get a bottle of wine,' said Aunt Yvette, turning towards the house. Bernard said that he would help her with the glasses. I watched them walk up the path, their heads close together. Bernard said something and Aunt Yvette laughed. My father had explained to me that Bernard was a good person who wasn't interested in women in the usual way, but he was so gentle with Aunt Yvette that sometimes I wondered if he was in love with her. I glanced at Uncle Gerome, but he was too busy boasting about the new still's capacity to notice.

'It is the type of still that is being used by the large distilleries in Grasse,' he said. 'It's more efficient than the portable ones we've been using.'

From the way he was talking, anyone would have thought the still had been his idea. But he was the financier, not the dreamer: he had provided the money for the expensive still and would take half the profits. But my father and Bernard had calculated that if three successive lavender crops were good, the still would be paid off in two years and the farm in another three.

Odile sniffed the air and sidled up to me. 'The oil smells good,' she whispered. 'I hope it makes us all rich and gets your father out of debt.'

I nodded but said nothing. I knew too well the shame of my family situation. The land had been divided between the two brothers on the death of my grandfather. When my father was away at war, Uncle Gerome lent my mother money to keep our farm going. But when my father returned maimed, and the meagre war pension was not enough to pay off the debts, Uncle Gerome reclaimed my father's half. After my father recovered, Uncle Gerome said he could buy his farm back in instalments with interest each year. It was a shameful thing to do within the family, when even the poorest in our village had left baskets of vegetables on our doorstep while my father was sick. But you could never say a word about his older brother to my father. 'If you had seen how our parents treated him, you would understand,' he always said. 'I can't remember either of them giving him one word of kindness. He reminded our father too much of his own father. From the time Gerome was a boy, he only had to look at our father to get a boxing around the ears. By rights, the entire farm should have been his, yet for some reason our parents always favoured me. Don't worry, we will buy our share back.'

'Who else will be bringing you their lavender to distil?' Jules asked my father.

'The Bousquets, the Nègres, the Tourbillons,' he answered.

'The others will come too when they see how profitable it is,' said Uncle Gerome, sticking out his chin as if he were imagining himself a successful distiller-broker. Monsieur Poulet raised his eyebrows. Perhaps he thought Uncle Gerome was imagining himself as the new mayor.

My mother's face pinched into a scowl and I could guess what she was thinking. It was the first time Uncle Gerome had sounded positive about the success of the project. While he would be taking half the profits, my father was taking all the risks. Our farm had been turned over almost entirely to lavender while Uncle Gerome was still planting oats and potatoes. 'In case it doesn't work out and I end up having to feed you all,' he'd told us.

⌘

When the lavender harvest was over, the driver returned with the wagon to take the workers to another farm. I stood in the yard and watched the Spaniards load their belongings. It was the same process as the morning they had arrived, only in reverse. Rafael hoisted up sacks and trunks to Fernandez and José, who crammed them towards the front of the wagon so they could sit at the back and keep the load balanced. When all was packed, José picked up his guitar and strummed a melody while the driver finished the wine my aunt had poured out for him in a tall glass.

Goya danced around his mother's legs. I took the lavender sachet I had kept in my pocket during the harvest and gave it to him. He seemed to understand that the gift was to bring him luck and pulled a piece of string from his own pocket and looped it through the ribbon. When he was lifted on top of the wagon to sit with his mother, I saw that he was wearing the sachet around his neck.

If Uncle Gerome had had any doubts about the profitability of the oil, they were dispelled a few days later when, on Bernard's recommendation, a company in Grasse bought the entire yield.

'It's certainly the best-quality oil I've come across in years,' Bernard said, laying the bill of sale on the kitchen table. My father, mother, aunt and I gasped when we saw the amount scrawled at the bottom of the note. Unfortunately Uncle Gerome was out in the fields and we didn't have the pleasure of seeing his surprise.

'Papa!' I cried, throwing my arms around his neck. 'Soon we will have the farm back and then we will be rich!'

'Goodness,' said Bernard, covering his ears. 'I never knew that Simone had such a loud voice.'

'Didn't you?' said my mother, her eyes twinkling with laughter. 'The night she was born, her grandmother declared she had an extraordinary lung capacity and predicted that she would be a singer.'

Everybody laughed. Underneath her reserve my mother had a mischievous sense of humour. And just to give her back what she was handing out, I stood on my chair and sang 'À la claire fontaine' at the top of my voice.

❧

Every month my father made a trip to Sault to buy supplies that we couldn't get in the village and to sell some of our produce. My father handled the mule and cart well on the farm, despite his missing eye, but the road to Sault was slippery limestone rock and ran alongside the precipices of the Gorges de la Nesque. Any error of perspective could be fatal. In October, Uncle Gerome was busy with his flock of sheep so our neighbour, Jean Grimaud, agreed to accompany my father. He needed to buy some harnesses and rope in town.

The morning mist was disintegrating when I helped my father load the almonds he would sell in town into the cart. Jean called out to us from the road and we watched his giant figure make its way towards us. 'If Jean were a tree he would be an oak,' my father always said. Indeed, Jean's arms were thicker than most people's legs and his hands were so large that I was sure he could crush a rock between his palms if he wanted to.

Jean pointed to the sky. 'Do you think there might be a storm?'

My father considered the few wispy clouds floating overhead. 'If anything, I think it might be hot. But you can never tell this time of year.'

I stroked the mule while my mother and aunt gave my father a list of supplies to buy for the house. Aunt Yvette pointed to something on the list and whispered in his ear. I turned towards the hills, pretending that I hadn't noticed. But I knew what they were talking about; I'd listened in on a conversation between Aunt Yvette and my mother the previous night. My aunt wanted to buy material to make me a good dress for going to church and for trips into town. I knew that she wanted me to have a different life to hers. 'A man who truly loves a woman respects her mind,' she often told me. 'You are intelligent. Never marry beneath yourself. And don't marry a farmer if you can help it.' While my father always said that I could choose a husband for myself whenever I thought the time was right, I suspected that Aunt Yvette had the sons of the doctor or notaries in Sault in mind for me. I wasn't at all interested in boys, but I was interested in a new dress.

Uncle Gerome appeared in the yard in his leather leggings with a hunting gun over his shoulder. 'Careful on the road,' he warned my father. 'The rains have washed some of it away.'

'We'll take it slow all right,' my father promised him. 'If we think we won't get back before dark, we'll stay overnight.'

Autumn in Provence was as beautiful as spring and summer. I imagined my father and Jean travelling past the jade pine forests and the flames of Virginia creeper. I would have liked to go with them but there wasn't enough room. The men waved us farewell and we watched the cart bump and sway down the road. My father's voice rang out in the air:

> Those mountains, high mountains
> That fill the skies
> Stand up to hide her
> From my longing eyes.

My mother and aunt headed back towards Aunt Yvette's kitchen, which we used more than our own because it was bigger and had a wood-fired stove. I followed them, completing the last verse of my father's song:

The mountains are moving
And I see her clear
And I'll soon be with her
When my ship draws near.

I thought about what my mother had said about my grandmother's prediction that I would be a singer. If that were true, then I could only have inherited my talent from my father. His voice was as pure as an angel's. Bernard said that when they were knee-deep in mud in the trenches, with the smell of death all around them, the men used to ask my father to sing. 'It was the only thing that gave us hope.'

I scraped my boots and pushed open the kitchen door. My mother and aunt were setting out porcelain bowls on the workbench. There was a basket of potatoes near the table and I sat down and began to peel them. My mother grated a block of cheese while my aunt chopped garlic. They were going to make my favourite dish, *aligot*: puréed potatoes, cheese, sour cream, garlic and pepper, all stirred into a savoury mash.

With Uncle Gerome out hunting, we were free to be ourselves. While we cooked my aunt told stories from books and magazines she'd read and my mother recounted village legends. My favourite one was the story about the *curé* who became senile and arrived at church naked one morning. I sang for them and they applauded. I loved my aunt's kitchen, with its mixture of orderliness and clutter. The woodwork was imbued with the scents of olive oil and garlic. Cast-iron pots and copper saucepans of every size hung from beams above the fireplace, which was blackened from years of use. A convent table stood in the middle of the room, its benches laid with cushions that sent up puffs of flour whenever somebody sat on one. Mortars and pestles, water jugs and straw baskets lined with muslin were scattered on every spare shelf or bench.

As my father had predicted, by midday the weather was hot and we sat at the table in the yard to enjoy our little feast. But in the afternoon, when I went to collect water from the well, the clouds were beginning to cast grim shadows over the valley.

'Just as well they took wet-weather clothes with them,' observed Aunt Yvette, throwing the potato skins to the chickens. 'They must be on their way back by now. If the storm breaks they will be soaked through.'

A light rain began to drizzle but the clouds in the direction of Sault were more sinister. I sat by the kitchen window, willing my father and Jean a safe journey home. There had been a sudden downpour the day I went with my father and Uncle Gerome to the Lavender Fair in August, and one of the wheels of our cart had become embedded in mud. It took us three hours to free it and get moving again.

A flash of lightning buckled across the sky. The clap of thunder that followed made me jump.

'Come away from the window,' said Aunt Yvette, reaching out to close the shutters. 'Watching the road won't bring them here any faster.'

I did as she said and took a seat at the table. My mother was slumped in her chair, staring at something. I looked over my shoulder and saw that the clock on the mantelpiece had stopped. My mother was as pale as a sheet.

'Are you all right, Maman?'

She didn't hear me. Sometimes I thought she was like a cat, vanishing into the shadows, able to see but not be seen, only reappearing from the darkness when she willed it.

'Maman?' I whispered. I wanted her to speak, to offer me some word of hope, but she was as silent as the moon.

At dinner Uncle Gerome stabbed his vegetables and tore his meat. 'They must have decided to stay in town,' he muttered.

Aunt Yvette assured me that Uncle Gerome was right, and the men had decided to stay the night in the cartwright's barn or the blacksmith's shed. She made me a bed in one of the upstairs rooms so I wouldn't have to run out in the rain to get to my own house. My mother and Uncle Gerome sat by the fire. I could tell by Uncle Gerome's gritted teeth that he didn't entirely believe in his own supposition.

I lay in bed listening to the rain on the roof tiles and softly sang to myself. I must have fallen asleep soon afterwards because the next thing I knew there was a loud banging on the kitchen door. I jumped out of bed and ran to the window. The mule was there in the rain but there was no sign of the cart. I heard voices downstairs and hurriedly dressed.

Jean Grimaud was standing near the door, dripping water onto the flagstones. There was a gash across his forehead and blood was oozing into his eyes. Uncle Gerome was as grey as a stone.

'Speak!' he said to Jean. 'Say something.'

Jean looked at my mother with tortured eyes. When he opened his mouth to speak and nothing came out, I knew. There was nothing to be said. Father was gone.

TWO

'There will be no arguments,' shouted Uncle Gerome, slamming his palm on the kitchen table. 'Simone goes to work for Aunt Augustine in Marseilles.'

My mother, Aunt Yvette and I jumped from the force of his anger. Was this the same man who had stood over my father's grave the week before, his face contorted with grief? He seemed to have recovered from the shock of his brother's death the way another man might have got over influenza. For the past two days he had been studying his ledger books and tallying up figures.

'I don't need two housekeepers,' he said, turning towards the fire and poking at it with a stick. The flame rose and died, turning the room darker. 'If Simone can't manage farm work then she needs to make her living elsewhere. She is not a child any more and I have enough mouths to feed. Perhaps if Pierre had not left so many debts . . .'

Uncle Gerome rattled off the cost of lavender cultivation, the price of the still, the money owing on the farm. My mother and I exchanged glances. Uncle Gerome was going to profit from the project my father's imagination had conceived. What did those costs matter now?

A picture flashed into my mind. It wasn't something that I'd seen but an image that had haunted me for a week: my father, lying on his back on a rock ledge in the Gorges de la Nesque. He and Jean had waited in Sault until the afternoon storm had passed before guiding the mule down the slopes. After negotiating the most difficult stretches of road, they had stopped to give the mule a rest and to eat some bread. But no sooner had Jean unhitched the mule and led it to a grassy patch than he heard a *crack*. Scree, loosened by the rain, rushed down the slope. A tree branch knocked Jean and the mule sideways. My father and the cart were washed over the side.

'Bernard will help,' said Aunt Yvette. 'If you are going to send Simone to Marseilles, at least send her there to get an education. Not to be some sort of slave to your aunt.'

It was the first time I'd heard Aunt Yvette stand up to my uncle and I feared for her. Although he had never struck any of us, I couldn't help wondering if things would change now that my father was gone. As head of both our households, Uncle Gerome's position was powerful and we had no recourse against him. But he only sneered, 'Education is wasted on a woman even more than it is on a man. And as for Bernard, don't fool yourself that he has any money. Anything he's made in his life has already been spent on cars and the Côte d'Azur.'

That night, my mother and I lay in each other's arms, as we had every night since the day of the accident. We listened to the mistral howl. The wind started as a draught under the door, then turned into a fitful ghost that bent the cypress trees and wailed across the fields. We had both wept so much since my father's death that I thought I would go blind from the tears. I squinted at the outline of the crucified Christ near the door then turned away. It was cruel that my father should have survived the injuries from shrapnel only to be struck down by nature. 'It was so quick, he wouldn't even have known what happened,' was the only comfort the *curé* could offer us. It had been so quick I still couldn't believe it was true. I saw my father everywhere: his outline bent over the well or sitting in his chair, waiting for me to join him for breakfast. For a few joyous seconds I would be convinced that his death was merely a nightmare, until the image faded and I realised that I had seen nothing more than the shadow of a tree or the outline of a broom.

My mother, always quiet, retreated further into her silence. I think she wondered why her powers had failed her, why she had not been able to foresee my father's death and warn him. But even she had said there were things that we were not meant to know, things that could not be read or prevented. I touched her arm, her skin was like ice; I closed my eyes and fought back more painful tears, fearing the day when I would lose her too.

At least my mother would have Aunt Yvette. Who was Aunt Augustine? My father had never mentioned her. All Uncle Gerome would tell us was that she was the sister of their father and had married a sailor, who died soon afterwards at sea. Aunt Augustine ran a boarding house, but now that she was old and arthritic she needed a maid and cook. In return I would be given food but no money. I wondered where my father's open heart and hand had come from. All the other Fleuriers seemed to have descended from Judas: prepared to sell their relatives for thirteen pieces of silver.

❧

Bernard arrived a week later to drive me to Carpentras, from where I would catch a train to Marseilles. Aunt Yvette cried and kissed me. 'Don't worry about Olly,' she whispered. 'I'll take care of him.' I could barely bring myself to look at my cat, who was spraying on Bernard's car tyres, let alone my mother. She was standing by the kitchen door, her mouth turned down and grief in her eyes. I squeezed my nails into my palms. I'd promised myself that, for her sake, I wouldn't cry.

All I had to take with me was a bundle of clothes tied in a cloth. Bernard took it from me and put it in the car. My mother stepped forward and pressed my hand. Something sharp pricked my palm. When she withdrew her fingers I saw that she had given me a locket and a few coins. I slipped them into my pocket and kissed her. We lingered in our embrace, but neither of us could bring ourselves to say anything.

Bernard opened the car door and helped me into the passenger seat. Uncle Gerome stood in the yard watching us. His expression was severe but there was something odd about the way he was standing. His shoulders were hunched and his mouth was twisted, as if he were in pain. Was there some sort of demon inside him that made him act so spitefully? Perhaps he wished he could be a man more like my father and less like himself? The illusion was shattered when he called out, 'Work hard, Simone. Because Aunt Augustine won't tolerate any nonsense, and I won't have you back here if she throws you out.'

❧

The station at Carpentras was a moving market. The first- and second-class passengers boarded the train in a civilised manner, but the third-class passengers squabbled over where to sit and where to put their chickens and rabbits and whatever else they planned to take with them. Noah's Ark, I thought, stepping around a pig.

Bernard showed the conductor my ticket. 'She is travelling alone,' he told him. 'She's never been on a train before. If I pay the difference in the fare, can you put her in a second-class carriage with some ladies?'

The conductor nodded. 'She'll have to travel third class to Sorgues,' he said. 'But after that I can get her a seat to Marseilles in second class.'

Why was it that Bernard thought of my comfort and safety, when my own uncle was happy to send me third class to who knew where?

Bernard slipped the conductor some money and the man helped me up the stairs and into a seat near the front of the carriage. The train whistle sounded and the pig screeched and the chickens clucked. Bernard waved to me from the platform. 'I'll find a way to help you, Simone,' he said through the open window. 'Next time I make some extra money, I'll send it to you.'

A billow of soot and smoke wafted across the station. The train shunted forward. I didn't take my eyes off Bernard until we had passed out of the station. When I sat down I remembered the locket my mother had given me. I pulled it from my pocket and flicked it open. Inside was a picture of my parents on their wedding day. I had been five years old when my father left for the Great War and I could barely remember what he had looked like before his injuries. The handsome, alert face that stared back at me from the photograph brought tears to my eyes. I turned towards the window, watching the farms and forests flicker by. After a while, overcome by the heat inside the carriage, the smell of unwashed bodies, and grief, I nodded off to sleep. The train clacked over the rails in a steady rhythm, the descent so gradual that I barely perceived it.

We arrived in Marseilles in the early evening. The journey in third class had been more enjoyable, despite the noise and animal smells, than the time I had spent in second class. When we reached Sorgues, the conductor accompanied me to the omnibus train travelling to Marseilles and told the conductor there to give me a seat in a compartment. He put me with two women who were returning from Paris.

'She is on her own,' he explained to them. 'Please keep an eye on her.'

I couldn't help staring at the women's clothes. Their dresses were silk with V-necklines instead of round ones. Rather than pinching in at their waists, their belts were loose and dropped to their hips. Their skirts were so short I could see their shins when they crossed their legs. But their hats were plain and floppy, and made me think of convolvulus flowers. When I asked the women if they could tell me something about Marseilles, they pretended not to understand me. And I saw them roll their eyes when I pulled out the garlic sausage Aunt Yvette had packed for my lunch.

'Let's hope she doesn't give us lice,' one woman whispered to the other.

I stared at my lap, my cheeks burning with shame. I was a poor girl but I had scrubbed myself and put on my best dress for the journey. But I forgot about the women's nastiness when the train pulled into Gare Saint Charles; I had never seen so many people gathered in one place. Surely that was the entire population of my district bustling about on the station? I watched women hurrying back and forth, identifying their luggage; pedlars selling flowers and cigarettes; sailors lugging canvas bags on their shoulders; children and dogs perched on top of suitcases. But it was the array of languages babbling around me when I stepped onto the platform that most surprised me. The Spanish and Italian accents were familiar, but not those of the Greeks, the Armenians and Turks. I opened the map Uncle Gerome had given me and tried to figure out how long it would take to walk to the Vieux Port, where Aunt Augustine lived. It wasn't long until sunset and I didn't fancy tramping through a strange town at night.

'It's too far to walk,' a sailor with a cigarette slung in the corner of his mouth told me when I showed him the map. 'You'd better get a taxi.'

'But I can't afford a taxi,' I said.

He edged closer to me and smiled with teeth like a shark. I could smell the whisky on his breath. A shudder ran through me and I slipped back into the crowd. There was a woman near the station entrance peddling miniatures of the Basilique Notre Dame de la Garde, the domed basilica whose bell tower was topped by a gilded statue of the Virgin. I knew that the Christ mother was supposed to watch over those lost at sea. If I'd had the money, I would have bought one of the miniatures in the hope that she would watch over me.

'Take the streetcar,' the woman told me when I asked her how to get to the old port.

I made my way to the spot outside the station where she had said to wait. A noise as loud as a thunderclap made me jump and I looked up to see a streetcar hurtling towards the stop. Clinging to the sides and running boards were dozens of bare-footed children with dirty faces. The car came to a stop and the children jumped off. I handed the conductor one of the coins my mother had given me and took a seat behind the driver. More people piled into the car, and new children — and some adults too — climbed up onto the sides. I later learned that you could travel for free that way. The streetcar took off, gradually gathering speed and rocking and bucking from side to side. I clung to the windowsill with one hand and the edge of my seat with the other. Marseilles was a place I had never seen before and I was sure that I could never have imagined it. It was a patchwork of grand buildings with tiled roofs and elegant balconies alongside houses with shabby wooden shutters and water stains down their walls. It was as if an earthquake had squashed together a jigsaw of different villages.

There was no glass in the windscreen of the streetcar and a cool breeze prickled my scalp and cheeks. It was just as well the ventilation was good because the man sitting next to me reeked of onions and stale tobacco. 'Did you just arrive?' he asked, observing the worried expression on my face when the streetcar squealed and lurched around a corner. I nodded. 'Well,' he said, his sickly breath in my face, 'welcome to Marseilles — home of thieves, cut-throats and whores.'

I was glad when I finally arrived at the Vieux Port. My legs trembled as if I had been at sea for months. I slung my bundle of clothes over my shoulder. The last rays of the sun glittered on the

Mediterranean and the sky was aquamarine. I had never seen the ocean before and the sight of it and the seagulls screeching overhead made my toes tingle.

I walked along the Quai des Belges, past Africans selling gold and ochre-coloured spices and brass trinkets. I knew of black people from the books Aunt Yvette had given me to read, but had never seen them in real life. I was fascinated by their white fingernails and pale palms, but I remembered how the two women on the train had treated me and was careful not to stare this time. I followed the port around to the Quai de Rive Neuve. Cafés and bistros were opening for the night and the air smelt of grilled sardines, thyme and tomatoes. The aroma made me hungry and homesick at once. My mother and aunt would be preparing the evening meal now, and I stopped for a moment to imagine them laying the table. I had left them only that morning and already they were beginning to seem like people in a dream. Tears filled my eyes again and I could barely see my way through the maze of crooked streets. The gutters were littered with fish bones and the cobblestones reeked of human waste. A rat scurried out of a crevice to feast on the garbage.

'Don't walk here!' a gruff female voice called out behind me. 'This is my corner!'

I turned to see a woman lurking in a doorway. Only her torn stockings and the red glow of her cigarette were visible in the gloom. I quickened my pace.

The Rue Sainte, where Aunt Augustine had her boarding house, was the same eclectic mix of architecture as the rest of the city. It consisted of grand houses from Marseilles' prosperous maritime days and squat terraces. My aunt's house was one of the latter, and was joined to another house from which a blend of incense and laundry soap wafted. Three scantily dressed women leaned out of one of the windows, but thankfully none of them shouted at me.

I stepped up to the door and lifted the knocker, letting it go with a timid thud. I looked up at the salt-encrusted windows but there were no lights in any of them.

'Try again,' suggested one of the women. 'She's half deaf.'

I was too shy to look at the woman but I took her advice. I grabbed the knocker and swung it. It hit the wood with a bang so forceful that it rattled the window frames and ricocheted along the street. The women laughed.

This time I heard a door opening inside the house and feet clumping down stairs. The latch clicked and the door swung open. An old woman stood in front of me. Her face was all angles with a beaky nose and a chin so sharp I could have tilled the vegetable garden with it.

'There's no need for such noise,' she scowled. 'I'm not deaf.'

I stepped back, almost tripping. 'Aunt Augustine?'

The woman examined me from the part of my hair to my feet and seemed to come to a displeasing conclusion. 'Yes, I am your Great-Aunt Augustine,' she said, folding her meaty arms over her bosom. 'Wipe your boots before you come in.'

I followed her through the parlour, which contained a worn rug, two chairs and a dusty piano, to the dining room. A table, a glass cupboard and a sideboard were crammed into the space. Paintings of seafaring adventures clashed with the striped wallpaper. The only natural light came from the adjoining kitchen's window. There was a fringed lampshade dangling over the table and I expected Aunt Augustine to turn the light on for us. But she didn't and we sat down at the table in the gloom.

'Tea?' she offered, pointing to the pot and the mismatched cups next to it.

'Yes, please.'

My throat was parched and my taste buds sprang to life at the thought of a soothing tisane. I could almost taste silky chamomile gliding over my throat or the refreshing snap of rosemary against my tongue.

Aunt Augustine grabbed the pot handle with her gnarled fingers and poured. 'Here,' she said, pushing a cup and saucer towards me. I eyed the dark liquid. It had no aroma and when I sipped it I found that it was cold and tasted like stale water. It must have been left over from the morning or even earlier. I drank the tea because I was thirsty, but tears pricked my eyes. Couldn't Aunt Augustine even make me a fresh pot for me? Part of me had dared to hope that she might be more like my father and less like Uncle Gerome.

Aunt Augustine sank back in her chair and tugged at a hair on her chin. I squared my shoulders and sat up straight, determined to give her another try. Surely she understood that we were both Fleuriers, each other's flesh and blood. But before I could open my mouth, she announced, 'Three meals a day. And watch what you eat, you're not a guest.'

She pointed to a piece of paper nailed to the doorframe. 'The others leave their names on that to let you know if they will be in for their meals. Monsieur Roulin is always in, and *that one* upstairs is never in. But I wouldn't have such a person to the table anyway.'

'That one?' I asked.

Aunt Augustine rolled her eyes to the ceiling and I followed her gaze. But whereas I saw only cobwebs, the scowl on her face gave me the impression she was referring to something evil. The ominous ring of 'that one' lingered in the air.

'Now,' said Aunt Augustine, snatching my empty cup away and placing it upturned on its saucer, 'I'll show you to your room. I want you up at five o'clock tomorrow to go to the fish markets.'

I hadn't eaten anything since my sausage on the train, but I was too afraid to say that I was hungry.

My room was at the back of the house and directly off the kitchen. The door was warped, and when I pushed it open the trim scraped the floor. I could see by the semi-circular scratch on the boards that this was its usual pattern of movement. My heart sank at the sight of the cement walls. The only furniture was a rickety-looking chair in the corner, an armoire and a bed, the cover of which was spotted with mildew. Through the grime on the barred window I could make out a lavatory shed and a herb garden in need of weeding.

'I'll be back in an hour to explain your duties,' said Aunt Augustine, closing the door behind her. She was not like a relative at all. She was nothing more than an employer.

On the back of the door was a list of chores. The paper it was scribbled on had turned yellow with age. *Clean tiles with linseed oil and beeswax. Beat bed linen. Mop floor* ... I wondered how long it had been since anyone had done those things or a maid had occupied this dingy room. I lowered myself into the chair and stared out the window, tears rolling down my cheeks when I compared the warmth of my father to the coldness of my great-aunt. I glanced at the sagging mattress. The simple bed I'd had at home suddenly seemed like a divan fit for a queen. I closed my eyes and imagined myself lying in it, curling my knees to my chest and disappearing into a foetal ball.

The first meal I had to prepare was lunch the following day. The kitchen was as depressing as my bedroom. The flagstones and the walls held in the chill, which was made worse by the draught blowing through a cracked window pane. Aunt Augustine squeezed herself into a straw chair to supervise me, her swollen feet submerged in a pail of warm water. I poured in a few drops of lavender oil, telling her that it would soothe the inflammation. The scent wafted up and fought against the mouldy dishcloth stink of the kitchen. I imagined the lavender fields rippling in the breeze, their layers of purple swishing in the dappled sunlight. I could hear my father softly singing 'Se Canto', and was about to join him for the chorus when Aunt Augustine broke the spell: 'Pay attention, girl!'

I lifted a pan off its hook. The handle was greasy and inside the bottom was encrusted with food. I swiped it with the dishcloth when Aunt Augustine wasn't looking. I'd hated it when she'd sent me to the cellar earlier to fetch some wine. The door to the *cave* creaked open and all I could see was a web with a black spider hanging in it. I removed the spider with a broom and crept into the airless space with only a lamp to guide me. The cellar reeked of mud and there were rat droppings on the floor. My skin crawled and I jumped from imagined nips. I was terrified of being bitten by a rat because Marseilles was legendary for its diseases, a hazard for any port city since the days of the plague. I had grabbed the first two dusty bottles I saw without even bothering to check the contents.

I collected water from the pump outside the kitchen door then peered into the basket of vegetables on the bench. I was surprised by the quality of the produce. The tomatoes were still firm and red for so late in the season, the aubergines were weighty in my hands, the leeks were fresh and the black olives looked succulent. In the dirty kitchen, the fragrance of good produce was as welcome as an oasis in a desert.

Aunt Augustine sensed my admiration. 'We have always eaten well here. I was famous for it. Of course, I am not the cook I once was,' she said, holding up her clawed hands.

I studied her, trying to find the woman behind that grim face, the fiery young girl who had disobeyed her parents and run away with a sailor. It lingered in the set of her broad shoulders and her manly chin, but in her eyes I saw only bitterness.

Once I had assembled the ingredients, Aunt Augustine shouted her instructions above the sounds of the steaming pots and hissing pans. At each step I had to bring the food to her for inspection: the fish to show her that the skin was cleanly off; the potatoes to prove that I had mashed them properly; the olives to demonstrate that they had been finely chopped despite the bluntness of the knife; even the garlic to show that it had been crushed to her specifications.

As the cooking progressed, Aunt Augustine's face became flushed. At first I thought it was because nothing I did seemed right. *Take that back, you've shredded those leaves just like a peasant. Too much oil, go and wipe it for goodness sake. How much mint did you put in this? Did you think I was asking you to make mouthwash?* I thought it was a lot of fuss from a woman who couldn't be bothered to serve fresh tea. But as the temperature of the room rose, and her instructions became more frenzied, I saw that the blush in her cheeks was the inner passion I had searched for earlier. She was a conductor whipping her notes of fried fish, butter and rosemary into a gastronomic symphony. And the aromatic vapours seemed to draw the lodgers from their rooms. I heard voices and footsteps coming down the stairs almost half an hour earlier than the specified time for lunch.

When the table was set there were five of us in all. Besides Aunt Augustine and myself there was Ghislaine, a middle-aged woman who worked as a fish vendor, and two male boarders: Monsieur Roulin, a retired sailor, and Monsieur Bellot, a junior teacher at the boys' *lycée*. Monsieur Roulin had a gap where his two front teeth should have been, his hair had retreated to a few wisps on the back of his sun-spotted neck and his left forearm was missing, sliced off at the elbow joint. He waved the puckered end of his stump, speaking in a voice that sounded like an engine in need of oil. 'It's nice to have a young lady at the table. She is as dark as a berry, but pretty nonetheless.'

I smiled politely, understanding from my position at the lower corner of the table, near the kitchen door, that I was a servant and should not put myself forward in the conversation.

Monsieur Bellot pulled at his earlobe and said nothing beyond 'please' and 'thank you'. During the meal, which Monsieur Roulin declared was the best they had eaten in months, Monsieur Bellot's face changed from puzzled to dreamy to stern, as if he were carrying on some animated inner dialogue. Whatever Monsieur Roulin lacked, Monsieur Bellot seemed to have double in quantity: his teeth were long like a donkey's, his hair was a wild halo around his head, and his limbs were so long that he didn't need to stretch to pick up the water jug even when it was at my end of the table.

Ghislaine was seated next to me. I was surprised that someone who worked at the fish markets could smell so clean. Her skin gave off the mild scent of a fresh peach and her hair smelt like the rich olive oil used in Marseilles soap. Her eyes crinkled into a smile when Monsieur Roulin caught me looking at his stump and cried out, 'A shark as big as a cruise ship off the coast of Madagascar!'

I sensed from the laughter and exchanged glances of the others at the table that the story wasn't true. The angle of the amputation was too clean and had either been the result of an accident with a machine or surgery performed by a doctor. I hadn't been looking at his stump with repugnance, just interest. The gnarled scar of my father's eye had taught me that a warm heart was not changed by outer disfigurement.

After I had washed the dishes Aunt Augustine set me to the other daily chores, including emptying the bucket upstairs with the lid on it into the lavatory in the courtyard. Then she ran her finger along the sideboard in the dining room and examined the streak of dust collected on the tip. 'Dust from the ground floor up,' she said, as if I were somehow to blame for the slovenly state of the house. 'Do Monsieur Bellot's room first, then sweep Ghislaine's floor once she leaves for work. Monsieur Roulin's room is cleaned by his daughter. Don't worry about the fourth floor. *She* doesn't want her things "interfered with".'

She? So I could put a sex to the mysterious being on the fourth floor, the mere mention of whom seemed to cause Aunt Augustine discomfort, although she didn't mind taking her money for rent.

'I rest in the afternoons but I'll be back down to supervise supper,' Aunt Augustine said, grabbing the banister and inching her way up the stairs.

The kitchen floor was gritty under my feet when I went to fetch the broom. I cringed at the thought of cooking another meal in that unsanitary room. Despite Aunt Augustine's instructions to start with the dusting, I cleaned the kitchen first. I filled a bucket with water and heated it over the stove, then scrubbed the table and benches with soapy water, trying to picture the secret guest upstairs as I worked. At first I imagined a shrivelled woman my aunt's age, bedridden and with a hollow, ailing face. She was a former rival, either in love or gastronomy, who had fallen on bad times and Aunt Augustine was leaving her to languish in dirt and starvation. As I progressed to cleaning the floor, the old woman's face softened and the wrinkles disappeared. One of her legs withered and she transformed into a crippled woman from a rich family who was ashamed of her affliction and paid Aunt Augustine to keep her. My mind ticked over. Perhaps she was a relative — an unknown Fleurier — whom Aunt Augustine kept hidden away and refused to acknowledge as her own flesh and blood.

I was so rapt in my fanciful scenarios and the *chhh! chhh! chhh!* sound my scrubbing brush made on the flagstones that at first I didn't register a door creaking open, then slamming shut. Then I heard someone humming. My hand stopped mid-motion and I looked up. The voice was light and hopped from note to note like a butterfly flitting from flower to flower. It was the kind of rolling tune that an accordion man would play at a fair. In rhythm with the humming, footsteps skipped down the stairs. *Tap! Click! Tap! Click!* The steps of a woman but too light to be Aunt Augustine or Ghislaine. The footsteps reached the landing. I could make out the tinkle of jewels and a rattle like rice being shaken in a canister.

I leapt up and brushed down my hair and skirt. My apron and hem were soaked through, but I couldn't resist the chance to see who it was. I squeezed the water out of my apron and wiped my shoes on the rag that I had been using to mop up, and ran towards the front room. But as I crossed the dining room my heel snagged on the carpet. I tripped and crashed into the sideboard, scattering the cups and saucers but luckily not breaking any. I righted myself and straightened the china, but reached the parlour a second too late. All I caught was a glimpse of an ivory beaded dress swinging out the door. A hint of ylang-ylang lingered in the air.

❧

The breeze off the ocean was reddening raw in December, as were my fingers from sloughing the layers of dust and grime off the shelves, cupboards and floorboards of Aunt Augustine's house. My muscles were stiff and my shoulders ached from dragging heavy furniture to reach dust balls and swiping at cobwebs that had hung from the cornices for years. Ghislaine nodded her approval at the polished parlour and the gleaming bathroom tiles, still reeking of the bleach I had used to kill the mildew wedged in the grout. Aunt Augustine merely jutted out her chin and said, 'The door knobs are tarnished and I can still see the scum stain in the bath.' I tugged up the frayed cuffs of my winter dress and knelt to scrub, polish and soap all over again, too afraid of my aunt to tell her that parts of her house were so dilapidated that no amount of sponging and sprucing could fix them up.

My grief over my father's death healed slowly, but more from being exhausted by hard work than from acceptance. At night I huddled under my thin blanket, listening to the radiator spit and hiss erratic heat into the air. My hair stank of salt and linseed oil lingered on my fingertips. I scraped the muck from under my nails and combed the dirt out of my hair each night, but the bath I was allowed once a week didn't rid me of the salt and linseed smells. They seemed to be seeping out of my pores.

There must be more than this, I would tell myself. The few minutes before I drifted into slumber were the only time I had to think and make plans. Aunt Augustine said that I cost her 'an arm and a leg' in board and that was why she didn't pay me anything. I didn't even have money for soap or to send a letter to my family. It occurred to me that I was under no obligation to stay with Aunt Augustine, except that my mother and aunt had begged me to make the best of it. 'I've heard that terrible things can happen to girls who are alone in Marseilles,' Aunt Yvette had warned me. 'Wait until Bernard can send you some money.'

I longed for beauty but all around me was drabness. The first things I saw on awakening each morning were the bars in the window, the cracks creeping down the walls, the stains on the floorboards. On the farm I had opened my eyes to a view of fields and been caressed awake by breezes scented with wisteria and lavender. In Aunt Augustine's house, the reek of seawater rose up through the floor so that I sometimes dreamed I was trapped in the hull of a ship. On the farm I had been careless about housework because natural beauty could not be marred by scattered clothes and a lumpily made bed. But in Marseilles my surroundings were so ugly that I became obsessed with order, although my attempts at beautifying the house were frustrated at each turn. It seemed that no matter how much I plumped and straightened, the furniture still looked shabby, and because Aunt Augustine insisted that the shutters remain closed even in winter, everything was depressingly dark. Ghislaine was respectful of my efforts, but even though Monsieur Bellot looked about him in admiration, it didn't stop him from treading muddy boots on the carpets or Monsieur Roulin from spitting his olive pips onto the steps I had just swept.

In all the weeks I had been with Aunt Augustine, I had not seen the mysterious guest from the fourth floor. I often smelt her: a hint of patchouli in the bathroom; a drift of woody-sweet incense seeping from under her door. And sometimes I heard her: feet tapping across the floorboards when I cleaned Aunt Augustine's room; the faint strains of a voice crooning from a gramophone, '*Je ne peux pas vivre sans amour*'. But I never saw her. She seemed to follow a timetable of her own. When we sat down to lunch, I heard the bathroom taps groan. When I was washing the dishes in the kitchen, her stealthy tread slinked down the stairs and evaporated with the bang of the front door. Sometimes, if I was still awake in the early hours of the morning, I would hear a car pull up outside the house and a chorus of excited voices. Her laughter rose above them all. It was a light, airy laugh that tickled your skin like a spring breeze.

Ghislaine filled me in with what information she could: the boarder's name was Camille Casal, she was twenty years old and worked as a showgirl in a local music hall. But I failed so many times to catch a glimpse of her that I simply gave up.

THREE

Spring arrived early the next year and by late March the air was already tinged with warmth. I examined the herb and vegetable garden, fingering the tangled tomato vines and pulling up the grass runners that had strangled the lettuce heads. There were twigs of fennel, rosemary and thyme, badly dehydrated but perhaps salvagable. If the leaves turned out to be too tough for eating, I could dry them and make sachets. I tugged a rusty spade from the clutches of the clematis, which had climbed the fence from the garden behind us, and braved the cellar to find a pitchfork. After supper, when the air was cooler, I jabbed at the compacted ground and mixed in vegetable scraps to enrich the soil. Ghislaine brought me seeds for coriander, basil and mint. I sowed them in raised mounds, thinking how my father would have laughed to see his 'flamingo' toiling in the dirt. Every morning I watered my garden and remembered one of his favourite sayings: 'Good things come to those who sow and wait patiently.'

By the end of April it seemed that all my days had rolled into a depressing monotony of cleaning, sweeping, digging and sleeping, until one afternoon when I was rehanging the curtains in the front room after airing them. I was despairing at the moth holes and faded spots in the fabric when I heard a yap and then Aunt Augustine's shrill scream. I fell off the stool and landed with a thud on my bottom.

'Who does this monster belong to?'

Whatever Aunt Augustine was referring to, it yapped again. I stood up and righted the stool, then hurried to the landing to find out what was going on. Someone was laughing. The sound sent pins and needles over my skin and I knew instantly who it was.

'You grumpy old bag! It's my puppy,' Camille said. 'Monsieur Gosling gave it to me after I received five curtain calls.'

'For showing off your fanny and titties,' scowled Aunt Augustine over the yaps. 'I told you no pets!'

I blushed to hear an old lady use such words. But my embarrassment didn't curb my curiosity. Prepared to face my aunt's wrath for eavesdropping, I advanced up the stairs.

'He's so small he's more like a plant than a dog. You're being a cow because he frightened you.'

'I don't want any mess!'

'You seemed quite content to live with it until your niece came along.'

This was followed by silence and I stopped on the first-floor landing, straining my ears to listen for what would be said next. It occurred to me how bold Camille was to speak to Aunt Augustine like that, and how greedy Aunt Augustine was to keep someone she loathed. But I knew from the ledger book my aunt had left open on her desk one day that Camille paid twice as much board as the others, even though she never took her meals at the house.

'He won't make any noise when I'm not here,' Camille said. 'That girl of yours can take him for a walk in the evenings. He'll sleep after that.'

'She'll do nothing of the sort! She's busy enough as it is,' Aunt Augustine snapped.

'I'm sure she will ... if I pay her. And I'm sure that you will take half of it.'

The conversation paused again. I guessed that Aunt Augustine was thinking the issue over. She'd prefer money over the house being clean. But would she give in to someone she despised? I itched at the idea of getting paid for something, even if Aunt Augustine did take half of it. It seemed to me that some money would herald the beginning of better things. I sucked in a breath and crept up the next flight of stairs. But the sound of footsteps heading towards me stopped me in my tracks. It wasn't Aunt Augustine's clumsy gait but the strut of a lioness. My first instinct was to turn and run. Instead, I found myself with feet as immovable as lead. The most I could do was to stare down at them. The footsteps came to a halt above me.

'There you are!'

I looked up. For a moment I thought I was experiencing a vision. Leaning over the balustrade of the landing above was the most beautiful woman I had ever seen. Her blonde hair fell in waves across her crown, her eyes were crystal blue and her nose was as sculptured as those of the statues in Palais Longchamp, which I had stopped to admire one day when I passed it on an errand. She looked like a rose in her pale mint dress with a corsage of scarlet petals. Her long fingers held an animal to her throat. From the size of it, I thought it was a honey-coloured rat, but when it turned to me and blinked bulging eyes and stuck out its pink tongue I realised it was the tiniest dog I had ever seen.

Camille stepped down towards me and placed the wriggly animal in my arms. 'His name is Bonbon. He's a chihuahua. Which I guess means that he cost a fortune.'

The dog licked my face and wagged his plume-like tail so vigorously that his whole body shook. I stroked his silky coat and let him nibble my fingers, forgetting for a moment that Camille was watching me.

'And see,' she said, 'he likes you better than me already.'

I looked up at her. 'You want me to take him for walks?'

'God, yes,' she replied, stroking her chin and studying me from head to foot. 'I'm no good with animals.'

I cradled Bonbon in my arms, rolling him onto his back and tickling his tummy. It was then I realised that Bonbon was a girl, not a boy.

⁊

Aunt Augustine took half of the fifty *centimes* Camille Casal paid me to walk Bonbon for an hour. But I didn't care because of the chance it gave me to be out of the grim house. Each time I stepped out the door and Bonbon pranced ahead of me, leading me through the crooked streets and out on to the quays, I felt that I was living again. We listened to restaurant hawkers plying their dishes and the gypsies playing violins. Bonbon and I strolled along Marseilles' main boulevard, the Canebière, stopping to sniff the roses bursting from buckets in the doorway of a florist or to 'window lick' outside the *chocolaterie*, where we watched pralines being packed into boxes tied with gold bows. Whether we passed the men drinking *apéritifs* in the sidewalk cafés or the women in their hats and pearls, sipping their *cafés crèmes*, they all lifted their eyebrows to see a girl in a faded dress walking a dog with a diamanté collar.

One afternoon when Bonbon and I returned home, the prostitutes from the house next door were standing on their doorstep, waiting for the evening trade. They shrieked when they saw me with Bonbon.

'What's that you've got on the end of your string? A rat?' the one closest to us laughed.

Although Aunt Augustine had told me not to speak to our neighbours, I couldn't help smiling at the women. I picked up Bonbon and held her out to them. They scratched her under the chin and stroked her fur. 'She's a cute one. Look at those ears — bigger than she is,' they said.

It was only close up that I realised the women were much older than they appeared at a distance. Their wrinkles and blotched skin showed through the layers of powder and rouge, and the rose water scent that wafted from their hair and clothes could not hide the musty smell of their skin. Although the women were smiling and laughing, they made me sad. When I looked into their eyes, I saw broken dreams and thwarted chances.

As soon as Bonbon reached the doorstep of Aunt Augustine's house her tail drooped, and I was sure that if I'd had a tail it would have been drooping too. I bent down and scratched the ruff around her neck and tickled her ears.

'I'll have her as a boarder,' I heard Aunt Augustine say as I stepped into the front room, 'but I won't have such a woman wandering about the house or bringing home men.'

I closed the door as quietly as I could. Bonbon's claws scratched on the floorboards and she plunked herself down, staring at me with her intelligent eyes. I swept her up and tucked her into my pocket, then crept towards the kitchen to hear more of what Aunt Augustine was saying. There was a tilted mirror on the picture rail in the dining room and reflected in it was my aunt sitting at the kitchen table with her feet in a bucket. Ghislaine was cleaning some mussels, tossing the empty shells into a basket. Aunt Augustine lowered her voice and I had to strain my ears to hear her.

'They wear practically nothing. *Nothing!*' she hissed. 'The women stick a piece of material over themselves with spirit gum and the men put padding ... well ... you know where.'

I clamped my hand over my mouth to suppress a giggle. How did Aunt Augustine know all this?

Ghislaine waited until she had shelled her last mussel before she answered. 'I don't think Simone will be corrupted just by walking Camille's dog.'

❧

Although Marseilles had frightened me at first, I came to like the city on my walks with Bonbon. The Vieux Port was picturesque in the long Provençal twilight. At that time of day there was none of the harried toing and froing that there was at dawn when the fish market opened. The evening walkers promenaded at their leisure. The barkers were out in force, luring people into their restaurants from which the smells of garlic and fish stew wafted in spicy currents. Gypsies gathered on the quays, selling woven baskets and tinware or enticing passers-by to have their palms read and fortunes told. Ghislaine had told me they were arriving from all over Europe for the annual festival of Les Saintes Maries de la Mer and would spend most of the summer in southern France. The air was alive with violin music and singing. The yellow and red skirts the dancers wore made me think of the wildflowers that dotted the hillsides in Pays de Sault, and reminded me that now I had a bit of money I could reply to Aunt Yvette's letter and tell her and my mother how I was keeping.

I passed one stall with what I thought were plucked birds strung up between two posts. The meat smelt gamy and I asked the seller what it was. He scratched his head and tried to draw the creature in the air with his finger before he remembered the French term: *le hérisson*. Hedgehog. I recoiled and scurried away. The bodies resembled Bonbon too much for my liking.

A seagull squawked overhead. I followed its path through the sky and watched it land on the dock. At the same time I noticed Camille standing at a fruit wagon on the corner of Rue Breteuil. She held a bunch of irises wrapped in newspaper in one arm, and pointed out some grapes to the grocer with the other. Her blondeness stood out amongst all the dark faces like a streetlamp in a dim alley. She was wearing her green dress with an Indian shawl draped over her shoulders and her hair swept back from her face with a ribbon. After collecting her purchase, she glanced in my direction. But if she saw me, she gave no indication of it and turned in the direction of the Canebière.

She must be on her way to the music hall, I thought. Bonbon wriggled in my arms and I set her down on the ground. She scampered her way through the tangle of legs, running towards Camille and tugging me after her. It was a strange thing for Bonbon to do, for she was much more attached to me than to her mistress. I wondered if she understood how much Camille stimulated my curiosity and was giving me a chance to talk to her away from the house.

The Canebière was crowded at the best of times but it was especially so that night because of the gypsies. For once I was thankful for my unfeminine height because I could just make out Camille's blonde head bobbing among the sea of others in front of us. She turned into an avenue shaded by plane trees; Bonbon and I followed behind. The street was crowded with well-turned-out women walking arm in arm with their sophisticated companions. Food vendors lined up their carts against the gutters and ripe melons and peaches scented the air. Bonbon pranced on, ignoring the bejewelled poodles and fox terriers that wagged their tails and sent her longing glances. Had she travelled this way before? I wondered. Was she remembering her way home?

It seemed devious to be following Camille but I couldn't get close enough to her to call out. At each corner I hoped that she would turn around and see me, but she never did. She marched on, fixed on her destination. After a while, she turned into a narrow street whose houses blocked the last rays of sun. The cobblestones reeked of alcohol and vomit. The façades of the houses — those that weren't covered with ivy — were eyesores of peeling paint. Prostitutes, much scrawnier than those who lived next door to us, peered from the doorways, beckoning to the groups of sailors loitering on the streets. I picked up Bonbon and glanced over my shoulder, wary of going any further into the side streets but too scared to turn back either.

Camille disappeared around a corner and I broke into a run to keep up with her. I found myself in a square with a fountain in the centre. At the end of it was an enormous stone building with four columns and a carved panel of dancing nymphs on either side of its double doors. *Le Chat Espiègle,* the sign above it read. The building was grand in size but dilapidated in detail. The columns were cracked and stained and the reliefs, probably once white, were black with grime. I reached the fountain in time to see Camille enter an alley at the side of the building. I bolted across the square in pursuit, and was about to call out to her when she ran up some stairs and disappeared through a door. I hesitated a moment, wondering if I should follow her. I climbed the steps and turned the latch, but the door was locked. The faint strains of piano chords and a *tappety-tap* sound drifted out through an open window on the second floor. Bonbon pricked up her ears and I stopped to listen.

Footsteps echoed on the cobblestones and I jumped down the stairs and hid behind some crates of rubbish. I was just in time to miss being seen by a procession of women coming towards us. They were young and slender with short hair and pretty faces. I eased myself further back into the scrunched newspapers and empty bottles. The air smelt of gin and fish. Bonbon lowered her ears and pressed her head close to my chest.

A redheaded girl strode up the stairs and rapped on the door. The others slouched on the railing or sat down. They wore fashionable dresses, cut just below the knee, but even from where I crouched I could see that the lace was stiff and the dull beads were cheap.

A girl with peroxide-blonde hair took a comb out of her bag and ran it through her fringe. 'I'm hungry,' she moaned, bending forward and wrapping one hand around her stomach.

'That's what happens when you don't eat,' the girl next to her said. Her accent was stilted, and although she had elegant features she spoke 'washerwoman' French.

'I can't eat,' replied the first girl, looking over her shoulder at the redhead who was banging on the door again. 'The rent's due tomorrow.'

'*Mon Dieu!* The heat!' complained a dark-haired girl, dabbing at her florid face with a handkerchief. 'I'm wilting like a flower.'

'It's died down a bit,' said the hungry girl. 'It was worse this afternoon. I was dripping greasepaint. They won't turn on the fans for rehearsals.'

The redheaded girl turned around. 'Marcel dropped me during the Arabian dance.'

'I saw!' exclaimed another girl. 'You fell right into the puddle of sweat at his feet.'

'Lucky I didn't drown!' the redhead roared.

The other girls giggled.

The latch clicked and they sprang up into a line, as if by force of habit. The door swung open. '*Bonsoir*, Albert!' they sang out one by one before disappearing into the darkness.

Bonbon wriggled and licked my fingers. I was about to stand up when I heard more footsteps on the cobblestones and ducked down again. I peeped between the piles of rubbish to see a matronly woman heading towards us with a stack of hatboxes in her arms. The boxes were so high that she had to peer around them to see where she was going. Two swarthy-looking men with instrument cases tucked under their arms followed not far behind. The threesome came to a stop at the door and one of the men knocked. As with the girls, they waited a few minutes for it to open before disappearing inside. Although my calves and feet were aching, and Bonbon was squirming in my arms, I was mesmerised by the parade of people passing by. Compared to my life of drudgery, they possessed mystery.

The door opened and I jumped. A man stepped out and cast an eye over the street. I was sure that he would see me, but his gaze stopped short of my hiding place. Despite the heat he was wearing an overcoat that reached to his heels and the collar of his shirt was turned up. The man propped the door open with a brick and leaned on the railing for a moment before reaching into his pocket and assembling a cigarette. My right ankle was burning from crouching and I shifted my foot to ease the cramp. My shoe knocked a wine bottle and sent it rolling into the gutter where it came to a stop with a *clink*. The man wheeled around and our eyes met. My breath caught in my throat. 'Well, hello there,' he said, scratching the stubble on his chin.

'Hello,' I replied, standing up and straightening my dress. Then, unable to think of a reason to be hiding in the rubbish, I said, 'Good evening' and ran off down the alley.

❧

Intrigued by what I had seen, and having no other entertainment, I returned to the theatre the following night. But when I reached the alleyway it was deserted. I thought that perhaps Le Chat Espiègle didn't have a show on Saturday nights and raced around to the cashier, who assured me that they did and pointed to the ticket prices. I returned to the alley. There were strains of a violin warming up and I was reassured that I would be entertained again by the arriving performers. I found an empty crate amongst the rubbish and set it under the awning of the junk shop opposite the stage door. I sat down on the box with Bonbon in my lap, clasped my arms around my knees and stared expectantly at the corner. I didn't have to wait long before the chorus girls showed up, giggling and parading like a line of ducklings on their way to the pond. The redheaded girl spotted me first. *'Bonsoir!'* she called out, not in the least surprised to see a girl sitting on a box with a dog on her knee. The other girls nodded or smiled as they passed. They knocked on the door, it opened and they disappeared into the darkness.

A while later, three men and two women appeared from around the corner. I was struck by the way they marched rather than walked, their broad shoulders pushed back and their chins pointing skyward. The men's arms were as thick as tree trunks while the women's limbs were sinewy and their faces taut. Two of the men carried a trunk between them. When they were closer I could see the words 'The Zo-Zo Family' painted on the side along with a picture of six trapeze artists balanced on a tightrope. The rope was strung over a river of crocodiles and in the background I could see mountains and prehistoric-looking trees. There were six acrobats in the picture and five people in the group. I wondered what had happened to the sixth performer.

One of the women knocked on the door. It opened and this time I could see the figure of the doorman lurking in the shadows. After the acrobats had entered, he stepped out on the landing.

'I thought it was you,' he said. 'You're early. Usually we don't let fans in until after the performance. And then only if they've paid to see the show.'

My heart pounded. I had a terrible feeling that he was going to send me away. I stammered that I only wanted to see the performers arriving, and that I didn't have money to see the show itself, but that if I did have the money I would certainly pay to enter his fine establishment. The doorman's eyes twinkled and the corner of his mouth twitched.

A man wearing a battered suit with worn knees and a white shirt with a grey tinge to it walked towards us. His eyes were fixed on a crumpled piece of paper he was holding. His other hand was jammed into his pocket.

'*Bonsoir*, Georges,' the doorman called out. The man stopped for a moment and glanced up but didn't return the greeting. He mumbled something to himself and climbed the stairs. The doorman raised his voice and repeated, '*Bonsoir*, Georges.' When the other man still didn't respond, the doorman blocked the passageway with his body and crossed his arms over his chest. 'It's bad manners enough to not greet me,' he said. 'But can't you at least say "*Bonsoir*" to the young lady and her dog over there? They've been waiting to see you.'

The man lifted his eyes to the doorman, then turned around and threw me a fearsome glance. Bonbon recoiled and yapped.

The man's brow wrinkled as if he had just woken from a dream. '*Bonsoir*,' he nodded sternly at us before slipping past the doorman into the darkness. His pock-marked complexion and hollow eyes made a macabre impression on me. I wondered if he was one of those black magicians I had read about, the ones who cut pretty girls in half with a saw.

The doorman watched the man disappear. 'That's the comic,' he grinned.

The sound of heels echoed on the cobblestones. *Tap! Click! Tap! Click!* All three of us looked up. Camille was walking down the alley, her legs stockingless because of the heat. She was wearing a red dress and her hair was swept to the side with a comb. Perched behind one ear was an orchid. She picked grapes from the bunch she carried in her hand and slipped them into her mouth one by one, chewing each globe thoughtfully while staring into the distance. Heavier footsteps followed behind her. I saw a man in top hat and tails turn the corner, a bunch of roses tucked under his arm. I was wondering what his line of entertainment was when he let out a moan of pain: 'Caaamiiille!'

I shivered with the sound of it. But if he was hoping for a reaction from Camille, he didn't get one. She strolled on with her eyes fixed on the stage door, not even seeing me. The man's face reddened and he bit his lip. He was about thirty years old but his puffy cheeks and weak chin made him look like a baby.

'Camille,' he pleaded, running up behind her.

Her brow pinched and she turned to face her pursuer. 'Can't you leave me alone for even a minute?' she snarled.

The man paused and swallowed, then took a step forward. 'But you promised.'

'You're boring me. Go away,' she said, her voice rising. The man stiffened. He shot a glance at the doorman who returned the look with an expression of sympathy.

'You'll meet me after the show, won't you?'

'What for?' Camille shrugged. 'So you can give me another dog? I gave the first one away.'

Bonbon pricked up her ears. I assumed that the man must be Monsieur Gosling, the admirer who had given Bonbon to Camille after she received five curtain calls. He looked out of place in the surroundings.

'Listen to me,' said Camille, jabbing her finger into his chest. 'I don't let people treat me like a toy. I don't have time for anyone who's not serious.'

She pushed him out of her way and was halfway up the stairs when Monsieur Gosling let out another groan and dipped at the knees. I thought he was either going to faint or crawl after her. He pulled out the roses, which he had been holding under his arm. I was sure that it was the wrong time to make the gesture to Camille. Her mouth formed into a cruel smile. She looked as though she was about to spit out a scalding remark, when she paused and stared at the flowers. Something she saw in them made her change her mind. Her face softened like a bud opening to the rain.

'Monsieur Gosling,' she purred, brushing her fingers over her neck before sinking her hand into the petals and pulling something out. It glinted in the sunlight. A diamond bracelet.

Monsieur Gosling's confidence lifted when he saw the delight on Camille's face. Her voice turned from cool to husky when she said, 'That's better,' and kissed him on the cheek. He was like a puppy who had pleased his mistress by peeing in the right place.

'After the show ...?' he said, trying to sound manly and demanding, but it was still a question.

'After the show,' replied Camille, before slinking past the doorman and into the darkness. The doorman rolled his eyes. Monsieur

Gosling skipped down the stairs but started when he saw me or, more precisely, Bonbon.

'Is that ...? I must ask ... Is that ...?' he stammered, edging towards me.

'Yes,' I told him. 'This is the puppy you gave to Mademoiselle Casal. I walk her every day.'

His eyes opened and he started to laugh, showing his crooked teeth. I would have run away if the doorman hadn't been standing there. Monsieur Gosling slapped his hands together and turned his face to heaven, his mouth breaking into a beaming smile. 'She loves me after all!' he shouted, loud enough for the whole of Marseilles to hear. 'She loves me!'

⁂

I missed going to the theatre the following night. I had Bonbon at the door, ready to go, when Aunt Augustine called down the stairs to say she had an urgent note for me to take to her lawyer. 'You can combine the two trips,' she said. Not really, I thought, knowing that I couldn't walk all the way to her lawyer on Rue Paradis and go to the theatre.

The next day, as I was fitting Bonbon's lead for our walk, Aunt Augustine called out that she had a letter she wanted me to deliver to the pharmacist. I hoped that she wasn't going to make a habit of these combined errand/dog walks. After dropping the letter into the pharmacy, I ran all the way to Le Chat Espiègle. When I reached the alley, my heart leapt with joy to see that my crate had been set up for me, along with a jar of water for Bonbon. I took my seat and poured some water into my palm, which Bonbon lapped up. But after waiting a quarter of an hour still no one had arrived. I leaned back against the wall, trying to contain my disappointment. I was half an hour later than I had been the first couple of nights and had missed them all. I was about to get up and leave when the stage door swung open and a familiar voice called out, 'I thought you weren't going to show up.'

I looked up and saw the doorman smiling at me.

'Have I missed them?'

He nodded and my heart sank.

'That being the case, Mademoiselle,' he said, 'I suggest that you come inside and watch from the wings.'

I jumped up, scarcely able to believe my ears. My legs trembled so much I could barely move.

'Come on,' the doorman laughed.

I needed no further encouragement. I ran up the stairs and plunged through the doorway where I had seen the others pass before me. At first I was dazed from the contrast of the sunshine outside and the darkness within, but after a few seconds my eyes adjusted and I saw that we were standing in a stairwell crowded with stuffed armchairs and panels painted with scenes of a Turkish bath.

'My name is Albert,' said the doorman. 'And you are ...?'

'Simone. And this is Bonbon,' I said, holding her up to him.

'I'm pleased to meet you both,' he said, gesturing for me to follow him up the stairs then down a narrow hallway. 'Now, Simone and Bonbon, it's very important that you be quiet otherwise the management will not be impressed.'

He pulled aside a curtain and pointed to a stool sitting under some stairs. I edged my way past more panels of scenery, a chandelier lying on a broken sofa and a bucket of sand, then eased myself into the space and perched Bonbon in my lap. My nose itched from the smell of dust and paint but I didn't care. Albert pressed his finger to his lips and I nodded my promise to be quiet. He smiled and disappeared.

I peered through a crack in the curtain and squinted at the bright lights that shone like four suns towards me. I discovered that I was in the wing closest to the backdrop, which was a painting of buffaloes stampeding across a plain. In the distance a wagon train was weaving its way alongside a river. I had a view down the stage into the orchestra pit and beyond to the first three rows of seats. In the middle of the stage was a towering wooden pole with primitive faces carved into its sides. The band was warming up and a man with spindly legs and a moustache with the ends waxed into curlicues darted about, yelling at someone in the front wings to close the curtains.

'We're about to let the audience in,' he shouted, running his fingers through his slicked-down hair. 'What do you mean the cord is tangled?'

He was answered by several grunts and a scraping sound. The curtains jerked from the wings but came to an abrupt halt a metre from each other. Further grunts sounded from the front wing, followed by a string of curses.

The tall man stared at a spot on the backdrop for a moment before sighing. 'What do you mean they won't close any further? I told you to check them at rehearsal. It's too late to oil the runners now.'

There was a bang and the scenery wobbled. Bonbon yelped but luckily the sound had been so loud that its echo drowned her out. I rubbed her back and squinted through the crack. The totem pole was lying on its side. Two men in overalls with hammers in their back pockets rushed onto the stage and righted it, fixing a support at its base. The curlicue man's eyes bulged and his hands clenched into fists by his sides. He seemed to be on the verge of exploding, but after the totem pole had been secured and the two stagehands returned to the wings, he let out a slow, whistling breath, threw his arms in the air and shouted, 'On with the show!'

The stage went black and I wondered what was going to happen next. I could make out a row of lights around the orchestra pit and a circle of light shining from a lamp in the front wing.

After a while, there were voices. The sound grew louder. My nose twitched: tobacco smoke drifted in the air. I peered beyond the gap in the curtains and made out the silhouettes of people pouring down the aisles and filling the seats. A few minutes later, a man's voice echoed around the hall and the chatter abruptly ceased. 'Ladies and gentlemen, welcome to Le Chat Espiègle ... '

A shiver ran all the way down my spine to the backs of my legs. Bonbon pressed herself against me and pricked up her ears. A circle of light flashed on the stage in front of the curtains. The audience clapped. The vibration of the applause shook the floorboards under my feet and made the chandelier tinkle. The band struck up a romantic melody and a man in a striped shirt and beret stepped into the spotlight. He turned and I caught his profile. His face was covered in white make-up and his eyes and lips were circled in black. He held out his hand, pretending to smell a flower. After admiring it, he offered the bloom to imaginary people passing by. I had seen mime artists at the Sault fair, but this one was more convincing. Each time his offer of the flower was rejected, his shoulders drooped and he bowed his head in a way that made me feel his disillusionment. I couldn't see his facial expressions but the audience burst into laughter and stamped their feet at his performance, which ended when someone accepted his flower and he skipped down the stage steps towards them.

The percussion instruments burst out with an explosion of drums and rattles. The curtains flew open and light flooded the stage. A stampede rumbled on the stairs above me and the stage filled with chorus girls dressed as American Indians. Their tan stockings shimmered under the lights and their plaited hairpieces swung around their faces as they bucked and stomped around the totem pole, singing out their war cry. The audience stood up and cheered. Some whistled and others made catcalls. With the brighter lights I could see them more clearly than before. They were nearly all men in dark suits and caps, or sailors, but dotted among the crowd were showy women in sequins and feathers and about half a dozen out-of-place men dressed like Monsieur Gosling. On stage, the dancing turned wilder. Indian braves arrived with a canoe, but were overrun by the squaws who wrestled them to the ground and stole their moccasins.

Then, as quickly as they had appeared, the girls departed like ants before a storm, fleeing into the wings or up the stairs. The sound of their fading voices ricocheted around me. The lights blacked out again. Bonbon quivered in my arms. My own heart thumped in my chest. Seeing the performance was like being hit by lightning. My skin burned and my temples throbbed. I had never experienced anything like it before.

I peered through the curtain again and blinked. Ghostly beings were scuffling around on the stage. They hoisted something over the backdrop; it unfurled with the *thump* of a sail opening into the wind. They pushed the totem pole into the wings and in its place set out objects that looked like trees. A few minutes later their shadowy shapes retreated, like assassins slinking away. I became aware of a muffled voice and saw that another act was taking place in front of the curtain. The rounded shoulders and grim posture were familiar and I realised that it was the sullen comedian. I couldn't hear what he was saying because he was projecting his voice towards the audience, but whatever it was they didn't like it. They were booing and banging the sides of their chairs with their fists.

'Bring on the girls!' a surly voice shouted above the riot.

Whether the comedian had finished his act or not I didn't know, but a few moments later a harp began a lilting melody. A flute joined in and weaved around the notes like a serpent. Golden light spread over the stage. The audience gasped and so did I. The scene was ancient Egypt with a backdrop of sand, pyramids and palm trees. The chorus girls stood or knelt before a staircase that disappeared into the rafters. They were dressed in white robes fastened at the shoulder with a silver clasp and all looked alike in ebony wigs and with eyes elongated with black liner. Eunuchs stood on either side of the stage, waving fans of peacock feathers. The chorus girls chanted and their voices were answered by a warbling one from up in the flies.

Feet bejewelled in silver anklets appeared at the top of the staircase and began to descend. They were followed by slim legs and a torso. When the woman came fully into sight a breathless hush fell over the audience. Draped over her hips was a swirl of muslin fastened at the waist with a clasp in the form of a cobra. She shimmered with jewels. They glistened at her ears and wrists and on each upper arm she wore a gold band. Over her chest dangled strings of beads which scarcely hid her pert breasts. One foot in front of the other she glided down the stairs. It was only because of her elegant walk that I recognised her. Camille. She had transformed from a pretty woman into an exotic temptress. Suddenly I understood Monsieur Gosling's fever.

Camille reached the bottom of the stairs and moved towards the footlights where she began snaking her arms and gyrating her hips in time to the music. A man in the front row clamped his hand over his mouth but couldn't take his eyes off her. The rest of the audience didn't move at all. They sat clutching their seats. Camille rolled her shoulders and hips and turned in a circle. I caught the flash of her eyes, her haughty expression. Everyone else on stage faded into insignificance. Her voice was thin but her stage presence was formidable. A boat with a purple sail slid out from the wings and stopped at the foot of the staircase. Flanked by the chorus girls, Camille stepped into it. She turned and gave the audience a last cheeky swing of her hips before being spirited away. The lights went out. The dance was over. The audience stood up and roared, their applause louder than a thunderstorm. I clutched Bonbon to me, both of us quivering.

After several encores, for none of which Camille appeared, I realised that it must be getting late and I would have to miss the second act. I stood up to go home.

Albert was smoking on the landing and I thanked him for letting me see the show, but I barely heard my own words, so fresh was the memory of music and applause in my ears. I wandered down the Canebière in a dream, Bonbon's paws pattering on the cobblestones beside me. Camille's act played before my eyes again; it had impressed me more than anything I had ever seen. It wasn't lewd or vulgar, as Aunt Augustine had described. It was spellbinding. And in comparison to it, my life seemed even more dreary.

I reached the front door as the sun was setting and lifted the latch. But the girl who had left the house that evening was not the same girl who returned to it. I knew then that my life would have to be the stage, or it would be nothing at all.

FOUR

———

Le Chat Espiègle was not a high-class music hall with a large production budget and an audience that included dukes and princes. But it was a place of magic to me. I thought that the lights and music, the bright costumes and the chorus girls, were the height of glamour and excitement. I had nothing to compare it with. I was blind to the tattered curtains, the shabby seats, the near starved faces of the performers. I lived for those evenings when Bonbon and I walked to the theatre and Albert sneaked us into our secret place in the wings.

Sometimes acts were changed from the second to the first half of the program, and once I saw the Sunday matinée when Aunt Augustine was down with a migraine and told me not to disturb her or make any noise around the house. In this way, I had a chance to see the other performers. The artists and the impresario, Monsieur Dargent, discovered me from time to time but said nothing. Even Camille turned a blind eye to my presence, remaining aloof but not giving me away to Aunt Augustine and continuing to pay me to walk Bonbon.

The mime's name was Gerard Chalou. Although I only saw his back during his performance, I often stumbled across him backstage, practising a shoulder stand against a wall or lying flat on his back, contracting and relaxing his stomach muscles. He would sometimes warm up in the wing where I sat, and often spent four or five minutes just rolling his eyes.

'They convey everything,' he replied to my puzzled expression. 'They must be limbered up too.'

During the interval Chalou gave me and Albert a performance of his sketch about a poodle who would not behave. To emphasise the comedy he froze in some of his positions. I scrutinised his lips and chest, searching for some telltale sign of breathing, but couldn't find any. Madeleine and Rosalie, two chorus girls who appeared nude in the show except for jewel-studded *cache-sexes*, begged Gerard to teach them his special 'immobilisation' technique.

'Practise by running around,' he said. 'Then stop in a pose. You must not move a muscle. But you must not look dead either. Your eyes should convey inner life.'

Madeleine and Rosalie pranced around like ponies. When Gerard shouted 'Freeze!' they came to a stop, doing their best not to teeter on their high heels and holding their feather boas out behind them like wings. But for all their earnestness, each time they tried something would give them away. An earring would rattle against a headdress; a bracelet would slip down an arm; or their breasts would continue to bounce. For women who were supposed to be nude, their 'costumes' were often heavier than those of the chorus girls who appeared clothed.

Monsieur Dargent, passing by, watched their attempts with interest. 'It will never do even if they manage to freeze,' he said. 'Not with all that running around.'

Albert explained to me that, according to the law, nude showgirls could appear in the program as long as they only paraded and posed. If they danced or moved too much, they would be considered strippers and the police could close down the production.

Claude Contet, the magician, was dazzling. He had the luminous skin and pale eyes of a mystical conjurer. When he paraded across the stage, his cape glittered and sparked with electricity. I watched him sweep his wand over the bird cage three times and tug away the purple scarf. The canary was nowhere to be seen. The audience clapped. Claude held out his palms to their enthralled faces. 'You see, my hands are empty.'

When the Zo-Zo Family appeared everyone backstage came out to watch, their painted faces, and my unpainted one, turned towards the spotlights while Alfredo, Enrico, Peppino, Vincenzo, Violetta and Luisa dusted their hands in chalk and scaled the rope ladder to take their positions on the platforms.

'Oh my! Oh my!' Madame Tarasova, the wardrobe mistress, would mutter into her handkerchief.

Violetta and Luisa leapt for their swings and swept over us like spangled birds, moving back and forth to gather momentum. The Zo-Zos performed their act without a net and the groan of the trapeze under their weight added to the tension. Often there were gasps and the occasional scream from the audience. Sometimes when the strain was too much, I'd have to look down at the musicians in the pit. There was no music for the act: the wrong beat could be fatal. The conductor would have his eyes squeezed shut. The violinists sat with their heads bowed, like monks at prayer. Only the brass section was brave enough to keep watching. I'd lose my breath the second before the transition and my heart lurched in my throat. Suddenly the women were spinning, somersaulting through the air like silver dolphins. A sensation in my stomach made it seem as if they were falling, swooning towards the deadly edges of the stage. But with a *slap!* their hands clutched those of their catchers with such split-second timing that for a moment the audience remained dazed. Then the sound of applause roared through the hall. Those whose legs weren't still trembling stood up to shout their admiration. Somehow, from that point on, I knew that the Zo-Zo Family would be safe even though their pirouetting and passages became increasingly complicated as the act progressed.

Although I saw the act several times, each time it ended and the band played the victory tune tears blurred my vision. The performance stirred my sense of beauty and loathing. Beauty because the act was more about trust than tricks; loathing because of the snatches of conversation I heard backstage. 'Not this time, I guess,' muttered as a sigh. When all the Zo-Zos had scaled back down to the stage and taken their bows, the collective exhalation of relief that went through the other performers contained a tinge of dissatisfaction: the same disappointment as among onlookers when a suicide decides not to jump.

But my greatest fear was that Aunt Augustine would find out where I was going each evening and forbid me to walk Bonbon any more. I was not a natural liar and the double life of deception took its toll. I was fearful of getting home late, and as evening approached I never knew until the last minute if Aunt Augustine was going to give me an errand to do and a whole day's anticipation of going to the music hall would come to nothing. If I ever wanted to work in show business, it was clear that I would have to leave Aunt Augustine's first.

It was in this matter that Albert came to the rescue.

'Madame Tarasova needs help with the costumes,' he said. 'Go see her.'

I pinched my wrist to make sure it wasn't a dream and found my way to the backstage area where the wardrobe mistress was stacking headdresses on a shelf.

'*Bonsoir*, Madame,' I called out. 'Albert said you need help. And I need a job.'

Madame Tarasova was a Russian *émigrée* who always wore a loose corduroy dress and a scarf fastened at her throat with a brooch. She smiled at me and cooed to Bonbon. 'What a beautiful doggie,' she said, stroking Bonbon's chin. 'We must make sure we don't put her on someone's head instead of a wig.'

We both laughed.

A blonde girl, a few years older than me, appeared with some dresses on hangers. She nodded to me and hung the dresses up behind a curtain.

'That is my daughter, Vera,' said Madame Tarasova, pulling some needles from a cushion and pinning them to my blouse. She slipped a spool of cotton and a pair of scissors into my pocket. 'Can you sew?'

I told her that I sewed well because on my family's farm that was one thing that I *could* do.

Madame Tarasova nodded. 'I need you to do repairs quickly,' she said, gesturing for me to follow her up the staircase. 'And to help set out the costumes. The headdresses are too awkward for the girls to run up the stairs with, so we collect them as each performer comes off the stage, clean them, then pack them away downstairs. If you come earlier tomorrow, you can help Vera set them out for the first act.'

We stopped outside a door with the number six painted on it. The chirping of female voices came from the other side. Madame Tarasova pushed the door open and a tableau of chaos unfolded before us. The chorus girls were perched on stools side by side in the cramped room.

They were staring into mirrors and rubbing their faces with greasepaint sticks and rouge. The air reeked of *eau de cologne*, brilliantine and sweat. Madame Tarasova took Bonbon from me and placed her in a hatbox on a chair, where someone discarded a kimono on top of her. Bonbon peered out from the material then slipped under the chair to watch the goings on from behind the safety of the legs. The redheaded girl I had seen before recognised me. 'Hello again!' she called out, smearing her eyelids with purple shadow. 'Helping out Mama Tarasova?' It was then I realised why her French had sounded so strange; it was because she was English.

'When the girls are on stage,' said Madame Tarasova above the commotion, 'you and Vera should come up here and straighten out the room.' She stopped to help a girl with the ties of her Indian costume and shook her head at a dress lying on the floor. 'They are good girls but sometimes they forget to hang up their costumes. Don't they, Marion?'

The girl grinned and continued rouging her cheeks.

A bell rang. 'Ten minutes until showtime,' called out Madame Tarasova.

The pace in the dressing room quickened. The girls flung off their kimonos and slipped on their costumes. Madame Tarasova and I ran between them, helping to straighten tights and smooth down wigs.

'Look,' said a pale-skinned girl, whom I recognised as the one who had complained of hunger the first night I had watched the performers arrive at the stage door. She pointed to a tear under the arm of her smock. 'I'll fix it,' I said. She tugged off her costume and handed it to me. I tried to ignore her bare breasts and mound of pubic hair jutting towards me and threaded my needle. I wasn't shy, but I wasn't used to the sight of female nakedness paraded so casually either.

I heard applause and the bell rang again. I helped the girl back into her costume and watched her flee after the others down the stairs. Madame Tarasova followed. The clamour of the chorus girls' feet and the war cries they shrieked as they ran down the stairs made the floor vibrate and the walls shake.

'Simone!' Madame Tarasova called over her shoulder. 'Come back tomorrow night. I will go to the office tomorrow and sign you up for the payroll.'

I guessed that meant I was hired.

Madame Tarasova said that I could live in the backstage area until I found a room of my own. Monsieur Dargent had let her and Vera stay there when they first came to Marseilles after fleeing Russia, and I understood why they were so loyal to him when they could have got better jobs elsewhere. The day after I was hired, I couldn't wait to get my things and tell Aunt Augustine that I was leaving. It was only when I had gathered my belongings and bundled up my clothes that I noticed Bonbon sitting by the door of my room with her ears drooping.

I picked her up. I had forgotten that if I left I would not see her any more. I climbed the stairs to Camille's room and knocked on the door. Camille opened it, dressed in a kimono. Her pretty face was ethereal without her stage make-up.

'I'm leaving,' I told her. 'I've got a job at Le Chat Espiègle.'

'I know,' she said.

'But I'll still take care of Bonbon if you bring her to the theatre with you. For free.'

'Take him,' Camille said, yawning. 'What am I going to do with a dog?'

Bonbon's ears pricked up and she wagged her tail. She must have sensed the happiness that ran through me. It was a good start to a new life: my little companion could stay with me.

Aunt Augustine was sitting in the parlour, reading the newspaper. I'd already sent a letter to Aunt Yvette that morning, telling her and my mother that I was leaving and that I had found work as a seamstress with a music hall. I had to contact them first, because who knew what lies the old woman would tell my family if I didn't. I could not think of one redeeming quality that made me feel sorry for Aunt Augustine. She had not shown me any kindness. She had not 'taken me in' after my father's death. She had done nothing but exploit me.

Aunt Augustine's face turned red and her nostrils flared like a maddened bull when I told her I was leaving. 'You ungrateful little hussy!' she screamed. 'Have you got yourself pregnant?'

'No,' I said. 'I've got another job.'

Aunt Augustine was stunned for a moment but quickly recovered. 'Where?' she asked, then her eyes fell to Bonbon who was sitting by my bundle. 'So you've joined with that slut upstairs, have you?' she spat. 'Well, let me tell you this. She'll have work as long as she is young and pretty but then she'll end up like those women next door.' She nodded in the direction of our neighbours. 'But you,' she laughed, 'you're not even pretty enough for that now.'

Her insult stung because there was truth in it: I was not as pretty as Camille. I would have done anything to have her hypnotic, catlike blondeness, but I was a black-eyed giraffe. Before Aunt Augustine could say anything else to discourage me, I swept up Bonbon and my baggage and walked out the door. In the end, what kind of looks did a seamstress need?

Aunt Augustine rushed to the doorstep after me and the women next door stepped out onto their balcony to see what the commotion was about.

'Simone!' Aunt Augustine shouted. I turned to see her pointing at the prostitutes. 'That's what happens to plain girls without talent who try their luck in the music hall. Look, Simone! That's your future staring back at you!'

I tucked Bonbon under my arm, slung my bundle of clothes over my shoulder and fixed my eyes firmly in the direction of Le Chat Espiègle.

⬥

A few weeks after I started work in the wardrobe department at Le Chat Espiègle, a neighbouring music hall called The One-Eyed Sailor closed down and Monsieur Dargent bought some of the sets and costumes from the debt collectors. He created a new show titled 'On the Seas'. The first act was a sketch about three sailors who find themselves shipwrecked on an island of Hawaiian beauties.

Because the costumes were simpler than those of the previous show, I could sometimes snatch a moment to watch the act from the wings. I began to understand the difference between the chorus girls and Camille. The chorus girls sang and shook their legs because they didn't want to starve. Dancing in a music hall was better than working on the streets and the audience paid them more respect, if only slightly. It was a cut above working in a laundry or a bakery or in domestic service where the burden of their labours would soon wear out their greatest asset: their youthful prettiness. In the theatre they could hold out a little longer, hoping that some night there would be a rich suitor among the men hanging around the stage door after the show. It was well known among the chorus girls that Madeleine, after a liaison with the heir to a shipping fortune, had been forced by the young man's father to have an abortion and that the previous year two girls had to leave the theatre after contracting venereal diseases. It was not an aspect of theatrical life that I had anticipated and it shocked me. I had not heard of La Belle Otero, Liane de Pougy or Gaby Deslys — women of the stage who were mistresses to kings and princes. Although the chorus girls did sometimes receive jewels and clothes for their favours, Madame Tarasova was quick to point out that no one at Le Chat Espiègle had ever been whisked away to matrimonial heaven by a prince, or even the manager of an olive oil company, and did her best to educate everyone on the benefits of *les capotes anglaises*, rubber sheaths that men wore over their penises to prevent conception and disease. But her advice fell on deaf ears; getting pregnant was still seen as a viable way of trapping a husband.

But Camille was different. From her eyes down to the sway of her hips, she cast out magic over the floodlights and towards the hungry crowd. The audience clamoured and clapped for her, as if trying to grab hold of prime produce at the markets, while she stood remote in her mysterious beauty. When Camille exited the stage, she took the enchantment with her and left the audience longing for the taste of it again. Camille might not be interested in performing any more than the other girls, but I was certain that she would never starve.

Sometimes, when the wardrobe area was empty, I would pout and pose in the mirror, trying to be Camille. I imagined slipping open my cape and letting it fall to the floor to reveal my 'Garden of Eden' glory. But I was as successful as night imitating day; as dusk pretending it was the dawn.

One evening I returned from tidying the dressing room to find Madame Tarasova slumped in a chair and Vera standing above her, fanning her with a song script. Madame Tarasova's cheeks were flushed and her arms hung by her sides.

'What's happened?' I asked.

The wardrobe mistress glanced at me. 'I can't take it any more,' she whimpered. 'I'm exhausted.'

I was surprised to hear Madame Tarasova say such a thing. Her boundless energy had always made her seem indestructible. Even when Vera and I were dead on our feet, Madame Tarasova could keep going. 'Sit there until you feel better then,' I told her. 'Vera and I can look after the girls tonight.'

Madame Tarasova and Vera exchanged glances and laughed. Madame Tarasova sat up. 'I'm not exhausted from the work,' she said. 'It's that damn song.' She slapped her knees and in an affected voice sang, 'Aloha! Aloha! Aloha!'

The song was the motif for the first act. When Monsieur Dargent bought the costumes and props from The One-Eyed Sailor, he'd used up his budget for a songwriter and so had to write the scores himself. The Hawaiian number wasn't a hit. Members of the audience often shouted at the girls to 'Get on with it!', and on opening night someone had hated it so much that they'd hurled a bag of cement onto the stage, knocking over a palm tree and sending the girls into a panic.

I couldn't stop laughing at Madame Tarasova's imitation even when she stopped. Then a girlish sense of *joie de vivre* overtook me. I picked up one of the leftover hibiscus flowers and tucked it behind my ear then flitted my way around the room, swinging my hips in a mock hula dance. 'Aloha! Aloha! Aloha!' I sang, flinging out my voice like a café-concert singer.

Madame Tarasova and Vera laughed and clapped. 'Belle-Joie!' Madame Tarasova called. 'Stop it! You'll make me bust my girdle.' Belle-Joie was her pet name for me. She said she called me that because I made her happy.

Spurred on by their enjoyment, I raised my voice and danced more wildly, knocking my knees together and turning down my lower lip to make a silly face. 'Aloha! Aloha! Aloha!' I sang, twirling around the room and rocking my hips more violently.

I glanced back at Madame Tarasova and Vera, but they were no longer laughing. Vera's face was as purple as a grape and she was staring at something behind me. I whirled around to see Monsieur Dargent standing in the doorway. I stopped dancing and fumbled with my hands. He was not smiling. His eyes narrowed into slits and he tugged on the ends of his moustache.

'Good evening, Monsieur Dargent,' I said, my knees buckling. I thought I might faint where I stood.

Monsieur Dargent did not reply. He merely grunted and walked away.

Bonbon and I cut sorry figures the following evening when we walked from Le Panier — where I now rented a room — to the theatre. I trudged along, barely able to lift my eyes to see where I was going, while Bonbon, sensing my mood, pattered along beside me, her tail at half-mast. Our air of unhappiness aroused the curiosity of some children playing in the street and they stared at us with open mouths. Even sailors and drunkards hurried out of our way, as if in danger of being tainted by our misery. I was sure that when I arrived at the theatre, Monsieur Dargent would fire me. He was the son of a respectable doctor who had defied his parents to become an impresario. Everyone had warned me that he was sensitive and did not like being mocked so I had brought disaster upon myself, prancing around the wardrobe space and making fun of his choreography. If he were to fire me, Bonbon and I would be in trouble. I had barely enough money for my rent as it was. The room I had found in Le Panier wasn't much better than the one Aunt Augustine had given me, but I had been so happy at the theatre that I didn't care. And even though the quarter was squalid, there were street musicians and artists on every corner.

I found Madame Tarasova and Vera at work setting out the headdresses for the first act. They greeted me as if nothing were amiss. I had no choice but to go to the dressing room and set it up. On my way, I passed Monsieur Dargent running down the stairs. I froze on the spot but he didn't notice me. He rushed by, shouting instructions to a stagehand, then disappeared down the stairs and onto the stage. I shrugged; maybe I was the one who was too sensitive? It seemed that I was going to live to fight another day at Le Chat Espiègle.

∽

A few nights later I turned up at the theatre to find the stage door open but no sign of Albert. It was unlike him to leave the door unlocked when he wasn't at his post. A chill fluttered over my neck and back and I sensed something was wrong. Bonbon pricked up her ears. As I peered into the darkness, muffled sounds floated down the stairwell. I listened, but they were too faint to distinguish. They could have been anything from water running down a drainpipe to gagged cries for help. There had been a shoot-out at a music hall in Belsunce the previous day and it was rumoured that the Marseilles mafia was moving in on the theatres.

'Albert?' I called out. There was no answer. I hesitated, wondering if it would be wiser to go to the front entrance and see the cashier, but my anxiety won out and compelled me up the stairs.

There was no sign of the stagehands or electricians who were normally busy with the sets. My feet creaked on the floorboards. The sounds I'd heard earlier were coming from the floor above: voices. A picture of Monsieur Dargent and the chorus girls tied to their chairs floated into my mind. I dismissed it. We weren't that influential and our profits weren't big enough to steal. I tiptoed to the stairwell.

This time Monsieur Dargent's pleading voice filled the air. 'You can't do this to me! The show starts in three-quarters of an hour!'

'I can and I am,' a female voice answered him. 'Look at my eye. You stand on stage and sing that stupid Hawaiian number you've come up with and see what it's like to get fruit thrown at you!'

Something clattered to the floor and I heard footsteps coming towards me. The English chorus girl, Anne, hurried down the stairwell, a bulging suitcase tucked under her arm. There was a dark smudge under her right eye and swelling near her nose. When she reached the landing she turned to me and muttered, 'Goodbye, Simone. Good luck. I'm going back to London.'

I watched her reach the bottom of the stairs and rush out the door. I was sorry that she was going; she had been my favourite chorus girl.

'Things were all right until you introduced that stupid number,' another female voice piped up. 'It will ruin us all. The audience hates it!'

I climbed the stairs to the third floor and was surprised to see all the cast and crew, except for Camille, assembled there. The chorus girls wore long faces. Monsieur Dargent was leaning against the door to their dressing room, one hand clenched by his side and his brow twitching in an effort at self-control. Albert glanced over his shoulder to where I was standing and waved me towards the group. I had never seen him looking so grim. 'We might have to close the show,' he whispered. 'The lead chorus girl has just walked out. We are taking losses — the audience doesn't like the first act.'

I caught the eye of Madame Tarasova who held a lei in her hands and was fidgeting with its flowers. She sent me a nervous smile.

'We can get jobs at the Alcazar,' said the hungry chorus girl, whose name was Claire. 'Their girls are always getting offers from Paris.' She shook her skinny fist and turned to the other chorus members, trying to muster their support. A couple of the girls nodded bravely, but I noticed Claudine and Marie purse their lips. They both had children to support and had more realistic views. The Alcazar was Marseilles' top music hall. No one from Le Chat Espiègle was good enough to perform there.

'What we need,' said the lighting director, 'is a whimsical, humorous act. Like the ventriloquist was in the last show. That made the audience laugh. It opened them up.'

'I can't get the ventriloquist,' Monsieur Dargent said, his eyes pleading with us. 'He was snapped up by a resort in Vichy.'

'Nothing's going to save the first act,' snarled Claire. 'It's a dud!'

A murmur of agreement buzzed around the room.

'Humour will do it!' the lighting director shouted above the voices.

Monsieur Dargent lifted his eyes as if he were praying. Then he dropped his gaze and studied each of the performers. I wondered if he felt like Julius Caesar, about to be betrayed by his friends. Hadn't he given each of these people their break in show business? Madame Tarasova always said that Monsieur Dargent had a gift for spotting talent, he just wasn't any good at running a business. He fiddled with his jacket pocket and pulled out a cigarette. He tried to light it, but his hand shook and it fell to the floor. He bent to pick the cigarette up and as he did he saw me. A strange look passed over his face.

My breath caught in my throat. Oh God, I thought. He's remembered my parody of the opening number. He's in a bad enough mood to fire me now. I tried to squeeze behind Albert, but the room was too crowded and, to my horror, I ended up being pushed even closer to Monsieur Dargent.

'Humour?' Monsieur Dargent muttered, tapping his foot. 'Humour!' He clicked his fingers and the whole room jumped. He rushed at me, grabbed my shoulders and pressed his face into mine.

I was terrified. What on earth did he intend to do? 'Aloha! Aloha! Aloha!' he sang, peering into my eyes.

Madame Tarasova caught on faster than any of us. 'We have half an hour,' she cried.

'Quick, get her clothes off!' shouted Monsieur Dargent, pushing me towards a stool and make-up mirror. No one thought to question him. His voice had taken on a Napoleonic tone of command and everyone sprang into action.

Madame Tarasova grabbed Bonbon from me and put her on a chair. Albert shooed the other performers away before running back to his post at the door. 'Get her a costume from downstairs,' Madame Tarasova called after him. 'Anne's one will do — she won't be needing it any more.'

Madame Tarasova tugged off my dress while Vera pulled at my shoes. Marie dabbed at my face with a greasepaint stick. 'She doesn't need any on her body,' Claudine advised, brushing back my hair. 'She's as brown as a nut.'

It finally dawned on me what they were intending to do. I wanted to laugh and scream at the same time. If it wasn't for the giddy feeling that overwhelmed me as people pulled pieces of clothing off me and covered me in oily lotions, I might have been embarrassed. The only man left in the room was Monsieur Dargent, and he was so engrossed in making notes on his song script that he didn't seem to notice that the wardrobe assistant was being stripped naked. Someone pulled off my chemise and pushed my breasts into a coconut bra with the same sensitivity a greengrocer might use to pack his goods for the market.

'Aloha! Aloha! Aloha!' Monsieur Dargent sang to himself.

'Shouldn't you get her to do this tomorrow?' asked Madame Tarasova. 'When she's had time to rehearse!'

'No,' he said, shaking his head. 'We've lost our lead chorus girl. We have to save the show tonight or not at all.'

My arms and legs were trembling so much that I could barely stand up when Madame Tarasova needed to take in my skirt. I still didn't believe what Monsieur Dargent wanted me to do.

The stage bell rang. 'Ten minutes until show time,' Vera called out.

Madame Tarasova fitted my wig and Vera pinned it in place. I stared at myself in the mirror. My face was alive with colour: my eyes had green arches over them and my lips were painted ruby red. My eyelashes were so stiff with mascara they looked like twin centipedes.

'Now,' said Monsieur Dargent, leaning towards me, 'when I give you the signal, I want you to appear out of the left wing and dance and sing on the mountain plateau exactly as you did in the wardrobe area the other night. I want you to mimic the chorus girls. You are going to be our comedian.'

I swallowed but the lump in my throat didn't disappear.

The chorus girls lined up on the stairs, waiting for their cue to go on stage. The pre-show music was a tinny carnival tune with accordions and guitars that put my nerves on tenterhooks. Madame Tarasova and Vera led me to the left wing. The place where I had viewed the show for the first time had been cleared out and there were some wooden steps leading up to the stage and out onto the plateau where I was supposed to dance.

'Wait at the top of the stairs,' said Madame Tarasova, giving my wig a last brush. 'Good luck!' The tone of her voice and the way she patted my shoulder made me feel as if I were about to be fed to lions. Of course I was doing what every performer dreads, although I had no idea what to call it then. I was going on cold.

I climbed the stairs and waited on the top step for the next signal. I cast my eye over the backdrop of smoking volcanoes and low-slung clouds. Below me, where the chorus girls were to dance, rubber palm trees and a water tank suggested a blue lagoon. Monsieur Dargent appeared in the wing opposite. The way he was chewing his bottom lip and fingering the hair at the back of his head did not inspire my confidence.

The curtains opened. The spotlights flicked on. A drum roll thundered through the hall and the orchestra burst into the first act's theme song. The girls rushed onto the stage.

'Aloha! Aloha! Aloha!'

My throat tightened. Beads of sweat sprang up on my lip, but I was too scared to wipe them away in case I smeared my make-up. Any desire I'd had to work in the theatre drained away from me. The girls danced around the lagoon, swinging their hips. Claudine and Marie strummed ukuleles. The situation was surreal. Monsieur Dargent didn't even know my name, but the success of the evening now depended on me. Only a short while ago I had been worrying about my rent, now I was about to appear on stage for the first time in my life, with coconuts for breasts and a wig that was in danger of slipping from my head. Many of the seats in the audience were empty, but enough were occupied to make me shiver. The faces loomed at me out of the dark. I realised that the girls were on the last line before the chorus and Monsieur Dargent was signalling to me. 'Now!' he mouthed.

I lifted my trembling leg to step onto the platform and ended up stumbling onto the stage. The brightness of the lights was a shock. I stood there, dazed, unsure of what I should do.

A man with a coarse voice roared with laughter. A woman cackled. My skin smouldered. I was sure my face was glowing. Another man joined in the laughter, but his voice held something besides mockery. Anticipation? Somehow that laugh loosened me and woke me from my stupor. 'Aloha! Aloha! Aloha!' I sang in a warbling voice that mimicked the chorus girls. At first I wasn't sure the voice was mine; it carried itself past the orchestra pit and echoed back to me, much fuller than the thin voices of the other girls. More people laughed and some started to clap. 'Aloha, Mademoiselle!' someone shouted. 'What next?'

I dared to look out at the audience. Two men in the front row were watching me with interest. I smiled at them and shimmied. The audience went wild. I didn't dance with any finesse, but the more the audience cheered and clapped, the more my body relaxed and the more wildly I jiggled. My self-consciousness vanished and I moved easily and gaily, bowing my legs and batting my eyelids, letting my arms and legs do whatever the music told them to. A thrill ran over my skin. Every face in the audience was looking at me.

We had been in such chaos before the number that no one had told me how to end the dance. I gyrated in a circle and when I faced the front again the chorus girls had left the stage. I threw my arms up in the air and posed like a statue, incongruous with the performance but a gesture of Camille's from her Egyptian number that had impressed me. The curtain came down and a tidal wave of applause burst from the audience. I ran off the stage, barely able to breathe.

Monsieur Dargent, Madame Tarasova, Albert and the others were waiting for me in the wing. Albert lifted me up, sat me on his shoulder and paraded me around. Monsieur Dargent was grinning from ear to ear. Madame Tarasova rushed forward and grabbed my cheeks. 'You know what you did is what every performer wishes for. You got them, Belle-Joie! *You got them!*'

FIVE

At my first dance rehearsal with Le Chat Espiègle I felt like an imposter. As part of my contract, I was to practise with the chorus girls each afternoon at two o'clock in the basement beneath the stage, except for Thursdays and Sundays when there was a matinée to perform. The room was kept locked and I sat on the dust-flecked stairs along with the other girls until Madame Baroux, the ballet mistress, arrived with Madame Dauphin, the accompanist. When she did, the girls scrambled from their slouched positions and I followed them. Only Claire and Ginette dragged themselves up with the listlessness of participants in a funeral procession, but if Madame Baroux noticed she didn't show it.

'*Bonjour*, ladies,' she sang out, leaning on her walking stick. She tugged a key on a piece of string from around her neck and pushed it into the locked door.

'*Bonjour*, Madame Baroux,' the girls answered, their voices ringing out like students in a convent.

Madame Baroux's eyes turned to me and she nodded. I assumed that Monsieur Dargent had explained who I was. The chorus girls were required to train every day to keep themselves supple, but that wasn't Monsieur Dargent's intention for me. He wanted me to understand what the girls were doing so I could mimic them on stage. Also, he wanted me to gain elementary dance training in case I was required for the next show or to fill in for someone who was sick. I had to earn my pay.

After several shoves, courtesy of Madame Dauphin's shoulder, the door creaked open and we trailed into the room after Madame Baroux. Madame Dauphin sat down at the piano and lifted the battered lid. She warmed her fingers on the keys with a tune that made me think of butterflies skimming over long grass. Her unkempt curls and floral dress were the antithesis of Madame Baroux, who wore her hair swept up with combs and kept any individuality tucked away beneath the crisp white blouse and crocheted shawl of an elderly Frenchwoman.

'Stretch!' Madame Baroux commanded, banging her stick on the parquet floor.

The girls threw themselves to the floor, transforming into a sea of sprawling limbs, their twisted figures doubled in mass on account of the mirrors that lined the basement walls. I dropped down too. The grit on the boards stuck to my palms and I brushed my hands down the sides of my tunic before studying what the girl in front of me, Jeanne, was doing.

'Like this,' Jeanne whispered, stretching out her leg and bending her chest towards her knee. Her mouth twisted and her cheeks turned red. I followed her example and, to my surprise, accomplished the pose without too much difficulty. I was congratulating myself when I felt Madame Baroux's stick tapping into the small of my back. 'Keep your spine straight. You are a dancer not a contortionist. All your movements must flow gracefully from your vertical axis.'

Although they were chorus girls and not ballerinas, most of the girls were experienced in classical dance. I was lost among them. What was I doing here? What *was* my vertical axis?

'Yes, Madame,' I said, correcting myself as best as I could. But when I glanced up, Madame Baroux had already moved on.

'Not much grace required in her act,' I heard someone in the front row mutter. I peered through the mass of headbands, tights and slips to see who it was. Claire? Paulette? Ginette? I may have saved the show, but that didn't mean that there wasn't resentment at someone from wardrobe being given a featured role.

'To the barre, ladies!' cried Madame Baroux. I looked up and saw that the rest of the class were waiting in position by a wooden railing along one of the walls. I trotted after them and took a place in the row. Madame Baroux sent me a grimace, barely passing it off as a smile.

'Arabesque,' she said.

I glanced at the girl next to me and extended my leg backwards in imitation. Madame Baroux moved along the line, pushing back shoulders and lifting hips. I gripped the splintery bar and imagined the vertebrae from my neck to my tailbone lined up like marbles. I held my leg steady, ignoring the burn in the back of my thighs. But Madame Baroux walked past without a glance in my direction. It wasn't that I was perfect; it was that I wasn't worth correcting.

'She looks like a baby in that get up,' Ginette whispered to Madeleine loud enough for me to hear. I compared their sleek jersey leotards to my calico tunic, pieced together from some cloth I'd brought with me from the farm. 'Well, she has been put in the show to make people laugh,' Madeleine giggled.

I bit my lip and fought back tears. Wasn't this what I had wanted — to be in the theatre? Yet I'd never felt more awkward, ugly or alone.

❧

The tension between me and the chorus girls came to a head some time later. We were crammed in the dressing room, getting ready for a performance. I had been allocated a spot in the back corner, squeezed between a painted-over window and a withered palm. It had been hot during the day, and although all the unbroken windows had been flung open there was still no breeze. Our costumes were due for laundering but Madame Tarasova was overrun and someone, possibly Marion, hadn't washed her feet since rehearsal. The air was loaded with a stomach-turning concoction of cologne, clammy skin and dank shoes. Only three of the ten bulbs on my mirror worked. It is just as well, I thought, shaking my head at the smears of colour above my eyes. I hadn't got the hang of make-up, although Madame Tarasova had done her best to teach me. I was trying to blend in the greasepaint at my jawline when Claudine pulled up a stool beside me.

'The show is going well because of you, Simone. I heard Monsieur Dargent say that he has just broken even,' she said.

I picked up my eyebrow pencil and nodded. I liked Claudine but I was wary of Claire, who sat behind me. She had taken Anne's place in the line and made no secret of the fact that she thought I was one person too many in the dressing room. No matter how careful I was, each time I pulled out my stool I seemed to knock the back of hers. 'Watch it!' she'd snap. 'If you tear my tights, you can pay the fine.'

Sure enough, she spun around now and growled at Claudine. 'The first act is terrible. It needs to be scrapped immediately!'

'Why?' asked Claudine, shifting her stool to face Claire. 'A new act would mean weeks of unpaid rehearsals.'

Marie glanced up from her mirror. 'It's unnecessary now anyway,' she said. 'Simone has saved the show. The audience numbers are up and last night we were filled to capacity.'

I bent down to fasten my anklets and avoid anyone's gaze. Everyone had been friendly to me when I was a dresser, but getting a role in the show had changed things. The girls were divided in their opinions of me. Claudine, Marie, Jeanne and Marion, who treated their role in the chorus line as a job, were happy to have me join their act because it meant they didn't have to be away from their children to rehearse a new one. But some of the other girls, like Claire, Paulette, Ginette and Madeleine, had ambition. They wanted to be stars, and I was a threat.

Claire wrinkled her nose. 'Bah!' she huffed, dismissing Marie with a wave of her hand. 'The numbers are up because the Bastille Day celebrations are over and people are looking for something to do.' Some of the other girls murmured their agreement.

'I think we should speak to Monsieur Dargent after the show,' said Paulette, wrapping her greasepaint-stained gown around her shoulders. 'The audience comes because they want to see beautiful girls dancing. Simone makes us look like fools.'

'You spoke to Monsieur Dargent last week,' tittered Claudine. 'And he fixed the problem by hiring Simone.' She patted my shoulder and beamed at me. I knew that she meant well but wished she would stop. 'And what's more,' she said, 'he is so pleased with Simone, he's thinking of putting her name on the billing for the show.'

The hum of voices in the room ceased. All eyes turned to Claudine. No one looked at me.

'It's true,' Marie said, rouging her cheeks. 'I heard him talking about it with the cashier yesterday. People have been asking if this is the show "with the funny girl in it".'

Paulette turned back to her mirror and tore her brush through her hair. Madeleine and Ginette exchanged a look.

'If she gets her own billing, I'm out of here,' said Claire, hunching her skinny shoulders. 'She's nothing more than a dresser. She won't last long on the stage. It's not enough to behave like an idiot. You have to be able to dance.'

'She's no beauty either,' said Madeleine, her nose in the air.

I stood up and rushed to the door, stepping over slippers and bags. Once in the safety of the hall, I dabbed my forehead with the back of my wrist and leaned against the balustrade. The nastiness of the chorus girls had bruised my confidence. Perhaps they were right and I wasn't cut out for the theatre.

But my mood changed the moment the stage bell rang. I rushed down the stairs to take my place in the wing. I could sense the audience before I saw them: the air was charged. The voices of the men and women entering the hall buzzed and crackled like sparks of static electricity before a storm. I pressed my hand against the rear wall to ground myself. The building itself seemed to be pulsating. Tonight was going to be a full house.

A drum roll echoed around the hall. The orchestra struck up the opening number and my foot stroked the ground in time with the Hawaiian guitars. I no longer needed Monsieur Dargent to time me in; I knew my cue by heart. At the end of the second verse I leapt onto the stage and into the lights. The crowd screamed and applauded.

'Aloha! Aloha! Aloha!'

My voice rang out above those of the other girls' even more than usual. It had become stronger from nightly practice. I was able to force the sound out further without losing the tone. Claire's shrill soprano struggled to reach over my part but she couldn't sustain it and dance at the same time. I scanned the audience, an ocean of transfixed faces. I forgot about Madame Baroux's pinched-faced admonitions to watch my 'vertical axis' and wiggled my hips and swung my legs out in all directions. The audience roared and applauded. Their laughter rolled towards the stage like a wave breaking on the beach. In an instant, the whole front row leapt to its feet and cheered. 'Bravo, Mademoiselle Fleurier! Bravo!'

They knew my name? Butterflies trembled in the pit of my stomach. The vibration travelled up through my chest and flowed out my fingertips. 'Aloha! Aloha! Aloha!' I sang, with all the power my lungs could give me.

'Only two weeks and you are already a hit!' Madame Tarasova cried when I came offstage. 'You've taken to the music hall like a duck to water. You're a natural!'

'We miss you down here,' said Vera, taking my wig from me.

'I'll get changed then come straight down, all right?' I told her, turning towards the stairs. 'Monsieur Dargent wants me to help you until he has more parts for me in the next show.'

I raced up the stairs to the dressing room but stopped short when I saw the mess outside the door. I stood dazed for a moment, staring at the make-up brushes and pencils scattered there. A rouge jar lay tipped on its side, a block of mascara had been crushed to a greasy pulp on the floorboards and rice powder was sprinkled over everything like snow. A dressing table and cracked mirror were propped against the wall. I gaped at the destruction for a few seconds before I realised that the objects were mine.

I crouched down to pick up the cosmetics and noticed that the rose-bud kimono I had inherited from Anne was wedged in the door. I tugged at it, but it was stuck and wouldn't budge unless I asked one of the girls to help me. Someone giggled and shadows moved in the wedge of light from the crack under the door. I imagined Claire and her accomplices watching me through the keyhole, congratulating themselves on their cleverness. I let go of the gown; I would rather come back for it than give them any satisfaction by begging for it.

I picked up the rouge bottle and cleaned up the rest of the mess as best I could, wiping the containers with the fringe of my grass skirt. Madame Tarasova had scraped together my make-up kit from lost and odd items that she had collected over the years. I was relieved to find the powder container was still half-full. I left the mascara; it was ruined and I couldn't afford to replace it. If I complained to Monsieur Dargent those responsible would have their pay docked for disruptive behaviour. But if I did that, it would make the bullying worse. And there were more chorus girls against me than for me.

I scooped up the collection of spoiled cosmetics and looked around the corner. Down the hall, near the lavatories, was an alcove.

The urine smell from the toilets was rank, but the alcove itself was clean and it had a frosted skylight as well as an electric light. I dragged my table and mirror there and arranged what was left of my make-up on the bench.

'Well, Simone, it's good to see you are making friends.'

I glanced in the cracked mirror to see Camille standing behind me, dressed in a tunic for her Helen of Troy number.

'Welcome to show business,' she went on.

I kept my face turned to the mirror. I didn't want her to see me cry.

She put her hand on my shoulder and squinted. 'Who taught you to do your make-up?'

'Madame Tarasova showed me some things and I've been copying the others.'

'Your face looks like a map of the world.'

My hand flew to my cheek. I knew that as much as I had tried, I hadn't quite achieved the art of blending colours. I was glad that the audience didn't see me up close.

'Come on,' said Camille, tossing her head in the direction of her dressing room. 'I've got fifteen minutes. I'll show you how to do it properly.'

Camille's dressing room was cluttered with beautiful things along with some grotty ones. A lopsided cane chair sat next to a polished rosewood bureau and a Persian rug crisscrossed with a grubby cotton one on the sloping floor. The daybed was covered with Spanish shawls while the dressing table was littered with perfume bottles without stoppers. My nose twitched from the smell of the room: a concoction of incense, dust and bath soap.

Camille sat me on her sateen-covered stool and wiped at the slick of greasepaint that had gathered around my chin and nostrils. It was easy to see the mistakes in her brightly lit mirror. My eyeliner departed my lashes at different angles on each lid and my mouth sloped to the side. Another shade darker on the face and a shade lighter under my eyes and I would have looked like one of the 'blacked-up' jazz singers from America.

'Look,' said Camille, tugging my hair back into a scarf and dabbing at my face, 'you need to take your greasepaint right up to your hairline and back over your ears so there's no edge. And even though you've got olive skin, you need to use something darker. Everything washes out under the lights.'

I glanced up at Camille. The charcoal around her eyes brought out their blueness. Her greasepaint blended with her skin and the red on her lips was smooth. The colours enhanced nature. She looked as perfect as a piece of waxed fruit in a bowl. I shifted on the stool self-consciously. Why couldn't I look like that?

Camille flipped open her cosmetic box and hunted through its contents. 'Here,' she said, holding up a pot of pearly cream. She opened the lid and smeared the substance under my eyebrows and lower lashes. 'Always highlight your assets and downplay your faults,' she said, patting out the two circles of rouge that I had applied to my cheeks and replacing them with sweeps of colour along my cheekbones. She wiped her powder puff on the back of her hand and patted it over my face. 'Humans are only animals with clothes,' she said. 'When those girls pick on someone, they are either trying to eliminate the weakest beast in the herd or scare away a new member they consider a threat.'

I fingered the violet that sat in a saucer on her dressing table. 'Are you from Marseilles?' I asked her. Camille was blonde and fine-featured like a northerner. No one at Le Chat Espiègle knew very much about her. She had a reputation for keeping to herself and never talking about what she had done before she joined the theatre.

Camille let out an exasperated sigh. 'You're a busybody,' she said. 'Now look up so I can get those clumps off your eyelashes.'

I did as I was told and she brushed my lashes with a tiny comb. 'How's that?' she said, turning my head towards the mirror. I looked like a doll in a shop window with long lashes and Cupid's bow lips.

'Thank you,' I said, not so much thanking Camille for the make-up as for five minutes of her kindness; as a young girl on my own I needed it.

Camille nodded. 'Don't be a weak animal, Simone,' she said. 'My mother was a weak animal. That's why she let my father beat her before working her to death.'

I wondered why Camille had confided that in me. Perhaps she was tired of her rich suitors and the 'stage-door Johnnys' who hounded her every night after the show.

⌘

Camille must have told Monsieur Dargent what had happened because the following evening I was moved to dressing room number three. The room was occupied by Fabienne Boyer, the show's buxom *chanteuse*, and acrobats Violetta and Luisa Zo-Zo. It was divided down the centre by a row of oriental screens and a piece of lattice, and we had to be careful not to slam the door otherwise the whole flimsy construction would collapse. Fabienne dressed on one side of the barrier, and the Zo-Zo sisters and I on the other. On the rare occasions we were all in the dressing room at once, it was a congenial atmosphere. Violetta and Luisa were sometimes solemn before their act but chatty afterwards, and Bonbon was welcome to sit in her basket by the door whenever she wasn't with Madame Tarasova in the wardrobe area.

'The audience is *fantastico*!' the Zo-Zo sisters would announce, bursting into the dressing room. I found the red welts on their palms and the backs of their legs unnerving, but the rope burns didn't bother them. They wiped the sweat off with towels and rubbed an olive oil and lavender salve into their skin.

'It's because it's the tourist season we have such a large audience,' Fabienne told us through the lattice. The division had been her idea, but it wasn't because of haughtiness on her part. Rather, she had made it out of consideration for us because she received so many visitors. The screens didn't stop sound though, and the Zo-Zo sisters and I would have to stifle our laughter when Fabienne practised her warm-up exercises. 'Ma ... Me ... Mi ... Mo ... Mu. Maaa ... Meee ... Miii ... Mooo ... Muuu ...'

The only quality her squeaky voice possessed was an ability to stay reasonably in tune, but no one came to see Fabienne for her singing. It was her pert face and fabulous figure that drew the crowds. Flat-chested flappers may have been the rage in women's fashion, but men drooled over her 38–28–40 figure. Her dressing table was always covered with flowers.

While the conversation Fabienne's callers made was discreet — 'Mademoiselle Boyer, your appearance on stage fills my heart with joy, you are magnificent' — there was something presumptuous about the men that made my skin crawl. They would bid Fabienne good evening, kiss her hand and swagger to the door, turning for a final bow, always with a glint in their eyes that made me think of wolves. A few minutes later, Fabienne would feign a yawn and say that she was going home.

'They will be coming for you soon, Simone,' Fabienne said one evening, squirting her lilac perfume into the air. It was her polite way of camouflaging the onion-tinged smell of sweat that the Zo-Zo girls brought back with them.

I thanked Fabienne for her encouragement although the attention of men wasn't first in my mind. I wasn't a prude. I'd been born on a farm and, unlike the stories the English chorus girls told us, my parents had never forbidden me to be in the fields when the animals were mating. I had always known 'the facts of life'. But the story about Madeleine being forced to have an abortion, and the idea of having my fate pegged to the whims of a man, filled me with terror. If that was the cost of being with the opposite sex, I didn't want it.

Nevertheless, I had a desire running in my veins as strong as sex. Each night I lusted for the sound of the audience's applause, and was not satiated until I had received at least two encores. I was about to turn fifteen but I already knew what I wanted in life — and it wasn't to be a second-rate comedian chorus girl. If I couldn't be a great stage beauty, then at least I could be a famous singer.

❧

On the second-last night of the 'On the Seas' show, I came off stage to see Camille peeking out from behind an artificial palm in the stairwell. 'Meet me in my dressing room,' she said, sweeping the edge of her tunic into her arms and disappearing like a goddess who has given her command.

I tramped up the stairs, narrowly missing Claude the magician who was negotiating his way down them, his bird cage balanced in one hand and a card table tucked under the other arm. I waited in my dressing room until I heard Camille humming in the corridor and the sound of her latch clicking. I had no idea what we were being so secretive about.

'Come,' she said, waving me inside when I knocked on her door. She shut it behind me and I stopped short. For a moment I thought we were standing in someone else's dressing room. There was nothing of Camille's usual clutter: no underwear draped over chairs; no feathers and shoes scattered across the floor; no strings of beads and scarves tumbling from the dressing table drawers. The only item of clothing visible was a crimson dress hanging on the armoire door.

'You've tidied up,' I said, noticing the suitcase beside the dressing table.

Camille turned to where I was looking. 'Oh that,' she said. 'I always like to pack things away at the end of a run. Then I pull everything out again on the opening night of the new show.'

I nodded. Every performer had a superstitious ritual. Mine was to kiss the locket holding my parents' photograph before I went on stage. Fabienne crossed herself before her act, and the Zo-Zo sisters slapped their hands and stomped their feet. Albert once told me that the impresario Samuel 'The Magnificent' turned up to opening nights in a moth-eaten hat and with a two-day growth. He thought that dressing for the occasion would bring the company bad luck. Our lives were so precarious that some sort of ritual was necessary for a sense of stability.

The muffled voice of the male singer, Marcel Sorel, penetrated the wall. He was talking to Monsieur Dargent. 'In the next show I want the last slot in the first act,' he said.

'Why?' asked Monsieur Dargent. 'Do you have an engagement at another music hall? That is breaking your contract.'

Camille lowered her voice. 'Listen, Simone, Monsieur Gosling wanted me to ask you to have dinner with us tomorrow night.'

'Me?'

'Yes,' she said. 'He's very taken with your act and wants to meet you.'

'Me?'

'We'll be dining at Nevers.'

Camille had meant to entice me but her words had the opposite effect. Nevers was one of the finest restaurants in Marseilles. I had a vision of the elegantly dressed women I'd seen in the restaurants along the Canebière when I used to walk Bonbon there.

'What's wrong, Simone?' she asked. 'If you want to be a success it's not enough to perform on stage. You have to mingle with the right people. People who can help you.'

Although I found it hard to believe that Monsieur Gosling had any interest in me, it was my clothes that were worrying me. I didn't have a dress good enough for church, let alone Nevers. I glanced down at my feet and Camille threw back her head and laughed.

'Is that the problem?' She walked to her armoire and grabbed the crimson dress. 'You can have this. I'm tired of it anyway. And I've got shoes to match. You can stretch them if they're too small.'

I remembered the dress Aunt Yvette had intended to make for me. The material for that had gone over the side of the Gorges de la Nesque with my father. Despite my enthusiasm for the theatre, not a day went by when I didn't miss him or think about my mother, Aunt Yvette and Bernard. I worried whether the lavender cultivation was succeeding and how my mother was faring under Uncle Gerome's control. Camille mistook my sadness for stubbornness.

'What is it now?' she asked, folding the dress over my arm. 'Nevers. A pretty dress. Dinner at the invitation of the heir to one of the largest Marseilles soap fortunes.'

'Why are you being so secretive about it?' I asked.

Camille arched an eyebrow. 'Because I thought you had caused enough jealousy around here.'

She didn't sound convincing, but I owed her a favour for being kind to me when the chorus girls had kicked me out of their dressing room, so I agreed to go.

⟨⟨⟩⟩

The following night, Camille greeted the doorman at Nevers with a wave of her hand and a shrug of her shoulder, and paused in the entranceway between two urns of ferns. I stood behind her, feeling more like a thief than a customer. I'd washed my hair and scrubbed my face, but even in Camille's dress I didn't feel up to the atmosphere. The light from the gas lamps bounced off the crystal glasses and silver cutlery. Women with jewels in their hair sat opposite men with gardenias in their buttonholes. At first I thought we must be waiting for the *maître d'hôtel*, but even after he had welcomed us Camille lingered long enough to catch the eye of every man in the room. When she was sure she had their attention, she nodded to the *maître d'hôtel* and strutted to the table where Monsieur Gosling sat smoking. He snuffed out his cigarette and jumped to his feet.

'This is Mademoiselle Fleurier,' Camille said, easing herself into the chair the *maître d'hôtel* pulled out for her.

Monsieur Gosling kissed my hand, then turned back to Camille. 'How was tonight's performance, *ma chérie*? I am sorry I missed it, but I had arrangements to make.'

Camille flashed him a smile and rested her fingers on his wrist. She was more interested in him than she had been the first night I had seen them outside Le Chat Espiègle.

'Simone gave a good performance tonight,' she said.

'Really?' said Monsieur Gosling, swivelling towards me. 'I've never seen the first act. I can never make it that early to the show.'

I glanced at Camille but if she was aware that she had been contradicted, she didn't show it. 'This is a nice place, isn't it, Simone?' she said.

A waiter brought us an *apéritif* of white wine and cassis. Camille lit a cigarette and passed it to Monsieur Gosling.

'We should have the bouillabaisse,' he said, before embarking on a lecture about Marseilles' signature dish and how no two people could agree on how to prepare it. 'Our cook insists the secret is white wine,' he said. 'But my grandmother throws up her hands in horror at that suggestion.'

Camille rested her chin in her hand, seemingly fascinated with Monsieur Gosling's speech, while I did my best not to yawn. What was I doing here, stuck between the edge of the table and a bust of Julius Caesar? Maybe Camille had wanted my company to make the time spent with the drivelling Monsieur Gosling bearable.

I was relieved when the waiter brought the bouillabaisse, although it wasn't what I had expected. I examined the mix of seafood perched in a pool of orange sauce. From Monsieur Gosling's description I'd thought it was a soup or a broth, but the dish was not either. Apart from the whiting and mussels, I didn't recognise the other seafood, even the fish that had been served with its head still attached. But when I breathed in the steamy aroma of fish, saffron, olive oil and garlic, my stomach rumbled in anticipation. I lifted my knife and fork and sliced a piece of fish.

A waiter strutted past and raised his eyebrows. I realised that I was slouched over my food while Camille and Monsieur Gosling sat with their spines pressed against the backs of their chairs and their faces far away from their plates. I jolted upright and a piece of fish smothered in sauce dropped from my fork onto the tablecloth. I dabbed at it with my serviette but the ochre stain spread out further and now I had a soiled serviette as well. I peeked at Camille and Monsieur Gosling, but they hadn't noticed. They were gazing into each other's eyes.

'I have good news, Simone,' Camille announced when the waiter brought the cheese and fruit. 'Tomorrow Monsieur Gosling and I are leaving for Paris.'

'Paris?' I almost choked on a cracker.

'Monsieur Gosling is setting me up in Paris with an apartment and a couture wardrobe,' Camille beamed. 'I'm going to star at the Eldorado.'

'But what about the new show at Le Chat Espiègle?' I asked. 'Rehearsals start tomorrow.'

Because 'On the Seas' had made a profit, Monsieur Dargent planned a more lavish show for the next season. I knew he had spent a fortune on the glittering costumes Madame Tarasova and Vera were working on. I also knew that he was counting on Camille Casal to be his star.

Camille's smile faded for a second. She rubbed her arms. 'How could I tell him?' she said. 'He gave me a start. But Paris ...' Her eyes lit up again. 'That's where you go if you want to be a star. The Adriana, the Folies Bergère, the Casino de Paris, the Eldorado. I can't stay in Marseilles, Simone. But every time I tried to tell Monsieur Dargent, I couldn't bring myself to do it.'

A niggling doubt about the truth of Camille's words prickled me but I ignored it. I couldn't resent her wanting to go to Paris. It was the place everybody said you had to go if you wanted to be a real star. But I was worried about what Camille's departure meant for the rest of us. Monsieur Dargent might have to cancel the show.

'He'll find someone else,' she said. 'Believe me, he's good at it.' She reached into her purse, pulled out an envelope and pushed it towards me. 'I trust you with this, Simone. It tells him everything that is in my heart and begs his forgiveness. When he gets this letter from me, he will understand.'

I breathed a sigh of relief. So Camille *had* given Monsieur Dargent's feelings some thought.

'You will give it to him, won't you, Simone? And not until tomorrow?'

'Yes, of course,' I said.

I should have known something was wrong. The warning was there in the way the shoes Camille had given me pinched my toes and rubbed my heels, and the look in Fabienne's eye when I passed her on the steps of Le Chat Espiègle.

'You weren't at the cast party last night,' she said, glancing over my dress. I wondered if she recognised it as Camille's.

'Cast party?'

'At the end of a run there is always a party. Everybody was there, except for you and Camille.'

I hadn't known anything about a party. Why hadn't Camille mentioned it?

'Well, next time make sure you go,' Fabienne sniffed. 'It doesn't look right if you run off with Camille and snub the others.'

It was hot inside the theatre. The walls of Le Chat Espiègle had a way of absorbing and retaining heat that was phenomenal. I wiped at the droplets of sweat on my neck. It was the first time I'd noticed how splotched the wallpaper in the foyer was from water seepage. The whole crumbling structure was riddled with cracks and the carpet reeked of mould. The cashier sat in her booth, stamping tickets for the next show. The fan in the metal cage on the cupboard was turned off. 'The stupid thing blows the tickets around if I turn it on,' she complained. I asked her where Monsieur Dargent was and she cocked her head towards the auditorium. 'With the stage manager, planning out the new show.'

The doors to the auditorium were propped open. A murmur of men's voices floated out from the darkness. A light on the stage was beaming towards the doors and I had to squint past it to see inside. Monsieur Dargent was leaning against the stage telling Monsieur Vaimber something about the lighting. My shoes clicked on the floorboards. Monsieur Dargent broke off mid-sentence and looked up. His eyes met mine and he relaxed. I had the impression that he had been expecting someone else.

'Yes? What is it?'

'Mademoiselle Casal asked me to give you this,' I said, holding out the envelope.

Monsieur Dargent regarded me for a moment and his brow furrowed. 'Bring it here,' he said. The uneasy expression returned to his eyes.

I shuffled down the aisle towards him. Monsieur Vaimber turned around to see what was happening.

'When did she give you this?' Monsieur Dargent asked, snatching the letter from me.

I clenched my toes. 'Last night.'

'Where?'

I wondered why he didn't just open the envelope instead of asking me so many questions. 'At Nevers.'

Monsieur Dargent glanced at Monsieur Vaimber, then hooked his finger under the flap and ripped open the envelope. I watched him unfold the paper and read it. It couldn't have been more than a few sentences long from the speed with which he finished it.

'What does it say?' asked Monsieur Vaimber.

Monsieur Dargent thrust the paper at me. 'Read it out to him!' he said. I took the letter and stared at it for a few seconds before I could bring myself to believe what it said or, more precisely, *all* that it said:

> *Off to bigger and better things.*
> *Au revoir*
> *C.*

'There must be something more,' I said. 'She promised a full explanation.' I took the envelope from him and searched inside it. But there was nothing.

Monsieur Dargent hissed. 'Camille has been trying to get out of her contract for a while now. I told her that she could go after this next show. And she promised me that she would stay. This is a disaster. I have no star.'

Monsieur Vaimber looked down his nose at me. 'It seems you knew about this?'

'No!' I said, clenching my fists. 'Not until last night. That was the first I'd heard that she was going to Paris.'

'You should have come straight to me last night,' said Monsieur Dargent. 'Not waited until the middle of the day. Don't you know what this means? It means we don't have a show.'

Despite his warning that without a star there wouldn't be a show, Monsieur Dargent didn't call off the afternoon rehearsal. Instead, he waited for everyone to assemble in the auditorium before clambering up onto the stage, running his hands through his hair and announcing that Camille Casal had abandoned the show. A gasp ran along the chorus line and came to an abrupt stop with Claire, who folded her arms across her chest and snickered.

'You find that amusing, do you, Claire?' Monsieur Dargent asked.

She shrugged. 'Camille wasn't *that* magnificent. You can find another person to do what she did.'

Monsieur Dargent scrunched up his face. In his white suits and coloured shirts, he usually looked like a dandy, if a little worn down at the heel. But on this occasion, with his hair standing out in two cones because he kept running his hands through it, he looked like a crazed dandy.

'The only solution, besides cancelling the show, is to entice someone with "a name" from another show. And for that I need money. Will you still think it is so amusing when I have to skim that money off everybody's wages?'

Claire's face dropped. A murmur ran through the group.

'You can't do that,' said Madeleine. 'We've got contracts.'

'I've learned that they don't mean much,' said Monsieur Dargent, sounding more hurt than angry now. 'Which do you want more — a contract or a job?'

Although Monsieur Dargent didn't mention my association with Camille's betrayal, I noticed the looks the others were casting at my dress. It wouldn't take long before they started to put a picture together. The thought of their already pathetic wages being cut soured the atmosphere, which was foul enough with the benzene stink of the cleaned costumes and the paint the artists were using to create the backdrops for the next show.

I watched Monsieur Dargent storm out of the auditorium. I was furious at Camille for turning me into her stooge, but even more angry with myself for letting her. Why had she invited me to Nevers? She could have left the envelope in her dressing room. Or was she worried somebody would find it *before* she left for Paris? Camille's departure couldn't have come at a worse time because I needed Monsieur Dargent and the cast on side. True to his word, Monsieur Dargent had given me more parts in the new show which was based around the story of Scheherazade. I appeared in five of the seven chorus acts, and even had a vaguely glamorous role in the pantomime as a reclining odalisque in the Palace of Shah Shahryar. I was sufficiently employed not to have to work as a dresser, and Monsieur Dargent had hired a mulatto seamstress to replace me. But what I really wanted to ask him for was a singing part.

'Simone!' Gilles, the choreographer, called out to me. 'Join the chorus girls on stage and I'll walk you through your routine.'

I made my way up onto the stage. Gilles had been Camille's dance partner in a *pas de deux* in 'On the Seas'. He was nineteen years old with skin as smooth as chocolate. All the girls swooned over him, even though he preferred the company of the male members of the cast and crew.

The opening number was set in a harem. The chorus would perform the dance of the 'seven veils' — or Gilles' interpretation of it — dropping each veil to eventually appear in sheer harem pants and jewelled satin brassieres. My comic role was to shimmy along with them in the beginning, but to have one continuous veil which I could never quite unravel. Claude had used his magic skills to create the required prop: a bolt of silk hidden in the trunk of a palm tree with one end wound around me, giving the appearance that the more I tugged the veil, the more material appeared. Monsieur Dargent thought the idea so amusing that he had scripted me to appear in several scenes afterwards, including an intimate one between Scheherazade and the Shah, still trying to unravel my veil.

'At first you must look like a regular chorus girl, Simone,' Gilles said. 'But then ... with your eyes and a little twist of your mouth, you give a signal that all is not right.'

Gilles shimmied and gyrated his way through the routine, stopping every so often to point out something of importance. 'If you roll your shoulders at the same time as you snake your arms, it is more sensuous.' He looked feminine when he danced, although his bare chest and back were muscular.

'Okay, now you try and I'll watch,' he said, wiping the sweat from his forehead with the back of his hand. He nodded to Madame Dauphin who began an oriental tune on the tinny rehearsal piano.

We moved in time to the music and Gilles flittered among us, calling out directions and correcting our positions. I imagined how the music would sound with the pipes and drums of an Arabian orchestra and let my limbs and torso flow with the rhythms and arcs the music suggested.

'Nice,' Gilles whispered in my ear. 'You're a natural dancer.'

If only Madame Baroux could hear him say that, I thought.

The doors to the foyer slammed open, sending a shudder through the hall and loosing a sprinkle of plaster from the ceiling. Madame

Dauphin froze on a chord and the chorus girls stopped mid-twirl. The figure of Monsieur Dargent loomed like a phantom against the daylight from the foyer. Even from where I was standing I could see that his face was red.

'Scandal!' he shouted, his voice echoing around the space. He held up a newspaper in his fist. 'SCANDAL!'

Claire glared at me. I held her gaze. I may have delivered Camille's bad news but I had nothing to do with any scandal. And yet a niggling feeling in my stomach told me that if something dreadful wasn't going to happen to me, it was certainly going to happen to someone else.

'Simone Fleurier!' Monsieur Dargent shouted. 'Step forward so I can see you!'

I froze to the spot at the sound of my name, but the cast shuffled to the sides so that Monsieur Dargent was looking at me down a human corridor, like Moses standing before the opening of the Red Sea.

'Have you seen this?' he asked, brandishing a copy of *Le Petit Provençal*. I shook my head. He unfolded the newspaper so I could see the front-page headlines:

Heir to Soap Fortune Runs Away With Music Hall Star
Steals Family Jewels
Lovers Helped by Comedian Chorus Girl

'I did no such thing,' I protested.

'Shh!' said Monsieur Dargent. He began reading the article in a theatrical voice.

As well as withdrawing money from his trust account, Monsieur Gosling stole a diamond necklace, bracelet and tiara from his mother's jewellery collection, claiming in his farewell letter that he would destroy the heirlooms if his family attempted to stop him. It appears that the heir to the Marseilles soap fortune intends to put the full force of his wealth behind helping Mademoiselle Casal launch herself in Paris. According to diners at the exclusive restaurant Nevers, the couple was not acting alone. A young girl, believed to be the comedian chorus girl from Le Chat Espiègle, Simone Fleurier, seems to have assisted the couple in their flight. They have been dubbed 'The Romeo and Juliet of Marseilles' for defying the Gosling family and finding true love in each other's arms.

Laughter sounded throughout the auditorium. I felt a lump in my throat and couldn't have spoken even if I had thought of something to say. The Romeo and Juliet of Marseilles? Camille was using Monsieur Gosling.

'Fire Simone!' Claire screeched. 'Before she ruins the rest of the show.'

'Good riddance,' agreed Paulette. 'She has been nothing but a nuisance from the beginning!'

Monsieur Dargent knitted his brows. 'Fire her? Are you insane? This is a SCANDAL! And do you know what a scandal means? PUBLICITY!'

Six

―――

It is one thing to get your name on the billing because you have earned it with your talent; and quite another for it to be there because you have been involved in a scandal. Each time I saw my name on Le Chat Espiègle's billboard, I cringed. Monsieur Dargent had created a new role for me: I played a handmaiden who helped Scheherazade's younger sister and the Shah's brother to elope. The characters, played by Fabienne and Gilles, risked their lives for love in the mood of misogyny and terror that the Shah had unleashed in the palace, and they turned to a handmaiden to help them escape. 'Just as she helped "The Romeo and Juliet of Marseilles" in real life,' the publicity read. I was interviewed by *Le Petit Provençal* and, with Monsieur Dargent twisting my arm, went along with the story that I had assisted in the love tryst.

My unearned billing made me more determined to speak to Monsieur Dargent about a singing part. After the first rehearsal of the pantomime sketch with Gilles and Fabienne, I caught him before he left the auditorium.

'Can I speak with you?' I whispered, glancing over my shoulder.

Fabienne and Gilles were still on stage, discussing some changes to their blocking. Paulette and Madeleine were near the wing, heads close together, gossiping. They hadn't been required in the skit but had hung around from the earlier chorus line rehearsal. Paulette looked up and glared at me. I turned back to Monsieur Dargent. I would have preferred to wait until everyone had left, but with the show going into production I needed to speak to him as soon as possible.

'What is it?' he asked.

'Have you found a Scheherazade yet?'

He tucked his notes under his arm and fiddled with his cravat. 'I am going to Nice tomorrow to see someone. Why? Have you heard from Camille?'

I drew a breath. 'No, I'd like to try out for the part.'

Monsieur Dargent shook his head. 'I don't have understudies in this show. I can't afford them. And everyone is fully occupied.'

'I meant for *the part*.'

Monsieur Dargent frowned and ran his finger down the side of his nose. I was taking the chance that he would at least humour me. I wasn't expecting to get the role of Scheherazade; I was trying for a chance to show him what I could do and perhaps get a solo singing part. I hoped that if he liked my voice he would give me Fabienne's role and let her play Scheherazade, but I had become savvy enough to know that if I asked to try out for her role directly, it would only cause trouble.

Monsieur Dargent reached into his pocket and glanced at his watch. 'Go and find Madame Dauphin,' he said. 'Pick a couple of songs and I'll be back here at four o'clock to listen to them.'

I wiped my palms on my tunic. 'Thank you, Monsieur Dargent,' I said. 'Thank you!'

The news of my having approached Monsieur Dargent for the lead part spread throughout the cast in minutes. On the way to see Madame Dauphin, I passed the chorus girls' dressing room and overheard Claire say to the others, 'Simone is getting too big for her boots. I'd like to fix her.' I hated the bitchiness of backstage life. After I had been given a billing for the show, even Jeanne had stopped speaking to me. Such was the jealousy and insecurity of our lives. Only Marie, with her rosy cheeks and effusive charm, remained friendly.

'Good luck,' she said, slipping into the hallway when she saw me heading down the stairs. 'I can't stay after the rehearsal to watch you but I know you'll do well.'

Madame Dauphin was waiting for me in the room under the stage.

She opened a satchel and dumped a pile of sheet music on the floor. 'Take your pick,' she said. 'Whatever you think you'd be good at.'

I bent down to examine the pile. 'I can't read music,' I told her, shooing away a beetle that had fallen out with the mess of paper. 'Perhaps you can help me choose?'

'Oh?' Madame Dauphin said, squinting at me over the top of her pince-nez. I didn't let her tone of disapproval discourage me. I knew that Fabienne and Marcel couldn't read music either and that they learned everything by ear. Madame Dauphin took a folder from the top of the piano and shuffled through the song sheets. 'I'll choose something from the score then,' she said, flicking through the music for 'Scheherazade'. 'We will try two numbers. One upbeat and one slow, so you can show your range.'

I listened to the first number, and joined in as soon as I understood the melody. My voice resonated in the empty basement. It sounded clear and pretty. But Madame Dauphin didn't compliment me; in fact, she showed no expression the entire rehearsal.

Who cares? I told myself. I won't let her put me off.

I was pleased with my performance and after an hour left to attend the chorus line rehearsal with Gilles, confident that I would impress Monsieur Dargent with my audition. I tried to keep my thoughts from straying while Gilles took us through the harem routine until he was satisfied that we rolled our hips and undulated our stomachs with ease. 'You're as stiff as a corpse,' he said to Claire, who screwed up her nose at him as soon as he turned his back.

At four o'clock the dance rehearsal ended and Monsieur Dargent made his way into the hall with Monsieur Vambier. They slipped into seats in the second row. Madame Dauphin turned around and nodded to them. She shuffled through her notebook on top of the piano and unfolded it at the first song we had rehearsed that afternoon. Monsieur Dargent took out his watch and placed it on his knee. I glanced around the room. To my dismay, the other girls showed no sign of leaving. Madeleine, Ginette and Paulette took seats a few rows behind Monsieur Dargent and whispered to each other behind their hands. I wondered why Monsieur Dargent didn't send them away. Perhaps he wanted to see how I performed in front of an audience.

'Whenever you are ready, Simone,' Monsieur Dargent called out.

Even on that first night, when I was pushed on stage for the Hawaiian number, I hadn't felt as nervous as I did now. I didn't have anything to lose then. The stakes were higher this time: if I failed the audition I wasn't likely to be allowed to try again.

Madame Dauphin ripped into the song's introduction without waiting to see if I was ready. She played it an octave higher than the one we had practised in and I had no choice but to start singing:

> It's up to me — don't be frightened
> It's up to me — I'll bewitch him
> It's up to me — I can do it . . .

In the wrong key, my voice sounded tight. I strained to lift it higher. I'd planned to give the song a warm, sweet tone. Instead, I was singing like a shrill bird. But Monsieur Dargent didn't appear displeased. He was leaning forward, studying me. If I get through this okay, I thought, he might let me try it again in the right key.

Madeleine and Paulette sank lower into their seats and giggled. I did my best not to let them intimidate me. Monsieur Vaimber was staring at the ceiling. But that wasn't a bad sign; if he didn't like me, he would have stopped me before now. My body loosened and my confidence increased.

> Other girls have gone to their deaths — but not me
> I'm stronger
> Other girls have lost their heads — not me
> I'm smarter
> He might be the ruler
> But I am a woman.

The curtain in the wing next to me fluttered. I thought it was the breeze, then lost concentration for a moment when I saw Claire lurking in the opening. She was in full view of me but hidden from the audience. 'You won't get it,' she muttered, just loud enough for me to hear. 'You're awful and you're as skinny as a bean.'

Irritation swept over me but I resolved to carry on. If I stopped the number, Claire might get in trouble but it would end my audition too. Monsieur Vaimber was a stickler for continuing to sing no matter what. 'Performers need to know how to hold the attention of a hostile audience as well as a friendly one,' he often said. Le Chat Espiègle certainly had its share of hostile audiences. Even towards the end of its run, when 'On the Seas' had full houses, the success of the show didn't stop rowdy hecklers throwing cigarette butts and programs rolled into missiles at the chorus girls. But Monsieur Vaimber made it clear that we were to go on despite the hooting and catcalls.

A burning sensation seared my throat and my eyes watered. I tried to blink away whatever it was that was irritating them. A stinging vapour filled the air. Through my blurry vision I saw Claire pouring something from a bottle onto the floor. It ran towards my feet in an oily line. In the heat, the smell was noxious: ammonia. My hand flew to my mouth and I missed a beat. I tried to take in enough air to complete the chorus but I couldn't breathe. My voice went off key. Monsieur Vaimber shook his head and Monsieur Dargent frowned. I tried to struggle on but it was no use. The blood pounded so loudly in my ears that I could barely hear the music.

I was on the verge of crying when I reached the final chord. But before I could catch my breath, Madame Dauphin launched into the next number. Monsieur Dargent held up his hand. 'I think that's enough for today,' he said.

'But Monsieur Dargent,' I gulped. 'It's not fair ... I can do better. It's just that —'

'It is one thing to start well but you need to be able to finish a song well too,' he said. 'Otherwise how can you perform a whole show?'

It was not said unkindly, but there was no need for him to say anything more.

❧

The following morning, I woke to see that the sky had turned grey. Water gurgled down the drainpipes. Rain that alternated between downpour and drizzle splattered the houses and turned the streets into dank-smelling channels of mud. The spring rains had been so brief as to be barely noticeable and the summer had been dry. I hadn't seen rain like this since the day of my father's death and for a moment I thought I was at home again on the farm. A trail of subdued light fell across Bonbon, who was still asleep by my leg. I ran my hand over her silky fur. Long rehearsals and late nights had made me a heavy sleeper but I couldn't sleep any longer that morning. I pulled the covers around me and listened to the water drip from the roof tiles. I thought about the letter I had received from Aunt Yvette when I returned from the theatre after my disastrous audition.

> *Dear Simone,*
>
> *I am very worried to hear about you working in a music hall ... I know that you are a good-hearted girl but I have heard bad things about those kinds of places and am concerned about you ... Bernard will come to see you as soon as possible. He thinks he can find you work in a factory in Grasse.*
>
> *PS I have also enclosed a message from your mother.*

I was sure that the job Bernard had suggested was light, clean work — probably with perfume — but Aunt Yvette's letter could not have come at a worse time. I needed her to have confidence in me because I had lost it in myself.

The enclosed message from my mother was a picture she had drawn of a black cat. I had smiled at that through my tear-stung eyes. She was telling me 'good luck'. I had always been closer to my father than my mother, although I loved them both. Now my father was gone, my mother's mysterious messages meant more to me than ever.

'You did not inherit my gifts, Simone,' my mother had once told me when scrying into the fire. 'You are too logical. But my, what marvellous gifts you have been given. And what a glorious flame you will ignite when you are ready to use them.'

I squeezed my eyes shut and wondered what face-saving stratagem I would have to use to make myself go back to Le Chat Espiègle for the rest of the show. What hope was there of achieving a better life if I was never going to be anything more than a chorus girl kicking my legs to make seventy francs a week so I could pay the rent on my single room with a communal cold water tap and a lavatory down the hall?

'But you would have done a great job if it hadn't been for Claire,' Marie whispered while we waited in the wings for the harem dance rehearsal that afternoon. 'She's the one who spoiled your chance. You should still believe in yourself.'

'No,' I said, shaking my head. 'If I was really good, I would have ignored her.'

'You are too hard on yourself,' Marie said, touching my arm. 'Wait a while. You're still young. There will be another chance.'

I put on a cheerful smile and wiggled my hips and arms as if I didn't have a care in the world although the rehearsal was torture. When Gilles called out instructions he either avoided looking at me or stared at me too long. Once I saw him flinch when I caught his eye. The sympathy in his gaze hurt me more than if he had ignored me. While I practised my solo part, the other girls sat in the front row to watch. Claire made a show of yawning until she was sure that she had caught my attention, then she smiled. I ignored her. She was nothing to me. But my hardened attitude was a day too late.

Monsieur Vaimber supervised the rehearsals while Monsieur Dargent was away in Nice negotiating the contract with the new star. One afternoon, a few days after my audition, he took us through the final number. The whole cast was in the scene, including the Zo-Zo Family who were to be giant birds swooping overhead as Scheherazade and the Shah declared their love for each other. The couple were to be spirited away on a magic carpet, thanks to an illusion involving ropes and mirrors which had been designed by Claude. The scene was to wind up with a frenzied dance by the chorus girls, a song by Fabienne, and me finally unhooking my veil. Madame Baroux filled in for the part of Scheherazade. Most of the time she posed like a prop rather than a performer, but for the final scene she made the effort, despite her walking stick, to strut down the rehearsal staircase on her spindly legs, her vertical axis so perfectly straight that I could almost see the 'imaginary piece of string' she so often talked about running from the top of her head to the ceiling. Suddenly, the auditorium door opened and slammed against the wall. We all turned to see Monsieur Dargent standing in the aisle next to a woman with yellow hair.

'Ladies and gentlemen, gather around,' Monsieur Dargent called out, waving to us to move forward. We wiped our faces and necks with handkerchiefs and towels and crept towards the edge of the stage.

'I would like to introduce Mademoiselle Zephora Farcy — the new star of the show.' Monsieur Dargent took the woman's hand with exaggerated courtliness.

It took a few seconds for the cast to recover from their shock and greet her. The skin on Zephora's forehead was so smooth she couldn't have been more than thirty but the rolls of fat on her chest and upper arms were so matronly she could have been anyone's mother or even grandmother. Her breasts were like two sandbags hanging from her chest and her rotund stomach was barely contained by her girdle.

'She must be a good singer,' Gerard whispered.

The stage lighting caught the fuzz on Zephora's cheeks and made me think of dandelions. Framed by her red lips, her crooked teeth were sensual and her mildly crossed eyes glistened. The smile she flashed at Monsieur Vaimber and the other men in the room was full of feminine charm, but her face turned stony and her mouth pinched into a scowl when she laid eyes on the rest of us.

'She's no Camille,' Fabienne muttered to Marcel but he didn't hear her. From the way his eyes were shining, he was as taken with the new star as Monsieur Dargent.

It is just as well, I thought. He's playing the Shah. He has to kiss her.

Oblivious to our stunned expressions, Monsieur Dargent clapped his hands and announced that Mademoiselle Farcy had recently completed a run with Madame Lamare's Theatre in Nice and before that had performed at the Scala in Paris.

Madeleine and Paulette exchanged glances. The mention of Paris made it more understandable why Monsieur Dargent had chosen Zephora to replace Camille. Having performed in the capital gave her kudos. All Monsieur Dargent would have to do to draw audiences was mention that he had a 'Paris star'. It wouldn't matter, at first, if she were any good or not.

Later that afternoon, we rehearsed a scene from the second act that included Zephora, Marcel, Fabienne and myself. Those not in the scene milled around the wings, curious about the new addition to the cast. 'What's she doing here when she could be in Paris?' Claude asked Luisa. 'Something seems fishy to me.'

'The chorus girls aren't needed in this scene any more,' Monsieur Dargent called from his place in the front row of seats.

'What?' asked Claire.

'Mademoiselle Farcy doesn't dance, so we don't need you in the scene. Simone's dance will be enough.'

The other girls didn't care either way. They shrugged and left the stage. Only Claire remained, her fists clenched by her side. It was the number where she cartwheeled and danced all the way from the backdrop to the front of the stage; it was practically a solo. She bit her lip and jutted out her chin. For a moment I thought she was going to cry. But she dropped her shoulders and seemed to think better of it. After all, she had rent to pay and the change in schedule wouldn't affect her wages, only her ego. She flashed her eyes at me and stormed off the stage. I listened to her stomp up the stairs to the dressing rooms. Where had all Claire's tricks got her now? I could dance. So could Fabienne. If either of us were playing Scheherazade she could have kept her part.

Zephora was unmoved by the chorus girls' departure. She sat on a bench, reading over the score, oblivious to the rest of us.

Marcel eyed her curiously before sidling up to her. '*Bonjour*, Mademoiselle Farcy,' he said, bowing. 'We haven't been properly introduced. I am Marcel Sorel, your leading man. It is a pleasure to meet you.'

Zephora glanced up at him but didn't smile. 'I think we should stick to what's on the page, don't you?' she said.

Marcel gaped, puzzled over whether he had been slighted or not. Zephora picked up her score again and gave no indication that she was aware of his existence. He slouched away like a beaten dog.

From the haughty way she looked at me, I knew better than to approach Zephora directly. I took all my instructions from Monsieur Dargent. But I did have to read some lines with Zephora and it surprised me when I heard her shrill voice and muffled enunciation. Up until then I had been feeling embarrassed about being on the stage with a performer whose part I had tried out for and had failed so miserably to get. But any sense of superiority I had was dashed when Zephora sang. Marcel and Fabienne's jaws dropped open with awed respect.

Zephora had a commanding voice. It was a touch brassy, and her tremolo was so exaggerated that the floor vibrated with every rolling 'r', but when she sang you were drawn to her, like a fish being reeled in to shore. And even though the flesh on her hips wobbled when she shifted her weight from foot to foot, she oozed charisma rather than obesity. Zephora was a beehive dripping with honey. I knew that she was going to be a success with the men in the audience. And considering that about ninety per cent of the people who came to see shows at Le Chat Espiègle were men, that was what really counted.

The following day I had an appointment with Madame Tarasova to be fitted for my costume.

'Why the gloomy face?' she asked, glancing up from her sewing machine. Her hair was plaited and coiled on top of her head in a style that was more fetching than her usual tight chignon. I wanted to leave the subject of my failed audition alone and tried to change the conversation by complimenting her on her hairstyle. But Madame Tarasova saw through my tactic and persisted. 'Well?' she asked, arching her eyebrows. 'Who died?'

Vera was hanging costumes on an upper rail with a stick. 'She's upset about the audition,' she said.

Madame Tarasova scoffed. 'It was your first audition and you were foolish to try one without any preparation. You might be able to get up and sing at a wedding, but it's not like that on stage. You must practise and practise.'

She stood up from the machine and pulled the measuring tape from around her neck. 'Why don't we adjust the costume Camille was supposed to wear?' she said. 'The new leading lady is going to need one in an entirely different size.'

'What should I have done for my audition?' I asked Madame Tarasova, when she bent down to measure my legs.

'I was wardrobe mistress with the opera in St Petersburg,' she said. 'Believe me, good performers practise for hours to make what they do look easy. You just don't stand on stage and become a star, even if they make it seem that way.'

Vera held a scarf against my hair. 'You'd make a much better Scheherazade than Zephora if you trained your voice,' she said.

'You think so?' I asked, my mood lifting.

'Your tone is good,' she said, 'but your voice is untrained. There is no way you could sing for a whole show.' She drew in a breath and sang a phrase from one of the 'Scheherazade' songs, holding the last note before letting it fade away. The sound was even and pretty.

Vera laughed at my astonishment. 'I was planning to be a singer myself, but the Bolsheviks had other ideas.'

'You could help Simone with her voice,' said Madame Tarasova, slipping her tape measure around my waist. 'Although she will need proper lessons eventually.'

'We can practise on the piano in the basement,' agreed Vera. 'We can do the songs from "Scheherazade" before anyone else comes along for rehearsals.'

I chided myself for being so easily defeated. The problem was not me; it was a lack of experience. And Madame Tarasova and Vera seemed to think that if I worked at it, I could be a good singer.

∽

'Scheherazade' was Le Chat Espiègle's most successful show. By the end of the second week word had spread and the crowd lining up for seats spilled from the cashier's desk, through the foyer, down the steps and along the square. The patrons weren't even deterred when the skies opened and a torrent of rain poured down. They merely raised their umbrellas and chatted beneath them while waiting for their tickets. As well as our regular clientele of sailors and factory workers, the publicity had attracted shipping clerks, teachers, doctors, hairdressers, town officials and other respectable inhabitants of Marseilles. Monsieur Dargent was aglow with his first real success. The gauntness that had sucked in his face since Camille's departure vanished in a matter of days. He slapped our backs, pinched our cheeks and took to smoking cigars like a true impresario.

The success of the show didn't put a stop to the backbiting, however. If anything, it became worse. Gerard watched from the wings, rubbing his hairy knuckles and muttering about everyone else's shortcomings. And even though Claire's cartwheel dance was put back in the show, it didn't stop her scowling at Monsieur Dargent or hissing at me. There was a rumour that Paulette had replaced Madeleine's spirit gum with honey and that was why she had lost her *cache-sexe* during the Wednesday night show and had to be pulled offstage by Monsieur Vaimber. In retaliation, Madeleine had mixed sand into Paulette's cold cream, and now Paulette was nursing grazes on her cheeks and chin. But, somehow, all those egos vying for the limelight improved the performance of the cast.

Zephora remained aloof and her coldness even began to extend to Monsieur Dargent. Before and after the show she would retreat to her dressing room and refuse callers. One night Monsieur Dargent begged her to show her face to the fans waiting at the stage door and he received the curt reply, 'Go away! I'm too tired!'

Fabienne and I were sent down to make conversation with Zephora's eager fans instead, although I had no idea what to talk about with the multitude of babbling men outside the stage door. Fabienne, who took adulation as her lot, helped me. 'Oh, don't harass her. She's far too young for you. Come over here and talk to me.'

Although we were rushed off our feet, Vera wasted no time in getting down to work on my voice. No matter how late we finished the night before, we met every morning at eleven o'clock in the basement. She played notes on the piano for me to sing to, moving higher and higher as far as I could follow.

'You have a delightful mezzo-soprano voice,' she told me. 'And your projection is good. I don't know what happened at your audition. Perhaps it was nerves.'

Vera explained that I could overcome my nerves if I breathed properly. 'Don't take in any more air than you would need to sniff a rose, then let your voice glide over that cushion of air,' she said. We sang all the songs from 'Scheherazade' and she demonstrated how to phrase them properly and put the right amount of emotion into each one.

I was enjoying my lessons and performing so much that, instead of feeling jealous of Zephora, I tried to learn from her. I studied her whenever I could, from the wings or during rehearsals. Although her voice had a different quality to mine, I memorised her delivery of the songs, imitating her when I was on my own. Then when I met with Vera, we adapted the songs to my own style.

During one matinée I was surprised when Zephora gave a listless performance. Her voice sounded hoarse and, despite her make-up, there were circles under her eyes and a feverish tinge to her cheeks.

'Please take me with you to the Shah's palace,' I said, giving her the cue for her song. She stiffened. For a moment I thought she had forgotten her lines and tried to mouth them to her but she did not respond. Fabienne tried to get Zephora's attention by stamping her foot, but that didn't work either. The conductor lifted his arms and directed the orchestra to play a few bars of the song before going back to the beginning. His trick succeeded: Zephora snapped out of her dream and began singing. Fabienne and I let out a sigh, but Zephora's heroic song about going to the palace to outsmart the Shah came out more as a whimper.

'If you ask me, she's taking opium,' said Fabienne later in the dressing room. 'I hope she pulls herself together for tonight's performance. It's shaping up to be our biggest night yet.'

'Ah,' sighed Luisa, 'she'll come to no good if she takes drugs. Where we performed in Rome, one of the chorus girls used to snort cocaine. One night she fell asleep on the rail tracks.'

'What happened?' I asked.

'She was squashed like a tomato!' replied Luisa, slapping her hands together.

Fabienne and I grimaced. I had heard that in the fancier clubs, audiences were sometimes served drugs on platters, and occasionally a chorus girl at Le Chat Espiègle received a bag of crystalline powder from an admirer. Often I would go into the laneway to escape the heat of my dressing room and find groups of men there, huddled together or staring at the sky, their noses streaked with white powder. Once, during interval, I saw a man screaming that he had cockroaches crawling under his skin. His pupils were dilated to twice the normal size and he was sweating and shaking. Albert threw a bucket of water over him and told him to go away. The man responded by vomiting all over our feet.

The chorus girls who took cocaine said it made them feel 'on top of the world'. For me, just going out on stage was enough of a rush.

'Zephora certainly covers up for such a vamp,' said Fabienne, wiping away her greasepaint with a cloth. 'Mind you, I would too if I had those size thighs.'

I cut a peach into quarters. It was sour but I was too hungry to care. I wasn't interested in maligning Zephora; I was worried about what would happen if she pulled out of the show, as Camille had.

'I bet she was kicked out of Paris,' said Fabienne. 'Otherwise why would you want to play at this theatre when you could be strutting your stuff before millionaires at the Scala?'

'I hear there will be a few reporters in the audience tonight,' I said, trying to change the subject. 'I hope they give us good reviews.'

'I hope there will be a few rich men in the audience,' laughed Fabienne, clutching her breasts and pushing them skyward. 'And I hope that they will give me good reviews too.'

I sat in front of the mirror and watched my hand tremble. I put on my eye make-up, rubbed it off and daubed it on again. The liner was still crooked and the flicks at the corner of each eye were too curly. My shadow and eye-black looked like bruises on my lids. I sighed, picked up my facecloth and charcoal pencil, and poised to try all over again.

I had received a telegram from Bernard saying that he was coming to tonight's performance. The last letter I had written home had been to tell them I was working as a seamstress. I hadn't said anything about performing on stage. I was sure Bernard was coming to see if Le Chat Espiègle was a legitimate establishment and to allay some of Aunt Yvette's fears. What a shock he was in for.

'Why are you here so early?' asked Madame Tarasova, flitting into the room with the Zo-Zo sisters' costumes.

'I couldn't sit still at home,' I told her. 'Look!' I held up my hand.

'You've got the jitters. It's nothing,' she said, hanging the costumes on a hook. 'It means you'll give a good performance tonight.'

She smiled reassuringly before darting out the door. I closed my eyes. *Slow breath in and slow breath out. Slow breath in and slow breath out.* I opened my eyes. The tremble was still there only now I was light-headed as well. 'This is useless,' I mumbled, examining my grubby facecloth. I needed to wet it again if I wanted to clean off the mascara I had smudged over my cheek. I pulled my kimono around my shoulders and headed towards the bathroom.

When I passed Zephora's dressing room I heard a crash. The door swung open and Zephora stumbled out, clutching her stomach. She took two steps before doubling over and dropping to her knees.

'Zephora!' I rushed towards her. Her face was pale. 'I'll get Madame Tarasova,' I said.

She grabbed my arm and dug her nails into my flesh. 'No!' she spat. 'I don't need your interference. I'm all right. It's just ... something I suffer from time to time.' She let out a dry, spiteful laugh.

Her manner was more severe than her usual brusqueness. She was shivering although it was hot in the theatre. I stared at her, trying to think what I should do. I couldn't leave her there like that. I rushed to the bathroom and wet my facecloth, intending to give it to

Zephora to put on her forehead. When I returned she was sprawled on the floor, her face covered in a film of sweat.

'Oh God,' she moaned through chapped lips.

I knelt down and wiped her face. She stared back at me, clenching her teeth. There was something in her eyes that frightened me.

'I will get help,' I said.

Madame Tarasova was backstage, brushing down costumes with Vera and Martine, the new dresser. 'Something has happened to Zephora!' I told them.

The three women followed me up the stairs but Zephora was not in the corridor. 'She's in here!' said Vera, pointing to the open dressing room door. Somehow Zephora had managed to drag herself back into the room and was lying on the floor, clutching the legs of a chair. Madame Tarasova's eyes widened. She crouched down beside Zephora. The singer rolled onto her back, her hands gripping her stomach.

'It is something she ate,' said Martine, stepping forward. 'My brother and I had something like that when we first came to Marseilles. It was terrible.'

Madame Tarasova frowned and pressed her hand to Zephora's stomach. She looked up, alarm on her face. 'Quick!' she said. 'Help me pull that couch from the wall and get her onto it!'

Martine and I dragged the divan to the centre of the room and Madame Tarasova and Vera lowered Zephora onto it. It was no easy feat for them, as Zephora was a few stones heavier than either woman and didn't seem able to exert any strength of her own. She curled up on the couch and stuck her fist in her mouth to stifle another groan.

'Zephora,' Madame Tarasova said, shaking her shoulder. 'Is it what I think it is?'

The muscles in Zephora's face tightened and she let out a wail which was drowned out by a blast of music from the rehearsal room. The spasm passed and she nodded. 'It's coming.'

Vera and I exchanged glances. Madame Tarasova hissed out a breath, readying herself for action. 'Vera, go get a doctor! Quick!'

Martine grabbed my arm. 'What is it?' she asked. 'Her appendix?'

'No,' said Madame Tarasova, propping a pillow under Zephora's head. 'Our star is about to have a baby.'

I stood outside Monsieur Dargent's office, tying and untying the knot of my kimono. Somehow, in the chaos that followed Madame Tarasova's announcement, it had been decided that I should be the one to break the news of Zephora's impending motherhood to him. I knocked on the door.

'Come in,' he called out.

I was greeted with a mist of cigarette smoke. Monsieur Vaimber and two men I hadn't seen before were sitting with Monsieur Dargent. From the relaxed expression on Monsieur Dargent's face, I assumed that the men weren't creditors trying to retrieve their money nor had they anything to do with the mafia.

Monsieur Dargent jumped up from his chair and ushered me into the room. 'Ah, Simone, come in,' he said. 'Let me introduce you to Monsieur Ferriol and Monsieur Rey. They have come all the way from Nice to see the show.'

'*Enchanté*,' said Monsieur Ferriol, rising from his chair and kissing my hand. Monsieur Rey followed suit.

'If they like the show, they will invest in it,' whispered Monsieur Dargent.

My stomach twisted but I did my best to feign delight. 'Monsieur Dargent,' I said, smiling. 'I need to speak to you for a moment.'

Monsieur Dargent gave me a puzzled look but didn't seem alarmed. His carefree attitude made me all the more sorry for what I was about to tell him. He followed me to the cashier's booth, which was empty.

'Investors, Simone! Can you believe it?' he said as soon as we were out of earshot. 'Le Chat Espiègle has never had investors before ... only me.'

'Monsieur Dargent, I have ...' I clenched my toes. How *was* I going to tell him? I grasped for the right words but he didn't give me a chance to speak.

'My time has come!' he said, squeezing my arms. 'The day my father threw me out of home he said that I would die penniless in the gutter. What will he say now?'

'Oh God, Monsieur Dargent — I have terrible news!' There: it was out. He looked at me askance, his lips thinning into a frown.

'Zephora is having a baby,' I said.

Monsieur Dargent's eyes bulged and he took a step back. At first he did not seem to believe me; then his face lit up with understanding.

'No wonder she left that show in Nice. She probably figured she would get away with it in a smaller theatre. I've had pregnant performers before, but if she puts on any more weight I'll have to fire her.'

'You don't understand,' I said. 'She's having her baby *now*.'

At that moment Vera rushed into the foyer with the doctor. 'Are they still in the dressing room?' she asked. I nodded. Vera signalled for the doctor to follow her.

Monsieur Dargent's face turned white. He pulled out his watch and stared at it. 'It is an hour to the show. Can't she wait until afterwards?'

'It doesn't work like that,' I told him.

He squeezed his eyes shut and collapsed into the cashier's chair. 'We are ruined,' he said, banging his head on the desk.

Monsieur Vaimber stepped into the booth. 'What is taking you so long?' he hissed. 'I sent the gentlemen away. They will come back for the show.'

I explained the situation to him and was grateful when he took the news more calmly than Monsieur Dargent. 'We shall have to cancel the show tonight,' he said. 'There's nothing else we can do.'

'We can't cancel the show!' cried Monsieur Dargent, tugging at his hair so viciously that I thought he was going to pull it out. 'Those investors will go straight back to Nice. They aren't going to wait around in Marseilles until we find a replacement.'

'You don't need to find a replacement.'

We turned around to see Madame Tarasova standing behind us. 'You have someone who can stand in for the part right there,' she said, pointing at me.

Monsieur Dargent looked from Madame Tarasova to me and back again. He shook his head. 'She can't carry it.'

Madame Tarasova crossed her arms. 'She can do the part. I know. Vera has been teaching her. Marie can take over the handmaiden's role.'

Monsieur Vaimber took his handkerchief from his pocket and wiped his forehead. 'There is no way we can put —'

'What choice do you have?' Madame Tarasova cut him off. 'You either take the chance or let those investors go for ever.'

Monsieur Dargent stopped pulling at his hair and looked up. 'Okay!' he said, wobbling to his feet. 'Okay! She saved us once before — maybe she can perform that miracle again. She's on!'

I don't suppose that as long as I live, I shall forget that night at Le Chat Espiègle. Even as I stood in the wings, listening to the orchestra play the lead-up to my first number, I couldn't believe I was there. I had wanted a singing part and now I had one; albeit with no notice. I was going on cold again.

Monsieur Vaimber waited with me for my cue. Sweat dripped from his forehead and the way his hands trembled did nothing to calm my own nerves.

'Okay,' he said. 'You're on.'

I braced myself and swept onto the stage. The crowd sighed and clapped. I stretched out my arms and they applauded more. It was a good sign that they were cheering, but it could only have been for the beautiful costume I was wearing, because I had missed my first line and hadn't sung a note. Luckily the conductor was used to covering mistakes and led the musicians into the introduction again. I glided towards the stage apron, bordered on either side by the chorus girls twirling in the harem dance. Marie winked at me and Jeanne smiled. Claire nodded. Had I really seen that? Perhaps she was grateful, understanding that I was risking my all to save everybody else.

The spotlights sent down a stream of white heat across my face and shoulders. I could only see as far as the first few rows of smiling faces, but I sensed that Bernard was out there somewhere. Oh God, I prayed, my legs shaking beneath me.

> Other girls have gone to their deaths — but not me
> I'm stronger
> Other girls have lost their heads — not me
> I'm smarter
> He might be the ruler
> But I am a woman.

The audience cheered again. My voice rang out over the noise, clear and strong. I had no trouble keeping my breath. My legs stopped trembling and I wiggled and swirled and improvised a dance to go with the words. Something fell at my feet and my heel clamped down on it. *Squish.* Oh no, I thought, they're throwing food at me already. I glanced at my foot but instead of a tomato, which had happened before even when they'd liked my act, I saw a rose. I bent and picked it up. Still singing, I held the flower to my nose, as if I were appreciating its scent, then passed it to Claire with a flourish. I didn't miss a note. The cheers sounded louder.

'Mademoiselle Fleurier!' a man shouted from the audience. Other voices joined him. '*Other girls have gone to their deaths — but not me, I'm stronger.*' The song that had caused me so much pain a few weeks ago was now my battle cry. When I hit the last note, unwavering, and threw my arms up bravely for the finish, the roar from the audience told me that I had won.

The rest of the show was a blur: two and a half hours flew by as if they had been only two minutes. Each time I raced upstairs for a costume change, Vera was ready with an update on Zephora's labour. 'The doctor says she hasn't long to go. It won't be too bad for her. She's built for it.'

I tried to sit still while Martine pinned on my wedding headdress. 'The doctor has been listening to you between the contractions,' she told me. 'He says you are very good and that with a voice like yours you could sing anywhere.'

I stood up while Madame Tarasova and Martine checked my hooks and pins. There were so many sequins and diamantés on the wedding gown that it took all my concentration to keep my balance. When I stepped out the door, I heard a long moan come from the direction of Zephora's dressing room and, seconds later, the sound of a baby crying.

It was all Martine and I could do to stop from laughing. 'Two new people have been born tonight,' she said.

The curtain came down after the ninth encore. The adrenaline that had sustained me for the show plummeted. My heart pounded and pins and needles prickled my feet and fingertips. Marcel took my arm and squeezed it. He had been shocked to find out that I was going to be his leading lady, but the surprise had improved his performance. I struggled to get my bearings. The rest of the cast flocked around us.

'Well done, Simone!' cried Claude.

'You look beautiful,' gushed Marie.

Monsieur Vaimber and the stagehands called out 'Bravo!' from the flies and even Claire's clique was solicitous. 'You look so different. I can't believe it is you,' said Paulette. 'It's amazing what a nice costume can do.'

Monsieur Dargent appeared in the wings and the others parted to let him through. 'Simone,' he said, throwing his arms around me and kissing my cheeks. 'Who would have thought? You have taken to the part of the star like a duck to water.'

He ushered me upstairs to the dressing room. The corridor was crowded with fans and well-wishers. Women in dresses with plunging necklines leaned on the arms of men with pencil moustaches. They seemed to sparkle and shimmer before me like a river in the sunshine. Their mouths moved rapidly, discussing their reactions to the show, but they fell silent when they saw me.

'*Bonsoir*, Mademoiselle Fleurier!' someone shrieked. That started everyone up again. 'Bravo, Mademoiselle Fleurier!' they shouted. 'What an act!'

I searched for Bernard amongst their faces, but couldn't find him. Despite what Monsieur Dargent had said about me taking naturally to the role of a star, I was paralysed by so many people paying attention to me. I would have liked to have run away, but I didn't want to let Monsieur Dargent down. I signed autographs in a daze, kissed cheeks and shook hands, doing my best to maintain the appearance of bravado when all I wanted to do was lie down.

'I can't see Bernard,' I whispered to Monsieur Dargent. I had told him earlier that a family friend was in the audience that evening.

He patted my arm. 'Go to your dressing room and I'll see if I can find him for you.'

Monsieur Dargent turned to the well-wishers and clapped his hands. 'Mademoiselle Fleurier needs a rest. She will meet you again tomorrow night.' The crowd began to move away. Several people shouted out that they would return. A trio of men in tuxedos and top hats lingered a while longer, the tallest one eyeing me. But whatever message he was trying to convey was lost. I was on the verge of collapse.

I closed my dressing room door and sank to my knees, too exhausted to think of removing my shoes or my headdress. Fabienne and the Zo-Zo sisters were still downstairs and I was grateful to have a few minutes of peace before they returned. The room smelt of lemon and mint, and something else ... Tobacco? I opened my eyes and started when I noticed the man sitting in my make-up chair. At first, I thought it was Bernard, but this man was a few years older although he was as impeccably dressed.

He stood up. 'I am sorry to surprise you, Mademoiselle Fleurier,' he said. 'I had to avoid the frenzy to get to you. I am Michel Etienne.'

He announced it in a way that suggested I might know of him. He certainly had the autocratic air of someone whose favours were sought after. But I had no idea who he was. He was of medium height and wiry, with wispy blond hair receding from his forehead. His accent was silky and nasal, and I'd heard it a few times in Marseilles now. He was a Parisian.

'You made an impressive debut for a young girl,' he said. 'If you can come to Paris I might be able to do something for you.'

He reached into his jacket pocket and pulled out a card. I took it from him.

Michel Etienne
Theatrical Agent
Rue Saint Dominique, Paris

I was bewildered as well as intrigued. 'Paris?' I mumbled.

Monsieur Etienne gave me a fleeting smile and indicated that I should let him pass. I dragged myself up and moved out of the way. He nodded to me and closed the door behind him.

Paris? I examined the cream and gold card, imagining elegant cafés and dormer windows like those I had seen in the magazines Bernard used to bring for Aunt Yvette. I pictured lights sparkling on the Seine and romance and intrigue on every street corner. 'If only,' I sighed, tucking the card under my make-up tray. The train ticket to Paris alone would cost more than I could save in six months.

A knock at the door made me jump. I opened it to see Bernard's face beaming at me.

'Bernard!'

He rushed into the room and threw his arms around me. 'What a surprise, Simone!' he laughed. 'What is this story about being a seamstress? You are the star of the show!'

'I was a seamstress,' I told him. 'It's a long story about how I got this part.'

'Your father would have been proud to see you. The audience was dazzled.'

I took his hand and led him to the couch on Fabienne's side of the room. My mind was still racing with the night's events and I found it hard to concentrate, but Bernard's enjoyment of the show gave me more pleasure than anything. I had been worried that he might not approve, but here he was telling me that my father would have been proud. If that were true, then I was sure my mother and aunt would see it the same way too. I was about to tell him about the Paris agent when I looked more closely at his face. His smile was tense and there were circles under his eyes.

'Bernard! What is it? What's wrong?'

'I have something to tell you,' he said, taking my hands and lowering his voice. 'There has been a misfortune at the farm. You must come home as soon as possible.'

SEVEN

When I told Monsieur Dargent that I had to leave the show because Uncle Gerome had suffered a stroke, he received the news more calmly than I expected.

'What can I say?' he asked. 'You stepped in at the last minute for two of my shows and saved the day. I have investors now, thanks to you. I can hold the role for a week if you come straight back.'

From Bernard's description of Uncle Gerome's condition, I sensed that I wouldn't be returning to Marseilles any time soon, so I agreed to play Scheherazade for two more nights to give Fabienne time to prepare herself for the role.

Madame Tarasova threw a party for me in the wardrobe area with Russian cakes and wine. The news of Uncle Gerome's illness had come as a shock and stirred complex feelings in me. I had never loved him. I thought he had cheated my family, and he had sent me away from home after my father's death when I needed my mother and aunt most. And yet, I found myself bound to return to Pays de Sault out of deeper emotions than duty. I was worried about my mother and aunt, and conscious of what my father would have expected of me — but to my surprise I also felt grief for my uncle. I remembered the pained expression on his face when I was leaving the farm for Marseilles. He was a man torn within himself. And yet, when I looked at the smiles of the people who had been kind to me at Le Chat Espiègle — Madame Tarasova and Vera, Albert, Monsieur Dargent and Marie — my sympathy was tinged with guilt. This was the life for me now. How could I just leave it?

'Your uncle is severely incapacitated,' Bernard explained, in the car en route to Pays de Sault. 'Your mother and aunt have been caring for him but it is taking a toll on them.' Bernard was driving the same car he had arrived in for the lavender harvest, although his suit was not as elegant as the one he had worn then. There was something countrified about it, and at first I thought he was wearing my father's Sunday best, although I realised that he couldn't be because we had buried my father in those clothes.

'What exactly happened to Uncle Gerome?' I asked.

'He was playing *pétanque* in the village. Albert Poulet was there, along with Jean Grimaud and Pierre Chabert. They say that one minute he was standing, taking aim, and the next he had collapsed to his knees. He couldn't move his legs or speak.'

We reached Pays de Sault early the following afternoon, having slept for a few hours in the car overnight. Bonbon sat on my lap, eyes darting back and forth, taking in the fields and mountains. As soon as I saw the pine forests and gullies on either side of us, I knew the location of our farm as if my heart were a compass. The twin farmhouses came into view and I bit my lip to resist the urge to cry. Although my father was no longer there, I sensed him in the sunshine and the breeze that stirred the treetops.

Bernard pulled up in the yard. A dog barked. Chocolat, the fur on his ears and tail bleached orange by the sun, bounded towards us. Bonbon wriggled out of my arms and the two dogs touched noses and circled each other, wagging their tails. I looked around for Olly, but knowing his habits I suspected that he was sleeping off his lunch somewhere.

Swarms of insects buzzed in the trees. The ground was sun-scorched and crackled. Summer had been dry. It was hard for me to believe there had been a time when the farm and I had shared the same calendar, when my daily life had been dictated by the changing seasons. For the past few months I had lived my days according to rehearsals, performances and costume fittings.

'Simone!' Aunt Yvette called out from the kitchen doorway. I ran towards her and we embraced. Her collarbone poked into me. 'Are you all right?' I asked her. 'I hope you are not working so hard that you don't eat.'

My mother appeared from the distillery and ran up the hill towards us. Bonbon broke away from Chocolat and dashed towards her. My mother stopped and stared at the little dog, then turned to me.

'Bonbon,' I said.

My mother crouched down and patted her thighs. Bonbon sprinted to her, leapt into her lap and started licking her chin.

'This is not a dog,' she said. 'It's a fox pup.' My mother put Bonbon down and threw her arms around my neck. Her hair tickled my cheek when she kissed me.

Aunt Yvette linked her arm with mine. 'It was God's will that this should happen,' she muttered. 'It was God's will.'

I stared at my hands, puzzled that Aunt Yvette could feel sorry for a man who had treated her so badly.

'Come on,' said Bernard, ushering us into the house. 'Let's talk over some food. Simone and I are starving.'

Aunt Yvette unlatched the kitchen shutters and threw them open to the afternoon air. They hit the outside walls with a thump and a rattle. Olly appeared on the windowsill. I slipped my hands under his back and cradled him in my arms. After handling featherweight Bonbon for so long, Olly felt like a sack of potatoes. He purred and rubbed against me so vigorously that wisps of his fur spun into the air. I scratched his stomach then placed him down on the flagstones. Chocolat and Bonbon fell asleep next to a potted geranium, the smaller dog curled up in the curve of the larger one's stomach.

My mother poured dried figs, almonds and milk biscuits onto a plate.

'According to the notary, if Gerome doesn't recover, both farms will belong to you,' said Bernard, pushing a glass of wine towards me. 'But even if he does live, he will never be the same.'

I took my mother's hand when she sat down next to me. Once, when Uncle Gerome had spoken particularly cruelly to Aunt Yvette, I had asked my mother why she didn't hex him.

'I am a healer, Simone,' she had replied. 'I must do what I can to mend life, not to harm it. If Gerome is the way he is, then there is a message in it.'

I wondered what message the stroke had sent to Uncle Gerome.

I glanced at my mother, who stared back at me with pride. I had filled out a little more in Marseilles and had learned to take care of myself. The thought that she was admiring my transition into womanhood warmed my heart but made me self-conscious too. I looked around the kitchen. The silence of the house was unnerving. No creaks on the floorboards, not a cough or a sneeze. I wondered where Uncle Gerome was.

'How will we manage the farm?' I asked them. 'You know that I'm useless at it.'

'Bernard is going to move here,' said Aunt Yvette. 'He will manage the farm as well as act as lavender-broker for the village.'

I couldn't hide my surprise and Bernard blushed from his throat to the tips of his ears. 'I am happier here than I am anywhere else,' he said, careful not to look in Aunt Yvette's direction. 'You are like sisters to me.'

With a scarf knotted at his throat and his slicked-back hair, Bernard was the film star version of a Provençal farmer but I had no doubt he would make a success of the farm. Since my father's death, he had put aside his leisurely ways. Now Uncle Gerome was sick, he wanted to take us under his wing and I loved him for that. Besides, he was intelligent with a good knowledge of modern farming methods, and my mother would be an asset to him with her understanding of the seasons and plants. When we had driven through the village earlier, the men had nodded in greeting. Despite the fact that Bernard was not interested in women, his hard work and willingness to improve the profitability of lavender production in our area seemed to have won him friends. Still, it was difficult to picture him playing *pétanque* with the village men or drinking liqueurs with Albert Poulet and Jean Grimaud under the plane trees in the square.

'We will hire labour for the physical work,' said Aunt Yvette. 'There is enough money for that. Gerome has been stashing it in the fireplace for years. I need a hand with the meals because it takes so much time to look after your uncle. He can't do anything for himself. It will be good to have you back, Simone.'

I saw the red curtain of Le Chat Espiègle close and my heart sank. There had been a time when I could not have imagined anything better than cooking with my aunt in her kitchen. What had changed?

Bonbon woke up, stretched and jumped into my mother's lap. 'She is a worldly one,' my mother said, ruffling Bonbon's fur but looking at me. 'She's meant for bigger things.' I did not understand what she meant.

'Can I see Uncle Gerome?' I asked my aunt.

Aunt Yvette hesitated. 'I don't know if he will recognise you.'

'I'd like to see him anyway,' I said.

I followed Aunt Yvette upstairs to the bedroom at the end of the corridor. She pushed the door open and gestured for me to go inside. Uncle Gerome was lying on the bed, supported by a mountain of pillows and covered to the waist with a quilt. The floorboards creaked under my feet. I glanced over my shoulder, expecting Aunt Yvette to still be there. But she had gone, leaving the door ajar. I heard her rejoin my mother and Bernard downstairs.

I inched towards the bed, expecting Uncle Gerome to stir or to glance in my direction. But he didn't move. There was a crucifix above the bed and a photograph of my father on the side table. It took a few seconds for me to gain the courage to glance at Uncle Gerome's face. He had been shaved clean but even if he'd still had his moustache I don't think I would have recognised him. He lay prostrate like a corpse, the colour bleached out of his face and his gaze fixed on the ceiling. The only signs of life were the rise and fall of his chest and a flicker in his eyes. It was the left side of his body that had been affected. His mouth was twisted as if his lip was being tugged by an invisible thread. The muscles around his eye had collapsed. His left knee was bent out to the side and his fist was clenched next to it. I faltered, my hands turning to ice. His resemblance to my father was overwhelming. I had to steady my breath before I could take another step.

'Uncle Gerome,' I whispered.

His eyes wavered in my direction but there was nothing I could read in his expression. The sinews in his neck were rigid, his arms and hands were skeletal. I had no idea if he was pleased or horrified to see me, or if he even knew who I was.

A rattle rose in his throat, as if he were trying to speak. A towel had been tucked up around his neck to catch the drool that slid from his mouth to his chin.

'Uncle Gerome,' I said again, although I had no idea what I wanted to tell him.

The rattle sounded louder. The man on the bed was not fierce now. He was frail. The stroke had been a bomb, detonated within him.

The way his body was contorted and twisted out of shape, he seemed like a man who had been turned inside out. Perhaps what I was seeing was his tortured soul, brought to the surface.

❧

The following afternoon I visited my father's grave in the village cemetery. His was the newest stone amongst the weather-beaten tombs and lopsided vaults. A lizard, sunning itself on a nearby rock, scurried away when I crouched down in the dry grass.

I breathed in the cemetery's scent — an odd combination of mildew, rosemary and thyme — and thought about how close my father had come to fulfilling his dream and how quickly his life had been snatched away. Although I was happy to see my family again, I despaired at the idea of staying at the farm for good. Life at Le Chat Espiègle had changed everything, and seeing Uncle Gerome had helped me understand that if you didn't take chances in life when they presented themselves to you, perhaps you never would.

I closed my eyes, imagining my father's smile. 'Paris,' I whispered. *Go*, I heard him tell me. *Go and take a chance on your dream.*

I opened my eyes and looked around me. There was no one to be seen but the voice had sounded distinct. I ran my finger over my father's name on the headstone — Pierre Gustave Fleurier — then contemplated the surrounding tombstones, some humble, some grand. I had come to the cemetery searching for an answer and I had found it.

❧

I watched my mother cut the artichokes for dinner. My aunt was the cook and artist in the kitchen, but my mother was the sorcerer. She sang to the water boiling over the fire and coaxed the vegetables to perfection. She had a way of bringing magic to even the most mundane things.

Every so often my mother would turn and tell Bonbon something in *patois* about the farm, about lavender harvesting or about what she was doing. 'I peel the artichokes like this and cut them as evenly as possible, see?' she said, holding out a slice for Bonbon to inspect. My mother talked more to Bonbon than I had ever seen her talk to anyone else.

'Maman, Bernard told you about my performance at the music hall in Marseilles, didn't he?'

My mother glanced over her shoulder. 'He told me that you were very good.' There was no judgment in her voice. For a woman who had spent all her life in the country, my mother found little to approve or disapprove of. She seemed to accept everything for itself.

I told her about how I had come to work in the music hall, about Bonbon and Camille, about Monsieur Dargent, Madame Tarasova and Zephora. Then I told her about Michel Etienne and his offer to manage me if I went to Paris.

'I am like Bernard,' I said, glancing at my hands. 'Only the opposite. I don't belong here. I belong in the city.'

My mother nodded towards the lavender fields. 'You do belong here, Simone. This is your home. The soil you come from. You will always belong here and you will always be welcome. But I know what your father would have wanted, and so I will tell you the same. Go to Paris, go and take a chance on your dream. There is some money left over from the harvest for a train ticket and to help you out with rent for a few weeks. But if it doesn't work out, I want you to promise me that you will come back here.'

I threw my arms around her and buried my face in her neck. She had said the same words I had heard in the cemetery. She knew my father so well it was uncanny.

'What about Bernard and Aunt Yvette?' I asked. 'How will Aunt Yvette manage without me?'

'Stay for the winter, if you can,' my mother said. 'After that, there are plenty of girls looking for work. We will get help for the house if we need it. Don't waste your life on Uncle Gerome; you don't owe him anything.'

That evening at dinner my mother announced that I was going to Paris in the early spring. Although Aunt Yvette was shocked, she soon changed her mind when Bernard described my performance in Marseilles.

'Well, if that's the case,' Aunt Yvette said, shaking her head and trying to take in the news, 'I have some town clothes I won't be needing that I can give Simone for the journey.'

I kissed my aunt. On another occasion, I might have felt sorry for her. I knew that she had never wanted to live on a farm. But these days she seemed content in the company of Bernard and my mother.

I did feel a twinge of sadness over my mother, however. Just as we were growing closer, I was going away.

Bonbon let out a yelp. My mother smiled at her and tickled her behind the ears. 'Bonbon says you can go to Paris on one condition,' she said, mischief dancing in her eyes.

'What's that?' I asked.

'She wants to stay. She likes it here.'

We all laughed at that.

Part Two

Part Two

EIGHT

———

I arrived in Paris in February 1924 to a grey sky and a dankness in the air that did nothing to disenchant me. I stood on the platform at the Gare de Lyon, watching the porters darting about and loading their trolleys with the baggage of women in silver fox stoles and men in hats and deerskin gloves. My nostrils burned with the soot from the train and my ears buzzed with the excited voices of lovers embracing, families reuniting and businessmen shaking each other's hands. Apart from Monsieur Etienne, who had replied to Bernard's letter with the advice that I come to Paris with enough money to last a month, I knew no one in the city. But my heart was filled with the certainty that my life was about to change for ever.

I glanced at the scrawled directions Monsieur Etienne had sent on how to get, by the *métro*, to his office on the Left Bank. But one look at the line snaking outside the ticket office and the crowds jostling each other through the gates and I lost heart. At least on the streetcar in Marseilles I could see where I was going. I would need time to get used to the idea of travelling through an underground labyrinth like a mole burrowing through the earth. I opened my purse and checked my franc notes, although I knew perfectly well how much was there, then looked around for the taxi rank. Paris deserved to be seen first by taxi, even if I had to skip four meals to afford it. A train guard pointed me in the direction of the front entrance. My 'first day in

Paris' extravagance did not include the price of a porter, so I dragged my trunk by its straps towards the doors. When I had left the farm for Marseilles, I had taken only clothes. But for Paris, Aunt Yvette had insisted that I take blankets and other household utensils with me. She wanted to save me money, but the ache in my arms and shoulders from lugging the trunk around made me realise what a burden thriftiness could be.

There were only two men and a young couple waiting in line for taxis and it wasn't long before one pulled up for me.

'Rue Saint Dominique,' I said to the driver, who stepped out of the taxi to help me with my luggage. He lifted my trunk into the boot and scrunched up his face. '*Pardon*, Mademoiselle?'

I repeated my request and, when I saw that he still didn't understand, showed him the address.

'*Ah, oui*,' he said, touching his cap. 'You must be from the south. I didn't understand you.'

I wondered how it was then that I had understood *him*.

The warmth of the taxi was a cocoon from which I could view the world flashing by outside. I craned my neck to look at the ornate buildings with their wrought-iron railings and slanted roofs. Paris was more sombre than Marseilles, but more elegant too. Marseilles burned into my mind in shades of turquoise and sunflower yellow, while Paris was hues of pearl and oyster. With the bare plane trees lining the boulevards and the slickness of the cobblestones, there was something funereal about the city. Indeed, we passed more shops selling urns, tombstones and marble angels than I had ever seen in the south. But I hadn't come to Paris to die and soon my attention was captured by the brighter sights of the city. We passed through streets lined with shops. A grocer stepped outside his store and glanced hopefully up and down the street. He blew into his hands and called out to a passing group of women in scarves and coats. They returned his wave and stopped to inspect his leeks and potatoes. In the store next door, a florist was busy arranging flowers in the window. The hyacinths and bluebells looked as vibrant and juicy as the carrots and spinach in her neighbour's store. The sight of the two shopkeepers going about their daily business delighted me, like patches of sunlight on a cloudy day.

My pleasure doubled when we passed the palatial Louvre, and again a few minutes later when we crossed the taupe waters of the

Seine. Excitement brought the blood to my face. I'm here, I thought. I'm here.

The Parisians were out in force on the Left Bank. Pairs of men strode down the sidewalks in navy blue coats and beige scarves, their shoes polished to a high shine. The women wore coats belted at the hips, with shawl collars or appliquéd at the sleeves with Russian swirls. I had thought I looked smart in Aunt Yvette's pleated skirt and wool coat, but compared to the people outside I was as drab as a pigeon among peacocks.

Despite the cold, a table of men huddled around a brazier at a sidewalk café, savouring their *cafés crèmes* as if they were drinking the finest cognac. One man's empty sleeve was pinned to his shoulder, another's crutches were propped up behind his chair. Even the waiter who served them was missing an ear. I had seen many of the war-wounded in Marseilles, but I would see hundreds more in Paris. To me, they were a reminder of my father; to others, a reminder of the horrors of war in a country that wanted to forget.

'Rue Saint Dominique,' said the driver, pulling up in front of a building with massive carved window frames and a blue slate roof. I didn't baulk at the fare, although it was twice what I had thought it would be, and tipped the driver generously. I will be making real money soon, I told myself, stepping out onto the street and taking my first breath of Paris air.

The front door was oak and as solid-looking as a president's coffin. There was no buzzer or bell to press, so I put one hand on the door and pulled my trunk after me with the other. It took a few moments for my eyes to adjust to the gloom of the foyer. At the far end of the space, working at a piece of knitting, was the concierge. Despite the noise my trunk made when I dragged it over the doorstep and the bang of the door, she didn't look up from her task.

'*Pardon*, Madame,' I called out, smoothing down my skirt and coat. 'I am looking for Monsieur Etienne.'

The woman glanced over the top of her spectacles. 'Apartment three, fifth floor,' she mumbled before returning her attention to her knitting.

Her reply was so brief — no 'Mademoiselle' or '*Bonjour*' — that I hesitated. I wanted to ask if she would mind looking after my trunk so that I didn't have to lug it upstairs. 'May I leave this here?' I asked.

This time there was no break in the click of her needles. 'Take it with you,' she said. 'This is not a hotel.'

There was a cage elevator in the foyer with a strip of red carpet on the floor. I pushed open the door and struggled to keep it open while dragging my trunk in after me. I pressed the button for the fifth floor. Nothing happened. I dreaded asking the concierge for assistance and gave the button a forceful jab. The lift jolted and I lost my balance, falling against my trunk and tearing a hole in my stockings. The cage shuddered, rattled and jerked its way to the fifth floor, where I opened the door and dragged my trunk out before it had a chance to trap me again.

There were only three apartments on the floor so Monsieur Etienne's office was easy to find. I stood at the door for a few moments, straightening my stockings and fixing my hair, before pressing the button. The door was opened by a young woman with blonde hair smoothed down over her scalp and wearing a jacquard dress trimmed in ostrich feathers. The fragrance of orange blossom drifted around her.

'*Bonjour*, Mademoiselle,' she said.

The woman was so chic that I assumed she must be one of Monsieur Etienne's Parisian clients on her way out. I was surprised when she introduced herself as Mademoiselle Franck, his secretary.

She helped me move my trunk in the door and then led the way along a short corridor into a reception room. The space was not much bigger than a train compartment, but tastefully furnished with two Louis XVI chairs and blue curtains with gold tassels. I took a seat by the window and Mademoiselle Franck handed me a form before returning to her desk. While she commenced typing, I studied the questions. The form had a segment for hair colour, shoe and dress sizes and other physical descriptions, and another for personal details such as known illnesses and next of kin. Each time Mademoiselle Franck paused to read over her typing, I heard Monsieur Etienne's voice vibrating through another door which I assumed led to his office. 'That's how it goes, Henri. That's how it goes,' he said.

I completed the form and waited while Mademoiselle Franck answered a telephone call from the Scala about an audition. 'Yes, we have several good magicians,' she said. 'I can send you two this afternoon if you like.' She put the receiver down and a few minutes later the telephone rang again. From the way her cheeks flushed and her voice took on a girlish giggle, I sensed that the call was not entirely professional. 'Ah, you will have the desk here this afternoon? It is beautiful? He will be so pleased.'

I studied the signed photographs of women in feathers and sequins that adorned the walls, and began to feel even more ungainly. I promised myself that as soon as I could afford it I was going to buy a dress as nice as the one Mademoiselle Franck was wearing.

About half an hour later, Monsieur Etienne stepped out of his office. He handed a stack of files to Mademoiselle Franck and caught sight of me. He stared for a moment before clapping his hands and exclaiming, 'Ah, yes. The girl from Marseilles. Come in, come in!'

I followed Monsieur Etienne into his office, which was smaller than the reception room and not nearly as elegant. He moved a stack of papers from a worn leather chair and directed me to sit down, taking his own place behind a desk scattered with files and photographs. He seemed less commanding than he had that night in my dressing room at Le Chat Espiègle; in his business suit he appeared more like an overworked accountant than a creator of stars. But from his puzzled look in the reception room, he had probably thought the same thing about me. In my aunt's hand-me-downs, I didn't look like a potential star.

Monsieur Etienne switched on a lamp and searched his desk for something, lifting papers and shuffling folders. He called out to Mademoiselle Franck that he couldn't find my file and she told him it was near his telephone.

'Ah,' he said, picking up a file with my name written in the corner. He opened it, flicked through the two or three sheets that were in it and handed a copy of a schedule to me. 'There, that's what I have for you this month. I don't charge anything until you get an engagement, except for your photographs, and after that I charge twenty per cent of whatever you earn.'

I glanced at the schedule. It was a list of auditions with various music halls and nightclubs along with the times and parts being tried out for. They were all for chorus roles or the last slot in a nightclub, when most of the patrons had already gone home. I was instantly deflated.

'Monsieur Etienne,' I said. 'There are no leading parts.'

He cleared his throat and sat back in his chair. 'How old are you, Mademoiselle Fleurier? Sixteen?' he asked, glancing over the form I had filled in. His finger tapped my date of birth. 'No, still only fifteen. You will get leading parts but you have to work for them. It is not as if in Marseilles you were performing at the Alcazar or the Odéon. If it had not been for the review in *Le Petit Provençal*, I wouldn't have bothered to go to see you.'

'I didn't come to Paris to be in a chorus,' I said, trying to keep the tremor out of my voice. Wasn't I good enough to be something other than a chorus girl? Wasn't what I had achieved in 'Scheherazade' enough?

Monsieur Etienne smiled. 'Mademoiselle Fleurier, in Paris it is better to be an usherette at the Adriana or the Folies Bergère than to have ten seasons as the star of a third-rate vaudeville show. Unlike many phonies in this city, I am an honest agent. I'm not going to call a girl away from her family unless I think she has potential. But for potential to become reality, it requires hard work and experience.'

I studied his face. He had a thin, stern look about him but not a misleading one. I sensed that he was telling me the truth.

Assuming that the matter had been resolved, Monsieur Etienne moved on. 'I have an apartment in Montparnasse for you. It has just been given up by one of my other clients who is now touring London. It is cheap and you can travel by the *métro* to your auditions. You can find something better once you start working.'

He stood up, signifying that our conversation had come to a close, then shook my hand and walked me to the door. 'Let Mademoiselle Franck know when you can have your photographs taken,' he said. The telephone on his desk rang and Monsieur Etienne rushed back to answer it, giving me a final wave before Mademoiselle Franck shut the door.

Mademoiselle Franck opened her diary to book the photographer and wrote down the studio address on a card for me. 'This photographer is reputable, so you won't have any problems,' she said, handing the card to me. Then, glancing over her shoulder at the closed door to Monsieur Etienne's office, she added, 'If he says you have potential, Mademoiselle Fleurier, he means it. I know: he is my uncle.'

❧

I boarded a crowded bus to Boulevard Raspail — the address in Montparnasse that Monsieur Etienne had given me. Fortunately, Parisian men were gallant and I was helped at both ends of my journey: first by a middle-aged man who heaved my trunk up the bus steps; and by a couple of rosy-cheeked students who yanked it down again when the bus approached my stop on the intersection of the boulevard and Rue de Rennes. 'Mademoiselle, we will help you,' they said, hoisting the box onto their shoulders and insisting on carrying it all the way to the iron gate of the building.

'We can take it up the stairs for you,' offered one of the students. His companion nodded, but I was too embarrassed to ask for any more help, so I lied and told them I had a friend in the building who would help me.

'Well, goodbye,' the students waved, turning back to the street. 'Good luck in Paris.'

'*Merci beaucoup!*' I called after them. 'You are very kind!'

The iron gate was unlocked and lurched on its hinges when I pushed it open. I wiped the rust from my hands and dragged my trunk after me. The courtyard was shaded by the buildings around it and full of old shoes and broken pots. The garden beds were a tangled mass of withered plants and ropy vines, so far gone that I had no idea what they once had been. I covered my nose against the stench of dog excrement and the sewer. I was tempted to leave my trunk there while I searched for my room, but one glance at the broken windows and the raggedy washing hanging on lines slung from their frames, and I decided against it.

The studio numbers were painted in lopsided numerals on each of the buildings circling the courtyard. Apartments seven to fourteen were at the rear. I crossed the yard and entered the building through an archway. The foyer was dimly lit and smelt even more pungently of dog piles and mildew, along with the added stink of sour wine. I inspected the stairwell and braced myself to drag my trunk up the narrow stairs, hoping that no one would be coming the other way. Someone was singing and I felt heartened by the richness of the voice. But then I cringed as I made out the lyrics:

> *I love to sit by my window day after day*
> *Here in Paris, so lovely and gay*
> *Watching the girls running along the street*

I want to give them a special treat
Come here, my pretties
And show Grandad your titties . . .

The door to apartment number nine was half-rotted with strips missing from the wood around its base. I patted my coat pocket for the key Monsieur Etienne had given me, and turned it in the lock. The door was stiff and I had to push my weight against it before it gave way and I tumbled into the room. The first thing I saw was pigeon droppings oozing down the window.

The room was both better and worse than I had expected. Better, because compared to my gloomy room in Le Panier, it was filled with light from two tall windows; worse, because of the chill that seeped through the walls. I had been hoping for somewhere cosy to rest but the room was colder than the air outside. At least the stench of the courtyard didn't reach up to it; rather, the air was tinged with the scent of stale water and camphor.

I dragged my trunk to the iron bed frame, grit crunching under my feet. The bed was the only piece of furniture besides a washstand. Monsieur Etienne had told me that there was a toilet on each level but the building didn't have a bathroom. If I wanted to wash, I would have to walk three blocks to the public baths and pay a few francs for a twenty-minute soak. But I already knew that Parisian women were famous for emerging from their apartments fresh and perfectly groomed after washing themselves with nothing more than a flannel and a bucket of water. The 'tart's bath' they called it. I would be fine with that, I thought, except how would I heat the water? There was a long pipe that stretched from the ceiling to the floor between the two windows. I touched it; it was lukewarm. I resigned myself to the fact that it was the only heating for the room and prayed that the heat would be turned up higher in the evenings.

I lay on the bed even though there was no mattress on it. The springs creaked with my weight. I turned on my side, and tucked my legs underneath me. I had only been in Paris a few hours but I was exhausted. I picked at a spot of dust and released it into the air. The dust spun for a moment before floating to the floor. Loneliness crept over me. I thought of my mother, Aunt Yvette and Bernard. They were miles away from me now. I closed my eyes, still feeling the motion of the train rocking me. I had only intended to lie down for a few minutes but I drifted off to sleep.

I awoke with a shooting pain in my right arm where it pressed against the springs. The temperature in the room had dropped several degrees. I rubbed my eyes, swung my legs to the floor and groaned. The sun was setting over the rooftops and chimneys. I had planned to clean the room and buy a mattress but it was too late now. My stomach growled. The best thing to do, I decided, was to get something to eat.

The traffic bustling down the street reignited my excitement at being in Paris. I wandered down the Boulevard Raspail, breathing in the aroma of the roasted chestnuts that the street vendors sold in newspaper cones. I stopped for a moment near the entrance to the Vavin *métro* station, sure that I could feel the rumble of a train passing underground, before walking on to the Boulevard du Montparnasse, where the cafés were crowded and the patrons spilled out onto the terraces, downing plum liqueurs and warming themselves around the braziers. The intersection rang with their conversations and the tinkle of wine glasses. When I passed the Café Dôme I caught a whiff of steaming mussels and melted butter. From the fine clothes of the patrons, I assumed that even a *café crème* would be out of my reach there.

I ambled on, my hands thrust into my pockets and my head full of visions of pumpkin soup, accompanied by a half-carafe of red wine to step up my circulation. My mouth was watering with the anticipated grainy sweetness of the pumpkin when I found myself in front of a café with an inexpensive menu in the window. Inside, it was packed shoulder to shoulder with students, their orders for drinks and fried potatoes echoing around the room. The air was hot, but whether that was from the heating or the bodies crowded together, I could not tell. There was a pile of woollen coats and berets on the pegs near the door. I unbuttoned my coat but decided not to take it off until the chill had thawed out of me.

A waiter who looked Spanish showed me to a table in the corner near the newspapers and periodicals stand. Pumpkin soup wasn't on the menu and he suggested that I have onion soup instead, and try *pâté* with my bread. I accepted his advice and looked around me. The lower floor of the café consisted of a zinc counter, stools and some tables. The mezzanine level had convent tables and benches.

I craned my neck to see how far the second level stretched, and was surprised to find a group of students huddled together with books and notepapers propped in front of them. I wondered how they could concentrate with the noise from the crowd below. Perhaps they lived in rooms as cold as mine and found it easier to study in a noisy café than to shiver in the quiet.

My meal arrived. Even though I was hungry I ate slowly, letting the soup's warmth spread to my fingers and toes. I stayed in the café for as long as I could make my food last, dreading the thought of walking out into the freezing air again. There were more people jostling in the door, and some patrons took up residence on the stairs. But even when I'd scraped my plate clean, the waiter didn't move me on. It was only when a trio of boys sat down at the table next to me and starting making eyes in my direction that I decided it was time to leave. I may have been young, but I was too serious to think about romance. I had other ideas in my head.

◈

My first audition was for the chorus at the Folies Bergère. I spent the morning running over a song from 'Scheherazade' and reading *Le Figaro*. The audition was for the next season's show, '*Coeurs en Folie*: Hearts in Folly', which was going to feature the high-kicking John Tiller Girls and costumes by the Russian designer, Erté. *Le Figaro* said that the amount of fabric to be used in the revue was enough to stretch from Paris to Lyon and that the theatre's proprietor, Paul Derval, was so superstitious that the titles of all the shows had to have thirteen letters. I put the paper down and counted the letters in my name. Fourteen. I wondered, with mounting anxiety, if the same rule applied to their chorus girls.

I allowed myself time to negotiate the *métro*. It took me a few minutes to pluck up the courage to venture down the stairs into the darkness of the station. Finally, I joined on to the back of a group of students and followed them. I bought my ticket from the booth and found myself being jostled with the crowd down a tunnel. On the platform, I studied the map and became confused by the mess of coloured lines twisting around each other and ending in far-off suburbs. An old lady explained that I would need to change at Châtelet in order to get to Cadet.

I stared at the abyss of the tunnel until two headlights like fire in the nostrils of an ancient dragon lurched out of the darkness and a train clattered towards the platform. I was bustled into the carriage and took a seat as close as I could to the door, terrified that I would miss my stop and end up lost in the maze of tunnels. The doors rattled shut, a bell pinged and the train took off. Under other circumstances, I would probably have enjoyed my first ride on the modern *métro* but I was too worried about my audition. At each stop, more people joined the train and I found myself straining to read the station names through the mass of heads and arms. *Saint Germain des Près. Saint Michel. Châtelet!*

I followed the crowd off the train and somehow managed to find the platform for trains heading north. The next train was just as crowded as the first and this time I didn't get a seat. I tugged my coat collar; with all the bodies pressed together the carriage was steaming. But there was hardly room to move, and I couldn't have taken off my coat if I had tried. The *métro* may have been modern, but I saw it as an unnatural way to travel: lurching blindly through a tunnel, my sense of direction taken from me. The train came to a stop and I saw the sign for Cadet. I made my way to the door, thankful there was someone in front of me to open it. If I had been by myself, I would still have been standing there when the train pulled out, not realising that although the doors closed automatically the latch had to be raised in order to get out.

I emerged from the station into the afternoon light with as much relief as an animal escaping from a trap. The ramshackle combination of cafés, butchers, grocers, trinket shops, restaurants and bars was less planned than Montparnasse. I opened my bag and reviewed the directions to the Folies Bergère. Still disorientated from the *métro* ride, I set off up a street in the opposite direction to where I should have been heading.

I admired the pink and green houses covered with bare ivy vines. The area would have had the atmosphere of a village if not for the seedy characters stinking of booze and cigarettes lurking in doorways. When I reached the traffic on the Boulevard de Rochechouart, I realised that I was lost. A policeman gave me directions to get back to the Rue Richer. I passed some street performers on my way, including an India-rubber man twisting himself into knots on a mat for the amusement of the patrons of a nearby café. Although he managed to cross both his legs behind his neck, I heard the crack in his joints and shivered. It was too cold for feats of flexibility.

I reached the Rue Richer and took a deep breath outside the glass doors of the Folies Bergère, dazzled by the plush carpet, wood panelling and sparkling chandeliers. A doorman with gold braid on his shoulders informed me that performers were to use the stage door on Rue Saulnier for the audition.

I turned the corner and my heart skipped a beat. There were about fifty women milling around the stage door. The management was only looking for three chorus girls to replace those who weren't continuing on from the previous show. Why were they auditioning so many? Some of the women had struck up conversations, but most were either sitting on the steps or standing around on their own, going over the words of their songs, smoking or staring into space. I leaned against a lamppost and reconsidered my audition tactics. I knew that getting a part in the chorus for one of the most prestigious music halls wasn't going to be easy, but I hadn't expected it would be *so* competitive. I had ended up on stage at Le Chat Espiègle by accident, and even then I had known the impresario and most of the cast beforehand. In Paris it looked as if I was going to have to work hard and get used to going into things cold. While I was recovering from my shock, a blonde girl with golden eyes glanced in my direction and yawned. I studied the women around me. Most were blondes and nearly all had their hair fashionably bobbed. There were only a few very tall girls and there was certainly no one as dark as me.

After a while, a woman with severe eyes appeared in the doorway. '*Bonjour*, ladies,' she said, clapping her hands. 'Nudes on the left. Chorus on the right.'

Along with the other girls I jumped to attention. We shuffled ourselves into two lines. I was relieved to see the girl with the golden eyes line up for a nude part, but there were still eighteen other girls trying out for the chorus. 'I heard it's Raoul who's going to be taking us through the steps,' a girl with a Russian accent said to her French companion. 'He's tough but good.' Her comment left me feeling even more isolated and inexperienced. Was I the only one who didn't know what went on at a proper audition?

After we had handed in our music, the woman took us to a room to change into our rehearsal costumes. As outer clothes were flung off and tights, chemises and tunics were tugged on the air became rank with the smell of nervous sweat. My fingers trembled when I tied on my dancing shoes, but I reminded myself that auditions were part of becoming a real performer.

'Hurry, this way,' the woman called out when she saw that we were ready. She shooed us into a rehearsal room with a scuffed wooden floor and mirrors on the walls. A black man in tights and a singlet stood at the front, his arms crossed over his chest. The woman took a seat at the piano. When we were all in the room, the man shut the door. 'I'm Raoul,' he said in a squeaky voice that was at odds with his muscular frame. 'I want you to organise yourselves into pairs for the dance segment. You will be auditioning in sets of two. It makes things faster.'

We did as he instructed. I joined a leggy girl whose sleek bob concealed half her face, knowing that standing next to a diminutive girl would only exaggerate my height further.

Raoul strode into the middle of the group. 'Now, I'm only going to show you this routine twice,' he said, holding up two fingers. 'This is part of your audition too, because if you can't learn steps quickly then you have no place at the Folies Bergère. Understood?'

Any face that had been smiling up to that point became as crestfallen as the rest of the group. My heart thumped in my chest so loudly that I didn't think I would be able to hear anything Raoul said. He demonstrated a quick cross step, which was probably the only useful thing I'd learnt from Madame Baroux, with Egyptian arms and a few kicks at the end. I was surprised that I picked up the routine faster than anyone else, including my partner who shuffled her feet, her steps blending into one shaky movement. I would have been happy to show her how to do it correctly, but we weren't allowed to talk to each other. Fortunately for her, we were given another ten minutes to practise on our own, by which time most of the girls had grasped the routine.

After the dance practice we were taken to the hall where the stage was lit with working lights and a man sat at the rehearsal piano sorting the music from a list of names. Raoul directed us into the wings and told us to be quiet. As we filed past the front row of seats, I noticed two men sitting there and assumed they were Monsieur Derval, the proprietor, and Monsieur Lemarchand, the producer. The sight of them did not calm my nerves. Both men were immaculately dressed: Monsieur Derval with a black jacket over pinstriped trousers; and Monsieur Lemarchand looking every part the *bon viveur* in his double-breasted suit with a handkerchief in the pocket.

I felt sorry for the pair of dancers who were called up first. One was a statuesque girl with strawberry blonde hair who was incongruously coupled with a petite redhead in a skimpy chemise. I peeked through the curtains to watch the reaction of the judges. After Raoul had introduced the girls and Monsieur Lemarchand had noted their names, the pianist struck up a tune. The tall girl was a natural dancer; her body rippled to the music. Her smile wasn't forced, but I knew she couldn't really be having the time of her life considering the nature of the audition. Her partner was a good dancer too but her style bordered on risqué. She added hip gyrations where there were none and kicked her legs a fraction too wide for modesty. Monsieur Derval noticed but his expression showed neither pleasure nor disgust. Monsieur Lemarchand kept his eyes fixed on the other girl.

The routine ended with a graceful pose but, just before they reached it, the tall girl slipped and almost fell off the stage. She quickly recovered her balance but not her composure. Her companion was dismissed with a 'Thank you, that will be all, Mademoiselle Duhamel,' but the tall girl was asked to perform her song. Despite having been asked to continue, she could not get over her mistake. Her voice was good but her eyelids twitched as if she had something stuck in her lashes and she didn't look at the men. The girl next to me smiled. She was pleased that the tall girl was becoming unravelled, but it unnerved me. I performed better when the people around me were at their best.

'That was nice, but not for this show,' said Monsieur Lemarchand. The girl thanked the men and left the stage. I felt the tremble in her legs when she brushed past me on her way out. I thought I was going to be sick.

The next pair of girls fared better. They ended their routine with true showgirl flair, posing with concave stomachs and pointed toes, a hand on one hip and the other reaching gracefully towards the ceiling. Monsieur Derval was delighted with them. When they had finished their songs they were asked to stay. The next two girls were good dancers too, but while one was classically beautiful with a radiant smile, the other was heavy in the legs. The second girl was the better dancer: she moved with the music, while the first girl kicked her legs mechanically. But the more beautiful girl was asked to stay on for the next part of the audition and the other one was dismissed.

My heart lurched in my throat when I was called up. My partner and I took our places on the stage but the pianist didn't start the tune because Monsieur Derval and Monsieur Lemarchand had their heads together in discussion. We were left standing with frozen smiles on our faces and our arms in the air. The room began to sway and the lights burned into my eyes. I thought that if we didn't move soon, I would faint.

Monsieur Derval whispered something to Raoul who nodded then turned to us. 'As the singing parts are causing the most problems, we've decided to change the order. We'll do the songs first and then do the dance segment,' he said. He gestured for my partner to move towards the front of the stage to perform her song. It took all my effort to keep still. Her voice was so high that it was childlike, but rather than being horrified by the earsplitting noise, Monsieur Derval seemed charmed by it. The girl was asked to wait for the dance segment.

Okay, this is it, I told myself when I was called forward. I tried to remember the feeling I'd had the last night I sang at Le Chat Espiègle. To my delight, my voice came out confidently and with a vibrancy that resounded through the hall. I forced myself to look around the room as if I were singing to a real audience, and particularly at the two men. Monsieur Lemarchand smiled back at me, but Monsieur Derval wasn't watching, he was picking at a loose thread on his sleeve. Although we were only required to sing a few bars for the first round, neither man stopped me so I continued with the chorus. It was only when the first verse repeated itself that Monsieur Derval held up his hand.

'Thank you, Mademoiselle Fleurier,' Raoul said. 'Move to the back of the stage and we'll see you dance.'

I was nervous from singing but threw myself into the dance alongside my partner. I needn't have bothered; Monsieur Lemarchand and Monsieur Derval weren't looking at us. They were having an argument about something, leaning over the backs of their chairs so they couldn't be heard, but their conflict played out in a series of hand gestures and shakes of their heads. Even when my partner and I came to our finishing pose, the men continued their discussion. Monsieur Lemarchand glanced in my direction and I understood that they were talking about me. My partner and I had no choice but to hold our poses. Raoul folded his arms and strode back and forth across the stage in front of us, trying to distract attention from the discussion, but I caught the telling phrases.

Monsieur Lemarchand said, 'She's charming. Different. What a voice!' To which Monsieur Derval replied, 'She's not beautiful enough for the Folies Bergère.'

The discussion ceased and Monsieur Derval turned back to us and smiled. 'Thank you, Mademoiselle Fleurier, that will be all,' he said.

❧

Not beautiful enough for the Folies Bergère! The voices of the other *métro* passengers faded while I played the audition over again in my head, turning it into more of a catastrophe than it actually had been. The girls in their rehearsal costumes became lurid stripes of pink and black; the piano music sounded tinny and distorted; Raoul transformed into a lurking giant; and the faces of Messieurs Derval and Lemarchand melted together into one grotesque mouth shouting 'Not beautiful enough!'

I coughed and stared out the window at the black spinning past me. Hadn't Aunt Augustine warned me that I didn't have Camille's music hall looks? A hunger spasm clenched my belly and I thought about the cold room waiting for me in Montparnasse. Then I imagined my mother and Bernard sitting at the kitchen table on the farm. Aunt Yvette was cooking potatoes in the fire. The light from the flames flickered on the walls and reflected on the glasses of wine on the table. Wouldn't it be easier to go back?

I shrugged the thought away. It *would* be easier to go back and be surrounded by people who loved me, to sleep in a warm bed and to have a full stomach. But the girl who had been content with wandering the hills of Pays de Sault and dreaming of the lavender harvest didn't exist any more. I wanted to be on stage.

By the time I reached Châtelet to change trains, I had exhausted myself with dramatic thoughts and had turned into a paragon of stoicism. I decided that I had to forget the Folies Bergère audition. Hadn't I failed my audition at Le Chat Espiègle and still got the part in the end? And hadn't Monsieur Lemarchand, one of the greatest artistic directors in Paris, praised my voice?

The train for Vavin pulled into the station. Besides, I thought, taking a seat in the middle carriage, I do not want to be some feathered bird strutting around the stage, no matter how prestigious Monsieur Etienne thinks that is. I opened my purse and took out the audition schedule. The next one was for the following evening at a nightclub in Pigalle.

There, I said to myself, glancing at the number of singers used in the show. There are only three singers, not sixteen. It is practically a solo part!

NINE

I left for my audition the following night in good spirits. I had spent
the morning scrubbing the walls and floor of my room. I had then
caught the *métro* to Ménilmontant to buy some blankets at a market
there and a thin cotton mattress over which I would put a second
mattress when I had more money. I had rested in the afternoon,
preparing myself for the audition and running over the ballads I had
chosen from 'Scheherazade'. I thought a smaller venue would want a
more intimate performance.

It was almost ten o'clock when I exited the *métro* at Pigalle. I was
amazed to see how much the village atmosphere of the Right Bank's
entertainment quarter changed in the evening. The tumbledown
streets were jumping with music: accordions, violins and guitars;
soprano and contralto voices; songs in French and English. The
music bellowed out of cafés and throbbed out of clubs. Foreigners
crowded the streets — Scandinavians, Germans and British. But
more than any of those combined were Americans. One man, too
young for the cane he was leaning on, was talking to a group of men
and women in evening wear. He began his sentences with '*Yawl*'
while they all ended theirs in '*schure*'.

'*Yawl. Schure,*' I repeated to myself, walking along Boulevard de
Clichy. The women of the night were out in force, their skirts girded
up despite the cold. I passed a bar with a sign, 'Café des Americains',

above the door. People were sitting on the windowsills and spilling out the door. Music blurted from the windows. I was struck by the energy and dynamism of it — a piano, drum set, trumpet and trombone. They sounded like a marching band, but less orderly. The singer started up. *Boo-boobly-boo-boo.* I couldn't tell if he was singing in a foreign language or simply making sounds. But I liked the way he bent his voice then returned it to pitch.

The nightclub I was looking for was off the main street, down an alley that stank of cat urine. I had trouble finding the door, but when I did I realised there was no handle. I knocked and waited. Nothing happened. I wondered if there was another entrance from the main street. I checked but there wasn't. I returned and this time pounded my fist against the door. After a minute it opened and I found myself face to face with a woman with her hair coiled into a bun on top of her head and a chin that sagged to her neck.

'I'm here for the audition,' I said.

The woman jerked her thumb over her shoulder. 'Come inside.'

I followed her through a corridor into the club. A cloud of tobacco smoke stung my eyes and it took me a few seconds to register the murky brown walls and the bottles lined up on the counter. The club was full of men, alone or in small groups, huddled over their drinks or card games. One of them glanced over his shoulder and scowled at me. I turned away and found myself looking at what I guessed must be the venue's stage: some boards propped up on a couple of fragile-looking trestles. The dip in the middle wasn't reassuring.

'Hey, René,' the woman shouted to a man cleaning glasses behind the counter. 'Your performer's here.'

The man flipped open the counter and stepped towards us. I did my best not to stare at his stomach which was straining the buttons of his shirt. 'The cellar,' he said, hissing his vinegary breath into my face. 'The audition's in there.'

He pointed to a flight of stairs that descended into a dimly lit room. If I hadn't been so desperate for a job, and so disorientated by Paris, I might have had the sense to leave then. Instead, I felt my way down the stairwell, pressing my hands against the damp walls. When I reached the bottom step I saw that the room was lined with barrels. I thought that I must have taken the wrong stairs, then I heard a man's voice behind me. 'Ah, you're here.'

I turned around. Sitting at an upright piano was an old man, as dusty as his surroundings. 'Deirdre will join us soon,' he said, smiling through stained teeth. 'You're the only one trying out tonight.'

The man's translucent face and bloodless lips made him seem unreal: a ghost trapped in the cellar with his piano. If it hadn't been for the sound of a table crashing to the floor upstairs and men's voices fighting to bring me to my senses, I might not have been able to speak at all.

'I have music,' I said, handing him my songs.

He took the sheets from me and flicked through them. He was holding them upside down but that didn't seem to bother him.

'Merde!' I heard the proprietor's voice shout upstairs.

'Very nice,' said the old man, handing the music back to me. 'But we have our own songs here. I'll sing you the song and then you sing it after me, all right?'

I nodded.

The man's fingers hovered over the keys for a minute before he began playing. The piano was out of tune.

> *My doggie's tail, it wags*
> *Tra-la-la-la*
> *My landlady's mouth, it nags*
> *Tra-la-la-la*
> *The Eiffel Tower, it stands*
> *Tra-la-la-la*
> *Ah Paris, isn't it grand?*

The man lifted his hands from the keys. 'Now, do you think you can sing that?' he asked, wiping spittle from the corner of his mouth. 'Let's try. Sing along with me.'

He played the tune again. I sang along as best I could, twisting my hands behind my back. My bewilderment came through in my wavering voice.

'Nice. Very nice,' the old man said, smiling. 'But how about making it a bit more jolly. Our patrons like their fun.'

A bottle smashed upstairs. Something heavy fell to the floor. Footsteps clumped on the steps. A few seconds later the woman with the bun, who I assumed was Deirdre, stepped into the cellar.

'Is she ready?' she asked.

He nodded. 'She's got a good voice. Sweet.'

Deirdre threw her head back and glared at me. 'Are you going to wear that outfit?'

My hand fell to the dress Camille had given me. 'Yes,' I stuttered, dumbfounded at how my best dress could be met with such disapproval. It was nicer than the smock Deirdre was wearing.

She reached into her sleeve and pulled out a card. 'If you get the job, you'll need to wear a black gown. Here's the name of our costume-maker.'

I took the card and nodded, too inexperienced to know about the racket run by disreputable café-concerts. Naive performers with stars in their eyes were made to buy costumes from dressmakers who gave the café manager a cut on the deal.

'Do you know your song?' Deirdre asked me.

The old man let out a spooky laugh. 'She does. Well enough.'

'Come on then,' Deirdre said, gesturing for me to follow her. 'If you pass the audition you can keep any tips you make tonight. Remember, it's only when I leave the stage that you or one of the other girls step in. I'm the star.'

'Other girls?' I asked, following Deirdre's enormous girth up the stairs. I had thought that the club only had three singers.

Deirdre turned around when we reached the top of the stairs. 'If the girls are busy talking with customers, then you get up there and sing. And if not, you let them. They were here first. Got it?'

I nodded although I wasn't sure if I had 'got it' at all. My heart was beating so violently that it was making me sick. It dawned on me that my audition was going to be before an audience.

Deirdre pointed to the four stools that had been set up on the stage and told me to sit on the one on the left. I did as I was told, slipping my bag and coat under it. I looked out at the audience. Amongst the men there were now women watching the card games or sipping drinks. The smell of unwashed bodies and musty clothes was suffocating. A man with a scar down the side of his face bawled at a waiter to bring him a drink. When it was sent to him he turned his attention to me, his gaze moving up from my feet to my breasts. I stared at the picture of the hog on the back wall, trying to avoid his eyes. To my relief, two other girls stepped onto the stage and took their places on the stools and the scar-faced man turned his attention to them. One of the girls was a brunette with pimples on her chin. Her eyes were swollen as if she had been crying. The other was a bleached blonde whose black eyebrows stood out like stripes on her forehead. The ghost man came up from the cellar and sat down at a piano near the stage. He ran his fingers over the keys. To my relief the instrument was in tune.

Deirdre hitched up her skirt and wobbled her massive bosom. My heart sank as soon as she hit the first note. Her voice was a cross between a parrot and a goat and for most of the song she was a couple of bars ahead of the piano. She shook her legs and shimmied her hips. No one paid her any attention, except for the scar-faced man who continued to leer.

An argument broke out at one of the tables. A man with a stain down the front of his shirt turned around and yelled at Deirdre, 'Shut up, you ugly mutt! I can't hear the call.' Another man, sitting by himself at a table near the front, spat an olive stone at her. It missed Deirdre and hit me on the chin. I wiped away the residue, not quite able to hide my disgust. But if Deirdre was concerned at the lack of respect given to her star position, she didn't show it. She continued for three more songs, including a shrill version of 'Valencia' to which she also performed a sort of bobbing dance that reminded me of a pigeon pecking for food, before bowing and stepping off the stage.

I was thankful to see that the other girls were still on their chairs. The brunette stood up and sang 'Mon Paris' in a throaty voice that wasn't too bad except it didn't carry. That kept the card players happy while the rest of the audience ignored her or called out, 'Sing up!' Even the scar-faced man transferred his attention to a broad-shouldered streetwalker. The brunette finished her song and stepped off the stage, sitting down next to the man who had spat the olive stone. He grinned, showing a gap where his front teeth should have been, and threw his arm around her the way a man might do if he were trying to headlock a vicious dog.

I turned back to the stage and noticed that the blonde girl wasn't there — she was sitting on the lap of a card player — and that the pianist was nodding at me. I slipped off my stool and edged my way to the front of the stage. I smoothed down my dress and cleared my throat. 'My doggie's tail, it wags. Tra-la-la-la.' I was so terrified, my arms and legs stiffened and I sang the entire song frozen to the spot.

But this was an audition I didn't care if I failed; I only wanted to get out of that place alive.

When I reached the end of my number, I made a grab for my stool but the pianist played the tune over again and I had no choice but to sing it again. To my horror, everyone who wasn't playing cards stopped talking and turned to watch me. '*The Eiffel Tower, it stands. Tra-la-la-la. Ah Paris, isn't it grand?*' My voice didn't sound like my own, it was strained with nerves. But compared to the other girls, there was no arguing that it was good. The scar-faced man clapped. 'Sing it again,' he shouted. A table of people sharing a bottle of wine joined in his applause. One of the men stepped forward and tossed a few coins in the jar on the piano. The other men at his table followed suit. René glanced up from the bar and winked. The pianist whispered, 'They like you. You're really good.' For a moment everything seemed fine. I never wanted to set foot in the place again, but tonight at least there might be money for a new dress or a rug for the floor. I sang the ditty again, this time more boldly, and lifted my voice to carry through the room.

A man with a broken nose who was playing cards turned around and shouted, 'Will someone make that bitch shut up? I can't think!'

'Yeah,' slurred his female companion, lifting her head from her beau's shoulder. 'She stinks.'

'Not like you, ya mongrel,' the scar-faced man shouted back at her. 'You stink like a rotting fish.'

A few people in the audience laughed. The broken-nosed man rushed to the bar and seized the scar-faced man by the throat. But his target was too fast — before the broken-nosed man could strangle him, the scar-faced man flattened him with a blow to the stomach. More punches flew. The broken-nosed man's friends ran to his aid. The proprietor swept the bottles from the counter; he was just in time. The card players picked up the scar-faced man and threw him over the counter into the mirror. His supporters retaliated by picking up chairs and smashing them across the backs of the card players.

The pianist smiled at me and continued playing my tune. I stood at the front of the stage, too scared to move. Something sharp jabbed into my stomach. I glanced down. The olive-spitter had a blade pressed against my ribs. His eyes were bloodshot. I stared at his cavernous mouth, his ruby-red lips. I was sure he was going to kill me for no reason other than it was something to do.

'Get out, bitch,' he said. 'You squawk like a dying bird and nobody likes you.'

I gave a cry and tried to get off the stage, but my feet wouldn't move. The man made a swiping action with the blade. The gesture spurred me into action. I grabbed my bag and coat, jumped to the floor and ran through the crowd, dodging flying bottles and chairs. I raced through the door and up the boulevard, nearly knocking people over in my panic to get away. It was only when I reached the brightly lit *métro* station that I stopped to catch my breath.

Back in my freezing apartment in Montparnasse I threw myself onto my bed, covered my head with a pillow and wept.

⌘

By the following morning, the events of the previous evening were beginning to seem like a deranged dream. Grotesque faces with scars, broken noses, missing teeth and double chins loomed up before me and I felt the sharpness of a blade pressing into my skin. Had any of that actually happened? I found it hard to believe that a reputable agent would have sent anyone to such a disreputable establishment, and I walked all the way to Rue Saint Dominique with the intention of telling Monsieur Etienne so.

To my surprise it was Monsieur Etienne, and not Mademoiselle Franck, who answered my impatient ring of the buzzer.

'Now then, what's wrong?' he asked, ushering me into the reception room. 'Something's the matter — I can tell by your face. And you missed your audition last night.'

'I did not!'

Monsieur Etienne raised his eyebrows and gestured for me to take a chair. 'What is going on, Mademoiselle Fleurier?' he asked, folding his arms. 'You didn't go to your audition at the Café des Singes last night after I had talked about you to the manageress. She rang me this morning to ask why you hadn't showed up.'

'But I was there,' I insisted.

I described my audition, including the stools and how we were to be paid only in tips. Monsieur Etienne's face blanched when I told him about the blade in my ribs.

'I've never heard of such a thing,' he said, looking at me as if he were trying to ascertain if I was mad. 'I would never send a client of mine to a place like that.'

He was cut off by the sound of a key in the door. Mademoiselle Franck sauntered into the room with a stack of mail clutched under her arm. She was even more chic than the first time I had seen her, wearing a georgette dress and crocodile-skin shoes.

'What's wrong?' she asked, looking from Monsieur Etienne to me.

Monsieur Etienne repeated what I had told him about the previous night's audition and her mouth dropped open. 'But, Mademoiselle Fleurier,' she said, waving her hand and sending the fragrance of orange blossom floating through the air, 'the place you describe sounds nothing like the Café des Singes. Monsieur Etienne and I have known the manageress for years. She runs a classy bar. That is why we thought, with your voice, you would do well there.'

'Manageress?' I repeated. 'The nightclub I was in last night had a manager and a piano player. Unless of course you are referring to Deirdre?'

'Deirdre?' Mademoiselle Franck knotted her brow and turned to Monsieur Etienne. 'The manageress's name is Madame Baquet.'

I reached into my bag and pulled out the schedule. 'Look, this is where I was last night at ten o'clock. The manager there was a man. His name was René.'

Mademoiselle Franck took the paper from me. 'Number twelve?' she muttered, hurrying to her desk and flipping through a card file. She found what she was looking for and gave a cry, her cheeks flushing crimson. '*Mais non!*' she said, holding up the card. 'The street number of the Café des Singes is twenty-one. The numerals are switched. A typing error!'

'Number twenty-one is over the other side of Boulevard du Clichy,' Monsieur Etienne said, running his hand over his forehead. 'It sounds as if the place you were in was a café-concert.'

We stood in the reception room looking at each other. Mademoiselle Franck's face turned a darker shade of red; even the backs of her hands were blushing. I thought of the ghostly pianist, of Deirdre calling herself 'a star', the appalling clientele and the frenzied eyes of the psychopath pressing the blade into my skin. I hadn't been where I was supposed to be at all. I must have auditioned in place of a performer who had never turned up. The coincidence was so horrible it was funny: I started to laugh and couldn't stop. For a moment, my anxieties about money and the cold became absurd. I tried to say something, but Monsieur Etienne had such a bemused look on his face that I doubled over with more laughter.

'Ah,' puffed Monsieur Etienne, straightening his jacket and attempting to re-establish decorum. 'Mademoiselle Fleurier, if only everybody could take a mistake like that as good-naturedly as you have.' A smile twitched at the corners of his mouth. 'I have no idea what to say or how to apologise for it. Perhaps my niece and I could make it up to you by inviting you to lunch?'

❧

Monsieur Etienne and Mademoiselle Franck lived in an apartment two buildings down on the Rue Saint Dominique. Their maid greeted us at the door.

'We have a guest for lunch, Lucie,' Monsieur Etienne told her. 'I hope that's not any trouble?'

The maid shook her head and reached out to take our coats and scarves. She was young, perhaps only nineteen, but had the lumpy elbows and rotund stomach of a matron.

Like the reception room of his office, Monsieur Etienne's apartment was elegant but compact. We took turns washing our hands in a bathroom the size of a closet, with mauve fittings and wallpaper in the pattern of blue hyacinths. Afterwards we passed through a drawing room, where I caught a glimpse of myself in a mirror and despaired at the mop the weather had made of my hair, and then to a dining room, where curtains softened a view of a wall scarred by drainpipes.

'It is hot in here,' said Monsieur Etienne, cracking open the window. With the heaters and the fireplace, and the steaming food Lucie was laying on the table, the room was hot, but I liked it that way. It was the first time I had been properly warm in days.

Monsieur Etienne indicated for us to sit down while Lucie served us soup from a tureen. There was a painting behind Monsieur Etienne that caught my attention because it was at odds with the formal decor of the apartment. It depicted a group of patrons spilling out of the Moulin Rouge. The lines weren't straight, the faces were exaggerated and the colours weren't realistic. I didn't know enough about painting then to understand much about dimension or perspective, but the patrons appeared to be moving. I could almost hear them chatting about the show. Monsieur Etienne noticed where I was looking.

'That is one of Odette's,' he said, indicating Mademoiselle Franck. 'Her parents live in Saint Germain en Laye which is too far away for her to commute to her art classes, so she stays with me and helps out at the office.'

'I like it,' I said.

'I have told Odette to speak to an art dealer acquaintance of mine,' said Monsieur Etienne. 'She has talent.'

Mademoiselle Franck swallowed a spoonful of soup. 'I don't care if my pictures are hung in galleries,' she said. 'I just enjoy painting.'

'My niece's ambition is to get married,' said Monsieur Etienne with a sigh.

'And my uncle's is to avoid it,' Mademoiselle Franck retorted.

They laughed good-naturedly at each other.

The main meal was roast chicken. The amber sweetness of the butter sauce melted on my tongue. It was my first real meal in Paris.

'What happened with the Folies Bergère?' Monsieur Etienne asked me when Lucie had cleared away the dishes. 'I know you didn't get a part, but how was the audition?'

I told him about Monsieur Derval saying that I wasn't beautiful enough for the Folies Bergère.

Monsieur Etienne lit a cigarette and leaned back in his chair. 'No,' he said, after a few moments' thought. 'You're a good-looking girl with a nice figure. Monsieur Derval isn't keen on types and you've got the exotic looks he usually likes to scatter amongst his blondes and redheads. I think this time around his decision had to do with the show featuring English chorus girls with a particular look. We will send you for the auditions for the next show and see what happens. Meanwhile, we have to find you a job, yes?'

'I think the Café des Singes will be just right for you,' said Mademoiselle Franck, passing the cream for my coffee. 'You will like Madame Baquet. Everyone does.'

'She is looking for someone to sing the two o'clock morning session a couple of times a week,' said Monsieur Etienne. 'That will pay your rent and you can keep it up even if you get something in the music hall. A lot of girls do that and make good money. Unfortunately, they spend it just as quickly.'

Mademoiselle Franck rolled her eyes. 'Uncle is always telling his clients to save a third of everything they earn. He does the same thing to me. Only I don't even get to see my third before he deposits it in a bank in Switzerland.'

Monsieur Etienne shrugged. 'If you are wise you will do the same thing, Mademoiselle Fleurier. Youth, beauty and popularity do not last. I have seen too many good women, used up by men and by life, ending their days in cheap hotels.'

I remembered the first time I had seen Monsieur Etienne in my dressing room in Marseilles. I had been intimidated by him then, but now I saw that the opinion I had formed about him was wrong. Sitting in his dining room he wasn't commanding or arrogant. He was everything a good uncle should be: worldly, level-headed and kind. Mademoiselle Franck was lucky to have him.

'What have you got to sing for your audition?' Monsieur Etienne asked.

I told him about the ballads from 'Scheherazade' and he shook his head. 'That is too music hall for Madame Baquet. She will want something more personal. What else have you got?'

I explained to him that I didn't have any music. He asked me how I had got the part of Scheherazade and when I told him the story of Zephora he opened his eyes in astonishment. 'I didn't realise that you had no experience with auditions. Odette and I will come to see you audition at the Café des Singes when that is reorganised. Meanwhile, she can take you to buy some sheet music. Don't worry about the money. You can fix that up later when you start working.'

I understood that Monsieur Etienne did not make friends of all his clients; he was too professional for that. And yet, when he smiled and shook my hand before Mademoiselle Franck and I headed out the door, I sensed that he had made friends with me.

~~~

Mademoiselle Franck took me to a music store on Rue d'Odéon. We bought two popular songs at three francs each, a couple of club standards and one from the discount bin at the back of the shop. I flicked through the yellowing pages. The song was titled 'It's Him I Love'.

'You can arrange it differently and make it your signature song,'

Mademoiselle Franck said, handing the music sheets to the sales clerk and opening her purse.

I glanced at the words.

> *It's him I love*
> *Though he's far away*
> *It's him I love*
> *But I should live for today.*

The frothy numbers of 'Scheherazade' had come easily to me, but I wondered if I was going to be able to sing convincingly about a broken heart when I had never fallen in, or out, of love.

'How fast do you think you can learn them?' Mademoiselle Franck asked when we stepped out onto the street.

'I can learn the words today,' I said, 'but how will I learn the tunes? I can't read music.'

'Most of our singers can't read music,' said Mademoiselle Franck, adjusting her scarf and pulling on her gloves. 'There is a piano teacher in the apartment below us. We don't complain about the noise his students make and in turn he gives our clients a discount on practice sessions. I'll set up an appointment with him tomorrow morning if you like.'

Mademoiselle Franck suggested that we have a hot chocolate in the café next to the music store. The space was crammed with people and we had to squeeze our way past legs and elbows to reach a table near the counter. I noticed the way men looked at Mademoiselle Franck — not in the lustful way they looked at Camille, but with admiration. She was lovely to look at, her walk was lovely, her voice was lovely; being with her made me want to be lovely too.

The café was unpretentious, with white walls and polished floors. The only decorative pieces were the engraved glass domes that covered the cakes, and two brass chandeliers hanging from the ceiling.

'They have different patterns etched in the glass,' observed Mademoiselle Franck, squinting at the frosted globes of the chandeliers. 'The one above us is patterned with olive trees and the other one with wreaths.'

'You're right,' I agreed, impressed by her eye for detail. I wouldn't have noticed the difference if she hadn't pointed it out.

I thought about the song we had bought. *It's him I love, though he's far away; It's him I love but I should live for today.* 'Have you ever been in love, Mademoiselle Franck?' I asked.

Her face flushed. 'I am in love now,' she said, pressing her palms against her cheeks to cool them. 'His name is Joseph. He works in a fine furniture store. Antiques, rare woods, that sort of thing.'

I thought of the telephone conversation I had overheard on my first day at the office and grinned. 'So he has an artistic flair, like you?'

She lowered her eyes, a smile tickling the corners of her mouth. 'We both like beautiful things, although Joseph doesn't have any money. He says that we must wait until he opens his own business before we can marry.' She looked up, a worried frown breaking across her forehead. 'That is why you must promise not to tell Uncle, Mademoiselle Fleurier,' she said, grasping my hand. 'Joseph is a good Jewish boy and there is no reason not to approve of him. But sometimes my uncle is an intellectual snob, and Joseph is no intellectual. We have to wait until the time is right, otherwise he will put my parents offside.'

That must be real love, I thought: when you see someone's shortcomings but love them just the same. I squeezed her hand back. 'I won't mention it until you do,' I promised.

The waiter took our order and a few minutes later our hot chocolates arrived. I breathed in the aroma of almonds floating up through the cream and sipped the velvety fluid with as much pleasure as a cat lapping a saucer of milk.

'I'm sure you will do well at the Café des Singes,' said Mademoiselle Franck, stirring her chocolate. 'My uncle is a good judge of star potential. I swear he does it by intuition rather than by logic, although he argues otherwise. He says it doesn't matter how vibrant someone appears to be on the surface or how good their voice is, at their core they must be hardworking and serious. That is how he summed you up, anyway.'

I smiled. I had never been described as 'hardworking and serious' when I lived on the farm. Perhaps I had found my *métier*.

'The audience at the Café des Singes is sophisticated,' Mademoiselle Franck continued. 'Some French and a lot of foreigners. But not tourists. Mainly American writers, German photographers and Russian painters. They will expect a lot from you but they will support you in return.'

I explained to her that I had known only two types of audience: the rowdy Marseilles working class and the audience I had experienced last night. 'I'm not sure I am refined enough for the Café des Singes,' I confessed.

'Oh, but you are,' exclaimed Mademoiselle Franck, putting down her glass. 'Much more than you think. But I would like to make a suggestion, if you don't mind.'

'I don't mind at all,' I assured her.

'You have beautiful eyes and cheekbones, but they are diminished by the way you wear your hair. I think you should cut your hair short. It would be much more chic and Madame Baquet would love it.'

Styling advice from someone as well groomed as Mademoiselle Franck could not go unheeded. 'I would,' I said, 'but I have no one to do it for me here. My mother trimmed my hair at home.'

Mademoiselle Franck shook her head. 'You must have a professional cut it. You don't want to end up looking like a boy. I can take you to my salon, if you like. We can go now.'

We caught the *métro* to Tuileries and walked across the Place Vendôme because, although the wind had turned icy, Mademoiselle Franck insisted that I see it. The massive space was surrounded by buildings with classical pediments and columns. Mademoiselle Franck told me the names of the cars parked around the Colonne Vendôme in the centre. 'That is a Rolls-Royce, that is a Voisin, and that is a Bugatti.' Then she tugged my arm and pointed to the window of a jewellery shop. 'Look at those,' she cried.

My eyes nearly popped out when I saw the velvet bust bedecked in diamonds — real diamonds. Minute spotlights reflected off a mirror behind the bust and added to the chimerical effect of the stones. Next to the jeweller was a *couturier*. The mannequins in the window were draped in *crêpe de Chine* dresses with fitted sleeves and gilt buttons.

'That is the Hotel Ritz, over there,' said Mademoiselle Franck, pointing to a palatial building to the left of the square.

The decadence all around sent me into a panic. 'Mademoiselle Franck, I don't think that I will be able to afford your hairdresser.'

'Please, call me Odette,' she said, linking her arm with mine and tugging me forward. 'The hairstyle is my treat. I wanted you to see the Vendôme because this is where you will shop when you are rich and famous. When you appear at the Casino de Paris, then you can return the favour to me.'

∞

Madame Chardin's salon was on Rue Vivienne. While it wasn't the Place Vendôme, one look at the gold fittings and the marble reception table and I could understand why Monsieur Etienne put away a third of Odette's income. The customers were not bunched together, the way men are in barber shops. Each woman sat in an individual cubicle created by Japanese silk screens. I caught a glimpse of a customer with a Pekinese on her lap and her hair in rollers. In the cubicle next to her a woman was having her hair brushed into a lofty bouffant by a girl in a white uniform.

'*Bonjour*, Mademoiselle Franck!' called a woman wearing a taupe dress with a pearl brooch in the shape of a peacock. She strode across the tiled floor and welcomed Odette with kisses. The woman was about forty with chestnut hair sliced straight across her forehead and graduating in length from the nape of her neck to her chin.

'*Bonjour*, Madame Chardin,' Odette returned. 'I want you to do something wonderful with my friend's hair.'

Madame Chardin glanced at me. Next to Odette I must have appeared miserable in my country dress and worn coat, but if she noticed, Madame Chardin had the good manners not to show it.

'Of course.' She clapped her hands. 'I can even do it myself because I am free right now.'

Madame Chardin steered us to a cubicle at the far end of the salon. She slipped on a white cosmetician's coat and laid out some bottles and combs on a tray. I eyed her curiously. Most women her age were turning matronly, but with her slim figure and effervescent manner she maintained a sense of the *gamine* about her. Odette lowered herself into a seat while Madame Chardin perched me on a stool. She grabbed a comb and tugged it through my knotty hair. Far from being appalled at my disorderly tresses, Madame Chardin seemed to grow more excited with each strand she managed to untangle. Perhaps such a challenge did not come her way often. I must have been to Madame Chardin what Africa was to an explorer.

After she had finished combing my hair, Madame Chardin brushed it back from my face and traced a shape in the mirror with her finger.

'Good cheekbones,' she muttered. 'A pretty mouth and a strong jaw. We don't want anything too short. What's needed is a soft fringe and some curls to frame your face.'

'Exactly!' agreed Odette, leaning forward in her chair and clasping her knees.

Madame Chardin picked up a pair of scissors and snipped lengths of about ten inches from my hair, dropping them into a basket by her feet. I gulped as the reality of what was happening hit me. I couldn't remember ever having short hair. If the style was a disaster, I had no idea how long it would take to grow back.

'It is a rich colour,' said Madame Chardin. 'My husband once had a racehorse —'

The bell on the salon counter tinkled and a voice boomed around the space. 'Can somebody do my hair? I'm in a hurry.'

We turned to see a girl standing by the reception desk. She wore a cloche hat, a mauve dress with hibiscus flowers embroidered on it and brocade shoes. One of Madame Chardin's assistants greeted the woman and led her to a cubicle.

Madame Chardin resumed cutting my hair but leaned forward to whisper to us. 'I like those American girls. They speak their minds and they're fun. But *oh la la*, they have no idea how to dress!'

'So many colours on a large girl isn't flattering,' agreed Odette.

'Let us hope no one mistakes her for a sofa,' said Madame Chardin and winked. 'Mind you, I didn't learn how to dress properly until I was already married.'

'Tell Simone about Mademoiselle Chanel,' Odette urged her.

Madame Chardin stretched my hair between her fingers. 'When my husband and I first moved from Biarritz to open my salon here, I was nervous about Parisian women and desperate to please. Mademoiselle Chanel, the *couturière* whose salon is around the corner on Rue Cambon, was one of my first clients. She had cut her hair short before anybody else did and came to me because she had heard from her Biarritz clientele that I was good.

'One day she arrived in a terrible mood because she'd had an argument with some buyers. She wasn't happy with the cubicle I put her in, complaining that my hands were too cold and that the chair was too low and it was hurting her back. While her hair was setting I had to sneak out for a sip of *fine à l'eau* to stop my hands from shaking. When I returned she was raving about what awful dressers the Americans were and that you couldn't teach them anything. "We are a country of restraint," she moaned. "They wallow in excess."

'That day, because I knew Mademoiselle Chanel was coming in, I had worn my best dress and thought that I looked *très chic*. I didn't put on my cosmetician's coat, as I normally do, because I wanted to impress her. In her bad mood she didn't notice anything, so I tried to humour her by asking, "And how would you dress the Americans, Mademoiselle Chanel?"

'She sprang from her chair and seized my scissors, her eyes ablaze. For one terrifying moment I thought she had lost her mind and was going to cut my throat. She pointed the scissors at me and snipped the baubles off my collar. Then, before I could register what she was doing, she cut off the lace from my waistline and the ruffles from my sleeves. The only thing she left was my gardenia corsage. My four thousand franc dress was in ruins.

'"There," she said, oblivious to the tears in my eyes. "Always take away, pare down. Never add! The Americans wear too much of everything."'

'That's terrible,' I cried, not quite able to imagine what a four thousand franc dress would look like. 'What an awful woman! Did you make her pay for the dress?'

'*Ma chérie*,' laughed Madame Chardin, 'it was the best lesson I have had in my life. Decoration must have no purpose other than to set off simplicity.'

I stared at Madame Chardin. She was speaking a foreign language. 'I thought decorations were to make things pretty.'

'Look at this,' said Madame Chardin, stepping back and opening her coat to reveal her dress and elaborate brooch. 'The line must be plain and perfect. Then you choose one decorative thing so that, like a diamond on a piece of velvet, it will stand out. The Americans can never make up their minds between the pair of red shoes, the African beads, the jade bracelet. *They wear them all!* But in order to be stylish, you must know where to draw the line. Choose one decorative item and one only. That is the secret of looking *chic*.'

When Madame Chardin had finished cutting my hair, she heated a curling iron and put waves into my side locks and ends. I stared at my reflection, unable to take in the transformation. I was stunned but pleased. I pictured myself drinking a *café crème* at the Rotonde. I could go anywhere in Paris with hair like this.

'Goodness,' said Odette. 'You are stunning. Wait until my uncle sees you!'

Outside, the sky had turned grey and it was beginning to sleet. 'We'll get a taxi,' said Odette, waving one down. The car came to a stop and I clambered in after her.

'Galeries Lafayette,' Odette told the driver.

'Why are we going to the Galeries Lafayette?' I asked.

Odette rolled her eyes. 'For the new dress you need to go with your hair.'

If one thing became clear that day, it was that Odette and I were as impractical as each other. I lived in a room with no heating and one thin mattress. I needed a rug on the floor and curtains at the windows to keep the cold out, otherwise I would soon be dead from pneumonia. But instead I paid everything I had for a black dress, knowing that if I had shown it to my mother and Aunt Yvette, they would have looked at its straight lines, the V-neck, the velvet on the cuffs and the fine *crêpe de Chine* material and asked: 'Whose funeral?'

TEN

The entrance to Café des Singes was a door at basement level under a bedding store. I pushed the buzzer and waited for an answer, checking my hair in the reflection of the brass plate. No one answered so I tried the buzzer again. When there was still no answer, I turned the door handle and was surprised to find it unlocked.

'Hello?' I called out, pushing open the door and staring into the gloom.

I hesitated by a potted palm and wrinkled my nose: the air was congested with the faded smells of tobacco, mint and anisette. The only natural light source was frosted panels on either side of the door, and the club's decor of brown carpet, leather chairs and wood-panelled walls conspired to absorb the little illumination they gave. The club was what was called a *boîte de nuit*; squashed into the space was a bar with no stools and a wall-length mirror behind it. In the opposite corner to the door was a platform with a piano. Scattered in front of it were a couple of tables for groups of six and about a dozen for pairs. Beyond the tables was a swing door which I assumed led to the kitchen. I projected my voice towards it.

'Hello?'

There was a sign informing patrons that while drinks and food could be consumed during a performance, they could only be ordered between the acts. Clearly this was a club that took its musicians seriously. I ran my tongue over my lips, pleased and nervous. Monsieur Etienne must be taking me seriously to suggest that I audition here. I hoped that I wouldn't disappoint him.

There was a menu lying on a table. I glanced at it. *Cassoulet — 15 francs*. My mouth dropped open. I had paid three francs for an entire meal of bread, mutton cassoulet and wine at the student café. I ran my hand over my dress, glad that Odette had made me buy it, and shuddered to think that I would have come wearing my old dress to a place where people paid fifteen francs for a meal.

I examined the menu again: *Pâté de foie gras truffé — 25 francs; coq au riesling — 20 francs*. My stomach growled. I opened the flap and found another menu tucked inside. *Menu Américain*. Corned beef — 15 francs; fried chicken — 16 francs.

A woman's voice bellowed in the darkness. 'You hungry?'

I looked up. The woman was standing near the kitchen door, garbed in a sequined hobble skirt. She stood with her stout legs planted on the floor, in heels as high as her feet were long. Her red hair was cut short around her heavy jowls and decorated with a beaded headband.

'Yes. I mean, no!' I stuttered, dropping the menu.

The woman gave me a sideways smile. 'We'll feed you soon enough,' she said with good-natured scorn. 'When Eugene finishes stuffing his own face in the kitchen, we'll do your song.'

From her gravelly laugh and beaming presence, I knew that she had to be Madame Baquet. She told me to take off my coat and sit down at a table. She sat opposite me, the chair creaking under her weight.

'See anything you like?' she asked, pointing to the menu.

Although it was the most luxurious menu I had ever seen, my nerves got the better of me. All I could say was that an omelette would be nice.

She threw her head back and sent a laugh thundering around the room. 'We'd have to go down the street for one of those. How old are you? You're younger than I thought you'd be.'

For a second I considered lying, then thought better of it. She was too sharp for that. Stretching the truth was better. 'I'm almost sixteen,' I said.

'A baby, just as I thought.' She made a clucking sound with her tongue. 'It's a long time since I was your age. Still, Monsieur Etienne said you were exceptional, and if anybody understands that term he does.'

The sound of pans crashing to the floor burst from the kitchen. Madame Baquet swivelled around and shouted, 'Eugene! Are you coming or are you just destroying the place?'

'Coming!' a man's voice answered from beyond the swing door.

The buzzer sounded and Madame Baquet got up to answer it. I was relieved to see Monsieur Etienne and Odette waiting on the step.

'*Bonjour*,' Madame Baquet said. 'I've just been speaking with your singer. Eugene's working on giving himself indigestion in the kitchen but he'll be out in a minute.'

No sooner had Monsieur Etienne and Odette greeted me than the kitchen door swung open and a black man wiping at his lips with a serviette rushed into the room. He flung the serviette down on one of the tables. 'Hello,' he said, reaching out a sticky hand and grabbing mine. 'What a lovely-looking lady you are. Why, your face just says joy all over it!'

He took Monsieur Etienne's hand and said something I didn't catch because he mixed up English words in amongst his French sentences. From the crystal clarity of his voice I took him to be an American.

'*Parlez-vous anglais?*' he asked me, sensing my confusion.

Of course I didn't speak English, but as everyone else seemed to understand him, and I was so eager to please, I answered, 'A little. I know *Yawl* and *Schure*.' I did my best to imitate the American accents I'd heard on my first night in Pigalle.

Madame Baquet roared with laughter and slapped the table. Eugene sent me a cheeky smile and rolled his eyes.

'She's funny, Monsieur Etienne,' said Madame Baquet. 'I like them cute and funny, and as she's brought her music along I think we'd better get her to sing.'

I followed Eugene to the piano. He wiped his fingers on his pants and took my music from me. 'These all French songs?' he asked, flicking through them. 'Nice. Yep, now we've got someone to sing in English, someone to sing in German and someone to sing in French. We should change our name to Café des Singes Internationales.' This time I understood his joke and laughed. I was beginning to see that there was a lot of laughter at the Café des Singes.

Eugene picked out the music for 'It's Him I Love'. I was glad he'd chosen that one because it was the song the rehearsal pianist and I had worked on the most. The pianist had emphasised that for a *boîte*, delivery was as important as technical skills. I had solved my problem of never having been in love by thinking of my father when I sang the song. I might not understand *l'amour* but I understood loss.

> It's him I love
> Though he's far away
> It's him I love
> But I should live for today

Eugene's hands sprang over the keys. For a moment I was mesmerised by them; the movement was so fluid, his touch so agile and light. Luckily, my concentration returned fast enough that I didn't miss my first line. From the instant I sang my first note, I knew that I had Madame Baquet on my side. When I sang, she couldn't sit still. She fidgeted in her chair and tapped her foot, her teary eyes gazing at me all the time with wonder. When I finished the song everyone clapped. Monsieur Etienne and Odette beamed with pride.

'Sing another,' Madame Baquet called out. 'You've got us wanting more now!'

Eugene began another number: '*La bouteille est vide*. The Bottle is Empty'. It was about a man who loves champagne so much that he drinks himself to ruin, the cynical words contradicting the upbeat tune. Eugene played it faster than I'd rehearsed it but I did my best to keep up. Madame Baquet hummed along at first, then started singing in a husky voice when she caught on to the words. She drifted from singing along with me to discussing my contract with Monsieur Etienne and then back again without a break.

'Monsieur Etienne, I want you to make up a contract this afternoon. I don't want any other club grabbing this girl. I can start her on eighty francs for two performances a week, plus tips. And I'll give her a good meal after each show to fatten her up.'

I kept singing even though I was on the verge of fainting on the spot. Eighty francs for two performances a week *plus* tips? I had estimated that, living frugally, it was going to cost me at least four hundred francs a month for my rent, meals and *métro* tickets. Assuming that I could double what Madame Baquet was paying me with tips, and deducting Monsieur Etienne's agent's fee, I was going to be making almost five hundred francs for just two nights' work! I continued singing my song, dizzy with thoughts of what I was going to buy with the extra money, completely missing the irony of the words or the warning in them: *The more you get, the more you want, you want and want, and then it's all gone.*

⟨⟩

Although I normally wouldn't be required to arrive at the Café des Singes until half past one, Madame Baquet suggested I get there earlier on the first night. 'You can watch Florence and Anke and get to know the place,' she said.

I caught a taxi on the Boulevard du Montparnasse, feeling pleased that I didn't have to take the *métro* just to save money. When the driver stopped in front of the Café des Singes, I was startled by the difference in atmosphere from when I had seen it during the day. The mesh shutters of the bedding store were closed and spotlights flickered around the entrance of the club. A man in a coat and velvet hat worked the door.

'It's as crowded as a can of sardines in there, Mademoiselle,' he said, his Russian accent rolling the 'r's even more deeply than Zephora's tremolo. 'Are you alone?'

I explained who I was and he waved me inside. All I could see at first were the backs of the people huddled in the entranceway, waiting for a table or just some space. 'Excuse me,' I said to a man still padded up in his coat and gloves. He scrunched up his face. I thought he was annoyed but then realised he was trying to get enough elbow space so he could lift his arm up for me to pass. The club was full and most people were standing. A wispy woman was on stage, singing a blues number in English. Her voice quivered like her black skin under the lights. Madame Baquet, with a dress of white fringes and a feather in her hair, was flirting with a young man wearing a monocle. She caught my eye and waved, although we had no chance of reaching each other through the crush. She pointed to a stool by the piano and I understood that I was to take it. I zig-zagged my way through the crowd and let out a sigh of victory when I reached the stool and plunked myself down on it. I was surprised to see that the piano player, who I had assumed to be Eugene, was not

Eugene at all. He was black and thin with the same protruding eyes, but was younger.

The singer, who I guessed must be Florence, delivered her songs with heavy-lidded eyes and down-turned lips but closed each number and introduced the next one with a beaming flash of white teeth. I didn't understand a word she said, but when she sang her voice bounced off the walls and vibrated through me.

When her session ended, the audience clapped and showed their appreciation by stuffing notes into her jar. A crowd converged on the bar to order the next round of drinks. French, I thought, listening to their cheerful babble. They are nearly all French. I wondered where the Americans were.

Eugene stepped out of the kitchen with a tray balanced on his shoulder and served dishes of *pâté de foie gras* and shrimp cocktails to a table by the piano. He caught sight of me and winked. 'That's my brother, Charlie,' he said, thrusting his chin towards the young man at the piano. 'We take turns waiting tables and playing. It gives us a break. You want anything?'

I shook my head. 'I don't like to eat before I sing.'

He nodded, patting his stomach. 'Good thing about being a piano player — you can always eat.'

Although it was true that Vera had told me that a singer should never perform on a full stomach, my not wanting to eat had more to do with my nerves. I'd been comfortable singing at the audition, but as soon as I'd stepped into the taxi on my way to the club I was hit by shakes and sweats. Seeing the sophisticated audience up close did not help. Was I good enough? What did they expect? Certainly I couldn't sing as well as Florence whose enchanting voice could bend a note without breaking it. Not yet, anyway. I wondered if the churning in my stomach, the nausea, that tightness in my throat, would leave me once I became a seasoned performer. Or would I have to live with them for ever?

Madame Baquet sang a quirky song about a man who gets caught by his mistress trying to seduce her mother, before announcing that the patrons should take their drinks and settle down because it was time for 'the fabulous Anke' to come up on stage. This is the German, I thought.

A man in tails and a top hat pushed through the crowd to the stage. The spotlight settled on his back. Charlie hit the first note and

159

the man spun around. I blinked. He had smooth skin and blue eyes smudged with black eyeliner. The singer was a woman. She'd made herself look like a man by brushing her short hair away from her face and the way she'd swaggered onto the stage. A hush fell over the audience and the woman started to sing. Her voice was as androgynous as her appearance, discordant and strange. She cupped her face in her hands, flicking out her green-painted nails like claws. I grimaced. Her act was disturbing. Her German words crawled over me like spiders. *Vernichtung. Warnung. Todesfall.* By her third number my skin was itching and I could barely stay in my seat. Yet the rest of the audience was spellbound — not one clink of a glass, not a murmur nor a cough.

When Anke finished she didn't bow or thank her spectators. She rushed from the stage and shoved her way through them to the door, as if they had made her angry. When she didn't come back to accept her tips, the audience rose to their feet and applauded wildly, leaving me to wonder what I could do to match her act.

There was a flurry of activity around the cloakroom girl, who stood in a booth not much bigger than a closet. The tables emptied and so did the space around the bar. No one is staying to watch my act, I thought. I couldn't take it personally. I was hardly 'a name' in Paris and the audience was probably rushing off to another show, or to meet friends for supper or more drinks. That was the way of things in Paris. There were so many restaurants, music halls, cafés, bars and theatres, so many distractions to be had in the city, that staying in one place for a whole evening was not an option.

But no sooner had the café emptied than it started refilling. The new audience rushed towards the bar, shouting greetings at each other and passing drinks over the sea of heads. Madame Baquet greeted the arrivals in English, and stopped for a moment to chat to a girl in a purple dress with roses on the sleeve and neckline. Eugene swapped places at the piano with Charlie and warmed up the atmosphere with a jazz riff. The Americans had arrived.

Eugene leaned across the piano. 'You've got a good crowd tonight. That's Scott Fitzgerald and his wife, Zelda,' he said, indicating with his chin a man and woman entwined in each other's arms. They were attempting to dance in the crowded space, splashes of whisky spilling from their glasses. The man's features were fine and his mouth so delicate that he looked almost feminine. His partner's face was more severe. Her salmon pink gown had silver straps across the back and flared out from her hips into a bell-shaped skirt. I wondered if that was what a four thousand franc dress looked like.

'They always run with the "in crowd",' said Eugene, not missing a note on the piano despite talking to me. 'If they like you, they'll spread the word.'

I rubbed my hands over my dress as if trying to press imaginary creases out of it. The tremble in my legs grew worse. 'Showtime,' Eugene said, and smiled. It took two attempts for me to stand. I eyed the bright faces. For some reason I had thought the supper crowd would be more subdued, but this throng was like a lit-up Christmas tree.

I clambered onto the platform, nearly losing my balance. I glanced at a table of six sitting in the far corner and wondered why I hadn't noticed them before. Everything about them — the carnations in the men's buttonholes, the charcoal painted under the women's eyes, the restrained way they sipped their drinks — gave them away as Parisians. The man at the end of the table caught my eye. His skin was a shade of gold not usually seen on city men and was like honey against the sable colour of his hair and eyes. He was sitting next to a woman with a beauty spot near the corner of her nose. She reminded me of an elegant Siamese cat, sleek and perfectly formed with even features and skin like cream. I'd thought I looked good in my dress, but compared to her I was as unkempt as an alley cat.

The man with the sable eyes turned in my direction and we locked gazes. My heart gave a jolt, as if I had reached for a light switch and touched a live wire instead. Did I know him? No, I had never seen him before, yet something inside me *recognised* him. I forgot where I was, and would have stood there for ever if Madame Baquet hadn't leaned across the table to welcome them and blocked the man from my view. I took advantage of the pause to think about something the rehearsal pianist had told me about capturing an unsettled audience. 'Sing to your home crowd,' he had said. By that he meant that I should sing to the friendliest face in the audience, then gradually draw the others in too.

Was the sable-eyed man my 'friendly face'? Madame Baquet slipped back into the crowd and I saw that the man was leaning across the table admiring one of his female companion's bracelets which she held out for him. Perhaps my songs wouldn't be refined enough for him. The Americans, on the other hand, were ready for some fun. *Who should I sing to?* Eugene glanced at me, waiting for my signal. I swallowed but couldn't get rid of the lump in my throat. I caught sight of Zelda Fitzgerald. She was draped over her husband and flirting with another man next to him, her cigarette holder drooping from her mouth. There was something in her frail arms and vicious mouth that said she was not long for this world.

'"*La bouteille est vide*",' I said to Eugene. 'We'll start with the champagne song.'

Eugene introduced me and I launched into the song with gusto, but my effort was met with indifference. I squinted into the darkness. No one was paying attention to me, not even the sable-eyed man. Who was I supposed to sing to in order to draw in the others if *no one* was interested? The French table was drooling over its *hors-d'oeuvre varié*, the Americans were lighting each other's cigarettes and swapping tales. Madame Baquet weaved her way among them, trying to draw their attention to me, but it was the role of the performer to captivate the audience, not that of the hostess. She was only responsible for making sure her guests had a good time, irrespective of me. Please look at me, I begged the sable-eyed man. But he continued to eat his artichoke with relish. I was having trouble making myself heard above the babble. I could have been singing anything in any language and no one would have been any wiser. I glanced at Eugene but he was too wrapped in his music to notice that I was in trouble.

It's up to me. The words from the 'Scheherazade' song flashed into my mind. *It's up to me.* I remembered how terrified I had been the day I was catapulted into the starring role at Le Chat Espiègle because of an emergency.

I began singing my opening number from 'Scheherazade', leaving Eugene to carry on with the champagne song. A rowdy bunch of Americans might be able to drown out a nightclub singer, but they would have a hard time competing with the lung capacity of a music hall performer. I took a breath, and let them know just how powerful my voice could get. In less than a moment the conversations ceased, knives and forks were laid down, glasses steadied, and all eyes turned to me.

At first, the sudden change from bedlam to silence unnerved me. Eugene, unfazed by my switch to another song, continued to play the champagne tune. For a few bars we were discordant but then I thought of Madame Baquet drifting from singing with me to discussing my contract with Monsieur Etienne, and I faded back into the champagne song as if that had been my intention all along. I finished the number with the feeling that I had either destroyed my chances at the Café des Singes or I had made an impression. My heart leapt to my throat when I realised that the sound in my ears was no longer my blood pulsing but applause. *'Elle est superbe!'* someone shouted. 'She is terrific!'

I completed my repertoire reeling from the warmth beaming towards me from the audience. They rose after my encore to applaud more loudly and shout 'Bravo!' My first performance in Paris was not just a success: it was a triumph. The Americans rushed forward, clasping my hands and shouting at me in their casual French. *'Tu es magnifique!'* There were so many notes being thrust into our tip jar that Eugene had to ram his fist into it to push them down. Zelda Fitzgerald dropped in a pearl ring. 'For good luck,' she said, touching my cheek with an icy finger.

I had a feeling that someone was watching me and turned to find the man with the sable eyes standing behind me. 'A memorable performance, Mademoiselle,' he said, smiling, and slipped a roll of notes into my jar.

It was as if someone had smashed a champagne bottle over my head and I was struggling to see through the sweet fizz. I opened my mouth to speak, but nothing came out. He said something else but I missed it because of an explosion of laughter from the Americans who were taking another round at the bar even though it was almost closing time.

'Au revoir,' he said, still smiling. 'I hope I will see you perform again.'

My eyes did not leave his back. I watched him join his companions, who were busy collecting their coats. When he turned around and sent me one more glance before walking through the door and into the night, I sensed that I had met someone who would one day change my life.

ELEVEN

I made three times more in tips than I had been expecting at the Café des Singes that night. Never having had money before, I had no idea what could be done with it besides spending it. The next day, inspired by Odette's sense of style, I went shopping. I traipsed through the dress, shoe and cosmetic sections of the Galeries Lafayette, my legs quivering and my mind racing from one thought to the next. But it wasn't the money or the shopping that caused those feelings. I savoured the sable-eyed man's smile in my mind. Was it possible that a few words exchanged with a stranger could have made me feel so ... what ... ? Alive?

I didn't return to my room until after dark. I tipped the taxi driver for carrying the bags and boxes to my door. He eyed the clutter of rotten brooms, pails and rubbish at the end of the landing. I had been so caught up in my acquisitions that it hadn't occurred to me to be embarrassed about the dilapidated state of my building. The driver must have wondered what someone with so many parcels from the Galeries Lafayette was doing living in such a dump. I watched him make his way down the stairs, his nose pinched against the odour of mould and dog piles that infused the air.

I laid out my treasures on the bed. I could hardly believe that the emerald dress with the elbow-length sleeves was mine and that I had bought it with money that I'd earned singing. My most expensive purchase was a jacquard coat. Just throwing it over my shoulders warmed me. I put on all my new clothes, including the linen chemise I had bought to replace my frayed one, and opened the box that contained the silver mirror and stand. I set the mirror up on the bed and stood back as far as I could, trying — unsuccessfully — to catch my full reflection.

≋

I had intended to dine at the Italian *crémerie* on Rue Campagne where I'd eaten the previous night after my show. The owner, a former artist's model, served soups for only a few sous. Artists who didn't have money could pay by pinning their pictures on the walls. But when I walked past the golden lights of the Café de la Rotonde, I decided to celebrate my success there.

The sound of laughter and the aroma of coffee liqueur swelled around me as soon as I entered. Two men at the bar looked me over. A waiter showed me to a table near the door, although judging by the chatter coming from the back room, that was the place to be. A spirited argument was taking place, so lively that I caught snatches of it above the sound of the clinking glasses and cutlery.

'The Surrealists! The Revolution!' a voice shouted.

There was a laugh of derision. 'We shall see about that!'

Two women leaned on the wall near the door to the room. One of them puffed on a cigarette holder. Her face was made up like a painting: bright moons of green shone above her eyes and her lips were blood red against her pale face and black hair. When she laughed, the point on her nose became sharper and made her face even more arresting.

'Kiki! Kiki!' her blonde companion laughed, dabbing at her eyes with a Chinese handkerchief. 'You are bringing me to tears.'

I ordered a Pernod and sipped at its liquorice milkiness while trying to choose between a plate of raw oysters and steamed mussels. I decided on the mussels cooked in white wine. While I ate, I watched more people file through the door: men in scruffy suits with paint on the cuffs and couples in evening wear. They were French, German, Spanish, Italian and American. The American women still lit cigarettes even though there was a sign on the counter to say that ladies weren't allowed to smoke in the café. Odette had told me that many of the city's famous artists and entertainers gathered at the Rotonde, or the Dôme opposite, but I had no idea if the faces I was looking at were those of celebrities or not. I finished my meal and paid the bill. I dreaded using the chilly lavatory in my apartment building, so I decided to visit the ladies' room before I left.

After tipping the attendant, I stopped to check my appearance in the mirror. The lighting was brighter than in my apartment. I took out my compact and made a few swipes at my nose, then became aware of somebody standing next to me.

'Was he angry when you told him?' the woman said. She seemed to be addressing her reflection. I assumed that she was drunk.

'Are you angry at me, Simone, for making you do it?'

I spun around. I knew that profile: the fine cheekbones, the perfectly straight nose. 'Camille?' With all that had happened since I last saw her, I had forgotten my anger at having been duped. But gradually the memory of being made a fool of returned to me.

'Perhaps I can make it up to you,' Camille said, still smiling at the mirror. 'Would you like to join me and my companions for dinner? They are some of the wealthiest men in Paris.'

Something about her coy manner caught me by surprise and I accepted her invitation without thinking.

I followed Camille to a table in the back room. Three men in dinner suits rose to their feet. The first introduced himself as David Bentley; he was a sturdily built Englishman who spoke French well. The two other men were Parisians. With their thin faces and opaque eyes, they could have been brothers. But they weren't: they introduced themselves as François Duvernoy and Antoine Marchais.

When we had all sat down, David Bentley — who insisted that I call him Bentley because that was his 'name among friends' — asked me how I knew Camille. I explained that we had appeared together in a show in Marseilles. I told myself that I was being gracious in not mentioning how Camille had deserted us. Bentley wrapped his fingers around Camille's wrist and stroked the translucent skin with his finger. She was wearing a diamond bracelet; much larger and more elaborate than the one Monsieur Gosling had given her. I only had to glance at Camille's silver beaded dress and fox-fur wrap to guess that she had replaced Monsieur Gosling with a wealthier man.

'You haven't told me about Monsieur Dargent's reaction when I left,' she said, slipping her wrist away from Bentley's explorations. 'Or whether you have forgiven me for making you deliver my news.'

It was difficult to gauge her tone but I sensed that she was more interested in what Monsieur Dargent had said about her leaving than whether she had put me out or not. I told her that there was nothing to worry about. The scandal had done us good and the show had been a success. She pursed her lips and I realised that wasn't the answer she had been expecting. She assumed that the show had collapsed without her.

'The season would have been better if you had been Scheherazade ...' I began, then paused. The show had been a success when *I* played Scheherazade, but somehow I couldn't bring myself to tell Camille that I had performed the part. What was it about her that made me so subservient?

Bentley asked us if we wanted champagne. 'Yes,' said Camille, then turning back to me asked, 'What are you doing in Paris?'

'I sing at the Café des Singes,' I said. 'But only two nights a week. I'm looking for other work.'

The champagne arrived and Bentley ordered the waiter to pour us each a glass. 'We are here to celebrate Camille's success,' he said, pushing a glass towards me. 'She's going to star at the Casino de Paris.'

'The Casino de Paris!' I cried. 'That's as good as the Folies Bergère!'

'Better,' said Bentley, leaning towards me. 'They have superior singing and dancing at the Casino. The Folies Bergère is spectacle and nudes.'

I felt sorry for him. He was in love with Camille, but from the detached way that she spoke to him I suspected he would be replaced when someone even wealthier came along, just as Monsieur Gosling had been.

'Let's have a toast,' said François, holding up his glass. 'To Camille.'

'To Camille,' we repeated, clinking our glasses.

Camille turned to me. 'They haven't found someone to fill my original slot in the first half,' she said. 'I could speak to the manager about giving you an audition. It's only a one-song and dance slot but it *is* the Casino de Paris.'

I was grateful for her offer but after what had happened at the Folies Bergère audition I wasn't confident that I would succeed. The

Casino may have been less frivolous than the Folies, but their standards for beauty would be just the same.

'It's time to move on to dinner,' said Antoine, signalling to the waiter for the bill. 'How about Le Boeuf sur le Toit? They have good jazz.'

'No,' said François. 'It's too loud. Let's go to Fouquet's.'

Bentley shook his head. 'You'll just be following this crowd there. I say the Tour d'Argent.'

'I've already eaten,' I said, as pleasantly as I could. The Rotonde had been a splurge for me. I might be new to Paris but I was informed enough to know they were naming some of the city's most expensive restaurants and, despite my growing visions of grandeur, I still had limits.

'Then eat again,' laughed François, pointing at me. 'You could do with some more weight.'

'Bentley will pay,' Camille whispered to me.

'I still think we should go somewhere with music,' said Antoine.

'Le Boeuf sur le Toit is full of South American playboys. We'll lose Mademoiselle Fleurier to them — I'm warning you,' said Bentley.

They hooted with laughter. I smiled too, although I didn't get the joke.

We squashed ourselves into a taxi: Camille and Bentley in the front and me in the back between Antoine and François. The bulk of our overcoats, scarves, hats and gloves pressed against each other as if we were a load of clothes in a garment-maker's truck. The taxi crossed the Seine to the Right Bank. We passed by the Egyptian Obelisk in the Place de la Concorde.

'This is where Louis XVI was executed,' Antoine said, tapping the window with his knuckle. 'And later on, Queen Marie Antoinette and Robespierre.'

'It doesn't seem the kind of place where something like that could have happened,' I said. I imagined a revolutionary crowd gathered on the cobblestones, shaking their fists and shouting, 'Off with their heads!'

'It certainly doesn't,' said Bentley. 'When you look at the pretty lights it's easy to forget the bloodthirsty history of Paris.'

We arrived in Rue Boissy d'Anglas and filed into Le Boeuf sur le Toit one after the other. It was so crowded inside the nightclub that we could barely move. I thought we would be jammed near the door for ever but the waiter managed to find us a table. The sommelier brought champagne in an ice bucket. The jazz music thrummed in my ears. From where we sat, we could see the band on stage with their glistening trombones, clarinets and saxophones.

'Everyone is here tonight,' said Camille. 'Look, there's Coco Chanel!' I followed Camille's gaze to a dark-haired woman with a wide, sensuous mouth. She was wearing a dress that draped over her body in scalloped tiers. She wasn't what I'd expected from Madame Chardin's description. Her dress was uncomplicated and floated around her each time she moved her arm to sip her drink. But she wore chunky earrings and strings of baroque pearls around her neck.

'I thought her theory was to pare things down,' I said. 'One decorative item only.'

Bentley glanced at me. 'She is a designer,' he chuckled. 'She makes her money by setting a fashion and then changing it.'

'There's your friend,' said Antoine to Camille, nodding his head towards a man with a crooked smile.

Camille turned to me. 'Maurice Chevalier. He performed at the Casino de Paris in the previous show and made two thousand francs a night.'

'Two thousand francs! What does he do?' I asked.

'He dances around the stage with a straw hat, tells jokes and sings songs full of innuendo. They say he's going to be snapped up by Hollywood.'

'Hollywood?'

'America. The movies,' Camille said, amused by my ignorance.

'They say he's ruthless,' said Bentley, cutting the end off a cigar with a pair of gold clippers. 'He dumped Mistinguett after she risked her life to save him from a prisoner-of-war camp.'

Mistinguett, I knew, was 'Queen of the Paris Music Hall' and France's most famous singer.

'You have to be ruthless to succeed,' said Camille.

Bentley smiled, although I was not sure why. I sensed a bad end for him if he were truly in love with Camille.

I turned to the dance floor and watched the couples twirling around it in a lively shuffle.

'Would you like to dance?' François asked me, putting down his glass.

'I would like to,' I said, tempted more by the music than the note of flirtation in his voice, 'but I don't know this dance.'

'If you can walk, you can foxtrot,' he said, reaching out his hand to escort me. There was barely enough space for us on the dance floor in between the other couples, but somehow François was able to guide me through the steps. It was surprisingly easy to pick up the slow-slow-quick-quick rhythm of the dance. The slow parts were long and graceful, the quick ones short and lively. We moved around the floor, sometimes bumping into other couples who were too in love or too tipsy to notice. We passed one elegantly dressed man with pouches under his eyes. 'That's the Prince of Wales,' François whispered in my ear. 'His grandfather was a great lover of this city and its women. He was heartbroken when he had to give up being a Parisian in order to become king. I wonder if this prince will feel the same.'

The music changed tempo. Half the couples fled the dance floor and were replaced by others rushing onto it. 'I can't do this one,' said François. 'You have to be a good dancer.' The people around us were kicking their heels and flapping their arms like birds to the syncopated rhythm. It was the most energetic dance I'd ever seen and it made me laugh because it was so full of *joie de vivre*. François excused himself but I remained in the frenzy. The dance could be performed as a couple but there were half a dozen people dancing it on their own. The footwork wasn't difficult for me. I had the knack of breaking dance sequences into steps quickly and I couldn't resist joining in the fun. Before I knew it I was shimmying and criss-crossing my knees along with the rest of the crowd. I even improvised a few hip slaps and head turns of my own.

After a couple of fast numbers, the dancers slowed down or left the floor and the band slid back into a foxtrot. I returned to the table just as the waiter arrived with a tray of dishes.

'We didn't know what you wanted to eat,' said Antoine, 'so we ordered fish in champagne sauce for you.'

The waiter placed a succulent-looking piece of cod before me.

'Your Charleston was amazing, Mademoiselle Fleurier,' said Bentley. 'Everyone in the room had their eyes on you.'

'The Charleston — is that what it's called?' I asked.

François lifted his eyebrows. 'It's American,' he said. 'You've never danced it before?'

I shook my head.

'Doubly amazing,' laughed Bentley. 'I still haven't got the hang of it and I've had lessons. It's so big here that it's difficult to get a job as a waiter if you can't do it. You have to be able to teach the customers if they ask you.'

Camille leaned towards me. 'There's someone who hasn't taken his eyes off you all evening,' she said.

'Who?'

She turned to a table at the edge of the dance floor. I looked up and saw the young man with the sable eyes staring back at me. I smiled but he didn't return the greeting. He was dining with the same people I had seen him with at the Café des Singes. The Siamese cat woman touched his shoulder and whispered something in his ear. He glanced at me again and laughed before turning away. Were they mocking me?

'Do you know him?' Camille asked.

'The champagne is going to my head,' I said, feeling too foolish to talk about the crush I'd had for the past twenty-four hours. Why didn't he even have the courtesy to return my smile? Hadn't he praised my performance the previous night?

Camille shrugged her shoulders then turned to say something to Bentley. I ate the fish with my eyes glued to the plate. Obviously the Siamese had a greater hold on the sable-eyed man than I had counted on. And why not? She had sultry eyes lined with thick black lashes. Her figure was petite and she had tiny hands and feet. Even from a distance she managed to make me feel like a giant. I wanted to send the object of my fantasies a glare that would tell him that I would never think of him again. But by the time I had worked up the courage to turn around, I found myself staring at someone's torso. I raised my eyes and looked straight at the sable-eyed man.

'*Bonsoir*. I hope you are well this evening,' he said to Antoine. The Siamese clung to his arm, resting her weight against him. He glanced from Antoine to me then back again. 'I was hoping you would introduce us to your friend. We saw her perform at the Café des Singes last night. She was magnificent.'

Those eyes were set in an arresting face. He had angular cheekbones and a largish but straight nose. If he were an animal, I thought, he'd be a Doberman, like the majestic canines that guarded the doorways on the Champs Élysées.

Antoine frowned. 'Mademoiselle Fleurier,' he said. 'This is Mademoiselle Marielle Canier and Monsieur André Blanchard.'

'I am enchanted,' said André, taking my hand to kiss it. I returned his compliment and glanced at Mademoiselle Canier. She murmured a greeting but looked over my head. Clearly the introduction had not been her idea. A tingle reignited in me.

'We were wondering if you might give us Charleston lessons?' André asked, his eyes fixed on me. 'Mademoiselle Canier and I have been invited on a jazz cruise and we don't seem able to do the dance with any flair.'

The tingle fizzled like a firecracker in the rain. Mademoiselle Canier's hand slid down André's arm and disappeared inside his palm. I did my best to ignore their intertwined fingers and wished that I were invisible.

'Why don't you go to Ada Bricktop for lessons?' suggested François. 'If she is good enough for Prince Edward, surely she is good enough for you? Mademoiselle Fleurier is a performer not a dance instructor.'

André laughed. It was a good laugh that came from deep in his chest. It made his eyes sparkle and showed off his straight teeth. 'Quite right. I apologise, Mademoiselle Fleurier. It is just that when you dance it, you look like you own the world.'

I noticed the subtle change in his eyes; something in them mirrored the disappointment I was feeling. He hovered for a moment, glancing at his feet, before apologising for interrupting our meal and guiding Mademoiselle Canier back to their table.

'Who was that?' Camille asked Antoine.

He waited until Bentley had turned away to summon a waiter before answering. 'André Blanchard of the Blanchard fortune. One of the families who control the French economy. But don't even think about it, Camille. He is the sole heir. Believe me, his father will not let him put a foot wrong.'

'And she?'

'Mademoiselle Canier? Just a society girl. Petted, pampered and spoilt. Nothing special about her except her looks.'

Camille's eyes lingered in the direction of André's table before turning to me. 'It will be a lucky girl who snags him,' she said.

❧

True to her word, Camille arranged an audition for me at the Casino de Paris before the end of the week. She was taking the place of a British singer who had broken her contract to make a movie in America, and because they needed to fill Camille's old slot quickly, it wasn't an open audition. And this time I had the friendly faces of Monsieur Etienne and Odette encouraging me from the front row. Léon Volterra, the owner of the Casino de Paris, sat next to them. He was a curious man with a twinkle of mischief in his eyes. He asked me if I knew the Charleston and I explained that I had taught myself the dance.

'That's exactly what we want!' he cried, raising his arms to the ceiling. Turning to the choreographer, a woman with the emaciated air of an aged dancer, he added, 'The Casino de Paris wants theatrical dancers not technical robots! Isn't that right, Madame Piège?'

Madame Piège replied that she couldn't agree more and patted him on the arm. It gave the impression that she was trying to stop him from saying anything further.

'Wonderful! Wonderful!' Monsieur Volterra's voice boomed out of the darkness when I had finished my dance and then performed '*La bouteille est vide*'. There was applause from the lighting men in the flies too. I glanced at Monsieur Etienne who sent me a pleased nod.

Monsieur Volterra rose from his seat and leaned his elbows on the front of the stage. 'Come back here today at two o'clock for rehearsals,' he said. 'You're hired.'

Once Monsieur Etienne, Odette and I were outside the theatre, I couldn't contain my excitement. 'I can't believe it!' I said. 'The Casino de Paris!'

'Well done,' said Monsieur Etienne. 'Your voice gets better every time I hear you.'

'And she looks so pretty,' said Odette, giving me a secret smile.

'Monsieur Volterra is a character, isn't he?' Monsieur Etienne said, signalling a taxi. 'You know he can't read?'

'He can't read?' I cried, stepping into the taxi as Monsieur Etienne opened the door for me. 'Didn't you say that he was the most successful impresario in Paris?'

Odette and Monsieur Etienne climbed in after me. 'Not a word. His partner taught him to trace out his signature on contracts,' said Monsieur Etienne.

'It's hard to believe, isn't it?' said Odette. 'The man who, at one time or another, has owned the Ambassadeurs, the Folies Bergère and now the Casino de Paris can't even write his own name.'

'He was an orphan. He never went to school,' explained Monsieur Etienne.

'He must be clever!' I said.

Monsieur Etienne smiled. 'He has entrepreneurship in his blood. He once told me that when he was seven years old he used to pick up discarded evening papers on park benches and around the *métro*. Then the following morning, he would stand on the corner yelling out fictional — but very enticing — headlines. By the time his unsuspecting customers opened their papers, the rascal's legs had carried him a few blocks away.'

'Goodness, I hope he won't cheat me!' I said.

Monsieur Etienne nodded. 'Oh, he will,' he said. 'Volterra cheats everyone, big or small. He's famous for it. But luckily you've got me.'

❦

I returned to the Casino de Paris that afternoon in high spirits. Although my name wasn't going on the billing that didn't stop me from fantasising about fame and rave reviews. But my illusions of grandeur were deflated the moment I stepped into the auditorium. Madame Piège and the rehearsal pianist were waiting for me.

'I believe you are a comedian,' said Madame Piège, her cheeks crinkling when she smiled. 'So we are going to work with that.'

Comedian? A comic part wasn't what I had been expecting. I thought I had left that behind in Marseilles. I wanted to be sophisticated now that I was in Paris.

'Mademoiselle Casal gave you quite a talk up and Monsieur Volterra says that you have a natural sense of timing.'

I remembered that Camille had never seen me perform in 'Scheherazade' or at the Café des Singes. Her only knowledge of me was as the crazy chorus girl. I realised what had happened: Camille had talked Monsieur Volterra into giving me a comic role by mistake. She probably thought that I didn't have any serious material.

'I do a different act now, Madame Piège,' I said. 'I sing in a nightclub.'

But Madame Piège didn't hear me. She sorted through some sheet music and handed a piece to the pianist. 'We'll go with this,' she said.

The pianist played the tune and my mind sprang into action. I would telephone Monsieur Etienne straight after the rehearsal, I decided, and ask him to explain the situation to Monsieur Volterra, who in turn could give Madame Piège new instructions about my choreography. It would mean one wasted rehearsal but everyone's feelings would be spared. Monsieur Etienne had been adamant that all negotiations with the Casino de Paris should be made through him.

'I liked the way you did the Charleston,' said Mademoiselle Piège, giving me a copy of the song. 'It is marvellous how quickly you pick things up. That is a sign of talent.'

I sighed. I had a feeling that, under other circumstances, I would have enjoyed working with Madame Piège. She took a seat in the front row and called out instructions as I went through the routine. 'Shimmy a little more there and give us a sweet smile, *ma chérie*,' she said. 'Then carry on those shuffle steps for longer than necessary, as if you have slipped on a banana skin.' I did as she asked. 'Keep doing it until the audience gets the joke,' she giggled, amusement lighting her eyes. The happier she looked, the worse I felt. I was beginning to feel guilty about my intention never to actually perform the act.

After the Charleston, Madame Piège wanted me to strut the stage swinging a cane and singing a song that wasn't so much funny as cute, which made me hate it even more.

> La! La! Boom! Here comes Jean
> In his new Voisin.
> La! La! Boom! He asks, 'What are you doing?'
> What am I going to tell him?
> La! La! Boom! That I'm hanging out the washing?

'Now each time you sing "Boom!" let your cane bang on the floor and bounce back up. The drum will play a beat for you at the same time. And when you catch your cane, the cymbalist will make a strike for you,' said Madame Piège, rising from her seat. I could not bring myself to look into her eyes. She was enjoying it too much.

Although I learned the song and the dance steps within half an hour, we rehearsed the act for another two hours, ironing out bumps and adding more comic elements. The orchestra joined us to go over the number together. I did my best to remain animated throughout the rehearsal although my insides were twisting into knots.

A messenger came to tell Madame Piège that the chorus needed her to fix a flaw in their routine. She turned to me. 'We have done all we need to with you, Mademoiselle Fleurier. You are perfect. You can go on tonight.'

'Tonight?' My voice croaked.

'Hmmm,' Monsieur Etienne said, when I called him from the theatre office. 'I am surprised too. I didn't think Camille Casal had been performing a comic number and I didn't expect that you would be either. I had the impression that you would be doing her old song.'

'They want me to go on tonight!'

'Hmmm,' said Monsieur Etienne again, thinking for a moment. 'In that case, you have no choice. You will just have to do it. They will replace you if you are too troublesome.'

'I hate it!' I protested.

'You don't have a big enough name to make a fuss,' said Monsieur Etienne. 'Do a good job and we'll see what we can get you next time. Just think of the money you are making. It's more than the Café des Singes and for only one song and dance!'

I hung up, knowing he was right, but when I had passed the audition I had been elated. Now I felt ridiculous. 'When I am famous, I am going to make a fuss about everything and no one is going to tell me what to do,' I promised myself, buttoning my coat and pulling on my hat before heading home to rest prior to the show.

The dress for my Casino de Paris number was covered in polka dots and had flounces around the neckline and skirt. The white dance shoes had bows on the straps. Madame Chardin would have choked if she had seen me. In my dressing room, which I shared with the dog trainer and her two poodles, I glanced over the program. My act was a 'filler' to allow the chorus girls time for an elaborate costume and set change.

When I stepped onto the stage and danced the Charleston, I swung my limbs with gusto even though my heart wasn't in it. I could see the audience clearly and, luckily for me, they were smiling. I grinned, shimmied and wiggled in the right places and sang my song with a smile on my face. They in turn laughed and applauded, and I exited into the wings convinced that rich Parisians were easier to please than working-class Marseillaise.

But once I was off the stage, there was no Madame Tarasova, Monsieur Dargent or Albert to congratulate me on how well I had done. I passed Monsieur Volterra on the stairs and he patted me on the shoulder as if he couldn't quite remember who I was. I wanted to stay to see Camille's performance in the second half of the show but the stage manager told me that 'minor acts' were not allowed to hang around the theatre once their numbers were done and so I found myself back in my icy room in Montparnasse by nine o'clock with no one to talk to. Such was my debut at the Casino de Paris.

TWELVE

The show at the Casino de Paris was a success and looked like running into the summer. Camille was launched into stardom. The reviewers couldn't drool over her enough: *'Camille Casal is so vibrantly beautiful that one's skin tingles the minute she steps onto the stage.'*

I managed to see Camille's performance by purchasing a matinée ticket and taking a seat in the audience after my act in the show. Camille was more sophisticated than she had been in Marseilles. She had toned down the obvious sexual slinking and sighing in her act and had become more remote ... and even more beautiful. The audience held its breath as spotlights criss-crossed the stage and the music for her signature song, *'Quand je reviens'*, started up. Camille slipped through the curtains, clothed in a figure-hugging dress with sprays of pearls and sequins fanning her breasts and hips, and a matching cape trimmed with ostrich feathers. As she stepped towards the audience, she let the cape slip from her shoulders and fall to the floor like a cloud of snow. Perched on her shapely legs, she surveyed the audience and did not move again until she was sure that everyone had taken in how sublime she was. When the audience was stilled to a complete hush, she started to sing. Her voice was still thin, but after her memorable entrance nobody noticed.

My act didn't receive a mention except in an obscure entertainment newspaper which stated: '*The program showcases some new talents, including the vivacious Simone Fleurier, a charming brunette who dances engagingly and whose voice has personality.*' But I didn't allow the lack of attention to make me sour. I sent Camille roses to congratulate her on her success and to thank her for getting me an audition.

Despite the addition of curtains and rugs, my room in Montparnasse was still cold and Odette suggested that I move into a hotel with reliable heating. I found one on the Rue des Écoles in the Latin Quarter. The manageress was Madame Lombard, a war widow. She checked my age twice on the reference Monsieur Etienne had given me. I was the average age for a Parisian chorus girl but I knew I looked younger.

'Come this way,' she said, handing back the reference and leading me down a corridor.

The ground floor room was furnished with a single bed, a desk and a coat rack with bent wire hangers dangling from it. Although the curtains and walls were shabby there was a steam heater under the window and a shared bathroom on the same floor. All I really needed was a warm place to sleep and dress, and to hang up my expanding collection of clothes. The rent was only two hundred francs a month more than my current room and I was about to accept it when Madame Lombard mentioned that she had a nicer room upstairs.

This one had a low ceiling that sloped down to a dormer window which looked out over the street, and as well as a bed and a heater it had a chest of drawers and an armoire. Although the rate was twice as much as the room downstairs — and well over my budget — I said that I would take it.

'Good,' said Madame Lombard, pleased but not smiling. Her gaze fell to my crocodile-skin shoes and silk stockings. 'No men in the room at any time. Visitors can be met in reception.'

'No,' I stuttered. I was always taken aback when people assumed that because I worked in the music hall, I was a girl of easy virtue.

⌒∽⌒

One evening, Camille sent me a note: 'Meet us back at the theatre after the show. Bentley is taking us out for dinner.'

Although Camille had done me some favours, I couldn't say that I found her a particularly warm friend. And yet I always accepted her invitations with the dutiful obedience of a mousy younger sister. I was fascinated by Camille and drawn to her because I saw her as possessing something I never would: the power of perfect beauty. On top of that, I was alone and adrift without my family and ready to cling to anybody for company.

I arrived at the Casino de Paris as Camille, Bentley and François were coming out of the stage door. I was surprised to see that Antoine wasn't with them; I had formed the impression the last time I saw them that François and Antoine went everywhere together. Bentley's driver stepped out of the idling Rolls-Royce to open the doors for us. Unlike the taxi, there was plenty of room in the back.

Bentley had booked a table at Fouquet's on the Avenue des Champs Élysées. One smile from the tuxedoed *maître d'hôtel* and a glimpse of the tables with their white cloths bathed in amber light from the chandeliers, and it seemed ridiculous that I had ever thought of the Rotonde as 'fine dining'. The chain of command for the floor staff was like a choreographed ballet: the coatroom girl swept away our outer garments; the *maître d'hotel* glided between the other guests in their evening suits and diamonds to show us to our table, before reading out a menu that included ratatouille, salmon terrine and wild boar served in pepper sauce; when he left, the sommelier arrived to take our order for pre-dinner drinks; the waiter followed, wanting to know if we had decided on our dishes; after we made our selection, the dining room assistant lurched forward to fill our water glasses and dish out the bread rolls; then the sommelier returned to recommend wines to go with our courses; once that was taken care of, the waiter reappeared with new cutlery to add to the impressive array of knives, forks and spoons already surrounding our plates; then the sommelier came back with his assistant to pour the champagne. And yet, despite all the activity, the restaurant was several decibels quieter than the Rotonde. The other customers chatted quietly or didn't speak at all.

I stared at the new knife the waiter had placed before me. It resembled a letter opener and was as much a mystery to me as the small fork on my left. I assumed that the two extra goblets on my right were for red wine and white wine. I would have been confused to see four glasses on my right if two had not already been filled with water and champagne. The time we had eaten at Le Boeuf sur le Toit, I had worked out the difference between the salad fork and the meat fork, the soup spoon and the dessert spoon, the butter knife and the cheese knife, by sneaking glances at François or Antoine. But the display of cutlery at Fouquet's was overwhelming.

I was conscious of François's eyes on me. I looked up and smiled, determined to show him that I wasn't ill at ease in such opulent surroundings. Hadn't Madame Piège said that I was quick to pick things up? His gaze fell to the rhinestones around my neck. I shifted in my chair and crossed and uncrossed my legs. Of course the stones were only glitter; they weren't real diamonds like Camille's bracelet. But why did he have to stare at them like that?

Fortunately the *hors-d'oeuvre* arrived and François turned his attention to his plate of snails. Watching him extract them from their shells with a pair of miniature tongs and a fork made me glad that I had ordered the *foie gras*.

'Did you see Cocteau in the audience tonight?' Camille asked Bentley, picking at her plate of shrimps with her knife and fork. I noticed how she approached her food gingerly while Bentley poked and stabbed at his cold cuts with flair. She is as out of place as I am, I thought.

After the restaurant we danced at Claridge's, drank more champagne, then went to François's apartment to listen to his jazz records and share a final drink. If I had been impressed with the luxury Fouquet's offered, then I was astounded by François's living arrangements. His apartment was on the Avenue Foch, near the Arc de Triomphe. The building was nineteenth-century cut stone with wrought-iron balconies, slanted roofs and a gilded elevator that lifted us to the fifth floor. A maid greeted us at the door and ushered us into a foyer as large as the floor space of the Dôme. The rose pink walls and chrome light fittings were a stark contrast to the decorative exterior of the building. A gold sarcophagus stood in the corner. So this is how rich people live, I thought, eyeing the polished stone replica of a sphinx perched in a fountain in the middle of the space and the Egyptian motifs on the tiles. And I thought I had gone up in the world with heating and a shared bathroom!

I followed the others into a drawing room where an ebony piano gleamed alongside the leather *chaises longues*. Paintings of tigers and elephants hung on the walls. François opened a set of glass doors that led out to a balcony with carved tables and chairs and sculptured hedges in planter boxes. 'During the day you can see the Bois de Boulogne from here,' he said, sweeping his hand towards a dark patch amongst the sea of lights. He had directed this comment to Camille but his eyes drifted in my direction. Was he trying to impress *me*? I dismissed the thought. He was too rich and I was far too easy to impress for there to be any challenge in that.

'It's not so cold out tonight,' said Bentley, stepping past François onto the balcony. Camille followed him. I was about to go outside as well when François placed his hand on my shoulder and let the door swing shut. 'Why don't you help me select the music?'

He flung open the doors to a cupboard and pulled out a sliding shelf with a gramophone sitting on it. He set the needle and jazz music filled the room. Then, he stepped towards me and clasped me in position for the foxtrot, our fingers intertwined and his right foot interlocked between my feet. We started to move and François pulled me closer. When we danced at Claridge's we had been a pair in a crowd of dancers. But dancing with François in his drawing room was uncomfortably intimate.

He brought his face to mine. 'You have been distracted all evening,' he said. His hand slid from my shoulder blade to the small of my back, which was bare because of the cut of my dress. I stiffened and he removed it to my waist. The record ended but François made no move to put on a new one. His eyes fixed on my lips and his mouth twitched. I tried to wriggle away, but he gripped my shoulders and pressed his lips to mine. The kiss happened so fast that I froze. His tongue wormed into my mouth. I flinched when our teeth clashed but I could not make myself move until he slid his hand down my neckline and brushed his fingers over my breast. I pulled away and fled behind a coffee table.

'Now you understand,' he said. 'It is not too late for you to go home. Or you can stay and look at my pictures while I change my clothes.'

He turned and left the room. I flew through the balcony doors and almost landed in Bentley's lap. He and Camille were sitting at a table blowing puffs of cigarette smoke at the sky.

'Where's François?' Bentley asked. 'You're not dancing any more?'

'He is changing his clothes,' I said. My heart thumped in my chest and my mind raced. Had I done anything to encourage François?

'Well, he's a fine host,' said Bentley, stubbing out his cigarette on a saucer. 'What's he doing — putting on his pajamas?' He rose from his chair. 'I'll find the maid and organise drinks for us. It was François's suggestion we come here for a nightcap. Surely he can at least offer us a glass of port.'

After Bentley left, Camille glanced over my dress. I looked down and realised that in my struggle with François the skirt had twisted around the waistline and one of the shoulder straps had slipped down.

'François is besotted with you,' she mused. 'He thinks you're beautiful.'

'He hardly knows me!'

It didn't occur to me that I could just leave. For some reason, when I was with Camille I thought I needed her permission before I could do anything.

Camille blew a stream of smoke into the air. 'He is more than wealthy, you know. This is his city apartment. He has a *château* in Neuilly. He could do a lot for your career.'

My mind slowed enough for me to study Camille. Her eyes were bloodshot. We'd had the same amount of wine at dinner and the same amount of champagne at Claridge's, but Camille was drunk. I thought back to when I met her and the others at the stage door. Perhaps they had started drinking straight after the show.

'You are a virgin, aren't you, Simone?' Camille asked, stubbing out her cigarette. 'Well, you will have to decide whether you want to be a virtuous girl or a star. You can't be both.'

I glanced over my shoulder; I had felt safer with Bentley there. 'What do you mean?'

Camille leaned back and squinted at me. 'Do you think I could have got where I have without Bentley? Or Monsieur Gosling for that matter? Do you think girls from our background can become anything without some assistance?'

I didn't answer; I was too surprised by the tone of her voice. The way she spat out Bentley's and Monsieur Gosling's names, it sounded as if they disgusted her. I knew that she used them but I couldn't see what there was to loathe about them.

'I was discovered by a theatrical agent. I came to Paris on my own and I have two prestigious singing positions,' I said. 'I did all that without a man.'

Camille lit another cigarette and looked at me gravely. 'Yes, but you have only yourself to worry about,' she said. 'Do you think I do this for my health? I have a child to think of.'

This piece of information stunned me. I stared at Camille, waiting for an explanation.

'She is in a convent. In Aubagne,' she said. Her voice was so full of controlled emotion that a lump formed in my own throat. 'She will have no more of a chance than I did as an illegitimate girl if I don't make a fortune.'

Suddenly I had a different perspective on Camille's way of life. My cheeks burned with shame that I had ever thought of her as an opportunist.

'Her father was a coffee merchant who didn't even stick around for her birth.'

'What about Bentley?' I asked. 'He seems taken with you. Won't he make you his wife?'

Camille lifted her eyebrows and laughed. She seemed to enjoy my naivety. 'Simone, men like that don't marry girls like us! We have to take from them what we can and then make a life of our own. Besides, I don't think his wife would approve of me marrying him.'

'Is Bentley married?' I realised that I had assumed he was a young bachelor about town, seeking out amusement and life. And possibly love.

'Of course,' Camille sniggered. 'His wife is in London, organising charity balls and calling on society dowagers and doing all the things required of a good married woman.'

She was about to say something else when Bentley returned with the maid and a tray of drinks. François shuffled along behind them, now wearing a smoking jacket and a cravat. His amorous mood seemed to have passed and he smiled at me before reaching into his pocket and taking out a small bag. 'Leave the tray,' he told the maid after she had served the drinks.

When the maid had gone, François removed the bottles and wiped the tray dry with a serviette. He opened the bag and tipped a pile of cocaine onto the mirrored surface.

'Ah, a deck of snow,' laughed Bentley. 'You're a better host than I thought, François.' He reached into his pocket and opened a silver case, took out a calling card and handed it to François.

'Most appropriate,' said François, using the card to divide the powder into four lines. When he was finished he reached back into his pocket and pulled out four straws, handing us each one.

Bentley pushed the tray towards me. 'The first one to greet the dawn wins,' he said.

'You go first,' said Camille, sliding the tray back towards Bentley. 'I'm sure Simone hasn't done this before.'

'Is that right?' said Bentley, bending his head to the tray. 'Then she hasn't lived.'

He put the straw to one of his nostrils and, sealing the other with his finger, snorted the powder like an anteater sucking up insects. He sat back in his chair and blinked his watering eyes. Camille inhaled next, followed by François. Camille started to laugh but clenched her fists so tightly that a trickle of blood threaded out from where her nails dug into her palms. François moaned and pushed the tray towards me, but all I could think of was the man outside Le Chat Espiègle screaming that he had cockroaches crawling under his skin. I slid from my chair and opened the door to the drawing room.

The maid helped me with my wrap and gloves in the foyer. 'Would Mademoiselle like to leave a message for Monsieur Duvernoy?' she asked. I shook my head.

Out on the avenue, the morning was already breaking. The sun glistened on the roofs of the buildings and the branches of the tallest trees. There wasn't a taxi in sight so I set off on foot towards the Arc de Triomphe, looking for a *métro* station.

THIRTEEN

When Monsieur Volterra began planning the next show, Monsieur Etienne negotiated a better singing and dancing part for me — modern rather than comic. Most of the theatres in Paris, including the Casino, closed in August with rehearsals for the new shows starting in September. I could have joined one of the troupes touring the provinces over summer or expanded my nights at the Café des Singes. I chose to do neither, and gave up my job with Madame Baquet's nightclub. I wanted to make a trip back to the farm for summer. I was lonely. Because of my age and what I did, I was isolated from normal life and even the other performers around me. The chorus girls didn't want to know me and I wasn't a big enough name to hang around with the stars. As my night at François's apartment had shown, Camille and I were worlds apart. Odette was my only true friend, but because of her work and art classes and my odd hours, we rarely saw each other. I loved Paris, but it was time for a trip home.

I caught the overnight train to Pays de Sault, splurging on a second-class sleeping compartment so that I wouldn't have to endure the discomfort of sitting upright all night. Bernard met me at the station, not in a sports car but a motor truck.

'*Bonjour*, Simone. Welcome home,' he said, and smiled. Bernard lifted my luggage into the tray then opened the passenger door for me before climbing into the driver's seat and revving up the engine. The southern sun burned through the windscreen. It was dazzling after the anaemic light of Paris. The pines shimmered under the blue sky and larks sang. The road was so bumpy I imagined the glass of milk I had drunk on the train churning into butter in my stomach.

I told Bernard about Montparnasse, the Café des Singes, my spot at the Casino de Paris and my dinner at Fouquet's.

'We have swapped lives,' he said, a grin breaking out on his sun-bronzed face. 'You have become civilised and I have gone wild.'

My gaze travelled from his hobnail boots to his cap. A film of perspiration glowed on his cheeks and forehead. He was a farmer now but he was anything but wild. His work trousers were pressed with a crease down the front of each leg, and the reek of scorched leather in the cabin was lifted by the scent of cologne floating up from his shirt collar.

The lavender harvest was over. Bernard told me it had been a success and that they planned to buy another still the following year. They were also hoping to purchase the Rucarts' abandoned farm from the only heir, who lived in Digne. The old house was beyond repair but they wanted to restore the orchard and prepare the other fields for lavender.

'A contact in Grasse says their scientists are developing a hybrid that is hardier than wild lavender and yields ten times as much oil,' Bernard explained, sounding like my father in one of his entrepreneurial moods. 'If it works out, we will need more land.'

We arrived at the farm in the afternoon. The cypress trees cast shadows over the sizzling road. My mother was standing in the yard with her hand shading her eyes, Bonbon on guard at her feet. Even from that distance I could see the little dog had put on weight; no doubt spoiled by Aunt Yvette's cooking. We cleared the grove and my mother called out. Aunt Yvette burst through the beaded curtain in the kitchen doorway, a pan in her hand. Chocolat and Olly scampered after her.

Bernard pulled to a stop in the yard. I didn't wait for him to open the door for me; I jumped out and ran to my mother. She rushed forward and clasped my head in her hands, punching kisses onto my cheeks. Her eyes brimmed with tenderness — and a hint of surprise, as if I were an apparition that had appeared out of the forest.

'It is good to see you, Simone. But you won't be staying long, will you? Not yet,' she said, giving me one of her mysterious smiles.

'Simone! Is that you?' Aunt Yvette cried, leaving the pan on the windowsill and fiddling in her pocket for her glasses. She slipped them on and squinted at me. 'Look at your hair!' she said. 'What have you done to it?'

I had forgotten that she might be shocked. The women in my village kept their hair long from childhood to death, and wore it tied up.

'So the lavender harvest went well again?' I asked, trying to deflect the attention away from my hair.

'Even better than last year,' beamed Aunt Yvette.

'Where is Gerome?' asked Bernard, lifting my suitcases from the truck and carrying them to the doorstep. 'He would probably like to see Simone.'

'He is sleeping just now,' said Aunt Yvette. Turning to me, she explained, 'We have converted the front parlour into a room for him. That way he can join in at mealtimes and watch the farm work without us having to drag him up and down the stairs.'

'He's better then?' I asked, taking the glass of chilled wine my mother handed to me and sitting next to her on a bench in the yard. The trellis sagged with the weight of the wisteria blooms which dangled above me like bunches of grapes. The sugary scent attracted swarms of bees. One landed on my skirt, drunk with the sweetness of the nectar. It floundered on the material for a few moments, wings and legs flailing, before soaring off again.

'He is improved,' said Aunt Yvette, pulling up a chair. 'He can sit up by himself and even says a few words now and then. We didn't need to get extra help in the end. Your mother and I can cope with him.'

My mother passed me a slice of melon and looked into my eyes. 'Go and lie down before dinner,' she said. 'You look tired. We can talk more after you have rested.'

I lay down in one of the bedrooms in Aunt Yvette's house, so exhausted by the journey that I didn't bother to take off my dress. Bonbon jumped up on the bed and nestled next to me. I ran my fingers through her fur. She gazed at me before stretching her mouth into a yawn. She was my mother's companion now, but I was pleased to see her again. I napped restlessly, the heat inducing a string of disjointed dreams about dancing at the Casino de Paris to the sound of a train's squealing brakes.

'Simone!' my mother's voice called from downstairs. I jolted upright, my heart thumping in my chest and my back damp with sweat. Bonbon had disappeared. Outside, the sun had set and a blue tinge glimmered in the early evening sky. I must have been asleep for hours.

I made my way downstairs, towards the sound of plates being set on the table and the scent of rosemary chicken. When I opened the kitchen door the flame in the hurricane lamp made me blink. Uncle Gerome sat at the head of the table. His expression was less contorted than the last time I had seen him, but one of his eyes was still clamped shut and his hair, always salt and pepper, was a shock of white.

My mother carved the chicken on the bench. Aunt Yvette, who was serving soup into bowls, paused the ladle mid-air and stared at me. 'Simone, are you all right? You are so pale.'

'I'm fine,' I said. 'It's the heat. I had forgotten what it was like.'

Bernard poured a glass of wine and held it up to Uncle Gerome's lips so he could drink. I cleared my throat. 'Hello,' I said. I had spent most of my life fearing or hating Uncle Gerome but the sight of his twisted body threw me into confusion. I wanted to cry.

Uncle Gerome tilted his head. Rivulets of wine dribbled down his chin. His expression was glassy and it was impossible to tell if he had understood me or not.

'Why is his arm in a sling?' I asked Bernard as I took my place at the table.

'He can't feel it,' Bernard said, wiping Uncle Gerome's chin with a serviette. 'He forgets sometimes that it is there so we have to bind it to prevent him catching it on something and wrenching it out of its socket.'

Uncle Gerome emitted a groan then muttered, 'Pierre?'

'No, it is Simone,' Bernard corrected him. 'Your niece.'

'Pierre?' Uncle Gerome repeated. 'Pierre?' He began to sob. The plea in his voice wrenched my insides. I glanced at my mother and Aunt Yvette. They sliced tomatoes and garlic cloves as if nothing were wrong. How could they not be unhinged by that pitiful sound?

'Don't be upset, Simone,' Bernard whispered. 'He is not unhappy. The doctor said it is normal for stroke victims to cry for no reason.'

I winced. Bernard and I both knew that wasn't true. We were listening to the sounds of a man buried alive, trapped in the coffin of his body. What Uncle Gerome was suffering was worse than death. He didn't have the peace of unconsciousness. He was aware of all his regrets; they paraded before him each day and he was impotent to do anything about them.

My mother and Aunt Yvette served the food. Aunt Yvette spooned the soup into Uncle Gerome's mouth and he quietened down. After dinner he stared at his hands and didn't say anything else for the rest of the evening. Bernard tried to lift the mood by asking why I had brought three suitcases from Paris. 'Did you think we would be going dancing at Zelli's each evening?'

I laughed. 'When we clear the table I will show you what is inside those suitcases.'

⊂∞⊃

My mother and Aunt Yvette refused to let me help clean up after dinner. But once they were done, I unpacked the gifts I had chosen before leaving Paris. 'It is the latest thing,' I said, holding out the black and white packets for my mother and aunt.

My mother opened the box of perfume and examined the square bottle and the bold print on the label: Chanel No 5. The design was everything that was chic in Paris: sleek, unfussy and modern. She unscrewed the lid and took a sniff of the amber liquid then recoiled. Her nose wrinkled and her eyes watered as if she had smelt an acerbic onion. She sneezed so hard that the empty box flew off the table.

Aunt Yvette dabbed some of the perfume on her wrist and trailed it past her nostrils. 'Yes, it is unique, isn't it?'

Bernard, with his ability to pull scents apart, was the most appreciative of my choice of fragrance. 'Neroli and ylang-ylang,' he said, dabbing some of the fragrance onto the back of his hand. 'Jasmine and rose.' He waited a few minutes before sniffing his skin again. 'Sandalwood, vetiver and vanilla.'

'It contains some synthetics too. They make the fragrance last longer,' I said.

I thought of the gifts of single flower perfume Bernard had brought from Grasse over the years, with their ribbed glass bottles, tapered necks and stoppers decorated with porcelain flowers or birds; and also of the herbal sachets and candles my mother anointed with lavender or rosemary oil for special days of the year. Chanel No 5 might be the fashion in Paris but I realised how things that were sophisticated there could be incongruous with the south. Bernard suited the emerald necktie I had bought for him, but the mustard-yellow waistcoat I had given Uncle Gerome was too bright against his muted clothes and made him look like a ghastly clown.

Aunt Yvette wrapped the kimono I had bought at Galeries Lafayette over her farm dress and served the coffee in it. The crimson silk billowing about her as she moved from the bench to the table gave her the appearance of a harlot pacing the Rue Pigalle. But it was my mother who I managed to make the most foolish. I had spent a week's wages on the silver fox fur which, despite the heat, she now wore around her neck. Against her tanned complexion and fuzzy hair the accessory lost all its sleekness and looked exactly what it was: a dead animal wrapped around a woman's throat. My misjudgment showed me how different our lives had become, and it made me sad. Was this the result of going out into the world and carving a life of my own? Since my father's death I had felt a new closeness with my mother, but now we were going our separate ways. I wondered if we would even recognise each other in a few years.

❧

My two weeks in Pays de Sault passed slowly at first, but when the fortnight came to an end I felt as though the time had flown by too quickly. At first, with none of the bustle and distractions of Paris, I had to relearn the habit of doing things slowly and with purpose. Water needed to be fetched from the well each day, vegetables plucked from the garden, distances covered by foot or by bicycle rather than taxi. My body had to get used to the rhythm of farm life again: rising early and going to bed after dark. I helped in the kitchen and with the animals, but whenever I offered to help with the farm work everybody laughed.

'You were bad at it before,' Bernard said, patting my back. 'I can't imagine you have improved at all in Paris.' Considering his miraculous adaptation to rural life, how could I argue?

Each day, I visited my father's grave in the late afternoon. Bonbon came along with me, the only time she would leave my mother's side. One day, as I was planting some lavender near his tombstone, the words to '*La bouteille est vide*' drifted into my mind. It was true that the more we got, the more we wanted. If someone had told me that one day I would be wearing department-store clothes instead of homemade hand-me-downs, that I would be living in Paris and making my living by singing, I would have thought that was the grandest life imaginable. Suddenly I found that I wanted more. I wanted *haute couture* clothes like Camille; I wanted an apartment like François's; and I didn't just want to be a singer any more — I wanted to be a star. More: I wanted all of those things on my own terms.

I decided that I was going to take risks and stand or fall on my own. I would not rely on men as Camille did. André Blanchard's face came to mind. If I was going to be with a man, it would be because I loved him.

❦

When the morning came for Bernard to take me back to Carpentras for the return trip to Paris, I realised that my visit had been more than a rest from the demands of my life in the capital. It had allowed me to take a breath before ascending the mountain of success.

Aunt Yvette and my mother propped Uncle Gerome in a chair near the door so he could watch the drama of me and Bernard running up and down the stairs with my suitcases, and me flying back up to my room for things I had overlooked in my packing. When everything was loaded into the truck, I kissed Uncle Gerome's cheeks.

'Good,' he said, fixing his eye on me before lapsing back into his own thoughts.

Aunt Yvette threw her arm around my shoulder, kissed me and guided me towards the truck. 'Hurry along,' she said, 'or you will miss your train. I don't want Bernard negotiating that road like a racing driver.'

I patted Olly, Bonbon and Chocolat in turn. Bonbon looked up at me with guilty eyes; perhaps she sensed that I was lonely in Paris. But

Chocolat had adopted her, and my mother adored her, and there was no way I would separate them. I rubbed Bonbon's ears so she would know that I understood. 'You are just like Bernard,' I told her. 'You have fallen in love with the countryside.'

Bernard started up the truck. 'Come on, Simone,' he said, 'this is your curtain call.'

I laughed and kissed my mother. She grabbed my hands in hers and squeezed them. There was soil ingrained in the lines around her knuckles and her skin was rough; they were honest hands, hardened by honest work. The sight of them filled me with love.

❧

When I arrived back in Paris, Madame Lombard handed me a letter which threw my plans into chaos. My act in the new season's show at the Casino de Paris had been scrapped. Not because it wasn't good enough, Monsieur Volterra's assistant tactfully wrote, but because the show was running overtime and Monsieur Volterra couldn't cut any of the material belonging to the comedian star, Jacques Noir.

I collapsed onto my bed. What would I do now? After my spending spree on gifts for my family, I had only two hundred francs left and my rent was due the following week. And I no longer had a slot with the Café des Singes to fall back on.

The situation was ironic, given the resolution I had made in Pays de Sault. Instead of getting more than I already had, I was about to lose the little I had got. My dreams of becoming a star were further out of reach than ever.

❧

The next afternoon, Madame Lombard asked me to come downstairs to take a telephone call. It was Monsieur Etienne on the line. He told me to go to the Casino de Paris immediately.

'What's happened?' I asked, keeping my voice low because Madame Lombard was hovering in the reception area, arranging a vase of tulips and fluffing the sofa cushions.

'Miguel Rivarola's wife walked out on him last night. They have to find another tango partner for him today or he has threatened to return to Buenos Aires.'

I twisted the telephone cord around my wrist then let it spiral out again. The tango had been popular in Paris ever since Rudolph Valentino had danced it in the film *The Four Horsemen of the Apocalypse*, and I had seen it performed in cafés and at *bals musettes*. But there was a huge difference between how couples danced in cafés and at afternoon teas to how Rivarola and his wife performed the tango for an audience. I had seen them dance at the Scala once and been mesmerised by the sensuality of their movements and the power in their limbs. They were two flames burning up the stage.

'Isn't Rivarola more concerned about finding his wife right now?' I asked.

'No,' laughed Monsieur Etienne. 'He is a professional artist. No matter what, he gets on with the show. Don't forget that it opens in three weeks.'

Who could match Maria? I thought, smoothing down my collar. The depth of feeling required for tango wasn't something you could learn in a day. The fact that the Casino was asking me to try was a sign of how desperate Monsieur Volterra was.

Madame Lombard brushed by me and sat down at the desk, sorting through the day's mail. I told Monsieur Etienne I would be at the Casino in less than half an hour. I wasn't going to argue if Monsieur Volterra offered the part to me; I needed the money.

When I arrived at the Casino de Paris I was piqued to discover that Monsieur Volterra was not only trying me out for the role of Rivarola's dance partner but the entire chorus line and some other minor female acts as well. The first three rows were filled with women in loose dresses and dancing shoes. Sophie, the lead chorus girl, was sitting next to Monsieur Volterra, a rose clutched between her teeth. I was about to turn around and walk out again when Monsieur Volterra caught sight of me and waved. I smiled back and took a seat. For the sake of smooth relations in the future it would be wiser to stay.

Rivarola was on stage, trying out a tango figure with one of the chorus girls. He manoeuvred like a stalking cat, painstakingly and deliberately. Suddenly he pounced. 'No, no, no,' he muttered, pulling away from his partner and addressing Volterra. '*Esta chirusa no me sigue!*'

As Rivarola didn't speak much French and Volterra spoke no Spanish, the remark was translated by the lighting technician who was from Madrid. 'He says that she doesn't follow his lead,' the boy explained.

'But she is lovely,' protested Monsieur Volterra, pulling his handkerchief from his pocket and patting his forehead. 'Surely that is something she'll learn if he teaches her. It's not as if we can just pull another Argentine tango dancer out of a hat for him. And, after all, we do have a contract.'

There was a moment's delay while the technician translated for Rivarola. The dancer folded his arms across his chest and shook his head. '*Esta mina salta como un conejo,*' he growled, shaking his fist towards the flies. '*Yo quiero una piba que sepa deslizarse como un cisne.*'

The lighting technician shifted from foot to foot and picked at a loose wire around one of the footlights, obviously avoiding translating the last comment.

Seeing there was no use pursuing that line of argument, Monsieur Volterra sent the chorus girl back to her seat and called up another one, who stepped gingerly onto the stage like a virgin to a sacrifice. 'No wonder his wife left him,' one of the chorus girls near me whispered to another. 'He is too difficult to please.'

Although I had resigned myself to the fact that the audition was going to be a waste of time, I was intrigued by Rivarola's method for trying out potential partners. He started by demonstrating a tango figure for the girl to follow. Once he was sure that she knew the pattern, he would turn and nod to a stagehand waiting in the front wing. The man would lower the gramophone's needle onto a record and tango music wafted up into the air. Rivarola would then step forward and clasp the girl with his hand tucked into the small of her back and his torso pressed against hers. The embrace was suggestive but there was not a trace of intimacy in Rivarola's stony face. He stood in that position, not blinking his eyes or twitching a muscle for at least a minute. If the girl squirmed, giggled or shifted her feet, she was dismissed.

I leaned forward and studied Rivarola. He was in his late forties at least; even though his body was as lithe as that of a boy, his age showed in his face. There were puffy bags under his eyes, and his neck, while firm under the chin, was goose-fleshed. Yet somehow those faults were surpassed by the flicker of his hooded eyes and the curve of his pursed lips. Every turn of his head and bend of his legs oozed sensuality. I began to suspect that his tight embrace was to test whether his partner would be burned by the flame smouldering under his skin or whether she would fuse with it. After what Camille had said about me being so obviously virtuous, I knew I would not be chosen. Yet I was curious to see who would be.

If his potential partner passed the embrace test, Rivarola performed the tango figure with her, propelling the girl around the stage and frequently changing direction. I noticed that dancers were not discarded for muddling their footwork; Rivarola didn't seem to be looking for perfection. I was intrigued by the way he guided his various partners — hovering over them, occasionally flinching from them or sniffing the tops of their heads — as if he were choosing flowers at a market by their perfume. But after more than an hour of try-outs, none of the girls pleased him.

'*Esto es como bailar con troncos!*' Rivarola spat out just before Monsieur Volterra called me up on stage. I had no idea what he had said but knew from the tone that it wasn't good. His insults were unjustified: he'd had the choice of some of Paris's best chorus girls, many of whom were trained in ballet. I took my place opposite him and braced myself for the test by imagining the chocolate éclair I intended to devour as soon as it was over.

Rivarola stared at my ankles then bent over and stroked them like a man choosing a racehorse. He seemed intrigued by the shape of them although no one had made any comment about my feet before. He brushed his hands over the bridges then slipped his fingers under my arches. I fought the tickle that irritated my windpipe; I was determined not to laugh. I wanted to make it at least as far as the second test before Rivarola declared me unsuitable. I was curious to discover how he made his decisions.

The stagehand dropped the gramophone needle and Rivarola clenched me to his chest. I stifled a cry. Something like a lightning strike jumped from his chest into mine. I shook with the force of it but didn't budge from my position. Rivarola stared into my eyes. Somehow I managed to hold his gaze. This is what it must feel like to be seduced by a gypsy, I thought, although of course Rivarola was no gypsy. He was a full-blooded Argentine.

Rivarola guided me backwards but the power that sparked from his legs gave the sensation that I was being shoved back into a wall of air. It took me by surprise and I didn't resist. Then the force of gravity around my body seemed to dissipate; my legs fluttered as if they were floating. It was not what I had expected from the tango, which I had imagined to be weighted down with drama and despair. Maria had always danced with her arms draped around Rivarola's neck, like a shipwreck victim clinging to a piece of wood. Now I wondered if she had been trying to stop herself being swept away. Rivarola dwelt on each step as if he were testing bathwater with the tip of his toe. And yet everything he did was smooth. The music separated into layers and Rivarola danced to each one. Sometimes we followed the melody of the piano, then the nostalgic voice of the singer, then the violins. I had never paid such careful attention to the details of music when dancing, only its overall beat and rhythm. I had seen music as the accompaniment to my dancing, but with Rivarola it was the core.

He suddenly stopped and thrust me away. I realised that in thinking about the music I had lost my concentration on the movements. Rivarola's face contorted and he rushed towards Monsieur Volterra so swiftly that I thought he was going to punch him in the face. The impresario must have thought the same thing because he threw himself back in his seat.

'*Esta piba acaricia la música como una diosa bailando sobre las nubes!*' Rivarola shouted.

Monsieur Volterra gaped from Rivarola to the lighting technician. The boy's face blanched and he wobbled on his feet. The needle slid off the record and the room turned deathly silent. Everyone seemed to be holding their breath, waiting for the technician to interpret what Rivarola had said. The boy crept to the front of the stage.

'Rivarola says she is perfect,' he told Monsieur Volterra, who had turned as white as a sheet. 'He says that she caresses the music like a goddess dancing on the clouds.'

❧

Within a day, I went from being unemployed to being part of a duo with the world's most renowned tango artist. Rivarola and I even had a billing, because we danced in several scenes and our act was the subplot to the show's theme of forbidden love. It was the first time I had seen my name in lights since Marseilles, and this time it was at the Casino de Paris! But I worked for every letter of it. With only three weeks to the opening, the rehearsal schedule was punishing: three hours of tango lessons each morning and a rehearsal proper from two to six o'clock every afternoon.

'*Necesitas mas disciplina pa' ser una bailarina seria que pa' ser una cantante de comedia!*' Rivarola would shout at me at least three or four times each session. 'To be a serious dancer takes more discipline than to be a singing comedian.'

Having picked up English phrases by working at the Café des Singes, I was now becoming proficient in Spanish too — a necessity when spending several hours a day with an Argentine who refused to speak French — and I understood what Rivarola meant better than he ever gave me credit for. It was easy to hide behind cute lines; much harder to bring out what was deep inside for all to see. I knew that if I wanted to leave the childish songs and unglamorous costumes behind for good, then I had to make a success of the act. Monsieur Volterra was even having our portrait painted for the wall opposite the poster of Camille and Jacques Noir!

'*Che, prestame mas atención. No bailes pa' la gente!*' The lighting technician, who acted as interpreter during rehearsals, had written that one out for me and I had posted it on my dressing room mirror. 'Stay focused on Rivarola. Do not play to the audience.' The instruction went against everything I had ever been taught as a singer, but it was the only way for a dancing duo to captivate a crowd. The people who saw us perform had to believe they were observing a real-life romance between a man and a woman.

Whether Rivarola knew how seriously I followed his instructions, I couldn't tell. I never took my dancing shoes off until I reached my room at the hotel, and when I did I had to peel the inners away from my bruised and blistered feet. With a scream of relief I would plunge them into a bowl of cold water. Often, after rehearsal, I examined my face in the mirror. Under Rivarola's constant shouting, my eyes were growing haughty and my mouth was developing a rebellious curve. My cheekbones and chin were sharper than they had been when I first came to Paris. It was as if Rivarola was transferring something of himself into me. We usually danced cheek to cheek, but sometimes when we practised he would press his forehead against mine. '*Asi podemos leer la mente del otro,*' he said. 'So we can read each other's thoughts.'

I cringed the first time Rivarola pressed me so tightly to his chest that my breasts felt like they were being crushed into his ribs, but I didn't protest. Nor did I say anything when during some of the patterns he rubbed his leg between mine when he was leading me backwards. Perhaps I saw it as the best way to rid myself of my virginity and still remain true to my art. To lose my innocence on stage was infinitely preferable than to surrender it for money to men like François. Purity did not suit the style of tango. If I was to be true to it, I had to convey at least a hint of lust and carnal desire, and it was in that, as much as the dance, that Rivarola was instructing me.

When the audience and gossip columnists saw us perform together on stage, they assumed that Rivarola and I were lovers in real life too. Those who saw us backstage knew better. For the minutes we danced together, Rivarola and I smouldered with desire in each other's arms. But as soon as the curtain came down and we ran to the wings, he discarded me like the sweaty shirt he tossed to the wardrobe assistant. In between acts he hid himself away in his dressing room, drinking whisky and smoking cigars. He was not interested in me beyond what I became for him on stage. I don't think he knew my name until several weeks into the performance. And yet, from the first night, our dancing moved the audience to standing ovations and reviews that were full of admiration. The critic for *Paris Soir* wrote: '*The sublime teaming of Rivarola with newcomer Simone Fleurier is one of the highlights of the show. The distinctive performance by Rivarola is enough to send anyone's pulse racing and his partner matches him in every way with her grace and precision.*'

Monsieur Etienne was pleased with my success and, as a treat, took Odette and me to dinner at La Tour d'Argent.

'It is one thing to be a great singer,' he said. 'And another to be able to dance the way you do.'

'I don't think there is anybody else in Paris who is a genius at both,' gushed Odette.

Monsieur Etienne raised his champagne glass. 'Paris is your tango partner, Simone. She is within an inch of your grasp.'

Until then, Monsieur Etienne's assessments of me had been positive but reserved. The fact that he was handing out such high praise gave me the boost in confidence I needed. From him, I could be sure it wasn't flattery. But while I might have been on the verge of conquering Paris, not everyone was enamoured of me.

FOURTEEN

The best thing about being lifted from the status of minor act to principal player was that I was included in the grand finale. The set was a Spanish villa, complete with pots of cascading geraniums, and a Moorish courtyard with a fountain as the backdrop. The audience sighed with admiration when Camille made her entrance, lowered from the flies on a chandelier like a deity descending from the heavens. She landed in the arms of the principal male dancer, who wore a matador's suit with pants tight enough to raise every woman's temperature. Camille's costume was daring too: a Spanish dress cut away at the front to reveal a corset and knickers and a lace mantilla sprouting from a comb on her head and spilling around her shoulders. The chorus girls, in little more than sombreros and sequins in strategic places, swirled around the couple, waving feathered fans. The clowns, playing the part of the matador's *banderilleros*, chased and were chased in turn by two clowns dressed as a bull. Just before Camille made her appearance I danced a kind of Frenchified flamenco, which Rivarola refused to perform because it had nothing to do with Argentina, but which the whole chorus line mirrored behind me. My exit came when I was swept away by a *picador* on horseback — a real horse's back. The animal was named Roi and was the offspring of one of Monsieur Volterra's racing thoroughbreds. After Camille and her lover danced and sang their triumphant number, the chorus girls broke out into a cancan. The dance had nothing to do with Spain, but the audience loved it.

Although she was a star, Camille did not have the top billing for the season. That place went to Jacques Noir, 'the most adored comedian in the whole of Paris'. 'Adored' was the right word: whenever he appeared on stage, my dressing room trembled with the earthquake force of the audience's applause. Once my photograph of Fernandel — which he had autographed for me after I had seen him perform at the Folies Bergère — fell off its hook from the violent vibrations and smashed on the floor. The glass cracked straight across the comedian's dopey smile. Poor Fernandel, I thought. Although he was one of Paris's most talented singing comedians, I doubted that with the dark circles under his eyes and his equine face he would ever be described as 'adored'.

Once Rivarola and I had settled into our act, I asked the stage manager if I could watch Noir's first set from the wings. Because of the schedule I had never seen him perform. Noir appeared in the grand finale after me, when the stagehands were too busy trying to manoeuvre me, the *picador* and Roi outside before the horse splattered droppings where the other performers would step in them. Despite not being fed for six hours before a performance, a bowel movement was Roi's usual reaction to his post-performance euphoria.

'Only Noir's wife sits in the wings during his performance,' the stage manager informed me. 'He doesn't like distractions.'

'I'll be discreet,' I promised. 'I can't see him at rehearsals. They are always closed.'

'That's so people don't steal his material before he performs it.'

'I'm hardly likely to do that,' I said. 'Unless you think Rivarola and I have potential as a comedy act?'

The stage manager relented and led me to a section of the left wing where there was a wooden stool. It was splintery and prickled my legs, but I smiled as if nothing were wrong.

The stage manager put his fingers to his lips. 'I don't want you to even breathe,' he said.

I peered through the darkness and saw a woman sitting in the opposite wing, a circle of light falling in her lap from a table lamp perched on a shelf above her. That must be Jacques Noir's wife, I thought, taken aback by the woman's appearance. For the wife of one of the richest entertainers in Paris, she was dressed dowdily in a grey dress. Apart from the wedding ring on her finger there was not a glimmer of jewellery anywhere on her person. And if the stage manager was so worried about me breathing, I wondered what he made of Madame Noir's knitting. The click of her needles was audible even from where I was sitting. Her birdlike neck and the wrinkles on her forehead made her look more like Noir's mother than his wife. I had heard that Noir was only thirty-two years old.

The chorus girls opened the act with a jazz dance performed on a chessboard floor with extra dancers dressed as kings, queens, bishops and knights. As the dancers were fleeing the stage via the staircase, one of them flipped up the crown of a giant rook. The chess piece opened and out stepped a man in tails and a top hat. He was as obese as a hippopotamus with three chins and beady eyes peering over his snout of a nose. Despite his expensive English suit I thought he was the most unattractive man I had ever seen. I was sure he was one of the clowns in extra padding and make-up until the crowd went wild and the women started calling out, 'Jacques! Jacques!'

My breath caught in my throat. If I had been surprised by his wife's appearance, I was shocked by Noir's. This was the most adored comedian in the whole of Paris? Maurice Chevalier was more handsome and bursting with Gallic charm. Even Fernandel didn't seem so unattractive next to Noir. I thought about the poster in the foyer: the artist had taken some liberties in improving Noir's appearance there. But from the reaction of the audience, he had a much more positive effect on them than he did on me.

'Ladies! Ladies!' Noir called out. 'Please! What will your menfolk think?'

The restless women giggled and settled down.

'At least you have the good taste to be at the Casino de Paris tonight,' he grinned, swaggering across the stage, 'and you haven't gone to see Mistinguett at the Moulin Rouge.' He stopped, eyed the crowd and rolled his tongue in his cheek. 'You know the difference between Mistinguett and a piranha, don't you?'

The audience tensed, waiting for the punch line.

'The lipstick.'

The crowd roared with laughter and clapped. Noir quickly followed up with, 'What is the first thing Mistinguett does when she gets up in the morning?' and, after a staged pause, answered his own question, 'She puts on her clothes and goes home.'

This joke brought more hoots of laughter and applause. I wondered if I was hallucinating. Could that obese man really be Jacques Noir? *He* was being paid over two thousand francs a performance? He was appalling.

I glanced across the stage to his wife. She didn't appear to be paying attention to her husband's performance; she looped and stitched at her knitting as if she were waiting for a train instead of sitting in the wing of a music hall. Meanwhile, Noir moved on from savaging Mistinguett to humiliating Chevalier who had featured in the gossip columns that week with the rumour that he had tried to kill himself. 'You know what happened there, don't you?' laughed Noir, eyeing the audience. 'They say it was because of his bad war memories. Hah! It was because of his bad New York memories. He was trying to sell himself as a big star on Broadway when a kid and his mother approached him and the kid asked, "Mister Chevalier, would you sign my autograph book?" "Sure, kid," said Chevalier, loud enough for everyone within a mile radius to know that *someone* had recognised him. Well, the kid pulled out this tiny notepad, no more than two inches by two inches, that he'd bought at a five and dime store somewhere. "Gee, kid," Chevalier said, "there's not much room here. What would you like me to write?" The kid thought about it a moment and then his eyes lit up. "You know, Mister Chevalier, perhaps you could write out your repertoire."'

The joke brought the house down. Noir's rapport with the audience baffled me. Was I missing something? Had working with Rivarola cost me my sense of humour? I wondered what Monsieur Volterra made of Noir's digs at Mistinguett and Chevalier; after all, they were two of his biggest stars at the Casino de Paris. I wondered if after tonight they would ever perform there again. But Noir had something in store for Monsieur Volterra too.

'How do you tell if an impresario is dead or not?' he quizzed the audience. 'You wave a thousand franc note past his face.'

With that the orchestra started up and Noir burst into song. The whole mood of the act changed and I understood what was so appealing about him. Noir hummed, half-sang and half-talked his way through the song in a voice that was the best I'd heard from a male singer in Paris. It was more resonant than Chevalier's argot, and more agile in its jumps and skips than Fernandel's. If you closed your eyes, you could forget the song was being sung by so hideous a man. The voice belonged to someone dashing. But even with my eyes open, Noir's appearance improved when he sang. There was something magnetic about him. I tried to pinpoint what it was, because I feared it might be that elusive 'star quality' I was desperately seeking myself. Perhaps it was the confidence that radiated from every pore of his generous body. He was good and he knew it.

I was so swept away by his song about a dandy who loves his mistress's maid that I forgot about the splintery stool and the cruelty of his earlier jokes. Noir's voice smoothed his rough edges the way the sea blunts sharp stones. But the next instant, I was jolted out of my pleasure. Noir picked up a cane and skipped around the stage, bouncing the stick in time to music I recognised.

> La! La! Boom! Here comes Jeanne
> Checking out my new Voisin.
> La! La! Boom! She asks, 'What are you doing?'
> What am I going to tell her?
> La! La! Boom! I'm warming up my little machine . . .

Noir was parodying the song I had sung in last season's show, only his version was full of double-entendres. But worse than just parodying the song, he was lampooning me, bouncing and skipping and wiggling his behind as I had been made to do by Madame Piège. I looked from Noir to the audience; they were laughing, their mouths open like hundreds of dark caverns. I had hated that number myself but that didn't lessen my humiliation. Noir turned my previous trivial act into a truly embarrassing memory.

If Noir had left his parody there, it would have been humiliating enough. But to add insult to injury he finished his act in a tango pose, blew a kiss to the audience and cooed in a mock-sexy voice with the extended vowels of a southern accent, 'I've come a long way, haven't I, darlings? Just look at me now.'

The curtain fell and the audience went wild. Horror overwhelmed me and I couldn't move. After three encores Noir exited and the stage manager shooed me off the stool to make room for the stagehands to change the set. I stared at the manager but he didn't pay me any attention. Was he so insensitive that he hadn't connected me to Noir's act before he let me watch? I rushed to my dressing room, so blind with fury that the other performers hurrying along the corridors appeared as blurs in my vision. I slammed the door. Bouton and Rubis, the poodles, jumped from surprise. Rubis yelped. Madame Ossard, their trainer, swung around.

I threw myself down at my dressing table and tore a comb through my hair. I didn't want to have to go through with the finale. I wanted to go home.

'What's the matter with you?' asked Madame Ossard, adjusting the lace on her jumping hoop.

I avoided her gaze and exchanged the comb for a powder puff, dabbing furiously at my forehead.

'Oh,' she said. 'You've seen Noir's act?'

I threw the puff down and shrugged. It occurred to me that the other performers had known of the parody all along. Why hadn't anybody said anything?

Madame Ossard clucked her tongue. 'He's a bastard for doing that to someone who is just starting out. Especially a fellow performer at the Casino.'

'How could they let him?' I asked, my voice quivering. 'It's not fair.'

Madame Ossard slipped a handkerchief from her neckline and passed it to me. The cloth smelt like the tar soap she used to wash her dogs. 'Take it as a compliment,' she said. 'It hasn't put the audience off your act, has it? If anything, it is good publicity for you.'

'But he makes me look silly,' I protested. I realised then what had upset me so much. By making fun of me, Noir had reduced me to a singing comedian again. In that moment I realised how difficult it was to 'grow up' on the stage. There would always be someone to remind me of the things I had done to get ahead.

Madame Ossard clasped my chin between her fingers and lifted my face so that I looked into her eyes. 'Simone, I think there are a few people at the Casino who are jealous of the attention you are getting. Being satirised by the most famous entertainer in Paris is not necessarily a bad thing.'

One evening, a few weeks before the Christmas season, Rivarola's wife returned. I caught sight of her on my way to the wardrobe mistress to fix a tear in the hem of my skirt. She was standing near the stage door with her hands clasped in front of her, staring straight ahead. Despite the heating, a chill stung the air and the skin on my scalp prickled. It was like catching a glimpse of a lurking theatre ghost. I had secretly feared this would happen, but the last I had heard, Maria was in Lisbon with a German playboy. The way her scarlet-lipped smile curled and she narrowed her glance to the dress in my hand spelt doom for me and Rivarola.

When the time came for our first set, despite three calls and stagehands searching everywhere, Rivarola was nowhere to be found. The stage manager and one of his assistants broke open his dressing room door, but all that remained was a trace of tobacco scent in the dusty air and a record snapped into pieces and scattered on the floor.

'I don't want to let you go, Mademoiselle Fleurier,' said Monsieur Volterra. 'The audience and the reviewers adore you — even more than they liked Rivarola.' He leant back in his chair, which creaked from his weight, and tapped his pen against his chin. 'Give me a week,' he said. 'I'll see what I can do.'

Of course, with Monsieur Volterra that was going to be an unpaid week, but I didn't have much choice. All the big shows were already in production and wouldn't be holding auditions any time soon.

'He is speaking with Madame Piège about the choreography for a new piece,' Monsieur Etienne told me when I hadn't heard from Monsieur Volterra for ten days.

'Great,' I muttered. 'Another polka dot song and dance number.'

I was called into the Casino de Paris a few days later and was immediately ashamed of my cynicism. Monsieur Volterra had engaged, at considerable expense, a writer to compose songs for me. 'We need something impressive to replace the tango as the subplot,' Monsieur Volterra explained, showing me into his office.

My jaw dropped when I saw the man with the dark suit and pencil moustache who was waiting for us. Vincent Scotto rose from his chair and stepped forward. 'It will be a pleasure to work with you, Mademoiselle Fleurier,' he said, gazing into my face with his melancholic eyes. 'I have some ideas that will suit your beautiful voice.'

I was surprised by his tone of deference. This was the man who had written songs for some of the greatest stars in Paris: Polin, Chevalier and Mistinguett. And Monsieur Volterra had commissioned him to write specifically for me!

There was an even greater surprise in store when I visited the wardrobe department to be fitted for my costume. Erté, the Russian costume designer, had created a dress for me. Even though he had a contract with the Folies Bergère and had recently been working with MGM studios in Hollywood, somehow Monsieur Volterra had persuaded him to create a one-off costume for the show. When the wardrobe mistress swept the organza cover aside I was delighted by the whimsy of the dress. It was made from shimmering lamé with key holes cut away around the ribs and the rise of the hips. The seams were trimmed in pearls. The costume draped the dress dummy like a waterfall, there was no flounce in it. It simply glistened. I was to wear a pair of feathered wings with it that stood half a metre above my head and a pearled headdress topped by plumes.

'It has taken two seamstresses and a beader five days and nights to complete it this quickly,' the wardrobe mistress explained.

'I can believe it,' I told her, handing my coat to one of the assistants and kicking off my shoes. I couldn't wait to try everything on.

It required two assistants to help me into the costume, and as soon as I felt the weight of it I understood why Casino de Paris chorus girls were statuesque. It took strength and a firm posture to wear a towering headdress and move with any sort of grace. I tried a few turns to the left and right and nearly toppled over. But I was determined to master the costume, even if it meant a stiff neck and headaches. One look at it and I knew it was the costume of a star.

If I had worked until my feet bled for Rivarola, then I worked until my lungs burned for Scotto. I sensed that I was walking down a magical corridor where all the doors were flung open. I could take any path I chose. To sing popular songs of the day was one thing; to sing material composed for you was quite another. And an impresario, especially Monsieur Volterra, was not going to spend money on a composer and five thousand francs on a costume if he didn't see me as an investment.

'This is your big chance, Simone,' I told myself each day when I arrived at the Casino. 'If you can't launch yourself with all of this, you never will.'

The thought chilled me, but it spurred me on to work hard too.

Scotto wrote and perfected the songs with lightning speed. As each number was completed and choreographed, I rehearsed it until it met the approval of Monsieur Volterra. Then it was immediately inserted into the show, because Rivarola's exit had left gaps in the program that needed to be filled.

From my first night on stage the critics were ecstatic. Jacques Patin, the reviewer for *Le Figaro* wrote:

> *A few months ago she was launched by the Casino de Paris as a key dancer. Now she is one of the principal singers. Simone Fleurier delivers. She puts more emotion into one line of a song than most performers put into a lifetime of work. She has a remarkable voice which, because of her age, I expect will develop further. This is a girl with a formidable future.*

I bought several copies of the paper and sent the article to my family and to Madame Tarasova and Vera in Marseilles. I kept a copy under my pillow and read it first thing in the morning and last thing at night. *A formidable future.* Jacques Patin did not say such things about anyone. He had hammered Jacques Noir; although that didn't seem to have made any dint in the comedian's popularity — the show was still sold out every night. I was no longer seen as a sweet girl singing ditties in a ruffled dress, or Rivarola's stage skivvy. A sublime energy inflated me from my toes to the top of my head. I became more self-possessed, and when I walked or danced I was like a caterpillar that had emerged from the cocoon and surprised everyone with her transformation.

∞

By Christmas, all my songs were included in the program. One afternoon in the New Year, I arrived at the Casino de Paris for my rehearsal and was heading towards the stage door when Jacques Noir came out, his wife scuttling a few paces behind him.

'*Bonjour*, Monsieur Noir,' I said. In the heady blur of my success I was filled with goodwill for everybody and I had forgotten that Noir had ever performed a parody of me. I wasn't greeting him because he was the show's star; I would have been delighted to meet anyone in my joyous state.

I didn't try to engage him in conversation or pester him in any way. I even stepped aside so he and his wife could go past me first. Noir gave me a frosty stare while his wife scowled. They ran down the steps to where the chauffeur held open the door of Noir's Rolls-Royce. I shrugged and stepped inside the theatre, barely registering the couple's surliness. I was too excited about practising my songs for the evening performance.

But the following afternoon when I arrived at the Casino for rehearsals, there was tension in the air. I felt it in the doorman's churlish greeting and the irritable way the stage manager handed me changes to the program. Outside the dressing rooms, I found the chorus girls and two of the clowns gathered around the notice board. From the indignant way they were standing with their arms folded and their feet apart, I assumed somebody had been unfairly penalised for something. Minor acts were often given fines for tearing a costume, turning up late to rehearsals or performing with scruffy shoes or a missing button.

'He's got a hide,' one of the clowns muttered.

Sophie, the lead chorus girl, shook her head. 'Whoever it was should have known better. Now we'll all have to walk around on tiptoes.'

I couldn't resist the temptation to find out what the issue was. The normal reprimands always caused grumbling, but this sounded like something interesting. I waited in my dressing room until I heard the chorus girls go down the stairs for their rehearsal, then I stuck my head into the corridor to check that it was clear. There wasn't much on the notice board: a couple of changes to schedules and some advertisements for rooms for rent. Then my eye fell to the memorandum, which I could tell was new because of the whiteness of the paper. The message had been typed in capitals. The words shouted off the page at me:

> MEMO TO ALL PERFORMERS
> IT IS NOT NECESSARY FOR SUPPORTING ACTS OR
> EXTRAS TO GREET MONSIEUR NOIR. REFRAIN FROM
> DOING IT. HE FINDS IT ANNOYING AND RUDE. IT IS
> ALSO AGAINST C.D.P. PROTOCOL FOR MINOR ACTS TO
> APPROACH THE STAR.
>
> THE MANAGEMENT

I stood in the hallway with my mouth open. It took a while to register the words. It was the preposterous request of a megalomaniac, but the way the memo was worded, the way the print seemed to be stamped on the page rather than typed, and the fact that the culprit — me — had not been directly approached, made it seem as if a heinous crime had been committed. I burned with shame. I felt as humiliated as the stagehand who had been reprimanded for defecating on the toilet seat.

I did my best to put the memo out of my mind and concentrate on rehearsing, but that became more difficult as the afternoon wore on. I soon discovered that the memo had not only been posted on the notice board. There were copies all over the theatre: in the rehearsal rooms; near the stairs; in each of the wings; even on the back of the toilet stall doors. To make things worse, I kept overhearing the other performers talking in hushed whispers about it. The memo was the news of the day and was discussed with as much passion as a scandal. *Who do you think it was? I bet it was that sly ballerina ... No, it was Mathilde. She's always trying to get a step up in the show by crawling to the stars.*

At one point when we were rehearsing the grand finale, I was tempted to call the cast to silence and confess that I was the offender. But I couldn't bring myself to do it. My bubble had been burst. Jacques Noir would have told Monsieur Volterra exactly who the culprit was, but instead of coming to see me himself Monsieur Volterra had dictated a memo to his secretary. Why? Because Monsieur Volterra was a busy man and the memo was expedient. It meant he could reprimand me and warn the other performers at the same time. If I had been the star that I thought I was, Monsieur Volterra would have come to my dressing room and explained the situation. 'I don't want you to worry about this, Mademoiselle Fleurier,' he would have said, putting a fatherly arm around me and acting as if the incident were a joke between us. 'I know it's petty, but Monsieur Noir is the leading star and we have to accommodate his idiosyncrasies. You understand, don't you?'

And what did the wording 'minor acts' mean? Despite all the money that had been spent on me, and the favourable reviews, was that all I was in the end?

When the rehearsal was over, I consoled myself by inviting Odette to join me on a shopping trip. I wanted to furnish my new hotel room. One of the first things I had done after *Le Figaro* praised me was to move from the Latin Quarter to a hotel in the Étoile area where I had two rooms and my own bathroom. The hotel itself wasn't much fancier, but the area was more suitable for a rising star. The streets of the eighth *arrondissement* were lined with prestigious hotels, grand limestone buildings and cafés that served champagne in crystal glasses. Camille was on the Right Bank too, in an apartment in the luxurious Hôtel de Crillon, paid for by her new lover, the playboy Yves de Dominici.

When Monsieur Etienne heard about my change of address, he didn't openly chide me about not saving money. He commented that I was following in the footsteps of Picasso, who had moved to the area with his Russian wife, Olga Khoklova.

'What are you suggesting?' I asked.

He smiled wryly. 'Well, he started off in Montmartre, moved to Montparnasse and now lives in the Étoile Quarter. It seems to suit his wife's social-climbing aspirations.'

'No, Monsieur Etienne, you are mistaken,' I answered, flashing him a cheeky smile. 'I have never lived in Montmartre.'

He handed me a letter of introduction to his banker. 'Monsieur Lemke will be happy to help you invest some of your money, should you ever decide to do so.'

I didn't tell Monsieur Etienne that I had met Picasso. When the gnarly Spaniard appeared at my dressing room door, his wife hovering nervously in the background, I was too ignorant to grasp how important a person he was. His intense eyes and the sloppy way he spoke French reminded me of Rivarola, though of course Rivarola spoke no French at all. The artist was wearing a dinner suit with a red cummerbund, but he seemed as out of place in it as my mother was in the silver fox stole. He said that he would like to paint me and gave me his card. I thanked him but forgot about him as soon as I closed the door. Monsieur Etienne would have been delighted to hear that an artist who never painted portraits wanted to do mine. *Think of the publicity!* he would say. All I knew was that on the same day *Le Figaro* had reviewed me, they had also announced that Picasso had discovered Surrealism, and I couldn't see the appeal of appearing on a gallery wall with a distorted nose and my insides in my lap.

After buying some silk sheets at the Galeries Lafayette, Odette and I went to the furniture store on the Boulevard Haussmann where

Joseph had just been made manager. Joseph wasn't as handsome as I had expected but there was something appealing about him. His boyish face lit up when Odette and I entered the store, and he greeted me with a warm handshake and three kisses. The look that passed between him and Odette was full of love and it made me smile.

'I am pleased to meet you at last, Mademoiselle Fleurier,' he said, pushing his steel-rimmed glasses further up on his nose and guiding us past bronze sculptures and Empire mahogany games tables. 'Odette speaks so highly of you that I am going to see you perform at the Casino on my first day off.'

Joseph took us to a back room and pulled aside a packing crate. 'I have been keeping these for you,' he said, pointing to two Louis XV chairs upholstered in leopard skin. 'As soon as I showed these to Odette, she said they would be perfect for you.'

I ran my hand over the sleek fur. The chairs were the most beautiful objects I had ever seen. I glanced at the price tag. They were outrageously expensive, even with Joseph's best discount, but I had to have them. After we had agreed on the price, Joseph dragged out an oriental screen.

'It will cover the battleship grey walls of your room,' said Odette, stepping closer to examine the gold leaf and abalone shell etchings.

'I'll take it,' I said, my head light with the excitement of spending so much money on luxuries.

After the purchase, which the three of us toasted with a glass of champagne, Odette and I returned to my hotel room. Odette directed the delivery men where to place the chairs and screen — a decision that was changed several times before she was satisfied that they had been positioned exactly where they should be in the room.

'You would be in a lot of trouble with your uncle if he saw you doing this,' I told her. 'He thinks I shouldn't be spending so much money.'

Odette shook her head. 'If you want to be a star you have to live like one.'

'I don't know if your advice is any wiser than your uncle's, but it is more appealing,' I said.

'I am coming to the show tonight,' Odette said. 'I haven't seen it since all your songs were included.'

I was glad for her friendship. While the performers at the Casino de Paris were extroverted on the stage, they were bitches and tyrants off it. It seemed that once you were past the third-rate stage, there was no comradeship in show business; only rivalry.

FIFTEEN

The show at the Casino de Paris was so popular that it was scheduled to continue until May the following year. Despite the success, it was a lonely life for me. Aside from Odette, the effusive applause of the audience was the only companionship I knew. When I looked out past the floodlights and saw the rows of enchanted faces night after night it was like meeting with friends — an illusion I could maintain as long as the spectators remained anonymous to me. I would return to my dressing room to find it flooded with flowers and bottles of Amour-Amour. There were always cards attached, expressing the sender's esteem and requesting a rendezvous. I was mindful to be charming and polite with my admirers but I knew those men — and some women too — were not really interested in giving me anything. Rather, they were hoping to take something away.

'Men are *ruthless*,' Camille told me one evening when she invited me to supper in her apartment. 'That's why, if you are smart, you will take what you can while you have the opportunity. Only fools feel sorry for them. As if they are acting with any morals! When a man makes a decision to get rid of a woman, you can be sure he won't take pity on her.'

I cut a slice of Neufchâtel and spread the velvety cheese on a piece of bread. I had been flattered at first by Camille's invitation — after all, she was a real star — but as the evening wore on I began to feel like a nameless audience to her philosophies on life and men. I could have been anybody. And yet I listened with rapt attention because I wanted her to like me. Or if not like me, at least approve of me. I was too inexperienced to agree or disagree with Camille on the subject. My knowledge of men — other than my father, Uncle Gerome and Bernard — was negligible. And out of the three of them, only Uncle Gerome could have been described as ruthless.

'Their decisions aren't made in the heart, no matter how in love they appear to be,' continued Camille, breaking a piece of bread and taking some cheese for herself. 'They are not even made in *le pantalon*, as the chorus girls say. When they get an idea, it is made impassively in the head, with themselves as the sole beneficiary.'

Camille called in her maid and asked for another bottle of wine to be brought to us. I studied the room. The Aubusson tapestry and the *bronze d'oré* chandelier belonged to the hotel but the giltwood *chaise longue* and the chairs with arms carved in the shape of lion heads were Camille's. She certainly was amassing a few things for herself from Yves de Dominici. There was even a rumour that he was intending to buy her a house at Garches on the Seine outside of Paris, where many of the French set had villas.

After the maid had poured the wine, Camille turned her attention back to cutting the cheese. I studied the delicate pallor of her hands and, when she looked up, stole a glance at her sapphire eyes. Did she really think that all men were ruthless? I wondered about Camille's daughter, but when I had enquired about her earlier in the evening, Camille had told me not to mention the child as the maid was a busybody and she didn't want people to know about her. Was it being left to take responsibility for a child on her own that had made Camille so jaded?

I didn't avoid my admirers because I was sure they were ruthless, but rather because I couldn't see how anything they could offer me could be more exciting than the music hall. I didn't find the real world as beautiful as a set designed by Gordon Conway or Georges Barbier. And even if my admirers bought me dresses worth thousands of francs, where else but the stage could I wear angel wings and a towering headdress studded with pearls? At each rehearsal I strove to perfect some aspect of my dancing or voice, and was thrilled when with each show my performance improved. Such things were much more enticing to me than being wined and dined in restaurants with too much cutlery and then carted from party to party like some kind of showpiece. Besides, I was making my own money and buying my own luxuries. Although it would have been nice to live in the Hôtel de Crillon, I wasn't prepared to do so at the cost of my liberty.

There was one exception to my lack of interest in the opposite sex: André Blanchard. Although I hadn't seen him since that night at Le Boeuf sur le Toit, it didn't stop me thinking about him. Sometimes when there was a break at rehearsal or I arrived back at my hotel too pent up to sleep, I would imagine conversations between us. We would talk about the music hall, about the things we liked best about Paris, about what foods we liked to eat. It was a strange thing to do, seeing as he and I had never exchanged more than a few words. But I was too inexperienced to understand the feelings he stirred in me or the chemistry of attraction. I tried not to think about Mademoiselle Canier, who I saw as an obstacle to my fantasies. I remembered the *curé* at home giving a sermon in which he insisted that 'to think about doing something is as bad as actually doing it'. I didn't see how that could be true. I couldn't control all the thoughts floating through my head at any one time, but I could control my actions. But something my mother often said proved true: whatever you think about most will eventually manifest itself.

One evening during the interval I opened my dressing room door, with the intention of calling Blandine, my dresser, and found that André Blanchard had manifested himself in the hall.

'Good evening,' he said, holding out a bouquet of roses.

I stood in the doorway with my mouth open.

He gazed past me and gave a slight cough. I woke from my dream and invited him into my dressing room, the first man ever to cross the threshold while I occupied it. I wasn't used to receiving guests and I kicked a pair of panties under the skirt of my table and cleared some stockings off a chair for him. The chair creaked and wobbled when he sat on it. I didn't have a vase for the flowers so I put them in the water jug.

'It is the Casino de Paris for you now, Mademoiselle Fleurier,' said André, perching as far forward as possible on the chair so that it might stop its embarrassing *eek* and *prrrf* sounds. His eyes fell to my jewelled brassiere with the tissue paper stuffed in the cups, which was hanging on the arm of the chair. He glanced away, searching for somewhere he could look other than at my face. 'Your new act becomes you.'

I sat down opposite him, unnerved by his sudden appearance. I hadn't seen him for weeks. My dressing area was tiny and our knees bumped. I was surprised to feel that his were trembling. Mine began to shake too, in sympathy. There was a case of cigarettes in my drawer and I took it out and offered him one. André shook his head. 'I only smoke one a day,' he said. 'And don't crave another until the following day.'

I opened a packet of spiced pecan nuts instead, the only food I had in the room, and poured them into a bowl. The nuts had been given to me by an admirer, along with some chocolates, but I had never opened them. Nuts are anathema to a singer's vocal cords.

I wondered how old André was. There were no wrinkles on his golden skin and he didn't look more than twenty. For someone with such a high social position, he didn't seem very conscious of it. But he spoke with maturity and carefully measured words, which made me think he was older than he looked. I put his age at twenty-five.

My thoughts were interrupted by a crunching sound. André had taken a handful of nuts and was tossing them into his mouth one at a time, the way a dog might snap at a treat thrown to him by his master. It wasn't a refined mannerism. It wasn't the way Antoine or François would have eaten nuts. André must have forgotten himself and it was all I could do not to laugh. I was dazzled by his wealth and presence, but his temporary lapse put us on a more even footing.

'Who is your manager?' he asked.

'Michel Etienne.'

André nodded. 'Ah, good. Conservative but experienced and thorough.'

'Do you know much about the music hall?'

'I am interested in business – and it is show *business*,' he said, smiling. 'I would pay a million francs to be able to sing like you, but that's not likely to happen. I would have liked to have been an actor but my parents thought that was ridiculous. So it is factories and imports and exports for me, like my father.'

'Don't you like enterprise?' I asked him.

He threw back his head and laughed that wonderful laugh, then looked at me with sparkling eyes. 'I love it, Mademoiselle Fleurier.

Taking something and making it a success thrills me. But I suppose that with the figure of my father looming over me, I feel I have a terrifying potential to fulfil.'

I had a sense that the previous times I had seen him, André had been hiding behind a public façade. Now he seemed to be letting that guard down a little.

'Do you have brothers and sisters?' I asked. Being an only child, I had a fascination with the idea of siblings.

André's face darkened. 'My older brother was killed in the war so I am the only male heir.'

'I'm sorry,' I said.

'Don't be,' André answered. 'My family is not the only one to have suffered a loss from the war. I have a sister who is married and behaves more like an aunt towards me. I also have a younger sister, Veronique. She is the rebel of the family and acts like a boy. She prefers frogs to dolls.'

'Each to his — or her — own,' I said, smiling.

'Unfortunately, rebels are not welcome in the family,' André said, taking another handful of nuts. 'Veronique will be bundled off to a finishing school if she doesn't change her ways.'

There was an edge to his voice when he spoke about his family. He had seemed happier when we talked about business so I asked him about the Blanchard enterprises.

'My grandfather started out selling ribbons and eventually became the owner of the biggest textile mill in Lyon,' he told me. 'But diversification was his dictum and his sons were expected to develop their own business interests, which they did: in newspapers, gas, railways and imports.'

André paused and gave me a disarming smile. I felt so taken into his confidence that the intimacy made me lose my nerve. I blurted out, 'And how is Mademoiselle Canier?'

'Mademoiselle Canier is well, thank you,' André answered, turning red around the ears. 'She is on the Riviera at the moment, with her mother. I shall be joining them next week.'

I could have kicked myself. There had been such a friendly ease between us; why had I sabotaged it by mentioning 'the Siamese'?

André was about to say something else when Blandine burst in the door. Not used to seeing me with visitors, her eyes opened wide. '*Pardon*,' she said and retreated.

André rose. The chair creaked and *prrrf*-ed again. 'Not at all,' he said. 'Mademoiselle Fleurier must be needed on stage again soon, and I should go.'

He turned to me. 'I have to travel with my father on business to Venice and Rome. I wonder if I may call on you again, when I return?'

I nodded, wondering what *this* visit had been about if Mademoiselle Canier was still in the picture.

After André had left, Blandine turned to me. 'Was that André Blanchard?' she asked. 'What's he doing visiting you?'

'I have no idea,' I told her.

<hr />

One evening, in the middle of March, the stage manager knocked on my door. 'Mademoiselle Fleurier, please go to the wardrobe mistress before your next slot,' he said. 'Your headdress was coming loose in the last act and they want to refit it before you go back on stage.'

'Of course,' I called out to him. 'I didn't notice. I'll go straightaway.'

I listened to his footsteps fade down the hall. There was another forty minutes before I had to appear on stage again, but I knew better than to keep the wardrobe mistress waiting. She wasn't a motherly figure like Madame Tarasova; she was a despot who wasn't afraid to slap a fine on someone for having a dog hair on their tights or for losing a sequin. Besides, I didn't want the wardrobe assistants, who were always frantic during and just after the interval, to be put under more strain because of me.

On my way to the wardrobe mistress's room, I came across the stagehands struggling to fix a set whose hinges had come loose. It was for the knife-thrower's act, which was scheduled straight after Jacques Noir, so they didn't have much time. Although they were blocking my way, I could tell from their red faces and the carpenter's exasperated curses that it would be wiser not to disturb them. I decided to go around through the wings. The chorus girls had just gone on stage for their chessboard number and as long as I was careful to count the number of wing segments as I went through, I thought I would be able to avoid appearing before the audience in my dressing gown.

It was forbidden to be in the wing area during a performance without the stage manager's permission, so I tried to crawl behind each curtain as discreetly as possible. I was making good progress towards the exit door when I slipped through what I thought was the last curtain and found myself face to face with Jacques Noir. I froze. The rook prop entrance had been discarded because Noir claimed that it made him claustrophobic, but I had been sure that he made his entrance from stage right, where his wife usually sat, and we were standing in the left wing. I squinted in the dark and realised that Noir had not seen me. He was bent over a bucket, gagging. It was only then that I noticed the acrid smell of vomit.

'Oh God!' he moaned, his shoulders trembling as if he had a fever.

I glanced to the opposite wing. Madame Noir wasn't there but her knitting needles and a ball of wool were perched on her empty chair. Perhaps she is on her way here, I thought, almost praying she was, because it was clear that something was very wrong with Noir. My mind flew back to Zephora at Le Chat Espiègle. At least I could be sure that Noir wasn't having a baby.

He let out another moan and clutched his chest. As much as I loathed the man, I knew I had to do something quickly. Someone had once told me that vomiting could be a sign of a heart attack. Or perhaps he was having a stroke, like Uncle Gerome.

'Monsieur Noir,' I whispered, stepping forward and putting my hand on his shoulder. 'Can I help you? Do you want me to get your wife?'

Noir bolted upright and fumbled for his handkerchief, patting his face and wiping the cloth across his mouth. When he recognised me, a shudder passed through his body. 'You stupid girl!' he snarled. He charged at me and punched me so hard in the chest that I fell to the floor.

I looked up at him, my eyes smarting from the pain. He has lost his mind, I thought. Noir glowered and I was sure he was about to attack me again when the orchestra started up the music for his act. Then I questioned if it was I who had gone mad because Noir transformed in an instant. He threw away his handkerchief, straightened his suit, donned his top hat and leapt out onto the stage exactly as he had done the last time I saw him perform.

'Ladies, ladies. Please! What will your menfolk think?'

I stared at the stage, unable to believe my eyes. I glanced at the opposite wing. Noir's wife was back in her seat, knitting.

I picked myself off the floor and staggered to the wardrobe mistress's room. Fortunately, she had been called away for another emergency and Agnès, her senior assistant, had taken it upon herself to start working on my headdress without me.

'Good!' she said, standing on tiptoe to slip the headdress on and fasten it behind my ears and at the nape of my neck. 'It fits properly now. Hurry! We must go to your dressing room and get you ready.' She peered at my face. 'Your mascara is running.'

I touched my cheek and examined my fingertip. It was chalky black. I wondered what I looked like. I couldn't believe what had taken place with Noir. If it wasn't for the throb in my chest where he had hit me, I might have thought it was a dream.

'Quick!' said Agnès, pushing me out the door. 'There are only seven minutes before you go back on stage.'

Agnès's warning spurred me into action. I couldn't explain what had happened with Noir, but there was no time to think about it now. I had an audience to entertain.

✎

What had happened became clear the next day, however, when I arrived for my rehearsal and found Monsieur Etienne waiting outside the stage door.

'They want to fire you,' he said. 'You are accused of trying to sabotage Jacques Noir's act.'

I dropped my purse. It clattered down the steps and my compact and lipstick tumbled out. Monseiur Etienne's announcement had stunned me so much that I couldn't speak.

'You have a contract and I am going to argue the decision with that,' said Monsieur Etienne. 'But you had better tell me what happened last night before we go to face Monsieur Volterra.'

Monsieur Etienne was an impeccable dresser but that morning the knot in his tie was crooked and his hair was dishevelled. It occurred to me that I had never seen him look so agitated. The blood rushed to my head. Fire me? Lose my beloved act at the Casino de Paris after less than three months?

'It is a lie, Monsieur Etienne.' I sank down on the stairs and tried scooping up my lipstick but my hand was trembling so much I ended up knocking it further down the steps.

'Oh, I am sure of that!' said Monsieur Etienne.

The tone of his voice calmed me a little. If Monsieur Etienne didn't doubt that I was innocent, perhaps once I'd had a chance to explain what had happened, Monsieur Volterra wouldn't either. I told Monsieur Etienne why I had been in the wings and about Noir.

Monsieur Etienne clenched his fists. 'I knew it would be something like that,' he hissed. 'This is not the first time Noir has pulled a dirty stunt. He gets rid of any talent that he perceives as a threat.'

'But we don't do the same act,' I said.

'You got a better review than him from the same reporter,' said Monsieur Etienne. He reached into his pocket and passed me his handkerchief. I wasn't crying, but the fear of being fired was stinging my eyes. If Jacques Noir sullied my reputation at the Casino de Paris, I would have difficulty getting work anywhere else.

'Was he pretending to be sick?' I asked. 'Was that a trick?'

Monsieur Etienne shook his head. 'That part is real. It is his nerves. That is why they had to get rid of the rook prop. Only a few people know about it, and Volterra turns a blind eye because he figures it helps Noir's routine. It is unfortunate that you stumbled across him like that. He is trying to use it as ammunition against you before you can use it against him. If you go to the gossip columnists with the story, he will say it is sour grapes because you got fired.'

Monsieur Etienne decided it would be best if he explained the situation to Monsieur Volterra himself, in case the discussion became heated. My nerves were on edge and it was taking all my reserves even to talk coherently. I returned to my hotel by taxi and, as soon as I opened the door to my room, collapsed into the nearest chair. Kira, my kitten, was sleeping on the windowsill. She lifted her head and blinked. She must have sensed something was wrong, because she stretched back on her hind legs and leapt from the windowsill into my lap, sacrificing her sunny position in order to comfort me. I glanced at the hands of the clock on my bureau. It was already three. How much time would Monsieur Etienne need? I closed my eyes, dreading the thought that I might not be performing that night — or any night — at the Casino de Paris. It had become my life.

'*Murr*,' meowed Kira, rubbing her chin against my hand. I massaged her back, my fingers sinking into her lavender fur. I had bought my little friend from an old woman I met one morning when I was walking around Parc de Monceau.

'A companion is what you need,' a voice had called out. I turned to see an old woman smiling at me and pointing to a cage draped with a blanket that she had propped on the bench next to her. Unable to resist my curiosity, I approached the woman and she lifted a corner of the blanket. Four kittens stared back at me. I stuck my finger through the wicker bars to play with them.

'A cat is the best cure for loneliness,' the woman said.

She had looked at me with her faded blue eyes as if she were trying to see into me and discover what kind of person I was. I wondered if my loneliness was that obvious or whether that was her line to draw people in. She was dressed in an olive-coloured coat with black trimming and her grey hair was tucked under a velvet hat. I guessed that she was about seventy, but her hands trembled with the frailty of a much older woman. All in all, she didn't seem like someone who was on the make, and if she was, she had chosen the wrong place. The only people she was likely to meet in Parc de Monceau at that time of day were the wealthy, who were not taken in by sob stories, or the nannies of children of the wealthy who were instructed not to talk to anybody. Then again, she had also met me and I didn't fall into either of those categories.

'I'll take all of them then,' I laughed.

'Only one per person,' the woman answered. 'They each require special attention. And I have to see where you live before I make my decision.'

Showing a stranger where I lived didn't sound like a sensible idea, although the woman seemed harmless enough.

'What kind of kittens are they?' I asked.

'Russian Blues. Their father is a descendent of Vashka, the favourite cat of Tsar Nicholas I.'

She had made the last statement so matter-of-factly that I couldn't tell if she was tricking me or not.

I played with the wriggling balls of fur. They reminded me how much I missed the company of my pets on the farm. I had a warm room now and could afford to feed another mouth. Maybe a kitten would be a good salve for my loneliness. All of them were sturdy-looking and healthy but there was one who did not take her eyes from me.

The woman let out a laugh that ended in a cough. She reached into her coat for a handkerchief. When she shook it out the scent of lily of the valley trailed in the air. Holding the lace to her mouth, she cleared her throat, and when she had recovered, she said, 'That's Kira and she has chosen you. She is a perceptive little one. She knows you will be good to her.'

I was lost to Kira's sweet face. 'I'll take her,' I said.

'She is five hundred francs,' the woman said.

I opened my eyes in surprise. It was twice my fee for a performance. Did people really pay as much as that for a cat? Maybe the woman thought that because I was in Parc de Monceau and well-dressed that I was richer than I was. Still, I reasoned, because I had my heart set on the kitten now, I had paid much more than that for the leopard-skin chairs. And Kira was a living thing.

I nodded. 'Do you want to see where I live now?'

The woman patted my hand. 'No, I shall come tomorrow at this time. Here,' she said, opening a notebook and handing it to me. 'Write down your address.'

I did as she told me. 'I am Madame Ducroix, by the way,' the woman said, holding out her hand.

'I am Simone Fleurier,' I replied, reaching out to take it.

'Oh, I know who you are,' the woman said and winked.

Madame Ducroix had arrived the next morning with Kira sitting in a cane basket with a red bow around her neck. 'Very nice,' Madame Ducroix had said, looking around my room.

Straight after leaving the park the previous day, I had gone shopping and bought rugs, a floral tea set and a crystal platter on which I had just placed a fig tart from the patisserie near the park, supposedly the best in Paris. I had no idea why I was going to so much trouble to impress Madame Ducroix. After all, I was going to pay five hundred francs for her kitten. And yet, when I thought of Kira's wise eyes peering out from her fluffball of a face, I was convinced that I was taking on responsibility for something more than a cat and that somehow I had to earn her.

'The suite is warm and sunny. And the doors are secure, so Kira won't get out on the balcony,' I told Madame Ducroix, bemused at the tone of desperation in my voice. I was acting like a hopeful bride-to-be trying to win the approval of her future mother-in-law.

'I am sure you will take good care of her,' said Madame Ducroix, lowering herself into the seat I offered her. 'I sense these things and Kira does as well. Cats are psychic, you know.'

Madame Ducroix's face became downcast and I wanted to ask her what she meant. But then she brightened again and began serving the tea and cake, although she was my guest. Despite my doubts of the previous day, I concluded that Madame Ducroix's intentions were honourable. She asked me about stage life but gave only brief answers to questions about herself. The most I could glean from her was that she was a widow, she lived near the park and one of her grandparents had been Russian. After about an hour, she stood up and patted Kira then bent over to kiss the top of her head. '*Ya zhelayu schast'ya tebe, moy malen'kiy kotyonok,*' she whispered in Kira's ear. I was about to joke with her that I hoped Kira spoke French as well as Russian, but stopped myself when I saw the tears in her eyes.

'This is for you,' I said, handing her the five hundred francs we had agreed upon.

Madame Ducroix pushed the money back towards me. 'No,' she said, shaking her head. 'That was a test. I need to know if the people who take my kittens really want them or not. Anyone who is prepared to pay five hundred francs for a cat understands their true value.'

I walked Madame Ducroix to the front of the hotel and hailed a taxi for her. 'I would like very much for you to come again and see Kira. Or perhaps I could visit you?' I said.

Madame Ducroix's face lit up. 'Visit? I would love you to. Please, here is my address,' she said, handing me her card.

The driver helped her into the taxi and Madame Ducroix waved before the car set off. She looked as happy as a child leaving for the summer holidays.

A few weeks later, when I hadn't heard from Madame Ducroix, I decided to pay her a visit. Her apartment was on Rue Rembrandt. There was no concierge in attendance so I went up the stairs myself. I rang the buzzer to Madame Ducroix's apartment, but no one answered. I expected that she would have a maid, so I waited a few moments before trying again. I was about to leave when the door across the landing opened and a well-dressed woman in a cream suit looked out.

'Can I help you?' she asked.

'I am looking for Madame Ducroix,' I told her. 'But she doesn't seem to be home.'

A startled expression passed across the woman's face and she said, 'But, Mademoiselle, Madame Ducroix died last week. The apartment is up for rent.'

I gripped the banister. I hadn't been expecting anything like that. Madame Ducroix had appeared frail, but she had been so lively the last time we had met.

The woman stepped forward, leaving the door to her apartment open. 'I am sorry, Mademoiselle. I have given you a shock. Won't you come inside for a moment? Are you a relative?'

I shook my head. 'No,' I said. 'She gave me one of her kittens a few weeks ago and I came to tell her how well she is doing.'

The woman nodded. I was about to head back down the stairs when, as an afterthought, I turned around and asked, 'Do you know if Madame Ducroix found homes for all her cats?'

A smile broke across the woman's face and she pointed to her feet. Poised on either side of her were two adult cats, one larger than the other. From their regal bearing and vivid eyes, I knew they must be Kira's parents. 'Oh, you can be assured of that,' she said. 'Madame Ducroix wasn't prepared to go until she had found homes for them all.'

I was remembering these things when Monsieur Etienne knocked at my door. It gave me such a start that I jumped up and sent Kira flying onto the rug, but she was quick to forgive and chased me to the door. Before I opened it, I squeezed my eyes shut and made a wish that I would continue to sing at the Casino de Paris. I opened the door full of hope. But I only had to look at the drawn expression on Monsieur Etienne's face to know that he wasn't bringing me good news.

Sixteen

Paris was at its most beautiful in the spring, but even in the Jardin du Luxembourg, with its chestnut trees bursting into clusters of white blossoms and the flowerbeds teeming with irises, anemones and tulips, the glory of the season was lost on me. I was out of work and out of luck.

I sat on a bench under the branches of an early blooming lilac, barely noticing the syrupy perfume that enveloped me from its panicles of purple flowers. What had happened with Jacques Noir at the Casino de Paris was a disaster. Although Monsieur Volterra had insisted that he believed my story, he had also insisted on firing me, because if he didn't, Noir had threatened to leave the show. Monsieur Volterra had paid out my contract but only after deducting the expense of my costume and Vincent Scotto's fee. I'd had to return to my hotel in the Latin Quarter, to a smaller room than the one I had rented before. I sold one of the leopard-skin chairs, the oriental screen and some of my clothes. The chair I kept was an apology to Kira for dragging her with me into lowered circumstances. But if she minded that we now shared a narrow bed in a shabby room, she never showed it. As long as she received a saucer of milk and could nestle into the crook of my arm, she was happy.

The blow of losing my spot at the Casino de Paris would have been softened if Monsieur Etienne had been able to find me a part somewhere else. But even though Monsieur Volterra never publicly announced that I had tried to sabotage Noir's act, the comedian spread the story everywhere he could. The Folies Bergère was already in rehearsal for 'La Folie Du Jour', in which they were going to launch Joséphine Baker, the American singer. After spending a fortune on over a thousand different costumes and music by Spencer Williams, they weren't willing to do anything that might upset their temperamental star. The response from the director of the Moulin Rouge was the same. They had just paid over half a million francs to the Dolly Sisters over a dispute with Mistinguett, and were not going to put the diva's nose out of joint again by hiring competing acts. Only the Adriana expressed any interest, but their singing and dancing roles were filled for the next two seasons.

A child in a red coat skidded on the gravel in front of me, sending the pigeons scattering in fright. The girl crouched on her knees, her eyes wide with astonishment. She burst into tears the moment her nursemaid swept her into her arms. 'Didn't I tell you not to go running so far ahead of me?' the nursemaid chided her, brushing the dust off the girl's coat.

I watched the woman and child angle off the path and disappear amongst the trees. The day was sunny and the park was full of people strolling through the formal gardens and terraces. Everyone seemed lively, happy that winter had melted away into a vibrant spring. The laughter of children came from the direction of the pond. And above that noise rose the sound of somebody singing.

I gazed at my feet. If I couldn't succeed at the Casino de Paris, where could I succeed? Was it all over? Was it time to admit defeat and go home?

The singer moved closer, his voice grew louder. The tone was rich but he sang off key.

> The more you get
> The more you want
> You want and want
> and then it's all gone.

I sat up straight and looked around.

'What's wrong?' a man's voice asked. 'You look dejected.'

I peered through the lilac. The speaker had positioned himself so that his face was hidden by the leaves. I could see only that he was tall and wore a camel coat and well-polished shoes. One of his hands rested on the bough of the tree, smooth and brown like an Indian's, but I knew the speaker couldn't be from the subcontinent because the hand was too large. Besides, the voice was familiar.

André Blanchard.

The hand reached up and brushed aside the leaves. Those eyes that always sent the blood rushing through my veins looked back at me. For a moment I forgot my woes and I didn't have to force myself to smile.

'I've heard the gossip,' he said, manoeuvring himself around the tree. 'Imagine trying to sabotage Jacques Noir's act.' When he gave that resonant laugh I could almost forgive him for making fun of my predicament.

'I think I have lost my chance,' I said. I would never have admitted defeat to anyone else, but there was something about André that made him impossible to lie to.

His face grew serious, as if he had read my thoughts. He stared at the space on the bench beside me. 'May I?'

I nodded and he sat down. 'Jacques Noir doesn't need someone to sabotage him,' he said. 'He is bad enough as it is. It is just that he has made good connections. That line, "The most adored comedian in Paris" — he made it up himself. He is good at publicity.'

'Good for him, bad for me,' I said.

André rubbed his chin. 'It is not always easy to explain why one thing takes off in Paris and another doesn't,' he said. 'Singers are sought after for more than their vocal ability. Take Camille Casal — we can understand her stardom because she is a beauty. But Fréhel? Now, who can explain that?'

'I don't know who Fréhel is.'

'No?' he laughed. 'Well, we shall have to go and see her some time. She is middle-aged and ravaged and sings in a hoarse voice about prostitutes and doomed lovers. And Paris loves her.'

The tips of my ears felt as though they were alight. Had he really said, 'We will have to go and see her some time'?

'I was surprised when I saw Mistinguett perform,' I said. 'Her voice is flat, she wobbles when she dances and she is not particularly beautiful.'

'No,' he agreed. 'But everyone thinks of her when they think of France. She is as essential to Paris as coffee and *croissants*.'

I bent to pick a blade of grass and twirled the sprig between my fingers. André leaned over and mirrored my action. 'And there you are,' he said. 'You can sing, you can dance and you're pretty too. And you're out of a job.'

He fixed his gaze on my face and smiled. The burn in my ears and cheeks spread over my entire body.

'If you are free this evening, Mademoiselle Fleurier, I would like to take you to dinner,' he said.

❦

Maxim's had changed from the grand days of the Belle Époque, when the kings of England, Spain and Belgium entertained courtesans such as La Belle Otéro and Cléo de Merode in style there. Nevertheless, in 1925 the restaurant still retained its Art Nouveau opulence with curving lines of mahogany pillars, plush banquettes and statuettes of windblown damsels. As the *maître d'hôtel* led us to our table I gazed up at the glass ceiling decorated with flowers, fruit and lemon tree leaves. The *maître d'hôtel* pulled out a chair for me and slipped the handwritten menu into my fingers. I glanced around the dark salon, lit by miniature lamps on each table, and at the elegantly coiffured women whose diamond earrings and necklaces sparkled. The patrons were no longer aristocrats but they still glittered: Well-to-do artists, writers, entertainers, journalists and politicians. Maxim's might be more respectable now but it was still not the kind of place a man brought his wife. I understood why André had chosen it: there was a kind of complicit discretion among the patrons. It was one of the few places in Paris where we wouldn't be stared at.

'They have the best beefsteak in Paris,' André announced, glancing at the menu which included *caviar osciètre* and a cassoulet made with frogs' legs.

I still hadn't recovered from the shock of being asked to dine with him and tried to cover my self-consciousness with chatter. 'I haven't seen you around Paris for a while,' I said. 'Have you been travelling?'

'I was in Rome, Venice and Berlin,' he answered. He shifted in his chair, turning to look for the waiter. I couldn't tell if it was because I was boring him already or whether he just found it hard to stay seated.

'What were you doing there?' I asked.

'It is my training,' he said, taking a sip of champagne. 'My father has acquired hotels in those cities and was showing me how they are run.'

The fluid in our champagne and water glasses was vibrating. I looked down and saw it was because André was bouncing his leg against the table. Bernard used to do that around Uncle Gerome whenever the older man made him nervous. André hadn't come across as fidgety before; was something worrying him?

The waiter set down our *entrées*. I stared at the blinis on my plate and wondered how to eat them. I watched André pick up a spear of asparagus with his fingers and dip it in the bowl of sauce. I shrugged; I might as well be adventurous and guess. I rolled the blini closed with my fork and ate it in one bite. The nutty flavour of the caviar exploded in my mouth. Whether that was the correct way to eat blinis or not, André didn't seem perturbed.

'Are you and your father very similar?' I asked him.

My intuition could have answered that for me. Ever since I had met André, I had read everything in the paper I could find about the Blanchard family. In his business dealings Monsieur Blanchard came across as a formidable character, confident to crush strikers protesting against low wages and to use foreign immigrants as labour in the face of public opinion. André, from what I had seen of him, was ambitious but also warm and fair-minded.

He shook his head. 'We are different people. I thrive on change while my father has a horror of it. He lives his life by clockwork, disappearing into his office at the same time each day, eating his meals precisely on the hour and going to bed at exactly twelve minutes past midnight. When they were first married, my mother made the mistake of rearranging his office. I don't think he has ever forgiven her for that.'

I was unsure whether to laugh or sympathise. André was smiling, but something in his eyes told me that his father's exacting behaviour was not as humorous as he made out.

'My father has a theory that money is made in the first and second generations and lost in the third and fourth,' he continued. 'He is determined that I won't follow that trend. He has said I can have all the fun I want and hone my entrepreneurial skills on any business I care to, until my thirtieth birthday. Then I must marry and take over the business.'

'You must feel under pressure,' I said, beginning to understand André's fascination with the music hall. Life was beautiful on stage and unpredictable off it. There was a sense of living on the edge. Doing exactly the same thing every day because that was what you had done for years didn't seem like living to me.

'I have more than a decade yet,' said André, the lightness returning to his voice. 'I am only nineteen. I like people much more than I like machines. I am going to show my father that what he considers my hobbies are things I can make financially successful. I am not going to lose the family fortune, but I am determined to live differently to him.'

'I have a feeling you will succeed,' I told him. My words were sincere but I was trying to hide my surprise at his age. So he was nineteen? He was only a couple of years older than me but seemed worldlier. Perhaps that was the way wealthy people were, because they had less insecurity in their lives.

Something behind me caught André's attention. 'Now there is a sight you should see,' he said.

I turned to find a black woman standing in the entrance of the grand salon. She had expressive eyes and a shiny helmet of hair. I knew instantly who she was; I had seen her poster everywhere. Joséphine Baker. She stood motionless until one by one the tables grew quiet and every eye turned to her. Then she flung the chinchilla coat she was wearing to the floor — sending the cloakroom girl scrambling for it — to reveal a scarlet gown with a neckline slashed to the waist.

While the *maître d'hôtel* showed Mademoiselle Baker and her hangers-on to their table, the music hall star batted her eyelids and wiggled her hips for the diners at every table she passed on the way. *'Bonsoir, mes chéries,'* she called out, sweeping her arms about her and blowing kisses. 'How wonderful you all look this evening.' Although it wasn't considered the done thing to interrupt people while they were eating, no one was affronted by her behaviour. Smiles lit up as she passed by. The whole mood of the salon had transformed. Instead of the subdued whispering of earlier in the evening, the conversations were animated and laughter burst from all the corners of the room.

'Did you see that?' André whispered, amusement twinkling in his eyes. 'She is not half as talented as you. But she knows how to play the part of the star.'

'Is star quality something people just have? Something they are born with?' I asked.

André shook his head. 'You wouldn't suggest that if you had seen her before. She has learnt from watching what others do and added her own touch.'

'And I haven't learnt it,' I said. 'That is what you are trying to tell me.'

André leaned forward. 'I am trying to tell you that if you cultivate it, you will be formidable. You should take what Jacques Noir did to you as a compliment. If he thought you were nobody, he wouldn't have bothered. You threatened him.'

I looked down at my plate. 'How will I cultivate it?'

André reached across the table and brushed a speck of caviar from my chin with his thumb. 'I could help you,' he said.

I clutched my serviette in my lap, rolling it into a tight ball. My skin burned where he had touched me. I had thought about André often enough to know that I liked him. He was every showgirl's dream — handsome, young, rich and willing to help my career. And yet I could feel my feet pressing into the floor as if I were slamming on brakes. I did not want to be one of a succession of girls on his arm. I imagined Camille taking me by the shoulders and shaking me: *What do you expect, Simone? Love?*

'Rivarola and I weren't lovers,' I said. I was taken aback by the tone of my own voice. The coldness in it made the meaning clear. I lifted my eyes to meet André's. If he was disappointed, he recovered quickly.

'I have entrepreneurial blood in me,' he said, pushing his plate aside. 'One thing an entrepreneur can't stand to see is wasted potential. And when I look at you, that's what I see: millions of francs' worth of stardom going to waste. A potential French icon floundering on the river bank like a dying fish.'

The image of a fish struggling to breathe startled me. I laughed and the atmosphere between us relaxed.

'Listen, you will be my apprenticeship in enterprise and I don't expect any more from you than that,' André said. 'This is my plan: I will take you out of Paris and together we will work on creating a new style for you. Then, when you have a unique angle to offer, we will come back here.'

His firm tone assured and disappointed me at the same time. Did I want a *purely* professional relationship? I should probably have asked more questions — after all, it was my life he was discussing — but I was intrigued by André Blanchard and flattered by his interest in my career. When he mentioned that Mademoiselle Canier would come too, I resigned myself to the fact that perhaps he truly was only looking for something adventurous in which to invest his entrepreneurial skills.

'Where do you propose we go?' I asked.

'Berlin,' he said, as if there were only one answer to the question.

I stared at him. Berlin? When I thought of Germany, I thought of Anke screeching her distorted songs and the country whose army had almost blown my father to pieces.

'We will go to all the cabarets and music shows. You will work hard and you will learn,' André said. His shining eyes appealed to my sense of adventure. Was that the bond between us? That we were two people who loved a challenge?

'I don't speak German,' I said.

'Not even *"Guten Abend meine Damen und Herren"*?' André asked.

'No.'

'Not even *"Wir haben heute sehr schönes Wetter"*?'

'No.'

'Not even *"Sie sind sehr hübsch und ich würde Sie gerne küssen"*?'

I shook my head.

André's face broke into a grin. 'Is there anything else that worries you about going to Berlin, Mademoiselle Fleurier?'

'No ... I mean, yes,' I said, taking a gulp of champagne. 'Can my cat come too?'

⌘

I explained to Monsieur Etienne that I was going to Berlin for a while to develop my talents, and wrote to my family with the same news. Then, a week later, André and I left Paris. We arrived at Potsdammer Station just after dusk. While André took a taxi ticket from the policeman at the exit, I slipped Kira into her wicker cage.

She blinked at the people rushing by and at the porter pushing our trolley of suitcases. She wasn't even perturbed when a man walked past us with an Alsatian straining on a lead; she merely yawned, rolled herself into a ball and fell asleep.

André showed the taxi driver the ticket and the porter packed our suitcases into the boot. I gazed out the taxi window, lost in a dream. Along the boulevard, garlands of electric bulbs adorned the doorways of theatres, restaurants and cabarets with names like Kabarett der Komiker and Die Weisse Maus. The terrace cafés were crowded with men and women sipping glasses of beer. So this is Berlin, I thought. Apart from the signs in Gothic German print, the city did not look so different to Paris. And yet, somehow, it was. I realised it would take further observation to be able to see exactly where those differences lay.

The taxi stopped outside a building with stone columns on either side of the doorway and a bronze plaque that read *Hotel Adlon*.

André paid the driver. 'This is where we are staying,' he said to me, slipping his wallet back into his jacket pocket.

We had two days alone before Mademoiselle Canier joined us. We had taken breakfast with her before departing Paris and the most I had been able to draw out of her was '*Oui*' or '*Non*'. For someone who had everything — including André — she appeared discontented with life. She had looked around the elegant restaurant with the intention of finding something displeasing, whether it be the consistency of the butter or the buttons on the waiter's shirt. Every so often I sneaked a glance at André, wondering if he was really attracted to her. To my vexation, André gazed at Mademoiselle Canier as if he could not believe what he was seeing, and constantly patted her hand or stroked her arm. She was beautiful, but how could a man of his vitality and intelligence spend his time with such a sourpuss? For her part, Mademoiselle Canier accepted his attentions with a wan smile. The real insult, however, was her nonchalant attitude towards me: although I was going to be alone in Berlin with her male companion, Mademoiselle Canier did not even perceive me as a threat.

A bellboy with hair so short that he could have been a young military officer took our bags from the taxi. I thought it strange that we should be staying at the Adlon when André had told me that his father owned the Ambassadeur and had shares in the Central.

'Why are we staying here if it is not one of your father's hotels?' I whispered, my heels sinking into the reception area's plush carpet.

'To compare,' he answered. 'The Adlon is considered the best hotel in Berlin. But I think with a few changes at the Ambassadeur we can outdo it.'

While André organised our rooms, I studied the marble foyer and gilt chandeliers. I turned to look at a bronze statue and caught the eye of a man standing by the elevator. He ran his fingers through the slashes of grey hair around his temples and smoothed his moustache. His expression was half-stern and half-amused.

After André had registered, the bellboy led us to the elevators where the man was waiting. His eyes narrowed on André. 'Good evening, Monsieur Blanchard,' he said, in French. 'It is always a pleasure to have a man of your high standards come to stay with us.'

'Good evening to you too, Herr Adlon,' replied André, a wry smile on his lips. 'May I introduce Mademoiselle Fleurier?'

'*Enchanté*,' said Herr Adlon, leaning forward to kiss my hand. 'I trust that you will enjoy Berlin and your stay at the Hotel Adlon.'

Once inside the elevator, André stared up at the ceiling, trying not to laugh. As soon as the doors opened and the bellboy walked ahead to show us the way to our rooms, André whispered to me, 'There was a time when Herr Adlon would have thrown the son of one of his competitors out of his hotel. But with the war and the German economy the way it is, he has to accept anyone who can pay.'

'Perhaps he takes it as a compliment,' I said. 'Most performers think that if another star turns up at their show.'

I had thought that the glamour of the stage had no equivalent in real life, but I changed my mind as soon as the bellboy opened the door to my room, switched on the lights and gestured for me and André to go on ahead of him. My eyes followed the line of the French pilasters up to the high ceiling then down again to the marble fireplace and the two onyx candelabras on either side of it. There was a bowl of plums and a vase of long-stemmed roses on the side table. The air in the room was a mixture of their heady scents combined with the smell of fresh linen. If Mademoiselle Chanel could have bottled the amalgamation she would have discovered a perfume more profitable than Chanel No 5. The bellboy opened a set of double doors to reveal a bed so sumptuously dressed in Rudolf

Herzog linen that I felt like sinking into it as soon as possible. I set down Kira's cage next to the sofa.

André stepped to the window and peeped through the curtains. 'You can see the Unter den Linden and the Brandenburg Gate from here.'

'The Unter den Linden is the most famous boulevard in Berlin,' the bellboy explained in precise French. 'It is named after the lime trees on its strip.'

He placed my suitcases near an armoire. Kira stretched her paw between the bars of her cage and tapped my shoe. I undid the latch and she sprang out and scampered across the carpet. She sniffed at the Constantinople rug and the gilt skirting boards, inhaled the scent of the table legs and twitched her whiskers around the sofa. Suddenly her tail and ears pricked up. For one terrifying moment I thought she was going to claw it but she bolted past me and through André's legs in a burst of kittenish energy. She did three whirlwind turns of the room before jumping onto the sofa and settling down there. I wagged my finger at her and she looked at me as if to say, 'This is much better. This is what I had been expecting all along.'

After the bellboy had showed me how the bathroom taps worked and where the light switches were, he wished me a pleasant stay and headed towards the door. André followed him. 'I'll let you settle in,' he said over his shoulder. 'Let's eat in the hotel restaurant and get an early night. We can start on Berlin tomorrow.'

The Adlon's dining room was a Venetian palace with a mural on the ceiling and bronze candelabras on the walls. André ran his palms along the arms of his chair. 'Did you know these are jarrah-mahogany? From Australia?'

Australia? I wasn't sure where that was. Somewhere near South America?

André's eyes scanned the room, taking in the details. 'Did you notice that there are no bells anywhere? They use flashing lights to summon the chambermaids so as not to disturb the other guests.'

I had never stayed in a hotel that used bells let alone flashing lights. When Madame Lombard wanted to summon me she would stand at the foot of the elevator and bellow, regardless of the other residents.

I glanced at my menu. I had been curious to try German food but the dishes were French or English: truffled capons; fish in caviar sauce; roast beef; woodcock. I peeked at André's sable eyes, which looked even more brilliant in the soft light. No, I told myself, if you want to be a star then you must be professional. You must focus. But why was it that when I was with André, my mind said one thing and my heart another?

'They have one of the most efficient kitchens in the business,' André said, nodding towards the kitchen doors. 'The chef's secretary is a genius. They serve the finest dishes but there are never any leftovers, never any waste. She and the larder steward run the storeroom with military precision.'

I stared at André, not sure of his point, but I didn't have to wait long for an explanation.

'A hotel makes as much from its banquets and restaurants as it does from its guests, so it is important to be efficient. Many a brilliant hotel has gone down because of losses in the kitchen.'

I turned back to my menu, wondering if the analysis of the hotel's features and its administration was going to be the theme of our entire conversation. André's enthusiasm reminded me how young we both were. Compared to the dignified guests sitting around us, we looked like two children who had escaped from their parents and were playing at being grown-ups for the day.

After we had ordered our food, the wine steward arrived and conferred with André about what to drink with our meal. When he left, André turned to me and said, 'Their wine cellar is worth millions. If one of the chefs orders wine for the ingredients of a meal, the steward puts salt in it, to make sure the kitchen staff don't drink it.'

I knew I had to humour André because he was doing so much to help me, but I was in a new city and I wanted to talk about Berlin, about the stage, about what we were going to do and see. I wasn't interested in the industrious operating procedures of the Hotel Adlon. But then André surprised me. He pointed to the glasses the steward was setting down before us. I was readying myself for another fact regarding the Adlon's wine cellar or the quality of the crystal, when he said, 'I have ordered the best vintage champagne, and claret that used to belong to the Kaiser's cellar. We are going to celebrate our first night in Berlin, our partnership and the beginning of your new career!'

I awoke the next morning as daylight was breaking across the sky. The maids had drawn the nightshades and curtains when they had turned down the bed the previous evening, but I had been unable to sleep and had opened them again to watch the car headlights streaming down the boulevard. I propped myself up on the pillows and stretched my arm behind my head, catching a whiff of almonds. I sniffed my wrist. The scent of the hotel's luxury soap still lingered on my skin.

Kira was crouched on the windowsill, her eyes darting to and fro. I wondered what she was looking at and untangled my legs from the sheets. 'You silly kitty,' I said, looking over the boulevard, which was empty apart from a few bread trucks and bicycles. 'There's nothing there.'

I ran my fingers through her fur and let out a yawn. The excitement of being in Berlin was playing havoc with my body clock. This was the time of day I would normally be arriving home, not waking up. I lay down on the bed and rested my cheek against the cool silk of the coverlet. The hotel was quiet. No taps being turned on and off, no noisy footsteps on the stairs, no chamber pots being emptied into the latrines. It wasn't at all like my hotel in the Latin Quarter. But I was too awake now to go back to sleep and, even though André and I had dined well, I was voraciously hungry.

I sat up again and flipped through the room service menu. I can eat something now and eat again with André later, I thought. I picked up the telephone receiver but before I could say anything a gentleman speaking French with a German accent wished me good morning by name and asked me what I would like for breakfast.

'*Guten Morgen*,' I said, keen to use at least one of the phrases André had taught me on the train. I ordered some rolls with honey and jam. Kira jumped from the windowsill into my lap. 'And some herrings and a saucer of milk,' I added.

I was drying my hair when the waiter arrived at the door with a trolley. While he set the breakfast table, Kira lifted her nose to the air then manoeuvred herself as close as possible to the table by sliding her bottom along the windowsill. When she was parallel to the table, she crouched, her tail swishing. I caught her as she leapt.

'*Danke schön*,' I said to the waiter, bouncing Kira in my arms.

'You are welcome, Mademoiselle,' he said, eyeing the thwarted kitten. 'Have a pleasant meal.'

I ate the rolls then glanced at my watch. It was only seven o'clock. I opened the door to my room and looked down the hall. André's shoes had been polished and placed outside his door. There was no light coming through the jamb and I assumed that he was still asleep. I returned to my room and slipped on my shoes. Kira had finished eating her herrings and lay on the sofa, licking her paws.

'I am going for a walk,' I told her. 'If I find something nice, I will bring it back for you.'

I passed the dining room where the waiters were busy setting out the plates and cutlery for breakfast. The aroma of brewing coffee mingled with the sweet scent of melting butter and fresh toast. The combination had such a cheering effect that I felt as if I were walking on my toes.

'*Guten Morgen*,' the concierge greeted me when I reached the front entrance. 'May I get you a taxi?'

I shook my head. 'No, thank you. I am going for a walk.'

He lifted his eyebrows but then nodded and smiled. 'To see the Brandenburg Gate, *ja*? If you can wait until after breakfast, the hotel guide or Madame Adlon can take you.'

I was keen to explore the street on my own and the awkwardness of being accompanied by Herr Adlon's wife didn't appeal to me any more than a guide. I thanked him and walked out the door. Was going for an early morning stroll such an unusual thing for a guest at the Adlon to do?

The air was fresh and cool. It had been a long time since I had smelt the air at the beginning of the day. By the time I ventured into it on my way home, my nose was too besieged by tobacco smoke and dressing room dust to notice.

As soon as I stepped onto the Unter den Linden, I realised that Berlin could not be mistaken for Paris at all. Although some of the buildings were from similar eras, those in Paris, with their ironwork and curvaceous roofs, seemed to have been fashioned to delight, while their counterparts in Berlin, with their sharp angles, Prussian statues and domes, had been built to command. I walked past the British Embassy and shops selling hand-painted music boxes and filigreed picture frames. I read the signs above the stores, trying to work out what they meant. But *Bank* and *Schuhladen* were the only ones I was sure about. *Bank* because it sounded so similar to the French word, and *Schuhladen* because the only things on display in the store's window were shoes. I stopped to admire the goods in the window of a store for gentlemen: jade letter openers, shagreen pencil cases, leather wallets and even a cuckoo clock.

'*Laden, Laden, Laden.*' I repeated the German word for 'store', trying to memorise it. My education had been sporadic to say the least, but I loved learning languages. My English had progressed almost by osmosis rather than conscious effort, thanks to Eugene and the clientele at the Café des Singes. From Rivarola I had learnt more than a smattering of Spanish, albeit most of it how to express displeasure. But German was so different to French — so precise, so definite, so many impossibly long words — that I was determined to learn as much as I could of it while we were in Berlin.

I continued along the boulevard to Pariser Platz and the Brandenburg Gate, stopping to admire the gate's towering series of columns, which I had read had been built to evoke the Acropolis in Athens. I gazed up at the bronze Goddess of Peace driving forth her chariot of four horses. There were a few people wandering around the Platz: a woman pushing a wheelbarrow; a young man sitting on a bench, sketching the gate into his notebook; and a couple of soldiers in uniform. I was careful not to stare at them as I passed for they were both in wheelchairs, their empty trouser legs pinned as far as their thighs. One had lost an arm as well and was using a mechanical claw to steady his chair.

I crossed the Platz and found myself facing the French Embassy with its red, white and blue flag drifting in the breeze. I remembered my father's horrific injuries and the stone in our village that commemorated the war dead. What was the use of it all? I wondered. What did the Great War achieve?

I shrugged off my sudden melancholy and continued my stroll along the opposite side of the Unter den Linden. There were more stores selling German luxury items, and some food shops whose traders were rolling up their grilles. I turned a corner and found myself standing in front of a toy shop, its window display a feast for the eyes: teddy bears, gingerbread houses, hand-painted building blocks, dolls in Bavarian dress and with eyes that opened and closed. There was a basket of brightly coloured balls inside the door. I glanced at the opening hours and decided to come back later to buy some for Kira. Madame Ducroix had said that Russian Blues were good at entertaining themselves, but I thought that now Kira was a first-class international traveller staying at the Adlon, it was time for her to move up from bits of screwed-up newspaper and balls of wool.

Something tugged my arm. I looked down and jumped back with fright. A face stared up at me but it took me a moment to realise that the creature touching me was a child. Her eyes bulged like a frog's under her puffed forehead. The rest of her was skin and bones. A pair of rickety legs poked out from her ragged dress. She slipped her hand into mine.

I glanced up and down the street to see where she had come from. I didn't have far to look: there was a woman lying in a doorway on the opposite side of the street, between two boarded-up shops. She was clutching another child, miserably swaddled in rags, to her chest. I had seen poverty before but theirs was far more misery than I had seen in my life. They weren't just poor, they were dying of starvation. I hadn't brought many marks with me because I didn't think there would be anything open, but I was determined to give them whatever I had. I opened my handbag and rummaged for my purse, but in the instant I grabbed it I felt more eyes on me.

Two youths came out of the doorway where the woman was lying. One of them stepped over her body as if she were no more than a sack of flour and stood staring at me with his hands on his hips. A vicious smile slashed across his face like a rip in his skin. If I give the woman money, I thought, he'll just take it from her. I had seen enough of the pimps in Montmartre to know how those types worked.

'I'll be back,' I said to the girl. 'I will come back with food. Wait for me.'

She shook her head and clutched my skirt, begging me with her eyes to stay. 'I'll be back,' I said, pulling her fingers gently from me. From the desperate look on her face, I saw that she didn't understand.

Ignoring the youths, I ran down the street and back onto the Unter den Linden. I tried to remember how far along the bakery I passed earlier had been. '*Bäckerei, Bäckerei*,' I repeated to myself, squinting at the windows, although deep down I knew that all the bread in the world couldn't save that girl and her family. They needed to be cared for in a hospital. Mine was the ineffective gesture of someone who had no idea what to do when faced with so much human misery, but hoped that doing something was somehow better than not doing anything at all.

I found the bakery and rushed inside. There were two customers ahead of me, but when they saw me pointing like a mad woman to the bread and emptying my purse onto the counter, the women stepped aside, hoping that the sooner the shop assistant dealt with the crazy foreigner, the sooner she would be on her way. I had heard that German bread was nutritious, and could even replace vegetables in winter, so I pointed to every variety available — black, brown and white — and left the store with two armfuls of loaves.

I ran back down the Unter den Linden to the street where the toy shop was located. The doorway where the mother had been lying was empty. I looked up and down the street but couldn't see her or the girl anywhere. They couldn't have gone far, I thought, not in that condition. I was tempted to call out but was afraid that would only bring the two youths out again. I walked up and down the street in both directions, then put the bread in the doorway where the woman had been lying and rubbed my hand across my eyes. I could not get the tortured expression on the child's face out of my mind. She must have thought I was running away from her.

I left the bread in the doorway, although I didn't know who it would benefit there apart from the mice. I thought of the rolls I had ordered for breakfast that morning, and the pieces I had left unfinished on my plate, and felt guilty. I turned to walk back down the street and found myself face to face with one of the youths, the one with the vicious smile. He looked even worse up close. The whites of his eyes were glazed, like those of a dead man, and he stank of tobacco and sweat. Before I could move he grabbed my arm.

'*Française?*' he demanded, pressing his fingers into my skin. 'Are you French?' He didn't wait for me to answer before he spat into my face. His spittle had an acidic sting to it and was enough to shock me into action. I tugged away from him and ran up the street. I had passed a policeman on my way back from the bakery. He wouldn't be far up the boulevard if I needed to scream for help.

But the youth didn't pursue me onto the boulevard. He stopped at the corner and began singing what sounded like a war song. *'Siegreich wollen wir Frankreich schlagen ...'*

I was still running, but everything drifted into slow motion. What is he singing? I thought. He is younger than me. He was never in the war. I reached the next corner and turned around to see if he was following me. The youth shouted out in French for my benefit. 'We will defeat France! We will drive her to the ground! There will be no more France! No more French! We will spit on her like a used whore!'

SEVENTEEN

André, dressed in a shirt and trousers with a robe over the top, opened the door to his room and beamed at me. '*Bonjour*, Simone!' he said, putting his cologne-scented cheek to mine. 'How are you this morning?' We had dropped the formality of 'Monsieur' and 'Mademoiselle' the previous night, comfortable enough together now to use each other's first names.

Before I could answer, he had picked up his shoes from the doormat, placed his hand on my shoulder and was leading me into his room. 'I've just finished shaving,' he said, clearing the morning newspapers from the sofa and gesturing for me to sit down. 'I didn't expect you to be up for hours yet.'

He dropped his shoes to the floor and glanced about for his jacket and tie, which he found hanging on a suit rack near the armoire in his bedroom. He returned to the drawing room and laid the articles of clothing over the back of a chair. 'I thought I had a whole morning to catch up on the news and write some letters. Was I wrong in thinking that show business people never get out of bed before noon?'

When I didn't answer he looked at me more closely. I could feel my eyes brimming with tears. This was not what I had planned. Before knocking on his door, I had washed my face and changed my dress. But all my music hall bravado couldn't stop the ache in my heart caused by the sight of the starving child and her family.

'What's wrong?' André asked.

A hot tear rolled down my cheek. I tried to speak but all that came out was a rasp.

'Simone,' he said, rushing towards me. He sat down next to me on the sofa. Before I knew what I was doing, I leaned my head against his chest. I could smell the citrus scent of his shirt and feel the warmth of his skin beneath the material. It wasn't until I told him about the starving girl and her family that I was aware of his arm around me.

'How awful!' he said, squeezing his arm tighter around my waist. 'If there is one thing to be grateful for, it is that starving children are less common a sight in Berlin than they used to be.'

I glanced at him.

'France held the blockade against Germany for months after the armistice was signed and hundreds of thousands of people died of cold and starvation. It is seven years since the war, but in many ways Germany is still a mess.'

I shuddered. The sight of one tormented child was enough for me, let alone thousands. André removed his arm from my waist and reached for his shoes. I watched him yank up the tongues before slipping the shoes on and tying the laces. What had I been thinking in letting him hold me?

'I am going downstairs to talk to the manager,' André said. 'The concierge shouldn't have let you go out alone. Something dreadful could have happened.'

'Please don't,' I said, patting my eyes with the back of my hand. 'It's not the concierge's fault. He suggested I take a guide.'

'Take a guide?' said André. 'He should have warned you.'

'Warned me about what?'

André didn't answer. His expression was drawn, no longer the happy face that had greeted me at the door. I wished I hadn't said anything and had kept the incident to myself.

'In a way, you can't blame France for wanting to cripple Germany so that it couldn't attack us again,' he said. 'But can we blame them for hating us?'

'I am more upset about the girl than I am about the youth,' I told him. 'She was pitiful. He was just your usual thug, the kind you meet anywhere.'

It was true that I had been more shocked by the state of the child and her family than by the youth, but I knew he was more than just another thug. I remembered the hate in his voice when he belted out his war cry. No, he was something much more menacing than that.

André shook his head. 'I'm sorry. I should have warned you that Berlin has some extreme types. I didn't expect you to get up so early, let alone to go off unaccompanied.'

André's emphasis on the last word unsettled me. I sat up. 'Unaccompanied?' I repeated.

André glanced at me; I still had no idea what he'd meant. 'What are you talking about "unaccompanied"?' I asked. 'How do you think I get around Paris?'

But as soon as I had spoken, I realised what he had meant. And I could see by the way his gaze shifted from me to his lap that he had realised too. Women of André's class did not go anywhere without some sort of escort, even if it was only their maid or their chauffeur. It was protection against the 'corrupting' things that could happen to a woman if she went wandering about on her own. Had he forgotten what I was — a showgirl? Although I had never danced naked, many of my colleagues danced bare-breasted and sometimes completely nude. What kind of corrupting thing could happen to me?

'If I had to wait around for someone to accompany me, I would never go anywhere,' I told him. It amused me to think that Mademoiselle Canier and her friends might be shocked at the idea of a young woman travelling around Paris on the *métro* or going to Pigalle on her own.

André's face broke into a smile. He glanced at me then looked back at his lap. 'I guess sometimes I forget that there are women and then there are *independent* women,' he said.

'Which sort do you like better?'

'Oh, the independent ones, definitely,' he answered.

We both laughed at that.

～

André and I strolled along the paths by the lakes of the Tiergarten and past statues of famous Germans like Goethe and Bach, trying to

247

find an antidote to the morning's unpleasantness. The weather was sunny but cool and the Berliners were out in force, walking in groups or in solitary contemplation. As a race, Germans were taller than most French people, with a sternness about their expressions that was different to the Gallic vivacity or Mediterranean hot-bloodedness that I knew. They were not all blond and blue-eyed, however; like French people, they came in many colours. The variety of appearances was further magnified by the many foreigners enjoying the park: Russian families stretched out on picnic blankets; two Italian ladies speaking by a fountain; a flank of American students riding bicycles and calling out to each other in their strident accents.

We reached the Zoological Gardens and selected a restaurant whose terrace was shaded by birch trees. André ordered an ice called *cassata* for me. It arrived in a crystal glass and tasted like champagne sorbet.

Despite the peaceful surroundings, the wasted body of the starving girl remained in my mind. But my distress made me more open to André: I wanted him to comfort me. And because of that, I began to see beyond his dazzling exterior and really look at *him*. He had told me that he knew a woman who worked with the poor in Berlin and that he would make enquiries about the girl and her family through her and see what could be done to help. That simple offer meant more to me that morning than if he had told me he adored me.

'The French economy almost collapsed too,' André said, continuing our conversation about the state of Germany. 'But the French took the wrong path if they wanted peace.'

I remembered my father's bandaged face, the way he looked when my mother brought him home from the military hospital. A few years later, I had heard him tell her that the man who had been in the bed next to him had lost his entire face to burns. He had no eyes, no nose, no lips and no tongue. He suffered so much that two nurses held a pillow over his face until he ceased breathing. No one stopped them. In those days, the French prime minister's catch cry had been: 'There are twenty million Germans too many'. Even as a child I had felt the rage against their race burn within me. But who could hate all Germans when they looked into the face of that starving girl?

'You lost your brother in the war,' I said. 'Yet you don't hate the Germans.'

'I have seen too much suffering on both sides for that,' André answered. 'Laurent never wanted to go to war. He was a good businessman but preferred a quiet life of reading and walking his dogs. My father thought that becoming an officer would make him more of a "man". Well, he's not a man at all now.'

A picture loomed up in my mind: a dark-haired boy peering out a window, watching his older brother leave for the front. The older boy gave one last heart-rending wave to his brother before disappearing for ever. But there was something else besides grief in André's tone.

'Are you angry at your father?'

I was surprised at myself for asking such a personal question, but André didn't seem to mind. He shrugged. 'I think my father suffers enough on his own without me adding to his guilt. Who could have known that the Great War was going to turn into the biggest bloodbath mankind has ever experienced? He lost his son ... and my mother. She gives him the respect of a good wife, but she avoids his eyes when he looks at her. My brother died a hero at Verdun, doing everything he could to save his men, but that does little to heal my mother's pain at having lost her firstborn son.'

I gazed at the genteel people wandering in the park. Everything seemed tranquil in the soft sunshine. André's father sounded like a hard taskmaster, driving himself and his sons towards manly perfection. I remembered the way André had stroked and petted Mademoiselle Canier in Paris before we had left. Perhaps André was used to giving and getting nothing in return.

'There will never be a war like that one again,' I said.

'Everyone in France says that. It is what we would like to believe,' André replied.

I looked at him. 'You can come here and do business. Herr Adlon might object to you being the son of his competitor, but he doesn't object to you being French.'

André lit a cigarette, his one and only for the day, and took his time to answer. 'Business is business between men like Adlon and my father, irrespective of nationality,' he said. 'German mothers don't want to see their children die any more than French mothers do. The Sorbonne will invite German intellectuals to lecture there, and

German directors will star French actresses in their plays. It is not from those people that war arises and yet, when the wheels start turning, many of them will rally to it.'

We turned our heads to follow the zigzagging path of a couple on a two-seater bicycle. Just as it seemed they were going to correct their path, they lost their balance and tumbled into a hedge.

'French politicians are imbeciles,' said André, flicking ash from his cigarette into a tray. 'They are more concerned about their seats at the Ballets Russes and where to place their Directoire furniture than economics and international politics. But in the end, at least they care about their popularity. I sometimes think there are dark forces in Germany that would kill their own people if it served their purposes.'

I had never heard anyone say the things André was telling me. 'What do you mean?' I asked.

'My father says that the reason inflation never became as bad in France as it did here was because of good luck rather than good management, but my uncle disagrees. He says that what happened to the German economy was more than post-war chaos. They did it to themselves.'

'Why would they do that?'

'It was good propaganda. The German press screamed that France's demands for reparation payments were the sole cause of the problems. Certainly, money going out of a country doesn't help an ailing economy. But at the height of inflation, when a loaf of bread cost two hundred billion marks, the government kept printing more money. Now why would they do that? Economic ignorance?' André shook his head. 'When they stablised the mark three years later, the problem was solved overnight. They were doing it to get out of paying reparations. France couldn't siphon off anything from an economy that was dry.'

I was puzzled. 'If so many people hadn't suffered from that approach, I would have said it was a smart strategy. But the German government wasn't trying to help their own people, so what did they want the money for?'

André pursed his lips and shook his head. He touched my arm. 'Come on, Simone, this is gloomy talk. This is not the reason you and I came to Berlin. And who knows? Things might get better.

Especially if men like the one we are going to meet this afternoon are allowed to run the country.'

'Who are we meeting?'

'Count Harry Kessler. He is the French-born son of a German-Swiss father and an Irish mother. He was educated in England and served as the German ambassador to Poland. He is a publisher and writes himself, but most of all he loves talented artists and entertainers. And when he meets you, he is going to think all his wishes have been granted at once!'

~

I didn't know enough about Berlin to know that the Romanische Café was the meeting place of the city's literary and cultural elite, but I did know enough about cafés to be astounded by how large it was. It had seating for over a thousand customers and was more the size of a dance hall than a café. A *portier* stood by the revolving door and welcomed us. I couldn't help noticing his name tag: Nietz. It sounded to me like the English word 'neat', which made me smile because it summed up everything about him, from his highly shone boots to his shaved hairline.

I was looking forward to meeting Count Kessler after André had called him 'the best-connected man in Germany' and told me that he was friends with everyone from Max Reinhardt to Einstein. I recognised the Count without ever having seen him before. He was seated at a table for regulars and looked as I had imagined him and more: an elegant man in his late fifties, with tapering fingers, appraising eyes and a thin but friendly smile.

From the moment the Count stood up, greeted us in genteel French and shook our hands formally but heartily, I was fascinated by him. His contradictions were intriguing. It was as if he had taken the best of all the cultures he had been exposed to: the precision of the Germans and Swiss; the tact of the British; the charm and wit of the French; and the lively earthiness of the Irish. He was a truly cosmopolitan man.

'I have taken the liberty of ordering the strawberry cake for us. I can promise you that it will be very good,' the Count said, grinning at me. His skin had a sallow tinge around the eyes, which suggested ill health, but his face was alert and his movements were so vital that he could have been the same age as me and not forty years my senior.

The Count's gaze moved over me, taking me in. 'André has told me that you are an exceptionally talented singer and dancer.'

I glanced at André. At first I was tempted to deny it, at least out of modesty. But then I thought, why should I? That was what I wanted to be and André was determined to make it happen. 'I'm sure I will be, if André has anything to do with it!' I said.

'She reached some sort of plateau in Paris,' André explained. 'But what's amazing is how far she went on her own before that happened. She hasn't even had proper training. I am hoping that in exposing her to different styles and a different city, she will return to Paris refreshed.'

'There are exceptional teachers in Berlin,' said the Count. 'I can write letters of introduction for you if you like.' André and I enthusiastically accepted his offer.

The Count nodded. 'Berlin is different to Paris, Mademoiselle Fleurier,' he said. 'I can imagine that the French would be taken with not only your talent but your energy. I could tell you were French the moment you walked in the door, by the way your eyes shone and your body vibrated, as if every new experience in life were a strawberry cake that was making your mouth water. Germans are more cynical than that. But at the same time, I believe that exposing oneself to different cultures creates more depth in one's personality, and that can only help an artist.'

'I've just arrived in Berlin and I can feel that happening already,' I told him, more than pleased to be referred to as an 'artist'. I thought what he was saying was true. I had been born in Pays de Sault, but now I had a bit of Marseilles and Paris in me too. 'Perhaps Berlin will improve my concentration and discipline,' I said.

The Count leaned towards me. 'There are some things in Berlin that may shock you,' he said. 'In Parisian cabaret, the songs are about disenchanted love and poverty. In Berlin, cabarets are much more political ... and often nihilistic. Sex and death are the obsessions here.'

André also leaned forward and whispered conspiratorially, 'Fortunately, unlike the English and Americans, the French are not shocked easily.'

For some reason this comment amused the Count. His face flushed and he tucked his chin into his collar, trying his best to control his laughter. But it convulsed in his chest and escaped as a roar. The sound skimmed across the tables and bounced off the walls, far louder than the clinking of coffee cups and murmured conversations around us. The more the Count tried to restrain himself, the more crimson his face turned and the louder he chortled. Then André's deep bark of a laugh burst out, echoing after the Count's delight like a mastiff chasing a ball. I looked from one to the other, their faces scrunched up and their torsos shaking. They were a two-man band producing the music of mirth.

∽

Mademoiselle Canier arrived with her maid and three compartments full of luggage the following day. I thought she must be planning to move to Berlin permanently. When she saw me waiting on the station with André, a frown flitted across her face.

André helped Mademoiselle Canier down to the platform and she planted a lingering kiss on his lips. Her attitude seemed to have changed in the last few days. She behaved the way she had at Le Boeuf sur le Toit, clinging to André's side like seaweed to the bottom of a boat.

After sitting through a monosyllabic lunch, during which Mademoiselle Canier ate a pickle and pushed the rest of her food to the side of the plate, I was relieved to learn that she had to return to Paris in a fortnight for her cousin's ball. At least there would be some reprieve. When I was alone with André, he had been informal. As soon as Mademoiselle Canier arrived, he reverted to addressing me as Mademoiselle Fleurier. I saw that I was going to have to feel one way towards him and behave in quite another.

Count Kessler joined us to dine at the Adlon that evening. An amused grin lapped around the corner of his mouth when Mademoiselle Canier spoke to the staff in French. She ignored the Count and me unless André made a specific point of referring to us in the conversation. Afterwards, the four of us took a walk down Friedrichstrasse. Every building seemed to be a cabaret, a cinema, a brothel, a dance hall or a drug den. Prostitutes crowded each corner and lurked in every doorway. I was used to the tarts of Marseilles and the bawdy prostitutes of Montmartre, but the whores of Friedrichstrasse were confronting: they seemed brutal and dangerous in their feather boas, chains and tassels. One dominatrix paced her corner like a panther, cracking her whip and snarling with her teeth. Another woman sat on a fire hydrant, naked except for a pair of lace-up boots. But what surprised me the most was that the people walking up and down the pavements were not working-class hordes but men in bow ties and shirts with mother-of-pearl buttons and women in dresses of oriental silk. They were stepping out of Mercedes Benz limousines and taking in their surroundings with a voyeuristic amusement. Not everyone lost their money during the crisis, I thought. Tycoons, speculators and criminals seemed to have made fistfuls from it.

André and Mademoiselle Canier strolled ahead of us. The Count walked in step with me.

'Mademoiselle Canier takes an awfully long time to get ready, don't you think?' he whispered. 'I thought we weren't going to eat until midnight. I timed you both by my watch. You were down in twenty minutes.'

'I have been trained for quick changes in the music hall,' I told him.

The Count smiled, and we stopped to watch a half-naked street performer execute a head-stand. We caught an eyeful of pubic hair when the man swung himself back to his feet.

'You look as though you have had enough, Mademoiselle Fleurier,' the Count said. 'This really isn't my thing either. But lots of tourists like it, and at least you can say you have seen the Friedrichstrasse now.'

The Count called out to André, then stepped to the kerb and hailed a taxi. 'Let us take the ladies somewhere more fun. Somewhere Mademoiselle Fleurier might learn a thing or two.'

We drove down the Unter den Linden towards the Schöneberg district and stopped on the corner of Motzstrasse and Kalckreuthstrasse. I gazed up at the bright Art Deco lights of a club, the Eldorado, and the sign underneath that read, *You've found it!*

'We play a special game here,' said the Count, his mouth twisting into a smile. 'But I won't tell you what it is yet.'

We left our coats with the cloakroom girl and I had to take a second look at her milky skin and ruby mouth. She was extraordinarily beautiful, even more stunning than Mademoiselle Canier or Camille, and far too exotic to be just a cloakroom attendant.

'Good evening,' the hostess greeted us. 'A table by the stage?'

The Count nodded and the hostess led us through the smoky space. Her walk was a queenly glide. She would be marvellous on stage, I thought. Once we were seated I looked around the club; its decor of rose lighting and the glass bar seemed at odds with the round tables and kitsch salt and pepper shakers. The band climbed onto the stage: a pianist, trombonist, clarinetist and banjo player. They were all women and were as glamorous as the cloakroom girl and the hostess.

'I thought the women we saw around Berlin today were beautiful, but the employees at this club are striking,' I said to the Count. 'Is that the reason you like this place?'

'I believe they bring them from Bavaria especially for their beauty,' said the Count, turning away to signal one of the waitresses. 'Shall we order beer or champagne?'

'Let's try a German beer,' said André, coughing into his handkerchief.

I gave him a pat on the back which elicited a scowl from Mademoiselle Canier. 'It is smoky in here,' I said.

André nodded and dabbed his watering eyes.

'Yes,' said the Count. 'It is amazing how someone who smokes can be so sensitive to it himself.'

André let out what sounded like one of his laughs but it dissolved into a violent cough, hidden behind his handkerchief.

The waitress was very tall, even for a German woman, and when she returned from the bar and placed our drinks in front of us I couldn't take my eyes from her well-manicured but large hands.

'I thought Bavarians were like Austrians,' I whispered to André. 'More on the petite side.'

Before he could answer, he was shaken by another violent coughing fit and quickly sipped his beer. Mademoiselle Canier gave me a wary look, before taking out her compact and retouching her nose.

'Look over there,' said the Count to André, nodding towards the entrance. 'There's Herr Egermann, the banker, talking with Herr Stroheim from the Reichstag. I swear, anybody who is anybody comes to the Eldorado nowadays.'

It must be for the beautiful women, I thought. I was sure there were more elegant places in Berlin. A young boy brushed past me; his silk smoking jacket tickled my skin. I looked up and our eyes met. He wore his hair smoothed down and had slender shoulders and hands. I watched him join a huddle of similarly dressed boys leaning on the bar.

'Are you ready for our game now, Mademoiselle Fleurier?' the Count asked.

I nodded.

'Well,' he said, rubbing his chin, 'look around the room and tell me who the real women are and who are men.'

I noticed the smirk on André's face. He hadn't been coughing at all. 'None of them can be men!' I cried.

'Study them more closely,' said the Count.

'Well, the cloakroom girl maybe,' I said, thinking of her angular features. 'And the waitress has large hands. But I would never have noticed anything if you hadn't pointed it out.'

I smiled at Mademoiselle Canier. It was an olive branch gesture, to see if she would join in the fun. But she looked as uninterested as ever. If the transvestites at the Eldorado couldn't amuse her, what could?

'How do you tell?' André asked the Count. 'I've heard a lot of them have been castrated and that's why they have smooth skin and curvaceous figures.'

The Count shook his head. 'It has nothing to do with their skin or feeling for Adam's apples or looking between their legs. The real giveaway is when they are more feminine than the most beautiful girl. Only pansies know how to be truly erotic women.'

'It is a good lesson for an entertainer, I think,' said André, turning to me. 'The art of illusion. If you can convince yourself you are one thing, then other people will believe it too.'

Mademoiselle Canier fished a silver case from her purse and pulled out a cigarette without offering one to anyone else. 'A woman is a woman,' she said, inserting the cigarette between her lips and waiting for André to light it. 'Only an erotic woman can be an erotic woman.'

'So knowingly put,' said the Count. His tone was chivalrous but I saw the amusement dancing in his eyes. He nodded towards the bar. 'And what about those boys over there?' he said to me. 'Are they what they seem?'

I turned to the men lined up at the bar. The one who had bumped into me winked in my direction. I looked back to the Count. 'I can see now that they are women,' I said. 'They're not as convincing as the men.'

'They're not trying to be,' said André. 'Theirs is the art of suggestion not transformation. Somehow their outfits make them even more feminine.'

'I have to say that I find a woman in a tuxedo quite fetching,' said the Count, ordering more glasses of beer.

The show began and the master of ceremonies, whose face was chalked white, introduced the chorus girls in German, French and English: 'The incomparable ... the fabulous ... the like-nothing-else-in-the-world ... the Eldorado Fräuleins!' A line of statuesque 'pansies' appeared on stage in little more than corsets and boots.

For the next act, two of the 'boys' from the bar danced the tango. They glided, plunged and strutted tantalisingly but the iceberg expressions on their faces never changed. The sight of two women dancing the tango together made what Rivarola and I had done seem clumsy. We had danced with fire and passion, but the women's act had such a chill to it that the audience was left in an agony of expectation, and with the sense that something had been held back for later.

I watched with interest. I understood that by exposing me to these performers and ideas, André was enticing me out of my shell. The more I opened my mind, the more layers I would have to draw on for my own work. Berlin was a fresh scene with no associations and I was ready to absorb it all.

Most of the performances were good-natured spoofs of transvestism, but there was one strange act with a dwarf playing a musical saw. The long strip of metal, which he clutched between his knees, was longer than he was. But he brought his bow across the edge without strain, and skilfully bent the metal to produce high notes or released it for lower ones. The music he produced was a haunting vibrato, so ethereal that the audience remained still for the duration of his act, as if they were frightened that if they should move or talk they would be turned to stone. For a moment, the memory of the starving girl's face returned to me and I shivered. The Count was knowledgeable in German politics; I would ask him about it when Mademoiselle Canier wasn't around. From the little conversation I had managed to elicit from her, I had come to the conclusion that the only subject that interested her was herself.

We finished the night off with what was to become one of my happiest memories of Berlin. At the Residenz Casino — or 'The Resi' as it was affectionately known — the *maître d'hôtel* assigned us Table Number 14. The Count asked if Mademoiselle Canier and I minded if he and André talked privately at the bar for a few minutes. 'Business matters,' he apologised. 'Very boring.'

'Go ahead,' I told him.

Mademoiselle Canier excused herself to go to the powder room, obviously not interested in talking with me. She is not Odette, I thought, my mind turning to my friend who was as lovely on the inside as she was on the outside. Mademoiselle Canier was all veneer. She was certainly guarding André much more jealously than before, but as far as I could see there was no need. Nothing had changed in his feelings towards me.

I turned my attention to the buzzing crowd. There was a jazz band playing and couples foxtrotting on the dance floor. I noticed that all the tables had a telephone on them and assumed they were to call through supper and drinks orders — another example of German efficiency. Perhaps they were needed because the band was loud and the waiters couldn't take orders the normal way. I was surprised then when the telephone on our table rang.

'Hello,' I said into the mouthpiece.

The person at the other end mumbled something in German.

'I don't speak German,' I said.

'Ah, you are French,' the man said. 'You are beautiful. May I come over to your table?'

'What?'

'Wave to me,' he said. 'I am over here at Table Number 22.'

I looked up to see a young man with a moustache and a red bow tie waving his fingers at me.

'I am here with my fiancé,' I said. 'But thank you anyway.'

I rehooked the receiver. I didn't have a fiancé, of course, but I thought it was better to let the man down gently. A few minutes later the telephone rang again but I didn't pick it up. Eventually it stopped, and then sounded again. I stared at the band and acted as if I couldn't hear it.

'Your telephone is ringing,' the woman at the next table informed me. I gave her a dumbfounded look even though she had spoken to me in French.

A moment later, a boy in a blue uniform and cap made his way to me. 'A delivery from the Resi Post Office,' he said, placing a package wrapped in gold paper on the table. I was about to tell him there was a mistake when I noticed the card was addressed to 'Fräulein Table Number 14'.

'Who is this from?' I asked.

'The gentleman at Table Number 31,' he said. 'Do you have a return message for him?'

I shook my head. What was going on? I glanced around the room, careful to avoid Table Number 31. André and the Count were standing by the bar, looking in my direction and laughing. I waved them over.

'I am never going to survive your practical jokes,' I said to them. 'What kind of place is this?'

'It's fun, isn't it?' said the Count. 'No one need ever be alone in Berlin. If you see someone you like, you can call them or send them a gift of perfume, cigars or cocaine.'

It wasn't at all what I had expected of those stern-faced Berliners. How gay life seemed then. How beautiful and fun.

Mademoiselle Canier returned from the powder room smelling of lilies but otherwise as well-groomed as before. We stayed with the Count at the Resi until it closed, dancing to the jazz music and drinking champagne at prices that would have shocked even Parisians. I forgot about the youth who had shouted threats at me that morning and about what André had said about another war. I let myself slide into the gaiety of it all. I was doing what everyone else at the Resi was doing, losing myself in decadence and trying to forget the real world looming outside.

EIGHTEEN

I had envisaged my stay in Berlin as a holiday carnival, where I would skip from one amusement to the other, ice-cream in hand. André had other plans. I discovered that for a Frenchman, and a moneyed Parisian at that, he enjoyed working. What was more, he expected me to feel the same way. Of course, I wanted to be a star and was prepared to do what it took to become one, but I had no idea that my days in Berlin were to start so early, end so late and involve such a medley of lessons.

A few days after we had visited the Eldorado and the Resi, André informed me that the Count had secured me a place with Madame Irina Shestova, formerly of the Ballets Russes.

'Ballet!' I had no intention of reliving the nightmare lessons I'd had with Madame Baroux at Le Chat Espiègle.

'Not to dance on points,' laughed André, 'but for poise and grace. To make you a blueblood of the stage. Otherwise you will look clumsy when you perform with the chorus girls.'

The next morning, I caught a taxi to Madame Shestova's studio in Prager Platz, not far from the Kurfürstendamm. To my relief, Madame Shestova wasn't intent on turning me into a professional ballerina. She helped me improve my posture and balance with exercises at the barre. But her most important mission, it seemed, was to make sure I knew how to take a bow.

'Like a queen bestowing her munificence upon her cheering subjects,' she said, demonstrating a graceful bow with one foot slightly in front of the other and bending from her hips rather than her shoulders. 'Not like a bobbing child who hopes that if she pleases everyone she won't be sent to bed!'

After Madame Shestova, I was scheduled for a lesson with Louise Goodman, an American dance teacher who had studied at the Denishawn school in New York. Her style of dance was the one espoused by Isadora Duncan, where movements sprang instinctively from the body as opposed to being forced on it with formal steps. Her studio was larger than Madame Shestova's, but reeked of paint because she shared it with two artists who worked in the morning when the light was better.

'I don't know what I can teach you,' she said. 'You're a natural dancer already.' In truth she taught me a lot about the balance of opposites in dancing: moving up and down, stretching and relaxing, falling and rising. 'Yin-yang,' she called it.

But André's plans for my education didn't end there. After leaving Mademoiselle Goodman's class I would return to the hotel for a light lunch of bread and salad — light because I knew it was not good to sing, or run and jump, on a full stomach. And sing, run and jump were what I did at my voice production classes with Doctor Oskar Daniel, the voice coach of Caruso and Marlene Dietrich.

After making me hurdle over chairs and do cartwheels in succession, he ordered me to sing out a high C. 'Belt it out!' he commanded, beating his cane on the floor. 'Belt it out all the way back to Paris!'

'I have found you an English teacher,' announced André, arriving in my room one evening when Mademoiselle Canier was away at her cousin's ball. I was lying on the sofa with Kira curled up on my stomach, recovering from a session with Doctor Daniel where not only did I have to hurdle chairs and do cartwheels but I had to sing my high C *while* doing them.

'An English teacher?' I cried, lifting my head off the cushion before realising that holding it up took too much effort and dropping it down again. André was in his dinner suit. I hadn't even thought about what I was going to wear that evening to the Apollo Theatre.

'For fluency lessons on Monday, Tuesday and Thursday afternoons.'

'Why?' I asked.

'It is not going to stop at Paris, Simone,' he said. 'There is London and New York. And don't forget South America.'

Kira jumped from my stomach and tugged one of my ballet slippers along the carpet by its ribbons. She wasn't a destructive cat, but silky or shiny things were her weakness. If I didn't put them away, my underwear and earrings were always going missing, only to be found later in Kira's food dish.

I turned from Kira back to André and was surprised to see him sitting in a chair with his head clutched in his hands.

'André?'

For a minute, maybe two, he didn't move. It was such a sudden change of mood that I wondered what had happened.

'Simone,' he said, looking up. 'Do you ever get nervous before you go on stage?'

His eyes were red-rimmed and sad. I wanted to lean over and touch his beautiful face and tell him that whatever it was that was worrying him, it would be all right. But I couldn't. Instead, I said, 'Nervous? Where do I begin?'

He laughed and shook his head. 'You always look so confident. I can't imagine anything scaring you.'

Confident? Was that how he saw me? I would never have said that about myself.

'Are you worried about something?' I asked.

His gaze fell to the carpet and he nodded. 'About not being considered good enough.'

'By whom?' I asked, but I knew he meant his father. I thought of the other young men of André's class, like Antoine and François, and how foppish they were. André was nothing like them. I recalled how, when his friend had been able to locate the starving girl and her family, André had made a sizeable donation to the charity on my behalf.

André looked me straight in the eye for a moment then stood up and walked to the window. 'I shall never be Laurent,' he said, leaning against the frame. 'My brother would have been horrified to think that I live in his shadow, but that is how my father sees me. Sometimes I catch him staring at me and I think he wishes that it was me who died at Verdun, not Laurent.'

I followed André to the window. 'Surely not,' I said. 'Any father would be proud of a son like you.'

André shook his head and smiled sadly. 'Your success is important to me,' he said. 'I am not using you to impress my father. But I wish I could prove to him that I am as good as the son he lost.'

He turned to me, about to say something else, but was cut off by the ring of the telephone. He strode to the bureau and lifted the receiver.

'It's the Count,' he said. 'He is waiting downstairs in the lobby.' Then, glancing at his watch, he laughed. 'What happens to time when I am with you, Simone? There is no need to rush, I will have a drink with the Count. Just come down when you are ready.'

André walked to the door. Before opening it, he smiled at me and said, 'You know, they will work you harder than I do in New York — when you appear on Broadway.'

'Good,' I said, returning his smile. 'I look forward to it.'

My busy schedule made the rest of 1925 fly by. While André and Mademoiselle Canier made trips back and forth between Paris and Berlin, I performed at the White Horse Cabaret on the Kurfürstendamm. It was a small, smoky theatre but the clientele was chic: actors and actresses, bankers and business tycoons. As the night wore on, the pieces became raunchier and the dancing more lurid. In Paris, we alluded to sex and teased about it with our innuendos, but the German singers blatantly referred to masturbation and homosexuality. The lyrics to the songs I sang at the White Horse contained the occasional allusion to 'rubbing the magic lamp', but Ulla Färber, the raspy-voiced star of the show, belted out a number called '*Der Orgasmus*'.

If the Count hadn't warned me that Berliners were obsessed with sex and death, or I hadn't seen for myself the rawness of life on Friedrichstrasse, the vulgarity of my fellow performers might have overwhelmed me. Instead, I studied them with the keen eye of a scientist looking down a microscope at a newly discovered protozoan. I noted how the buxom Ada Godard, who wore a monocle and feather boa, dominated her audience with her wit, and how the chorus girls thrust out their naked breasts like weapons rather than objects of desire. Their ability to shock even the most decadent Berliners wouldn't work for my style. But I did become more confident and learnt to weave the audience into my web from the moment I stepped on stage. I did this by lowering my voice an octave and consciously slowing my speech. It had much more impact than my method at the Casino de Paris, which was to rush out on stage and hope that they liked me.

After the performance, the cabaret transformed into a nightclub. One night when I was out on the floor by myself, dancing the black bottom for the amusement of a table of bankers, I noticed an elegant woman in a white dress with a corsage of violets watching me. I found myself drawn to her like a pin towards a magnet. The band slowed to a tango as if she had willed it do so with her hypnotic eyes.

'You are beautiful,' she told me in French, her fingers lingering on her swanlike throat.

The woman took my hand in hers and hooked her other hand around my back. She was smaller than me, but she led me in the tango with the strength of a man. There was a steely coldness about her that reminded me of Camille, but when she pressed her chest to mine I realised that she wasn't wearing any undergarments and was taken aback by the softness of female flesh pressed against my own breasts. It was like hugging my mother, and yet not like that at all.

'You are like a feather,' she said to me. 'I could crush you in my fingers.' The woman was a skilful dancer who interpreted the music well. She seemed vaguely familiar to me, but I had no idea where I might have seen her.

When the dance finished, I thanked the woman and slipped from her arms, secretly wishing André was there to protect me. I did not usually find women approaching me threatening. And if the woman was beautiful, I sometimes even found it flattering. But something about this woman made me uncomfortable. I felt her eyes on my back the entire way to the bar.

'I see you have escaped the clutches of Marlene Dietrich,' said Ada, sidling up to me when I ordered some soda water. She laughed bawdily. 'You would be a marvellous act together, both on and off the stage. Your French charm and vivacity and her blonde aloofness.'

So, I had danced the tango with the famous Marlene Dietrich and not even known it. 'On the stage, perhaps,' I replied, glancing over my shoulder. But Marlene was gone.

⟨⟨⟩⟩

Count Kessler took me to Ciro's for dinner one evening, when André was in Paris with Mademoiselle Canier for his mother's annual charity ball. I enjoyed the Count's company whenever we went out. Although he was an aristocrat, there was something about him that reminded me of my father. Perhaps it was the curiosity that sparkled in his eyes, as if the wonders of the world could never grow dim in his sight.

After we had ordered our food, the Count turned to me and said, 'I think André is growing weary of Mademoiselle Canier, don't you? Let us hope he doesn't bring her back with him.'

The Count must have noticed my shocked expression because he let out a hearty laugh. 'Come now,' he said, 'admit it. You would rather spend a week in a stalled railcar than an hour with Mademoiselle Canier. I see how you politely suffer her. God, I've seen how *André* politely suffers her. She is like one of those stunning pieces of furniture you buy when you are in a foreign country. It has no practical purpose so you put it on display in a corner and after a while you cease to notice it.'

'But he is in love with her,' I said, remembering André's fond glances in Mademoiselle Canier's direction.

The Count regarded me with amused interest. 'You think so?' he said. 'She is the daughter of one of his mother's friends. Mind you, she is not any more empty-headed than the other girls in his circle. André probably made the best choice he could have ... at the time.'

The Count gave me such a pointed look that I blushed. I sensed that he saw right through me and my feelings for André. 'You are being callous,' I protested.

'Hah!' he laughed again. 'Don't think Mademoiselle Canier's feelings will be hurt. André is merely at the top of her list of eligible bachelors. She will move on to Antoine Marchais, one of the Michelins or the Bouchayer boy without blinking an eye.'

I wondered if what the Count said was true. He and André were close, so the Count, if anybody, would know what André's real feelings were.

'If I ask you something, Count Harry, will you kept it a secret and not make fun of me?'

'Make fun of you, Mademoiselle Fleurier?' the Count replied, feigning a scandalised expression. 'Never!'

'Do you think ... I mean ... would it be possible ... for two very unlikely ...'

I had muddled my beginning and now could not bring myself to finish my sentence. I suddenly realised how ridiculous it would be to declare my feelings. I was a music hall singer. André was the son of a powerful family. There was no reason why we should not mingle socially, but beyond that ... No, anything else was impossible.

'Mademoiselle Fleurier,' said the Count, tapping my arm, 'you haven't finished your question. You have me in suspense now. Two very unlikely what?'

I had dug myself into a hole and now I was going to have to climb out of it. 'Two very unlikely ... I mean ... Germany and France, for instance. Will they always be enemies?'

The Count seemed to find me funny at that moment, but he sat up straight and answered me seriously. 'The French and Germans have more in common than anybody else,' he said. 'During the Great War, the men in the trenches used to throw food to each other when the fighting for the day had ceased. No, the next time Germany decides to cause an international disaster it will be due to self-combustion. The most dangerous enemy is always the enemy within.'

I glanced at him. Why was it whenever anyone spoke about the future of Germany, it was in terms of another war?

'Now that the middle classes have been turned out of their homes and we have made beggars of small businessmen, who will keep Germany stable?' the Count asked.

The ominous warning in his words sent a shudder through me. I played with the bread on my plate. I knew that as long as I lived I would never forget that starving girl's face. Seeing first-hand what humans were capable of doing to each other had changed me. But what could I do about such suffering? The problem seemed overwhelming. I looked at the Count again. He was smiling.

'In answer to your *other* question, Mademoiselle Fleurier,' he said, 'let me say this. You are unusually self-possessed. One rarely sees that in someone your age and even more rarely among entertainers. You would make a more suitable companion for a certain young man than anyone else I know. Why, if I were thirty years younger, I would marry you myself.'

I leaned across the table and gave the Count a kiss on his cheek. I knew he was lying about the second part. He was Germany's most resolutely confirmed bachelor.

❧

The Count was correct in his prediction that André would break off his relationship with Mademoiselle Canier and return to Berlin alone. I didn't press André for information and he offered no explanation. But if I had thought that the elimination of Mademoiselle Canier would make any difference to André's feelings for me, I was sorely disappointed. If anything, André became more distant, treating me the way one business partner would treat another, warmly but professionally. He never spoke to me about his brother or of his feelings about his family again. After a few sleepless nights, I resigned myself to the fact that André Blanchard and I were never going to be anything more than friends. And, to take my mind off my disappointment, I threw myself into my work schedule.

André, Count Kessler and I welcomed in the New Year by attending a party hosted by Karl Vollmoeller, the playwright.

'Vollmoeller throws bizarre parties,' the Count warned me on our way from the Adlon to the Pariser Platz, where Vollmoeller lived. 'He invites his publisher and the Berlin theatre crowd, then he goes about in a taxi collecting any eccentric he can find "to add a bit of spice".'

'At his last party,' André added, 'I had Kurt Weill on my left and some nut Vollmoeller had picked up outside the Charité Hospital on my right. The whole night he wouldn't stop talking about the rate at which different parts of the human body decay.'

'Vollmoeller's girlfriend is attractive though,' said the Count.

'What is her first name?' asked André. 'Vollmoeller only addresses her as Fräulein Landshoff.'

The Count shrugged. 'If I ever knew, I have forgotten. She is the niece of Samuel Fischer, the publisher.'

We passed some children who were lighting firecrackers and sending them shooting up into the air. Golden sparks sprinkled across the sky with a succession of bangs that were louder than shots from a gun. I thought of Kira back in my hotel room. I had left her a saucer of milk and some chicken, but she would probably spend the night hiding under the bed.

Vollmoeller's party was under way by the time we arrived. Around the edges of the room, pushed to the sides like the furniture, stood men in evening suits and women with diamond earrings and matching necklaces — the kind of people you might find dining at Maxim's in Paris or taking in a show at the Moulin Rouge. But in the middle of the room, writhing around to jazz music from a gramophone, was a mass of naked bodies. In the middle of this orgy a petite woman danced on top of a coffee table. She wore a man's dinner jacket and a pair of horn-rimmed spectacles.

'There is Fräulein Landshoff,' said the Count.

'Where is Vollmoeller?' asked André. The Count shrugged.

A woman brushed past us wearing nothing but a string of pearls and a smile on her face. She was followed by a man with horns on his head and a horse's tail tied to his behind. I watched their buttocks wobble through the crowd before they disappeared into another room.

'Can I get you anything?' the Count asked us. 'Champagne? Beer? Cocaine?'

André and I settled for champagne.

A trio of boys was sprawled on a sofa near the door. Every so often, one of the dignified men would walk past and a few minutes later one of the youths would get up and follow him out. I thought about what the Count had said about Germany self-combusting one day, and about the poverty that lurked in Berlin's dark corners beyond the hedonism on display in this room. I also remembered the Count's comment that the Germans and the French had much in common. Didn't we also wash away our fears with fine champagne and lose ourselves in eroticism? I blinked the thoughts away and turned back to the party. What good would it do to worry about these things? I couldn't change anything. I had one life to live — I might as well enjoy it, I told myself. But the sensation that we were all teetering on the edge of an abyss niggled at me.

The Count returned with our drinks — not champagne but a potent German punch called *Feuerzangenbowle*. It was made of warmed sweet wine, orange and lemon juice and spiced with cinnamon and cloves. A stocky man with electric blue eyes and waves of grey hair sidled up to us.

'This is Max Reinhardt,' the Count said.

'The Count has been telling me that you are a talented young woman,' Reinhardt said to me in his rumbling Viennese accent. 'Perhaps one day you will come to my acting school and become a great actress.'

I was more amazed at having one of the most famous directors in Europe kiss my hand than I was by the naked people wriggling around me. But after a glass of *Feuerzangenbowle,* I was incapable of sensible conversation.

'Well, after she has conquered Paris, New York and the rest of the world with her singing and dancing, I don't see why Mademoiselle Fleurier shouldn't act as well,' André told Reinhardt.

At a quarter to midnight some of the guests braved the cold and ran out into the square to watch the fireworks created by the students from Humboldt University's chemistry department. The Count suggested that we stay in the apartment and watch from the windows. 'It is too cold out there and I am in no mood to lose an eye. At least one of those students manages to blow up himself — or some bystander — each year.'

Fräulein Landshoff — there was still no sign of Vollmoeller — instructed everybody to turn off the lights and blow out the candles. We huddled around the windows and counted down to midnight in unison. Just as the students let off the most impressive of their explosions, sending sparks whizzing by the glass, a body pressed close to mine. Hands grabbed my elbows then spun me around. I was crushed against a man's chest. His breath skimmed over my forehead then warm lips pressed against mine. From the height of the person and the clean smell of his skin, I was sure that it must be André. But before I could think whether to kiss him back or not, the person let go and the room was lit up by a brilliant green flare. Fräulein Landshoff cried out that she had dropped her glasses and someone turned on a lamp to help her find them. I looked around for André; he was with the Count at the window furthest away from me. I stared at the other men standing nearby. They were all tall and wearing evening suits. It could have been any one of them.

André glanced in my direction and lifted his champagne glass. I couldn't read the meaning of his smile.

❧

In January, André returned from a trip to Paris with good news. The impresario of the Adriana was planning a spectacle on a scale never seen before in the capital and was looking for someone sensational to star in it. He needed something novel to compete against the Folies Bergère, which was having unprecedented success with Joséphine Baker, and the Moulin Rouge, which was staging its most grandiose revue yet, 'Ça C'est Paris', with Mistinguett. The impresario had considered Camille or Cécile Sorel, but since André had talked to him about me, he wanted to meet me as soon as possible. We had to leave immediately.

Count Kessler came to see us off at the station. 'Remember me when you are a star!' he said, kissing my cheeks. I smiled to think how formal he had been when I first met him and how close we were now.

We had been having farewell drinks with Max Reinhardt and my teachers, and now we were running late. The porter sprinted ahead with our luggage, but the platform was crowded. André lifted Kira's cage onto his shoulder. We had just stepped through the platform gate when a man with bloodshot eyes thrust some pamphlets into our hands. 'Liberate Germany from the Jewish scum! They are destroying the country!' he shouted.

I was too taken aback to react, but the Count grabbed the pamphlets from the man's hands and ripped them to pieces.

'Liberate Germany from ignorant scum like you! You are the ones who will destroy the country!' the Count yelled at him.

The man screamed something back that I didn't understand. André pulled the Count away.

The porter called out to us: our luggage was on board but we still had to make the train. André and I clambered up the steps as the whistle sounded and the train started moving off.

'I shall see you both in Paris, soon,' the Count called, walking beside the train as it gathered speed. 'I'll come to see Simone star in her show!'

I blew him a kiss. He blew one back and his mouth twitched. A gleam of light flickered over him. For a moment I saw my father standing by the farmhouse, waving to me. But in a blink of an eye the image was gone and the Count was there again, waving to me from the platform. 'Goodbye, my sweet Simone,' he called out. 'Goodbye, André!'

A mist of steam blurred him from view. 'Goodbye, Count,' I called through the smoky shadow. A sense of gloom fell over me, but I shrugged it away and followed André to our compartment.

NINETEEN

The Adriana on the Champs Élysées was Paris's most modern music hall and its impresario, Regis Lebaron, one of the most daring entrepreneurs in Europe. Set back from the other nineteenth-century buildings on the avenue, the theatre's entrance was a chrome arch with columns on either side. The façade was opaque glass and in the foyer four figures representing Zeus, Aphrodite, Iris and Apollo held up giant globes of light. The decor was a blend of the ultra modern with Greek mythology and the seats in the auditorium were equipped with head and armrests. The chairs were said to be so comfortable that copies of them were found in many fashionable houses.

Lebaron, who had made his first fortune at the roulette table and his second as an impresario, spared no expense when it came to hiring the best. He used Italian scenic artists to create lavish palaces and Russian émigrés to recreate Tsarist ballrooms and courts. His technicians were British or American and his costumiers were French. The Adriana had been the first music hall to incorporate the medium of film into a show, using it as a backdrop to some of the dance numbers. Lebaron's personal motto was 'Better than the best' and he strove to make each show even more spectacular than his last triumphant success. Only now, according to André, there was a danger that the best of the best was running out of steam. It was going to be hard to match Paris's long-time favourite, Mistinguett, and its newest star, Joséphine Baker. Camille was the next biggest female star in Paris, but as Lebaron had said to André: 'Being beautiful will only take you so far and the novelty is starting to wear thin. I want to launch someone new.'

I had never thought the day would come when anybody would consider me over Camille Casal. She never seemed to doubt herself; her calm behaviour before the Casino de Paris shows confirmed that. To me that was the sign of a true star: absolute confidence in yourself.

I glanced at André who was leaning back in his train seat. The sun shining through the birch trees outside the window flickered stripes across his face so that he looked like a character in a film. He was puffing on a cigarette, the fourth he had smoked since we had left Potsdammer Station an hour before.

'Lebaron says that if you are half as good as I say you are, and twice as good as you were when you were at the Casino, he will take you on. He will make *you* the star. The comedian will get second billing.' André stood and rested his arm against the glass. 'Do you understand what that means, Simone? No more waiting in line and working your way up. You will be there!'

My heart dived into my stomach. I hadn't even auditioned yet. It was a long way to fall if I failed. I had been driven to work hard in Berlin not only by my own ambition but out of a burning desire to please André. I knew better than to express any doubts now. He had put himself on the line to get me an audition and, although he smiled at me, his face was tense. In many ways, my debut was André's debut, and that scared me. Perhaps the reality of what we had been aiming for was finally dawning on us.

André's driver met us at the station. It was drizzling and the buildings and cafés were cloaked in grey. It was strange to be back in Paris after being away for almost two years. The streets and the shops looked the same, but I was a different person, although I didn't quite understand that yet. We drove straight to the Étoile Quarter, only this time it wasn't a shabby *hôtel particulier* we pulled up in front of but an apartment building opposite the park.

'I hope you like it,' said André, searching in his pocket for the key. While he turned the lock I lifted Kira out of her cage. She fled into the apartment before André or I could get in and ran to the leopard-skin chair in the hall, the only piece of furniture that was familiar.

André put my suitcases inside the door and led me to the drawing room. The floor was inlaid with wood of different hues and my eye followed the lines of the rosewood furniture and the honey-coloured walls.

'I was intending to move here myself,' he said. 'But it is a nice apartment for a woman and I can find another place. Once you are a star, the press will want to come and photograph you here.'

The sofas and armchairs were strewn with oriental pillows and fur throws. The decor was sleek with touches of originality — everything André thought I should be.

André moved to the corner of the room and pulled up the blinds to reveal a round corner window that looked towards the park and the street. Even with the overcast weather, light streamed in through the panes.

'You can sit here when you want to read or learn your lines,' he said.

I followed him to the bedroom which was decorated in the same mixture of beiges, russets and blacks as the rest of the apartment. André threw a switch and light glowed from behind shards of crystal glass on the walls.

'I like it,' I said.

I thought the apartment was beautiful but I wasn't as awed by it as I would have been a few years earlier. I had grown accustomed to luxury at the Adlon and to having my needs taken care of by André. It did not occur to me that I was becoming spoilt, it had happened gradually.

Kira pattered after us, sniffing around the floorboards and the furniture.

'Your maid will come tomorrow,' said André, resting his hands on my shoulders. 'Now, try to rest and I will come back to pick you up at two o'clock.'

He is good to you, Simone, but he does not love you, I reminded myself.

I was so numb with nerves that I hardly felt André's lips when he kissed me goodbye. I shut the door and the burn of bile rose up my throat. I had been excited when we left Berlin, but now that my meeting with Regis Lebaron was only a couple of hours away, I was stricken with panic. I walked back into the drawing room and my eye fell on the drinks cabinet. I swung the door open and found a decanter of brandy. Perhaps a drink would calm me. I opened the stopper and sniffed the burnt sugar aroma. No, I thought, remembering how I hadn't been able to make decent conversation with Max Reinhardt after a glass of *Feuerzangenbowle*.

I sank onto the sofa and stared at the painting above the fireplace: a jaguar creeping through the jungle. A maid? I looked around at the glossy surfaces. You would need one here to wipe away the fingerprints. I remembered the roughly hewn furniture in my parents' farmhouse and the oak table in Aunt Yvette's kitchen. We wiped down the kitchen table after each meal and beat out the bed linen, but we rarely got around to polishing or dusting anything more than twice a year.

I stood up and moved to the bureau and opened the drawers. There were sheets of writing paper and a pen. I sat down and began a letter to my mother, Aunt Yvette and Bernard, telling them that I was back from Berlin and was now living in a big apartment, so they should come and visit me in Paris because it would be a while before I could get away to visit them.

I glanced out the window towards the rainy street. I remembered my mother in her farm dress with the silver fox fur I had bought her around her neck.

I folded my arms and rested my head on them. Pressure bore down on me and I could hear the blood humming in my ears. Loneliness, stronger than I had ever experienced before, clutched my heart. I was heading down a tunnel and there was no one to help me. I hadn't quite grasped it yet, but a new Simone Fleurier was being born.

I had worked myself into such a state by the time André came to collect me that I was afraid I might be sick in his car. I was careful to hide my anxiety, however, and my misgivings proved ridiculous when my 'audition' with Regis Lebaron and his artistic director, Martin Meyer, turned out to be nothing like those I had gone through at the Casino de Paris or the Folies Bergère.

André and I were greeted by two gentlemen in almost identical navy blue suits with brilliantined hair and cravats knotted at their throats. The taller of the two was Regis Lebaron; I recognised him from his photographs and those bulging golden eyes and thin lips. He was often described as bearing a resemblance to a frog, but the comparison told nothing of his exuberant personality. Martin Meyer was introduced by his nickname, Minot, a pet name given to him by school friends which had stayed with him through the years. He was slim with a cleft in his chin and seemed to have difficulty keeping his hands still. They opened and closed and reached towards all corners of the room when he told me how excited he was to meet me. They were temporarily stilled by a reproachful glance from Lebaron, after which Minot stuffed his hands into his pockets, only to have them escape again a few seconds later to form a theatrical gesture towards the auditorium doors. 'This way, please,' he said, ushering us inside.

The auditorium was dark except for the stage which was lit by floodlights and a spotlight beaming down onto its centre. André took my coat and laid it over one of the seats. I noticed Lebaron look me up and down and was pleased when a smile curved his lips. After various beauty treatments, make-up by Helena Rubenstein and having my hair trained into a sleek bob, I had hoped he would like what he saw.

There was a rehearsal piano near the stage but no pianist. I clutched my portfolio of music, hoping that one would arrive soon so we could get the ordeal over with. To my surprise, Minot took my music from me and flicked through the sheets. 'Oh, I do like this one,' he said, pointing to one of Vincent Scotto's pieces. 'When you sang it at the Casino, it brought tears to my eyes.'

'She has come a long way since then,' said André. 'She can really make her voice reach now, and dance without losing her breath.'

A door opened and a waiter sauntered in with a bottle of champagne in an ice bucket and some glasses on a tray. Lebaron instructed him to leave them on the stage. 'We'll get to them in a minute,' he said, then turning to me, he added, 'I already know that you have one of the best voices in Paris. I saw you at the Casino and cursed myself that I hadn't found you first. They were wasting you there. What I want to know is what we can do with your act.'

'Well, she's had dance lessons with two of the best teachers in Berlin,' André said. 'I have brought some records. Perhaps we can show you?'

Lebaron clutched his chin in his hand and glanced at André. 'I know she can dance too. Another year and they would have had to replace Rivarola with a better partner. You are forgetting that spotting talent has been my *forté* for years. What I want to know is how we can showcase her.'

André and I exchanged glances. I was about to say something but André put up his hand to stop me. If I had spoken, I would have asked Lebaron if that meant he had made up his mind to hire me. But it was apparent that he already had. Somewhere between talking to André and meeting me, he must have decided to take the risk. My heart lit up. It was as if the backdrop had changed and suddenly I was in a new scene. For the first time I didn't have to prove that I had talent or even that I was attractive enough. Those were being taken as a given.

'Perhaps Mademoiselle Fleurier would not mind to stand in the spotlight a moment,' said Minot, sweeping his hand towards the stage.

I did as he asked. I felt as if I were standing in a ray of sunshine, although my legs were trembling with all the adrenaline I had worked up. Lebaron and Minot moved around me shouting ideas to each other.

'I see a storm scene and the sky opening,' cried Minot. 'Then celestial beings ... No, Greek gods and goddesses moving up and down the staircase.'

'When they reach the bottom they will turn their reversible costumes and become flappers and young men arriving at a chic club,' said Lebaron, glancing from me to the rest of the stage as if the scene were unfolding before his eyes.

'Then the most beautiful girl of all will arrive,' said Minot, pulling me forward. 'And she will sing the opening song.'

Lebaron held his hands in the air. 'The posters will read: *Simone Fleurier, the most sensational woman in the world*.'

I looked to André who was beaming at me from a front row seat. Lebaron and Minot had already decided they needed a legend and I had enough talent to satisfy them. They were going to fuse legend and talent to create a star. And that star was going to be me.

❦

The preparations for the *'Bonjour Paris! C'est Moi!'* show were a trial by fire for me. As a key performer at the Casino de Paris all that had been expected of me was to turn up for rehearsals and costume fittings and to do my best in the performance. But now, as the star of a major production, I was involved in everything from the selection of the supporting acts, to the choice of the tableaux, to the poster design. I had to be, because everything revolved around me. I realised this fully at the auditions for the chorus girls.

'They will all be blonde,' exclaimed Minot, fanning his hands towards me. 'So that you stand out like a gorgeous black pearl.'

André was to be the co-producer for the show and had the task of overseeing everything from the sets and costumes to the stage machinery. Lebaron intended the tableaux of 'Bonjour Paris! C'est Moi!' to be the most sumptuous Paris had ever seen: they would include a ball at Versailles and a jungle scene with live monkeys and a tiger. One afternoon I visited André in his office at the theatre and found him studying the scaled models of each set complete with moveable flats and curtains for the changes of scene. He looked as happy as a boy playing with a train set.

'The engineer says he can design a waterfall,' André told me, pointing to the jungle set where I was represented by a cardboard doll.

André was a good choice for a co-producer because he worked thirty-six hours out of twenty-four and his energy and enthusiasm spread to the designers and carpenters, who were all trying to outdo each other to make the most spectacular sets possible.

'If you can do that, I think it will be a first for the Paris stage,' I told him.

'I have to prove to my father that my "special project" has been worth all the time and money I have lavished on it,' he laughed.

I assumed that he was teasing, but the joke hurt. It hadn't been easy for me to adjust to thinking of André as nothing more than my patron and friend. I managed to accept that he had never found me attractive, and that I had been misled. At least I had saved myself the humiliation of declaring my feelings. But acceptance of André's lack of interest did not prevent my own feelings from ambushing me from time to time. Even with both our noses to the grindstone, the sound of André's voice could make my heart flutter.

Sometimes I found some of the minor acts kissing backstage and once, when I was standing near the air vent in my dressing room, I heard the ecstatic sounds of a man and woman making love somewhere in the theatre. I pressed my ear to the hole, enthralled by the moans, pants and sighs. A throb burned in my belly but I could only dream what those touches might be like. I closed my eyes and imagined running my hands through André's hair and feeling his naked flesh melt into mine. But when such thoughts occurred I would splash my face with cold water or dab my temples with cologne. It was no use cherishing a desire that could never be fulfilled. I thought I was old for my age, and I was certainly older than the average music hall virgin, but André treated me with the familiar sweetness of a brother doting on his little sister.

I certainly felt like a 'special project' the first time I walked past Galeries Lafayette and saw my face looming on a billboard above Boulevard Haussmann. '*For skin as smooth as Simone Fleurier's use Le Chat Soap.*' Was that girl wrapped in a satin dress and clutching a wide-eyed, diamond-collared Kira to her bosom really me? André had arranged for me to represent several products as pre-publicity for the show and I appeared in advertisements for Helena Rubenstein cosmetics and Rivoire & Carret pasta. I eyed the Le Chat advertisement with suspicion. The girl's hair was glossy and smooth, her lips were rouged with dark lipstick and her eyes rimmed in kohl. She wasn't the person I felt inside. I was still treading on tiptoe, waiting for the chorus girls to turn on me and declare that I was a gawky comedian who belonged at the end of the line. But the success of the advertisements belied those doubts. Sales for all three products doubled in the first month. I was on the verge of stardom. All that I had dreamed of and had worked for was coming to fruition. Why, then, did I feel so lonely?

'We have an invitation,' said André, holding up a white card. 'Mother is keen to be in on my surprise for my father. She told me that in order to bring you the best audience we have to get you into the social pages. She has invited you to her enclosure at Longchamps. She says if a beautiful but unknown lady is seen at the races with Madame Blanchard, everyone is going to want to know who she is. But first I have to introduce you to her.'

❧

André and I arrived at his family's townhouse on Avenue Marceau the following morning for coffee and cake with Madame Blanchard.

Staying at the Adlon and dining at fine restaurants had smoothed out my country manners, and the Vionnet dress I wore did not make me look out of place on the granite portico where André and I waited for the butler to open the door. But as soon as I laid eyes on the foyer with its marble staircase, fountain and portraits by Gainsborough, I was thrown. The Adlon was a poor cousin compared to the Blanchard residence. I did my best not to gape at the swagged valances and oriental carpets, at the candelabras with their bronze roses or the dark wood furniture with its accents of gold. The house was everything the residence of a powerful European family should be: it was imbued with age and permanence. And it was intimidating.

Madame Blanchard was waiting for us in her parlour with André's younger sister, Veronique. His mother had pouch-like cheeks and was as blonde as a Swede. André had inherited his height and colouring from his father.

'My dear, you are as lovely as André described you,' Madame Blanchard said, taking my hand and guiding me to a chair upholstered in blue brocade. The curtains and sconces were turquoise, and everywhere I looked I saw tones of lapis lazuli and gold offset by vases of white orchids. The effect was like standing in an exotic seashell. The room was refreshingly different to the sombre tone of the rest of the house.

For some reason, Madame Blanchard had omitted introducing Veronique, but the girl was not going to be ignored. She rose from her seat, tossed her red hair over her shoulders and announced herself in a prepubescent voice, adding that I seemed 'much nicer than Mademoiselle Canier'.

'Veronique!' exclaimed Madame Blanchard, trying to suppress a smile. 'Compliment Mademoiselle Fleurier, by all means, but do not insult anybody else to do it.'

Next to me was a skirted table with a picture frame on it. The figure in the photograph was broad-shouldered and handsome in his officer's uniform. But the eyes had the soulful look of an artist, not a soldier. I glanced at the case of war medals on the shelf above. There was no need to ask who the man in the picture was.

I was conscious of Madame Blanchard watching me and turned to her. Although she did not refer to the picture, something in her eyes told me that she was pleased I had noticed it.

'The fashion writer from *L'Illustration* will do something on

Mademoiselle Fleurier,' she said, nodding to André. 'Talent is one thing; publicity quite another.' Then, once the maid had poured the coffee and served us each a slice of chocolate torte, she added, 'Mademoiselle Fleurier needs to be seen and photographed at the right places before opening night. And Longchamps tomorrow is an opportunity too good to miss.'

A Pomeranian puppy wandered into the room and took a seat under Veronique's chair. The girl bent down and fed him a piece of cake on her finger. I thought of how my family used to feed Olly like that, but the rustic kitchen in Pays de Sault was worlds away from Madame Blanchard's elegant parlour.

'Tell me about yourself, Mademoiselle Fleurier,' Madame Blanchard said. 'So you started your career in Marseilles?'

I explained to her about my family's lavender farm, my father's death and Le Chat Espiègle. Madame Blanchard listened carefully to my account of my humble origins and did not seem put off by them in the slightest. If anything she was impressed by my determination to succeed.

While Madame Blanchard and I made small talk, André spoke with his sister. Their voices had the affectionate ease of a history of childhood games and shared secrets. When Veronique finished her slice of cake, André cut her another piece, despite his mother's good-humoured scowl. I remembered what André had said about Veronique being the rebel in the family and I hoped that her father would not crush the girl's lively spirit — or André's either. Monsieur Blanchard was away on business in Switzerland, but I felt his dominating presence in the portrait above the fireplace. I knew who it was because he looked just like André, only sterner. I thought the family patriarch was an unusual choice for Madame Blanchard's parlour. Even when Monsieur Blanchard was not there, he seemed to be watching over the order of the house.

'My children are each so different,' said Madame Blanchard. 'Everything shows on Veronique's face, whether she is happy or displeased. André is another matter entirely. You can never tell what he is thinking. With him it is true that still waters run deep.'

We stayed with André's mother and sister for an hour. When we stood up to leave, Madame Blanchard placed her hand on my shoulder. 'I like you,' she whispered. 'You are not at all what I imagined.'

I liked Madame Blanchard too. I thought her kind and sincere. But there was a niggling doubt in her voice that made me afraid. I sensed that André's father would not be so easy to please.

~∞~

My contract with the Adriana included part of my performance fee upfront. As André was taking care of my material needs, I sent half of the fee to Bernard so that he could improve the farm. Then I went to see Joseph at the furniture store.

'Mademoiselle Fleurier,' he greeted me. 'Odette didn't tell me you were coming. Are you after something special?'

Ever since I had returned from Germany, I had noticed how forlorn Odette looked because her twenty-first birthday had come and gone and she and Joseph were still not married. Joseph was successful in his job with the furniture store but he hadn't been able to put aside enough capital for his own business. Without it, Odette's father would not give them permission to marry.

'My parents like Joseph very much,' Odette explained. 'But they want to make sure that he can support me. And Uncle agrees with them.'

I had to hide my smile. Odette had expensive tastes, even her middle-class parents discerned that. If Joseph did not have a good income, she would send him broke in a year.

'I want to help you set up your own store,' I told Joseph. 'I have a cheque for you in my bag.'

Joseph's eyes opened wide and he shook his head. 'No, Mademoiselle Fleurier, I can't ask that of you.'

'You are not asking,' I told him. 'I am giving it to you. Odette has been a good friend to me and I want you to marry her and make her happy.'

Joseph's shoulders relaxed and he beckoned me into his office.

'I do want to marry Odette,' he said, pulling out a chair for me. 'But I would be ashamed of myself if I were in debt. So I must refuse.'

'Don't be silly,' I told him. 'You won't be in debt. One day, when you are successful, you can furnish my family's farmhouse in Provence. They have simple tastes but I would like them to have some beautiful things too.'

Joseph's eyes lit up. 'It would give me great pleasure to do that. I could make a trip to Provence especially to buy what was needed.'

'So it is settled then?' I said, rising from my chair. 'I don't see any need for us to tell Odette what we have discussed.'

Tears filled Joseph's eyes. He was a sweet man and I was sure that he would be a good husband. 'You have no idea how happy you have made me,' he said. 'If Odette and I have a daughter, we will name her after you.'

'I would be honoured,' I said. 'But I don't hold you to that.'

I caught a taxi back to my apartment with joy in my heart. At first I had thought money could only be used to buy things, but now I realised that it could bring happiness too.

❦

By the end of March everyone was working full throttle, the accelerator of the show stuck fast to the floor. It usually took Lebaron and Minot six to ten months to prepare for a new spectacle, but, with André's help, they had almost done it in three. 'Almost' because by the time the final orchestrations of the songs had been completed, some of the dance tempos needed to be changed. There were also still costume alterations to be done and some of the sets needed amendments to work with schedule changes. Tempers flared. One of the electricians stormed out and a seamstress collapsed from exhaustion. Odette came along to help with the costumes and I developed even more respect for my friend after seeing her day after day with a needle in her hand and thread between her teeth, telling everyone, 'Calm down. It will all come together in the end.'

My dress for the finale was still tacked on a dressmaker's dummy in the workroom. I offered to help finish it but Minot opened his eyes in horror. 'No, no, no, Mademoiselle Fleurier! You must save your energy. You are the star. This show rides on your wings.'

I had been hoping to turn my mind to something else to settle my nerves. The show 'riding on my wings' was what caused me to have night sweats and dizzy spells. I didn't tell a soul about the panic attacks. The first one came after the book had been written and the scores composed. I was in my apartment going over some lyrics when my heart began to palpitate. I tried to focus on the score but my mind spun and everything turned white. The only way I could get rid of the nauseous feeling was to hide the score under a pillow. After that, I could only rehearse in the company of someone else, usually André or Minot.

'I can't memorise anything unless I am performing for someone,' I laughed, hiding my terror behind my smile.

With the strain everyone was under to put together the best show yet in half the time, I couldn't afford to dampen anyone's spirit or make them doubt me. I realised that the pressure I had felt at the Casino de Paris and Le Chat Espiègle had only been 'butterflies'. The stakes were much higher now. If the audience didn't respond, I would be taking a lot of people down with me.

It didn't help my state of mind when, in the last week of rehearsals before opening night, Lebaron lurked about the sets when I practised my numbers, wearing the expression of a condemned man. Even worse, by the last day he was shaking his head as if he had made a terrible mistake in taking a gamble on me.

'Ignore it,' whispered Minot, patting my shoulder. 'He is always like that at this time. It is his superstition. He thinks that if he tells you how fabulous you are, he will jinx the whole show.'

⬿

On opening night, I arrived at the theatre at half-past seven with Kira, my good luck mascot. André had sent his car but hadn't been able to come himself due to a last-minute change with a support act. My dressing room was filled with roses and there was a bottle of champagne in an ice bucket. Attached to the neck was a card from Minot which read: 'We shall be drinking this at midnight, my lovely!' Dear, sweet Minot. He thought of everything. He had even sent out a memo that I was not to be disturbed by anyone and all messages were to be conveyed to me either by the stage manager or himself. Although I was concerned this might put me in the same petty tyrant league as Jacques Noir, I appreciated it. I needed to gather my thoughts. Kira sensed my jumpiness. During the rehearsals she had slept on a blanket near the heater or amused herself by swiping my cosmetic pencils from the bench. But now she was hiding under my dressing table and refusing to come out. I couldn't blame her. If I could have, I would have done the same thing.

My hand trembled when I opened my greasepaint tin. My eyes were watering, something they always did when I was anxious. I stretched my head back and closed them, willing myself to relax. The previous night I had dreamt that I had gone on stage and forgotten the words to the opening song, which would have been ridiculous because there were so few of them.

After all the chaos and bustle of the previous weeks, the theatre was eerily quiet. I imagined everybody at their posts: dressers laying out costumes and counting wigs; the stagehands checking props and light switches; the musicians warming up their fingers or drinking their last-minute coffees.

My dresser was scheduled to come at eight o'clock. As soon as the hands of the clock on my bench struck the hour, there was a knock at the door. I opened it to find Odette holding up my dress for the first number. 'I thought you might need some moral support,' she said. 'From someone who hasn't yet turned purple in the face.'

'What's happened?' I asked.

'One of the chorus girls has put on weight and burst out of her costume.'

'They hardly wear anything,' I said. 'What could have burst?'

'A row of beads. But it was enough to send the wardrobe mistress into a fit.'

Although I didn't hear half of what Odette said about Joseph's purchase of a furniture store and how they were planning to marry the following year, her happy chatter soothed me like the sound of a record playing in the background. And she was patient too. I had to get out of my costume once she had hooked me into it for one more 'nervous pee'. By half-past eight I could hear the callboy knocking on the dressing room doors and a few minutes later the chorus girls tromping down the stairs. They weren't as boisterous as usual and I asked Odette if there was something wrong.

'No,' she said. 'That is in deference to you. Monsieur Minot ordered quiet on the stairs.'

When the callboy knocked on my door I almost jumped out of my costume again. Odette patted me on the back. 'You will be wonderful,' she said. 'Just do what you have been doing in the rehearsals and everything will be fine.'

I followed the callboy to the flies with the same cheer Marie Antoinette must have felt heading towards the guillotine. I could hear the string section warming up and the hubbub of the audience. 'Good luck!' the boy whispered to me. I ruffled his hair so he would know that I wasn't a stuck-up diva, I was just too nervous to speak. The key dancers were lined up at the top of the stairs, ready to make their entrance before me. The chorus girls were bunched up in the wings. A couple of them sent me cheerful smiles. I did my best to grimace back.

At a quarter to nine the *trois coups* — the three thumps of the staff on the stage to signify the show was about to begin — sounded. The audience fell silent and the orchestra started up. I beat my fist against the lump in my chest. My blood was humming in my ears.

The stage manager gave the cue and I watched the row of dancers move forward. They descended into the flood of light, their eyes ablaze, their faces glowing. Other celestial beings were lowered to the stage on glass platforms like genies on magic carpets. For a moment I forgot my nerves, everything looked so beautiful. The audience must have thought so too; I could hear their 'oohs' and 'ahhs' rising up towards me.

The music changed tempo and the audience let out a cheer as togas and wreaths were whipped away and the performers danced to the jazz tune. Some male dancers in top hats and tails arrived on the stage in a Hispano-Suiza sports car. The stage manager gave me a nod and a wink. I smoothed my dress and took a deep breath before moving to the top of the stairs and walking down them into the burning light.

> *Bonjour Paris!*
> *It's me!*
> *Tonight of all nights the stars will come out and shine,*
> *Shine for the whole of Paris to see.*

Although I'd had visions of myself toppling down the steep staircase and landing dead on the stage, my legs ceased to tremble as soon as I started singing. My voice carried so well that it surprised even me. I reached the stage and led the top and tail dancers in a Charleston, then everyone in a foxtrot, before the lights dimmed and the principal male dancer and I did a slow tango, a reference to my past. The audience cheered.

The lights changed to blue and a dummy grand piano was wheeled on stage. I was lifted onto it by the men and I danced the Charleston again, the lights flickering over me so I looked like I was dancing in slow motion on film.

The audience didn't wait for me to finish before they applauded. The light turned to gold and I could see their faces. They were beaming at me. But it was the expressions of four men sitting in the third row that pleased me most: Lebaron, Minot, André and a man who looked like André, only older. They were grinning from ear to ear. I sensed that if I could please the patriarch of the Blanchard family, I could satisfy anybody.

The cast rushed forward and we sang the refrain together. The audience clapped and cheered again. There was no doubt they liked what they saw.

Until the stagehands could reverse the set we were to hold our poses, but I could feel my right leg beginning to shake again. Standing on top of a piano in a short skirt, there wasn't much I could do to hide it. Something that Doctor Daniel had told me came to mind. 'Energy either goes inwards or outwards. With performers, if you let it in, it is fatal. Your energy must always go out.'

Although it wasn't scripted into the number, I flung my arms out and shouted, '*Bonjour Paris! C'est Moi!* Hello Paris! It's me!'

From the auditorium came a roar as the audience rose to its feet and shouted back: '*Bonjour*, Mademoiselle Fleurier! And welcome!'

From that moment on, I knew there would be no turning back. Paris loved me.

TWENTY

'*Bonjour Paris! C'est Moi!*' was the most successful revue ever staged at the Adriana or any of the other Paris music halls. It ran for over a year, a total of four hundred and ninety-two performances, with a short break before the commencement of the new revue, '*Paris Qui Danse*'. The reviewers of every major paper, from *Le Matin* to *Paris Soir*, were in raptures and as well as the usual audience of *Tout-Paris* and well-to-do tourists, we were honoured with the presence of VIPs such as the Prince of Wales, the King and Queen of Sweden and the royal family of Denmark.

If André and I had worked torturous hours before the revue, then we were firing on all cylinders during it. I rose at seven o'clock for a breakfast of orange juice and toast. Then I had my bath before my hairdresser, manicurist, masseuse and secretary arrived. I dictated correspondence to my secretary during my beauty treatments. Afterwards I headed to the Adriana for meetings with Lebaron, Minot and André to plan for '*Paris Qui Danse*'. Because of the success of '*Bonjour Paris!*' Lebaron was determined that the new revue was going to be even better. Afternoons were devoted to rehearsals, costume fittings and press interviews. In the evenings I was at the theatre by half-past seven and didn't leave until one o'clock in the morning. Every other spare moment was devoted to something that I would soon learn to hate: an exercise of contortions, false smiles, image manipulation and 'white lies' whose slogan was 'Talent is not enough for success'. That exercise was called publicity.

I had fallen in love with the music hall for its magic, and it was my joy to dance and sing for an audience, but I learned that being 'a star' was different to what I had expected. A star has to be in the public eye not only when she is on stage but off it as well if she wants to keep her edge. As my wealth increased — and, to Monsieur Etienne's delight, André invested some of it — I also learned the difference between being rich and being famous. Anyone who saw my *haute couture* dresses, my diamonds, my chauffeur-driven Voisin, my apartment, the handsome André who accompanied me to social occasions, must have assumed that I was living a wonderful life. But it wasn't a life; it was an image. There was no time to savour any of those things for myself. They were all for public consumption.

I had once heard Mistinguett say that she would never lose her diamonds to gain notoriety. But Mistinguett, Joséphine Baker and I were always having to out-sensationalise each other. Mistinguett insured her legs for a million dollars; Joséphine staged a marriage to a count, who was actually an Italian stonemason pretending to be a count; and my publicist 'leaked' that the secret of my vitality was to drink speckles of gold flakes in my coffee each morning and to bathe in milk and rose petals. He even had a milkman arrive at my door each morning with several vats of milk to prove it. It was the kind of frivolous nonsense that got us bad press in places like Austria and Hungary, where people had barely enough to eat. One communist paper claimed that the amount of milk I 'bathed' in each day would have kept ten children alive for a week.

Joséphine Baker and Mistinguett had an ongoing public battle of cattiness and rivalry. They even got into a spitting fight once at a film première at the Cinéma Apollo. The two divas had battled it out, digging their nails in each other's arms and scratching at each other's faces. Mistinguett tried her tactics on me one evening at the Rossignol when André and I went there for supper after the show. She was sitting at a table surrounded by young men, pearls strung around her still youthful throat, when she signalled to me and shouted, 'Hello, baby girl. Have they cleaned behind your ears yet? Why don't you salute me?' and grinned at me with her piranha teeth. You could almost see the columnist for *Le Petit Parisien*, who was sitting behind her, reaching for his pen.

'Good evening, Madame,' was my reply. She was more than thirty years older than me and I had been brought up to be respectful to my elders. The *maître d'hôtel* gave a sigh of relief but Mistinguett's face collapsed with disappointment.

'You are going to have to improve your one-liners,' André said, once we were seated. 'Otherwise you will be perceived as a snob who thinks she is too good for a catfight. If you and Camille Casal were smarter, you would have started one long ago. It would have helped her fledgling career and it wouldn't hurt you to be seen as her rival.' I was glad to see from the mischievous twinkle in his eye that he was joking.

There was a commotion at the door. Joséphine Baker, followed by her entourage — which included 'Count' Pepito de Abatino, her chauffeur, her maid and her pet pig — stormed into the restaurant.

André raised his eyebrows at me.

'I am too tired,' I said.

Although I didn't say anything to André, I had never seen Camille as my rival. I was in awe of her. A month into the show I invited her to dine with me at my apartment. For some reason I thought her approval of my transformation would give it the stamp of success. But as soon as Camille arrived, I realised that even with my groomed hair and stylish clothes I was still diminished by her physical perfection. She sauntered into my apartment wearing a mauve dress with layers of pearls circling her neck. The air around her was scented with Shalimar. It seemed impossible that anyone could have such chiselled features or such flawless skin.

'You're doing well,' she said, eyeing the rosewood bureau as if she couldn't quite believe that I lived in the apartment. Some days I couldn't believe I lived in the apartment either. Camille and I had travelled miles since we had been in Aunt Augustine's house in Marseilles. I glowed with pride from the indirect compliment.

I lead Camille to the drawing room and offered her a seat. She pulled out a cigarette and I leaned forward to light it.

'So you took my advice about men, after all,' she said, running her silver nails over the sofa. 'It seems André Blanchard has done a lot for you.'

'It's not like that,' I assured her. 'Our relationship is professional.'

The look of disbelief on her face turned into a frown. I noticed for the first time the circles under her eyes, cleverly powdered but present just the same. Her relationship with Yves de Dominici was over; he had married an Italian countess. But I had heard that Camille was seeing someone high up in the War Ministry. I wondered about her daughter, who would be turning five years old soon, but knew not to ask after the child. Camille had told me that she would take the girl out of the convent as soon as she found a rich enough — and permanent enough — patron. The man from the War Ministry was married to a woman who controlled the purse strings, so that wasn't going to happen any time soon.

'So the show is going well?' she asked. 'What will you do when it finishes?'

I wondered if she knew that she had been considered for the star role in '*Bonjour Paris!*' But as she didn't mention it, neither did I.

'André wants me to make a record.'

'André Blanchard must be very taken with you,' she said, glancing about the room. 'I can't believe a man would do so much for a woman and not expect something in return.'

I blushed, not so much from embarrassment as shame. It gave me a certain amount of self-respect that André truly believed in my talent and didn't expect sex in return for helping my career. But not to desire me at all when I was besotted by him? That made me feel like a wallflower and nothing at all like 'the most sensational woman in the world'.

My maid, Paulette, announced that supper was ready, saving me from having to explain my relationship with André further. I knew that Camille had the appetite of a small bird so I had asked the cook to prepare stuffed cabbage with tarragon sauce and champagne. During the meal Camille was distant, her mind somewhere else.

'I am leaving Paris,' she announced after a while. 'I'm going to make a film with GW Pabst.'

My heart skipped a beat. I knew then that no matter what I achieved, Camille would always be several steps ahead of me. I would love to star in a film. The medium was new but I found the idea of telling stories through images thrilling. And who better to work with than GW Pabst? The young German was already earning a reputation as a notable director.

'You will be a film star,' I said, sincerely happy for Camille's good luck but coveting a little of it for myself too.

After the meal, I walked Camille to the door where Paulette helped her with her coat. Camille kissed me goodbye and wished me well. I gave her a bouquet of roses to take home with her and a Chinese lacquer box. She complimented me on the fragrance of the flowers and the exquisite pattern on the box, but she left me with the impression that she had preferred my company when I was poor and out of luck.

❧

When the show had 'settled in', André's father invited us to visit the family *château* for the weekend. Because of urgent business matters, Monsieur Blanchard had been unable to meet me after the opening night performance, but he had sent word through André that he thought I was magnificent. The praise pleased André so much that he gave all the performers a bonus out of his own pocket.

On our way to the Dordogne Valley, André hummed tunes from *'Bonjour Paris! C'est Moi!'* and looked at me with such tender regard that I had to remind myself that he was not attracted to me. My feminine tricks to test the waters — standing close to him, letting my fingers linger on his arm a fraction longer than necessary — had come to nothing. Why should things change now? But while André was so clearly uninterested in me, there had not been any more Mademoiselle Caniers either. Perhaps he was just one of those men who preferred work to love.

'I was nervous,' he said, negotiating a tight bend in the road. 'I didn't know what my father would think of my foray into show business. But your talent has won him over. He has nothing but praise for you.'

'My success has as much to do with you as it does with me,' I said.

André laughed, his voice booming above the hum of the engine. 'I think you could have done it without me, Simone. But it was fun to watch you blossom.'

The Blanchards' *château* was surrounded by seventy-two acres of parkland and overlooked the Dordogne Valley, a picture of green fields and oak trees with a tranquil river winding through them. We arrived at the ivy-covered mansion in time for lunch and were guided by the butler to a terrace. The air smelt of freshly cut grass and jasmine. Veronique was throwing a stick to her dog on the lawn. Her instructions to the puppy and the animal's delighted yelps carried through the summer air. Madame Blanchard sat on a bench between a matronly woman and a bald man. But it was Monsieur Blanchard who moved towards us first.

'*Bonjour!*' he called out, waving to us. He had a voice like a naval captain, deep and used to giving orders. But a friendly smile danced on his lips and made him seem less intimidating than I had expected.

He clasped André's shoulder and André returned the greeting. I had expected to see them salute each other rather than embrace. Their relationship was not as cold as I had anticipated but there was still something formal about the way they approached each other. I thought of Uncle Gerome and my father. Uncle Gerome may have wanted to love his brother but he had never seemed able to work out how to show it. Deep hurt had destroyed the natural affection between them. I sensed this may be how Monsieur Blanchard felt about André.

'Now, tell me, Mademoiselle Fleurier,' said Monsieur Blanchard, taking my arm and leading me towards the others, 'how did my tone deaf son discover the best singer in Paris?'

He had the same sable eyes as André, but while his son treated me with the manners of a gentleman, Monsieur Blanchard fixed his stare on my breasts. I had the uneasy feeling that he was imagining me naked.

'André is not exactly tone deaf,' I said and laughed, more to cover my awkwardness than because I thought what he said was funny. 'He was simply the first person, besides my agent, to believe in me.'

'Come on, we are late for lunch,' called out Madame Blanchard, waving us to the table. 'We shall be in trouble with the cook if the salad goes limp.'

'Are we doing away with introductions?' asked Monsieur Blanchard, ushering us to a table set with white china and bouquets of field flowers. Madame Blanchard blushed but did not look at her husband. She introduced the woman and man with her: André's sister, Guillemette, and her husband, Felix. I greeted them but neither smiled. Guillemette had not inherited the attractive appearance of her parents, nor their dignity and composure. If André hadn't mentioned earlier that his sister had just turned thirty, I would have assumed she was at least ten years older than that.

Guillemette and I were seated diagonally to each other, with Felix opposite me, but I found conversing with either of them difficult. Eye contact with Felix was impossible; when he wasn't picking at his food, he was staring somewhere over my head. Guillemette, on the other hand, studied me intently.

'André tells me that you have a passion for riding,' I said to her, attempting small talk. 'Is it true that you ride in the Bois de Boulogne every morning?'

'Yes,' was her one-word reply. From her tone, you would have thought I had asked her for money. I sensed the undercurrent of resentment although I had no idea of the cause.

André was discussing a business deal with his father so I turned to Veronique for some relief but she was subdued in her older sister's presence. Later, when the main course was served, she sidled up to André to whisper to him but was cut short by a scowl from her sister. 'If you have something to say, Veronique, you should say it to everybody.'

Veronique's eyes filled with tears and her lip trembled. She was not the spirited child I had met in Madame Blanchard's parlour when André and I had visited there before the opening of the show. Guillemette had the ability to give an *al fresco* lunch on a summer's day the tense air of an army camp. I was curious to see her relationship with her father, but Monsieur Blanchard addressed all his questions to Felix.

'How is the hotel in London doing?' Monsieur Blanchard asked him.

Felix rubbed his head, which was so flat and hairless it gave him the look of a salamander. 'I shall need help setting it up,' he answered, flashing his eyes at André.

'You will have to seek it elsewhere,' said André, good-naturedly. 'I am taking Mademoiselle Fleurier on tour.'

Guillemette glared across the table at me. 'And what about the serious enterprises?' she said, turning to André. 'You seem to be neglecting the hotels.'

André had told me that when he went into business with his father, all the hotels would be handled by Felix. I guessed that was why Guillemette was so concerned about them.

'Ah, come now,' said Monsieur Blanchard, dabbing his lips with a serviette. 'There will be time for all that when André turns thirty. I have promised him that he has until then to enjoy himself in any way he chooses.'

Monsieur Blanchard smiled at me and winked. It was all I could do not to cringe. I glanced at André, but he appeared not to notice his father's behaviour. I was surprised to see how André was with his family. When I was with him, I found him lively and a good conversationalist. But around his family, he retreated into his own world.

Madame Blanchard, who had not spoken directly to her husband for the entire meal, turned the conversation to lighter topics. She chatted about the fortified town we would visit that afternoon and her charity work with orphans. I felt that she, André and Veronique were the welcoming side of the Blanchard family, while the others verged on hostility. I was so uncomfortable in the company of André's sister and brother-in-law that if Madame Blanchard had not made such an effort to include me in the conversation, I doubted I would have ended up saying anything at all.

'Tell me, Mademoiselle Fleurier, do you never get stage fright? You look so at home in the spotlights,' Madame Blanchard asked me.

How to answer a question like that? Stars were not meant to reveal their failings; unless they were 'publicity whimsies' such as a liking for fresh raspberries and cream after a performance or a partiality for smoking Indian pipes.

'I am always excited before a performance, Madame Blanchard,' I answered. André smiled into his fist but didn't look at me.

'Excited' was the euphemism André and I had coined for the shakes, sweats, watering eyes and endless trips to the bathroom I experienced before the first number of a performance. The opening night had been the worst, but the shortness of breath gripped me every night when I climbed into the car to make my trip to the theatre. I had developed a habit of taking Kira to the dressing room with me, although this did get us in trouble once when the dresser left my costume out and Kira, with her attraction for shiny things, chewed off all the sequins.

Part of my ritual to calm my nerves was to never dress until the last minute. When I received my stage call, I would open the locket with my parents' wedding picture in it and leave it that way on the dresser until after the final curtain call. During the breaks I lit a candle with my wish to give a good performance scribbled on the side of it — something my mother had suggested. The rituals and cups of chamomile tea did little to calm my nerves, however. The dizzy feeling and the churning in my stomach left me only when I stepped out on stage and sang the first note. Then, like magic, my head would clear and my limbs steadied like a boat sailing out of a storm into a calm sea. Everything would be fine after that.

'I have heard that Mademoiselle Fleurier is the most composed performer in Paris,' said Monsieur Blanchard. 'Most can't make themselves go out on stage unless they have had something to drink.'

'Mademoiselle Fleurier never drinks before a show,' said André, proudly. 'She doesn't let anything affect her performance.'

'They all start like that,' said Guillemette. Her tone reminded me of a priest delivering a sermon warning of impending doom. 'But the lack of sleep and always being in the public eye gets them in the end. Nobody has the nerves for living that fast for too long.'

'Thank you for the gloomy prediction, Guillemette,' said Madame Blanchard, smiling at me.

'That didn't go too badly,' said André, the following day on our drive home.

He had to be joking, I thought. Having grown up with Uncle Gerome and the strain of being in his debt, I couldn't claim that I had come from the happiest of families. But I had always been loved by my parents and Aunt Yvette. Poor André was adored by his mother and Veronique, but any light those two shed was snuffed out by the rest of the Blanchards.

'I don't think your sister likes me,' I said.

'Guillemette doesn't like anybody,' said André. 'It's my father's opinion that counts anyway. And you made a good impression.'

I thought Monsieur Blanchard had liked me too, but then I remembered the way he had looked at my breasts, and the wink, and I felt uneasy.

❧

In June I received a telegram to say that Uncle Gerome had died. Lebaron cancelled two shows so I could return home in time for the funeral.

'He died in his sleep,' Bernard told me on our way to the farm from the station at Carpentras. 'It was for the best. He had started to deteriorate again.'

The whole village attended the cemetery. There were also people from Sault and Carpentras as well as dozens of faces I had never seen before. There was even a photographer from the Marseilles press. Given the unpopularity of Uncle Gerome, it was clear they had come to gawk at me. I was embarrassed to stand by the graveside in my silk Charmeuse dress while my mother and aunt were attired in the same black cotton dresses they had worn for years.

At the wake, Monsieur Poulet stood up to give a speech. 'I want to say how proud we are of Simone Fleurier, and I hope that when she gets married she will come back to her village church and our little town hall for the ceremony.'

It was nice to be welcomed so warmly, but I thought it in poor taste to toast me when it was Uncle Gerome's funeral.

The following morning, I opened my shutters and saw my mother carrying buckets of water into the house. I ran downstairs to help her with the backbreaking task, and sat with her in the kitchen while she boiled a pot over the fire to make us coffee. There were strands of grey in her hair and a painful-looking vein snaked up her ankle. I thought of Mistinguett. She was old enough to be my grandmother, but compared to my mother's appearance, their ages could have been reversed.

'What if I bought you a house in Carpentras or Sault, or even Marseilles?' I asked Bernard while he brushed down the donkey and unharnessed it from the cart. 'Life would be easier for you all.'

'Easier. But not a life,' he answered. 'Not for us. We love it here. But I promise to use the money you have been sending me to make life more comfortable for your mother and aunt.'

The truth was that the pace of life on the farm, even the making of the morning coffee, was so slow that it gave me time to think. And thinking made me question if I were truly happy. Uncle Gerome's death drove home how terrible it was to live with regrets. I had thought that being a star would be glamorous and exciting, but, once the initial rush wore off, it was draining. I cared deeply for André, but my love had to remain buried, and there was little real fondness between me and his family. Furthermore, the gossip fuelled by his patronage of me was the lifeblood of the lowest Paris magazines.

Simone Fleurier must be as good in her boudoir as she is on stage, if the quality of the men who visit her dressing room after her show is anything to judge by ... How did this scrawny unknown become the toast of Paris? You would have to look between — the lines? — to know that.

Was this really the life I wanted to lead? Things were much simpler on the farm. There was gossip in the village but it was not usually the vindictive kind. Guillemette's words had stuck with me: '*Constantly being in the public eye gets them in the end. Nobody has the nerves for living that fast for too long.*' Hadn't I learnt that in Berlin? The Germans lived faster than anybody, and by the time I had opened at the Adriana, Ada Godard had collapsed on stage and died from a brain haemorrhage at twenty-two years of age. I might not drink to excess or take drugs, but there were days when the pressure made my heart palpitate.

I had to leave the farm the following morning to return to the show. 'Promise me that you will visit me in Paris,' I said to my mother and Aunt Yvette. Now that Uncle Gerome was gone, Bernard would be able to manage for a week or so on his own. I kissed my mother and aunt goodbye before getting into the car with Bernard. The women's faces were stony but their eyes shone with reserved strength. I could see they were proud of me.

I breathed in the lavender, rosemary and wisteria scents permeating the air. No, I thought, I love the farm, but I could never live there again. Paris had changed me.

❧

When '*Paris Qui Danse*' reached the end of its run in February 1929, I put some of my songs from the revue onto record before André and I set sail for New York on the *Île de France*. The famous Broadway impresario, Florenz Ziegfeld, had invited me to perform in his musical, 'Show Girl'. I didn't have the lead part; that was going to Ruby Keeler. I was to be a guest star in a scene titled 'An American in Paris'. But we took the opportunity to go to the United States to make contacts for the future and also to do a short tour of Brazil and Argentina afterwards.

When we arrived at Le Havre I gasped at the size of the ship. 'I have never seen anything so big in my life!' I told André. 'It is bigger than the Louvre or the Hôtel de Ville.'

'It is the most beautiful ship on the ocean,' he said. 'It is not the largest or the fastest but it is the most magnificent. You will see when we get inside.'

I gave my press conference on the pier, camera bulbs flashing, and announced that while I was excited to be going to America, France would always be my home. André and I made our way up the gangplank, stopping halfway and waving to give the press another photographic opportunity. The captain greeted us when we came on board and handed me a bouquet of lilac roses before the head purser led us to the grand foyer, where we could wait until the ship was ready to leave.

'I see what you mean about the elegance of it,' I said to André. I was used to luxury now but the ship was grander than anything I had seen before. The foyer was four decks high and extended almost the full length of the vessel. The angular furniture, sweeping columns and red pilasters were the essence of Art Deco chic.

'Other ships copy the interior design of manor houses and Moorish castles,' André explained. 'But the Île de France is unique. The decor mimics the ocean.'

'It feels more like a resort than a ship,' I said.

'That is why I chose it,' said André, his hand dropping to the small of my back and lingering there. The warmth of his skin burned through my dress.

'You have forgotten what you told me in Germany,' I said, shifting my feet. Was I imagining it or was he drawing circles on my flesh with his fingertips? André had touched me dozens of times before — a hand on my shoulder, chaste kisses on my cheek. But this was something else.

André raised his eyebrows and shook his head.

'You told me that they would work me much harder on Broadway than you did in Berlin, and since that's where you are taking me now, this may be my first and last holiday!'

The ship's horn sounded and I jumped from surprise. André laughed and grabbed my arm, pulling me out on the deck to join in the merriment of hoorays, whistles and rice-throwing as the ship left port.

'Things are going to be different, Simone,' he shouted over the noise. 'But we will talk about that over dinner.'

I looked at André's excited eyes and sensed that something between us was moving. If I was right, things were going to change for ever.

❧

That evening, André and I descended the *Île de France*'s marble staircase to the dining room. In my shell-pink gown I felt like a movie star sweeping her way onto a Hollywood set. With the number of Americans and their wives rubbing shoulders with Europe's social elite, I could have been. The dining room was long with square lights in the ceiling rather than elaborate chandeliers. On the menu there was Loire pike in clarified butter along with duck *à l'orange* and *ice bombe impériale* with Vienna cream.

'Perfect,' said André. 'The pike is the lead-in to what I want to tell you.'

I was still flustered from the way he had touched me earlier in the afternoon. Had they only been absent-minded caresses or was there something more?

'What is it you want to tell me?' I asked, not taking my eyes from his face.

He smiled. 'When I mentioned to my father that we were travelling on the *Île de France*, he told me about a friend of his who made one of the first voyages on the ship. As you know, the *Île de France* was designed to showcase the best of everything French. But the British and Germans are still competing against each other for speed. Anyway, on that journey, my father's friend was savouring his meal of Loire pike when a British ship, the *Mauretania*, raced past. A while later, the steward brought him a radio message sent by a friend of his who was on the passing ship. "Do you want a tow?" it read.'

I listened carefully, trying to decipher what meaning the story had for André and me. But it was a mystery.

André continued with his account. 'The Frenchman picked up his crystal glass and sipped some wine then took another bite of the pike before giving the steward his reply. "Please send back this message," he said. "What is your hurry? Are you starving?"'

'We shouldn't laugh,' I said, grinning. 'Look how we work — not like French people at all.'

'I want to change that,' André said.

'How?'

'I want you to marry me.'

I dropped my fork. It clattered to the floor. I had been aching for André to announce that he was beginning to find me attractive. I had not been expecting him to propose to me. I blinked at him, lost for words. Out of the corner of my eye, I saw the wine steward making his way through the tables towards us. I sent him a glance. The good thing about French waiters was that they had a sixth sense in knowing whether or not to interrupt a conversation. The steward did a spin on his heel and took another turn around the room.

'Are you so surprised?' asked André, reaching over and touching my hand. 'I have loved you ever since I saw you at the Café des Singes.'

I wanted to tell him that I had been dreaming of him for years, but I couldn't speak. Where was the sense in this? If he had loved me since first seeing me, why had he brought Mademoiselle Canier to Berlin? Why had he never responded to any of my hints?

'You forget that you were the one who said you only wanted a professional relationship,' he said, when I finally found the words to question him. 'I have been in love with you all along. But every time I tried to get close to you, I was thwarted.'

I thought back to André's visit to my dressing room at the Casino de Paris and my self-righteous speech at Maxim's, and couldn't help blushing. 'But surely you noticed my feelings had changed?' I protested.

'Yes,' he said. 'But there were things I needed to sort out.'

I was so lightheaded I thought I might float out of my chair and drift around the room. Was I dreaming? André was telling me that he loved me. 'What things did you have to sort out?' I asked.

'My father.'

My joy deflated. 'Your father?'

He turned away. 'I didn't want my father to think you were someone to amuse myself with until I married someone else. I respect you too much.'

I remembered the wink Monsieur Blanchard had given me when André and I had visited the family in the Dordogne. That was exactly how he had seen me. 'Has your father given his permission then?' I asked.

'Not exactly,' André said, looking at me again. 'But he likes you and respects your work, and that's a start. I am twenty-three now. If we wait faithfully until my thirtieth birthday to get married, my father can have no hesitation that we are meant for each other.'

I glanced at my plate. André sounded confident but doubt gnawed at me. I understood the power Monsieur Blanchard wielded, not only over his own family but over the whole of France. Marrying without his permission would be next to impossible.

André leaned across the table and pulled me towards him. 'I don't want to wait to hold you any longer,' he whispered.

I looked up at him. 'André, this is crazy!' I said. 'Do you realise how crazy this is? Nobody starts a love affair like this. We have known each other for three years and we have never even kissed.'

'That's not true,' he said. 'You have forgotten New Year's Eve in Berlin.'

'That *was* you?'

'I thought you might have guessed that.'

I shook my head. 'You surprised me. Besides, I could never tell . . .'

The wine steward headed towards us again. He raised his eyebrows and I shook my head. He gave a nod and disappeared to the other side of the room. André kissed me. The softness of his lips made my heart melt and my flesh burn. The flame spread from my lips to my spine and down my legs.

When the wine steward finally made it to our table, he would have found a note on it asking him to send champagne to us by room service. André and I had a lot of catching up to do.

❧

This can't be real, I told myself, as André slipped my camisole down my shoulders and nuzzled his mouth against my breast. His kisses sent tingles down my spine and the backs of my calves. I clutched his hair and breathed in his sandalwood scent. He lifted his eyes to mine and kissed my lips.

Most love affairs start with a passion that fizzles into friendship, if the lovers are lucky, or turns cold and dies if they are not. But André and I had taken the best journey of all. We were friends who had become lovers. We didn't have to build trust, it was already there. Every touch, every exploration, was only an extension of what we had felt for years.

I glanced at the mural of dancing nymphs on the wall in the cabin. I had heard the bawdy tales of sexual encounters from the chorus girls, and the horror stories of first-time experiences. But there was nothing frightening about being with André. I dissolved wherever he touched me. I ran my fingers over his broad shoulders and muscular arms, admiring his beauty. He slipped his hands under me and lifted my hips to his mouth.

'Does that feel nice?' he asked, his breath on my thigh.

'It all feels nice,' I told him.

I imagined myself sitting in a river on a hot day, the water tickling my flesh. André's lingering touches buoyed me up. 'I love you,' he whispered, lifting himself over me and planting kisses on my collarbone. I felt his hardness gently push against me. I opened my thighs wider to let him inside. I had waited for him so long that there was no resistance. I circled his hips with my legs. As he moved in and out of me, every nerve in my body sprang to life. I was filled with light. A burning sensation swept across my chest and an ache of pleasure pulsated from between my thighs, making me gasp and my back arch. André moved faster, his own breath coming quicker. I reached out and clutched a pillow, my nails tearing the material. The light became brighter and brighter before exploding into stars and floating away.

⌘

Apart from dining in the ship's restaurant or taking Kira out for walks on the deck, André and I spent the rest of the voyage in bed. We had agreed to be careful that I not fall pregnant until we were married, and André boasted that he had bought every *capote anglaise* that the ship's pharmacy stocked. 'Everyone else is going to have to hold off or tie a knot in it,' he laughed.

On the night I was to sing for the captain and first-class passengers, André and I woke up at eight and scrambled to bathe and dress before my performance at nine o'clock. I was trained for quick costume changes, but my problem was the bird's nest our afternoon's lovemaking had made out of the back of my hair.

'I will have to cut it,' said André, holding the ball of tangled hair and trying to tug a comb through it.

'No!' I said. 'I am not having a bald patch at the back of my head.'

'Maybe we can put a hat over it, or a scarf?'

'Neither will go with what I'm wearing.'

We tried to smooth it out with André's hair oil but that just made my hair look flat.

'Maybe we should use egg white from the kitchen?' he suggested, although we only had half an hour left to get to the dining room. Eventually we decided to wash it in the basin. After a rubdown with the towel I stood with my head out the porthole, letting the fierce wind blow it dry. The result was a wavy bob which hid the knot and didn't look too bad when we tamed the frizz with some hair cream.

I sang four numbers and was a success with the audience. I was also a success at the beauty parlour the next day, where the hairdressers were besieged by women requesting the 'new Simone Fleurier do'.

'It's really quite easy,' André told one woman who came up to ask for my autograph. 'But you do need to spend an afternoon on it.'

On the last day of our journey, André and I were up at dawn to join the other passengers waiting to sail into New York Harbour. We cheered when we passed the Statue of Liberty and the Manhattan skyline loomed up ahead. I felt a surge of joy and hope: André's tenderness had given me confidence in the future of our love. After all, hadn't Liane de Pougy married her Prince Ghika? And Winnaretta Singer her Prince Edmond de Polignac? They had lived much racier lives than I had. There was nothing André's family could reproach me for except not being born into money.

André and I kissed, as happy as a couple on their honeymoon. Although, of course, we were not married. Not yet.

TWENTY-ONE

The Ziegfeld Follies of New York were as famous as the Folies Bergère in Paris, but while Paul Derval adhered to the French dictum that 'uniformity breeds boredom', Ziegfeld was famous for his 'factory' of beauties with long necks, similar proportions and homogeneous height. 'The perfect Ziegfeld girl has measurements of a bust of thirty-six inches, a waist of twenty-six inches and hips exactly two inches bigger than her bust,' he was quoted as saying.

At the time Andrè and I arrived in New York, musical theatre was undergoing changes. Whereas the music hall had been born of variety acts, the American public liked musicals in which the songs and dances revolved around storylines. Ziegfeld had made himself a millionaire all over again the previous year by following the new trend with two of the most successful productions of his career: 'Show Boat' and 'Whoopee'. But when we arrived at the Ziegfeld Theatre on Fifty-Fourth Street, with its bowed façade that looked like a wedding cake, it didn't take us long to sense that something was wide of the mark with 'Show Girl'.

We were greeted in the foyer by Ziegfeld's secretary, Matilda Golden, who he always called 'Goldie'. She was a softly spoken woman who told us that Ziegfeld was in a meeting and had asked her to show us around the theatre until he was finished.

'It was designed by Joseph Urban, the same man who is designing the sets for the show,' explained Goldie, opening the doors to the auditorium. 'He's from Vienna.'

André and I followed her into the delicately lit space. I could see a resemblance to the work of the artist Gustav Klimt in the gold tones of the carpeting and seats. The colour flowed up the walls and blended into a mural of romantic figures from various epochs, including Adam and Eve. It covered the ceiling and formed a border around the stage. The hall had been built without mouldings and gave the impression that we were standing inside a giant decorative egg.

'Monsieur Urban is a true artist,' I said, my excitement growing at the prospect of working in such a breathtaking theatre.

Goldie curled a ringlet behind her ear. 'Mister Ziegfeld *never* compromises on beauty,' she said.

After showing us the music library and the dressing rooms with their bevelled mirrors and en suite bathrooms, Goldie took us to the seventh floor to meet Ziegfeld. My stomach fluttered in anticipation. Could this really be me, Simone Fleurier, here in New York and on her way to meet the great impresario Florenz Ziegfeld?

As it turned out, I heard him before I saw him. Goldie raised her fist to knock on the door to his suite but before her knuckles had a chance to touch the wood, a nasal voice roared, 'Damn it! Don't you dare storm into my office and give me drivel like that!'

I assumed that the voice was Ziegfeld's because he had said 'my office'. Later I would realise that his pinched voice was what they called the 'Chicago accent'.

Another voice answered. 'It would help if your genial Bill McGuire could get his rear end into motion. We could write songs so much faster *if* we had a script!'

The second man's voice was more resonant than Ziegfeld's. The accent was American too, but the way he stressed some of his syllables in odd places, he could have been Russian.

Ziegfeld roared again. 'Just do what I asked you to, George! Go to that trunk of yours and dig out a couple of hits!'

'Oh, dear,' said Goldie, ushering us towards her office. 'They're still at it.'

I didn't really want to be bundled off to Goldie's office — the conversation was interesting — but I followed dutifully.

'And you, Ira,' continued Ziegfeld. 'You've got nothing to complain about. I've got you Gus Khan to help with the lyrics.'

George? Ira? Ziegfeld must be talking to the Gershwin brothers — the songwriting duo famous for its energetic music and witty lyrics! I nudged André who nodded back at me. I hadn't known that they were the composers for the show. I wondered what kind of song they had come up with for me. Something sensual? Something urbane? Or maybe a clever play on words?

Goldie offered us seats next to her desk and shut the door. 'Mister Ziegfeld hopes to repeat Maurice Chevalier's success with you, Miss Fleurier,' she said, pouring us coffee. 'His guest appearance in "Midnight Frolics" was very well received.'

'Do you have a copy of Mademoiselle Fleurier's score?' André asked. 'We want to start rehearsing as soon as possible. The American scene is new for us and we want to make sure that she fits into the show smoothly.'

So much for our holiday, I thought with a smile. André was straight into business. Although this time, at least, we were sharing a hotel room.

Goldie took a slurp of her coffee and waved her hand in front of her mouth. 'Boy, that was hot,' she said, glancing at her telephone. Before André could repeat his question, Goldie swung around on her chair, reached for a plate piled with doughnuts and thrust it at him.

'Try a nut?' she said, stuffing one straight into his mouth. 'The hole's the best bit.'

The door to Ziegfeld's office slammed and footsteps thumped down the corridor. I hadn't heard Ira speak earlier but I assumed it was he who said to his brother, 'You know what I'm gonna answer next time somebody asks us "What comes first? The words or the music?"'

'What?' George asked.

'I'm gonna say, "The contract".'

Goldie's telephone rang and she picked up the receiver. 'Yes, I'll send them in right away.' She smiled at us. 'Mister Ziegfeld is ready for you now.'

I had heard from one of the American dancers at the Adriana that Ziegfeld was a tyrant and his manner of speaking to the Gershwin brothers supported that image. So when I followed Goldie into the impresario's office I was surprised to find a smiling man with the most fascinating eyes I had ever seen. Round and twinkling like a teddy bear's, they were the kind of eyes that never grow old.

'Mademoiselle Fleurier!' Ziegfeld gushed, lifting my hand to his lips. He nodded briefly to André before slipping his arm around my shoulders and guiding me to a cluster of easy chairs. His office was the size of a banquet hall and furnished with antique tables and cabinets. Everywhere I looked — on the shelves, on his desk, on a refectory table — I saw elephants made from jade, gold or silver. They were charging with their trunks raised.

'Ah,' said Ziegfeld, clapping his hands, 'you're observant, Mademoiselle Fleurier. They're my good luck charms. If the trunks were down that would mean bad luck.'

Despite the heated argument I had heard only a few moments before, Ziegfeld looked as cool as a member of the White Raj sipping on iced tea and being fanned by slave girls. He was dressed in white linen pants and a grey jacket with a gardenia in the buttonhole. Each time he moved the scent of Guerlain's *eau de cologne* seemed to float up around him.

'Mademoiselle Fleurier,' he said, glancing me over with those lively eyes, 'we have such magnificent ideas for costumes for your act. Magnificent! Magnificent! You will be like a beautiful constellation bursting out on the stage.'

'I am wondering about the score, Mister Ziegfeld,' said André. 'I would like to get Mademoiselle Fleurier settled into her rehearsal routine as soon as possible.'

I wasn't sure which word offended Ziegfeld the most: 'score' or 'routine'. He screwed up his face and turned as red as someone stuck in an elevator with a bad smell.

'Young man,' he sneered, 'I can see that you are new to the business. My productions are not born of scores, scripts and schedules. If you want those, perhaps you can find yourself a position as a business manager with the Shuberts. The most important thing to start with is a concept of beauty ... a dream.' Turning to me, he added, 'Mademoiselle Fleurier understands that. She understands it because she is an *artiste*. And *artistes* must not be bothered by mundane things like scores and routines.'

André glanced at me, bemused but not reproached. Even so, I was relieved when he didn't pursue the matter further. Otherwise I was sure that with Ziegfeld's temperament we would soon be out of the production and looking for a job with the 'Shuberts', whoever they were.

❧

'You know what they say about Ziegfeld, don't you?' said André, while we were snuggled up together in our bed at the Plaza Hotel a few mornings later. We had spent the previous day sightseeing: walking the grid system streets of the city hand in hand, our necks craned up towards the Art Deco skyscrapers looming overhead. It was the first modern city I had seen, and after Marseilles, Paris and Berlin, it gave me the impression that I hadn't just travelled to New York; I had travelled to the moon.

'You will have to tell me,' I said.

André made a comical face. 'They say that he is like a man who goes to a jeweller and can't decide what he wants, so he buys everything. It is only when he gets home that he sorts out what he wants to keep and what he has to discard. He is known to have thrown away yards of material and dozens of sets when he has changed his mind.'

'That sounds like an expensive way to work,' I said, propping myself up on my elbow and brushing a lock of André's hair off his forehead. 'How can he make a profit?'

André shook his head. 'I'm not sure that he always does. He is good at spending money, that's for sure. In the past few days I've learned that he spends as much time in court fending off lawsuits as he does in his office. On top of that, he is a compulsive gambler.'

It seemed to me that Ziegfeld was well suited to New York. When André and I explored the city we were taken by its pace: everyone spoke quickly, walked fast and listened to jazz, boogie and blues all at once. The architecture screamed of wealth and industry and the magazine racks were full of slick journals promoting the ideal Park Avenue lifestyle: *The New Yorker*, *Vanity Fair* and *Smart Set*. The energy was intense and the city's inhabitants seemed to do nothing by halves. But I knew that kind of frenetic energy could turn in on itself, because it never looked outward — or inward — closely enough.

'What have you got me into, André?' I laughed, then, imitating Ziegfeld: 'Scripts! Scores! Routines! You imbecile!'

André reached over to the bedside table and opened the drawer. He pulled out a document and placed it on the pillow next to me. '*Voila*,' he said. 'My father said not to leave France without a completed contract, but I trusted Ziegfeld's word and agreed to sign it when we arrived in New York. And it seems my hunch was correct.'

I was surprised that André had not waited for a proper contract before we had left France. He was usually fastidious about such things.

André grinned. 'For *artistes*, payment is not a problem. It is only stagehands, seamstresses and dirty business managers like me who are made to wait.'

I picked up the contract and glanced over it. To my surprise Ziegfeld had already signed it before giving it to André.

'The part for the payment amount is blank,' I said, glancing at André. It was careless of Ziegfeld to have done that.

André gave me a wry smile. 'Mademoiselle Fleurier, the space is blank because you are an *artiste*. You simply fill in the amount that you want to be paid.'

<hr />

As much as Ziegfeld's method of working amused us in the beginning, after six weeks of no score, no rehearsals and no word from the impresario, André and I became impatient. Ziegfeld had paid my fee and was footing the bill for our hotel room, so we weren't disgruntled over money. We were madly in love with each other and every moment we spent together was bliss, but there were only so many nightclubs, zoos, museums and galleries that we could visit before we wanted some routine back in our lives. We were annoyed that we were biding our time when both of us were itching to be working. For all the time Ziegfeld had wasted, I could have made another record in France.

By the seventh week, André was telephoning Ziegfeld twice a day. Each time Goldie told him that the impresario was out of the office.

'You try,' André said to me. 'I have the feeling that he is there, he just doesn't want to talk to me.'

Goldie put me straight through to Ziegfeld. 'Now, don't you worry, Mademoiselle Fleurier,' he reassured me. 'Your costume and the set — ah, they will be magnificent!'

I asked when I would start rehearsing.

'I'll give you plenty of notice,' he told me. 'Now, you get as much rest as possible. People pay a lot of money to see my shows and they don't want any of our ladies looking tired.'

'The problem is the writer,' André told me, after doing some checking himself. 'The Gershwins are complaining that McGuire turns up hoping to be inspired by their songs. The only problem is, they don't know what to write about until they see the script.'

'But the story is from a book,' I said. 'It's about a girl from Brooklyn who wants to become a Ziegfeld chorus girl. Why is it so difficult to write a script about that? What does McGuire need to be "inspired" for?'

André shrugged. 'I've never seen anything like it. I thought Lebaron and Minot were crazy, but at least in the end we had a schedule and we had a show.'

Another two weeks passed and nothing happened. André and I resigned ourselves to the fact that if Ziegfeld didn't call us in by the end of the week, we should leave for South America. The following day, after dutifully phoning Ziegfeld and being told he was out, André suggested that we go to Brooklyn. We went on the rides at Coney Island and spent the afternoon walking along the promenade.

We were surprised at the mix of nationalities of the people around us. Not just Americans, but Italians, Russians, Poles, Spaniards and Puerto Ricans.

'If you could live anywhere in the world, where would you live?' I asked André.

He pulled me close so I could feel his warm breath on my cheek and pressed his palm against my heart. 'I would be happy living anywhere as long as I always belonged here.'

I yielded to his touch. I am the luckiest woman in the world, I thought. I not only have the love of a man I adore but I respect him too. Part of me knew that in New York, away from the society pressures of Paris, André and I were living in a safe harbour. But I kept thoughts of trouble out of my mind and let myself tumble into love without hesitation or safeguards.

'You always will belong in my heart,' I said, reaching up to kiss his lips. 'Always.'

We returned to the hotel intending to make love, but instead found twenty telegrams from Ziegfeld demanding to know where we were.

Some were several paragraphs long and written in such convoluted English that I could barely understand them. 'Come to the theatre as soon as you receive this,' the last one read.

'Couldn't he just leave a telephone message?' asked André. 'These must have cost him a fortune.'

We changed our clothes and caught a cab to Fifty-Fourth Street. 'Something tells me this isn't going to get easier,' I said.

'Do you want to pull out?' André asked. 'I am happy to if you want to. We can refund the money. I am in no mood to be treated like a dog on a leash.'

André was right, of course, but I told him we should at least see what happened when we got to the theatre that afternoon.

We arrived to find Urban and the set designers at work. The technicians were trying out the lights on a set of night-time Montmartre. The scene was breathtaking and André and I stopped short when we saw it. Urban used a method called pointillage to create the colours on his backdrops. It was the same painstaking technique Impressionist painters used: proportions of pure colour laid side by side so that when the lights were directed at them the hues mixed into one shade. The effect was a more vibrant and lifelike set than could be achieved using flat colours.

'He wanted you to see it,' said Goldie, greeting us at the door to her office. 'It's the set Miss Fleurier will be singing in front of.'

'Is Mister Ziegfeld here?' André asked. 'We will tell him how much we like it.'

'No,' said Goldie. 'His wife called and he had to go home. It's his favourite dessert tonight: chocolate mousse with strawberries.'

With as much patience as he could muster, André asked if the rehearsals would begin soon.

'Try-outs are tomorrow,' Goldie told him. 'You'll start rehearsals in the afternoon.'

❦

Over the next week, André and I were called in every day for the promised rehearsal but all we ended up doing was sitting through other cast members rehearsing or endless chorus girl drills. I couldn't understand Ruby Keeler. She was a beauty with big eyes and pert features. She was also a dancer with a technical agility that would be hard to match anywhere. But whenever she appeared on stage, she seemed nervous and distracted. In one rehearsal, she was overcome with stage fright and froze at the top of the staircase. Her husband, Al Jolson, who was sitting next to Ziegfeld, stood up and began singing her song for her. He performed the melodic twists perfectly.

'That's great!' cried Ziegfeld. 'We'll use you in the show.'

It was a good ploy on Ziegfeld's part. Al Jolson was one of America's favourite entertainers. He had also been the first man to speak in the first sound feature film, *The Jazz Singer*. The inclusion of Jolson, however, only seemed to make Ruby more nervous.

'What is it with that girl?' André asked me. 'I know you get nervous before an audience, but not at rehearsals. Given that "Show Girl" is to be her first big role, I don't understand why she doesn't seem more excited.'

I could understand her nerves. I was lucky that for my opening show I'd had Minot, André and Odette to support me. 'Maybe Ziegfeld has worn her down,' I said. 'Or she's tired of always been shown up against her husband. The gossips say she only got the part because of him.'

'I think it is her husband that is the problem,' said André. 'I don't like him. He is too old for her and he dominates her.'

André didn't elaborate on that and I didn't ask. We had enough troubles of our own. In my scene, an American tourist wandered around Paris, dreaming of returning home. I was to play a singing street urchin who transforms into a beautiful goddess. Performing alongside me would be the ballerina Harriet Hoctor and the Albertina Rasch ballet dancers. When the Gershwins finally gave me the song sheets, it was a week before opening night and some of my rehearsals lasted ten or twelve hours or took place late at night and ran into the early hours of the morning. So much for not tiring myself out.

At the first full dress rehearsal, the orchestra played my music at the wrong tempo and a light that had not been properly secured crashed to the floor a few feet away from where the technical director was sitting. But Ziegfeld didn't notice. He stood up from his seat, his arms folded across his chest and a frown on his face.

'Bring me the costume designer!' he bellowed.

'I think he might be in bed,' one of the stagehands offered.

'I don't care,' shouted Ziegfeld, his face turning purple. 'Bring me someone from wardrobe then.'

A while later the stagehand returned with a young man whose bleary eyes were not amused. 'What's the problem, Mister Ziegfeld?' he asked.

'Look at the sleeves on Mademoiselle Fleurier's dress,' said Ziegfeld.

I held my arms up from my body so everyone could see my sleeves. The chiffon gown had seemed fine to me when I put it on. I glanced at André, who shook his head.

'What about them?' asked the young man. 'They are three-quarter length, like you wanted them.'

Ziegfeld's face turned a shade darker. 'Three-quarter length they may be but they taper towards her elbows when they should fan out like bells! She's supposed to be a celestial being not a peasant girl!'

'That's what you ordered,' the young man retorted.

Clearly he had not been employed at the Ziegfeld Theatre for long to give that kind of answer. And I feared from the way Ziegfeld's hands shook that he wasn't going to stay much longer either.

'You idiot!' Ziegfeld screamed, his voice booming around the auditorium. 'Get out! Get out! I said "celestial" not "peasant"!'

The young man gave a disgruntled shrug and bolted out of the theatre. An enraged bull was less frightening than Ziegfeld when he was angry.

The impresario ran up the stairs and onto the stage, his eyes fixed on me. I had muddled some of the words in the song. 'Eyes' was next to impossible for me to pronounce. It always came out 'aizzes'. *Paris is a feast for the aizzes. Come here and look into my aizzes.* I froze on the spot, awaiting his rebuke.

He stopped, took my hand in his and spoke in a tender voice. 'I'm wondering, Mademoiselle Fleurier, how you feel about this song? I'm wondering what the words say to you?'

His manner was soothing and such a contrast to his outburst that I was sure he was being sarcastic. I stared back at him. But he seemed oblivious to my confusion and fixed his intense eyes on me. 'What I want to know, Mademoiselle Fleurier, is what the song says to you. As an *artiste*.'

I was saved from having to answer by the director calling the comedy trio of Lou Clayton, Eddie Jackson and Jimmy Durante onto the stage.

'Show Mister Ziegfeld what you've put together,' he told them.

But the comedians had barely made it through their first sketch, in which they played stagehands between the scenes, before Ziegfeld told them to get off.

'Enough of that! Bring on the girls again!' he shouted, then turning to me said, 'I never understand comedians. I don't get their jokes. I'd get rid of them if I could but the audience loves them.'

❧

My nerves were no better on the opening night of 'Show Girl' than they had been in Paris. If anything, they were worse. Ziegfeld had been so adamant that I sing my part with reserve and poise that I had nothing of my real self, my French flamboyancy, to draw on. By seven o'clock my hands were trembling, and when I warmed up my voice I could barely keep it under control. I asked André to stay in my dressing room with me until the stage call.

'Simone,' he said, picking up Kira and placing her in my lap, 'you shouldn't get yourself so worked up. You know that the Ziegfeld opening night audience always comes twice: first to take in the sets and the costumes, and the second time to enjoy the performers.'

The music from the show, which had already started, surged up loudly then died away. Someone knocked on the door. André opened it and a man dressed in tails swept into the room. He had a round stomach like a pumpkin and his beard was shaved in three stripes down his chin. I didn't like the look of him. There was something sinister in his eyes.

'Can I help you?' André asked him.

The man shook his head and gave a snarling grimace. André and I exchanged glances.

'There is some mistake,' said André, assuming the man was a minor act who had come to the wrong dressing room.

'No mistake,' answered the man, inclining his head so that the light reflected in his sleek hair. He reached into his jacket and pulled out something long and black. For one terrifying moment I thought he had taken out a gun, and then I saw that he held a slim balloon in his hand. He pinched the balloon in sections between his fingers before twisting the sections so that the balloon resembled a string of sausages. The rubber squeaked under his touch but his fingers moved as nimbly as those of an origami master. André and I were mesmerised. The man folded the balloon and twisted the parts together, forming a neck and ears, two front legs, two hind legs and a tail. André and I let out a synchronised 'ahh' when he placed the figure of a cat on the dressing table.

The man gave us an idiotic smile and pulled a card with a ribbon in the corner from his pocket and hung it around the cat's neck. *Good luck*, the card read.

'The Zeigfeld Theatre wishes Mademoiselle Fleurier a wonderful performance,' said the man, giving us a bow before retreating out the door.

Kira slipped from my arms onto the dressing table and sniffed the rubber cat. André burst into laughter. 'He was a stooge,' he said. 'It is an American tradition. He is a special performer sent in to make the stars laugh so they are relaxed before they appear on stage.'

'*Mon Dieu*,' I said, sinking back onto my stool. 'I don't feel relaxed at all. I thought he was going to kill us.'

'Really?' said André, clasping my wrists. My hands were steady and my palms were dry. He laughed. 'I think I know what to get you next time you appear in Paris.'

Despite my fears, my performance was well received by the Americans. The Broadway audience was as sophisticated as the Parisians, although they applauded more easily and shouted out their approval before I had finished my number.

'Thank you,' I called out to them. 'It is wonderful to be here in your exciting city.'

I had forgotten myself. This was a musical, not the music hall, and I had stepped out of my character. But the audience loved it and I received a standing ovation.

Ziegfeld had been right: the Americans wanted sentiment not humour from a French singer. I was exhilarated when the *New York Times* reviewer described my voice as '*a liquid instrument with the notes spun from gold*'.

Sadly, however, the show was not a success. While the comedy trio — especially Durante who was affectionately labelled 'Schnozzola' because of his enormous nose — along with dancers Eddie Foy, Harriet Hoctor, the ballerinas and myself were praised for our performances, the critics panned everyone else, including Ruby Keeler. '*She limps along with as much fire as a box of wet matchsticks rather than a gal from Brooklyn determined to make the big time,'* said one review. Only a few weeks later, Ruby pulled out of the show, claiming ill health, and was replaced by Dorothy Stone. The Hollywood movie star upped the pace a bit but the show was pretty much as the critics described it — a slow, rambling farce where nothing much happens.

Ziegfeld blamed the Gershwins' 'hackneyed lyrics' for the show's failure and refused to pay them. The brothers sued him, but by the time the case came before a court the stock market had crashed and there was no money to take from Ziegfeld anyway. He and most of New York were ruined.

As André and I left for South America, the newspaper boys were screaming headlines like: 'Stocks Collapse: Nationwide stampede to unload'; 'Unexpected torrent of liquidation'; and 'Two and a half billion in savings lost'. The worst part was the stories of ruined businessmen leaping from windows thirty storeys high and from the Brooklyn Bridge.

'If they calmed down things would stabilise faster. They might even see opportunities for fortunes to be made,' said André.

I nodded my agreement. But I knew something that André didn't; something those businessmen might have known too. I knew what it was like to be poor — and that once you had become rich, anything was better than being poor again.

TWENTY-TWO

The Paris André and I returned to in January 1930 was anything but depressed. The economy was good, the war reconstruction work was completed and the franc had stabilised. The only noticeable effect of the Great Depression on the city was that the American tourists had disappeared. But the Parisians were as lively as ever and in the mood to amuse themselves.

André had some business to attend to in Lyon with his father, and left for the south the day after we returned from Le Havre. The first person I went to see was Monsieur Etienne, who I had left in charge of business matters while André and I were away. When I had left for Berlin, Monsieur Etienne had agreed that, while he would continue to handle my business affairs in Paris — including publicity — André could seek out engagements for me. Whether Monsieur Etienne had been happy with that arrangement in the beginning, I couldn't say. But things had worked out well for all of us after the Adriana shows, and the relationship between him and André was harmonious and cooperative.

'You look well, Mademoiselle Fleurier,' he said, opening the door to the office. 'And you have come back just in time. I have offers for you coming out of my ears.'

There was a dark-haired girl sitting at Odette's desk. She seemed familiar to me and I remembered that she was the daughter of the concierge. Not the one who had been rude to me on my first day in Paris, but her replacement. I looked around for Odette and saw that she was filing some papers in Monsieur Etienne's office.

'New staff?' I asked.

Monsieur Etienne's face turned glum. 'Oh, there have been changes here,' he said. 'Odette tried to reach you at the Ziegfeld Theatre, but I don't think her letter was passed on to you.'

'That doesn't surprise me,' I said. 'What has happened?'

'She is getting married.'

Odette came out of the office and placed some files on the desk. She stepped towards me and we kissed each other's cheeks. 'Married? To whom?' I asked, arching my eyebrows in mock surprise.

'To an old friend of the family,' said Monsieur Etienne. 'Joseph Braunstein.'

'Isn't he a nice man?' I asked, noticing his frown. 'You don't seem very happy for her.'

Monsieur Etienne shrugged. 'He is a wonderful young man. Very enterprising. It is more that I will miss Odette. She is like a daughter to me.'

'What does Joseph do?' I asked Odette.

'He runs a prestigious furniture store.' She smiled coyly. I had kept my promise never to mention Joseph until Odette did, but had Joseph kept his promise not to tell Odette about the money I had given him? I wondered. I had intended for him to propose to Odette as soon as he had bought a shop, but he had decided to wait until he was sure of the profitability of his business. Knowing Odette's spending habits, it had probably been a good plan.

'Ah,' I said, squeezing Odette's hand. 'She will send him broke, you know that, don't you? Then she will have to come back and work for you again.'

Monsieur Etienne's face brightened and he directed me into his office. Once we were seated he opened a folder crammed with letters.

'I have a very good offer from the Folies Bergère,' he said, passing me a letter from Paul Derval.

'I am not sure I have forgiven him for saying that I wasn't beautiful enough for the chorus line.'

Monsieur Etienne sat back in his chair and wagged his finger at me. 'You are going to have to move on from that. I doubt Monsieur

Derval even remembers auditioning you. As far as he is concerned, you are "the most sensational woman in the world".'

'How success changes things!' I said.

'I have good offers from the Adriana, who would love to have you back, and the Casino de Paris, now run by Henry Varna. The record company would like you to cut another disc and I have film offers from three different countries, including Paramount in America. So yes, you are right: success does change things,' said Monsieur Etienne. 'Now, tell me, what are you going to do first?'

'First,' I said, picking up my purse, 'I am going to Galeries Lafayette. Odette and I have to go shopping for her wedding present.'

We wandered around the Galeries Lafayette for three hours. Odette didn't want anything too practical like linen or a kitchen appliance. But as she and Joseph were going to live with her parents until they found a place of their own, we agreed that an unwieldy Chinese cabinet or a Grecian urn would be inconvenient. Finally, she chose mirrored placemats and silver bowls for fruit and nuts. She would be able to store those under her bed or in a cupboard until she moved. I organised for the store to have them delivered.

Odette — married? I thought, watching her scribble out her address for the clerk. It had taken a long time to get to that point, but now everything was moving quickly. Would it be the same for me and André? Perhaps patience *was* a virtue and things did happen in their own time.

Over coffee at La Coupole, I told Odette about what had passed between André and me on our trip to America and my worries about his family. She smiled knowingly. 'I can't say either of our parents would have made things easy if Joseph and I had rushed. Take your time and be patient. From what you have told me, André is very much in love with you and you should trust in that first.'

I took Odette's advice to heart. I decided to be proud of who I was and what I did, and I took up the prestigious offer from the Folies Bergère. Meanwhile, now we were back in Paris, André planned to introduce me to society. 'They had better get used to seeing us together,' he said. He was confident that, side by side, we would conquer not only the Paris audiences but the whole of *Tout-Paris*.

'Kira,' I said, placing her on the passenger seat of André's new Renault Reinastella, 'you have the Marquise de Crussol's poodle and Princesse de Faucigny-Lucinge's Great Dane to compete with. So show everybody how superior cats are and don't jump out of the window or do anything else flighty. Agreed?'

I turned to wave to André and his mother who were sitting in the stand. André waved back, smiling but with an anxious twist to his mouth. 'You don't have to win the *Concours d'élégance automobile*, Simone,' he had said, watching his chauffeur give the glass radiator cap one last rub. 'You just have to be seen.'

'What is the point of that?' I had ribbed him.

'What does he think I am going to do?' I muttered now, watching Comtesse Pecci-Blunt, the niece of Pope Leo XIII, drive across the field in her custom-made silver Bugatti. 'Puncture someone's tyre? We might be from the music hall but we do have some sense of propriety, don't we, Kira?'

Kira blinked at me. I hoped that having travelled several continents on trains and boats, she wouldn't be fazed by an automobile and fashion parade.

The official gestured to me to start up my motor. I checked over the knobs and controls although I knew perfectly well how to drive. André had organised lessons for me. Still, the Reinastella weighed a tonne and André had told me a terrible story the previous night over dinner. In one year's contest, the wife of a diplomat had got so wrought up that she had confused the brake and accelerator and crushed three spectators against a tree. I realised that was probably why some of the contestants today had their chauffeurs driving them.

I pressed the accelerator pedal and manoeuvred the car without incident to in front of the judges' stand. On the panel were André de Fouquières, a debonair Frenchman who seemed to be found wherever attractive women were; Daisy Fellowes, the daughter of a nobleman and heiress to the Singer sewing machine fortune; and Lady Mendl, whose lightly powdered skin and shell-pink dress gave no hint that she was almost seventy years of age.

'Mademoiselle Simone Fleurier,' an official announced through a megaphone. 'Driving Renault's Reinastella and accompanied by Kira.'

Another official rushed forward to open my door. I picked up Kira, held her under my chin and glided out, not like a society debutante, as the others before me had, but as the star of the Folies Bergère. 'The most sensational woman in the world,' I laughed under my breath. Despite the way I was promoted, I didn't really believe that about myself. I never once truly felt that I had 'made it'. With each step I rose, the harder I had to work to maintain my position. As Mistinguett had once confided in me: 'It is more difficult to keep your balance on top of the ladder than it is climbing up the rungs.'

The sight of so many people threw Kira into a panic. She pressed her paw against my chest and veered away from me. But the applause stopped her short. She froze and ceased wriggling long enough for me to parade around the car.

Daisy Fellowes' eyes lit up when she saw what I was wearing. Paul Derval had introduced me to a new designer, an Italian called Elsa Schiaparelli. She was nothing like Chanel or Vionnet, whose feminine gowns I still wore to opening nights. Schiaparelli was modern. Her clothes followed the planes of the body rather than the curves, which gave them a stylised simplicity. My navy suit had wide shoulders, a pinched waist and leopard-print piping. 'The cloche hat is dead,' Schiaparelli had informed me, crowning me instead with a tiny hat whose black plume was so bristly that I thought it resembled a hedgehog. I wouldn't have worn it if Paul Derval hadn't assured me that I looked chic. My shoes and handbag were leopard print too, and Schiaparelli had 'accessorised' Kira with a matching collar and miniature plume of her own. Luckily, Kira was so terrified that she hadn't noticed it or else she would have ripped it up like one of her toy birds.

I paused near the bonnet of the car for the photographer from *Le Figaro Illustré* to take a picture. Out of the corner of my eye I saw Janet Flanner scribbling the words that would appear in her column in *The New Yorker*:

> *The music hall muse, Simone Fleurier, stepped out of Renault's latest top of the range model and announced to the world with her sleek suit and long legs that the flapper era of androgyny is gone. She was all woman — dramatic, bold and assertively seductive.*

✥

'Come on,' I said. 'We are all champions here!' I swung my arm around the Marquise de Crussol's shoulder and clinked my glass against 'The Best in Show' cup sitting on my make-up table.

André, who was leaning against my wardrobe and chatting with Comtesse Pecci-Blunt, shot me a sly smile. My dressing room was full of the descendants of France's aristocracy. There were almost as many European 'titles' sitting on my zebra rug, nibbling on American fried chicken and drinking champagne, as there were chorus girls at the Folies Bergère. My hands-down victory at the *Concours d'élégance automobile* had elicited more than a few sulky glances and disgruntled comments about 'outsiders'. It was not what André had been hoping for. 'You were supposed to charm them, not humiliate them, Simone!' he had hissed while driving the Reinastella around the field for my victory lap. 'You were lucky my mother could get you an invitation at all. We are trying to get them to accept us as a sporting couple, not show them up.'

'I'll fix it,' I said, holding up my trophy and waving. 'Thank you, ladies and gentlemen!' I called out in my best music hall voice. 'I should like to invite the judges and all the contestants and their gentlemen for a champagne supper in my dressing room at the Folies Bergère after the performance tonight.'

A thrill of excitement ran through the stand. Daisy Fellowes and Lady Mendl exchanged smiles. An invitation to behind the scenes with a star was better than winning another *Concours d'élégance automobile* or the best hat at the races. For while many performers filled their dressing rooms with hangers-on, all of Paris knew that my dressing room was 'by invitation only' and that my hospitality in that area of my life was rarely extended.

In my dressing room that evening, the Marquise de Crussol clinked her glass to mine and tapped Daisy Fellowes, who was powdering her face in my mirror, on the shoulder. 'Daisy, you must have Simone to your next party! She is such fun!'

Daisy nodded and called out to a homely-looking woman who was trying on my Queen Nefertiti headdress. 'Elsa, you will make sure Mademoiselle Fleurier is on my party list, won't you?'

André brushed past me. 'I have nothing to teach you,' he whispered, squeezing my hand. 'Nothing to teach you at all.'

The American writer Scott Fitzgerald once said that the rich were different and I discovered the truth of this for myself when my first *Tout-Paris* invitation arrived. It was for a party to be held at the house of the painter Meraud Guevara in Montparnasse.

'What is a "Come as you were" party?' I asked André, when he showed me the invitation. I was lying in the bath. A long, luxurious soak was my post Folies Bergère performance ritual.

'One of Elsa's creative ideas,' he laughed, sitting on the edge of the tub. 'She is sending a bus around some time that day and when the horn sounds we are to leave our apartments and join it, exactly as we are.'

'So if I am in the bath then, I am supposed to get on the bus naked?'

André smiled, his gaze resting on my knees — the only part of me that was visible through the bubbles except for my shoulders and head. 'In theory,' he said. 'Some people will be waiting around in their underwear all day for that chance.'

I reread the invitation. Elsa Maxwell, the American, intrigued me. She was everything that wasn't chic. She was short, plump and had a face that scared children. And yet, even with her grating French, she was charming. Although she had no money of her own, she managed to persuade *Tout-Paris* to host 'her parties'. She was certainly full of ideas. 'It's quite okay to choose music and laughter instead of a husband,' she had told me the first time I met her, that night after the *Concours d'élégance automobile* in my dressing room. 'Never be afraid of what "they" might say.'

Unfortunately, I was a little too afraid of what *Tout-Paris* might say. André and I were lovers, but we still lived in separate apartments. Just like all the other hypocrites in that circle, we maintained an air of propriety. And even though on the surface we were welcomed everywhere, I was conscious of the backbiting that took place. I had heard it for myself once at a ball. I had gone to the ladies' room and, while in the stall, overheard one society girl say to another, 'Simone Fleurier is nothing more than a spiky southern weed trying to root herself amongst the roses.' I understood the jealousy. I had stolen one of France's most sought-after bachelors. I knew André didn't care as much as I did about what those people said; he was only hoping to impress his father by showing that I had class and could mix with the best.

I thought André's remark about people going to Elsa Maxwell's 'Come as you were' party in their underwear was a joke, so when the bus came to collect us from my apartment I was shocked to see that it was true. Daisy Fellowes leaned out the bus door to greet us holding a pair of lace panties in her hand. But she was one of the more decently dressed people on the vehicle; several young women were wearing negligées and nothing else. In the early evening sun, you could see their nipples through the sheer fabric and even the dark triangle of hair between their legs.

'*Bonsoir*,' said the Marquis de Polignac. 'Elsa has organised a bar. What would you like to drink?' He was wearing an evening suit, the sharply cut top and tails that Englishmen liked to wear, and looked the perfect 'man-about-town' except that he wasn't wearing any trousers.

I accepted a glass of champagne from the marquis but had no idea where to look. I was too embarrassed to stare at his bare legs and too uncomfortable to look at his face. I slipped my arm around André and pulled him down next to me into a seat. He had been lounging around on my sofa all day in his dressing gown and pajamas. I had taken the invitation literally and gone about my day as usual. Only that afternoon, despite the July heat, I had decided that I wanted to bake a cake, something I hadn't done in years. When the bus arrived, I was presentably dressed but my blouse and apron were covered in flour.

'As if we are going to believe Simone Fleurier cooks when she is at home,' said Bébé Bérard, the designer, blowing me a kiss. 'What were you doing, making a lemon tart for your man?'

Like André, Bébé was wearing a dressing gown but instead of having a book under his arm, he had a telephone attached to his ear and shaving cream on his chin.

'I have always loved baking,' I said.

'Your apartment must be well ventilated,' said Bébé, taking a sip of wine, 'if you could bear to cook in this heat.'

Coming from Provence, I couldn't understand why Parisians made such a fuss of the heat. Still, the bus was growing stuffy with dust and exhaust fumes. Elsa hadn't counted on us getting caught up in traffic. The party was supposed to start at seven but it was already eight o'clock and we hadn't even passed over to the Left Bank yet. The travellers resigned themselves to drinking the bar dry.

'We might have to walk the rest of the way,' slurred the Marquis de Polignac, peering through the windscreen at the procession of cars in front of us.

'He is as high as a kite!' I whispered to André. 'Does he really think we can walk? Look at what everyone is wearing.'

'Or what they are not wearing, you mean,' he replied, kissing my cheek. I curled my fingers around his hand. No matter what we were doing, I was always happy to be with André. Every time I looked at him, I was aware that the man who loved me was one in a million. He was privileged, but he was also decent.

'Hello, birdies,' called out the Countess Gabriela Robilant, standing up to wave her whisky glass at a group of men waiting to cross the road. Somewhere on the journey she had lost her skirt and we were treated to the sight of her panties and suspenders.

Countess Elisabeth de Breteuil stood up and pushed Gabriela down. 'Put on your skirt!' she screamed at her. 'This is disgraceful! Remember your position!'

Gabriela laughed, her head lolling to one side. The Countess de Breteuil's cheeks reddened. She jumped up and marched down the aisle towards the driver. 'Open the door!' she demanded. 'I refuse to travel with such scandalous company!'

The driver was about to let her out when Gabriela screamed, 'To the Bastille,' and lurched towards the countess. There was a ripping sound and, before we realised it, she had pulled the other woman's skirt down.

André and I looked away but it took all our willpower not to laugh. So this was the French nobility? These were the people I was supposed to impress?

⚬

In Paris, time sped up. It seemed as if we had no sooner welcomed in the new decade than three years had passed and it was 1933.

'Are you all right there under the lights, Mademoiselle Fleurier?' the assistant director asked me. 'It will take a while to frame the camera shot.'

'For the moment, thank you,' I said, although the lights were burning my skin and I was shading my eyes with my hand because I had promised the make-up artist that I wouldn't spoil my powder by putting on sunglasses between shots.

I had a philosophy of not complaining on film sets. I considered it a privilege to be there and no one's job was any more comfortable than mine. During the making of my first film, based on my show at the Folies Bergère, I had seen a camera man suspended from a track on the ceiling to get a 180-degree shot and in my second film, a romantic escapade, I had seen a sound technician knocked from a train platform. Luckily he wasn't badly hurt, but his microphone was bent out of shape and I dreaded to think what might have happened had he fallen a few inches further either way.

Most music hall stars who worked in films found my enthusiasm for the medium extraordinary. 'But you are boxed in by those chalk marks on the floor,' Camille Casal moaned when I told her that I wanted to make at least one film a year. 'And there is no audience to applaud you. How do you know if you are doing well or not?'

'The director tells you.'

'Yes, but after the shot,' she said, shaking her head. 'And how do you know that the audience will see what he does? He may be as disillusioned as you. All you have looking at you is that camera with its black eye.'

I was surprised at Camille's impatience with the process of film-making; she was, after all, one of Europe's most famous stars. She was doing less stage work these days but was in demand for the screen. '*It's easier to hide the wrinkles on film than it is under spotlights*,' a columnist had written about Camille's change of career. It was shallow bitchiness: at thirty years of age Camille was still a beauty, and there were much older stars still performing on stage.

I dropped my hand and glanced at Jean Renoir as he discussed the frame with the camera operator. 'We'll reblock the shot,' he said. 'I want to shoot through the window.' I get to work with geniuses, I thought. And humble geniuses at that.

Jean Renoir was the son of the painter and every inch a great artist, although in a different medium. His camera movements were carefully choreographed and he sweated blood over the cuts with his editor. Although my first two films had been commercial successes, I had cringed when I saw the way I batted my eyelids and swung my arms around. My gestures were too extravagant for the screen. But in this, my third film, I was transforming under Renoir's instruction.

'Underplay, Mademoiselle Fleurier,' he told me from the first day. 'You have real potential as a dramatic actress, only I don't want you to *act*. I want you to *think* and to *feel*. The slightest movement of your eyes on screen can say as much as twenty lines of dialogue or one exaggerated sigh.'

I was lucky that such a brilliant director believed in me, but then someone had once said that Renoir was so gifted he could teach a wardrobe to act.

I watched the technicians relighting the shot. Joseph de Bretagne, the sound man, sent me a smile. The previous week we had been shooting on location in Montmartre for the scene where my lover and I say goodbye outside a jazz club. Renoir hated dubbing and believed in the sound being recorded on location. The only problem was the level of background noise in the street, which on that day included a goatherd blowing his pipe to attract the attention of housewives — a shot Renoir could use — and a sewage wagon pumping the waste from a cesspool — something Renoir could not. Joseph had tried to dampen the background noise by surrounding me and my leading man with mattresses and hangings. None of that showed in the scene of course, but whenever I saw the film I thought of those mattresses propped around me like some sort of outdoor bedding store.

After the second take, Renoir was happy with my performance and Jacques Becker, his assistant director, called everyone to stop for lunch. Although my shooting schedule was only for the mornings — so I could rehearse for the evening shows at the Casino de Paris — I usually stayed for lunch. What I liked best about making films was the camaraderie of the cast and crew. Making movies was more fun in those days and more egalitarian.

'So have you got yourself a yo-yo yet, Mademoiselle Fleurier?' Jacques asked, filling my wine glass.

'Oh, please,' I said.

A craze had taken Paris by storm. You couldn't walk anywhere without seeing grown men, and some women, spinning yo-yos. They swung them on the *métro* platforms, on trams and buses, in cafés and even during the interval at the opera.

'Come on, Mademoiselle Fleurier,' laughed Renoir. 'I hear Cartier has made one in gold. Only two hundred and eighty francs.'

After three years of balls and candlelight suppers with the *beau monde* of Paris, I could believe anything. I loved fashion, interior design and food, but I wanted to talk about other things as well. Elsa Schiaparelli was more interesting than the people who wore her clothes, and I accepted invitations to dine at her apartment just so I could hear about the art movements and new technologies that influenced her. Whenever *Tout-Paris* tried to be interesting it was pretentious. The latest thing was to take 'adventure' holidays. No longer was it enough to holiday in Biarritz or Venice, you had to go hunting in Peru or Africa, fishing in the Kuban or swordfishing in the Canaries. My thirst for more substantial conversations was another reason I loved to make films with Renoir.

'What has come over Paris?' I asked him.

'Denial,' he answered, buttering a piece of bread. 'Frivolity has always been the Parisians' reaction to danger. We can't deny the Depression won't affect us any more. Our economy has slowed down and industry profits are falling. It's not so bad in Paris yet but it has already hit the other cities. The rest of Europe is going the same way. Hitler would not be chancellor if it wasn't for the state of the German economy.'

I sipped a spoonful of soup and gave the matter some thought. Perhaps that would explain the extravagance of *Tout-Paris* and their need for constant diversion. The previous month, André and I had attended a ball organised by his mother to raise money for the unemployed. When I spoke to some guests, I discovered they had no idea what the ball was for although they were more than happy to come. Eventually André and I learnt to not expect more of *Tout-Paris*.

'If it wasn't for my family's position, and out of respect to my mother and Veronique, I would give it all away,' André often said, when he was exasperated by the ignorance of the people in our social circle.

I wasn't sure that was quite true. Now that he was twenty-seven, André was taking on more of the business as his father prepared to retire and hand over the running of the Blanchard company to him. André had once told me that he was a born entrepreneur, and there was no denying it. He may not have been keen on mingling with *Tout-Paris*, but he loved his work. I could see the pride in his eyes when he surveyed the plans for a new manufacturing plant or a hotel. His work kept him up late and got him out of bed early, but he was never tired. He was as passionate about business as I was about performing. You couldn't separate the man from the talent, and to try to would be to kill his spirit.

'You were there, weren't you?' Joseph asked Renoir. 'When Hitler was made chancellor.'

Renoir's face clouded. 'I was trying to raise funds for a film. I thought I would stay to see history in the making but what I saw was a bunch of brownshirts forcing an old Jewish lady to crouch on the pavement and lick it.'

We fell silent. Renoir and I had shared many conversations about Berlin, because he liked Germans, despite having been wounded in the Great War, and I had fond memories of the city from my time there. 'Berlin is a city in which the best and worst flourish,' he told me. 'War destroys in a matter of minutes what a slowly evolving culture has taken centuries to create.'

The location secretary rushed in. 'Mademoiselle Fleurier, there is a telephone call for you,' she said. 'The gentleman says it is urgent. You can take it in the office.'

I picked up the receiver and was surprised to hear André on the line. 'Are you almost done?' he asked, trying to sound cheerful, but I caught the anxiety in his voice. 'Are you able to skip the rehearsal this afternoon?'

'Yes. Why?' I asked.

'Count Harry is here. And he needs to see us immediately.'

It wasn't the first time Count Kessler had come to Paris. He had seen all my shows but we hadn't heard from him for a few months. His health had not been good for a while but this time I sensed there was something more than that in his sudden need to see us.

'Something is wrong, isn't it, André?'

'Come as quickly as you can,' he said. 'I am sending my car.'

As I put down the receiver I was overcome by a feeling of darkness that I couldn't explain.

⌘

André and I met the Count in the apartment of one of his friends in Île St Louis. The place consisted of two rooms crammed with books on lopsided shelves, but it wasn't the disorganised clutter that shocked us, it was the appearance of the Count when he met us at the door. Was this the same man? The eyes that had once been so full of amusement now darted around like those of a frightened animal.

'I have good and bad news for you,' he said, ushering us into the apartment. 'The good news is that you will be seeing more of me than before, for a while anyway. The bad news is that I am in exile.'

André and I were too stunned to speak.

'I have been denounced,' said the Count, lifting his hand to his head. 'By my manservant, would you believe?'

'Denounced?' said André. 'What for?'

'Oh,' said the Count, gesturing for us to sit down at a table by the window, 'in a police state it doesn't take much.' He explained that he had come to Paris with the intention of staying until the elections took place in Berlin. He had opposed the terror tactics used by the Nazis to put Hitler in power, and had supported a Freedom of Speech congress at the Kroll Festival Hall. It would have been dangerous for him to stay while there were storm troopers in the streets. But a friend had contacted him and warned him not to go back to Germany. The Count's manservant, Friedrich, had informed on him. The Nazis had raided the Count's house and found a republican flag in the attic.

The Count glanced at me, tears clouding his eyes. 'It is a terrible thing to have to ... Well, it is a terrible thing to be betrayed.'

I put my arm around him. This was not a time for formality.

'I feel as if this is an evil dream and I keep hoping that I will wake up from it,' he said. 'I read, I go for walks, I meet old friends, but all the time I am aware of the pain in my heart.'

'Is it true they are persecuting the Jewish people?' I asked.

The Count nodded. 'They are being beaten in the streets and thrown out of their jobs.'

I thought about Monsieur Etienne and Odette. I was glad to be French. 'Such a thing could not happen here,' I said. 'The French people would not stand for it. Catholics, Jews — we are all the same.'

'We thought the same thing in Germany,' said the Count. 'But Hitler has persuaded people who normally would not hurt a fly to support his thuggery.' He covered his eyes with his hands. 'It makes me sick to think of that philistine ruling Germany. I ask myself, "How did this happen? Those of us who could have stopped it — where were we looking?" Suddenly artists, authors and intellectuals are delegated to second-rate citizenship and vendors of cheese and gherkins are the only ones who count any more.'

'People in high circles support Hitler too,' said André. 'How else could he have got the chancellery?'

'True,' agreed the Count.

I looked around the apartment and noticed that the only piece of furniture in the other room was an iron bed with a leg missing. The fourth corner was supported by a chair. Despite the ramshackle nature of the apartment, it was cosier than those I had stayed in when I first came to Paris, but it was not comfortable enough for a sick man. I wondered if the Count had sufficient money. And if he didn't, I wondered how I was going to get around his pride to ask him. André and I would be glad to provide him with a more suitable apartment.

André must have been thinking the same thing. 'What do you intend to do?' he asked the Count. 'I have an apartment on the Right Bank that you are welcome to for as long as you want.'

The Count patted André's wrist. 'I am lucky to have friends like you and Simone. But I am all right. I have given instructions for the sale of my home in Weimar. Then I plan to move to Mallorca. I have always dreamed of retiring on an island.'

He managed a wan smile before his composure broke down. 'No, that is not what I dreamed of at all,' he said, weeping into his hands. 'I wanted to live out my days in Germany.'

He said the name of his country the same way a mother might cry out for a lost child. It brought a lump to my throat. I glanced out of the window. The sky had turned overcast and reflected the grim mood of the day. A storm was brewing somewhere but I had no idea from which direction the tempest would come.

In 1934 my mother and aunt came to stay with me in Paris. I was busy with my show and it would be some time before I could travel to the farm again. It was not their first visit; Aunt Yvette loved Paris and took up André's offer of a car and driver so that she and my mother could make day trips to Versailles and Senlis. My mother was more reserved in her appreciation of the city, and I sensed from the way she eyed the flamboyant café waiters and froze whenever she found herself caught in a pedestrian rush that she would never have left Pays de Sault if not for me.

She refused to let me buy her new clothes and we visited museums and ate at brasseries with my mother wearing her traditional Provençal dress. When people stared at her, she stared back. And it was always my mother who won the match. André took it in his stride and usually accompanied us to Provençal-style restaurants so my mother and aunt would feel comfortable. I loved him all the more for it — and my mother and aunt too. For while the food never came up to the standard of their cooking, they always 'Mmm-ed' and 'Oh-ed' as if they were tasting the finest cuisine in the world.

One day we came across Guillemette and Felix in Parc de Monceau. Guillemette had seen us approaching and tried to steer Felix off on another path, but was foiled by a group of nuns coming from the opposite direction. Guillemette stared over my mother's head when André introduced her and even Felix, for all his snobbery, blushed at his wife's rudeness. But if my mother noticed, she didn't show it. She greeted Guillemette with the dignified manner suited to her own position as a village healer and owner of one of the most successful lavender farms in our region. Guillemette's eyes opened wide, unnerved at my mother having so easily seized the upper hand. To top things off, as we parted ways, Aunt Yvette whispered loudly to me that a tablespoon of olive oil a day was good for 'that sort of thing'. By which she meant a cure for what she had interpreted as Guillemette's case of constipation.

'My mother and aunt might seem harmless but they both have a wicked sense of humour,' I explained to André later, as he rolled around the sofa in his apartment laughing. He acted as if my mother's high and mighty attitude and my aunt's interpretation of Guillemette's pinched face was the funniest thing he had ever seen.

'They are so proud of you,' he said, wiping the tears from his eyes. 'It shows in how they look at you.'

Poor André, I thought. I knew how much he would have loved to see that same pride in his father's eyes.

One day, André took Aunt Yvette to the Louvre, leaving my mother and me to spend the morning alone together. I looked across the dining room table at my mother who was mending one of my nightdresses with her red thread. I might be a stage and film star but I was still the daughter of this quiet, mysterious woman.

I wondered why she and my father had not had more children. Maybe the Fleuriers were not fertile. Aunt Augustine didn't have any offspring and Uncle Gerome had never produced children with Aunt Yvette.

When I was a child, my mother was not like a normal woman to me. She had always been an enigma. But now that I was grown, I was curious to know more about her.

'Maman, how did you save Papa's life when the hospital had given him up for dead?' I asked.

My mother continued to sew. She took so long to answer that I thought she mustn't have heard my question. But finally she said, 'One night when there was a full moon, I crept into the hospital with a basket of thirteen eggs. Your father was dying of an infection that had spread throughout his body, so I opened the curtains to let in the moonlight and rubbed every inch of him with the eggs, chanting a healing prayer as I did so. I disposed of the eggs by burying them in various parts of the forest. In the morning, when the doctor came to see your father, he was sitting up in bed. Cured.'

'Why didn't his eye and leg heal?' I asked.

She looked up at me and smiled. 'I told you when you were a little girl that you were too logical. It is always black and white with you. That is why I am a healer and you are a singer.'

'But why, Maman? Didn't it test your faith when he did not heal completely?'

My mother tied off the thread and put her work down. 'It strengthened it,' she said. 'Who knows the wisdom of why things are the way they are? I have never sought to change what is meant to be. I have only ever sought the wisdom and beauty in what is.'

I sensed that she was trying to teach me something but I found her lesson hard to understand. She considered my troubled expression, and reached across the table and patted my arm. 'Your father was a good man from the beginning, but he became a better one because of his injuries. He may have had one eye less, but he saw things more clearly.'

'What do you mean?'

'He became more visionary about the farm. Remember, it was your father who decided to plant lavender. He was no longer content just to follow in the footsteps of his father. He became his own man in a way that Gerome never did.'

334

At the end of the visit, André drove us to the station and helped my mother and Aunt Yvette with their bags. My mother smiled at André then turned to me.

'I am getting old,' she whispered. 'I won't be around for ever.'

I was too happy to have spent time with her and Aunt Yvette to let her words trouble me. 'Maman, you are barely in your mid-forties.'

'Our time in this world does not always correspond to our age,' she said. 'Get married, Simone. It is bad luck for you and André to love each other but wait for so long to make it a sacred union. Your father's family was against me from the beginning, but we never let them stand in our way.'

I was flooded with gratitude and squeezed her hands. I had never told my mother about André's family and their attitude towards me, or how it hurt to be snubbed. She had guessed from the rude way Guillemette had treated her that all was not well.

The train whistle sounded and I waved to my mother and Aunt Yvette. 'I will see you at the farm in a couple of months,' I called. 'Give Bernard my love.'

My mother was right: the Fleuriers had opposed her as an outsider and yet my father had still married her. But there was some light ahead for me and André. He had broached the subject of his enduring love for me with his father, who had promised that if André and I were still together in the year André turned thirty, he would believe that I was a suitable match for his son. I told myself not to care about Monsieur Blanchard's condescending attitude towards me. No matter how rich I became in my own right, he treated me as some sort of frivolous gold-digger. I couldn't help wondering if Monsieur Blanchard would have relented at all if André had been his favourite son.

TWENTY-THREE

Camille had returned from Germany in 1930, when the film industry converted to sound and she couldn't get away with mouthing words any more. Whenever we bumped into each other at premieres and balls, we always said that we would catch up, but never did. That was, until the summer of 1935 when Camille was renting a villa in Cannes with her lover, Vincenzo Zavotto, of the Italian shipping family. She invited André and me to stay there in August.

'I have never understood why you have anything to do with Camille Casal,' groaned André when I told him about the invitation. 'She is so condescending when she speaks to you, it is like watching a cat torture a mouse.'

André's viewpoint surprised me. Was that how he saw us? When I was younger I had idolised Camille, but our relationship had changed over the years. My success had put us on a more even footing, although we were more like colleagues than friends. I would never confide in Camille the way I did Odette.

'I have known her for years,' I said. 'She got me my first part with the Casino de Paris. I would be embarrassed to refuse her now.'

'As you wish,' he said, running his fingers through my hair. 'I am happy to go with you. But be careful of her. She has a reputation of being a snake.'

André wasn't saying anything about Camille that I hadn't heard from other people. Her aloofness and opportunism hadn't won her many friends. But I knew about her daughter, and that made me interpret her motives differently. If I had given birth to an illegitimate child I would have had a family to help me. Camille had no one. She had been generous to me; I didn't think it was asking so much to be her friend, at least socially.

The contrast between the blue of the bay in Cannes and the white-walled villa on the hillside reminded me of the two colours I had always associated with Provence. Camille and Vincenzo were sunning themselves by the pool when André drove the car up the gravel driveway. Vincenzo, hair slicked back and bronzed all over, leapt up to greet us. Camille slunk after him.

Vincenzo introduced himself in an affected French accent. He was a playboy from head to toe with his square sunglasses, belted swimming shorts and manicured feet. But he was likeable nonetheless when he flashed his pearly smile. I had heard that Camille still carried a torch for the War Ministry official, and only saw Vincenzo to keep herself amused.

Camille called the maid to bring us a drink. 'You must be exhausted from the heat,' she said. 'I'm surprised that you decided to drive.'

'We took our time,' said André. 'We had a few rest stops along the way.'

'Very wise,' said Vincenzo. 'Come, have a seat. The maid will show you the rooms afterwards.'

We sat down at a table by the pool. The maid brought us glasses of Pernod. The aniseed flavour coated my tongue and took me back to Marseilles 1923, with me and Bonbon walking past the cafés of the Canebière. Bonbon was old now and her companions, Olly and Chocolat, were gone. Camille slipped off her sunglasses and rubbed her eyes. She was still beautiful but she was showing signs of age. Her skin wasn't pure cream any more; there were freckles on her cheeks and lines around her eyes. But to my mind, she was still the ultimate screen goddess.

After dinner that evening, Camille fell asleep in the armchair. 'She's had too much sun,' grinned Vincenzo. 'You two should take a walk on the beach.'

After driving the past few days, the thought of stretching our legs was tempting and we rallied to his suggestion.

'Smell this air,' I said to André, running across the lukewarm sand to the water. The waves bubbled like frothy milk around my ankles. 'And look at the sunset. It is so beautiful! I am sure that dusk in the south of France lasts longer than anywhere else.'

André stood behind me and put his arms around my shoulders. 'It's nice to be like this, isn't it? To be out in the open space.'

'It is,' I agreed. 'It reminds me of the first trip we made on the *Île de France*.'

He pressed his cheek against mine. 'Simone, I will be thirty in December. When we return to Paris, I am going to tell my father that we are getting married.'

I turned around and looked at him. 'Do you think he will give us his blessing?'

He kissed me lingeringly. 'Everyone knows that he will. *He* knows he will. I have chosen a beautiful and intelligent woman who speaks several languages and is an elegant hostess. You are three rungs higher than any of the daughters of his friends. The fact that you also love and understand me will make me a better businessman and a good father.' André rested his chin on my shoulder. 'He and the whole of *Tout-Paris* know that there has been no other woman except you.'

I turned back to the ocean. So this was it? How quickly life was changing! I had loved my time in the music hall and films but I couldn't go on at that pace for ever. I was almost twenty-seven and I wanted at least four children. I imagined tiny pairs of hands reaching up to mine and four upturned faces, two girls and two boys.

'I have already told my mother,' André said.

'What did she say?'

'She said that we should look for a house.'

The sun seemed to stop in its tracks and the water around my feet rippled away. 'Really?'

'Maybe in Neuilly or Les Vésinet. Somewhere we can have a garden but not too far from the city.'

So our patience and faithfulness had paid off. Monsieur Blanchard could not deny us the happiness we had earned. I smiled, thinking how wonderful it would be to finally live with André as man and wife. I had loved him ardently for all the years we had been together, but sometimes I'd had doubts that Monsieur Blanchard would really agree to our marriage. And yet, somehow, it had worked out. I was going to be André's wife at last.

André slept late the following morning, while I was wide awake before breakfast. I looked out the window at the teal blue ocean and was pleased to see Camille sitting by the pool, watching Vincenzo swim his laps.

'You look as happy as a cat that has just caught a bird,' said Camille, glancing up from her deckchair when I stepped onto the patio.

'André and I are getting married,' I said, forgetting André's warning to be wary of her. We had waited long enough; I wanted to announce the good news to everybody.

Camille looked startled, as if I had somehow insulted her. 'He asked you?'

I nodded. She turned her eyes towards the pool. 'Are you sure? He might love you but I don't see how his parents will approve. Those kinds of families marry for power.' Her voice was dry and hard. I hesitated, not sure how to react to her less than enthusiastic response.

'They have known for years,' I said. 'André's mother adores me and his father said if we were still together when André turned thirty, he would give us his blessing.'

Camille looked unconvinced. She cast her eyes over me, taking in my figure and clothes. I felt like a young girl standing before the headmistress. I was telling the truth but she made me feel as if I were lying. I realised that I was gaining what Camille had always wanted but never found: someone to give her and her daughter security. She had been ahead of me in every step in life, but in this one thing I was the winner.

'Has Monsieur Blanchard formally given permission? Has he made a public announcement?' she asked.

I shook my head. 'All that will happen when André and I return to Paris.'

Camille's face settled into a more serene expression but something lingered in her eyes. 'Do what you want,' she said, lying back in the deckchair and slipping on her sunglasses. 'I just wanted to warn you that I know about those kinds of families. I can only predict things ending badly for you, even if they do let you marry him.'

I realised a rift had opened between us. Camille was not used to having anything less than the upper hand in our relationship. But now that I was about to marry André I felt more secure and less needy for her approval. I shrugged and turned to walk down to the beach. I would be alone with my happiness if Camille would not share it. But I could not shrug off the chill of premonition in her words.

❧

As soon as we returned to Paris, André and I embarked on our search for a house. We marked our territory on a map and learnt the street names by heart. I kept my 'film work hours' but used them to contact real estate agents and inspect houses. We enlisted the help of Odette and Joseph, who we intended to put in charge of decorating and furnishing the house. The four of us travelled around Neuilly together. Paul Derval had suggested that we stick to street and house names with thirteen letters for good luck, but we let Kira be our guide. When we arrived at a house I set her down by the gate. If she lifted her tail and ambled inside, sniffing the path and following her nose to the house, then we continued too. If she didn't, there was no point in going any further.

'You will like this one,' said Joseph one morning as he drove us along a tree-lined street. 'The exterior and the garden are perfect. I will have the interior stripped out to create something beautiful for you.'

We pulled up outside a house with oatmeal-coloured walls and white shutters and columns. The garden was overgrown with lilac and wild rose.

'It is peaceful,' I said.

I placed Kira near the gate where she hesitated a moment, sniffing the air. She was getting matronly in her middle age and stubborn. But then she moved forward and sauntered down the path to the front door. We cheered.

'The interior colours are hideous,' said Odette, while Joseph slipped the key into the lock. 'Ignore them. Think of the layout.'

The entrance way was powder blue with gilt detailing and a black and white tiled floor. A chair sat in the corner with some dusty books scattered around it.

'Imagine it all in beige and white,' said Odette, leading us into the drawing room. 'With natural wood, sleek lines and a couple of Directoire pieces and Japanese vases mixed to give it a soft touch.'

'I like the sound of that,' André said as we climbed the stairs to the upper floor.

Joseph threw open some double doors and led us into a light-filled room with a marble fireplace and bay windows. 'The master bedroom.'

'It's huge,' I said. 'And it looks over the main garden.'

Joseph and André wandered down the hallway, opening the doors to the other rooms, while Odette and I circled the master bedroom and imagined the possibilities.

'Jean-Michel Frank made me a suite with dark wood and ivory upholstery,' said Odette. 'Something like that would look good in here.'

'Simone, come quickly!' called André from downstairs. Odette and I found the men in a room with French doors looking out onto the garden. André turned to me. 'Wouldn't this make a wonderful music room? Or a room for dancing? We could put in a polished floor and ... *voilà*!' he said, sweeping his arms into a waltz pose. Kira appeared from under a table, pranced across the floor and pushed on the doors before running out into the garden.

'Can you get it fixed up by the end of the year?' I asked Joseph.

'Of course,' he said, folding his arms and surveying the room. 'I would be delighted.'

André and I smiled at each other. All that remained was to tell Monsieur Blanchard formally, which André intended to do the following month when he and his father travelled to Portugal on business.

I reduced my performing engagements and put my energy into the house instead. There was little structural work to be done, so the decorating progressed quickly. Odette's colour scheme for the interior — butterscotch, vanilla, toffee, cocoa and cream — was so delicious-looking that sometimes I was tempted to lick the walls. The tones would 'warm up' the modern furniture which was to be finished in tortoiseshell, bronze and leather.

One afternoon, Odette and I were sitting on the terrace, mapping out designs for the garden. We wouldn't do much to it until the spring, but with the house well on the way to being finished we wanted to keep going.

'A visitor is here to see you, Mademoiselle,' my maid, Paulette, announced.

'Who?'

'Madame Fontaine.'

I glanced at Odette. 'André's sister.' I told Paulette to show Guillemette to the terrace and to make us some tea.

'Should I leave?' asked Odette.

I shook my head. 'She didn't make an appointment with me so why should you go? Besides, she is a dragon. I don't want to face her alone. I'm sure she is here to say something negative about the house.'

Paulette returned with Guillemette. She had three sons now and motherhood had not improved her figure or her temperament. She barely waited for Paulette to retreat and for me to introduce Odette before she pointed an accusing finger at me and blustered, 'So you think you have won, do you?'

'What do you mean?' I asked her.

She took a step closer, trying to intimidate me. She was powerfully built but I was taller and I disliked her too much to be threatened by her. 'You think you can wheedle your way into my family and drag us all down to your level.'

Odette let out a shocked hiss.

'I haven't wheedled my way into your family —'

'You intend to marry my brother, do you not?' she spat, making a gesture towards the house. 'It looks to me as if that is your plan.'

I folded my arms. I remembered the way Guillemette had treated my mother and it infuriated me as much as if it had happened a moment ago. André and I had been happy together for ten years. Yes, I had made my career as a performer, but I had never danced naked. André was the only man I had ever been with. I had enough money of my own not to need any of the Blanchard family fortune. I simply wanted to marry the man I loved.

'That,' I said, 'is none of your business.'

Guillemette's eyes turned red. Her face became so flushed I thought she might burst into flames. 'It is very much my business,' she screeched. 'I have three sons and I do not intend for them to have an immoral aunt. I have tolerated you long enough as André's companion but I will certainly not tolerate you as his wife.'

Odette stood up. 'Madame Fontaine, if you cannot speak calmly and with civility, I suggest you leave,' she said.

Odette's poise in the face of Guillemette's hysteria reminded me of those fairytales where a beautiful princess must match her wits against a wicked witch. Guillemette accused me of base behaviour, but Odette had shown her that the only vulgar person was Guillemette herself.

When Guillemette realised that she could not frighten us, she turned to leave. Before she did, however, she pointed her finger at me again. She was about to speak but stopped herself. Her face broke into a smile. She pushed past Paulette, who was stepping out onto the terrace with a tray, and stormed through the house. A few minutes later we heard a car motor start.

'*Mon Dieu*,' said Odette. 'I have never met anyone like that in my life.'

But I couldn't respond. I had been too unnerved by Guillemette's smile.

<hr />

On the day that André was due to return from Portugal I sat in the drawing room all afternoon, waiting for the sound of his car. I had received a telegram from him to say that he had arrived safely, but after that had heard nothing. He returned after nightfall, the car wheels crunching on the gravel and the headlights glinting through the window. I rushed to the door to meet him, and wrapped my arms around his waist, cowering against the stinging wind.

'It is blowing a gale,' he said, stepping into the hall and bringing a swirl of leaves and twigs with him. He handed his coat and hat to Paulette.

'Come on,' I said. 'There is a fire in the drawing room. I will get you a drink.'

André looked up at the ceiling then dropped his gaze to the walls and furnishings. 'These chairs,' he said, running his hands over the leather, 'they're fantastic. They make you want to sink into them.'

'Please do.' I handed him a glass of cognac. 'I can't wait to show you the rest of the house. All the main rooms are finished.'

'After dinner,' he said, taking a sip from his glass. 'I didn't eat on the train.'

'Well, after dinner then.'

I looked at André more closely. He was smiling but there was something else . . . a tension in his eyes.

'André, what happened?' I asked, kneeling by his side. 'Don't keep me in suspense.'

He stared at me, distracted. I had brought his thoughts back from miles away. It is because he is tired, I persuaded myself. Not because his father has changed his mind. No; André would have telephoned or written to me straightaway if that were the case. I had told him about Guillemette's visit before he left for Portugal and he had laughed it off. 'Guillemette reacts hysterically to everything. I've never known my father to pay attention to her,' he'd said.

'Let me show you the master bedroom,' I said. 'Then you can see the other rooms tomorrow after you've had a rest.'

I led him up the stairs, pointing out the mirrors and furniture Joseph, Odette and I had chosen. Although he was enthusiastic about each piece, he also seemed to be growing more miserable with each step. The fireplace in the bedroom was lit and Kira was curled on a rug in front of it. André stepped towards her. Whenever she saw him, Kira would roll over on her back so he could scratch her stomach. André bent down to her but stopped halfway and slid to the floor as if he had been shot. I rushed towards him. He was holding his face in his hands, crying.

'What is the matter?' I asked, cradling him in my arms.

André rubbed his face and stared at me. 'I love you,' he said. 'I want us to be together for ever.'

A gust of wind blew through the trees outside the window and somewhere I heard a branch snap.

André's face twisted. He pressed his wet cheek against my throat. 'It's all right,' I said. 'What happened? Did your father refuse?'

'It is worse than that,' he said, standing up and stumbling to the window. 'He says that if I go ahead and marry you, he will banish me from the family.'

I was too stunned to say anything at first. It was the most extreme thing a parent could do to a child. I tried to get my mind to slow down and think clearly. I would hardly have been shocked if Monsieur Blanchard had refused permission all along, but to suddenly retract his word? If he didn't take Guillemette seriously, what would have caused him to do this?

'What made him change his mind?' I asked.

André shook his head, staring at me with bewildered eyes.

'There must be some way around this,' I muttered. 'There has to be.'

'Not if I can't legally be with you.' André rushed to the bed and punched the mattress. No, I thought, please don't. Please don't say what I think you are going to tell me.

His voice was barely audible above the crying wind. 'He expects me to marry next year, but not you, Simone. He wants me to marry Princesse de Letellier.'

❧

The storm was still blowing the following morning when I opened my eyes and saw that the wind had stripped the leaves from the trees outside the window. My bones ached with exhaustion. My eyes were so swollen it was hard to blink. André was still sleeping, slumped against my shoulder like a man in a coma. We had cried for hours before falling asleep in the early hours of the morning, too spent to cry any more.

Why was Monsieur Blanchard doing this? Why couldn't he let us be happy together as we had been for the past decade?

I slipped out of bed and gazed through the window. I felt Monsieur Blanchard's betrayal like a slap in the face. Perhaps there had been some misunderstanding? I remembered Guillemette's smile. Had she told him some lie?

When André woke, he told me that he was going to his own office to sort some things out. I couldn't bring myself to look in his eyes. When I finally did, I saw that they were wild with fear.

'I don't care about the money, Simone,' he said. 'Or the power of my family name. I would give all that up for you. All of it. It doesn't mean anything to me.'

Yes, André, I thought. I know you would. But your mother and your sister? Could I ask that of you?

After André left, I dressed and went to the film studios. Renoir had asked me to play a small part in his new film. I had agreed as a favour because it was only one day of shooting, but when I saw the awe with which the other actors looked at me when I arrived on set, I regretted it. Did I have the strength to go through with this now? Just the day before I had been as blissful as any soon-to-be bride about to marry the love of her life. Now everything was falling apart.

I was determined that none of the cast or crew, not even Renoir, should see me cry. André and I weren't defeated yet. Whenever there was a break, I slipped from the set and walked down the corridor to the production secretary's empty office. There, I would slump in her chair and release my tears for a few minutes before collecting myself, powdering the blotchiness from my face and striding back on set as if I were the luckiest woman in the world.

After the shooting was complete, Renoir sat with me in the cafeteria and talked for an hour about an idea he had for an American–French production that would star me. Although he spoke with energy and I nodded enthusiastically, when the chauffeur came to pick me up and Renoir kissed my cheeks, I realised that I couldn't recollect a word of the conversation.

'Is everything all right, Mademoiselle?' Paulette asked me when I arrived home. The concern in her voice nearly caused me to break down. I tried to hold myself together, but the effort made me sound like I was choking. 'I am not feeling very well today. I am going to rest in my room.'

I lay down on the bed, fear creeping over me like a winter fog. I had never considered that money might be something that could break me and André apart, yet I began to see how it might. I had a fortune of my own and would have gladly set André up in business. But my resources did not match the wealth of the Blanchard family. If André was disowned by one of the most powerful families in France, it would not work in his favour. Businessmen needing the goodwill of Monsieur Blanchard senior would not show favour towards his son. André could go into show business management, but was that what he wanted to do? I knew how much he had loved his work over the past few years. Could he give that up and still remain André?

I glanced at my watch. It was four o'clock. I wondered if Monsieur Blanchard would still be at his office.

❧

I had expected Monsieur Blanchard to greet me with the same exasperation of a boss dealing with a dismissed employee who wants her job back, but he was merely evasive.

'Some coffee, Mademoiselle Fleurier?' he asked, after offering me a seat by his desk.

'You know why I have come.'

He nodded, his jaw set, steeling himself for a confrontation. It was not his usual approach; I was used to Monsieur Blanchard being smug. But the change in his behaviour was only temporary. He sat down, moved his pen from the left to the right side of his desk then back again, gathering his strength. 'Your coming here won't change my mind,' he said. 'A man in André's position cannot marry whomever he pleases. He has responsibilities. Marriage is not a frivolous thing. But I am prepared to hear you out.'

'Is love a frivolous reason to get married?' I asked. 'If it is, why didn't you refuse outright to let us marry years ago?'

'Marriage is about family, reputation and duty. It has nothing to do with love,' said Monsieur Blanchard, curling his fingers over and examining his nails.

My impression was right. He was being evasive. 'And what is it about me that suddenly offends your sense of family, reputation and duty that didn't only a year ago?' I asked.

Monsieur Blanchard rubbed his eyes. 'You seem to have misunderstood me, Mademoiselle Fleurier. I have always liked you. I do not object to André being fond of you. I do not object to you having a house together. I do not even object to you having children together, but those children will not carry the Blanchard name. For that André must marry someone from a reputable family. However, I see nothing wrong in a man having a beautiful mistress *and* a dutiful wife. In fact, I think it is necessary to a man's domestic happiness.'

My stomach rolled over. A terrible idea began to dawn on me. It was well known that Monsieur Blanchard had a mistress in Lyon. Was it possible that André, not a philanderer like his father, had misunderstood his father's intentions towards us? Maybe Monsieur Blanchard had given his blessing to our relationship but not our union.

'Go on,' I said.

Monsieur Blanchard glanced away from me, out the window. 'You must understand yourself that you and André are not a suitable marriage. Who are your family, Mademoiselle Fleurier?'

I had been around Paris society enough to know about class prejudice. My fortune was greater than that of Princesse de Letellier's, whose origins were not much more impressive than mine. Her maternal grandfather had been a sardine fisherman who had made a fortune and bought a fleet. Her mother had gained a title by marrying the impoverished Prince de Letellier. And yet my social position was considered lower than the Princesse de Letellier's because I had made my wealth myself, and self-made women were a threat to the status quo. Coco Chanel was the richest woman in the world, but she was snubbed as a 'tradesperson' in Paris's elite salons.

Whatever I had come for, I was not going to get it from Monsieur Blanchard, and until I spoke to André there was no point antagonising him further. I rose from my chair. 'I had an uncle like you, Monsieur Blanchard,' I told him. 'He was bloody-minded in his determination to have his way. He died with nothing but regrets.'

Monsieur Blanchard met my eyes. 'Do not fight this, Mademoiselle Fleurier,' he said. 'You will not save André by marrying him. In fact, you will destroy him.'

I left Monsieur Blanchard's office and didn't look back. But out on the boulevard, it occurred to me that Monsieur Blanchard had not been cocky or arrogant. He had spoken as if the decision were somehow out of his hands.

❧

André sat on the sofa in the drawing room, shaking his head in disbelief. 'So my father thinks you are acceptable as a mistress but not as a wife?'

For a man to have a regular mistress wasn't an unusual arrangement in upper-class marriages. The wives didn't like it, but they couldn't object unless they were prepared to lose everything under the Napoleonic code. Did I love André so much that I was prepared to share him with another woman? I flinched from the crushing pain in my chest, imagining myself waving goodbye to André as he drove off to return to his wife and legitimate children.

'It is impossible,' said André, stroking my hair. 'I love you too much. Imagine fathering children with you and not being able to give them a name?'

A few weeks later, André went to see Count Kessler in Lyon where he was staying with his sister. The Spanish War had arrived in Mallorca and the Fascists were executing German exiles, so the Count had moved back to France. One drizzly afternoon, I was sitting in the drawing room when Paulette announced that Madame Blanchard had arrived to see me. Since Monsieur Blanchard's refusal to let us marry, André and I had avoided his family. We had drifted between reality and a dreamlike state. There had been whole hours, at the opera or walking hand in hand in the park, when we forgot what we were facing and life seemed as blissful as it always had been between us. I sensed the arrival of Madame Blanchard was about to crack that fragile shell. Indeed, even before Paulette had left the room, Madame Blanchard collapsed onto the sofa, sobbing. 'He destroyed Laurent and now he is going to destroy André,' she said.

I had not been eating properly the last few days and almost swooned when I stood up. I felt sorrier for Madame Blanchard than I did for André or myself. She had to live with the self-conceited tyrant. 'Madame Blanchard,' I said, sitting down next to her and putting my hand on her knee. 'You have always been good to me. You wanted André to marry me, didn't you? You wanted us to be happy here.'

Her face twisted. 'I would have been proud to have such a lovely daughter-in-law,' she said. 'And I know how happy you have made André.'

'You see no possibility that Monsieur Blanchard will change his mind?'

Madame Blanchard shook her head. A shiver ran through me and I turned away. For the first time, I saw the possibility that I could lose André. At first, Monsieur Blanchard's refusal had brought out our unshakeable belief that our love could conquer all. But what next? How long before external pressures began to conspire against us?

'I had a terrible dream last night,' I said, half to Madame Blanchard and half to myself. 'I was standing on the beach at Cannes, watching André swimming. I could hear him laughing and see him waving to me. Suddenly the sound faded. I ran into the water but the waves knocked me back. André was slowly being sucked out into the sea and I was powerless to stop it.'

'My husband is as strong as an ox,' said Madame Blanchard. 'So it is not as if we can wait. He will outlive us all.'

In the midst of all the darkness, what she said struck me as comical. I laughed and wept at the same time. Monsieur Blanchard would carry out his threat to banish André if he married me, of that I had no doubt. I understood his temperament. Men like Monsieur Blanchard and Uncle Gerome did not see their families as people, they saw them as possessions.

'Is it impossible for you and André to be happy without being married?' Madame Blanchard asked. 'He will never love that girl as much as you.'

I had wrestled with that question day and night. I recalled the days in Berlin with Mademoiselle Canier and knew I could not continue to love André with my whole being while sharing him with another woman. I also knew in my heart that was how he felt about me. I shook my head. 'Now it is down to a choice between me and you and Veronique.'

Madame Blanchard reared back as if I had struck her. 'Do not take my son from me, I beg you, Simone,' she cried. 'He will choose you if you make him choose. Veronique and I will have no one. I lost Laurent. Guillemette is an abomination I cannot believe is mine, and I stopped loving my husband years ago. All I have in the world is André and Veronique.'

I stood up and went to the window, leaning on the sill. I couldn't stand the sound of Madame Blanchard's voice, so full of pain. She followed me and clutched my hands.

'I know you love André,' she said. 'But you are still young. One day there will be someone else for you to love. Then, when you have children of your own, you will understand the compassionate thing you did for me.'

I shut my eyes. 'I will never find another André, Madame Blanchard,' I said. 'Never.'

After Madame Blanchard had left, I stood in the garden, staring at my hands. It wasn't until I heard the front doorbell that I came to myself and realised that my fingers were turning blue. A minute later, Paulette opened the French doors to tell me that Monsieur Etienne was waiting in the drawing room. I thought how nice it would be to distract my mind from Madame Blanchard's visit. I asked Paulette to make us some coffee, but as soon as I entered the drawing room and saw the pained expression on Monsieur Etienne's face, I knew there was not going to be any comfort for me.

'You had better tell me what is going on, Mademoiselle Fleurier,' he said gently.

I had become so used to pretending nothing was wrong that my forced smile came naturally. But André and I had been missing social engagements, and there were rumours amongst the press. There would be time to speak to Monsieur Etienne about how to handle the newspapers later; I didn't have the strength to face them now. I had to face myself first and I wasn't doing very well.

'Nothing is wrong,' I said. 'I have been busy with the house.'

Monsieur Etienne saw straight through me. 'The Blanchard family are making announcements about an impending marriage and you and André are saying nothing,' he said. 'You had better explain it all to me. With Prince Edward and Wallace Simpson in the news, any whiff of this kind of thing is like the scent of blood to hounds. I want to help you, Mademoiselle Fleurier. You might be popular, but the press is going to be brutal.'

<hr />

That afternoon, I took a taxi to Boulevard Haussmann where Odette and Joseph had their shop. I hovered on the pavement for a moment, my legs trembling so violently that it took all my concentration to put one foot in front of the other and go through the door. I caught sight of my reflection in a mirror. My hair was wild from the wind and my pupils were wide with fear. I wore the same expression I had seen on Count Kessler's face when he had found himself exiled from Germany. I stared at a painting of maidens and satyrs, the colours blurring in my disorientated vision. What was I doing here? I sank to my knees.

'Simone,' said Joseph, pulling me up from the floor. He looked into my face, a worried frown on his brow. 'Come,' he said, putting his arm around me and leading me to his office. 'Odette is in the back room. I will fetch her.'

'What else has happened?' asked Odette, taking my hands and helping me into a chair. She glanced over her shoulder at Joseph who set about making tea. I had told her about Monsieur Blanchard's change of heart a few days before.

'I don't know why I am here,' I said, my hands shaking so much that I couldn't pick up the tea cup when Joseph set it before me. But even as I spoke I saw a black hole open and felt the chilly draught of my future blow over me. The dream I had kept in my heart for ten years was not going to happen. How could it? André and I had been living an illusion. I had trusted his judgment that our love could take on the world because he was older and more experienced. But now I understood he had been just as blinded by love as I had. *Tout-Paris* had never been for us, they had always been against us. Could I really ask him to give up his family and position, to never see his mother or Veronique again? Could even the greatest love stand up to so many sacrifices?

'If I hold on, I will destroy him,' I said.

As soon as the words left my mouth I saw the strong rope that bound me and André together begin to fray.

Odette squeezed my arm. I could not have imagined that such a delicate hand could contain such strength. 'You and André have loved each other for years,' she said. 'As long as you listen to that dear, true heart of yours, Simone, you will know the right thing to do.'

I put my hands to my eyes. Joseph sat down next to me. Odette stood up and threw her arms around me, weeping. 'Be strong, Simone. Joseph and I love you no matter what you decide.'

When I returned to the house, I walked into the dancing room, my heels clicking on the wooden floor. *Wouldn't this make a wonderful music room? Or a room for dancing?* I remembered André's face the first time I had seen him at the Café des Singes. I had wondered if he was the 'friendly face' I should sing to. Ten years of memories floated by me: dancing at the Resi in Berlin; my debut at the Adriana; our trip on the *Île de France* when we first became lovers. 'We were going to be so happy,' I whispered.

I turned and walked down the hallway, my hand brushing over the furniture. For a hazy moment I saw André striding towards me, four small children trotting alongside him, trying to keep up. I opened up my arms, but before they reached me, he and the children disappeared into thin air.

As long as you listen to that dear, true heart of yours, Simone, you will know the right thing to do.

André returned from his visit to Count Kessler a few days later. He was gaunt but smiling. His smile disappeared when he saw my suitcases in the hall.

'Simone,' he said, sinking into a chair.

I had intended to be cold and cruel. I wanted to make it easier for him to forget me. But when I looked into those sable eyes, and saw the tenderness there, I broke down and sank to the floor. André crouched next to me.

'Maybe it is best we don't see each other for a while,' he said, taking out a handkerchief and dabbing my face. 'Then we can think with clear heads and decide what is the best thing to do.'

Poor André, I thought. He is going to keep hoping until the last. I sat back and cradled his face in my hands. 'This *is* the best thing to do, André. We can't win.'

Kira rubbed against André's knees. He stroked her head and looked away. 'What about us, Simone? What about *our* happiness?'

We remained still for a few minutes. When André finally turned back to me, our gazes locked and our eyes brimmed with tears. In that instant we knew that our dream was over and our time together had come to an end.

'We had the love of a lifetime, didn't we, Simone?' André said, running his finger down my cheek. 'Something more precious than most people will ever know.'

The future André and I had pictured together had been snatched from us. But no one could take away what we had shared. The memories of those ten years together were ours to keep for ever. On our last evening at the house, André asked the chef to prepare Loire pike in honour of our first journey on the *Île de France*. Afterwards, we made love in the flickering light of the fire. I ran my hands over André's cheeks and chin, over every muscle and joint, savouring what had become familiar over the years. He brushed his fingertips over my skin and pressed his lips against mine. I drank the moment in, shutting out the future as best as I could. I did not allow myself to think that after tomorrow I would never feel the crush of his bare chest against mine or that I would never see those beautiful sable eyes grow old. 'My André' would no longer be mine; he would belong to someone else. He lifted me to him and I held on with all my strength, kissing him then burying my face in his hair. I did not want to see the morning come, the first silver light of dawn break across the sky.

After breakfast, which neither of us could touch, the taxi arrived and we watched the driver pack my suitcases into the boot. He placed Kira in her cage on the back seat then held open the door for me. André drew me close. We lingered for a few seconds in the embrace.

'Wherever you go, Simone, whoever you are with, you will always be in my heart,' he said.

'And you in mine.'

Slowly I pulled away and he loosened his grip.

The driver closed the door behind me. I wiped the mist from the window so I could see André through the glass. He was standing so formally, it looked as though he intended to salute me. Only his chin, held high, trembled as he fought to keep back his tears. The gates swung open and the taxi rolled forward. Kira meowed. André and I did not take our eyes from each other. I watched him until we turned into the street and he disappeared from view.

Part Three

TWENTY-FOUR

The months following my separation from André were bleak and colourless. I was torn apart. I could not taste the food I forced myself to eat, sometimes I could scarcely breathe, and each night I paced the floorboards of my new apartment off the Champs Élysées until I was exhausted enough to sleep.

Minot offered me an engagement at the Adriana and I threw myself into the show, afraid that if I stopped working I would not be able to get out of bed. But at each performance I found myself gazing into the audience, hoping that I might see André amongst the sea of faces. Ghosts of him appeared in my dressing room, sitting in his favourite chair and reading a book as he'd liked to do once a show had settled in. Sometimes I woke with a start in the night, sure that I could feel the brush of his skin against mine. But André was not there; not in my dressing room and not beside me. He had been ripped from my life like a photograph torn from a newspaper. All that remained was a gaping, jagged hole.

It was Monsieur Etienne who informed me of André's engagement. 'André told me himself,' Monsieur Etienne explained. 'He didn't want you to hear of it through the press.'

The news pierced me like a bullet. When we parted, André and I had agreed that we would get on with our lives. For him, that had meant getting married. I thought I had accepted that when I decided we couldn't go on, but the reality was a blow I had not expected. Nevertheless I did not see André's engagement as a betrayal. The decision to end our relationship had been mine, and he had only agreed because he feared what the situation was doing to me.

'Perhaps you should leave Paris for a while,' suggested Monsieur Etienne. 'You still have those offers from Hollywood.' I knew that he wanted to protect me from the French press. Even though Hitler's troops had stormed into the demilitarised Rhineland, violating the Treaty of Versailles and slapping France in the face, the newspapers would be all agog over a society wedding.

I declined his suggestion. Perhaps I thought that by staying in Paris, the sky might open one day and a miracle would bring me and André together again. My hope was as far-fetched as that of a condemned man who watches the dawn burst on the horizon and still believes a last-minute pardon is possible. The night of the wedding, I collapsed on stage with a burning fever. My press agent announced that I had pneumonia and was returning to my family in Pays de Sault to recover. But I hadn't contracted pneumonia; the world had simply become too much for me. I had suffered a nervous breakdown.

During Uncle Gerome's illness, my mother had stayed in Aunt Yvette's house along with Bernard. After Uncle Gerome died, she remained there. On my return home, my mother saw that I swung from a desire for company to a need for solitude and set me up in my childhood bedroom in my father's house. Each morning she lit the fire in the kitchen and I spent the day by it, with Kira sleeping in my lap. Sometimes I read to distract myself, but usually I just stared into the flames. I had a sense that I was falling into darkness and somehow the firelight gave me something to cling to. I fought against the question that constantly sprang up in my mind: what was André doing now? I knew where he was and it wasn't with me.

'Any creature in shock needs warmth,' said my mother, stoking up the fire. She had always been softly spoken, but during those days she only whispered to me. Her voice was imbued with healing spells; she wanted to soothe the pain in my heart.

At midday, Aunt Yvette would struggle through the chilly wind to bring me something to eat. One day it was ewe's milk cheese with warm bread, another it was anchovies and eggs. One bitterly cold day she cooked a stew and Bernard helped her carry the terrine to my father's house.

'You and Kira have come to look alike over the years,' Bernard said, setting the terrine on the table and sending steam, aromatic with red wine and bay leaves, wafting around the room.

Aunt Yvette gave him a sideways glance. It was the kind of look a wife might give a husband long after the passion has cooled but the love and regard remain. 'What are you talking about, Bernard?' she laughed.

Bernard smiled and ladled the stew into a bowl. 'They are both beautiful and graceful.'

I could have said the same thing about Aunt Yvette and Bernard.

In the nurturing company of my family I started to heal and by the time spring came I felt well enough to spend my days walking the fields. I watched baby rabbits leap up from their burrows and young goats stumble on their first steps. The tone began to return to my muscles and colour reappeared in my face. But my healing was nearly undone when a strange car sped up the road one day.

I watched from the farmhouse window as a slope-shouldered man stepped out of the car, holding something under his jacket. Bernard called out a greeting and hurried towards the stone wall, assuming the man was a stranger who had lost his way or a farmer looking to buy some land in the area. But after a brief exchange Bernard's voice lowered to a growl.

The man retreated but as he did, he caught a glimpse of me. He pulled the object out from under his jacket. A camera. I stepped back just in time to avoid having my picture taken. The man shouted: 'The Marseilles press would like to know if Mademoiselle Fleurier will be sending André Blanchard a congratulatory telegram now that the Princesse de Letellier is expecting a child.'

Bernard picked up a rock and aimed it at the reporter, who backed away to his car. It wasn't Bernard's nature to be violent, but he wanted to protect me. His threat was convincing because the reporter threw his jacket and camera into the car, revved the motor, and was soon nothing more than a speck on the dusty road.

After the reporter's visit, I retreated to the house again although the weather was turning warmer. André's first child. I hadn't allowed myself to even imagine that.

'I have wasted years of love,' I said to my mother when she tried to coax me out into the sunshine one day. 'I was destined to lose André.'

'Nothing is ever wasted, Simone,' she said. 'The love we give never dies. It only changes form. Never be afraid to keep giving love.'

Soon afterwards, I received a telegram from Monsieur Etienne informing me that I had been invited to sing at the World's Fair in Paris.

'It is an honour,' said Bernard, reading the telegram to my mother and aunt. 'Simone will be representing France.'

It was the highest honour that could be bestowed on any French entertainer, and it showed how much I had achieved. But I was the most famous singer in the country because of André.

'What is wrong?' my mother asked.

I lowered my eyes. 'I can't face Paris,' I said. I didn't need to look at her to sense her dismay.

That night the moon was full and the air was tinged with the warmth of early summer. I left my shutters open and let the moonlight fall over my skin. I breathed in the scents of my childhood: lavender and pine; cypress and cedar. Suddenly, out of the shadows, my mother appeared in a scarlet dress. She held a basket of eggs. I tried to sit up but my legs and arms were so heavy I couldn't move. My mother took the eggs one by one and rolled their cool shells over me, chanting under her breath. She moved the eggs across my forehead, along my arms and over my chest. I felt something drag up inside me, as if the darkness in my heart was being sucked away. She rubbed the soles of my feet then turned me over and caressed my back. I floated upwards, buoyed by a sense of lightness and joy that had escaped me ever since I had left André. I flipped over and sank down to the bed as lightly as a feather drifting on air. The mattress pressed against my back and my limbs were free to move. I glimpsed my mother disappearing back into the shadows and I fell into a peaceful sleep.

The next morning when I awoke and saw the sun shimmering over my bed, I knew I had to find the strength to return to Paris and rebuild my life.

The day after my performance at the World's Fair, Monsieur Etienne, Minot and I had dinner at one of the outdoor cafés on the grounds, sampling the food of the provinces and listening to the foreign accents buzzing around us. The tourists had returned to Paris and smiles lit the faces of the hoteliers and restaurateurs once again after years of the Depression. Afterwards, we wandered around the American and Spanish pavilions and visited the formal garden of fountains which spouted water shaped into trees, hedges and blossoms.

'Look at that,' I said, pointing to the fountains in the centre of the Seine which shot up water like geysers. Gold lights glinted on the river's surface.

'They have used a thin layer of oil sprinkled with gold dust to achieve that effect,' explained Minot. 'When the searchlights hit the river, the water glitters like tinsel.'

'It is very pretty,' I said. 'And so Parisian.'

'You are glad to be back then?' asked Monsieur Etienne, gesturing for us to sit down on a bench. He reached into his jacket and pulled out a newspaper. He handed it to me, pointing out an article from that morning's *Le Figaro*:

> Simone Fleurier, after being away from Paris for nearly a year, gave a triumphant performance at the World's Fair last night. She is, and will always be, our shining star; the brightest light in the City of Lights. Welcome home, Mademoiselle Fleurier. We are glad that you are back, lifting our spirits with your vibrant voice and thrilling us with your dancing.

'What a declaration of love!' I said. 'So Paris missed me after all.'

'We all missed you,' said Minot.

'You are sadder,' said Monsieur Etienne, pressing my hand, 'but it doesn't affect your performance. If anything I have never seen you sing with as much depth as you did last night.'

I sensed the sympathy in his words and was grateful that he had broached the subject of André so discreetly. We walked on towards the Pont d'Iéna and the Eiffel Tower. 'Look at that,' said Minot. Looming before us was the German pavilion, brilliantly lit with searchlights. At its entrance a tower soared above all the other pavilions. A golden eagle perched on top of it, clutching the swastika in its claws.

Monsieur Etienne clucked his tongue. 'You can see it from everywhere. I think it is in bad taste, considering Spain.'

I thought about the painting by Picasso we had seen in the Spanish pavilion. It was called *Guernica* and showed a woman crying out in pain, clutching her dead child; a disembowelled horse in its death throes; a figure falling from a burning building. It was Picasso's ode to the Basque town that had been brutally bombed by the Italians in planes supplied by the Germans. Italy, Germany, England, Russia and France had agreed on a policy of non-intervention in Spain, but Germany and Italy weren't playing by the rules.

'You would think that France would stand up for democracy,' I said. 'But we stand by and watch as the legitimate Republican government and their supporters are slaughtered by the Fascists.'

'Be careful, Mademoiselle Fleurier,' said Minot. 'You are speaking like a Jew. Don't you know that *L'Action Française* says that the Jews are pushing for another European war?'

'I am not pushing for a war,' I said. I understood why the French didn't want to get involved in Spain. My own father had suffered during the last war and I had seen enough widows, orphans and disfigured men to be sickened by the thought of more fighting. 'But many people say that France will find herself involved in a war anyway if she continues to shrink in the face of the Nazis.'

We turned from the German pavilion and walked through an archway, finding ourselves strolling by the Seine again.

'Camille Casal's agent has approached me,' said Minot, turning to lighter topics. 'He wants Mesdemoiselles Fleurier and Casal to do a show together. He thinks it will be novel to put two of Paris's most famous women on stage at the same time.'

'It would be interesting to have two rivals together,' agreed Monsieur Etienne, 'but Mademoiselle Fleurier is the bigger star. She will get top billing.'

He was thinking like a true agent, but the thought of performing alongside Camille made me uneasy. We hadn't spoken to each other since I had seen her in Cannes and told her that André and I were getting married. I had thought her warning about the Blanchard family was motivated by jealousy. Now I saw that she had been right.

'We can share the billing,' I said. 'It would make more sense.'

'Don't defer,' said Monsieur Etienne, lifting his eyebrows at me. 'Camille Casal's star has been falling for some time. I think her agent is hoping to boost her career by riding on your wings.'

Whether I was the bigger star or not, my old insecurity about being compared to Camille began to creep in again. When I was on stage by myself, I felt attractive. But next to Camille's glorious beauty, I was in danger of being swamped. Still, I thought, remembering Marlene Dietrich in Berlin, a petite blonde and a tall brunette could make an interesting combination.

'Let's do it,' I said. 'I will call Camille myself.'

Camille arrived at our first rehearsal in a gold Rolls-Royce. She had just returned from Hollywood where she had done screen tests for Paramount Pictures. 'Unless you want to lie around on set and mutter inane lines like "Look into my eyes, darling", I don't suggest you try to work in American movies,' she announced to the cast.

To my surprise, rather than being intimidated by Camille as I had expected, I was glad to see her again. And finally I understood why: she was a nostalgic link to my past, a reminder of a time when I didn't know what being a star was. My mind flashed briefly to a picture of myself in a worn dress, scrubbing Aunt Augustine's kitchen floor. That could have been the rest of my life. It was Camille who had inspired me to become an entertainer. I suddenly realised how much of my success I owed to her.

'It's good to see you again,' I told Camille, kissing her cheeks. 'You too,' she said. She looked me over but I sensed that it was not for signs of cracks as my other rivals did when they met me. 'You're doing very well,' she said. I knew she was referring to my life without André. But, to my relief and admiration, she never mentioned it.

Camille and I starred in the biggest show of that year. Lebaron spent four million francs producing 'Les Femmes' and recouped more than that in the first two months. Although it was a music hall show with variety acts rather than an American-style musical, the theme of female competition and solidarity ran throughout it, from the comedians to the chorus girls, from the clowns to the acrobats.

Camille and I did all our numbers together, and two of the songs became the year's greatest hits: 'Welcome' and 'Stone Around My Neck'.

Our reviews blew away all the others including Mistinguett and Maurice Chevalier. One paper described the show as *'Simone Fleurier's triumph and Camille Casal's comeback'*, although Camille saw things differently. 'I am going out with a bang,' she confided in me, as we ate supper one evening at Maxim's after the show. 'When the run is over, I will retire.'

I was shocked by her announcement. Working together on such a successful production, and sharing the limelight, I felt that we had finally become friends. In the old days, Camille would not have confided in me. But when I asked about her daughter this time, she told me she had taken her out of the convent and that she was staying with a piano teacher in Vaucresson to get a 'lady's education'. When I asked why her daughter was not living with her, Camille had answered, 'I can't let people know that she is my daughter. I want her to make a good marriage.'

I remembered what she had told me all those years ago in François's apartment: *men like that don't marry girls like us!* Even though André had wanted to marry me, the statement had proved true. No matter how successful we became, Camille Casal and I would always be on the outside of society.

'But you have been so well received,' I protested to Camille, regarding her decision to retire. 'You could do anything now. Make a record. Make another movie.'

She shook her head and gave me one of her wan smiles. 'I only ever sang and danced in order to find myself a rich patron for life,' she said. 'I have collected enough trinkets and apartments to last me until I am old, but I never did quite get that. Still, the show isn't over yet, so who knows what the future may bring.'

∽

One evening there was a knock at my dressing room door. It was the interval, so it wasn't likely to be the stage manager. And it didn't sound like my dresser's knock. I shrugged. My dressing room was still 'by invitation only'.

Whoever it was knocked again.

'Who is it?'

No answer.

I tugged the clip from my hair and let my tresses fall loose, smoothing them with my fingertips. If it was one of the stagehands then they were going to get a talking to. I tied my dressing gown at the waist and swung the door open. My heart nearly stopped when I found myself facing André. I had told myself that I had forgotten him, forgotten that I had ever loved him. But one look at his face and I knew that was not true.

'I'm sorry. I know that you don't have much time,' he said. 'But I haven't been able to reach you all day.'

Something about him seemed pitiable. His face was still young but the vitality had vanished from it. He was stiff and artificial.

I nodded for him to come inside although my heart was pounding. I could see by the uneasy way his eyes roved about the room that he was as unnerved as I was by this reunion. The chair that he used to sit in was no longer there so I invited him to sit on the sofa. I placed myself on a stool opposite him.

André took a few seconds to compose himself before asking: 'Did you know that Count Harry died?'

I could not believe what I was hearing. When André had returned from Lyon the year before, he had told me that the Count's health had deteriorated due to the upheaval of having to flee his home for the second time. But the Count had written soon afterwards that he was on the mend.

'I can't believe it,' I said. 'He was so full of life.' I looked up and noticed for the first time the leather folder tucked under André's arm. I wondered what it was.

'I am sorry to tell you this in the middle of your performance,' he said. 'But the funeral is tomorrow.'

I shook my head. 'I'm glad you did.'

André took the folder from under his arm and placed it in his lap. He stared at it, as if reluctant to tell me what it contained. But the sound of the call boy making his way down the corridor woke him from his dream.

'I never told the Count that we weren't together any more. He thought we were and bequeathed this to us,' said André, passing the folder to me. 'It's the pages from his diary where he wrote about us in Berlin.'

I was surprised by the weight of the folder. It had looked so thin. 'Berlin?' I whispered. I didn't know if I had the strength to remember those days: the Hotel Adlon, the Unter den Linden, the Resi. The past rushed at me and then receded. Seeing André again and hearing of the Count's death were two shocks too many.

'Berlin,' I said again. My mouth was dry and I could barely speak. I saw how uncomfortable and sad André was. I wanted to make this meeting easier for him, but I couldn't. Each time I looked at his face I couldn't help thinking of that first time he had come to my dressing room at the Casino de Paris. We had been so young then, just starting out on the adventure of getting to know each other. Now we were standing in the wreckage.

André's voice faltered. 'I think it is best if you keep them,' he said. 'It is not appropriate for me.'

I drew back. It was as if he had stuck a knife into me and now he was twisting it. But I knew André and understood that he would not do that on purpose. Of course it wasn't appropriate for him to keep them: he was married.

The call boy knocked on the door. 'Ten minutes.'

André rose from his chair. 'I am sorry, Simone,' he said. I had a sense that he wasn't apologising for breaking the news about Count Kessler so abruptly but rather he was apologising for our lives.

After André left, I opened the folder and read the first entry:

> Met a marvellous young woman today in the company of André Blanchard. Mademoiselle Fleurier approaches each new experience with the same wonder and enthusiasm of a child opening her Christmas packages. She has a spirit that reaches into me, making me feel young again. I am certain that she will accomplish great things: in the music hall and in the grander theatre of life.

That night, I sang my numbers as if in a trance. I had to block out my memories of Berlin. The Count was dead and, in a way, André was too. Our lives were so far apart from each other now that we might as well be living in different countries. Was the André I had seen this evening really the man who had made my career? The first man to have loved me? He was a stranger now. It took supreme effort to get through the show, and when the final curtain came down I retreated to my dressing room where I cried as forlornly as I had the night my father died.

The Count was buried in Père Lachaise cemetery. There was only a handful of mourners at the funeral. Where were all the artists the Count had supported? All the people who had called him 'friend' when he was rich and generous? I had only learnt the previous night from André that the Count had been unable to retrieve his paintings and other treasures from his house in Weimar because the authorities had permitted the local population to loot it.

I avoided meeting André's eyes. The Princesse de Letellier was with him. She was a waif-like woman with blonde curly hair and a wide forehead. Every so often she would turn and stroke André's arm, letting him know that she was there to support him. I would have preferred to avoid her too, but when I passed her in the aisle she reached out and touched my arm.

'I am sorry, Mademoiselle Fleurier,' she said. 'My husband has told me how much the Count meant to you both.'

The Princesse de Letellier would have known that André had wanted to marry me, but she behaved graciously. I sensed that her sympathy was sincere. I didn't know a lot about the princess except that she was well-educated and, unlike most of *Tout-Paris*, was the patron of many charities. André had married a decent woman. In other circumstances, perhaps the princess and I might even have been friends.

'Goodbye, Count Harry,' I whispered when they lowered the coffin into the ground. I tossed my roses to fall alongside the other dozen that lay over it. I remembered the Count's mischievous laugh and his sparkling eyes the night he played a joke on me at the Eldorado. Those lively eyes were closed now and he would laugh no more.

I thought of his diary entry and what he had said about his first impression of me. The Count had lived with backbone and, despite his ill health, had lived fully. I idolised him too much to ever put myself in the same league as him. I could not know that his faith in my ability to accomplish things in the grander theatre of life was soon to be put to the test.

TWENTY-FIVE

Jean Renoir invited me to the première of his film *La Grande Illusion* at the Marivaux Cinema in June 1937. Monsieur Etienne escorted me and we were both excited to see how French cinema had grown. The story was about three Great War pilots in a German prisoner-of-war camp and their relationship with the commandant. It was a love song between the French and the German soldiers, who could have been brothers if not for the war.

'Technically it is as good as the American movies,' said Monsieur Etienne when the lights came up. 'The picture isn't blurry and the sound doesn't scratch.'

Renoir's directing had always been able to override technical imperfections but now, without them, his vision was magic. I knew from working with him that he didn't like to fragment scenes in the usual way by having 'close-ups' cut into 'long-shots'. He preferred to shoot his actors in close-up then follow their movements, subtly passing from actor to actor in what he called a 'ballet of the camera'. In a way it mirrored the natural movement of the eye. Of course, only insiders knew this. To the audience, the movement was so flawless as to be imperceptible.

I congratulated Renoir at the party. 'It is a beautiful story, so gently told.'

He lifted his eyes. The lively spark I associated with him was not there. 'Simone, you and I are old friends so I can say this to you. Ever since I started making films, I have had only one theme: our common humanity. When I made this film I was hoping to stop a war. But I see now that art can't stop anything. It can only document it.'

The talk in the salons and cafés at that time was whether France was likely to be dragged into war with Nazi Germany. But wasn't France the most civilised country in the world? Didn't we, of all nations, truly know how to live? If we could not stop a war, who could?

'Do you think war is inevitable?' I asked him.

'We have traitors and fools to lead us,' said Renoir. 'The rest of us just look on in despair.'

❧

One morning, nearly a year after the première, I opened the paper and remembered Renoir's remark about traitors. The headline announced that there were doubts that the new premier, Edouard Daladier, would defend Poland and Czechoslovakia should they be attacked by Germany. Georges Bonnet, a Hitler sympathiser, had been appointed to the position of foreign minister.

But if the rest of Paris was worried, they didn't show it. The city was dancing and revelling more ardently than ever.

In July 1938, King George VI and his queen visited France for a royal tour so sumptuous that it cost France twenty-four million francs. I was asked to sing at a gala performance of the best of everything French, which followed a state dinner of *lobster à Marinier* accompanied by 1923 Château d'Yquem. As I sang I was aware that I was part of an expensive publicity stunt. All the pomp and extravagance, the parades through a cheering Paris, the laying of the wreath at the Tomb of the Unknown Soldier, were to show Hitler that Britain and France were allies. Surely the dictator would not be so foolish as to attack France when we had such a powerful nation on our side?

'They seem to be missing the point,' said an exasperated Minot. 'While we are throwing money at their royalty, the British prime minister is making appeasement deals with Hitler.' With André no longer in my life and Renoir overseas, Minot had become my companion in political discussions.

'*Not a widow, not an orphan for the Czechs*,' the newspaper headlines were screaming in September. Day after day *L'Action*

Française printed on its cover 'No! No War!' and repeated its claim that it was the Jews who were pushing for war because they didn't like Hitler's policies against them.

Hitler had demanded the cession of much of Czechoslovakia. He wanted to claim the Sudetenland, but it was clear that soon he would want the whole country.

'The idiots,' Minot said one day when we met for drinks at Café de Flore. 'Even if the French and British governments don't care about the shame of deserting an ally, they should at least think about the help the Czechs can give us if we are attacked. The Czechs have the most modern armaments factories in Europe and a well-planned defence along the German border. They are one of the few democracies left in Europe — and we aren't exactly surrounded by friendly nations.'

After my conversation with Minot at the Café de Flore, I returned to my apartment with a sense of rising fear. Paulette was out for the afternoon so I put the percolator on the stove myself to make coffee. There was a letter from Bernard on top of the other correspondence. When I opened it I found that Aunt Augustine had died and left her house to me. I sat down at the dining room table staring at the view of the Champs Élysées and sipping my coffee. Aunt Augustine hated me, I thought. Why would she leave her house to me? I imagined her torn between giving the house to a niece she despised or letting it go to the state. I must have been the lesser of two evils. Of course I would sell the place; I couldn't stand the miserable memory of it.

Down on the street, a newspaper boy was shouting out the afternoon headlines. People were cheering and calling out the premier's name, 'Daladier! Daladier!', praising him for his 'enlightened' policy.

I closed my eyes and remembered the youth who had shouted at me on my first day in Berlin.

We will defeat France! We will drive her to the ground! There will be no more France! No more French! We will spit on her like a used whore!

My skin turned cold. I could almost smell the acrid sweat and malevolence oozing out of the youth's pores. I rushed to the bureau in the drawing room, pulled out some note paper and began writing.

Dear Bernard,

War is coming to France. You may not feel it in the south yet, but as surely as I breathe I know that the German army is going to invade. I am sending you some extra money this month. Please use it to buy whatever you need long term for the farm. Regarding Aunt Augustine's house, I think I will have use for it. Please arrange to have it repaired and painted. Please do not discuss these matters with anyone.

I paused. My intuition was making plans ahead of my conscious thoughts. My family were in what was probably one of the safest places to be in France if war did break out — surrounded by rugged mountains and far from major cities, borders and the coast. And Marseilles was within sailing distance of Africa. If the Germans invaded from the north, the south was going to be the best route of escape. But it wasn't myself or my family I was worried about right now.

⤜⤏

'Simone!' laughed Odette, rubbing her pregnant stomach. 'You are making a drama out of nothing. Germany is not going to invade France. And even if they tried, the Maginot line is there to stop them.'

We were in the kitchen of her parents' house in Saint Germain en Laye. Odette and Joseph were staying there until after Odette had her baby. A sunbeam played through the lace curtains and shimmered on the table. The kitchen was painted sunny yellow and the furniture was white with blue trims. I watched the steam from the kettle on the stove rise up and arch into the air.

'I don't think anybody has faith in the Maginot line any more,' I said. 'The bunkers stop where the Belgian border begins.'

'Because Belgium is our ally,' she said, setting a cup of coffee and a slice of chocolate cake in front of me before sitting down herself.

'The Germans will march right over them, as they did in 1914.'

Odette flashed me a dubious look. 'So you are not a singer any more, Simone,' she said. 'Now you are a military strategist.'

'I can't see what it has to do with strategy,' I said. 'It's common sense. We French are supposed to be great thinkers, but we are being incredibly stupid.'

Odette's face stiffened and she shifted in her seat. 'Joseph has just opened his new shop, and when the baby is born I'm going to help him. He is my husband. If he says there is nothing to worry about, then I have to believe him.'

I glanced at my hands. A mere music hall star I may be, but was Joseph so naive that he didn't understand the implications for a Jewish family if the Nazis invaded? Surely he had read about the laws that had been passed in Germany? I had once thought that the way the Germans treated the Jews could never happen in France, but now I saw that wasn't true. The circulations of anti-Semitic newspapers had increased threefold in the last two years.

Odette sipped her coffee and hummed a tune under her breath. As sweet as she was, I knew her well enough to understand that she became obstinate in the face of confrontation. If I wanted to persuade her to leave Paris, I would have to do it over time and subtly. The problem was, I had no idea how much time we had. Odette was married and pregnant. I was facing the end of the world alone. Perhaps that was why I could see things more clearly. There wasn't much else for me to think about.

'So have you decided on a name for the baby?' I asked, changing the subject.

Her eyes lit up and a smile came to her face. 'Yes. Michel if it is a boy and Simone for a girl.'

My face flushed. I could feel Odette's love beaming across the table. I knew I was lucky to have a friend like her.

'Really?' I asked.

Odette nodded and put her arm on my shoulder. It was wonderful to be loved like that. My broken heart felt almost alive again.

❧

'I appreciate what you are saying,' Monsieur Etienne told me when I went to visit him at his office. 'And I am touched by your concern. But Joseph has a point too. The Germans have a superior airforce, one that has tested itself in Spain. They are just as likely to bomb our ports as they are to invade by land. But what if they are stopped before they even reach Paris? We will have given up our homes and businesses for nothing.'

I sat back in my chair. Was I being neurotic? Odette was staying outside of Paris. If the Germans were to bomb us, she would be safer there than in a house in the centre of Marseilles. For a moment

Count Harry's face on the day of his exile from Germany loomed up before me. I remembered the time I had spent in Berlin and the ominous feeling of darkness that pervaded the decadence. It seemed that the predictions for a second world war, more devastating than the first, were coming true. I had to do my best to warn my friends.

'Look,' I said, scribbling out the addresses of the Marseilles house and the farm in Pays de Sault, 'it is a gut feeling I have. Please keep these in case you need them. Who knows what will happen?'

❦

To my relief, I had no trouble persuading Minot to cooperate with my emergency plan. He had an elderly mother to think about. Lebaron had fled for the United States two months earlier, leaving Minot in charge of the Adriana.

'I have bought a car and am sending supplies to my family in Provence,' I told him. 'If the Germans invade, you and your mother are welcome to come and stay with us.'

'You are very kind, Mademoiselle Fleurier,' he said. 'I will send my paintings to the house in Pays de Sault in advance. I don't want the Krauts getting their hands on them.'

I smiled, imagining the walls of our twin farmhouses decorated with paintings by Picasso and Dali. Poor Minot, I thought, I hope he doesn't expect to be staying in a *château* with marble bathrooms. Maurice Chevalier and Joséphine Baker had country retreats, as did many wealthy French people. I had always thought it was something I would buy with André when we married. Such houses had been done up over the years and were no longer the ramshackle structures they had been when I was growing up. But Pays de Sault was still wild country and my family liked simplicity. Our houses were more rustic than chic.

'Make sure the paintings are packed in crates,' I told him. 'You don't want them to warp in the heat.'

Minot's cooperation gave me some peace of mind. I questioned myself every day as to whether my impulse was an over-reaction. How embarrassing if, after all this preparation, nothing happened. But how much worse if it did and we were unprepared. There was no hint of concern in the faces of the people who came to my music hall and nightclub appearances. Paris was shining more brightly than ever, with spectacular operas, plays, fashion shows and parties. The Polish ambassador hosted an elegant ball on the same night Odette went into labour and gave birth to a girl. The German ambassador was invited to the ball and we danced waltzes and mazurkas and finished the evening watching fireworks spinning into the sky. Wasn't that a sign that all was well?

As it turned out, the only mistake I had made was to panic one year too early. Two months after the ball, Germany invaded Poland. When the Franco–British ultimatum to Hitler expired, the French army was mobilised. People walked around the streets in a state of disbelief. Could this be real? Were we really at war against the Third Reich?

Minot and his mother moved in with me in case we found ourselves having to leave Paris in the middle of the night. Elsa Maxwell sent invitations to a party that, instead of an RSVP date, was inscribed with ICNW: In Case No War. It felt impossible to plan anything.

'How can I go on vacation?' my secretary moaned. 'My husband might be called up to join his regiment.'

But month after month dragged by before anything happened. The newspapers called this time the *drôle de guerre*, the phony war.

One Thursday afternoon, after the weekly air-raid drill, I met Camille at a café near the Ritz. Minot had organised for me to do a series of tours along the Maginot line to entertain the soldiers who were restless with boredom in their bunkers. I wanted to catch up with Camille in case she had left the city when I returned. The mannequins in the boutique windows in the Place Vendôme wore gas masks with ribbons tied at the neck. It was a joke, but the thought that we were preparing to face an enemy capable of dropping mustard gas on civilians did nothing to comfort me.

In the café, the chocolates and cakes had been moulded into the shape of bombs. 'It is good to see that not everyone has lost their sense of humour,' Camille said, opening her purse to pay the waiter as soon as he brought our drinks. That was the system in Paris now: the servers no longer waited for the saucers to accumulate; you had to pay for each drink as it was delivered in case the sirens went off and everyone rushed to the shelter.

'The city seems strange without children,' I said. 'The Jardin du Luxembourg is a ghost town without them. They are evacuating more today.'

'They should have sent the brats away a long time ago,' said Camille. 'I am enjoying the peace.'

It was an odd thing for a mother to say.

'What about you?' I asked her. 'What is your plan?'

'Well, the house in the Dordogne is there if I need it. But otherwise I plan to keep my room at the Ritz.'

'You can't,' I said. 'Imagine what the German soldiers could do to you if they storm the city?'

Camille raised her eyebrows. 'I've done nothing to them so why should they do anything to me? Besides, according to Comtesse de Portes, the French will be organising a welcoming committee.'

My skin turned cold. Comtesse Hélène de Portes was the mistress of Paul Reynauld, who had just replaced Daladier as the premier of France. She was known for her extreme right-wing views. Did Reynauld now share them?

'Camille,' I whispered, 'tell me that you are joking.'

'French or German, what does it matter?' muttered Camille, lighting a cigarette. 'As long as Paris remains Paris.'

I was taken aback by her nonchalant tone. Who had Camille been talking to in order to come up with that view? I inspected her more closely. Her face was pale and there were the beginnings of bags under her eyes. I had heard that she was having money troubles and there were rumours of lawsuits from debtors. Perhaps those things were weighing more heavily on her mind than the looming war.

'Haven't you heard what the Nazis are doing to the Jews?' I asked.

Camille's head snapped up and she looked me in the eye. 'You're not Jewish. When are you going to watch out for yourself?'

I flinched at the blasé way she said it. Some of the best people we had worked with over the years had been Jewish. Did she have no feelings for them? I remembered how, when I first met her and saw how she treated men, I had thought she was motivated purely by self-interest. Then I had found out about her daughter. But her comment about the Jews was ignorant and cruel. That wasn't the Camille I had come to know while working with her on '*Les Femmes*'. Or was it?

I found myself unable to tell. When we parted from our rendezvous, I was left with the uneasy impression that I didn't know the real Camille Casal at all.

TWENTY-SIX

I returned to my apartment to find a mound of sand heaped on the sidewalk in front of the building. A cat was digging into it, delighted to have found soft matter in which to do her business.

'What is the sand for?' I asked Madame Goux, the concierge.

She threw up her hands. 'An order from the city administrators. We are supposed to spread it out in the attic.'

'Why?'

'To prevent fires from travelling from the roof to the lower floors. But I can't be expected to walk up and down seven flights of stairs with buckets of sand.'

'Of course not,' I said. 'I will help. And I am sure the others will too.'

I would have offered Paulette's assistance but she had already returned to her village in the west of France.

Madame Goux scoffed at me. 'I mean, I am not doing it at all. It's not in my job description.'

'I'm sure the Germans will be very respectful of your job description when they drop a bomb on the building,' I said, before turning and walking up the stairs.

To my disappointment, the other people in the building weren't any more willing to help than the concierge. 'What a useless thing to do,' said the man on the floor above me. 'The *Boche* aren't going to make it any further than the border before we push them back. The Ardennes forest is impenetrable.'

Only the neighbour who lived below me, a violinist by the name of Madame Ibert, agreed to help. We covered our hair with scarves and for the next two hours lugged pails of sand to the roof. Each time we passed Madame Goux she shook her head and let out a *pfsst*! She wasn't the only one who refused to do as the administrators had asked. The piles of sand outside the other buildings on our street lay untouched, and some of the children who hadn't been evacuated were busy tunnelling toy trucks through them.

'I feel sorry for the blisters you will get on your hands,' I told Madame Ibert, watching her spread out the sand with a broom. She was about ten years older than me, skinny as a bird, with brown wavy hair and cobalt blue eyes.

She straightened up and gave me a rueful smile. 'It is a small price to pay for France.'

'There are fourteen people in this building and hundreds of people in our street,' I said. 'And we are the only two prepared to fight.'

When I closed my eyes that night, I worried that the ratio might be true of the whole of Paris. Even with the war on our doorstep, we seemed to lack the energy to take it seriously. I thought of André. His father had retired and André was now head of the family business. I wondered if he was going to fight or do something to contribute to the war. He spoke German as well as a native and knew how to drive a car and fly a plane.

It had been months since I had last seen him and I was surprised to find that I no longer felt the crushing hurt I once had over him. I could even see myself talking to him without going to pieces. I considered the drastic change in my feelings and wondered what had precipitated it. Perhaps now that war was coming, I knew we were facing something much bigger than the end of our love affair.

The following morning, I had no qualms about calling André at his office to find out what he was intending to do. But his secretary informed me that the Blanchard family, along with the heads of their companies and their families, had moved to Switzerland a month ago. I was disappointed with André's choice, but given that some of the Blanchard businesses were vital to the French economy, it had probably been the right thing to do.

❧

A few weeks later, Minot and I put his mother and Kira on a train to the south. We were sending them ahead of us in case we needed more space in the car. Bernard was going to pick them up in Carpentras and take them to the farm. As it turned out, we had acted just in time.

In early May 1940, the German army attacked Holland, Belgium and Luxembourg. Despite the efforts to bomb bridges ahead of the enemy, one by one those nations fell. If anyone in Paris had been living in denial about the reality of war, they now saw the evidence of it day after day on the streets. Thousands of refugees poured into the city from the north. I stood on the Boulevard Saint Michel and watched them pass by: a stream of cars, horse-drawn carts and bicycles whose occupants looked shell-shocked, weary, tearful. There was one car driven by a heavily pregnant woman with an old woman in the passenger seat and four young children and a cat in the back.

I rushed back home and gathered the tins and packaged food I had been storing. On my way down the stairs I met Madame Ibert coming out of her apartment. 'What are you doing?' she asked.

'Taking food to the refugees,' I told her.

'Wait!' she said, putting her key back into her door. 'I will come with you.'

We drove to the Jardin du Luxembourg, where many of the refugees had stopped to rest or to graze their horses, and handed out the food items to women with children. Some of them recognised me and asked me to autograph their aprons and handkerchiefs. It was a moment of normality in the midst of chaos. Madame Ibert and I returned home after dark. I was so exhausted that I didn't take my clothes off before I fell into bed.

The following morning I tried to telephone Odette but couldn't get through. I clutched the picture she had sent me of pretty Petite Simone and tried to think what I should do. Finally, I ran to Monsieur Etienne's office. When I found it closed I continued on to his apartment. He was at home, packing his bags.

'We are going to stay with Joseph's family in Bordeaux,' he said.

I was relieved they had decided to get out of the city, but Bordeaux was still France. I would have been happier if they were getting out of Europe entirely. I helped Monsieur Etienne pack his papers and some photographs into boxes, my heart cramping in my chest as I remembered the first day I had come to Paris. It was almost laughable to think that I had been so intimidated by the man I now thought of as a dear friend. I wondered what was going to become of us. Would we ever see each other again?

'Good luck, Mademoiselle Fleurier,' Monsieur Etienne said, kissing my cheeks. He always seemed so strong, so self-assured, but today I detected a tremble in his hand, a fragility that showed in his eyes.

'Won't you ever call me Simone?' I asked him, my voice choking up.

'No,' he said, smiling through his own tears. 'Besides, now I would only get you confused with my grand-niece.'

⸎

I returned home to find Minot in a panic. 'Mademoiselle Fleurier,' he cried, 'we must leave now.' He explained that a German parachutist had been seen landing on the Champs Élysées.

I rang a friend at *Le Figaro* to see if he could confirm the story. 'It was a falling observation balloon,' he told me. 'But we are getting reports of Germans dropping from the skies dressed as priests, nuns and chorus girls. Last night somebody called to say that a whole ballet troupe had descended.'

'So Paris is calm in the face of a crisis?' I said. Despite the situation, we somehow managed to laugh.

'Are you joking, Mademoiselle Fleurier?' he responded. 'The authorities cannot get the people of Paris to cooperate. They are acting as if the war is some sort of inconvenience, like a blackout or a strike. The city sounds air sirens to warn them and instead of running to their cellars they rush to their windows to see what is going on.'

'I am thinking of leaving Paris. Am I being neurotic?' I asked him.

There was a pause. A man shouted something in the background and I heard a buzz burst out in the newsroom. The reporter came back on the line. 'Mademoiselle Fleurier,' he said, his voice shrill. 'We've just got news through. The Germans have broken through the Ardennes frontier.'

The news would take several more days to be digested by the population, but it was a disaster as far as the defence of France was concerned. The Ardennes frontier was not impenetrable after all: Hitler's panzer tank divisions had ploughed through it with ease.

Unless our forces could cut them off, there was little now standing between them and a major invasion of France.

I knocked on Madame Ibert's door. 'My friend and I are leaving Paris tomorrow. Do you want to come with us?'

'Yes,' she said, clutching my hands. 'I have no family to go to.'

The car I had bought for the trip was a Peugeot. I had deliberately selected a middle of the range model in case we needed parts on the road. It was also the kind of family car that wouldn't attract attention. My planning had been sound up to then, but when Minot and I went to collect the car from the parking garage we discovered that the petrol in the tank had been siphoned off and the reserve containers I had stored in the boot had been stolen.

'*Merde!*' I cursed. 'I should have kept the containers in the apartment. But I was so terrified of a fire!'

'What will we do now?' asked Minot. 'Petrol is harder to come by than truffles.'

Minot, Madame Ibert and I spent the next week and a half on clandestine trips to buy fuel wherever we could. Petrol had been rationed during the 'phony war' and now it was very difficult to get hold of, no matter how much you were willing to pay. Everyone was holding on to a supply in case they needed it to escape. We each never returned with more than a couple of severely overpriced champagne bottles of the stuff.

'This is going to take too long,' muttered Minot, watching me funnel that day's collection into a storage tank in the bathroom.

The atmosphere in Paris was a combination of calm and terror. While some were seeing Germans dropping from the skies or lurking in the sewers, there were just as many people in restaurants enjoying oysters and vintage wines. Although I had no singing commitments, Maurice Chevalier and Joséphine Baker were still performing at the Casino de Paris and the cinemas were showing the latest hit films: *Ninotchka* with Greta Garbo, and *The Hunchback of Notre Dame*.

A few days after we discovered our petrol had been stolen, the summer sky was thick with smoke.

'What could it be?' I asked Minot. 'A smoke screen to protect us from air raids?'

Madame Ibert, returning from the Conservatoire de Paris where she gave lessons, set the record straight. 'They are burning the oil reserves so they don't fall into the hands of the enemy.'

There were smaller fires too; I saw them when I walked past the Foreign Ministry on my way to Gare de Lyon on one of my petrol-seeking missions. The ministers and their aides were burning sensitive documents. As I was passing the Hôtel de Ville, a half-ashed document fluttered on a drift of air and landed at my feet. In the corner were the words 'Top Secret'.

⟨⟩

While most of the occupants of the apartments in my *arrondissement* had fled, the working-class suburbs were full of people. When I went to buy petrol from a baker in Belleville, I was shocked to see so many children playing on the streets. Housewives were hanging out washing and commenting on how this summer seemed the hottest ever. Hadn't they noticed that the public buses were disappearing from the streets, used to move government offices out of Paris? *Tout-Paris* and the city's leaders were deserting their posts, leaving the ordinary people to fight the war they should have prevented.

'They are calling up the German nationals today,' reported Madame Ibert when I returned to the apartment to add my meagre acquisition to the tank. 'They are putting them in holding camps.'

'How stupid!' I said, sinking into the nearest chair. 'Many of those people are Jews who escaped here from Germany or people who opposed the Nazis. If they are trapped in holding camps and we are invaded, it will be like offering them up for sacrifice.'

'Like sheep in a pen,' said Madame Ibert, shaking her head.

'Do you really think Jews will be persecuted here the way they have been in Germany?' asked Minot, placing a glass of water on the table next to me. I noticed that he was wearing Paulette's apron but I was too tired to tease him about it.

'It worries me that so many French Jews think that what happened in Germany couldn't happen here,' Madame Ibert said. 'They think that they can simply change their names and paperwork and no one will tell the authorities.'

Renoir's story about the German youths making an old Jewish woman lick the pavement had stayed with me all these years. I sensed Madame Ibert was right. Hadn't those boys and the old lady once been neighbours too?

The following day, Minot and I assessed our supplies. We had enough petrol to make the trip to Pays de Sault only if we had a free run to the south, which wasn't likely considering the congested traffic of refugees on the road. We needed at least another two reserve cans.

'Should we go by train?' I asked Minot. 'Or you and Madame Ibert can go by train and I will follow after you?'

Minot insisted that we all go together by car in case we needed a vehicle once we got to the farm. We decided to continue our hunt for petrol a while longer.

Minot left to run some errands and see off friends. Madame Ibert and I had just sat down to lunch when we heard the hum of planes, followed a few minutes later by the howl of air-raid sirens. We ran to the window and stared up at the sky. A swarm of black dots swept overhead.

'We should go to the cellar,' I told her, remembering what my reporter friend had said about Parisians standing by their windows during air raids.

We walked calmly down the stairs to the cellar. The situation was too surreal for panic. Obviously everyone in the building shared that feeling because the only other person in the cellar was Madame Goux. She was peeling potatoes, dropping the skins into a bucket. I had a feeling this was her regular spot for peeling potatoes — it saved her lugging them up the stairs — and she had not fled to the cellar for safety.

There was a rattle of anti-aircraft fire. Madame Ibert and I cringed.

'They are just trying to scare you,' Madame Goux huffed. She said 'you' as if Madame Ibert and I were a different race of people.

'There were enough of them to do that,' I said, remembering the black shapes in the sky.

Madame Goux sneered at me. 'Do you hear bombs?'

I had to admit that the only things I could hear at that moment were the scrape of her knife and Monsieur Copeau playing 'Aux Îles Hawaï' on his gramophone at full volume. Obviously the air raid was not going to interrupt his listening pleasure.

But we were not so stupid to have taken precautions. When the sirens sounded again to signal that the raid was over, we found a badly shaken Minot waiting for us in the apartment.

'A thousand bombs,' he said. 'That is the estimate. They hit the

Renault and Citroën factories. And a hospital. There might be more than a thousand people dead.'

'A hospital!' I cried, exchanging a disgusted glance with Madame Ibert.

'That target may not have been intentional,' said Minot.

'We haven't reached our petrol mark,' said Madame Ibert, 'but may I suggest we leave now?'

I had no argument to give. We had all agreed that we would leave Paris when we were sure it was going to be attacked, and now it seemed that deadline had come.

Minot fetched the car from the garage while Madame Ibert and I carried our supplies and suitcases downstairs. We were relieved that Madame Goux was not at her desk to interfere. I left her a note to say that I was going to visit my family for a few days, and that my apartment was locked and under no circumstances was it to be used by unauthorised persons — by which I meant the Germans. Of course, such an instruction was useless. Would an invading army baulk at breaking into an apartment? Besides, if they were going to drop a thousand bombs at a time, perhaps there wouldn't even be an apartment to return to.

Although I had been preparing for war for almost two years, I had lost my advantage by departing Paris on the same day that half the city also decided to leave. The streets were blocked with overpacked cars, as well as coffee vendors' carts, taxis, bakers' trucks, horse carriages and hay wagons.

'Look at this traffic,' Minot hissed under his breath. 'We are going to use up our petrol before we even get to the Orléans gate.'

It was hot in the car. My hands dripped sweat onto the wheel. But inside I was as cold as a grave. I stared at the sandbagging around Cleopatra's Needle on the Place de la Concorde. Would the familiar monuments still be here when I returned? *If* I returned.

Why are you leaving?

I wiped my hand across my forehead and tried to push the thought out of my mind. It persisted. I reasoned with it: because I have to get Minot and Madame Ibert to safety.

Yes, but you? Why are you leaving?

My original plan had been to get Odette and her family out of France. It was also true that I wanted to help Minot and Madame Ibert. But the question of why I too was leaving started to bother me.

I went over my reasons: because the Germans were known for their cruelty in the Great War; because of the stories my father had told me of German soldiers bayoneting babies and raping women and girls.

The brightest light in the City of Lights.

I clutched the wheel. That was not a title I had bestowed on myself, the way Jacques Noir had described himself as 'the most adored comedian in the whole of Paris'. It was an expression the French public had given me. And now, as Paris was facing her darkest hour, 'the brightest light' was leaving.

We didn't get out of Paris and onto Route National Six until early evening. The highway south was crowded, but at least we were all heading in the same direction. At sunset we passed a church whose yard contained rows of freshly dug graves. We averted our eyes.

∞

We drove through the night, Minot and I taking turns at the wheel. When I awoke at dawn, I saw fields. 'Are we nearly there?' I asked Minot, yawning.

'Are you joking?' he asked. 'We are barely a third of the way.'

The sky was clear and the air was already hot. Madame Ibert made breakfast, cutting up bread on a board on her lap. In front of us was a motor truck with a dozen young children in it, along with a middle-aged woman and a teenage girl.

'I didn't see them earlier,' I said.

'We must have caught up with them some time during the night,' Minot said. 'The number plate is Belgian.'

'They can't all be that woman's children,' I said, looking at the little heads bobbing up and down. Some were dark, some were blonde, some red-haired. The children ranged in age from about four to seven years old and their weary faces pinched my heart.

'They might be evacuees from a school,' suggested Madame Ibert.

'Do we still have that bag of peaches,' I asked.

She reached under her feet. 'There is enough for one each,' she said.

'Oh, no,' said Minot. 'What are we going to eat if you and Mademoiselle Fleurier keep giving our food away?'

Madame Ibert handed me the bag, along with two loaves of bread, a block of cheese, a packet of chocolate and a bunch of grapes.

'We shall have more than enough to eat when we get to the farm,' I said. 'Those children may not have had anything for days.'

We weren't going fast enough for Minot to have to stop for me. I slipped out of the Peugeot and ran through the other cars and bicycles towards the motor truck.

The woman's face lit up when she saw me. She reached over the side to take my offerings. 'Thank you! Thank you!' she said, tears filling her eyes.

I asked if she was the childrens' teacher, and she said that she was. They had fled as the German army razed their town.

'Good luck, Madame,' I said.

'God bless you,' she called after me as I ran back to our car.

We continued along the highway at a crawl, passing a farmer selling water at two francs a cup and another selling petrol at a price that was inflated, even for war time.

'I guess there will always be someone ready to exploit a situation,' Madame Ibert muttered.

For the next hour we drove through open fields. Minot amused us with tales from behind the scenes at the Adriana, including gossip about the Paris stars, and I tried to lighten the atmosphere by singing a couple of numbers from my last show. I was crooning the theme from '*Les Femmes*' when a blood-chilling wail cut through the sky.

'*Merde!*' said Minot, peering up through the windscreen. 'What is that?'

The traffic stopped ahead of us. People leapt from their cars or dropped their bicycles and fled across the field towards a grove of trees. Those with carts dived under them.

The schoolteacher and her assistant jumped from the truck, pulling the children down after them. The driver rushed out of the cabin to help. I stepped from our car. A Dutch man in the field turned and screamed out 'Stukas! Stukas!' for the benefit of the French people who didn't understand what was going on and were looking at each other. Then I saw them: two German planes heading towards us.

But they were military planes, looking for military targets. They wouldn't fire on unarmed refugees. The planes lowered altitude. My heart cramped in my chest. Minot and Madame Ibert dropped to the floor of the car. 'Duck!' screamed Minot. But my eyes were fixed on the children trying to make their way to the trees, pushed and urged on by the teacher and her assistant. The driver was running with two toddlers under each arm.

'No!' I screamed.

There was a rattling sound like stones hitting the road. Dirt jumped up in puffs. The little bodies shook and dropped to the ground. The teacher froze, jerking to the left and the right, trying to shield a girl from the bullets before she and the child toppled face down. The assistant fell a moment later. The driver was still running ahead, weighed down by the children he carried. A man ran out from the trees towards them and grabbed one of the children. They had almost made it under cover when one of the planes turned back. It cut all four of them down in a hail of bullets before regaining height and disappearing into the sky on the tail of its mate.

My legs would only carry me as far as the edge of the road. Nobody else moved, terrified that the planes might come back. I stared at the huddle of bleeding bodies in the grass. At that low altitude, the pilots would have known their targets were children. They had hunted them for sport.

'Those bastards!' screamed Minot, running up beside me and shaking his hands in the air. 'Those child-killing bastards!'

The people who had fled to the trees ran back across the field. They rushed towards the bodies but it was clear from their solemn faces that there were no survivors. A woman fell to her knees and wailed over the body of the man who had gone to the aid of the driver. There was a discussion among the survivors; a few minutes later three men returned to their vehicles and took out spades. It seemed there was no way these bodies could be taken to a churchyard, they would have to be buried where they had fallen. A woman asked if there was a priest among the refugees and the message was passed down the line of cars. A cyclist rode ahead, calling out the request. A man in a priest's robe got out of a car and headed back towards the scene of the killing.

About twenty people remained behind to help bury the children and their guardians. The rest of the crowd returned to their vehicles. There was nothing for them to do but move on. From the conversation of two women who walked past me, I realised it was not the first time German pilots had fired on refugees. Now I understood why so many of the cars I had seen passing through Paris had mattresses tied to their roofs.

'Come on, Mademoiselle Fleurier,' said Madame Ibert, slipping her arm around my waist. 'We had best move on. There is nothing we can do here.'

I thought of the teacher's eyes when I had handed her the food. Who was that woman who had given her life for children who were not her own? Her assistant too, a young girl, so much younger than me, who had sacrificed herself? The driver whose face I never saw? I wanted to cry for the waste of innocent souls in the face of evil, but no sound came out. I retched but there wasn't enough food in my stomach to bring anything up.

Madame Ibert rubbed my back.

'Do you know how to drive?' I asked her.

'Yes,' she said.

I straightened up. 'Minot has a map to the farm. Can you share the driving with him?'

She nodded. 'You rest in the back. I can drive,' she said, turning towards the car.

I grabbed her arm. 'I mean, can you help Minot get to Sault? I am going back.'

She held my gaze.

'There is something I have to do,' I told her.

Minot, who had been listening to our conversation, came up behind us. 'Mademoiselle Fleurier, you are in shock. You are upset. Calm down. There's nothing you can do now.'

But Madame Ibert seemed to understand. She must have seen it in my eyes. The murder of those children had broken open a seed inside me, and it was beginning to grow. She reached into the car and pulled out a bottle of water and some food and put them in a straw bag which she handed to me. 'It will take you at least a day to walk back,' she said, slipping an army knife from her pocket into the bag. 'And it might be dangerous.'

Minot glanced from Madame Ibert to me, shaking his head. The ring of spades hitting dry earth broke the silence. I shut my eyes against the sound. When I opened them again, Minot was holding my hand. 'Send us word as soon as you can. I fear for you, but I see I won't change your mind.'

I watched Minot and Madame Ibert get back in the car and start up the motor. Then I turned away from them and began walking back along the road, in the opposite direction to the traffic. I couldn't have said what I intended to do once I got back to Paris. All I had was my shaky courage and the conviction that I could not run from this dark force that had swamped Germany and was now falling over France. Until my last breath, I was not going to give in to evil. I was going to fight.

TWENTY-SEVEN

It took me three days to return to Paris. I spent one night in a field huddled under a tree with the knife Madame Ibert had given me at my side. The other night I slept in a barn. Every so often I would stop someone on the road to warn them about the German strafing. One man on a bicycle looked at me with unbelieving eyes but promised to pass on the message. No one recognised me. In my ragged stockings and crumpled dress, my hair stiff with dust, I bore little resemblance to the glowing figure on the posters for the Adriana and the Casino de Paris. I was so tired, thirsty and hungry that I saw spots before my eyes. On the third morning, I managed to hitch a ride with a Red Cross ambulance, the only vehicle going in the opposite direction to the traffic.

The American driver handed me a canteen, her eyes flitting across my dusty, sweat-smeared face. She sensed my disorientation and said, 'Finish it. I've got more water in the back and you're dehydrated. Where are you going? Paris?'

I nodded.

'I'm driving through there to get supplies,' she said. 'The police estimate there's less than a third of the population left. Two million have fled.'

We didn't share much more conversation after that. She probably assumed I was going to Paris to collect a child or a parent. Every so often I would glance at her face. Her piercing blue eyes never left the road. Her jaw was set as if she was steeling herself for the grim and dangerous task that awaited her. She knows where she is going, I thought. But what was it that I was intending to do?

The City of Lights was pitch black when we drove through Porte d'Orléans. There were no streetlights and the windows were blacked out. The driver dropped me near the Arc de Triomphe. It was the first time I had seen the roundabout without traffic. Some policemen standing near one of the columns were the only living beings around. I offered to buy the driver dinner if there was anything open, but she shook her head. 'I must get my supplies and head north. There's no time to lose.'

I thanked her for the ride, then on impulse asked, 'Why are you here? You are American. Your country is neutral.'

Her face was invisible in the gloom but the whites of her eyes caught glints of moonlight. 'I've had a good time in your country, Mademoiselle. The time of my life. It would be wrong to leave France now that she is suffering.'

I thanked her again and made my way down the deserted Champs Élysées. The shutters on the apartment buildings were closed and the grilles were down on the shops and galleries. Any window without shutters was criss-crossed with tape and blocked with black curtains. The ghostly glimmer of the moon was the only light and, apart from the muted barking of dogs from inside the buildings, there was no sound. Had everybody gone? I thought of the American woman driving through the night to pick up mangled soldiers. A foreigner was prepared to fight. Why weren't we? Where was our will?

My apartment building was as gloomy and desolate-looking as the others in the street. I rang the bell although I held little hope that the concierge would be there. There was no light coming from her office or apartment. My feet were covered in blisters and I loathed the thought of walking all the way back to the Arc de Triomphe to ask one of the policemen to break in for me. I stared up at my apartment windows as if I was expecting Paulette to open one of them and call out a greeting to me. I ran my fingers through my tangled hair, searching for a pin. The next moment, cold metal poked into my throat. I caught a whiff of sulphur and something acrid, but after that I didn't dare breathe. The gun barrel pressed against my skin.

'Who are you?'

I recognised the voice of the concierge. I couldn't look at her because she had my head forced up with the gun and I was too scared to move.

'Madame Goux.' My voice was choked. 'It's me. Simone Fleurier.' This was not Paris. This was Chicago.

Madame Goux lessened the pressure then slowly removed the gun from my throat. I lowered my gaze. The barrel was still pointing at me, Madame Goux's finger dancing around the trigger. She squinted, trying to see who I was in the dark. Something must have registered because a few moments later she dropped the gun to her side.

'*Mon Dieu!*' she said, pushing me into the building and locking the door behind us. 'What happened to you?'

I told her about my journey, not even thinking to ask her why she was still in the building or how she had got the gun. But I stopped short when she switched on a lamp. Her skin sagged under her eyes and her expression was listless. She had never been a genial figure at the best of times, and the tenants had often joked about the dour-faced way she greeted people, but she was much more haggard than usual.

'What happened to you?' I asked her in return.

She glared at me then looked away. 'The *Boche* didn't just bomb military targets. They hit houses in the south-west of the city. My younger sister and her family are dead.'

I stared at the light, trying to block out the image of the children fleeing from the German planes. Now it seemed that more innocent people were dead. 'I am sorry,' I told her, remembering the nonchalant way she had sat in the cellar peeling potatoes during the air raid. It must pain her to think of that now.

There wasn't enough power to run the elevator so I climbed the stairs. Cramps pinched my stomach and my legs trembled. By the time I reached my apartment, my skin was burning and I collapsed straight onto my bed. I awoke a few hours later, twisted in the cover. There were thuds and explosions in the distance but I wasn't sure if they were real or I was imagining them. Somewhere in the cacophony sirens wailed and bursts of anti-aircraft fire split the air. I was sure those were real, but I didn't have the strength to go down to the cellar. I prayed to my father to watch over me. I wanted to live so that I could fight, but it was taking all my effort just to breathe.

The next thing I knew, the sun was on my face and Madame Goux was peering at me. 'The fever has gone,' she said, touching my forehead. 'Just as well you didn't shut the door behind you. I wouldn't have known you were sick. The hospital is full of soldiers and there is no doctor to come to you.'

I swallowed. My throat felt like sandpaper.

'You have been lying there for two days,' she said, moving to the window and peeking out of the curtains. 'You would have died of dehydration if I hadn't been here. I have been giving you sips of water through my douche hose.'

I did my best to forget what she had said and tried to sit up. Nausea swept over me and I collapsed back on the pillow.

'You won't be getting up until you've had something to eat,' she told me. 'So don't think about moving.'

Outside the street was quiet. But from somewhere in the building came the woof of a dog, answered by the yaps of another.

Madame Goux lit a cigarette and hissed out a stream of smoke. Combined with the airlessness of the apartment and stale sweat on my clothes, the smell made me gag.

'What is happening with the war?' I asked her.

Madame Goux raised her eyebrows as if my question was as stupid as someone asking about the health of a terminally ill patient. 'The government has left the city. Italy has just declared war on us.'

'Italy?' I tried to sit up again. This was a disaster. If Italy wanted to attack France, it would certainly start with the south. My family was far enough inland and away from the border to be safe for a while, but I thought of all those people travelling to Marseilles. How would they escape now?

Madame Goux stubbed out her cigarette and sat on the leopard-skin chair, the only piece of furniture that had been a constant with me. When André and I had parted, all the furniture had been sold with the house. I stared at the chair, seeing for the first time how incongruous it was that I, who loved animals, had once coveted their skin and fur for clothes and furnishings. The human species was the most treacherous of all — and now we were on the verge of destroying each other.

'Why did you come back?' Madame Goux asked.

'I wanted to fight,' I said.

It was a ridiculous statement for someone who couldn't even sit up, but Madame Goux didn't laugh. I told her about the American driver who had picked me up. 'We have foreigners fighting for us,' I said.

'If that's so,' glowered Madame Goux, 'she is the only one. The American president has sent us nothing but his sympathy.'

'But the British are still on our side,' I said.

'Hah!' she sneered. 'You haven't heard. They are withdrawing from the north. They are deserting us.'

I squeezed my eyes shut. Nausea swept over me again. Everything was getting worse.

I stayed in bed until early the following morning, when I couldn't stand the fusty smell of my skin any longer. Everything turned white when I stood up. I leant against the wall until my vision cleared, then wobbled to the bathroom to have a splash bath and to brush my teeth. Those two actions alone exhausted me and I lurched back to my bed.

I woke a few hours later to find myself covered in specks of soot. The sun was a fiery ball in the sky. I was sure that I was dreaming. Why was the sun so red and the sky so black? I shuffled to the window and looked out. Trucks were motoring down the street. Bedraggled men stumbled along the pavements, some of them bleeding from wounds to their faces and arms. One stopped and sat down in the gutter, laying his head on his folded arms and weeping. I peered at him more closely. He was wearing the uniform of a French officer.

'I am dreaming,' I told myself. 'The French army is the grandest and the most powerful in the world.'

Madame Goux came into the room, a bowl of soup on a tray. She put the tray on the bedside table and looked through the window over my shoulder. She was even more doleful than the last time we spoke.

'They aren't supposed to retreat through the city,' she said. 'They were ordered to go around it.'

Her presence brought a sense of reality to the nightmare and my head cleared, but it still took a moment for what she had said to sink in.

'Why around it?' I asked.

'I have heard a rumour that they aren't going to defend Paris,' she said.

'Not going to defend it? What does that mean?'

She clucked her tongue and gave a rueful laugh, shaking her head with her own disbelief. 'It means we are going to be hostages to the devil and there's not a thing we can do about it.'

～

The next morning I woke up feeling stronger, thanks to Madame Goux's care. It was ironic that we who had said so little to each other in all the years I had lived in the building were now companions in the unfolding tragedy of Paris. I climbed out of bed, washed and dressed, all in slow motion because I was still weak. I knew it wasn't a good state to be in at the beginning of a war, because wars brought rationing and famine. It would have been wiser to stay in bed for at least another day, but I couldn't. I wanted to find out for myself what was happening in the city.

On the landing I was hit by a putrid smell. I descended the stairs and the stench became overpowering. It was ten times the stink of meat gone bad. Whatever it was must have disturbed Madame Goux too because she had left the front door open, despite her paranoia about looting. I knocked on her office door. She called me in and I found her sitting at her breakfast table drinking coffee.

'What is that smell?' I asked.

'The whole city stinks,' she said. 'There are no garbage collectors. No sanitary trucks. The waste is piling up in the streets. Meat is going off in butchers' shops and the food is spoiling in the other shops.'

'But it seems to be coming from this building,' I said. 'Did the other tenants leave you their keys? It might be food rotting in their apartments.'

Madame Goux glanced at me. 'I think it might be Monsieur Copeau's dog,' she said. 'I haven't heard it bark for the past two days.'

At first I didn't make the connection. Monsieur Copeau's dog was a Great Dane. According to Madame Goux, Monsieur Copeau had left the same day I had. Then I remembered the barking I had heard during my illness and I understood.

'He left his dog behind?' I asked.

'They all left their animals behind, except for you.'

I ran over the apartments in my mind. Madame Ibert didn't have animals; neither did the family on the next floor because of their daughter's allergies. Monsieur Nitelet, the man above me, did though: a Maltese terrier called Princesse and a West Highland terrier named Charlot, after Charlie Chaplin. But the smell was of decay, not dog faeces.

'You let them starve to death?' I cried. 'Why didn't you let them out?'

'They are not my dogs,' she said. 'I've been throwing bones to the little ones but I couldn't do anything about the other one. He is a watchdog. If I had opened the door, he would have eaten me alive.'

Monsieur Copeau's apartment was on the ground floor. She could have broken a window, I thought, and let the animal out that way.

Madame Goux read my mind. 'I could have let him out but the police would have shot him anyway. A lot of dogs were left behind and the police have been killing them to prevent an outbreak of rabies.'

'*Mon Dieu!*' I said, remembering the stream of refugees. So many of those families with all their worldly goods piled onto wagons had taken their pets as well. What was wrong with the people of the eighth *arrondissement*? But I already knew the answer to that. They saw their animals as fashion accessories that could be discarded when they no longer suited them.

But something wasn't right. While Monsieur Nitelet was an arrogant man who could easily abandon an animal, every time I had seen the elderly Monsieur Copeau with his Great Dane he seemed to have real affection for the dog.

'I heard the ones upstairs yapping this morning,' said Madame Goux, taking a key out of her box and handing it to me. 'You seem to forget I have had my own grieving to do and that I was busy taking care of you.'

The key was for Monsieur Nitelet's apartment. I was aware that my concern for animals was beyond what most people considered normal, but I couldn't bring myself to apologise to Madame Goux. I didn't see Kira as an object to add warmth to my apartment whenever I needed it. I thought of her as part of my family. After all, I had sent her off to the south with as much concern as Minot had sent his mother.

The strength I had saved to go to find out what was happening with the war was spent mounting the stairs again. I opened the door to Monsieur Nitelet's apartment. It was empty of all its furniture and paintings except for a couple of chairs stacked in a corner. I caught sight of bones scattered across the floor. The two dogs scampered towards me. They were thin and looked at me with frightened eyes but wagged their tails just the same. To my surprise, a white cat with a ginger smudge above its eye and another smaller one near its nose sidled up to me. I hadn't seen it before.

'He took all his furniture,' I muttered, 'but he couldn't be bothered taking you.'

I lifted the cat into my arms — a female, I saw — and called to the two dogs to follow me to my apartment. They didn't hesitate and padded after me down the stairs. I had plenty of cans of sardines stocked up; in fact, I had so many that there hadn't been room for them when Minot and I had packed the car. I had planned to leave them outside the apartment in case anybody else needed them but I had forgotten in the rush. I opened three of the cans and scooped the contents into two bowls and filled another with water. Within a second three white balls of fur were lapping at the food.

'If you had been mine,' I told them, 'I would have taken you and left the furniture.'

I tied an apron around my waist and found an empty sack in the pantry, thinking of the dead dog downstairs. I had felt ill enough from dehydration. How awful to be left to die from starvation. It would have been kinder if the police had shot him.

Madame Goux was waiting for me in the foyer. Where would we bury a dog that big? I wondered. At ten months of age, he had only been a puppy but was as big as a man. I watched Madame Goux insert the key into Monsieur Copeau's front door and push it open. The smell was even more disgusting in the enclosed entrance way. I took the scarf from around my neck and tied it over my mouth.

'Ready?' asked Madame Goux, pushing the key into the lock of the second door. I nodded and she shoved the door open. The stench rushed towards us like a living thing, pressing its reeking claws into our faces and arms. Bile rose in my throat. Madame Goux ran to the window and threw open the curtains. She had trouble with the latch. I lunged towards her and cut my finger but managed to force it. Together we swung the windows open and leaned out, gulping mouthfuls of fresh air.

A 'woof' sounded behind us. We spun around to see the dog

lumbering into the room. His ribs were showing through his fawn coat and his eyes drooped, but he was alive.

'*Merde!*' spat Madame Goux. 'I should have brought my gun.'

But the dog didn't look as though he intended to attack us. As if to reassure me, he rested his muzzle against my thigh. What was the smell then? It had to be more than garbage and dog faeces.

'Did you see Monsieur Copeau leave?' I asked Madame Goux.

She shook her head. 'No. I just assumed he did, like everyone else. Why?'

I looked down the corridor from where the dog had come. It was gloomy and at the end of it was a half-open door that led to another room beyond.

'Do you think the dog killed him?' Madame Goux asked.

I shook my head. 'He's guarding him, that's all. He knows we've come to help.'

The dog whimpered and turned back to the corridor, glancing over his shoulder to see if we were following. Madame Goux and I inched down the hall after him. The smell was so strong it was seeping into our clothes and clinging to our hair. I could taste it in the back of my throat.

I pushed the door open. It was too dark to see anything. The window was blacked out; the only thing that gave it away was a glimmer of light through the side of the curtain. I stepped towards it, hoping that wherever Monsieur Copeau was, I didn't stumble on him. Something brushed my shoulder. I screamed. Madame Goux pushed past me and ripped down the curtain.

The dog let out a mournful howl and Madame Goux crossed herself. We gazed up at the body of Monsieur Copeau, suspended from the light fitting like a puppet on a string. I stared and stared but could not convince myself that it was a human being hanging there.

❧

The police didn't collect Monsieur Copeau's body until the afternoon. If he had left a note, we never found it. But the police said it was the eighth suicide they had picked up in the area that morning and that they could guess the reason. Monsieur Copeau had fought the Germans in the Great War.

While Madame Goux cleaned out Monsieur Copeau's room, I burned my clothes in the kitchen stove then scrubbed myself from head to foot. I could still smell the stink of decay, but once I had washed the Great Dane and rubbed him down with *eau de cologne*, I knew that the smell was more vivid in my memory than it was evident anywhere else. I fed the Dane meatballs from a can, before lying down on the sofa. The cat perched herself on top of a cupboard. She didn't seem afraid of the large dog but kept her distance just the same. The two smaller dogs inspected their new friend, sniffing his tail and leaning on his back. I tried to remember what Monsier Copeau had named his dog. It was something Italian and, I remembered thinking, a bit *kitsch*.

'Bruno,' said Madame Goux, coming in the door with a tray of bread and cheese. After all we had been through that morning I was surprised to find I had the appetite to eat it.

'Bruno,' I said, stroking the Dane's head.

'Don't get too friendly with him, I'm going to have to shoot him,' Madame Goux said, slicing up the bread.

Charlot and Princesse pricked up their ears.

'Why?' I asked, sitting up. 'He doesn't have rabies.' I was grateful to Madame Goux for helping me while I was sick, but in every other regard she got on my nerves.

Madame Goux passed me a plate before answering. 'He's too big. We won't be able to feed him.'

'I'll worry about that,' I told her. 'You are not to touch him.'

She turned down her mouth and made a *pfff* sound. 'Of course,' she said, 'we may want to keep him to shoot and eat *later*.'

⊗

The sight of Monsieur Copeau's body had been traumatic, yet the horror of it was eclipsed by my desire to find out what was happening in Paris. I stepped into the street at around four o'clock. The sun was still shining. It could have been a brilliant summer's day like any other in Paris, but there was nothing usual about the city itself. There was no one on my street and, as Madame Goux had warned me, the mounting rubbish on the pavements reeked almost as badly as Monsieur Copeau's apartment had.

I walked along the Champs Élysées towards the Grand Palais but could not find an open newspaper stand anywhere. I crossed Pont Alexandre III to the Left Bank to try my luck there. I had a sudden desire to revisit the area I had lived in when I first came to Paris and made my way down the Boulevard Saint Germain. A policeman was at work directing the refugee traffic. There were no more cars, just hundreds of bicycles and carts pulled by oxen or donkeys. Some people were on foot, pushing wheelbarrows and prams stacked with household goods.

I found an open kiosk and asked the vendor for *Le Journal*.

'There is no more *Le Journal*, Mademoiselle,' she said. 'Just *Edition Parisienne de Guerre*.'

I must have looked puzzled because she explained that the remaining volunteer staff of *Le Journal*, *Le Matin* and *Le Petit Journal* had all combined to produce the latest newssheet, *The Paris War Edition*.

I bought the newspaper. Like all the other papers that had been published in the last few weeks, it was a single sheet printed on both sides. The headline read: 'Hold On. All the Same'.

What did that mean? I sat down in a café that had no coffee but could offer me some weak tea, and read about the orders that were being given to bakers, pharmacists and food stores to remain operating or face prosecution. Factory workers had been told that they should not leave their posts or they could be charged with treason. 'Fine example,' I muttered, remembering how their bosses had fled to safety in foreign countries.

The interesting thing about the paper was that there were no blanks where the authorities had suppressed information. The censorship department must have left the city too.

I walked on towards the *métro* Odéon. It was obvious that not many store owners were paying attention to the authority's threats. Most had their shutters down or signs in their windows that read 'Closed until further notice'. I did find one place open and bought some extra cans of condensed milk and some more tins of meatballs. I had an apartment full of 'guests' to think about now.

There was a huddle of people gathered around the *métro* entrance. I stopped to look at what they were reading. A notice had been put up by the Prefect of Police saying that 'in the grave circumstances now being experienced in Paris' the Prefecture of Police would continue its work and was relying on the people of Paris to 'facilitate the task'.

'What does it mean?' someone asked.

There was a policeman standing nearby and a woman called out to him. He came over to the group and explained: 'The police are to stay in the city to keep order and peace. We are not to leave under any circumstances.'

I felt sorry for him. He was young — the right age for the army — and his voice trembled. Who could blame him for being nervous? What were the Germans likely to do to a Frenchman of military age?

I wondered if I would have been wiser to continue south rather than coming back to Paris. It would have been safer in Pays de Sault, and I knew my family would be worried about me. There was no way I could send them a telegram, all the post offices were closed. But it felt right to still be in Paris and my mother had always encouraged me to follow my instincts. I was bearing witness to a colossal event, or at least I was holding the hand of my beloved city while she gasped in her death throes.

❧

It was the following day, June thirteenth, that I finally accepted there was no hope that we could resist the Germans. I went to the newspaper stand in Montparnasse early, but it was shut. The vendor had left the latest bulletin pasted to the door:

Notice
To the Residents of Paris
Paris having been declared an OPEN CITY, the Military
Governor urges the population to abstain from all hostile acts
and counts on it to maintain the composure and dignity
required of these circumstances.

The Governor of Paris

So the rumour Madame Goux had heard was now official. We weren't going to blow up bridges, blockade the roads, 'pour oil down the city walls' so to speak. We were going to let the German army walk in. Was this some sort of military strategy? A trap for the Germans? Or was the government really handing over our beautiful city so it wouldn't be fire-stormed like Rotterdam?

When I returned to my apartment building, I found Madame Goux slumped over her desk, snoring. There was an empty bottle of wine next to her. A good bottle, something one of the apartment owners must have left behind. A trail of drool trickled down her chin and onto her copy of *Edition Parisienne de Guerre*. She was maintaining the appropriate 'composure and dignity' required of the circumstances. And if I had known where to find another bottle of Château d'Yquem, I would have joined her.

TWENTY-EIGHT

I opened my eyes at dawn the following morning, woken by the purr of a motorcar. The vehicle paused and idled under my window. Even though I had lived overlooking the busy Champs Élysées for several years, there were few cars left in Paris at that time and no buses, so the unusual noise disturbed me. I glanced down the bed. Four pairs of eyes shone back at me. The cat, who I had named Chérie, was curled between my thighs. Princesse and Charlot had tucked themselves under my arms. Bruno was stretched out over my ankles. Each animal had at least one part of their body — chin, paw, stomach, rump — resting on me. When I stirred, they stirred too. We were a pack of wolves, ready to move when the dominant animal decided there was danger. I resisted the urge to squirm under the heat and sardine breath generated by so many furry bodies, and tried to guess what kind of vehicle it was. But the car moved off again and the sound faded into the distance.

A few minutes later, Bruno growled. The smaller animals followed his lead, lifting their heads and pricking up their ears. I strained my own ears to listen. Chérie sprang up and leapt to the floor, her pupils wide and the fur on her spine and tail fluffed up. I could just make out a faint sound: a steady rumble. *Clod! Clod! Clod! Clod!* The noise grew louder and more menacing. I sat up. I knew what it was: boots pounding on pavement. *Thousands* of boots.

We had been told to remain indoors for forty-eight hours after the Germans entered the city. Only no one had told us when we should expect them. I slid out from under the animals and rushed to the window, ripping open the curtains. At first all I could see were rows of French policemen lining the avenue, their batons drawn by their sides. Had I been mistaken? Was it the police I had heard? But the policemen weren't moving and the sound was growing louder. I flung open my window and leaned out. My blood rushed to my feet. German tanks, four abreast, were grinding their way down the Champs Élysées. Marching behind them, for as far as the eye could see, were columns of German soldiers.

I shut my window and threw on a dress and sandals. Despite the warning to stay indoors, the sight was so terrifying that I couldn't. I had to see this catastrophe for myself, because until I did, I didn't think that I could believe it.

Madame Goux must have had the same idea. She was coming out of her office as I reached the foyer, dressed from head to foot in black like a widow. Out on the Champs Élysées, we found that other people were disobeying the order too. They had pale, grief-stricken faces and many of them were weeping. The policemen did not tell us to go back inside. Perhaps they were glad for our company. One policeman, standing to attention like the others, had tears rolling down his cheeks. I thought of the young police officer I had seen in Montparnasse. What an awful task these men had, to hand over the city and its people to the Germans.

The first of the tanks roared past us, grey against the morning rays of June sunshine. An armoured car with two helmeted soldiers followed afterwards. The passenger smiled at me. I turned away but the woman in front of me was excited by the victory parade. 'Look how smart the Germans' uniforms are!' she gushed. 'Look how handsome they are! Like blond gods.'

Madame Goux snapped at her, 'And some of those blond gods have slaughtered French people!'

The other bystanders glared at the woman, supporting Madame Goux's words with their icy stares. The woman shrugged, but was wise enough to stay quiet for the rest of the spectacle. The worst part was that in voicing what she had, she underscored our humiliation. The German army did look smart. Their uniforms were neatly pressed and their boots shone; a contrast to our own soldiers when they had retreated through the city a few days before, dishevelled, wounded, gabbling with despair. Still, even as I stood there watching the parade, I believed that while the French army had lost Paris, they were powerful enough to stop the Germans going any further south. That belief was the only thing I had to keep me going.

The Germans marched and paraded most of the day. In the late afternoon I walked to Montparnasse to see if I could find out more news about the progress of the war. I was sickened to see that the Dôme and the Rotonde were full of German soldiers. And, worse, that there were so many French citizens happy to share their tables and chat with the invaders as if they were some sort of tourist group in Paris for the day. Or perhaps the people were relieved that the German army was showing restraint. They were paying for their drinks, whatever pittance the franc was now worth against German currency, and didn't seem to have the intention of embarking on a looting and raping spree.

In the evening, Madame Goux and I listened to the radio, trying to find out what was happening in the south. But all the Paris radio stations had been taken over by French-speaking Germans, repeating the same message: the German army did not wish to harm the people of Paris. We had been deserted by our government and deceived by the Jews. The sooner France made peace with Germany, the sooner they could defeat the British, the real enemy.

'They don't intend to harm us?' I said, switching the radio off. 'They killed those children on the road. The eldest was barely seven years old.'

∞

The following morning, I found the dogs lined up by my front door. They had regained their strength and were itching to be taken for a walk. Madame Goux found Bruno's lead in Monsieur Copeau's apartment, but a search of Monsieur Nitelet's cupboards and drawers was in vain and I didn't have any pieces of rope or belts long enough to use as leads.

'Do you think I'll find a pet shop open?' I asked Madame Goux. 'Or a hardware store?'

'Try along the Rue de Rivoli,' she suggested, sarcastically. 'All the storekeepers there seem to be putting out their welcome mats for the Germans.'

I took Bruno with me to find leads for Princesse and Charlot. He was a formidable creature; even on all fours he was as tall as my waist.

The Germans had set up their headquarters in the Hôtel Crillon, on the Place de la Concorde, so I walked the long way, in the direction of the Arc de Triomphe. When I caught sight of the monument, my knees buckled under me. A swastika flag hung over it, big enough for the whole city to notice. It shouted the message I didn't want to hear: Paris now belonged to the Germans.

I turned down a side street and headed towards the Seine. Plastered on the wall of a building was a poster of a German soldier. He was holding a small boy in his arms while two girls looked up at him adoringly. The caption read: 'Abandoned people: have confidence in the German soldier'.

I thought about the radio broadcasts Madame Goux and I had listened to the previous night. This war will be fought in the mind, I told myself. We were abandoned people, forsaken by our army and government. But I had no confidence in German soldiers.

Two days later, Madame Goux knocked on my door. 'Marshal Pétain is going to speak on the radio tonight,' she told me.

Our government had fled to Bordeaux and the latest news we had heard was that Marshal Philippe Pétain, France's war hero of Verdun, had replaced Paul Reynauld as premier. The news had been greeted with joy but I wondered what an eighty-four-year-old man could do for France, apart from rallying the people. As it turned out, I was right. But what Marshal Pétain tried to get us to rally to was something that I could not accept.

Through the static we listened to Pétain's shaky voice: '*With a heavy heart I tell you that the fighting must cease.*' He was intending to call an armistice, to make peace with the Germans.

Madame Goux and I stared at each other, unable to speak. France had been defeated in a few weeks? Pétain was asking us to make the best of things and cooperate with the Germans?

'They handed Paris over like a gift and now they will do the same with the rest of France,' spat Madame Goux.

'I don't understand how he can —'

'Because he is a right-wing fascist himself, that's how,' she said, clenching her fists. 'I will not collaborate with the Germans. I will not cooperate with those people.'

Was this the same woman who had refused to spread sand in the roof? There was fire in her eyes now.

∞

It wasn't until the following morning that the full impact of Pétain's message hit me. France was now a Nazi satellite. All our industrial strength and resources, including ourselves, were available to the enemy. The Germans were right when they called us abandoned people. We had been abandoned, but I was not going to collaborate with a regime that murdered children and stripped people of civil rights because they were Jewish. I thought of Minot. He was probably safe at the farm for a while, and only a few hours from Marseilles by train if he needed to escape. But what about Odette, Monsieur Etienne and their families? I hoped they would go to Pays de Sault. It didn't matter that Pétain had said he offered himself to France in order to lessen her suffering. The way he had announced France's defeat seemed suspiciously hasty. If Pétain was a fascist then the Jewish people couldn't expect protection from him.

I had managed to buy leads for Princesse and Charlot and decided to take all three dogs for a walk. On that glorious summer day it seemed that Madame Goux and I were the only people who hated the German army. Paris, it appeared, had resigned itself to defeat and was now intending to 'get on with it'. After all, as I heard one waiter tell another when I passed by a café, 'The Germans are not so bad. Perhaps what we have been hearing about the Nazis were only lies from our own government.'

Certainly the soldiers I saw about the city were not what I had been expecting. They were fresh-faced and apple-cheeked. They smiled at storekeepers and young women, but did not fraternise. They took pictures of each other outside monuments and bought French perfumes and scarves to send home to their mothers. They gave up their seats to the elderly and women on the *métro* and lined up like everyone else for tickets to the Louvre. They were endearing themselves to the Parisians with their good manners.

'I saw them salute the Tomb of the Unknown Soldier,' Madame Goux confided in me when I returned home. We both agreed that these boys did not seem capable of gunning down children or forcing old Jewish women to drink from puddles.

'It's not right,' I said. 'I still feel something evil; a storm brewing in the distance.'

'When evil comes,' said Madame Goux prophetically, 'it usually comes on the wings of innocents.'

∽

The next week passed like a strange dream. I was over my illness but was listless. Getting out of bed became such a struggle that for several days I stayed in it. Madame Goux lapsed into her own kind of depression, smoking and playing solitaire in her office for most of the day. The only task that kept her going was making sure that the apartment building looked occupied. She watered the flowers in the planters, opened and closed curtains at different times of the day and also asked me to help lug some of the furniture from Monsieur Copeau's apartment into Monsieur Nitelet's apartment upstairs.

'I don't want the *Boche* to think that they can shack up here,' she explained. It was true that the German high command was requisitioning the finest hotels and apartment buildings for its personal use.

Many of the Parisians who had fled started to return. Shutters rolled up again on shops. There was food at the markets, theatres issued programs and banks recommenced business with limited trading hours. Some of those who returned were industrialists, but most were small business owners, many of them Jewish. They relied on Paris for their livelihood.

It seemed as though the Germans had been planning the takeover of Paris for years. Everything moved like clockwork. On the heels of the army came the civil servants. I received notification from the Propagandastaffel that I was to present myself at the office as soon as possible and register with them. All French entertainers would have their songs vetted and their backgrounds checked before they could work.

'I don't think so,' I muttered. I rolled the letter into a cone and used it scoop out Chérie's sand tray.

∽

The stream of refugee traffic returning to Paris from the south made me worry about Monsieur Etienne and Odette. I prayed that they would stay away from the city for their own good. Our telephone line had been cut for some reason, so I decided to go to Monsieur Etienne's office myself. There were no taxis available to the French public so I caught the *métro* to the Left Bank, something I hadn't done in years. The first carriage I got into was full of German soldiers, so I changed to another car at the next stop. But at the station after that, more German soldiers poured onto the train. I resigned myself to having to travel with the enemy. I sensed someone staring at me and glanced across the aisle to see two German officers diagonally opposite. They were looking in my direction and smiling. I had no intention of flirting with them and looked for something with which to seem occupied. I couldn't stare out the window as the line was underground. There was a folded newssheet tucked into the side of the seat. I pulled it out and pretended to read it. A slip of paper floated from the page onto my lap. My eye fell to the handwritten words:

To the people of Paris: Resist the Germans!

I quickly hid the note back in the fold of the newssheet so no one could see what I was reading. My eyes scanned the words. It was a transcription of a speech given by Charles de Gaulle over a week ago:

Is the last word said? Has all hope gone? Is the defeat
definitive? No. Believe me, I tell you that nothing is lost
for France.

I glanced up; one of the German officers was still looking in my direction. He whispered something to his companion. I tried to keep my face as neutral as possible while I read the rest of the message. Colonel Charles de Gaulle, now General de Gaulle, had been one of the critics regarding France's lack of preparedness for a war. It seemed that somehow he had escaped to London and was calling on all French soldiers who were in Britain, or who could make their way there, to contact him.

The flame of French resistance must not be quenched
and will not be quenched.

Tears welled in my eyes. My chin trembled. We had not been forgotten. There was a leader, someone who still believed in France. Resist? Of course I would resist, and with my last breath! But how? How would I find these people who still wanted to fight for France?

I got out of the *métro* at Solférino, so buoyant with joy that I ran up the stairs. We have not been forgotten, I told myself. Nothing is lost for France.

'Mademoiselle Fleurier!' a man's voice called out. I stopped, uncertain if I had heard my name or not. The accent was German. I turned around. Standing behind me were the two officers who had been sitting near me on the train. They were holding up a camera.

'Please,' said the taller of the two men, 'we would like a photograph with the famous Mademoiselle Fleurier.'

Of course, I cursed, the Germans would know who I was. I had refused to perform in Berlin after I had heard the stories about the treatment of Jewish people from Renoir and Count Kessler, but the Germans would have known me from my films and my records.

A crowd of people gathered around, keen to see what was going on. The officer repeated his request. 'Please, Mademoiselle Fleurier. A picture with you.'

I did not want to have my picture taken with German soldiers. My personal feelings aside, what if it appeared in one of the propaganda newspapers? *Simone Fleurier welcomes Officer Berlekamp and Officer Pätz to Paris.* I used the Parisian approach and pretended that I couldn't understand the question, although the officer spoke reasonable French. Unfortunately, a woman in the crowd decided that she would be helpful. 'They want to have their picture taken with you,' she said.

The officer held out his camera, teasing me with his smile. I lifted my chin.

'You want a picture of Simone Fleurier?' I said. 'Then take a picture of this.'

I turned my back on him and walked through the crowd. A couple of people gasped, the rest remained silent and moved out of my way. As I approached the corner I noticed a man leaning against a post, holding a newssheet. His eyes burned into me for a few seconds before he turned away. Did I read his message correctly? He seemed to be saying, 'Bravo, Mademoiselle Fleurier. Bravo.'

It was a foolish act of resistance that wouldn't change anything and, if the German authorities heard about it, would only get me into trouble. Yet it gave me satisfaction every time I thought about it. I was still buoyed by the memory of my defiance when I took the dogs for a walk a few days later. I was also pleased to have found out that Monsieur Etienne had not returned to Paris. Perhaps he and the others had gone to the farm after all. From there, I trusted that Bernard would assist them to leave the country.

Since Pétain's capitulation on our behalf, France had been divided into two zones. The northern part, including Paris, was run by the Germans. They claimed that they needed it to launch their attack on Britain. The southern part was to be administrated by Pétain and his Vichy government. Although the south was technically 'Unoccupied France', it was clear that Pétain was a puppet of Hitler. Correspondence was restricted over the demarcation line. There was no way I could explain to Bernard about Monsieur Etienne and his family. From Paris you could only send a form and tick the boxes to set answers: I am well; I am okay; I am not so well. All I could do was pray that everything would be all right.

I took my route towards the Seine. My heart leapt when I saw that the poster of the German soldier with the children had been scrawled over with a painted message:

Beware, Nazi assassins! We will overcome you!

'We will,' I whispered to my unseen kindred spirit. 'We will.'

I returned to the apartment building in good spirits, feeling more vigour than I had in weeks. I was about to run up the stairs with the dogs when Madame Goux darted out of her office. Her face was flushed and her pupils were black buttons in her grey eyes. At first I thought she was excited about the task I had given her of copying out General de Gaulle's speech. I was intending to slip the notes into newssheets and other places French people would find them. But when she approached me I saw that she was pale and trembling.

'Mademoiselle Fleurier,' she whispered in a hoarse voice. 'There are two men in your apartment. I tried to keep them downstairs but they refused to wait in the foyer. They wouldn't tell me who they were.'

I tried to think who might come and visit me, but there seemed no reason why anyone I knew would not declare themselves to my concierge. 'Are they French or German?' I asked.

'French, but sinister-looking,' she said. 'I wouldn't trust them.'

It sounded like a serious visit. But if the Germans were upset about my treatment of their officers or my failure to register with the Propagandastaffel, wouldn't they send their own men?

'I'll leave Princesse and Charlot with you,' I told Madame Goux. 'But I'll keep Bruno with me.'

The door to my apartment was open and as I approached I could see the two men sitting on the sofa. One was petite and peaky-looking; the other was older with pouches under his eyes and slicked-back grey hair.

As soon as he saw me, the younger of the two men leapt up and moved in my direction. Madame Goux had been right: there was something vicious in his bony face. His eyes narrowed on Bruno.

'You can leave the dog outside,' he said.

My pulse raced. I wasn't about to be ordered around my own apartment. 'Bruno is never left outside,' I said, surprised at the calmness in my voice. 'He becomes agitated if he is separated from me.'

A look of irritation flashed across the man's face. The older man stood up. 'All right then,' he said. 'But keep him on the lead.'

Something about the clinical tone of his voice made me shudder. The young man closed the door behind me. I heard the lock click. The older man sat down again in an armchair, but his eyes never left me.

'We have been sent by the Propagandastaffel to find out why you haven't registered,' the young man said, moving to the sofa and taking some papers out of a briefcase he had propped beside it. 'Then your concierge explained that you have been ill. Never mind, we have all the necessary forms here for you to fill in.'

As neither man had introduced himself, I invented names for them. The younger one I called Mouse because of the way his body twitched with nervous energy. The older man I called the Judge because of the way he held his chin and kept his hands folded on his knees. He emanated authority, yet seemed content to listen while the first man talked.

Mouse thrust some forms at me. 'We will wait here while you sign them,' he said. 'It will save you making the trip to the Propagandastaffel.'

I sensed that my future might depend on how I behaved with these two men. I knew that the music halls and theatres were opening up again, but I had no intention of performing for the occupation army. How could I express that in a way that wouldn't have me thrown into prison?

'I don't think it is necessary in my case,' I said.

Mouse's face grew taut. 'Not necessary?' he asked. 'All your colleagues have cooperated. Why should an exception be made for you?'

The animosity in his voice chilled me. He was seething with it.

It was a crucial moment. If I was to be useful in any way to those willing to fight for France, I knew that I had to behave more astutely than I had a few days before. If I was going to take risks then they had to count for something.

'I am not intending to perform any more,' I said. 'I have retired.'

The Judge raised his eyebrows.

'I am exhausted,' I explained. 'I am too tired to perform. And I have not been well.'

'I see,' said Mouse, nodding politely but without warmth. 'But that doesn't really help us with the other problem.'

'What other problem?' I asked.

Mouse folded his arms across his chest. 'We have checked your records. And what we have found is not very commendable. You refused to perform in Berlin and you have had close relationships with two anti-Nazis.'

I assumed that he was referring to Count Kessler and Jean Renoir. So the Germans had been spying on me? Bruno yawned. He was surprisingly calm in the face of Mouse's interrogation; normally he barked if anyone raised their voice at me. Once, on one of our walks, a paper seller had shoved a newssheet at me and screamed out the headline. Bruno had nearly taken the man's arm off.

Mouse stood up and circled the room. 'The Deuxième Bureau kept tabs on anyone who was crossing borders frequently. Unfortunately, when they fled the city they left some sensitive files behind. One of them was yours.'

I stared at him in disbelief. The Deuxième Bureau was the French secret service. I had been watched by my own country! Furthermore, they had been stupid enough to leave my file behind while they fled to save their own hides.

Mouse completed his circle of the room and came to a stop before me. I sensed that he was enjoying every moment of the tension.

'You see, Mademoiselle Fleurier,' he said, bringing his face close to mine, 'you are not really in a position to be antagonising anyone. You are Paris's most famous performer. The French need your light more than ever. The Germans need you too, to rally the people to collaborate.'

On the radio, the word 'collaborate' had a positive ring. But to me it sounded worse than the filthiest curse. I would rather die than collaborate. But Mouse had done his job: he had thrown me off balance.

'I will not rally to the Nazi cause,' I said. 'Nor will I encourage anyone else to. I will not align myself with murderers.'

The men exchanged glances. I was courting disaster but my feelings were out in the open now. If I was going to be thrown into gaol, then I was determined to go down kicking and screaming. If the French people were to receive any message from me about collaboration, it would be to fight to the death against it.

'That is not a very cooperative attitude,' said the Judge, brushing a speck of dust off his trousers.

'And you,' I said, pointing at him, 'you are a failure of a man! A Frenchman! You should be fighting for your country. Not kissing the feet of the Germans.'

Mouse moved towards me but Bruno growled and bared his teeth. Mouse leapt back.

'Get out of my apartment now!' I shouted. 'The both of you!'

To my disconcertment, neither man moved. Now what should I do? Call Madame Goux to get her gun? Then a strange thing happened: Mouse and the Judge seemed to transform before my eyes. Mouse's face relaxed and his focus softened. He began to look less like a mouse and more like a rabbit. The Judge seemed to grow taller and sprightlier. The two men exchanged a smile, a good-humoured smile — something I would have thought was beyond them.

The Judge shook his head. 'She is too fiery and big-mouthed,' he said to Mouse. 'I warned you that entertainers are overly emotional. What if she starts talking like that to the Germans?'

Mouse shrugged his shoulders. 'I can teach her to be more discreet. What is most important is that we can have no doubt whose side she is on.'

The Judge lifted his palms in resignation. 'All right,' he said. 'We don't have much time and much choice.'

Mouse turned to me. So quickly had his expression changed that I wondered if I was suffering from a hallucination. I sank down onto the sofa.

'Mademoiselle Fleurier,' Mouse said, sitting down next to me, 'we can't give you our real names but we are from the Deuxième Bureau not the Propagandastaffel. It is true that your file was left behind, but I can assure you that I have amended most of it and destroyed the rest, though possibly not with the same level of imagination you used to get rid of your Propagandastaffel notice.'

So he knew about that too? Had he gone so far as to rifle through my rubbish bins? When they said that they weren't from the Propagandastaffel, I could believe them. But wasn't the Deuxième Bureau now part of the Vichy government?

'Well, let us say that we have defected,' explained Mouse. 'And that we need your help. We need to get out of France to join General de Gaulle in England.'

My skin tingled with the sound of the general's name. I had wondered how I was ever going to find the people who were willing to fight against the Germans. As it turned out, they had come to me.

'If that is your mission then I am at your service,' I told them. 'I pledge myself to General de Gaulle.'

Mouse turned to the Judge, who nodded, then looked back to me. 'We need to get to the south so we can leave France either by boat or via the Pyrenees. We can get forged papers for ourselves and change identities, but it will still be difficult to get across the demarcation line, especially with our "parcels". But if we could travel in the employment of someone who might have a good reason to be going to the south of France, say to perform there, it would be easier.'

He gave the word 'parcels' a particular kind of emphasis but my mind was racing too far ahead to focus on it. 'You mean I could employ you both as my manager and my artistic director, for instance?' I suggested.

Mouse grinned. 'Exactly.'

After some discussion it was agreed that I should arrange to travel to Marseilles with a view to seeking out venues to stage a performance there. It would involve registering with the Propagandastaffel and seeming to cooperate with the Germans in other ways. But now that I was working in the interests of saving France, those things didn't matter as much. The Judge told me that he would make the arrangements for the following Wednesday. All I needed to do was to seek permission to travel, which he expected would be granted now that he had replaced my file with a more acceptable one.

Before they left, the Judge turned to me. 'Mademoiselle Fleurier,' he said, 'I have to warn you that the Germans will shoot anyone who aids the Resistance. But the Vichy government has an even more gruesome deterrent. They behead anyone involved in subversive activities. *With an axe*.'

He was testing my resolve, trying to gauge my level of fear. Later, when I got to know him better, I would understand that he was also making sure that I understood the ultimate price of what I was committing myself to. But I was not frightened; my mind was clear and calm. I thought of all the great moments in my life — my first appearance on stage, my leading role at the Adriana, the success of my first movie. None of them compared to this. This was not a performance. This was something much more important.

'I am willing to do whatever I have to in order to free France,' I said. 'Even if that means sacrificing my life. I will not rest or give in until the enemy has been chased out of our country.'

TWENTY-NINE

Mouse and the Judge returned the following Wednesday evening. I was surprised to see that they had brought two men with them. One was around six foot two with a shock of black hair falling across his forehead from a slight widow's peak. The other was short with blond hair so curly that it looked sewn to his scalp. The tall one gave me a nod before sinking into a chair. He had an air of quiet authority and self-assuredness. The younger one smiled with crinkles at the corners of his eyes. I assumed that they must be ex-Deuxième Bureau men too, but there was something not quite right about them. They were dressed in suits and carried their hats in their hands, but it was the way they moved that caught my attention. The one in the chair sat with his long legs splayed out; the other stood with his chin tucked into his neck.

'Our "parcels",' whispered Mouse, a note of pride ringing in his voice. 'Two RAF pilots who were shot down at Dunkirk. An Australian and a Scotsman. We are going to take them back to England with us.'

Of course, I thought, they aren't French. But if I had noticed the stiffness of their gaits and their lack of gestures, wouldn't the Germans too?

'Mademoiselle Fleurier,' Mouse exclaimed, 'we have more serious worries than that. The Australian speaks French well but with a slight accent. The Scotsman doesn't speak a word of it.' Mouse must have seen the alarm on my face because he quickly added, 'But we have cover stories to suit them. The Australian is now a Frenchman born in Algiers and the Scotsman is a Czech composer, although he doesn't speak Czech. But most of the Germans don't either.'

'I hope he plays the piano at least,' I said, trying to keep my sense of humour. If I didn't potentially have my neck on a chopping block, I probably would have found the situation highly comical.

'He does, in fact,' said Mouse, 'exceptionally well. He was a student at the Royal College of Music when the war broke out.'

'Are you afraid, Mademoiselle Fleurier?' asked the Judge. 'Are you having second thoughts? You had better speak up now if you are.'

The Australian stared at me. He had an intense, lean face but gentle green eyes. I guessed he was about the same age as me, somewhere in his early thirties, while the Scot was younger, not more than twenty-three or twenty-four.

'I am not afraid,' I replied. 'I am just determined to get you all over the demarcation line.'

'We had better get going if we are to make the train,' said Mouse, tapping his watch. He gave me a quick briefing on everyone's cover names and stories. He was Pierrot Vinet, my manager. The Judge was Henri Bacque, my artistic director. The Australian was Roger Delpierre, the stage director, and the Scotsman was a Czech composer by the name of Eduard Novacek.

The formalities over, I pointed to the line of suitcases and hatboxes by the door. We were travelling first class and Mouse had told me to pack like a star. Chérie was already in her cage and I opened my bedroom door and called the dogs. Mouse's face turned white when he saw Princesse, Charlot and Bruno bounding towards him.

'Oh no,' he said. 'They can't come.'

'Why not?' I asked, bending down to attach their leads.

He raised his eyebrows. 'We are leaving on a dangerous mission, Mademoiselle Fleurier. We can't be worrying about a menagerie of animals.'

'Well, they're not staying here,' I said, hooking the leads onto the dogs' collars and standing upright again. 'They have been abandoned once before. I am not abandoning them again.'

'Couldn't your concierge look after them?' suggested the Judge. 'Until you come back.'

'I won't be back for a while,' I said. 'And my concierge is the kind of woman who would eat them.'

I had another reason for taking the animals. I had decided that if I was going to go to the trouble of getting myself over the border, then once I had delivered the Deuxième Bureau men and their 'parcels', I would go to check on my family and see if the others had arrived. I was having trouble obtaining enough food for the animals in Paris and I knew the dogs and Chérie would be welcome on the farm.

The Scotsman was wandering about the drawing room, studying my photographs and the ornaments on the mantelpiece. But the Australian had not taken his eyes from my face the whole time.

'Well,' said Mouse, straightening his jacket, 'as leader of this mission, I am ordering you to leave those animals where they are.'

The skin on the back of my neck prickled. I could have told Mouse that, as financier of the mission and volunteer for General de Gaulle, the animals were coming with me or he and his mission could go to hell. But I did not want to do that. I wanted to help these men get to England. I wanted General de Gaulle to win back France for us. But when I looked at the trusting faces of the animals, I could not betray them.

'I will leave my luggage,' I said. 'But I must take them.'

'That won't do,' said the Judge. 'An entertainer without luggage will arouse suspicion.'

Bargaining wasn't getting me anywhere and I was tempted to resort to feminine wiles. But I was too angry to summon crocodile tears. It was inconceivable to me to leave the dogs and Chérie in Paris when there was no one I could trust to look after them. And I had no intention of abandoning them to the fate that their original owners had. But I could see from the way Mouse had set his feet firmly on the floor that he was girding himself for battle.

He was about to speak when 'Roger', the Australian rose from his chair. 'I think we are going to miss the train if this argument goes on any longer,' he said in carefully measured French. For a moment I was hypnotised by his voice. It was rich and fluid, like an actor on stage. 'If Mademoiselle Fleurier is prepared to risk her life for four men she doesn't know from a bar of soap, then I think we can let her take her animals,' he went on.

Mouse's face turned from white to crimson. But whether it was from the embarrassment of being outdone in chivalry or because he was being challenged, I couldn't tell.

'Come on then,' said the Judge. 'We will each take two pieces of Mademoiselle Fleurier's luggage.'

Mouse, chastised and annoyed, was the first out the door. Roger and I reached for the same suitcase. He smiled at me. The expression transformed his face: he was handsome rather than surly. I realised that he would probably have come across differently if he had not been a downed pilot, trapped behind enemy lines. My heart did a twirl in my chest. It startled me. I had experienced that sensation once before, many years ago. The blood rushed to the surface of my skin and I could feel my cheeks glow.

'I grew up with dogs. Four of them,' Roger said. He reached to pick up Chérie's cage with his free arm. 'I've never had a cat but I suspect I'll like her.'

He was self-assured in the way he spoke but his smile was shy. It melted my heart.

'I think a person who is kind to animals must be a good person overall,' I said, trying to regain my composure. I was acting as if I was sixteen again — and we were in the middle of a war!

'I agree,' he said, standing aside so I could go through the door first. 'And I think a woman who is loyal to her animals will not betray her friends,' he added in English.

Roger's voice was warm and rumbled like a tremor under the earth. He would make a good singer, I thought. The charm of it made me want to learn ... whatever it was they spoke in Australia. Australian?

We had chosen a day and time when Madame Goux normally visited her brother, so we all froze when we found her standing in the foyer. She was dressed in a travel suit with a suitcase by her side. The Judge glanced at me and Mouse gave me a nudge. It looked as though I was going to have to start with the cover story sooner than expected.

'Good evening, Madame Goux,' I said. 'I would like you to meet my manager, Pierrot Vinet —'

'My arse!' she spat, lifting her eyebrow at me accusingly. 'I know who they are. I heard through the air vent. Not as good spies as you think, are you?'

I was too surprised to say anything. I had told her that my two visitors the previous week were from the Propagandastaffel and she had given every sign of believing me.

'Madame, may I ask what you intend to do?' said the Judge. His voice was chillingly calm and I sensed that he was feeling in his pocket for a weapon. I was afraid that if Madame Goux said she was going to denounce us, he would kill her on the spot.

'As you see,' she said, pointing to her suitcase, 'I am coming with you.'

'Pardon?' asked Mouse.

'I am coming with you,' said Madame Goux. 'To fight for France.'

'Oh,' said the Judge, switching to a more gracious tone. 'You could do that so well from here, Madame. We need a Paris coordinator.'

'Don't give me that shit!' barked Madame Goux. 'I've got my papers in order. You can buy me a ticket at the station. I'm going as Mademoiselle Fleurier's personal assistant. Didn't it occur to you that it would look strange for her to travel alone with so many men?'

It hadn't occurred to me, but she was probably right. I glanced at Mouse who shrugged at the Judge.

'Come along then, Madame,' said the Judge, rolling his eyes. 'Before everyone else who knows Mademoiselle Fleurier wants to come too.'

❧

We arrived at the station to find it crowded with German soldiers and French civil servants. With the luggage carriage filled to capacity, the conductor agreed to let the animals travel with us, although he warned that we would have to move if the Germans objected to them or the dogs started barking. My being given a compartment in first class was clearly an exception: the Germans were given the best seats first and the French had to settle for whatever was left after that. There were six seats in our compartment and, as it turned out, having an extra member in the party was to our advantage. If Madame Goux hadn't come with us then a German soldier or French official would have taken the spare seat and maybe tried to make conversation.

Mouse and I sat opposite each other in the seats nearest the door. Roger sat next to me, with Charlot resting near his feet, and Eduard was placed by the window. The plan was that when the police came to check our tickets, Eduard would pretend to be asleep and I would speak for him.

I was aware that the compartment walls were thin and that we had Germans on either side of us, but I was fascinated by the two RAF men and wanted to know more about them. Especially Roger. I wondered what his true name was, but Mouse had forbidden me to enquire about any of the parties' real lives, in case I was caught. 'If they torture you, the less you know the better it will be for the rest of us,' he had said.

Eduard had already 'fallen asleep' so I whispered to Roger, 'You were born in Algiers?' If I couldn't have a real conversation with him, surely I could get myself better acquainted with his cover story.

Roger rose to the game. 'My sisters and I went to live with my grandparents there after my parents were killed in a train accident. My grandfather was a retired naval captain who had travelled to Algiers and never wanted to leave.'

Mouse frowned at me, then seemed to think better of it. Hadn't he said himself that a cover story should be practised until it was flawless and all questions could be answered without hesitation?

'And how come you are in France?' he asked Roger.

'My uncle invited me here to study law at the Sorbonne. I fell in love with Paris.'

'Why weren't you called up for military service?' I asked, knowing this would be the first thing the Germans would ask of a man his age.

'I'm diabetic,' he answered.

Goodness, I thought, I hope if he is ever caught and the Germans bring in a doctor, he can fake that.

I tried to pick out what was true and what wasn't in the cover story. I guessed that Roger probably did have two sisters. He may well have studied law, but not at the Sorbonne. What would be the use of knowing French law when you intended to practise in Britain or one of her dominions?

The ticket and papers check by the conductor when we boarded the train had gone without a hitch, but when we stopped at the demarcation line and four French policemen came on board, my pulse began to throb.

'*Bonsoir,* Mesdames and Messieurs,' said one of the policemen, peering into our compartment. 'Your papers, please.'

As planned, Roger slipped Eduard's papers from his pocket, put them on top of his and passed them to me. I handed all three of our passes up to the policeman, while Mouse did the same with his, the Judge's and those of Madame Goux. The policeman studied them much more carefully than I had seen anyone do before the war. He checked my picture against my appearance and did the same with the others. But he stared uncomfortably long at Eduard's.

'Wake him up, please,' he said, nodding his chin towards the Scotsman.

'Is that necessary?' I asked, laying my hand on the policeman's wrist. 'He has *la grippe* and has been sleeping since Paris.'

I hoped that my comment that Eduard had influenza would cause the policeman to leave our compartment quickly, but the expression on his stern face didn't change. To my horror, he leaned out into the corridor and called for the other policemen to come. I glanced at Mouse. Outwardly his face and posture were calm, but I could see how white his knuckles were on the armrest.

Three more police officers arrived, blocking the corridor. My eyes fell to the revolvers on their belts. 'There,' said the policeman, holding Eduard's papers towards them. 'This document has all the details filled out correctly. This is what the Germans want to see. This is what a genuine pass looks like.'

The other policemen glanced at the paper and nodded their approval. 'The French don't realise how they hold things up by not doing things precisely,' one of them said.

The first policeman handed back our papers, then touched his cap and wished us a good trip. We were careful not to relax our positions as soon as he left. It wasn't until the policemen got off and the train began moving again that we let out a collective sigh of relief.

'We will have to warn the forger you use in Paris,' the Judge said to Mouse. 'He might be too good.'

❦

The train trip to Marseilles was supposed to be an overnight one, but we had been warned that with all the checks the journey could end up taking two or three days. At each stop, I would have to take the three dogs for a toilet break and Chérie when she needed it too. I could see why Mouse had objected to me bringing the animals, but

I had to stand by my decision and find a way to manage. No wagon compartments had been available but we were content to sleep upright as long as we weren't disturbed. Madame Goux and Mouse shut the curtains. I posted Bruno near the door to warn us if anybody came inside. Princesse curled herself into my lap while Charlot remained at Roger's feet. Chérie seemed happy to sleep in her cage on top of the luggage rack.

On a train crowded with Germans, we weren't going to risk the dining car and my stomach rumbled as I drifted off to sleep to dream of policemen endlessly checking my papers. I must have been asleep for an hour or so when the train slowed down then came to a stop. There were shouts outside; the voices were German. I sat upright. The others did the same. The Judge peered through the curtains. 'Another check. A German one.'

A few minutes later the conductor knocked on our door. 'Everybody out. Leave your luggage in the compartment.'

'Okay,' Mouse whispered in English, 'Mademoiselle Fleurier and I will go first with everybody's papers. The rest of you stick close behind.'

I left Chérie where she was but took the dogs with me.

We stepped out of the carriage and found the platform overrun by German soldiers. Even though we had passed the demarcation line and were supposed to be in Vichy France, it appeared that the Germans were giving the local police some 'assistance' in checking travellers' papers. To my horror, the control desks were divided by language and there was one for Czech citizens. We were done for.

'Stay with us,' the Judge whispered to Eduard. 'Don't allow yourself to be separated. Whatever happens, keep calm.'

We were directed to a table where an officer sat waiting to check the French first- and second-class passengers. He was the most fastidiously dressed man I had ever seen. His boots glistened under the dim station lights as if he had just painted them. His buckles and buttons sparkled and there was not a crease in his uniform where one shouldn't be. While his colleagues were also neatly dressed, they looked wilted by the heat. But this officer was as cleanly shaven and fresh-looking as if he had just started work for the day. He gestured for us to step forward. My heart was pounding so hard I was sure that he would hear it.

'You are travelling on the train with these dogs?' he said, in perfect French. 'It is unhygienic.'

He looked like the kind of man who would call a dog hair on his trousers 'filthy'.

'They are clean dogs, I assure you. No fleas or worms,' I said. On cue, Bruno rested his chin on the table, a string of drool oozing from his jaws. I brushed him away. 'They are part of my act,' I said, trying to keep the tremble out of my voice. 'For my upcoming show in Marseilles.'

'Part of your act?' The officer watched Charlot relieve himself against a post. 'I have never seen you perform with animals.'

Jean Renoir had once told me that the best way to calm nerves was to act the opposite to what you are feeling. I did my best to act flattered. 'You have seen me perform?' I asked, tossing my head and smiling. 'Where did you see me?'

'In Paris in 1930. I saw your show sixteen times.'

'Well,' I replied, laughing, 'I guess that means you liked it.'

'We are travelling to Marseilles to design a new show for Mademoiselle Fleurier,' Mouse said, sounding as slick as any Parisian manager. 'You must come and see her perform there.'

The officer glanced at the two soldiers standing behind him and said to them in German, 'Can you believe that I have Simone Fleurier standing in front of me? And her manager invited me to her show in Marseilles.'

'You should search her,' replied one of them, licking his lips. 'You can't let a chance like that go by.'

I felt myself pale. I wasn't hiding anything on my person that could give the others away, but the thought of being searched by those men was terrifying. Then, an image of my mother flashed into my mind. I saw her staring down Guillemette in the Parc de Monceau when she had tried to intimidate her. I found myself giving the same look to the officer. He shifted in his seat although he would have assumed that I couldn't understand German. Nevertheless, he turned to the others and said, 'I can't search a French citizen of her standing without good reason. Besides, do you really think a spy would be travelling with such a zoo? I mean, look at them all. Especially that old woman. She has a face like a donkey's arse.'

The two soldiers laughed and the officer shuffled through our papers. He stamped them and handed them back to me. 'Till Marseilles then, Mademoiselle Fleurier,' he said, appraising me with the eyes of a man, not an officer.

I tucked the papers into my handbag and turned back to the carriage, calling the dogs to come too. The men and Madame Goux followed but we said nothing to each other until all the passengers had been checked and reseated. I felt in some way that although we were travelling together, each one of us was making this treacherous journey alone.

⤞∽⤟

By some miracle we arrived in Marseilles on schedule and without further incident. It was strange for me to be back in the city where I had first dreamed of becoming a star. The smell of salt and the screeching seagulls brought back memories of Aunt Augustine's house. I had travelled a long way since then.

I had reserved a four-bedroomed suite at the Hôtel de Noailles. After the waiter had delivered us a breakfast of omelettes, cheese, *croissants*, melon and champagne, we blocked the air vents and keyhole then toasted the success of the first part of our mission.

'Here's to getting out of occupied France,' said the Judge.

'I could have done just as well with bacon and eggs,' said Eduard, eyeing the feast set out before us. 'But this is splendid.'

It was the first time I had heard him speak and he didn't sound like a Czech at all. He had a high, lilting voice.

'You must have been bursting to say something,' I told him. 'I don't think I could have gone that long without saying a word.'

Roger laughed. Even Mouse and the Judge allowed themselves to smile. Madame Goux demanded to know what we were talking about and Mouse translated our conversation for her.

'I am impressed with your *sang-froid*, Mademoiselle Fleurier,' said the Judge, buttering a piece of bread. 'You are a remarkable woman.'

I turned to Mouse, keen to rub in what the officer had said about the animals. 'Bruno, Princesse, Charlot and Chérie turned out to be an excellent cover story.'

'All right then,' chuckled the Judge. 'We shall toast our animal friends too. But I had no idea that you could speak German. Where did you learn?'

I explained about my time in Berlin and about my lessons there. I had everyone laughing again when I told them about Doctor Daniel, who used to make me jump over chairs and sing high Cs.

'You must have had some bizarre teachers in your time too,' Roger said to Eduard.

The Scotsman put down his knife and fork. 'None to match that one,' he said. 'At least with the piano no one expects you to be able to run around and play it at the same time.'

'I hope I will hear you play before you go,' I said. 'I am curious to know how a concert pianist ended up in the RAF.'

'Ask the Squadron Captain,' he answered, nodding at Roger. 'I'm just an officer. He's the fighting ace. He shot down a number of the Luftwaffe before he got hit himself.'

Roger blushed and, because he was embarrassed, dropped his guard. 'I flew quite a bit in Tasmania,' he said. 'My grandmother told me that my very first word was "airplane" —'

Mouse coughed and we fell into an awkward silence. I realised we weren't supposed to go that far. It was hard for me to get used to the secrecy. It was still early in the war and our spirits were high. The thought of being thrown into prison and tortured, let alone executed, didn't seem real. But then, none of us knew anyone who had died that way yet.

'What is the next step in the plan?' asked Madame Goux. If Mouse had praised me on my coolness in the face of danger, then she deserved to be complimented too. Madame Goux had shown restraint the whole journey and had played the part of an efficient secretary well.

'We have a contact in Marseilles,' Mouse explained. 'Once we have spoken to him we are going to leave either by sea or cross the Pyrenees into Spain. But I'm afraid I can't tell you which one.'

The sea would be easier than the Pyrenees, which were rugged mountains and difficult to cross. Roger, Eduard and Mouse looked fit enough to make it, but I worried about the Judge.

'Please, gentlemen, eat up and rest well while you are here,' I told them. 'I will spare no expense for you. You must be strong for your escape.'

Roger lifted his champagne glass. 'I should like to propose a toast to Mademoiselle Fleurier,' he said. 'For being a good sport.'

I saw that Roger had the kind of energy that I had admired in André. When a job needed to be done, he was a machine, but in personal moments, he was soft.

The others held up their glasses and gave me a cheer.

'Thank you,' I said. 'I have known you all only a short time and I don't even know who some of you are, but I think that I shall miss you.'

I looked up, directly into Roger's eyes. He held my gaze for a moment before turning away. He was smiling.

⁓

The Judge stressed the importance of maintaining our cover stories to avoid suspicion. While he and Roger went about finding their 'contact' — which I had gleaned enough to guess was actually two people, someone high up in the French navy and an Allied soldier who had escaped from Fort Saint Jean — the rest of us were to keep up appearances. I had a piano installed in the suite for Eduard to play, which also gave us an excuse to leave the 'Do not disturb' sign on the door.

Meanwhile, Mouse and I went to see the artistic director of the Alcazar. 'Mademoiselle Fleurier, we have been trying to get you to perform here for years!' Franck Esposito exclaimed. 'And now you have come to us!'

As it turned out, Raimu was about to perform a show with the theatre but they were interested in having me do a few guest shows and spoke about putting together a special production for the next season. To my surprise, despite the war and his lack of experience, Mouse managed to negotiate a good contract for me.

Whenever we could, our party ate together in fine restaurants along the Canebière so as not to draw attention to ourselves by always hiding away in our suite. Marseilles had been bombed by the Italians but apart from that, the war and the Germans seemed far away. Something about the toughness of the Marseillaises told me they would put up more of a fight than the northerners had. One evening, a Spanish woman came into the restaurant to sell bunches of lavender. She looked so much like my mother that I was taken aback. I am homesick, I thought. With all the upheaval and fear, I longed to be with my family. But for the past few weeks I had put my country first. Had they known, my family would have implored me to do just that; but they didn't know where I was or what I was doing and it pained me to think I was causing them worry.

A week later, when we were gathered in the hotel suite, the Judge announced that Mouse, Eduard and himself were leaving that night on the train for Toulouse.

'What about Roger?' Madame Goux asked.

'He is staying,' said the Judge.

My heart skipped a beat. I couldn't bring myself to look at Roger. I had no idea who he really was, but being near him had become important to me.

'What for?' asked Madame Goux.

'There are hundreds of downed airmen in France,' said Roger, standing up and moving to the window. 'There are also escaped prisoners of war trying to make their way south on their own. Many are being recaptured. It's a waste of skilled men for the Allies. My contact is setting up a series of safe houses from Paris all the way south to get the men to the Pyrenees. But he needs help and people he can trust. I'm going to stay in France to assist with the network.'

I was in awe of Roger's bravery. There was so much self-seeking cowardice amongst the French and here was a foreigner prepared to risk his life to fight the enemy.

'I want to help,' I told him, 'in any way I can.'

'Me too,' said Madame Goux.

Roger's face lit up. 'Neither of you can imagine how valuable you are to the Resistance. But I'm afraid to ask any more of you ladies than you've already done.'

'Ask,' I urged him. 'What could be more important right now than saving France?'

Roger sat down next to me. 'The apartment in Paris — can we use it?'

'Of course,' I told him. 'I also have a house in Marseilles that I inherited. It is down in the Vieux Port. It is nothing grand but it has been done up inside and isn't in any way conspicuous.'

Roger clapped his hands. 'You speak German and English, and you have a house in Marseilles! What a find for the Resistance!'

He turned to Madame Goux. 'I am also impressed with you, Madame. I'd like to get you back to Paris so that you can keep watch over the building. We'll leave for Paris tomorrow.'

'Tomorrow!' I cried. I thought of my plan to visit my family once the escape party had left. I was anxious to find out whether Minot and Madame Ibert had arrived safely, and also whether Odette and her family were there. I explained my situation to Roger, who was enthused by the news.

'So you don't just rescue abandoned animals, Mademoiselle Fleurier,' he said. 'You're already practised in rescuing and hiding people!'

My face burned. Why was it that every compliment he gave me made me feel like a little girl? A Frenchman could never do that.

'Where is Sault?' he asked, unfolding his map of France. 'How do you get there?'

I showed him the train line to Avignon. Although the journey was about six hours with all the connections, he was excited. 'Would your family be willing to hide Allied servicemen? It's a secluded location if ever we need to wait things out.'

'My father fought the Germans in the Great War,' I said. 'My family will not stand for collaboration.'

Hearing that, Roger changed our plan. He suggested that Madame Goux should return to Paris as soon as possible, while he and I went to see the farm.

'*Achem!*' coughed the Judge, pointing to his watch.

I kissed Mouse, the Judge and Eduard goodbye as fondly as if they were my brothers.

'I hope that we will meet again, in better days,' I told them.

THIRTY

The next morning, Madame Goux, Roger, the animals and I caught the eight o'clock express train for the north. Roger and I were going as far as Avignon while Madame Goux was continuing on to Paris with my luggage.

After Kira arrived at the farm with Minot's mother, Bernard had written to tell me that my mother and aunt were thrilled with their new feline companion as Bonbon had passed away a few months before. What a surprise they would get when they saw four more animals! Still, sheltering animals was less dangerous than what Roger and I were about to ask them to do. The war was raising my threshold of fear. The pre-show nerves I had suffered for years seemed ridiculous in the face of the presence of mind I needed to work for the Resistance. I was prepared to go to any lengths in order to free France, but could I ask my family to take those sorts of risks too?

With reduced train services between the north and south, and because we hadn't made a reservation in advance, we had to make do with a crowded third-class carriage. The onion stink of the sweating bodies surrounding us, the screaming children in the aisles and the baggage jammed under our feet limited conversation between us. The dogs and Chérie had to travel in the luggage compartment, although the conductor was nice about it and promised to make sure they had enough water.

When the train slowed down for Avignon, we wished Madame Goux well and squeezed our way towards the door. As there was no longer a train service to Carpentras, Roger, the animals and I had to take the motor coach. The ruddy-faced driver let out a growl when he saw how many animals I had with me.

'It is against *Compaigne Provençale des Transports Automobiles* regulations to transport livestock,' he bellowed.

'Surely you don't regard my pedigree animals as livestock?' I protested. 'They are part of my stage act.'

'*Pfff!*' he scoffed, shrugging his shoulders. 'I don't care if you have sex with them. They are against the regulations, unless you want me to stick them on the roof along with the luggage.'

I sensed I would not be able to charm this garlic-reeking southerner the way I had the German officer by flirting with him. How could any woman? His eyes were bloodshot and there was dirt in the creases on his forehead. I decided that the solution was to pay more money. An offer which he gruffly accepted, charging me an adult fare for Bruno, children's fares for Princesse and Charlot and an extra tariff for Chérie as 'overweight' baggage.

'I hope that means the dogs will have a seat each,' Roger told him, tongue in cheek. 'You can't charge those prices and expect them to sit in the aisle.'

We arrived at Carpentras before midday and ate lunch in a café that stank of oil and cheese. With no sea breeze to relieve it, the heat was unbearable. My hair fell in limp strands around my face and when I patted my cheeks with my handkerchief I saw that my powder was melting into an oily mess. I had hoped to make it to Pays de Sault without attracting too much attention, but unfortunately the woman behind the bar recognised me and called out to her kitchen staff that Simone Fleurier was dining at their establishment. Roger and I had to eat our tomato and ham sandwiches under the curious eyes of the woman, the cook, a kitchenhand and a waitress. When we had finished, the woman asked me to autograph the restaurant's menu.

'And you,' she said, turning to Roger. 'Who are you? Are you a film star too?'

Roger shook his head. 'No, just one of Mademoiselle Fleurier's agents.'

It took all my willpower not to laugh at the double meaning. On our way down the street to catch the motor truck, I whispered to

Roger, 'You should have told her we had come to Carpentras to make a film about the town.'

'I know about small towns, Mademoiselle Fleurier,' Roger said, bringing his mouth close to my ear and sending a tingle through me. 'If I'd said that, we wouldn't have been left alone for a minute. Everyone from the mayor to the undertaker would have been vying for a part.'

The motor truck travelling to Sault that afternoon was a smaller vehicle than the motor coach had been, but the driver was jovial and made no objections to taking the animals. He greeted each dog as she or he bounded up into the tray. As the only other passenger was an old man with an accordion, the driver said he would drop us off near the farm rather than taking us all the way into Sault.

'So you grew up here?' Roger whispered to me, once the driver had started the motor. 'Amongst these people?'

'You seem to find that hard to believe,' I said.

'A little.' The corner of his mouth twisted into a smile. 'I saw you as the ultimate Paris sophisticate. But now I see where you get your determination and strength.'

I sat back and studied Roger. Was it possible that while I was so captivated by him, he was also a little in awe of me?

The driver dropped us off about half a kilometre from the farm. Roger and I had a small suitcase each. He carried both and I carried Chérie. The dogs walked. The sun was still high in the sky but fortunately the road was shaded by trees.

'Have you ever lived in Algiers?' I asked him.

'I've never even been there,' Roger answered. 'But the Deuxième Bureau men had me studying the French area and Kasbah down to the last rug shop and magazine stall. So I feel as though I have.'

'So how is it that you speak French so well?'

'My father served here in the Great War. He was a doctor. Afterwards he stayed on to help with the repatriation of soldiers. He returned to Australia such a Francophile that he hired an immigrant to be our tutor. From the time I was eight up until twelve we spoke French at home.'

I found the story amusing. 'Your father sounds charming and a little eccentric.'

'He was,' said Roger. 'I was telling the truth when I said my parents were killed in a train accident and I was brought up by my grandparents. I've kept up my French though, it's my way of remembering him.'

We walked on through a field, Bruno making a path for us through the grass and Charlot and Princesse leaping after butterflies.

'And what about Tasmania?' I asked after a while. I omitted that I had only worked out where the place was by sneaking a look at an atlas in a bookshop in Marseilles. I had thought it a separate country to Australia, like New Zealand, but when I read the commentary, I had learned it was Australia's southernmost state.

Roger glanced at me and raised his eyebrows.

'I'm sure you can tell me about Tasmania,' I said. 'If I am caught by the Germans I can give them a good travelogue.'

He let out a hearty laugh, as warm and rich as his speaking voice. 'I suppose that isn't giving away vital information, although the Germans may have plans to invade Tasmania.'

'And what will they find if they do?' I asked, switching Chérie's cat cage from my right arm to my left.

'Well, in the north-west, where I was raised, they will find rich farming areas with volcanic soil. Travelling south along the coast and inland they'll find mining towns as well as wilderness no one has ever touched. And in the north-east they'll find the biggest lavender farm in the southern hemisphere.'

'A lavender farm? Like those in France?'

'Very much so,' he said, looking around him. 'I've always wanted to see Provence. And now I am, courtesy of the Germans.'

'I thought Australia was a desert,' I said, pulling out every bit of information I had read in order to impress Roger with my knowledge of his country.

He shook his head. 'Some of it. But not Tasmania.'

'I would like to go there some day,' I declared, which was quite a statement for someone who had just discovered where the country was. 'Do they have music halls?'

'In Sydney and Melbourne, although we might have to finish the war first,' he said, smiling. 'How much further to go until we reach your farm?'

'Not long,' I told him. I wondered if I was annoying him by asking so many questions. But when he asked me about my childhood in Provence and how I had become a star in Paris, I assumed that he was enjoying the conversation too. I was surprised when he told me that he had seen me perform.

'That must have been in London?'

'Paris too. But twice in London,' he said. 'I've been working in my uncle's law firm there. My grandparents migrated to Australia and my father was born there. But my mother's side of the family is English through and through: pale, weak and inbred.'

'I don't think so,' I said, laughing. 'Look at what a passionate fight the British are giving. Besides, I admire Churchill.'

'You do?' asked Roger. 'He's a good friend of my uncle's.'

'He makes the French leaders who dragged us into this mess look small.'

'When I see him again, I'll tell him what you said,' Roger said. 'He'll be chuffed because I happen to know that he has seen every one of your films.'

∽

It was my mother who first saw us crossing the fields towards the house. She was throwing scraps to the chickens, her hair tied back under a scarf. When we reached the wall, she lifted her chin as if she smelt our scent on the wind, then turned, her hand to her forehead to shade her eyes.

'Simone!'

A few seconds later Aunt Yvette and Bernard appeared in the farmhouse doorway. A window sash was raised in my father's house and Minot and Madame Ibert leaned out. Before we even reached the yard, everybody was rushing towards us. My mother threw her arms around me.

'We have heard nothing from you in the past month,' Aunt Yvette said. 'We have been so worried.'

I explained about the post offices being closed during the invasion, and asked about Monsieur Etienne and Odette. I was disappointed to hear that they hadn't contacted Bernard. Then I realised that everybody was looking at Roger.

'This is my friend, Roger Delpierre,' I said.

I left my introduction there. I wasn't going to lie to them and say that Roger was my stage director or agent, but standing out there in the heat and with so much to catch up on, it didn't seem the right time to explain our mission. Bernard thrust out his hand to Roger and everyone welcomed him.

'And this is Bruno, Princesse and Charlot,' I said, introducing the dogs.

Roger took the cat cage from me and held it up. 'And this is Chérie, who Simone rescued in Paris.'

My mother glanced at me then bent down to pat the dogs. I could feel my cheeks burn. For some reason Roger had called me 'Simone' instead of 'Mademoiselle Fleurier'. Perhaps it was because I had introduced him as a friend, but the effect was to put us on a more intimate footing.

'Simone hasn't changed. She collects pets as she goes along,' said Aunt Yvette.

Aunt Yvette's kitchen had changed as little as she had over the years. As we bundled into its coolness I felt as though I were stepping back in time. There were still the familiar scents of rosemary and olive oil, and the multitude of pots hanging from the beams. How far away the war seemed here. Everything was the same as it had ever been. Minot's mother was sitting at the table, eating a bowl of soup. She was eighty-seven years old but her mind was still bright, although she had to be reminded who I was. Kira was perched on top of one of the cupboards. As soon as she saw me she let out a '*Murr!*' and ran towards me. I picked her up and she rubbed her chin against my cheek, purring. 'This is Kira, one of my oldest friends,' I said to Roger.

'We have never had so many people staying at the farm,' Bernard said, gesturing for us to sit down. 'Just as well we have plenty of room.'

Roger and I exchanged a glance. Bernard noticed it and gave me a puzzled look.

While my mother and Aunt Yvette prepared bread and dried fruit for us, Madame Ibert and Minot took water to the dogs outside. Kira and Chérie stayed in the kitchen, eyeing each other. Chérie was used to other animals and was fearless. She won Kira over by inching up to her and sniffing her nose. After that, everything was fine and they sat together near the door, watching insects flitter in the grass, their hunters' tails swishing in unison.

'We haven't seen one German here,' Bernard said. 'Despite what has happened in the north.'

'So things haven't changed much in the village?' I asked.

Bernard shook his head. 'Except that Monsieur Poulet received an order to remove the statue of Marianne and other symbols of the Republic. They are replacing the motto of "Liberty, Equality, Fraternity" with Pétain's new dictum: "Family, Work, Country".'

'Has the feeling here turned against the Allies since the Mers-el-Kebir bombing?' Roger asked him, picking up a fig. 'It has in Marseilles.'

I knew Roger was feeling his way, trying to gauge my family's loyalties for himself. Bernard glanced at me for reassurance. I could see he was perplexed by Roger's accent. It wasn't too pronounced but it couldn't be placed. He was clearly not from Paris or Marseilles.

'A lot of the sailors who were killed were probably from there,' said Bernard cautiously. 'But most people here think that it was to be expected. What could the Allies do? Pétain bailed out on them, and the British warned the French navy that it would be forced to destroy the fleet if they didn't hand it over themselves. They couldn't afford for the ships to fall into German hands.'

'Dirty *Boche*,' mumbled Madame Meyer.

Roger eyed Bernard. 'Your village must have a good news service,' he said. 'All they are getting in Marseilles and Paris is German propaganda.'

Bernard's face blanched. I understood his fear. In these times the wrong opinion could be fatal.

'It is all right,' I reassured him. 'Roger feels as you do.'

Bernard looked at me with such trust it twisted my heart. He leaned across the table. 'Our mayor managed to put together a radio set. We have been listening to the BBC.'

Tuning into an 'enemy' radio station was illegal and punishable by prison. I contemplated my family and friends with pride. They were born Resistants.

My aunt and mother served the wine, then sat down at the table with us. Madame Ibert and Minot came inside to join the discussion. I felt Roger's foot tap against mine. I trusted Roger and I knew the character of my family. Now was the time to put them together.

'I can vouch for my family's discretion,' I told Roger. 'And Minot and his mother are Jewish. Madame Ibert feels the same way I do about the Nazis. I think you might as well tell everybody what it is that you have to say. They will have to work together anyway.'

'I'm Australian,' Roger announced, and once everyone had got over their astonishment, went on to explain how he came to be stranded in France and what he was intending to do to build a Resistance network.

'And I thought you were Simone's fiancé,' my mother said, a smile dancing around her mouth.

The blood rushed to my cheeks. I was sure I must be glowing like a lantern. It was ironic that my mother, who hardly ever said a word, especially in the presence of strangers, should come out with something so embarrassing. Roger shifted in his seat. Neither of us dared look at each other. The best I could do was to send my mother a reproachful glance.

Bernard came to my rescue. 'Whatever we can do to assist France,' he said, 'I assure you that you will have our complete support.'

Roger studied each of the faces at the table carefully. There was no doubt that he had created a formidable team all in one afternoon. He had at his disposal a music hall star, a violinist, a lavender-broker, a theatrical director, two peasant women and an octogenarian.

Roger smiled and raised his glass. 'We have a new cell in the Pays de Sault region,' he declared. 'Mesdames and Messieurs, welcome to the network.'

❧

Although my mother and aunt asked us to stay longer, even another day away from Paris could mean losing an Allied serviceman to the Germans. Roger and I thanked them, but explained that we must return to Paris as soon as possible. It was decided that Madame Ibert would return with us, so that she could organise her apartment as a safe house.

I had become so attached to Chérie and the dogs that I was sad to leave them. But I saw how much they enjoyed running around the farm, and how much my mother liked them. I had intended to leave Kira too, but she rubbed against my legs and meowed so ardently that my mother suggested I take her with me.

'I don't think our work would be the same without at least one furry companion,' agreed Roger, loading the cat cage into the back of

Bernard's truck, then climbing into the tray to sit with Kira so that Madame Ibert and I could travel in the front.

'You shouldn't be annoyed at me for saying he was your fiancé,' my mother whispered to me. 'He is nice and he doesn't take his eyes off you for long. I don't want you to be alone.'

I pretended I didn't hear her. In another time and another place, I might have allowed myself to fall in love with Roger. But we were at war, fighting to save our countries. How could I involve myself in anything else?

Paris was sombre when we returned. The ingratiating farm boys of the first German advance had been replaced with more sinister officials and the true nature of the German occupation was revealing itself. Most of the shops around Gare de Lyon were open but there was hardly any food in the windows or on the shelves. Hardly any food for French people, that was. While Parisians had to stand in line for meagre rations of bread and meat, we saw one butcher loading up a German officer's car with packages. The occupation currency had been pegged at twenty francs to one mark. Before the war it had been less than four.

'A sophisticated way of plundering,' muttered Roger, reading the rationing notice posted in a baker's window. From other notices we learned that clothing and shoes were rationed too.

There were no taxis to transport us to the apartment. All the cars had been requisitioned for the German war effort. But there were too many Germans in the *métro* for us to feel safe. We were going to have to walk all the way from Gare de Lyon to the Champs Élysées.

We were dismayed when we reached the Place de la Bastille and saw that the street signs were in German. The only spot of brightness that made us laugh was when we passed a shop with a portrait of Pétain in the window. Strategically placed next to it was a sign that read: *Vendu*. Sold out.

To our relief, we found Madame Goux at her desk in our apartment building, and no Germans living there.

'I've been up and down the stairs every morning and night,' she told us. 'Turning lights on and off and shutting and opening curtains. But two doors down from us the *Boche* threw the occupants out of their apartments. They gave them receipts for their furniture — to be returned to them "at some future date" — and twenty-four hours to get out.'

'Two doors down?' I said, glancing at Roger. 'Isn't that a bit close?'

He shook his head. 'Sometimes the best way to fool the enemy is to work under their noses.'

The next day, Madame Ibert, Madame Goux and I worked zealously to ready the apartments for our 'guests'. We developed an elaborate series of signals, including crooked doormats, turned vases and taps on the drainpipes to warn of any German visits. Roger busied himself making contacts with the Parisian members of the network, and two days later we were sheltering eleven downed pilots. With so many able-bodied men coming and going from our apartment, we needed a good cover. Roger managed to find two doctors sympathetic to the cause and they set up their rooms in Monsieur Copeau's apartment: a psychiatrist by the name of Doctor Lecomte, and Doctor Capet who specialised in treating venereal diseases. If there were two things the Germans were terrified of, they were mental illness and contagious diseases.

During those days I woke with a start several times in the night, sure there was a German standing over me or that I had heard an intruder downstairs. I would patter in bare feet up to the floor above where whoever was on watch would reassure me that all was well. Sometimes the guard would open the door so I could peek in and see that the men were there, peacefully sleeping. My eyes sought out Roger amongst the prostrate bodies. He had a habit of lying perfectly still, with his hands crossed over his chest like an angel folded into its wings. When it was Roger who was on guard, I would take a bottle of wine and we would drink a glass each and talk until the dawn.

'Your mother is not the child of gypsies,' Roger told me one evening. 'She is the daughter of your grandparents.'

'How do you know that?' I asked.

'She told me the day we went to visit your family. After you went to bed, we stayed up and talked.'

'Hmm,' I said. I had asked my mother for the truth about her origins dozens of times and she had always evaded me. What had possessed her to tell a complete stranger things she wouldn't tell her own daughter?

'Your grandfather was a shepherd and your grandmother was an Italian from Piedmont,' said Roger, regarding my bafflement with amusement. 'Your father met your mother at the Digne fair.'

I knew about the Digne fair; my father had told me. But what about the other things? No one had ever mentioned that my grandmother was Italian. 'How do you know she told you the truth?' I asked him. 'My mother enjoys teasing people with mysteries.'

Roger reached out and touched my hair. 'It would explain your colouring. You could be Italian, you know.'

The skin on my neck tingled. I turned, wondering if he intended to kiss me. But Roger was already standing by the window, looking at the dawn breaking across the sky.

'We'll go south today,' he said, frowning. 'The weather is bad enough for it. Maybe the *Boche* will leave us alone.'

Roger, Madame Ibert and I took turns to accompany the men south with forged papers. Because I was more conspicuous, I usually accompanied escaped French prisoners of war or bilingual British servicemen, preferably ones with some sort of theatrical talent in case we were called on to prove their cover stories. With so many different men passing through our hands, it took a lot of money to get them French clothing, train tickets, forged papers and to feed them. Because we were limited in rations, we often had to purchase our food on the black market where items could be ten or twelve times the normal price. Madame Ibert and I were happy to give all that we could, but the Germans had limited how much money French citizens could withdraw from their bank accounts in any one month and, even though we resorted to selling our jewellery and some of our furniture, we were constantly falling short.

Although I would not perform for the Germans, I did do the shows at the Alcazar in Marseilles and in other cities in the unoccupied zone. I did my best to keep my cover as a big-spending star, while drinking ersatz coffee and eating soya-bean meat whenever I was alone so I could save money for the network. But as hard as I worked, it was never enough. By November it was clear that the greatest hindrance to the success of our mission, besides the Germans, was a lack of money.

In late November I was performing at a music hall in Lyon. One evening after the show, when I had put on my coat and boots to keep out the encroaching winter, I headed out the stage door and was startled to see a man standing near the steps. The streetlights were out but in the bluish glow of the sign above the door I could see his tall silhouette leaning against the balustrade. He was blowing out ghostly puffs of steam. My skin prickled. I knew the height and the lines of the figure but couldn't recall where from. The stage door banged shut behind me and the man turned around. André.

'Hello, Simone,' he said, the light glinting in his sable eyes. 'I saw the show. You were wonderful.'

I was so shocked to see him that the best I could manage was a mumbled 'Thank you', as if I were talking to a fan in the street, not the man I had loved for years. What was he doing here? Wasn't he supposed to be in Switzerland?

'Can I take you to dinner?' he asked. 'I am alone tonight and it would be nice to talk.'

The mention of food made my stomach pinch. I had been eating lavish lunches at Lyon's best *bouchons* to keep up the appearance of a star, and skipping my other meals to save money. But it was hard to do a show a night and sleep in an unheated hotel room on so little food. Perhaps it was inappropriate for me to accept the invitation of a married man and the father of two girls, but I was so alone and tired from my work that I threw caution to the wind and nodded.

André signalled to a car parked on the corner. It was a Citroën with a uniformed chauffeur. The only Frenchman who would enjoy such a privilege was one in the pay of the Germans. My God, I thought, my mind turning black. André is a traitor.

'It is strange that we should meet like this after all these years,' André said, helping me from the car when the driver stopped in front of a bistro. Inside, the restaurant was full of French officials and seedy-looking types in flashy suits. The food on the menu was black market produce: artichokes, cured pork sausage and pike quenelles. Food most French people had not seen in months.

I watched André while he gave our orders to the waiter, trying to find the man I had known so many years ago in the distinguished figure sitting opposite me. His face was as beautiful as it had ever been but there were patches of grey above his ears. I remembered the ache in my heart the last night at the house in Neuilly and realised that a touch of it still lingered there.

'I believe that's the first time you have performed in Lyon,' said André, turning to me. We made small talk about everything except the war — and our private lives. André and I were two spirits moving through a twilight world. The glittering France we had once shared was gone; the love we had once held for each other remained a subject too painful to mention.

'And do you still have Kira?' André asked, while the waiter filled our wine glasses. I laughed and told him that Kira was well and the conversation became easier between us. The heat in the restaurant thawed out my bones and the Burgundy wine began to swim in my head. I pushed away my wine glass, reminding myself to be careful. I had known André intimately once but that had been in a different time and place. Nobody knew anybody any more: parents did not know their children; husbands did not know their wives. One clumsy word to André and I could betray the network.

'So your factories in Lyon are still operating?' I asked. 'With the rationing I didn't think there would be a market.'

'I export to the Germans,' André said. 'I make uniforms for the army.'

His frankness shocked me. I found it impossible to hold his gaze. Was he so shameless? The André I had known would not have done such a thing. I glanced back at him and saw there were tears in his eyes.

'It is the only way I know to help France,' he said. He seemed to be turning something over in his mind. I realised with some surprise that he was contemplating whether he could trust me. He must have decided in my favour because he lowered his voice and said, 'After the Armistice, it didn't seem there was anything a man could do to erase France's shame. At least this way I can keep my employees in jobs and save them from being sent to labour camps. The men who work for me have families to feed. The women have husbands in prisoner-of-war camps and hungry children at home. It is the only thing I can do to help.'

The quiver in his voice touched my heart. Relief rushed through me. It was as if we were the young André and Simone of our innocent days, back when I never doubted that I could trust him.

I wanted to throw my arms around him. No, André hadn't changed. The rest of the world had gone insane, but André was the same. The table next to us let out a howl of laughter. Their faces were flushed and their eyes glazed with drink.

I leaned across the table. 'André,' I whispered, 'take my hand as if we are talking intimately. There is something I need to tell you.'

He looked puzzled but did as I asked, moving his chair so that he sat close to me. In revealing my secret, I could be condemning myself and the network to death. But without money, we wouldn't be able to keep it going. I had to take the risk. Besides, when André took my hand, I felt the same comfort and strength I had felt in his many years ago.

'There is something you can do to help,' I told him. 'I do not believe the war is over for France, that we are defeated. Have you heard of de Gaulle?'

André shifted in his chair. He studied my face; as he did, the brightness returned to his eyes. 'Simone,' he whispered, 'you have joined the Resistance?'

'Yes.'

'It is very dangerous. You will be executed if you are found out.'

'Yes.'

I had taken the leap and had no choice but to keep going. I explained to him the work I was doing with the network and about the problem of money. He was quiet for so long that for a few chilling seconds I wondered if my trust had been miscalculated. I half expected to feel the barrel of a Gestapo man's gun press into my neck. Then André awoke from his dream and looked into my eyes. 'I will not only help you with money but I can supply clothing as well,' he said. 'And if your contact thinks he might have use for my factories in hiding escapees, tell him to come and see me.'

André paid the bill. Outside, he told his driver that he was going to walk me back to my hotel.

'We must be careful from now on, Simone,' he said as we turned the corner at the end of the street. 'I am watched. Not only by the French and the Germans but by my sister.'

'What do you mean?'

'Guillemette is in Paris,' he answered, looking away, 'giving parties for the German high command. Most of *Tout-Paris* has turned like that. Some of the women are even sleeping with them, as long as it means they can continue to drink champagne and eat *foie gras*. My wife and I have dissociated ourselves from our families by moving here.'

The mention of his wife was a sudden reminder of why André and I could not be together. I recalled the princess at Count Harry's funeral. I had sensed then that she was exceptional. The fact that such a privileged woman was willing to turn her back on *Tout-Paris* made me admire her even more. I took André's hands and gripped them. 'Thank you,' I told him. 'What you have offered to do will help the Resistance enormously. Each time you send another batch of uniforms to Germany, you will know that the profits are helping France.'

He glanced at me. For a moment I thought he was going to lean down and kiss me on the lips. Roger's face flashed before me and I retreated a step. But André didn't make any move towards me. Instead he glanced over his shoulder then said, 'Don't thank me, Simone. It is I who am grateful to you.'

I watched him walk back down the street and disappear into the night.

THIRTY-ONE

The winter of 1940 was the coldest I had known in years. The Germans weren't willing to use their transport to bring coal to Paris, so our apartments went unheated, although the charcoal braziers in the establishments they frequented were always burning. Madame Ibert and I did our best to keep the men we hid warm. While André supplied us with blankets and overcoats, we knitted the men socks and gloves from the crude wool that was available. But food was still a problem. Even on the black market it was becoming scarce. Madame Ibert and I tried to put together soups, but some days the best we could do was chicken stock and water. I was glad that I didn't have the dogs with me. Kira ate half a can of sardines a day and spent the rest of her time curled in a lined hatbox in my wardrobe; her version of hibernation. The rest of us usually went to bed straight after the evening meal. It was the only way we could stay warm.

'We are doing better than a lot of other people,' said Madame Goux, coming in from the cold one day, four withered carrots in her string bag. 'People are burning their furniture and lining their clothes with newspaper.'

'It's still not as cold as Scotland,' said one of the men in our care.

I laughed, glad that he had kept his sense of humour. With the tensions of war, crowded conditions, the cold and the hunger, tempers were always in danger of getting out of hand.

On one occasion, Roger was up from the south for a dangerous mission. A ship's captain had agreed to secrete twenty men on board his vessel bound for Portugal. We had exactly twenty men in our care at that time, and the only way to meet the ship's departure time was to take them down south together. Transporting twenty men, none of whom spoke French, with only me, Madame Ibert and Roger to accompany them was risky enough, but added to the danger was the reason why we were looking after so many men in the first place. Four safe houses had been exposed by a double agent and the Resistants had been tortured with spikes driven through their hands before being shot. After a week of living in tense conditions, our attempt to take the men south in one group was aborted when we arrived at the station and found that pictures of some of them had been posted on the notice boards with rewards for their capture. The ship would have to go without them.

Having to return to a crowded apartment and wait until we could get new papers for them and, with the help of the Adriana's wardrobe assistant, change their appearances, was too much for some of the men. Fights started over petty things like someone spending too long in the toilet or snoring. Two men got into a punch-up over a card game. Some of them began to question Roger's leadership.

'If I lose their trust and respect, Simone, we may as well lie down and give ourselves up to the Germans,' he said. Roger, I had discovered, was the kind of person who thought big. 'Impossible' wasn't a word he associated with easily. So it was unusual to see him so down in spirit. He was facing a daunting task. I had seen the signs of exhaustion among the men even before we had set off for the journey south. Their postures gave it away: hunched forward, gazing at the floor, arms crossed over chests as if they were trying to stop their hearts bursting out. I thought of the stories my father had told me of the men who became shell-shocked in the trenches: trembling, whimpering, they walked straight into the enemy fire. The certainty of death was preferable to the constant waiting for it.

'It is battle fatigue,' I told him. 'They might be trained soldiers but it doesn't mean they don't feel it.'

Roger nodded. 'I sense they are ready to give up,' he said.

We lapsed into silence for a few moments, both of us

contemplating the situation. My mind drifted to André. I had tried to be strong when our relationship fell apart but everything came down on top of me in the end.

'People can't live under pressure for ever; something always cracks,' I observed.

'You and I have to be careful because we endure it too well.'

I understood what Roger meant. The adrenaline rush we felt getting past the German controls was useful for keeping us alert to danger. But we had done it so often now there was a chance of becoming desensitised and making foolish mistakes.

'Do you think that is what is happening now?' I asked him. 'That we are taking too big a risk in trying to get all those men south?'

Roger shook his head. He looked genuinely lost. 'I don't know, Simone. I'm starting to doubt myself.'

I leant back against the wall and caught sight of Kira sitting in the doorway, licking her paws. For some reason she reminded me of the 'good luck' cat the stooge at the Ziegfeld Theatre had made me to calm my nerves before the show. Suddenly the entertainer in me sprang to life.

'I have an idea,' I told Roger. 'Help me carry my gramophone upstairs.'

Roger carted the gramophone to Monsieur Nitelet's apartment, where the men were staying, while I followed with an armful of records. After we had set the gramophone down on a chair, Roger put on a tango record while I invited the men who knew the dance to take turns in partnering me. At first it was difficult to get anyone to join me, but after some cajoling I discovered two very good tango dancers among the men. One of them was so flamboyant with his dips and turns that it didn't take long before we captured the interest of everybody. I arranged the men into groups and gave them a lesson before telling them to partner each other.

'We're not pansies,' objected a New Zealander.

'The Argentine tango was originally danced between men,' I told him, 'in the days of imported labour when there was a shortage of women.'

Despite their initial protests, the men soon got into the spirit and danced with each other. Whether they were hamming it up or trying to master the dance with the seriousness they applied to military missions, I could see how much they were enjoying themselves. The

New Zealander teamed up with an Australian, pointing his nose in the air and wiggling his hips. 'This should be nothing new for you, mate,' the Australian ribbed him. 'You should be pretty used to doing it with sheep.'

Their laughter made me chuckle too, and I realised that it had been months since I had laughed so easily.

'May I?' asked Roger, holding out his hand to me.

'Of course,' I said, blushing like a teenage girl.

Roger was one of the most confident men I had ever met when it came to planning missions, yet he always seemed a little reserved around me. I thought he might be too shy to hold me but when he clasped me in his arms it was with such a passionate touch that my pulse quickened. He was an excellent dancer with an assured lead. Even more surprising, he began singing along with the Spanish voice on the gramophone in a tone that was beautifully melodious.

> You'll see in the fire
> All that is a lie
> And all that is true
> Let us dance this tango
> So when I'm far away
> I will be able to see you.

Rivarola had told me that when I danced the tango I should imagine myself as a sleek cat — beautiful, proud and graceful. I had never felt like that with Rivarola. But that was how I felt with Roger.

'You're not an ordinary woman, are you, Simone Fleurier?' Roger whispered in my ear. 'You're not only brave, talented and beautiful but you're smart as well. Things weren't going at all well but you've lifted everyone's spirits.'

The atmosphere in the room had certainly changed. The men were smiling and slapping each other's backs. I sensed that their improved spirits and comradeship would somehow get them through their dangerous journey safely.

'I wanted them to have a good memory of Paris,' I said.

Roger tilted my chin with his fingertips so that I looked directly into his eyes. 'You are my fondest memory of Paris.'

Warm sparks danced along my arms and a tingle ran up my spine. But I couldn't hold Roger's gaze and looked away.

'Come on,' said the Australian soldier, tapping Roger on the back. 'Mademoiselle Fleurier is the one who got this whole thing started so I should at least get a chance to tango with the sheila.'

Roger smiled and we reluctantly let each other go. Although every moment we spent together was precious, it was not the done thing to refuse a soldier a dance, not when there was a chance he could be killed the next day.

'When the war is over, I will give a concert especially for all the men here tonight,' I told the Australian.

'Better not get my head blown off then,' he grinned, leading me around the floor with the strength of a man trying to force open a door.

When everyone was warmed up and tired out, Roger called a stop to the evening. I kissed each of the men and wished them luck before returning to my cold apartment downstairs. But although my bed sheets were like ice when I slipped into them, I was warm inside. I closed my eyes and did my best to fight off thoughts of Roger. This was a war. It was not the time to fall in love. And yet, in the midst of terrible events and in the most unlikely of circumstances, I could not deny that a light — so long turned off in my heart — had been switched on again.

⁓

Within a few weeks of successfully getting the twenty soldiers across the demarcation line, we started receiving fewer servicemen at the apartment and more agents sent in by Britain to report back on enemy troop movements and military installations. We were also receiving radio operators and my journeys to southern France often involved hiding a transmitter or a headset in my luggage.

One afternoon I was walking along the Rue Royale after a rendezvous to pick up forged papers for three men Madame Ibert was accompanying south the following day. The air stung my cheeks and the cold from the frozen cobblestones penetrated the soles of my shoes. Leather was no longer available, and even the shoes in the upmarket stores had wooden soles that clacked on the streets like horses' hooves. The cold made my stomach ache and set my nerves on edge. If the winter was a trial for me, a wealthy woman who lived in an apartment with curtains, rugs and carpets, what must it be like for a poor family? Or for newborn babies? *What must it be like in prison?* My mind drifted to Fresnes prison. It was now empty of criminals — the Germans had jobs for thugs — but there were rumours of cries for help and screams of agony echoing into the night from its cells. The prisoners were Resistants who had been caught. Some of them were young students.

Someone called out my name. I spun around to see a blonde woman standing in the door of Maxim's and waving to me. She was wearing a blue dress, pinched at the waist, and a fur collar. It took me a moment to recognise her. Camille Casal.

'I thought it was you,' she said. 'Come in.'

Her hair was crimped and her face was made up with white powder and violet-black lipstick. My brain was so frozen with the cold that I wasn't thinking properly and I stepped into the entrance as she bid me to. Maxim's was no longer the opulent meeting place of artists and entertainers. It was the hedonistic den of the German high command and French collaborators.

'You are so thin,' observed Camille, eyeing me from my head to my shoes.

I barely heard her. The warmth and the smell of cognac were intoxicating. There was the delicious aroma of melted butter and roasted duck in the air.

'We were just about to eat,' Camille said, propelling me towards the dining room. 'You must join us.'

I found myself standing in the room I had once known so well. I looked at its stained glass ceiling and the Art Nouveau murals. It was a place where courtesans had entertained princes, but it was full of other kinds of prostitutes now. I recognised a number of people from André's old circle, including the daughters of several elite families.

A table of Germans in uniform stood up when we entered. They nudged each other and smiled as Camille introduced me. There were only five of them but the table was laden with enough terrines of soup and *foie gras*, plates of caviar and vegetables in butter sauce to feed an army. Most of the officers were young with pink in their cheeks, but the man who stood up from the head of the table and leaned forward to kiss my hand was in his fifties with grey running through his black hair.

'Colonel von Loringhoven,' Camille said, sidling up to him and slipping her arm through his.

My eye fell to the SS insignia on his collar. I pressed my purse with the forged documents tightly against my side. The SS was Hitler's elite fighting force. Roger had told me that they had shot the Allied prisoners of war at Dunkirk, ignoring all the conventions that were followed by the regular German army. The refugees from the north had said that the SS had burned churches and destroyed crucifixes on their way through villages, claiming that Jesus Christ was the son of a Jewish whore and that they were bringing a new religion to France. Von Loringhoven was a colonel? Then he was one of the men who gave those orders.

'He's dashing, isn't he?' Camille whispered in my ear. 'He saved me a room at the Ritz when they were kicking everybody else out.'

I glanced from Colonel von Loringhoven to Camille and remembered the conversation we'd had at the café during the 'phony war'. Was she so blind? This wasn't another playboy or man-about-town. This wasn't even an ordinary German soldier; this was a devil. Was the room at the Ritz worth her soul? The only excuse I could make for her was that she might be trying to provide for her daughter. I would have liked to take Camille aside and warn her, but I had Allied agents in my care and I had to think about safeguarding them first.

I turned to Colonel von Loringhoven and gave him the most charming smile I could manage. 'It has been a pleasure to meet you but I must go.'

He smiled in return, showing a row of lizard-like teeth. When I turned and walked towards the foyer, I could feel his eyes penetrating my back. I had a sickening feeling that he hadn't been fooled at all.

※

In June, we heard on BBC radio that Germany had invaded the Soviet Union. The radio operator staying with us that week was cheered by the news. She was a bilingual Englishwoman who had lived in Paris as a child, and had been sent by the Special Operations Executive to relay intelligence information to England. I asked her why Germany's attack on Russia was good news. Didn't it just mean another country under German subjugation?

'Ah,' she said, her eyes sparkling, 'you're French but you've forgotten. Napoleon attacked that inhospitable landscape and those hot-blooded people, and it was his undoing.'

I took heart from what she said but the subsequent reports filled me with shame. Not only was the ill-equipped Russian army fighting to the last man and woman, but their civilians were too. Why had France given in so easily?

In December, freezing again in our unheated apartments, we learned that the Japanese had bombed Pearl Harbor and that the United States had entered the war. At last, I thought. At last.

'Surely, with help from the Americans, we can win the war now,' said Madame Goux.

But any hopes we had of a quick end to the war were dashed by the summer of 1942. The Germans were on the verge of taking Stalingrad and, with it, the Caucasus and their oil fields. They were also in Africa: Alexandria and Cairo were almost in their hands. Despite the radio operator's confidence that the Germans were spreading themselves so thinly that they would collapse, they now had Iran, Iraq and India in their sights. Who would have thought that one European nation could spread so quickly, like a dark stain on the map of the world? Perhaps they would swarm over the United States as well.

If I had sensed an inkling of evil in my encounter with Colonel von Loringhoven, then Paris and the rest of France were soon to see it too. Even some of the self-seeking collaborators started to wonder what malevolent force they had invited into their country. In July, the Nazis banned Jewish people from attending cinemas, theatres, restaurants, cafés, museums and libraries and even forbade them to use public telephone booths. They could only travel in the last two cars in the trains on the *métro* and had to wait for rations at inconvenient times. To identify them, they were forced to wear the yellow Star of David on their outer clothing with the word 'Jew' in the centre.

On my way to a rendezvous in Montmartre, I ran into Madame Baquet, who had given me my first job at the Café des Singes. She was wearing a yellow daffodil in her hair and a yellow scarf around her neck. Her male companion, who she introduced as her new act at the club, was wearing a star on his jacket with 'Musician' embroidered in the centre of it. 'We've seen lots of interesting stars in Montmartre this morning,' Madame Baquet said. 'Buddhist ... Hindu ... Human Being.'

I embraced both of them before going on my way. This was the France that I wanted to believe in: irreverent, egalitarian, humane.

But the German high command saw nothing humorous in the gentle protest. One man paraded down the Champs Élysées wearing his war medals next to his star and was beaten up by some SS soldiers and shot in the head. The shame of what was being done to their friends and neighbours spread through the city's inhabitants as the man's blood spread out on the pavement. The fact that a French veteran was killed so openly and in cold blood was not lost on them.

A few days later, I received an instruction from Roger to cross the demarcation line and go to my family's farm, accompanied only by Kira. Suspicions were becoming aroused and it seemed likely that I would soon have to move south permanently. Although I had registered with the Propagandastaffel, questions were being asked about why I wasn't performing in Paris. With Maurice Chevalier, Mistinguett, Tino Rossi and others doing shows, it seemed my excuses were wearing thin. Adding to our problems was the fact that we could no longer receive radio operators in our building. Twice the German tracking vans had traced a signal in the area. Once we had been searched. Madame Goux hid the receiver by putting it into the cat cage and sticking Kira in front of it. The male radio operator and I stripped naked and jumped in the bath. We were so indignant when the Germans burst in that the red-faced soldiers withdrew quickly without noticing there was no water in the tub.

'Crikey,' laughed the operator afterwards, when we were tugging on our clothes, 'I'm standing here naked with Simone Fleurier. None of my mates will believe it.'

I arrived back in Pays de Sault when the wild lavender was blooming along the road and through the crevices in the rock faces. It filled the air with its sweet, uplifting scent. The road was dusty and Kira's cage was heavy under my arm. I rested every so often, sitting down on my small suitcase and swiping at my neck with a handkerchief. Two kilometres from the farm I realised that I wasn't going to make it if I had to carry Kira the rest of the way.

'You are going to have to walk, my friend,' I said, slipping her out of the cage and leaving it behind a rock.'

I expected her to sit on her rump and refuse to move. But she only gave a '*murr*' and scampered along beside me.

'If I had known you could be so cooperative,' I said, 'I would have discarded the cage long ago.'

We were passing the Rucarts' old farm when I heard a vehicle rattle up behind us. I turned to see Minot waving from the driver's seat of the Peugeot. '*Bonjour*,' he smiled, pushing open the door for me to get inside.

I put Kira on the seat and tossed my suitcase in the back. Minot was wearing rough cotton trousers and a checked shirt with sweat patches under the armpits. It was hard to believe he had once been the suave artistic director at the Adriana. But then, in my grimy dress and scuffed shoes, I wasn't exactly the Le Chat soap girl any more either.

'Is Roger at the farm?' I asked. I hadn't seen him for months as he had been busy getting people over the Pyrenees. I secretly hoped that in moving south I would be with him more often.

Minot shook his head. 'He is coming tomorrow with two agents he is taking to the *maquis*.'

The *maquis* were farmers who had taken to the hills to fight the Vichy *gendarmes* and the Germans. They performed acts of sabotage and attacked strategic posts. They were being armed by both de Gaulle and Churchill — who seemed to have had some kind of falling out — in night-time drops. Their numbers had been greatly increased the previous month, when the Germans had tried to force Frenchmen to go to Germany to work in munition factories and on farms. Tens of thousands of young men had escaped to the hills to swell the numbers of those willing to fight.

'I am worried about you and your mother,' I said. I told Minot what had been happening in Paris. 'The Vichy government is even more anti-Semitic than the Germans. It might be time for you to leave.'

He shook his head. 'I can't leave my mother. She is too old to even get on a ship. If worst comes to worst, we will have to hide her. I'll take to the hills and fight with the others.'

I thought about how Minot and I had once been and how we were now. There was a time when I had thought being a star and being rich was everything. Not any more.

'I am proud of you,' I told him.

'You should be proud of your village,' he said. 'They suspect that my mother and I are Jews, but not one of them has denounced us. Not even the mayor.'

When we arrived at the house, the dogs were sleeping in the garden. My mother and aunt were laying the table for lunch. I noticed the sprigs of cypress and bulbs of garlic hung around the door — the Provençal charm for protection. Bernard was seated at the table, talking to Madame Meyer. I hugged my mother and aunt. They were both much thinner than the last time I had seen them although in the countryside there seemed to be plenty of food to go around. My eye fell to the five extra plates on the table.

'I thought Roger and the others weren't coming until tomorrow?' I said.

Bernard's expression turned grave. He reached for the broom by the stove and made three knocks on the ceiling with it. Instantly I heard the scurrying of feet. I had thought the previous group of soldiers had already been taken to Marseilles to wait in the house there. Then I realised that the footsteps were light.

The children stopped in the doorway when they saw me: two redheaded girls of about seven and nine, and three boys of around the same ages. I was taken aback by the combination of their innocent faces and the terror in their eyes.

'I found them when I was settling the men in Marseilles,' Bernard said.

'Their parents were taken away,' Aunt Yvette whispered. 'A woman in the house next door to Aunt Augustine's hid them.'

'Come to the table,' my mother said to the children, stretching out her arm. 'This is Simone.'

As the children inched forward, she introduced them by name: Micheline, Lucie, Richard, Claude, Jean. Their eyes were globes in their heads. It pained me to see children scarred by mistrust. I called Kira over and picked her up so they could pat her.

'What is her name?' Claude, the youngest, asked.

'Kira,' I said. 'She is Russian.'

'She looks like Chérie,' Lucie told me. 'Chérie sleeps on my bed.'

The children patted Kira and scratched her chin, but their hands were trembling so much I wondered if they could feel anything at all. Anything, that was, except the cold, sharp sensation of fear.

After lunch, the children returned upstairs to play. I thought it strange that they couldn't play out in the open. The farm was miles from anywhere.

'The activities of the *maquis* mean that the *gendarmes* come by regularly to check that the people in the village and on the farms aren't hiding stashes of weapons or wounded men,' Bernard explained. 'I would keep the children here but I'm not sure how long they will be safe. I am hoping Roger will offer a solution.'

❧

Roger arrived the next evening with a weapons trainer and a female radio operator who looked no more than twenty. They had been parachuted into France the previous night. After dinner, we sent the trainer and operator to their rooms for a good night's rest in a bed, and Roger and I went outside to talk. He was still as handsome as the last time I had seen him, in Paris, but there were circles under his eyes and the lines on his forehead had deepened.

'You need a rest,' I said.

'So do you,' he replied, grasping my wrist and examining it. 'Look how thin you've become.'

I told him about the children Bernard had hidden upstairs in the house.

'I know,' said Roger, looking up at the moonlit sky. 'He told me about them in Marseilles.'

'Can we get them out?'

Roger leaned against the side of the house. 'We've been sending Jewish refugees along the line for some time now. But those children will never make it across the Pyrenees with only a guide.' He fell silent for a moment, turning the question over in his mind. 'There's a ship coming for the men in Marseilles in a few days' time,' he said. 'It will be dangerous, but it's the only way I can see that we can get those children out of the country.' He turned to me and his breath brushed across my cheek. 'I'll be going with them, Simone. I have to leave France.'

My heart dropped to my feet. He was leaving.

'Why?' I asked.

'I've been compromised by a double agent and I must break with the network so I don't lead him to any more people.'

Cold gripped my insides. How could I be so selfish? If Roger had been compromised then he was in grave danger. He had no choice but to leave. For a moment I considered asking if I could go with him, but I shook myself back to where I was. France needed me, and my family and friends had put themselves at risk at my persuasion. I had to stay in the country no matter what my personal feelings were.

'I'll miss you, Simone,' Roger said, reaching out and running his hand through my hair.

I turned away so that he would not see the tears glistening on my cheeks.

≈∾

At dawn the following morning, Roger and I took the two agents to the local *maquis* whom they would be working with.

When we arrived at the camp, the first people I saw were Jean Grimaud, my father's friend, and Jules Fournier, the brother-in-law of the mayor. It was only by their posture and eyes that I recognised them; both men had grown woolly beards and their clothes were mud-splattered and covered in pine needles. Their life of sleeping rough wherever they could had made them haggard, but the men greeted us in good spirits and invited us to share in their meal of wild mushroom omelettes. Roger and I declined; we knew that food was hard for the *maquis* to come by and that their wives and daughters took risks in bringing it to them.

While they were serving the meal, a young man with dark pools for eyes delivered a message to Jean from a neighbouring *maquis*. The boy looked familiar to me, but I couldn't remember how I knew him. He noticed my puzzled expression and smiled.

'Ah, it is you!' he said, in an accent that wasn't French. 'I have never forgotten your kindness to me.' He reached into his jacket and pulled out a sachet of lavender, grubby and withered with age and handling. 'It has been my good luck charm all these years.'

And then I realised who he was. Goya, the young boy who had come with his family the first year we had harvested lavender. He told me that his real name was Juan and we spoke briefly about our lives in the years since we had last seen each other. 'My mother always joked that you were not a girl made for farm work,' he said. 'And look — her prediction was true.'

We stayed with the *maquis* most of the day. Roger exchanged information and the agents discussed strategies for weapons drops and contact with the Allies. I watched the operator set up her radio.

Roger had told me that each operator had a special code to pass on to Britain to indicate if a message they were relaying was false. The operator would need it if she ever found a German gun pressed to the back of her head.

She probably has a lover and a family back home too, I thought, watching the set determination with which the young woman went about her task. If she was so strong-minded then I must be that way also.

In the late afternoon, Roger and I wished the radio operator and the weapons instructor good luck and said farewell to the *maquisards*. We reached the edge of my family's fields just as the sun was setting. The plants were lavandin now, the commercial hybrid, but Bernard had left a patch of wild lavender in the field closest to the house out of respect for my father. The soft light shimmered on the tips of the plants. My sadness at Roger's impending departure pierced my heart like a sharp stone.

'Shall we sit here for a while?' Roger asked.

I nodded and we sat down together on a boulder that was still warm from the sun. We were both long-limbed and our legs sprawled out before us in the chalky dust.

'That was your code name in the network,' Roger said. 'Wild Lavender.'

'I didn't know I had a code name. I never used it.'

He smiled. 'Well, that's how I always thought of you: tenacious and stubborn but also rather sweet.'

I was about to tell him I didn't like that description much when he put his hand on my shoulder. 'When this war is over, Simone, can I come back for you?'

His grip was gentle but energy flowed from it like a torch. I remembered how he had held me the night we danced the tango and drew closer. 'I don't even know if Roger is your real name,' I said, tracing his widow's peak with my finger.

Roger slipped his arm around me. 'It is,' he said. 'Roger is every bit as English as it is French. But my last name is Clifton not Delpierre.'

He exaggerated the roll of r's in his code name so much that it made me laugh. I pressed my cheek to his. The sun was still there in the heat of his skin. I breathed in his wonderful scent, like the smell of thyme simmering over the fire.

'And when I come back for you, Simone, will you marry me?'

My heart skipped a beat. Was this real or a dream? 'Yes,' I said, surprised at how quickly I had accepted. I didn't need to think about it. It felt natural to be with Roger, as if we were two pieces of a puzzle that fitted together.

Roger brushed his hand down my back. When he touched me I realised how the war had worn out my body, how tired and heavy I felt. But with each caress my skin tingled to life.

'Who would have thought it?' Roger said, laughing. 'France's biggest star and a boring lawyer from Tasmania. Only the war could have brought such an unlikely couple together.'

I remembered the way he had danced the tango and sung in Spanish. 'You are anything but boring,' I said. 'Besides, you are a hero. And I pray that this war won't last for ever.'

'Well, we have to believe that it won't now we are getting married,' Roger said, kissing me. The softness of his lips was divine. Kissing him was like pressing my lips to a peach. I could have lost myself in his kisses for ever but I broke away for a moment to ask, 'Where shall we live? In London or Paris? Or are you intending to take me to Tasmania?'

'We can go to Tasmania for our honeymoon. But when we are married I want to live here.'

I sat back and looked at him. 'In Provence? Or do you mean France?'

'Here on the farm,' Roger said, surveying the sky. 'It's so beautiful, I can't imagine why anybody would want to live anywhere else. I'd be happy growing lavender alongside your family and raising our children here. Law seems such a pathetic thing to practise after all I've seen. Law relies on order. All I've seen is chaos.'

I loved Pays de Sault and my family too, but I had never imagined living here again. 'I am not very suited to farming,' I said. 'I'm hopeless at it.'

'Who said you needed to do any farming?' he asked. 'You're a performer. If you want to go to Paris or Marseilles, I'll fly you there.'

Tears pricked my eyes. The dream was so beautiful that I couldn't bring myself even to imagine being that happy. I was afraid that if I did, the happiness would be snatched away, as had happened with André.

Roger brought his lips to mine and kissed me again. I pressed myself against him and he tugged me down onto the chalky earth.

'Don't put up barriers to happiness, Simone,' he said, stroking my face. 'After getting through this, I'm sure we can do anything.'

Roger's hand glided to the opening of my shirt and curved over my breasts. I closed my eyes, quivering with desire.

'Tenacious, stubborn but *very* sweet,' he whispered.

⟨⟩

At dawn the following morning, I slipped out of Roger's embrace, pulled on my clothes and ran across the yard to my aunt's house. My mother was in the kitchen, laying out plates for breakfast when I burst in the door. She jumped back a step, sending knives and forks clattering to the floor.

'Sorry,' I said. With the tension of the circumstances, it wasn't considerate to surprise people. But my mother wasn't annoyed.

'Roger asked me to marry him,' I said. 'He has promised to come back for me after the war.'

My mother smiled but did not respond. She kept her eyes on me.

I stepped towards her. 'Do you think it is all right to promise something like that while there is a war on?' I asked. 'He has to go back to London. We may never see each other again.'

My mother put down the plate she was holding and took my hands. 'We are still alive, Simone. We must act as though we are living. Promise to marry him. He loves you.'

I threw my arms around her and hugged her harder than I had in years. My mother was petite in stature but strong. I could feel the hardness of her bones moving under her muscles. She pushed me back for a moment and looked into my eyes. 'But is that what is really frightening you — the war?' she asked. 'Or is it something else?'

Under her gaze, I felt fourteen years old again. I didn't need to tell her what was in my heart.

'André?' she asked, raising her eyebrows.

I nodded. The way I had felt about him when I saw him in Lyon had stayed with me. Although he was married with children, and both of us were dedicated to the cause, there had been a sense of unfinished business between us. Could I honestly give my whole heart to Roger if I still felt that?

My mother's eyes softened and she kissed the top of my head. 'I have seen you and Roger together,' she said. 'You have fallen in love under a trial of fire. What you have between you is strong. That man will never desert you. He might be leaving for now but if he promises to come back for you, he will.'

'What if his family doesn't approve of me?' It was unlikely that Roger's family was as elite as the Blanchards, but if his uncle was friends with Churchill then they were clearly people of standing in society.

My mother shook her head. 'I am sure they would be proud to know that Roger wants to marry someone so brave and honourable. If your father could see the woman you have become, he would tell you exactly the same thing. The gifts you have, you inherited from him.'

Aunt Yvette's footsteps sounded on the stairs. We both turned to see her come into the kitchen, tying a scarf over her angel hair. She stopped short when she spotted us, her face twisting into a puzzled expression.

'Roger and Simone are getting married,' my mother told her. 'He is coming back for her after the war.'

Aunt Yvette's face relaxed into a broad grin.

THIRTY-TWO

The morning Roger and I announced our engagement, we all sat down to the happiest breakfast we had enjoyed in years. Even the children in our care seemed in better spirits than they had the day before. My mother rested her hand on Roger's arm as lovingly as if he were her own son. I told myself that the next time my mother and I had some time alone, I was going to ask her about my grandparents and if it was true that her mother was an Italian. I wanted to be as proud of my ancestors as I was of this gathering of family, friends and guests. Aunt Yvette and Bernard pulled out every childhood story they could think of to embarrass me in front of Roger, including telling him that my nickname used to be 'the flamingo' because of my long legs. But I didn't mind. I was content to know that, despite the situation we were in, we could be cheered just by imagining a better future.

I had one last task in Paris before I moved south permanently. Roger had a code that he needed delivered to a network member. I had memorised it so that if I was searched it wouldn't be found. The plan was for me to stay overnight in Paris, then to catch the first train back south. Roger and I would have one more night at the farm together before he had to leave France.

While I was packing my bag, my mother handed me a cloth pouch. 'Don't open it,' she said. 'You know what it is.'

I felt the spiky object and guessed it was a rabbit bone, for protection. 'You will need it,' she said. 'I can't watch over you for ever.'

I had long discarded my Provençal superstitions, but I tucked the pouch into my pocket with respect. My mother and I may have different weapons, but we were fighting the same war.

'I shall keep it with me always,' I told her, kissing her cheeks.

When I was ready to leave, I embraced my mother and aunt, Minot and his mother, Bernard and each of the children, and patted the dogs and cats, before following Roger out the door and into the sunshine. Kira tagged along with us until the stone wall, then watched as Roger and I headed through the fields towards the village, from where I would catch the motor coach back to the railway station.

When we reached the town hall, Roger and I kissed while the driver good-naturedly beeped his horn. 'Come on, you two, the motor coach now runs on Vichy time.'

'I love you, Simone Fleurier,' Roger said, tucking a sprig of wild lavender into the buttonhole of my dress.

From the back of the motor coach I waved goodbye to Roger. One night in Paris and I would return to him and my family. That was the plan. But it never happened like that. It never happened at all.

❧

I arrived in Paris late in the evening and caught the *métro* to the Champs Élysées. Even in the short time I had been away, I could see that the mood of the people had sunk even lower than it had been before I left, although I didn't yet understand why. Perhaps I was too tired to notice that the last two carriages of the train were empty.

Madame Goux opened the door for me. No sooner had I stepped inside than she poured out her story. 'They have been rounding up the Jews,' she said. 'Not just the foreign ones any more but French people as well. They are sending them to camps in Poland.'

'Who is rounding them up?' I asked, slumping into a chair by the office door.

'The Paris police.'

'So the Nazis are getting us to do their dirty work?' I said, leaning my head against the wall. To me, that was the most discouraging news of all. The Germans didn't have to worry about spreading themselves too thinly when they had so many French people to act as accomplices.

Madame Goux clucked her tongue. 'A dozen police have joined our network. They are disgusted by what happened at the Vélodrome d'Hiver.'

I looked up at her. 'What happened?'

Madame Goux sniffed. 'I saw the buses heading towards the sports ground when I was out on an errand. A crowd of us gathered near the entrance, wanting to know what was going on. Some of the police were ripping at the women's clothing, searching for jewels or money. They separated the men from the women and children, then took the men away. The women and children were left without food or water for three days.'

I covered my eyes with my hand. 'What happened after that?'

'One of our police recruits was here earlier,' Madame Goux went on. 'He said the Germans had given orders that they only wanted children old enough to work. So the police pushed the young children away from their mothers with the butts of their rifles and water hoses. He said the screams will live in his memory for ever.'

I took my hand away from my eyes. How could anybody do that? I thought about the policemen I had seen in the days when Paris was left as an open city. The last command given to them had been to keep order. But wasn't there a time for every person to question the instructions he or she was given?

'Where are those children now?' I asked.

'Some have been snatched up by the network, but most of them have been left to fend for themselves,' she said. 'The policeman believes they will soon be rounded up too.'

'Like hunted animals,' I muttered.

'A request has been sent to Germany that all children accompany their parents in the future. It is more humane,' said Madame Goux.

'More humane!' I cried. 'Those people are being sent to their deaths!'

When the foreign Jews were first rounded up and deported, most of us did not know about extermination camps, and the Nazis did a good job of propaganda by screening documentaries of Jews being settled in the east. Non-Jewish people even received postcards from their Jewish friends, assuring them that all was well. But the intelligence arms of the Resistance had been piecing together a different picture. Roger had told me about the suspected atrocities, but when underground papers such as *J'accuse* and *Fraternité* printed reports of genocide, people dismissed them as too horrible to believe or viewed them as Allied propaganda.

I thought of the five children Bernard had saved in Marseilles and the trouble Roger would have to go to in order to get them to safety. How was the Resistance in Paris going to save thousands of children, let alone their parents? We needed help. We needed Parisians to stop hiding behind the fiction that life was normal under the Nazis.

'Do you think we can conceal children here?' I asked. It was a heartbreaking question for me. I had committed myself to assisting Allied agents. If concealing children compromised the safety of those agents, the network would forbid me to do it.

Madame Goux's expression changed. 'You have two visitors waiting for you upstairs already. The woman wouldn't say who they were, but I think they need your help.'

I was expecting my visitors to be agents, so I was surprised when I found a woman sitting at my dining table with a small child clasped in her arms. The woman spun around when she heard me come in the door. She had the same terrified eyes I had seen on the children at the farm. But I knew her instantly.

'Odette!' I cried.

She stood up and rushed towards me. I put my arms around her and stroked Petite Simone's head. The girl was as pretty as her mother with a pert nose and luminous skin. But her eyes drooped wearily.

'Let's put her in my bed,' I said. 'Then we can talk.'

Petite Simone yawned and fell asleep as soon as her head rested on the pillow.

'Leave the door open,' Odette said, when she saw I was about to shut it. She sounded as if she were afraid that if Petite Simone was out of her sight for a moment, she would be snatched away.

We sat down on the sofa together and took each other's hands. 'Why are you in Paris?' I asked her.

A wild look flashed into Odette's eyes. 'I should have listened to you, Simone. They took Uncle and Joseph. They took my parents. They have rounded up the Jews in Bordeaux. We thought we were safe because Uncle found a *passeur* willing to take us across the line.

We were supposed to hide in the back of his clothing van. But he never showed up. He took nearly all our money but he never came.'

Tears welled in her eyes and she shook her head, as if she couldn't believe there were people capable of stealing from the desperate. 'The next day everybody was rounded up,' she said. 'Petite Simone and I were saved because we had gone to visit a Catholic neighbour. She hid us in her cellar until the raid was over. When I returned to our house, it had been turned upside down and everybody was gone.'

I buried my face in my palms. For the past two years I had given all my available resources and time to saving Allied servicemen and hiding British agents. Months ago we had been told that the Americans would swiftly end the war. Where were they all now? Couldn't they see that everything was getting worse?

I went to the kitchen to make Odette some of the real coffee I had stashed away. I had to admit to myself that my true disappointment was not with the Allies but with the French people. *Passeurs* who stole money from desperate Jews. Policemen who beat children until they let go of their mother's skirts. 'If no help is coming from the outside, then we must help ourselves,' I muttered.

'Odette, do you and Petite Simone have false papers or only your real ones?' I asked, when I set down the cup of coffee before her.

'The *passeur* was supposed to give us false papers,' she said. 'I have only our real ones, stamped "Jew".'

'How did you get to Paris?'

'I had just enough money left for a ticket for me and Petite Simone,' she said. 'I got on the train with our Jewish papers and nobody stopped me.' She gave a sharp, nervous laugh. 'Perhaps they figured if the Germans missed us in Bordeaux, they would get us in Paris anyway.'

My mind ticked over. I had only ever picked up false papers from another member of the network, never directly from a forger myself. The good ones were too precious to the network to be compromised, so access to them was limited. For years I had simply taken orders. I had no idea how to go about getting Odette and Petite Simone across the demarcation line myself. My mind drifted to Roger. There was no way I could contact him now to ask him what to do. He had severed his ties with the network. When I didn't turn up the following day, he might think that I had been caught. I hoped that it wouldn't stop him leaving. I didn't allow myself to think how disappointing it was that I wouldn't see him; I was too worried about Odette and Petite Simone. Nor did I allow myself to think about Monsieur Etienne or Joseph and what their fate might be. If I had, I was sure I would have broken down. I had to think as Roger did when he planned a mission. I convinced myself to be like a machine, churning forward with only one goal in mind: to get Odette and Petite Simone out of the country.

◈

The following morning, I made my rendezvous to deliver the code Roger had given me. I sat on a bench in the Jardin du Luxembourg, which was risky because a few people recognised me and asked for my autograph. Worse still, a German officer tried to flirt with me. I thought he was never going to go away, until I explained to him in German that I was waiting for 'my man'.

When the contact arrived, I was glad that the officer hadn't stayed around to see him. 'My man' had a stomach that was straining all the buttons of his shirt and three double chins. I gave him the code. He repeated it only once, perfectly. He was about to get up to walk away when I put my hand on his arm.

'I need papers,' I said. 'For a woman and a child.'

'Jews?'

I nodded.

'Do you have photographs? Money?' he asked. I handed him an envelope with the forger's fee and the photographs I had snipped from Odette and Petite Simone's real papers.

He slipped it straight into his pocket. 'Be back here in three days' time,' he said.

For the next three days, Odette, Petite Simone and I stayed inside the apartment. Odette drew pictures to calm her nerves while I kept Petite Simone occupied. I had never had a chance to get to know my namesake and I enjoyed making paper dolls with her and playing cats and dogs on the carpet as much as she did. I had been given a porcelain doll some years before by an admirer. It was from Holland and had eyes that opened and closed. Not being particularly fond of dolls, I had put it away in my cupboard. I went to fetch it.

'I would like you to have her,' I said to Petite Simone, holding out the doll which was still in its box.

Petite Simone took the doll from me, a frown wrinkling her forehead. 'She needs to come out of the box,' she informed me. 'Little girls need air.'

For the rest of the afternoon Petite Simone only had eyes for her new doll, who she named Marie. Odette and I played a game of cards. 'Petite Simone hasn't had much of a childhood,' Odette whispered. 'I am frightened that she will grow up thinking that hiding is normal.'

At night Odette and I slept in my bed, Petite Simone squeezed between us. The little girl had a habit of locking her chunky arm around mine. I listened to her soft inhalations and the faint whistling sound she made when she breathed out and was struck with a sad feeling that perhaps I would never have a child of my own.

The second night, Petite Simone asked after her father and uncle. I waited to hear what Odette would say.

'They are at work, my little darling,' she answered. 'Meanwhile you and I must go and find a new place to live, so they can join us afterwards.'

Odette sounded so calm that I could almost see Monsieur Etienne at his desk, making calls to theatres, and Joseph in his store. Where were my old friends now? What unspeakable things were they enduring?

❧

True to his word, the contact who had taken the code was waiting for me on the bench in the Jardin du Luxembourg three days later.

'These papers are not perfect,' he told me matter-of-factly. 'The Germans keep changing the requirements in order to catch people out. There are many Jews trying to leave the city. I made the woman your cousin. But if they catch you and check your birth certificates, you'll be finished.'

'I have no choice,' I said. 'I have to save her and the child.'

He glanced at me and nodded. Although his manner was abrupt, I could see the sympathy in his eyes. It encouraged me that I could look into the face of another person who had not lost his sense of humanity.

Given what the contact had said, I wondered if it would be wiser to keep Odette and Petite Simone in Paris, either concealing them in my apartment or taking them to one of the network's safe houses. I stopped at a café, to rest my feet and consider the matter. Like a chilling omen, no sooner had I sat down than I caught the conversation of two men sitting behind me.

'They are offering rewards for anyone who denounces Jews or reveals who is hiding them.'

'What kind of rewards?' his companion asked.

'You might get to keep their apartment and furniture.'

I tried to finish my chicory coffee as calmly as I could, but my heart was thumping in my chest. Was this what human beings had become? Greedy people who would denounce a family so they could sit on their sofa or admire the view from their apartment? I did my best to think clearly. Odette was known to many people in the entertainment business in Paris. Taking her and Petite Simone across the city with their false papers would be as dangerous as trying to get them onto a train south. But the final encouragement I needed to get them out of Paris was handed to me by Madame Goux when I arrived home.

'They put it under the door,' she said, passing me an envelope with my name written on it.

I opened it and found a leaflet inside. It was a notice from the Germans about the deportation of Jews. The line, 'Those who help the Jews will suffer the fate of the Jews', had been circled in red.

'Is it a threat?' I asked. 'Are we being spied on?' When I thought about it more, I realised it had probably come from one of the network members. Somebody was trying to warn me.

Odette and I wasted no time in packing and going directly to Gare de Lyon to catch a train south. To my relief, the station wasn't any more crowded than it had been the other times I had travelled with agents and servicemen. It seemed a mass exodus of Jews with false papers trying to escape Paris wasn't happening that night. Although we hadn't reserved seats, I was able to get us places in first class.

'Enjoy your journey,' said the ticket vendor.

'I'm sure I will,' I said. I smiled although my heart was racing.

This would be my last journey from Paris to the south. Every other trip I had made, I had been successful in getting my 'parcels' across the border. Odette and Petite Simone were less suspicious-looking than the men I had accompanied. I prayed that we would make it to Lyon safely. André would be able to help us from there.

Odette and Petite Simone were sitting on a bench waiting for me. I showed them the tickets. I admired Odette for the calm she was trying to project. She had a piece of sewing on her lap and worked at it as if she didn't have a care in the world.

'Let's go,' I said.

Petite Simone slipped her hand into mine and said, 'I love you, Tante Simone.'

'I love you too,' I told her, stopping a moment to kiss her cheeks.

The conductor greeted us without suspicion when we climbed on board the train. A German official checked our papers in the corridor. He gave mine a quick glance, but he read Odette's thoroughly and checked the picture.

'You are from the south originally?' he asked her, looking over her clothes. She was wearing a navy blue suit with satin lapels that I had given her from my wardrobe. She looked very Parisian but that was the idea.

'Yes,' she answered. 'But I have lived in Paris most of my life.'

Petite Simone held up Marie to the German. To my surprise, he smiled at her. He handed the papers back to Odette and waved us on.

Odette and I took our seats in the compartment, placing Petite Simone near the window. We were so terrified that we couldn't bring ourselves to speak. I took Odette's hand and squeezed it. Her skin was like ice. She picked up her sewing and continued, although her fingers were trembling. I glanced at my watch. Seven minutes to departure. There would be more checks on the journey, but I was sure that if we could get away from Paris we would somehow be all right.

More passengers boarded the train. Every time somebody walked past our compartment, my heart jumped. I closed my eyes and leaned back in my seat, trying to relax. I could hear the hiss of the engine. It wouldn't be long now. The door to our compartment rattled open. Four German officers glanced in, then realised that they had the wrong seat numbers. They apologised and moved on. I scarcely dared breathe. It would have been easier to travel third class, but because of my reputation that was impossible. I prayed with all my might that we should not end up with a compartment full of Germans. I felt in my pocket for the rabbit bone my mother had given me and realised that in our hurry to exit the apartment I had left it on my bed. I glanced at my watch. Four minutes to go.

I looked out at the platform. It was almost empty. We might even have the compartment to ourselves if we were lucky. I relaxed and stood up to get a book out of my travel bag which was on the rack above me. At that moment the door to our compartment opened. A cold shadow crawled up my back. I turned around. At first I thought my terrified mind had produced a hallucination, but the longer I stared the more the black hair and sharp teeth became real. Colonel von Loringhoven.

'Mademoiselle Fleurier,' he said. 'What a surprise. I thought I had the compartment to myself.'

He smiled at Odette and Petite Simone. His grin seemed to tighten the skin on his face, as if there were another person underneath trying to push himself out. I was proud of Petite Simone for not screaming, for that was the effect the colonel's smile would have had on me if I had been her age.

'Really?' I said, recovering as quickly as I could. 'We wouldn't want to inconvenience you. We can change if you need the compartment to yourself.'

I was careful that my tone was one of generosity on my part, rather than acquiescence. Stars never gave up their compartments; we never gave up anything. But in these circumstances it would have been a relief to sit in the coal carriage rather than travel with von Loringhoven.

'That won't be necessary,' he said. 'In fact, it is a delightful coincidence. I had always hoped that we could become better acquainted.'

His gaze drifted again from me to Odette and Petite Simone; there was something treacherous in it that I did not like. I did my best impression of a pleased smile and introduced Odette and Petite Simone. We had told Petite Simone that if anyone else sat in the carriage she must be very quiet. My heart melted when I saw how tightly she pursed her lips.

'I am charmed to meet you,' Colonel von Loringhoven said to Odette. 'I didn't realise that Mademoiselle Fleurier had relations in Paris.'

Odette did not miss a beat. 'We are very distant relations and have always thought of ourselves more as friends. I used to go to watch Simone sing when she first started out.'

Odette's fingers were steady in her lap but drops of sweat were pooling around her hairline. Would von Loringhoven notice?

I glanced at my watch. Two minutes to go. Once we were moving I could make an excuse for an early meal in the dining car, and after that we could pretend to sleep. The train let out a hiss of steam.

'Excuse me a moment,' said Colonel von Loringhoven, standing up. He gave no explanation of where he was going, but as soon as he was out of the compartment Odette glanced at me. Had von Loringhoven guessed something? But if we got off the train now it would look suspicious.

'Look,' said Petite Simone, pressing her face against the window. 'There's that man.'

I looked out the window and saw the colonel talking to two German soldiers and pointing in our direction. The whistle sounded and the train began to shunt forward. 'Thank God,' I said, and almost laughed. Colonel von Loringhoven was going to miss the train. But one of the German soldiers shouted out and the train came to an abrupt stop, its wheels screeching on the tracks.

'He knows,' gasped Odette.

'Let's go!' I screamed, picking up Petite Simone and running for the door. There were suitcases in the corridor but I struggled past them, bruising my legs and ripping my stockings. Odette scrambled after me. The conductor saw us coming. For a moment I thought he was going to block our way. Instead he said, 'Not out this door. Go through second class.'

We ran past the surprised-looking passengers and jumped from the train onto the platform. 'Come on!' I cried to Odette over my shoulder. 'Make a run for the entrance.'

I pushed past a ticket controller who was too surprised to react. I could see the station entrance ahead. Odette let out a shriek. I turned to see a German soldier wrestling her to the ground.

'Run!' she screamed at me.

For a dreadful second I was torn between stopping and running. 'Run!' Odette screamed again. There was nothing I could do to help her. The best I could do was to save Petite Simone. Turning my back on Odette made my heart tear like a sheet of paper, but I tucked Petite Simone onto my back, kicked my shoes off and propelled myself forward with every ounce of strength in my body.

'Maman! Maman!' Petite Simone cried, and struggled, but I held her tightly. I heard Germans behind me shouting to stop or they would shoot. But I knew that not even they would shoot in a station.

The entrance was a few metres ahead. My heart was cramping and I was struggling for air. I thought I was going to pass out but I was determined to escape. There wasn't a German in sight ahead of me.

We are going to make it! I told my trembling limbs. We are going to make it!

A blur of blue crossed my eyes. A French policeman who I hadn't noticed made a lunge for me. He crashed into my hip and sent me sprawling across the floor. Petite Simone tumbled forward. A German soldier caught up with us and picked her up by the scruff of her coat. She kicked and bit at him but he held her tightly. I reached towards her but the policeman brought his truncheon down on the back of my neck. I collapsed to my knees, the pain shrieking down my spine, but managed to get up again and stagger forward. The policeman dealt me another blow, this time above my ear. I called to Petite Simone but he hit me again and again on my shoulders and back until I lost consciousness.

❦

When I opened my eyes it was dark. My head throbbed and there was a stabbing pain in my shoulder. I was aware that I was lying face down on something hard and cold. A smell like rotting vegetation filled my nostrils. From somewhere behind me came the sound of dripping water. I tried to sit up but pain seared across my back. My arms gave way. I lapsed into unconsciousness again.

It must have been some hours later that I woke up. Flashes of morning light flickered on my arm. I raised my eyes and saw that the light was coming from a barred window. I was lying on a stone floor, its hardness pressing into my hips and knees. There was no sound other than the trickling of water down one of the walls.

I defied the agony and lifted myself up onto my elbows, wincing from the pain in my back and ribs. There was a straw mattress opposite the door. By sheer force of will, I managed to stand up. My head swam and my vision blurred. I swooned towards the bed and collapsed onto it, falling into a deep sleep.

The third time I woke I saw that the sun had disappeared from the window. But I could see a patch of blue sky and the air in the cell was warmer. I guessed it was the afternoon. I had no appetite but my throat was so dry that it was painful to swallow. There was no tap in the cell. Not even a pitcher of water. Just a putrid-smelling bucket in the corner. I pressed my face against the musty mattress and wept for Odette and Petite Simone. Were they here too? Or had they been taken away?

The grille on the cell door opened and a guard looked in. A few moments later I heard him push the key into the lock. The door squealed open and banged against the wall.

'Stand up,' he shouted.

I could see that protesting would not do any good. I forced myself to my feet but my legs gave way beneath me. I realised that my right knee was so swollen I couldn't close my legs. Compared to the other pains in my body, I had scarcely noticed it until then. The guard stood behind me and grabbed me underneath the arms. Another guard came in and clamped chains around my ankles.

'Walk!' the first guard ordered, shoving me forward.

With my full weight on my knee and the extra burden of the chains, walking was excruciating. I limped a few steps then fell. The guard who had chained me stepped forward. I instinctively covered my head, expecting a blow from a truncheon, but instead he grabbed me by the shoulders and yanked me up again. The other guard put his arm around mine and supported me. I shuffled alongside him down a dim corridor. The only light came from barred windows near the ceiling. I heard a shout then an explosion cracked the air. There was silence for a while before the sound broke the air again. I had not heard it before but I knew instinctively what it was: a firing squad. Was this how it was to be? I was going to be shot?

'Where am I?' I asked the guard who was walking in front.

'Shut up! Don't talk!'

I was taken down another corridor that ended with a flight of stairs. The guards had to lift me up them. Finally they dragged me into a room with only a chair and a light hanging from the ceiling. The guard who was holding me pushed me into the chair and handcuffed my hands behind me. Then they left without a word.

'It is a shame to see a beautiful woman in such a state.'

The portent of evil in the voice sent a chill through me. I knew it was Colonel von Loringhoven, but I couldn't see him. He stepped out of the darkness into the glare. My heart skipped a beat. I thought that must be how a pearl diver felt when he saw a flash of fin and tail emerge from the murky depths.

Von Loringhoven circled my chair, studying me from every angle. 'Can I get you anything?' he asked. 'Some coffee? A cigarette? Some ice for your knee?'

I glanced down. My skirt was ripped and my mottled, deformed knee was exposed. I shook my head. There was nothing I wanted from von Loringhoven.

He disappeared into the darkness then reappeared with a chair. He scraped the legs along the floor and propped it into position opposite me.

'The first time I saw you was in 1930 in Paris,' he said, sitting down and taking a silver cigarette box from his pocket. 'At the Folies Bergère. What a voice, I thought. What a magnificent voice. And, of course, you were very beautiful.'

He paused to take out a cigarette, light it and blow out a long puff of smoke. The stink of tobacco scraped down my throat. I did my best not to choke. Wherever this interrogation was going, I had to be careful. It was possible that Odette and Petite Simone had not been identified as Jews and that I had been arrested for something else. After all, Roger had warned me that the Gestapo were becoming suspicious of my activities.

Von Loringhoven gave me a long, considered look, as if he were waiting for me to speak. Roger had once told me that the most important thing was to keep quiet for at least twenty-four hours. That would give the network time to hear of the arrest and go into hiding. I was determined to remain silent for as long as I could.

A shadow appeared in the light. It was a man wearing a leather coat. He stepped forward as if he were going to greet me but instead delivered a blow to my cheek so forceful that my neck cracked and I saw stars.

'Not on the face,' growled von Loringhoven.

I looked up in time to see the man swing his fist again. His knuckles slammed into my chest. The chair skidded backwards and I crashed to the floor, falling onto my damaged shoulder. I howled in pain and wriggled backwards. I tried to tell myself that the situation was real and to think quickly. But the thug's violence was not a part of anything I had ever known or imagined. He made a run for me. I struggled to curl up but I couldn't defend myself with my ankles chained and my hands cuffed behind me. His foot smashed into my stomach. I heaved and gasped for breath, feeling as though my pelvis

475

had been shattered into pieces. He drew back his foot, ready to strike again. I closed my eyes, sure that the next blow would kill me.

'Enough!' ordered von Loringhoven.

The torturer uprighted the chair, with me in it, and left the room.

'You are a foolish woman, Mademoiselle Fleurier,' said von Loringhoven. 'The Germans and French work so well together. And you could have been free to carry on with your life as normal. But perhaps it is the company you have been keeping.'

I could barely hear him above the ringing in my ears. The air in my throat was making a desperate, rasping sound.

'Now,' said von Loringhoven, 'tell me what you know about Yves Fichot.'

'I don't know an Yves Fichot,' I gasped through the pain.

'What about Murielle Martin then?'

I shook my head.

Von Loringhoven paused. For an awful moment I thought he was going to call in the thug again. But I was telling the truth: I did not know who those people were. I had been deliberately kept in the dark regarding names. I lifted my head. It was the first time I had really seen Colonel von Loringhoven's eyes. They were dark and beady. The eyes of a snake.

He clucked his tongue. 'What about your dear friend, Roger Delpierre?'

My mouth turned dry and I swallowed. Von Loringhoven's face broke into a smile. He was pleased to have got a reaction.

'You see what I mean about your foolishness in who you choose for friends? Why would a glamorous, talented woman like you trust a lowlife like that?' he said.

Von Loringhoven stood up and paced around the circle of light. He came to a stop at my right side and reached his hand towards me as if he were going to caress my face. But the side of my cheek was bloody from the fall. He must have thought better of it and withdrew his hand to his pocket.

'Did Roger Delpierre tell you that he loved you?' he asked, with a slight chuckle. 'He has told every woman he has slept with the same thing. He has used you all for his own ambitions. We caught him three days ago trying to escape from Marseilles. We only had to threaten to cut off his balls before he blabbered everything he knew about you and the network.'

There was a taste like metal in my throat. I coughed and the pain racked my ribs. Roger? Roger had used me? The beating had deadened my senses. I forced myself to put one thought logically in front of the other, but the effort was like one of those dreams where you run and run but get nowhere.

Von Loringhoven returned to his seat, smug in the certainty that he had broken me. There was something about his hastiness that raised my suspicions. As I repeated Roger's name to myself, images of the work we had carried out together flooded my mind. Roger would never betray the network he had worked so carefully to build, even under torture. He had shown me once the cyanide tablet he kept in his pocket in case he was ever caught and felt himself in danger of 'giving vital secrets away'. Besides, if von Loringhoven had found out 'everything' why wasn't he using Roger's real surname? He must be lying, I thought. He is assuming that if I think all is lost for the network, I will tell everything I know. The idea gave me something to hold on to despite the searing pain. I had to outsmart von Loringhoven at his own game. I tried to emulate Roger when he was under pressure — slowing my breathing, calming my emotions, staying focused on the essentials.

'Then you know about Bruno and Kira?' I whimpered. 'The radio operators I took to Bordeaux.'

Von Loringhoven's eyes danced over me. 'Yes,' he said. 'Delpierre told us everything about them.'

Despite the horror of the situation, I had an urge to laugh. I hid it by tucking my head against my shoulder and pretending to weep. The Great Dane and my cat had many talents, but radio operating was not one of them. And I had not been to Bordeaux in years.

Von Loringhoven reached over and patted my arm. 'Perhaps your visit here will encourage you to make wiser choices in the future,' he said.

The colonel's voice prickled my skin. I was sure I was in the presence of the most evil man I had ever met, but his tone was almost fatherly.

Von Loringhoven called in the guards, who dragged me back to my cell. Later, I was given some watery soup and dry crusts of bread. Alone again, I had time to think over what had happened. Von Loringhoven had not asked me many questions about the network and none at all about Odette and Petite Simone. He had not even mentioned them. I had been beaten, true, but I had heard of the Gestapo burning people's feet, cutting off their fingers and toes, and gouging out their eyes. In the light of those tortures, I had escaped lightly. I wondered if that was a good sign, or whether they were going to keep me until they found an Agent Bruno and Agent Kira in Bordeaux? I could understand why even the most courageous people talked under interrogation. It was the uncertainty and waiting that weakened you as much as the beating.

❦

When I heard the guard unlock my cell door the following morning, dread fell over me. Would today's beating be worse than the one I had received yesterday?

I glanced up and saw Camille Casal looking back at me. The guard brought her a chair and dusted it off with his handkerchief before allowing her to sit down. She straightened her silk skirt over her legs and nodded to the guard that he should leave. It took me a moment to recover from her appearance. But then I guessed why they had sent her. They were hoping that as an 'old friend' she might be able to coax more information out of me.

'You are wasting your time, Camille,' I said to her. 'I don't know anything about the network. I was never told a thing.'

That wasn't strictly true; after all, I knew Madame Ibert and Madame Goux, the doctors, André and my family in Pays de Sault. But I was prepared to die rather than give away any of them.

Camille shifted in her seat and pulled her jacket over her shoulders, as if she had just noticed the chill in my cell. I was so numb I could barely feel anything.

'Your attitude towards the Germans is what has brought you to this, Simone,' she said. 'They know that you are nothing but a minor link in any Resistance movement. That you were exploited because you had fallen in love.'

Her statement stunned me. I sat back on the straw bed and leaned against the wall. Was it possible that the Nazis really did not know the extent of my involvement in the network? Perhaps the double agent had been playing a game, hedging his bets either way.

'You refuse to perform in Paris,' Camille continued, her voice booming around the cell. 'You are difficult with the Propagandastaffel, you snubbed Colonel von Loringhoven's hospitality at Maxim's and then you refused to share a train compartment with him.'

My sluggish, starved and dehydrated mind tried to keep up with this new development. I was in prison because I had hurt a Nazi's feelings?

'Why am I here?' I asked her.

'Because of your responsibilities,' Camille said, as if she were talking to a wilful child. 'You are a popular entertainer.'

I sensed she was speaking so loudly for the benefit of the guard in the corridor. But she had confirmed what I had been thinking: I was not in prison because of my involvement in the network or because I had tried to smuggle two Jews out of Paris. That didn't mean her statement stunned me any less.

'What is it you want, Camille?'

She lowered her voice. 'I want to help you. Colonel von Loringhoven would like to do something to please General Oberg to coincide with the victory parades later this month. He suggested that a concert given by the elusive Simone Fleurier would be appropriate. "When the world thinks of Paris, it thinks of the Eiffel Tower, of food, of love and of Simone Fleurier," he said. They need you to rally the people.'

My insides tightened. They wanted to use me the same way they had used Pétain, to make their despicable policies palatable to the French people. Karl Oberg was head of the SS in Paris. Under his command was Theodor Danneker, the SS officer overseeing the deportation of Jews. I had refused to sing for the Germans since they had occupied Paris and I had no intention of doing so now. Oberg and Danneker were as evil as the pilots who had slaughtered the Belgian children. They were cold-blooded killers. What message would I be sending out if I sang for them?

'No!' I said. They might be able to torture names out of me, but there was no way they could force me to sing.

Camille's eyes narrowed and she clutched my arm. 'I told you, I am trying to help you. You don't seem to understand the situation, Simone. If you refuse, you will be shot.'

'Then they will have to shoot me,' I said.

The conviction in my voice shocked me as much as it did Camille. It wasn't courage that made me say it. It was the thought of trying to live with myself after doing such a cowardly thing for no good reason but to save my own skin.

Camille rose from her chair and paced the room. 'Oh, there you go! You are so self-righteous, Simone. You always have been. Look at you, sitting there with your matted hair, your dirty clothes. Look what you have become. Look at where your self-righteousness has got you.'

'And look at you, Camille Casal,' I retorted. 'Look at what you have become: a whore for the Nazis!'

We stared each other down. It occurred to me how odd it was that Camille and I had come to this: two opponents with different allegiances, facing each other in a prison cell. Who could have foreseen it back in the days when we were only ever perceived as rivals on the stage? But nothing was normal any more.

Camille clenched her fists but her hands trembled. 'Perhaps you wouldn't judge me so harshly if I told you that the father of my daughter was Jewish,' she whispered. 'So far, no one knows.'

As I listened to Camille a realisation came to me. The Germans couldn't shoot me. If they were losing the support of the French people, how would executing a beloved national icon help? Although Maurice Chevalier was performing in Paris, he had avoided performing in Germany, despite repeated demands. And he had a Jewish wife. The strength of my bargaining power began to dawn on me.

I stood up as best I could, limped over to Camille's chair and sat in it. 'The woman and child who were arrested with me —'

'They were sent to Drancy. They will be deported to Poland.'

My heart sank. So Odette and Petite Simone had been found out. Drancy was a French holding camp with a reputation for cruelty. The agonising instant when Odette had been caught at the station flashed before me. I'd had to decide whether to leave her to her fate and serve another cause. I had done that once. Could I abandon her again? I closed my eyes. I was standing on the edge of an abyss. I had a chance to save my friend and her child, but I would have to betray my country to do it.

'Can they be saved?' I asked Camille.

'No,' she answered, folding her arms. 'The orders come from Germany.'

I opened my eyes and looked at her. 'Can they be saved if I agree to sing?'

Camille held my stare long enough for me to know that we understood each other perfectly.

THIRTY-THREE

The day after Camille's visit, a female guard brought me a bowl of soapy water, a towel and a clean dress. Later, a doctor came to my cell. He cleaned my cuts and diagnosed bruised ribs and a dislocated knee. He snapped my knee back into position, inflicting so much pain that if a Gestapo agent had done it, I was sure I would have confessed to anything. After the doctor left, the guards took me to Colonel von Loringhoven.

'I hear you have come to your senses,' he said.

'I have made a bargain,' I reminded him. He may have persuaded me to sing but I wanted him to remember that it was not willingly.

He ignored my comment and read out a list of conditions. I was to sing at the Adriana, which I knew was now run by a French collaborator. I was to wear a black evening dress and I was not to dance or to sing anything '*risqué*'. Even if I had agreed to dance, which I had not, it would have been impossible with an injured knee. To my surprise, he left me to choose my own songs, although I would have to have them cleared by the Propagandastaffel.

'You can have back-up cabaret artists but no naked chorus girls and no comedians,' von Loringhoven concluded. Karl Oberg, it seemed, did not have a sense of humour.

'And my friends?'

'The woman and child have been taken from Drancy. They will be kept in another location until you have completed your performance to my satisfaction.'

'I want them released *before* I sing,' I told him.

'You are not in a position to bargain,' answered von Loringhoven, raising his voice a notch. 'After your performance they will be taken to Marseilles and put on a ship for South America. It makes no difference to me, quite frankly, Mademoiselle Fleurier. Germany will soon rule the world. You have merely bought your acquaintances time.'

He had the same attitude as the Germans who had allowed Odette and Petite Simone to travel from Bordeaux to Paris. But time, I decided, was good enough for now.

'I will call a driver to take you home,' he said, standing up from his desk. 'But let me give you one last word of warning: you must pretend that you are singing of your own free will. If you tell anyone that you have made a bargain with me, your friends will be dead. And I will do it Vichy style. The mother will be beheaded in front of the child. Then I will kill the child too.'

He didn't have to say any more. I may have thought him stupid, but he was dangerously so. When I looked at him, I saw a mutated beast, something unnatural and without normal logic or restraint. I believed he was capable of carrying out the threat.

❧

I was driven back to my apartment building in a black BMW. The Gestapo agent who chauffeured me kept yawning, sending wafts of stale tobacco through the car's interior. I wondered if he had been up all night, beating someone to death.

When we pulled up in front of my apartment, he opened the car door, handed me a walking stick and dragged me to the front door.

'I'll be right here,' he said, pointing to the pavement. 'I'll be watching you. I'll see who comes and I'll see who goes.' Glancing at my leg, he let out a laugh and treated me to the stench of his breath again. 'But you won't be going anywhere with that knee.'

He unlocked the door and pushed me inside. It was gloomy in the foyer. I switched on the light.

'Madame Goux?' I called softly. But there was no answer.

I pushed open the door to Monsieur Copeau's apartment. The secretary and the doctors were not there. The furniture was overturned and papers were scattered over the floor.

'Who's there?' a voice behind me asked.

I turned around to see Madame Goux. Her eyes were black and her nose was crushed and swollen.

'What have they done to you?' I limped towards her and grabbed her shoulders. There were cigarette burns on her face and neck.

She shrugged. 'What have they done to you? You're a mess.'

I told her about my interrogation, then asked about the others, although I was afraid to know if they were still alive or not.

'The doctors cleared out in time. Madame Ibert got the warning and went south to your farm. She had tried to get a message to me but I walked straight into the trap. But they didn't get a thing. I acted the part of an imbecilic old lady.'

There was a burn near her eye that was weeping. I put my arm around her shoulders. The irony wasn't lost on me that before the war I could barely stand Madame Goux. And now I would be devastated if anything happened to her.

'It would take more than that to kill me,' she said, helping me towards the elevator which, by some miracle, was working.

∽

A few days after I returned to my apartment, I heard a man's muffled voice talking to Madame Goux in the foyer. Madame Goux had ordered me to stay off my knee until it was better and I was lying on the sofa with my leg propped up on cushions. I strained to listen, trying to discern who the man was.

'I have only stopped by for a moment,' he said. 'I don't want to intrude. I told them that I was going to manage her for the show.'

The concert for the SS was big news around Paris. The Propagandastaffel had not wasted time in having posters made: *The Brightest Light Sings for the New Paris.* What I didn't know then, and was later glad that Madame Goux hadn't told me, was that draped behind my image was the swastika flag.

'Go on up,' Madame Goux urged the visitor. 'She needs someone to brighten her spirits.'

It took me a few moments to register that the voice was André's.

There had only been a few occasions when our Resistance work had brought us into direct contact. For the most part, we communicated through messengers. Being seen together could have started rumours that may have aroused Guillemette's suspicions. André's footsteps drew closer. I smoothed my hair and rearranged my dressing gown. The door to my apartment had been left ajar in case I needed to call Madame Goux, but André knocked on it anyway.

'Come in,' I told him.

'Simone!' he said, rushing towards me. 'I am glad to see you are alive. I lost ten years off my life worrying about you!'

I was taken aback by his appearance. In his teal blue suit and red tie he looked dashingly handsome. His hair was slightly greyer than it been the last time I had seen him, but his eyes were as bright as ever. I told him that I was improving every day. He looked at me in a searching way, and I knew he was hoping for an explanation of why I was singing for the Nazis. I was heartsick that the people in the network would think that I was betraying them. I dared not imagine how Roger would feel if he ever found out. I could trust André with my life, but the dictum of our network was 'The less others know, the better'. None of us could say for sure what we would or would not reveal under torture. And after von Loringhoven's threat about beheading Odette and Petite Simone, I couldn't take the risk of telling anyone my reasons.

'Make yourself a drink,' I said, pointing to the bar. 'And please pour me a soda water.'

As I intended, André had to turn his back on me to walk to the bar and take the glasses out of the cabinet. It gave me a reprieve from having to look him in the eye when I felt so sullied. I could see him making the drinks in the reflection of the mirror on the opposite wall. The line of his shoulders and his straight broad back stirred an ache of longing that surprised me. Now I had promised myself to Roger, I had assumed those sensations were gone for ever.

'How are your wife and children?' I asked, astounded that I had brought up the subject so casually. Perhaps I was trying to change my focus. I loved Roger with all my heart and would never betray him. Why then did I feel the guilt of a wife who has been unfaithful to her husband?

'They are all well, thank you for asking,' said André, passing me the soda water and returning to his seat. 'And now, tell me, is there anything I can do for you?'

'Can you find out about Roger Delpierre?' I asked. 'I want to know if it is true that he was arrested.'

André stared at me but didn't say anything.

'You know the man I am talking about, don't you? The one who first made contact with you when you joined the network?'

'Yes,' said André. 'I remember.'

He looked at his drink for so long that my mind drifted to the night at the Hotel Adlon when he had told me about his relationship with his father. One minute André and I had been ribbing each other about my language lessons, and the next the mood had turned sombre. André glanced up. He was searching my face again, but this time he was asking a different question. His gaze glided down my neck and along the line of my body. I was taken aback by what I had failed to see in all the years since he had married the Princesse de Letellier. The lightning bolt of it pierced my heart. André Blanchard still loved me.

⟨⟨⟩⟩

After a week, the swelling around my knee subsided and I regained some of my strength. I realised that if I was going to perform to von Loringhoven's 'satisfaction', then I needed to rehearse. I sent a note to the artistic director of the Adriana telling him that I had a piano in my apartment and would begin rehearsing as soon as he could organise a pianist. As there would be no costume fittings and I chose to perform alone, there was no need for me to attend the theatre until the final rehearsal. I received a reply that afternoon, along with a bouquet of roses so profuse that the Gestapo agent had trouble fitting it through the door. The note read:

> Dear Mademoiselle Fleurier,
> It will be my greatest pleasure to have you sing at the Adriana to celebrate the union of France and Germany in the New Europe.
> Maxime Gaveau

I ripped the note in two. I had worked with Martin Meyer, Michel Gyarmathy and Erté. Who was this upstart named Maxime Gaveau? I threw the flowers in the kitchen sink, then remembered that the

Gestapo man might come back to my apartment so I stuck them in a bucket instead.

The truth was that Gaveau's note had brought home the gravity of what I was doing. I could not snub him when I had agreed to collaborate with the Germans too. He might be cooperating for his own self-seeking ambition, but I was giving my public name and face to the legitimacy of the Third Reich. Even worse, as a 'PS' to the note, Gaveau had informed me that the performance was going to be broadcast on Radio France, so not only would my betrayal of the Resistance be known in Paris but all over the country as well.

Later that afternoon, Madame Goux called from downstairs to tell me that André was on his way up to see me. My heart leapt at the thought that he might be bringing me good news about Roger. I limped to the door and swung it open. But André's grim expression hit me like a blow to the stomach.

'You had better sit down,' he said. 'I'll get you a drink.'

For a second I couldn't move. 'Don't keep me in suspense,' I said.

André gripped my shoulders. 'Roger Delpierre was arrested in Marseilles. But he wouldn't talk. So they shot him.'

I stared at André. At worst, I had been expecting to hear that Roger had been arrested. I had never considered that he might be dead. My legs buckled. André helped me to the sofa. Roger? Shot? The smell of lavender wafted around me; I felt Roger's caresses on my thigh. *Don't put up barriers to happiness, Simone.*

André gripped my hands. I sensed that I was tumbling down a dark tunnel. I remembered the first trip Roger and I had made down south with Mouse, the Judge and the others. We had all been on that dangerous mission together but each one of us had faced our own personal terror of being caught and executed. That loneliness was what I was feeling now. André could hold me as tightly as he wanted, but he couldn't save me from descending into the nightmare.

'I am sorry,' he said, tears in his eyes.

I knew that, whatever pang of jealousy he had felt the previous week, he was sincere.

'Could there be a mistake?' I asked.

'Roger Delpierre was head of the network,' he said. 'I cross-checked the story with two contacts. To the best of everyone's knowledge, the report is true.'

I thought of Roger sleeping, his arms folded like an angel's wings across his chest, and tried to get a grip of myself. Roger was a true military man, he would have told me that there was still a war to be fought and it was my duty to be strong no matter the sacrifice. I turned to André. 'The children and the Allied soldiers Roger had with him? Were they caught too?'

André shook his head. 'He was arrested alone, in a bar. It is believed he went there as a decoy. So the others could get away.'

I swiped at my eyes but was unable to stop the tears. This was what war did. It took good people from us. One of the pilots I had accompanied over the line had told me that he had lost so many friends that he never wanted to be close to anyone again.

André poured me a drink then called Madame Goux from downstairs. 'Simone,' he said, bending down to kiss my cheek, 'I have to go but I will come back to see you tomorrow. The best thing we can do to honour Delpierre's memory is to finish what he started. To defeat the Germans and win this war.'

~

For the next few days, I lay in my bedroom listening to the sound of my lungs struggling for air. André had said that the best way to honour Roger's memory was to finish what he had started. But I had agreed to sing for the SS high command. Could my betrayal of Roger be any worse? Somewhere in the audience would be the man who had given the order for his execution. What was the point of winning this war if I had lost Roger? He had opened doors in my heart that I had thought were shut for ever. After loving and losing him, what kind of life would there be to live? I stared at the ceiling, at the floorboards, at the furniture. But they had no answers for me.

'Maman!' I cried in the night. I was now under house arrest and asked André to tell my family what had happened. I begged him to instruct them, for their own safety and that of the agents in their care, not to contact me. 'Tell Maman, Aunt Yvette, Bernard, Madame Ibert and the Meyers that not a day goes by when I do not think of them.'

I was a ship breaking apart, full of leaks. There was no chance of retreating to the farm for comfort this time. I had to sail on. I had to sing for the lives of Odette and Petite Simone.

When Madame Goux announced that the rehearsal pianist from the Adriana had arrived, I was shocked to see Monsieur Dargent walk into my drawing room.

Nothing about him had changed since the last time I had seen him at the Le Chat Espiègle, sixteen years before. He was wearing a white suit with a pink carnation in his buttonhole and his curlicue moustache was as stiff and black as ever.

'Monsieur Dargent!'

'Look what has become of you!' he said, holding out his hands. 'The funny girl who danced like a savage!'

'I tried to get in contact with you a few times,' I told him. 'To thank you for giving me a start. But I have never been able to track you down.'

He laughed his wild man laugh. 'I have been travelling,' he said, hiding his mouth behind his hand. 'Avoiding debtors!'

There was something in his manner that made me uncomfortable. I guided him to the drawing room. 'So you are my rehearsal pianist?'

'No,' he said. 'I am the new director of the Adriana. These days I am Maxime Gaveau.' He bowed and made a flourish with his hand.

My heart sank. He was a collaborator. The rightful holder of that position was Minot, and he would still have had it if not for the Nazis. But I reminded myself that it would not do the Resistance any good to show my anger.

Monsieur Dargent straightened himself again and handed me some sheet music. 'These are songs from your previous shows. I thought we could do a retrospective set. I am having some new numbers written for you too — I'll get them to you early next week. They have to be approved by the Propagandastaffel first. That will give us a few days to rehearse them before the performance.'

I didn't warm to that news. It was humiliating enough to be singing for the enemy high command, but it had never been my intention to perform German propaganda.

When the package of songs arrived several days later, I opened it up with grim foreboding. I carefully read the words to each song. Much to my relief, they seemed harmless enough. But one stood out to me as mysterious:

When my love cools
I'll leave you for the heat of Africa
You'll look in the East, the West and the Centre too
But you won't find me in the darkness of Africa
Unless you bring me the light of your torch.

I had learnt over the years how to read music and played the melody now on the piano with one finger. It was a mellow tune. The Germans did not permit jazz; they called it 'nigger music'. The verses were haunting. I tried singing it through, working out what I would emphasise or sustain. I picked up my pen and changed 'Unless you bring me the light of your torch' to simply 'Unless you bring me your light'.

Monsieur Dargent came to rehearse with me the next day. He flicked through the music sheets and frowned when he saw the Africa song. 'Mademoiselle Fleurier, didn't I say not to change any of the words?'

'No.'

'Didn't I say that the Propagandastaffel had cleared them?'

I couldn't understand why he was getting worked up. Nothing I had altered made any difference to the meaning of the song. I couldn't remember him being so precious before.

'Surely the Propagandastaffel couldn't object to those slight changes?' I said. 'I changed the words to fit the way I want to sing them.'

A look passed across his face. I couldn't interpret it, but it seemed more like worry than anger. He said nothing more, but when he left after the rehearsal I barely heard his goodbye.

Monsieur Dargent's reaction disturbed me so much that I rehearsed the songs again that night on my own, making sure I did not change a thing. With the concert so close, and with Odette and Petite Simone's lives in the balance, I did not intend to antagonise the Nazis — or their collaborators.

⌖

My final rehearsal at the Adriana took place on one of those gloomy Paris days where the cloud cover turns everything a funereal grey. I cast my eye over the theatre's velvet curtains and Art Deco furniture, at the glass and steel doors. The first time I sang there, I had been shaking with nerves. Back then I had thought the most important thing in the world was to be a star. Now I could not concentrate on anything except how quickly I wanted the evening's ordeal to be over. And if I had asked myself whether I was pleased to have become famous, I would have answered that I wished I was anybody but Simone Fleurier, 'the most sensational woman in the world'. My stardom was a weapon the Germans were going to use against France.

I stayed only to rehearse my songs. Monsieur Dargent showed me the program but I was not interested in what the other acts were going to do. There were some Austrian trapeze artists — 'world class' according to Monsieur Dargent; an opera singer — 'the best in Germany'; and a troop of cabaret singers and dancers from Berlin. It was ironic that I, with my dark Mediterranean looks, was going to star among such fine specimens of the Aryan race. But that was the incongruity of fame in Europe: I was better known — and more venerated — than any of them.

Before the performance that evening, I sat in my dressing room listening to the creaks of the floorboards from Monsieur Dargent's office upstairs and the orchestra warming up below. There was no Kira with me to be my good luck charm, no Minot to send me a bottle of champagne. I was alone. Sitting in the star's dressing room brought back memories of '*Bonjour Paris, C'est Moi!*' It had been the most dazzling show Paris had ever seen. The sets and the costumes had been sumptuous and all the chorus girls had been blonde, so that I, as Minot had put it, would 'stand out like a gorgeous black pearl'. Now the black pearl would be standing in front of the Nazi flag. I rested my head in my arms and wondered where Odette and Petite Simone were. Did they realise that tomorrow they would be free? Roger, with his green eyes and sense of purpose, would be treasured in my heart for ever. But tonight I had to push thoughts of him to the furthest corners of my mind so I go could through with what I was about to do.

There was a knock on my door. I knew it wouldn't be a dresser; with only one black dress, I didn't need one. 'Who is it?'

'It's me, Gaveau,' answered Monsieur Dargent. 'I need to speak to you.'

I hadn't put on my dress or done my hair yet. I wrapped a kimono over my underwear and opened the door. Monsieur Dargent pushed straight past me and sat down on my make-up stool. His hands were trembling and his face was pale. I wondered what he could be so agitated about. It wasn't as if anything could go wrong with my performance, unless the Germans didn't like it. There were only a few new songs, no dancing, no scenery or props and no costume changes. I wasn't even going to make my usual entrance down the staircase, balancing an elaborate headdress on my neck. My damaged knee had put an end to that. And if something went wrong with the recording for Radio France, that wasn't the responsibility of either of us.

'What is the matter?' I asked, pouring him a glass of water from the pitcher on my table. Perhaps Monsieur Dargent was feeling out of his depth? This was the first major production at the theatre in years and, fond as I was of him, he was no Minot.

'I didn't have permission to explain our position to you the other day,' he said, sipping from the glass. 'But I do now. You sang the songs perfectly during the rehearsal but I am worried you will change something in the performance. I have to reiterate to you that you must sing the Africa song exactly as it is written.'

I leaned against my dressing table. He was placing far too much emphasis on the accuracy of the lyrics, which to my mind was not as important as the music to anyone except the songwriter. I was singing alone, so it wasn't as if I was going to put out back-up singers if I changed a word here or there.

Monsieur Dargent noticed my frown and let out a sigh. 'It could ruin everything,' he continued. 'That is why we have decided it is better to tell you. The words to that song are of prime importance to the war effort.'

I straightened. Now things were making sense. I recalled the lyrics, trying to work out what they could mean. They weren't specific enough to be any kind of propaganda. When I thought over them, they sounded more like strategic locations. Or a code.

'Whose war effort?' I asked. 'I don't intend to help the Germans in any way.'

Monsieur Dargent's eyes flashed. 'What are you talking about?' he whispered. 'We are on the same side. When you sing the words to the Africa song you will be informing the Resistance that the Allies and de Gaulle's Free French are about to strike. The Resistance must be ready, because when the Allies attack, the Germans will occupy the south of France too. Through Radio France the word will pass from the radio operators to the *maquis*.'

I eyed him suspiciously. He was a collaborator. I found it easier to believe that any message in the song had been put there by the Germans to confuse the Resistance, not to help them.

'You are using me,' I spat.

'*Mon Dieu!* What do you take me for?' cursed Monsieur Dargent, standing up. 'We are working for the same network.' He finished his water in one gulp and shook his head in disgust. 'Clifton said you might be difficult.'

A chill ran down my back. At first I wasn't sure that I had heard him correctly.

'Who? Who said that?' I demanded. I tried to keep myself calm but it did not work. My hands shook. Perhaps Clifton was a common British name.

Monsieur Dargent swallowed so hard that his Adam's apple slipped from his chin to his neck and back again. 'I wasn't supposed to tell you. It just came out.'

I rushed at Monsieur Dargent and grabbed his arms. 'Captain Roger Clifton? Code name: Delpierre?'

Monsieur Dargent squeezed his eyes shut. I dug my fingers into his skin. 'Captain Roger Clifton? Code name: Delpierre?' I repeated, my voice rising.

Monsieur Dargent pushed me away. 'He said you could be stubborn, Mademoiselle Fleurier. And he was right. It is as much for your own safety as for his that I don't tell you any more.'

My skin prickled. In my life there was only one person who had referred to me as stubborn. I was suddenly yanked out of the darkness into the light. I rushed at Monsieur Dargent again. He retreated but was trapped against my wardrobe. 'Roger is alive!' I cried. 'How? Where? How did he escape the Nazis?'

'He was never caught,' relented Monsieur Dargent. 'He heard of your capture and came to Paris to find you. The double agent spread the rumour of his arrest and execution to confuse the network.'

'Is he still in Paris?'

Monsieur Dargent shook his head. 'He is leaving on a plane for London tonight.'

The German stage manager knocked on the door. 'Ten minutes to curtain call.'

Only ten minutes? I hadn't put on my dress or done my hair. But Roger was more important than the performance at that moment. I was about to ask Monsieur Dargent if he could get a message to Roger before he left Paris, but he put up his hand. 'Enough, Mademoiselle Fleurier. Hurry and get dressed. If you upset the Germans, that won't get us anywhere.'

I turned to my mirror. Happiness bubbled up in me. Roger was alive! I drank in every sensation from the pins and needles in my toes to the blood rushing through my veins. I wanted to throw my arms out and sing the good news for everybody to hear, though of course I couldn't. Roger was alive and he had given me a gift — I was about to help the Resistance, not betray it!

'*Bonjour Paris!*' I sang out and waved my hand, entering the stage from the wings. The Germans applauded. Beyond the floodlights I could see rows of black SS uniforms rising up to the balconies, like hundreds of spiders waiting in their holes. But the repulsiveness of my audience and all that they stood for couldn't stop the light that was shining in me. It ran up my legs and spine. The joy was so hot that I thought I might burn up with it.

'*It's me. Tonight of all nights the stars will come out and shine. Shine for the whole of Paris to see.*'

The recording technician for Radio France was sitting in the orchestra pit. I sent him a smile, the biggest grin I had ever given to a collaborator. He and I were comrades tonight. Unknown to him, we were singing out good news to the Resistance.

The Germans liked what they were seeing so much that they clapped again. Despite the residual pain in my ribs from my Gestapo beating, my voice had never been so powerful. My soul was singing within me. It was the pinnacle of my life; one of those moments when the curtain opens and you suddenly know that you are doing what you were born to do, that you are fulfilling your purpose on earth. At that moment I was glad to be Simone Fleurier and thrilled that the Allies were able to use me.

Colonel von Loringhoven was sitting in the balcony with Karl Oberg and Camille. The orchestra slipped into '*La bouteille est vide*', and I directed my voice to them.

> *The more you get*
> *The more you want*

> *You want and want*
> *And then it's all gone.*

Karl Oberg smiled and gave a self-satisfied laugh. Von Loringhoven glanced at him, then looked back at me. He shifted in his seat, pleased with himself. Smile while you can, I thought. It is going to be over for you very soon.

> *La! La! Boom! Here comes Jean*
> *In his new Voisin.*
> *La! La! Boom! He asks, 'What are you doing?'*
> *What am I going to tell him?*
> *La! La! Boom! That I'm hanging out the washing?*

I wanted to laugh with the comedy of it. During the Voisin song I became so giddy that I had to remind myself not to seem too pleased because that might raise von Loringhoven's suspicions. I sang my tango songs with all the tragedy and soulfulness they deserved, but the only way I could sound authentic was to think of what had started my work with the network in the first place: the massacre of the Belgian children.

But it was the finale that was my greatest moment of all.

> *When my love cools*
> *I'll leave you for the heat of Africa*
> *You'll look in the East, the West and the Centre too*
> *But you won't find me in the darkness of Africa*
> *Unless you bring me the light of your torch.*

I sang those words with all my heart. The besotted SS men gaping at me must have been convinced that I was singing for them, but when I looked out at the audience I didn't even see them. I was singing for Roger, for Odette and Petite Simone, for my family, for Monsieur Etienne and Joseph, for General de Gaulle, for Minot and Mouse and the Judge, for André and all the Resistance. I sang for my father and I sang for France. I did not allow myself to think of the men in front of me, many of whom had tortured and executed Resistants.

Although I hated those SS men with every inch of my being, they adored me. When I finished the song, the audience rose to its feet.

I bowed graciously and slipped into the wings. 'Bravo!' they called out. 'Encore! Encore!'

Monsieur Dargent was standing in the wings. We exchanged a smile. The audience cheered and clapped louder.

'Go on!' Monsieur Dargent said. 'You're a performer. Give your audience what it wants.'

I rushed back out on stage and stood in front of the swastika backdrop. I sang the Africa song all over again.

The audience was still shouting for me when the fifth curtain finally came down. If I had dropped dead on the spot at that moment, I would have died the happiest woman in the world.

THIRTY-FOUR

In November, the Allies attacked the Axis powers in North Africa. The operation was a success, and gave the forces a base not only to rescue France but Italy as well. When André brought us the news, Madame Goux and I hugged each other, pressing our wet, tear-streaked cheeks together and laughing with joy. In the midst of the darkness that had fallen over our lives, there was a flame of hope flickering again. Of course we weren't aware then that the Allies would take another two years to enter France, and that life was going to get worse before it got better.

Just as Monsieur Dargent had predicted, the Germans rushed across the demarcation line and occupied the south of France to 'defend' us against the enemy. As morale soared throughout the Resistance, and Britain and de Gaulle stepped up their efforts to arm the *maquis* in preparation for an Allied invasion, so the repression by the Germans became more brutal. The Milice was formed: a French army at the command of the Gestapo and made up of the worst elements of society, including criminals who had exchanged prison terms for the chance to hunt down Resistants.

André and his wife had come under suspicion and, to avoid exposing the network, André had to sever his ties with it, although he still made payments through his sister, Veronique, who was living in Marseilles. Because he could no longer act as a go-between for information, I had no news from Pays de Sault. But André did have access to a radio at one of his factories, and from the BBC we learned that the Russians were advancing, forcing the Germans back towards Berlin. With the people of their conquered countries willing to cooperate, the Nazis had hoped that their satellites could run largely on their own. Although they had been right in many ways, they had not counted on the passion of the Resistance not only in France but in Austria, Denmark, Poland, Belgium, Holland, Czechoslovakia, Italy, Norway and even in Germany itself. Count Kessler would have been proud of the young German men and women who were fighting valiantly from the eye of the storm. Even if numbers were pitifully few, the underground rebels were prepared to fight to the death; proof that sometimes passion could be more significant than power.

In the last year of the war, I was woken each morning by the bone-chilling crackle of gunfire. For every German soldier killed by the Resistance in Paris, ten French prisoners, many of them Resistants themselves, were taken to the woods of the Bois de Boulogne and shot. While the Resistance members had always known that they might pay for their patriotism with their lives, the terror truly hit Paris when the Germans began running out of imprisoned Resistants and started rounding up civilians.

Each day when Madame Goux went to buy our rations, accompanied by a Gestapo agent, she read the death notices pasted on the bakery wall. That was how I learnt of the execution of Madame Baquet, the owner of the Café des Singes. She had been waiting at the Hôtel de Ville to renew business papers when the Gestapo rushed in, bent on revenge for an act of sabotage performed by the Resistance. They had emptied the local police station of prostitutes, homeless old men and drunk husbands but still did not have enough people to fulfil their numbers. So they rounded up the civilians in the foyer — a student, two housewives, a doctor, a librarian, a lawyer and Madame Baquet. The following morning the terrified huddle was marched into the dappled light of the woods. I never visited the Bois de Boulogne after hearing of the incident, but it was said that the bullet marks were still visible on the trees for years afterwards.

In the summer of 1944, the tide could not be held back any longer. André managed to smuggle a disassembled radio transmitter past the guards outside my apartment and together we listened to the crackly voice of de Gaulle announce: '*This will be your year of liberation.*' Something was happening at last.

Paris started to look like a city at war. German trucks rushed out of the city and a few days later they returned full of wounded soldiers. André and I met again to listen to the BBC but this time the signal was blocked. Food became scarce; there was no milk or meat in any of the shops. Our electricity and gas supplies were limited to certain times of the day. The *métro* stopped running. It was from Monsieur Dargent that we heard the thrilling news that the Allies had landed in Normandy and were pushing the German army back.

By August it was clear that the Germans were losing. They were no longer the proud force that had entered Paris. As most of the soldiers were evacuated, those left behind to guard strongholds moved about in groups, terrified of what might happen to them should they become separated from their unit. The women's auxiliary organisations and civil servants were evacuated in buses. Madame Goux recounted to me the story of one busload of German women, military wives, who waved tearfully at the Parisians lined up along the sidewalk, wondering what was going on. Madame Goux's parting shot was to suck up as much saliva as she could and project it at the bus's windscreen. The most telling detail, however, was that the German soldier accompanying her said nothing.

In the middle of the month, there were rumours that the Allies had landed in the south and, with the help of the *maquis*, were chasing the Germans and Milice out of their strongholds. The Paris police, seizing the moment to wipe out four years of shame, put away their uniforms but kept their weapons. The numbers of the fighting Resistance swelled. The police may have been left with the task of handing Paris over to the German army back in 1940, but now they were keen to show the enemy the way out.

Madame Goux and I clung to each other in my apartment, listening to the exchange of fire between the Germans and the Resistance. We kept a candle burning, although candles were not easy to come by, and prayed for Paris and the men and women who were dying. The French people took to the streets; not in our neighbourhood, but on the Left Bank and in the suburbs. They built barricades to stop the Germans escaping or patrolling the city in their tanks. Madame Goux and I ripped up sheets to make bandages for the Red Cross, and the German soldiers who guarded us now that the Gestapo had fled allowed us to take them to the hospital. Bound by the Geneva Convention, the Red Cross nurses were treating both Resistants *and* Germans.

Then one hot August evening, while I was taking a bath, the battle sounds ceased. The silence after so much violence was unnerving. A while later, the bells of Notre Dame began to ring. I dried myself and wrapped a kimono around me. I rushed to the window and threw the sash open. The bells of St Séverin joined in with those of Notre Dame and I peered into the black night, wondering what was happening. The lights of the buildings near the Seine lit up, flickered, then died. Suddenly the bells of St Jacques, St Eustache and St Gervais filled the night with sound.

I ran downstairs to find Madame Goux standing in the foyer, her face gaunt and her eyes wide. 'What do the bells mean?' she asked.

It was then I noticed that the two German soldiers who guarded us were gone. I rushed down the remaining stairs and threw my arms around her. I knew I would never forget that moment. The hug I exchanged with her hurt my ribs but lit my heart.

'It means the Allies have won!' I cried. 'Paris is free!'

∞

In the initial sweep of euphoria it seemed that our joy would last for ever. The tricolour flew from windows and doorways, some of the flags hastily sewn from whatever was available — a white tablecloth, a red petticoat, a blue shirt. Despite the glass that littered the streets and the stray bullets fired by German soldiers who had not yet received notice of their surrender, we could not stay indoors any longer. The summer air was filled with the stirring melody of the *Marseillaise*, once banned but now sung on every corner.

I walked Paris from street to street, as I had when I first arrived in the Twenties, but as I passed the cafés and the crowds gathered around monuments or the flower-strewn Allied tanks, it dawned on me that our happiness was a kind of charade. How could Paris be the same? There were bullet holes in many of the buildings and flowers laid on streets and pavements where a Resistant had offered up his or her life for France. *'Here died Jean Sauvaire, who fought bravely for his country.'*

But there had been pitifully few who resisted. What about those who had done nothing, or, worse, who had actively collaborated? Already I was hearing of women who had taken German lovers having their heads shaved and being paraded through the streets, and other collaborators being found dead in stairwells or floating face down in the Seine.

General de Gaulle was due to make his official appearance in Paris a few days after the Allies had entered it. We understood from the police milling around the Arc de Triomphe that he would be parading that afternoon along the Champs Élysées. I was eager to see the man who had been a disembodied voice in the war years, a voice that had so inspired me that I was prepared to risk my life for its call.

As my dining room had a balcony facing the avenue, I invited André and Monsieur Dargent to join us for lunch. Madame Goux and I set about scrounging together the best feast we could — tomatoes, some limp lettuce, bread and goat's cheese. We pushed the table close to the balcony doors and set it with serviettes of red, white and blue. After we had put the champagne on ice, I glanced at the clock and noted with surprise that André and Monsieur Dargent were half an hour late. André, especially, was usually so precise.

'Look at this,' said Madame Goux, calling me out to the balcony. She unfurled a tricolour that she had somehow managed to knit in the past few days. The sight of her woolly flag, curling at the edges, made me laugh.

I was about to offer her a drink when there was a violent banging on the door which made both of us jump. I rushed into the entrance hall and called out, 'Who is it?' But the caller only answered by knocking fiercely again. Certainly it wouldn't be André or Monsieur Dargent.

'I'll answer it,' said Madame Goux, undoing the latch before I could stop her.

She opened the door and three armed men rushed across the threshold, one of them brandishing a machine gun as if he were expecting to find an apartment full of Germans. They were unshaven and smelt of stale sweat but there was pride in their rugged faces. I glanced at the FFI armbands on their shirtsleeves. They were men of de Gaulle's French Forces of the Interior.

'Come in,' I said, assuming they must be searching for vantage points from which to detect snipers over the Champs Élysées. Some people had thought it premature for de Gaulle to parade out in the open when there were still pockets of fighting in the city. But he had insisted on congratulating the people of Paris for their contribution to the liberation. 'Please feel free to use whatever balconies or windows you wish. And help yourself to the food. We don't have much, but you are welcome to it.'

A flicker of surprise flashed across the face of the soldier nearest to me. 'Mademoiselle Fleurier?' he barked.

'Yes.' I was taken aback by the ferocity in his voice.

'By the order of the Paris police, I am placing you under arrest,' he said. 'You will come with us immediately.'

I didn't move. I was too stupefied to take in his orders. The soldier stared me down as if I were challenging him. 'You are charged with collaboration and will accompany us to the police station.'

I glanced at Madame Goux, whose gaping mouth showed that she was as shocked as I was. 'You must be joking,' she said. 'Mademoiselle Fleurier is not a collaborator. She is a Resistant. She was resisting from the moment the Germans occupied Paris. Why else would she have been placed under house arrest?'

The soldier shrugged. 'That is not what our report says. But if it is the truth then she can clear it up at the station.'

My head felt light. I tried to think clearly. The best course of action would be to cooperate. Surely I couldn't be found guilty of collaboration even if I had somehow managed to be charged with it? I would have to set things right.

I picked up my purse from the sideboard and put my hand on Madame Goux's arm. 'Don't worry,' I told her. 'There has been some mistake. Go ahead and celebrate with the others when they arrive. I am sure this will be cleared up and I will be back for afternoon tea.'

The police station the men took me to looked like a railway platform. Soldiers marched up and down the foyer with guns by their sides while the police checked the papers of bleary-eyed detainees, many of whom looked as if they had been dragged out of bed. I was led to a row of chairs and made to sit down next to an old lady in a dressing gown and slippers. I glanced around the waiting area and saw that Jacques Noir was sitting opposite, his head in his hands. Surely they couldn't mistake me for someone like him? Noir had gone so far as to perform for Hitler in Berlin. I glanced at my watch. If this whole misunderstanding was cleared up soon, I could be back in time for the parade.

After my papers were verified, I was taken to a cell. It was crowded with the most mismatched group of women I had ever seen. At least half of them were prostitutes, while the rest looked like shopkeepers and housewives except for three elegantly dressed women who were huddled together on a bed.

'What do you think they will do to us?' whimpered one of the women, tugging at her red curls. 'My God, what will they do to us?'

She seemed familiar to me and I tried to place her. Then I realised she was one of the women I had competed with in the *Concours d'élégance automobile,* a former friend of André's. He had told me about her war deeds. She had taken a perverse pleasure in denouncing Resistants and Jews, including her own housekeeper. She didn't do it for the reward, she never took the money. She did it because she thought it was an amusing game.

'I hope they shoot you,' said one of the prostitutes. 'Just so the rest of us can get some peace.'

I hoped that they *would* shoot her for what she had done, and was surprised at the vehemence that stung my blood. I hadn't known I was capable of such hate. I glanced at my watch: it was almost three o'clock. General de Gaulle would have started to march.

Some time later a soldier opened the door and called out my name. The way the other women trembled in his presence, he may as well have been calling me up for the firing squad. The soldier led me up two flights of stairs to a questioning room. I eyed the stiff-jawed lieutenant sitting at the table.

'Take a seat,' he said.

I did as I was told and the lieutenant read out the list of accusations against me. My skin prickled at the words 'passing intelligence information to the enemy' and 'treason'. Those were serious charges, much more than mere collaboration, and were punishable by death.

'Who denounced me?' I asked. 'There has been some mistake.'

He gave me a look that said he had been hearing that all day and for once he'd like to see someone admit their guilt. 'I can't give names, but you did perform for the Germans and the records at the Deuxième Bureau support the charge of treason.'

Merde! The records Mouse had 'amended'. But who had denounced me? A jealous rival trying to settle a score?

'I worked for a network,' I told the lieutenant, trying to sound as calm and factual as possible, although his attitude had dampened my confidence. 'I accompanied Allied servicemen and French soldiers across the demarcation line. I was assisted by my concierge, Madame Goux, and my neighbour, Madame Ibert.'

'And where are they now?' he asked, noting their names on a piece of paper. I told him that Madame Goux was at my apartment and that Madame Ibert was in the south.

'We can't reach the south yet but I will have Madame Goux interviewed. What was the name of your contact in the network?'

'Roger Clifton ... Roger Delpierre, I mean.' I hated the way my voice trembled. It dawned on me that it might not be so easy to prove my innocence as I had thought. I had assumed that Roger had either contacted the Special Operations Executive or rejoined the Royal Airforce when he had returned to London. But I had not seen or heard from him for almost two years. The war was over in France, but it was not over everywhere. It might be months before Roger could reach me. And with de Gaulle and Churchill fighting from separate camps, the FFI may not know who he was.

The lieutenant looked at me appraisingly. 'The Garrow–O'Leary line? That is quite a claim, Mademoiselle Fleurier. Besides your concierge, do you have any French persons in authority who can vouch for you?'

'I became involved with the network after being approached by two members of the Deuxième Bureau.'

'And what were their names?'

I was about to say Mouse and the Judge, when I realised those were not their real names. I had no idea who they really were. I tried to explain that to the lieutenant. He let out a sigh and leaned back in his chair. 'If you don't know their names, is there anybody else?'

'Yes,' I told him. 'André Blanchard.'

The lieutenant stared at me. 'André Blanchard has been arrested on serious charges. He supplied uniforms for the German army while his brother-in-law was manufacturing weapons.'

'André is a patriot,' I said. 'He gave money and clothing to the network. Without his help we would not have been able to save as many servicemen as we did.'

I sounded much more confident about André's innocence than I did about my own. It seemed to make an impression on the lieutenant. 'He will have a fair trial and so will you,' he said, standing up and opening the door.

He called out for a soldier then turned to me. 'What is most amazing,' he said, rubbing his hands together, 'is that all through the war there were never more than a few hundred people in Paris involved in the Resistance. But in the past two days, in this police station alone, we have interviewed over five hundred known collaborators who have insisted that they were really working for the Resistance. Now how could that be?'

◦⟋∞⟍◦

I was taken to Cherche-Midi prison, the same place where the Germans had interned me. Although I wasn't beaten this time, and was given adequate food and water, I was more terrified than I had been when I was imprisoned by the enemy. This time I was innocent and the people who were holding me were French. The new administration seemed bent on rounding up and punishing collaborators before they could escape. When I heard the crackle of bullets the following morning, I wondered how much time the police would allow for the collection of evidence supporting my case.

After a breakfast of bread and ersatz coffee, a guard led me out into the exercise yard. There were about ten other women there and the sight of them turned my stomach. They had shaven heads and swastikas tattooed over their bodies. One shivering girl wore nothing but a chemise. She tried to cover her nakedness by crouching in a corner. I was still wearing my clothes from the previous day and gave her my scarf so she could make herself a skirt. She glanced at me and I saw she was no more than fifteen. Sleeping with the enemy was not an honourable thing to do, but I didn't see it as the worst crime of collaboration. For many women it had been the only way to feed their children. Industrialists, like Felix and Guillemette, who had helped the German war effort were far worse. And what about the politicians who had abandoned the city in the first place?

There was a soldier guarding the entrance to the yard. I turned to him. 'Is this what I risked my life for?' I snarled, pointing to the girl. 'Is this my beloved France? If it is, then we are no better than the Nazis!'

'Be quiet!' he cautioned.

I was not about to be silenced. 'Why are these women here?' I screamed. 'Is it because you can't touch the real collaborators?'

I was whipping myself up into a frenzy and, despite the gun in his hand, the soldier looked alarmed. One of his comrades rushed up and twisted my arm behind my back. 'If you can't appreciate the fresh air, then you're going back inside.'

He dragged me by the hair to my cell. For the first time it occurred to me that what happened to those women might happen to me. Simone Fleurier, shaved and humiliated, marched through the streets of Paris for her crime of collaboration. The soldier shouted to the guard to open my cell door and then pushed me inside. I stumbled on my knee, which had never become quite strong again. The soldier picked me up and threw me onto the straw bed. Then, his adrenaline spent, he straightened and said, 'We didn't do that to those women. It was the mobs. We detest their behaviour and have made it illegal. But those women have been denounced by others and we must investigate their crimes.'

'Perhaps those who are denouncing them have much to hide themselves,' I said.

He stared at me, sizing me up. 'Perhaps,' he said, before turning and slamming the cell door shut behind him.

I rested my head on my knees. I had thought the war was over. How wrong I had been.

∞

I was still in prison a week later when I received a message from the guard that my trial would take place in a few days. I asked him if Madame Goux had been interviewed; if Monsieur Dargent's testimony had been taken; if the doctors who had used our apartment building had been found? The guard said he knew nothing, but I could answer those questions myself. If those testimonies had been taken, then they had not been strong enough for the charge of treason to be dropped.

On the day of my trial, I did my best to clean myself up. I couldn't do much about my dress which was crumpled and dusty. But I washed myself with a rag and some water and brushed my teeth with my finger. Perhaps if I had understood what was going on in the outside world, my plight would have been clearer. As the lieutenant had pointed out, there had been few active Resistants in Paris and yet since the liberation over 120,000 people had applied for official recognition for their work in the Resistance.

'*Septembrisards,*' I overheard an FFI soldier call them. September Resistants, who joined when they saw that the Germans had lost the war. The true Resistants were reluctant to come forward because of the shame of it. But where did that leave me?

A few hours before I was expecting to be taken from my cell on the day of the trial, the guard arrived and pushed open my door.

'*Vite! Vite!*' he cried, handing me my purse, which had been confiscated when I was imprisoned. 'Hurry! Hurry! Make yourself presentable.'

If I wasn't so surprised by his urgent concern with my grooming, I would have questioned the difference that powdering my face and smearing on lipstick made to my dirty clothes. But I did as he told me. I dabbed *eau de cologne* behind my ears and splashed some on my wrists. It was only when he pushed me out the door that it occurred to me what might be going on. The trial of Simone Fleurier would be an event. If I looked as if I had been mistreated, public sympathy might turn in my favour. But to my surprise, I wasn't taken out of the prison and rushed off to court with a police escort, as I had envisioned. I was taken downstairs to the office of Cherche-Midi's superintendent.

The guard stopped in the corridor, which was lined with FFI soldiers standing to attention.

'I present Mademoiselle Fleurier,' he said.

One of the soldiers knocked on the superintendent's door and was told to enter. He stood aside and ushered me into the office. The superintendent was an elderly man with a bald head who was shuffling papers on his desk and wearing a worried frown. There was another man by the window. The light was streaming in behind him. He was the tallest, lankiest man I had ever seen. He stepped towards me.

'Mademoiselle Fleurier,' he said. 'I apologise that your plight has only now come to my attention. You will be released immediately.'

A tingle ran down my spine. I had never seen this man before but I knew his voice. It was the voice that had called out to me four years ago, telling me never to accept defeat. General de Gaulle.

'When I was in London, I was aware of your courageous service in helping your countrymen join the Free French,' he said. 'It inspired me that not all the lights of Paris had gone out; that there was one still shining brightly.'

The great de Gaulle had found inspiration in me? I forgot my dishevelled appearance and thanked him for his compliment as if we were two guests who had just been introduced in an elegant salon. For his part, he seemed so caught up in victory that he didn't appear to register my dirty clothes or my surprise. Instead he nodded to the superintendent, who pulled out chairs for me and the General, and scurried about serving us tea like an eager-to-please maid.

'It is with great honour that I give you this,' said de Gaulle, handing me a small box. I opened it to find a gold Cross of Lorraine inside — de Gaulle's symbol of the Resistance. 'You will have other honours,' he said. 'But this token must do for now.'

The saying 'my heart swelled with pride' suddenly made sense to me, for that was exactly what was happening inside me. My centre grew larger and wider. The world seemed to be opening up for me. It was the proudest moment of my life.

The General put down his cup then rose from his chair. 'I hope that when things settle down, my wife and I can meet with you again, Mademoiselle Fleurier. But for now I have some urgent things which I must attend to.'

I stood and watched the superintendent rush to the door to open it for the General. Before he left, de Gaulle turned to me. 'I too was charged with treason by the Vichy government when my goal was to serve the true France,' he said. 'I hope that you will wear this terrible misunderstanding as another badge of honour.'

I nodded, although if somebody other than General de Gaulle had suggested that to me, I would have bitten them.

'*Vive la France!*' he saluted me.

Without thinking, I jumped to attention and returned the salute. '*Vive la France!*'

It was unheard of for a military man to salute a civilian, and the exhausted de Gaulle must have forgotten himself. But I understood the sentiment; he was a man who respected fighters above anyone else.

Upon my release, the first thing I had to do was to find out what was happening with André. Now that I had been officially recognised by de Gaulle, my testimony would carry weight. As it turned out, I was just in time. André's trial was scheduled for the following day. For some reason, he had been granted access to his own lawyer, while I had not. I stopped by my apartment for a bath and change of clothes, then went straight to his lawyer's office to give my testimony.

Monsieur Villeret was an elegant man in his mid-sixties who had known André since he was a child. 'You can't imagine how pleased I am to see you,' he told me, showing me to a seat. 'André has been charged with collaboration and treason. I doubt they will even try him now.'

'How soon can we get him released?'

'Maybe not until the day after tomorrow. Executions are fast but releases are backlogged.'

'I shall visit him this afternoon and tell him,' I said. 'So you can get to work on the release.'

'Are you aware that Camille Casal is also being held at Fresnes prison?' Monsieur Villeret asked me.

Something in his tone struck me as odd, but I assumed he was just letting me know the fate of someone with whom I had co-starred in a major show. Camille had been very public in her fraternisation with the Nazi high command. Although she was unlikely to be executed, she had too much weighing against her to escape prison entirely. I doubted whether any statement I could give would affect the outcome of her trial. But her connection with von Loringhoven had allowed me to sing the Africa song for the Resistance and to save Odette and Petite Simone.

'I can make a statement in her favour,' I said.

Monsieur Villeret looked startled. He raised his eyebrows. 'You are aware that it was she who denounced you to the FFI?'

I was so shocked that for a moment I forgot where I was. My mind raced to come up with excuses for Camille's conduct but I could find none. 'She denounced me? Why would she do that?'

'She has always been against you, Mademoiselle Fleurier.'

'That is not true,' I said, shaking my head. 'That is only how we were portrayed in the press.'

'You don't know, do you?' Monsieur Villeret frowned. He sat back and sighed, as if weighing up the consequences of what he was going to say next. 'Can I rely on your discretion?'

I was reeling too much from the revelation that Camille had denounced me to take in his question. She must have done it to protect herself — or her daughter. Perhaps she had thought that I would denounce her first?

I looked back to Monsieur Villeret. He pulled a box out of a cupboard and placed it on his desk with the gravity of a funeral director arranging an urn.

'When André was arrested, I went through his father's files to gather support of his innocence,' he said. 'I came across some old correspondence between Monsieur Blanchard and Camille Casal. She was blackmailing him.'

The room went out of focus. I had no idea that Camille had ever known André's father. 'Blackmailing him? When?'

'1936.'

That was the year André had turned thirty; the year we were supposed to get married.

'She wanted money?'

Monsieur Villeret shook his head. 'She wanted to ruin your happiness. She wanted Monsieur Blanchard to refuse to let André marry you.'

I thought the suggestion was ludicrous. Even if Camille had been that malevolent, I couldn't see how she could have had any power over Monsieur Blanchard. Contrary to his wife's prediction that he would outlive us all, he had succumbed to dementia soon after retiring and now lived under a nurse's care. But back in 1936 he had been arrogant and cocky. Even someone as manipulative with men as Camille wouldn't have been able to fool him.

'Why would somebody with Camille's fame and beauty want to hurt me?' I asked. But as soon as the question left my mouth the truth of what Monsieur Villeret was implying hit me. I remembered Camille's reaction to André's proposal to me in Cannes. And no one had been able to explain Monsieur Blanchard's sudden change of heart when he had already agreed to let André marry me.

'It was spite that made her do it,' said Monsieur Villeret. 'The workings of a jealous mind. There was a skeleton in the Blanchard family closet. She found out about it from someone high up in the military and she decided to use it against you.'

My eyes did not leave Monsieur Villeret's face.

'Laurent Blanchard did not die a hero at Verdun,' he said. 'That was a cover-up by the government in light of the Blanchard family's importance to France. Laurent Blanchard incited his men to mutiny. He was shot fleeing the battle by another officer.'

My breath caught in my throat. 'He was shot for treason?'

'He was shot without a trial,' Monsieur Villeret said. 'And what he did was covered up.'

I stood up from my chair, my legs unsteady beneath me, and stumbled to the window. Out on the street some American soldiers were supervising the clearing of a burnt-out building. Ropes had been tied around the frame and the soldiers were pulling on it. Camille had destroyed my happiness with André because she was jealous?

Through the haze of confusion in my mind, I heard Monsieur Villeret ask, 'Do you think that I should tell André?'

Onlookers gathered on the street to watch the Americans pull down the unstable building. At first it seemed as if the wood would not budge. But after a few minutes of determined tugging, the frame collapsed. The crowd cheered.

I turned to Monsieur Villeret, barely able to see him through my tears. If he told André about Camille, he would have to tell him about Laurent. I remembered the picture of the man with the soulful eyes in Madame Blanchard's parlour. I suspected that Laurent had not betrayed his countrymen, rather he had been like many of the young officers my father had described: intelligent men who could not see the point of sending thousands of soldiers to slaughter just because some general ordered it. But none of us would ever know that for sure. The accusation of treason and cowardice would stain Laurent if the true circumstances of his death were ever revealed.

I thought of that cold morning in Neuilly, when André and I were broken apart for all time. What was the use of him knowing now? What good could come of it? I thought of Princesse de Letellier and André's daughters, of Madame Blanchard and Veronique. André and I should have put our own happiness first all those years ago. It was too late to do that now. There were too many people to hurt. Part of me would love André for ever, and he might still love me, but I belonged with Roger.

'No,' I said. 'We must never tell him.'

I took a package of clean clothes, linen, soap and food to Fresnes prison for André. He was brought out to me in prison garb with chains around his ankles. I was startled by his haggard appearance.

'Simone!' he said, his face brightening. 'They let you out? Are you all right?'

I felt as if my own smile was forced. All that Monsieur Villeret had told me was weighing on my mind. I asked the guard if I could speak to André alone. Glancing at the Cross of Lorraine on my lapel, he nodded and left.

'You won't be tried, André. You will be released as soon as your lawyer can get the paperwork through.'

André gave a sigh of relief, and pressed his fingers to the grille of the window that separated us. I couldn't bring myself to lift my hand to touch his. In front of me was a man I had loved with my whole heart. I would never do anything to hurt him or his wife and children.

'Simone? What is it?'

'I had better tell your wife that you will released,' I said. 'She must be worried. Do you have a message for her?'

André bowed his head. I sensed something shifting between us. Like two tectonic plates realigning themselves into more stable positions. He looked up again and our eyes met. 'Only that ... I love her and the girls,' he said.

We both smiled.

'And you, Simone,' he asked. 'What is your plan now?'

'To go south to my family and wait for Roger.'

André frowned at the mention of Roger's name, but it was with concern this time rather than jealousy. 'Monsieur Villeret has been trying to track Roger Delpierre down. It was true that he was the contact for your song at the Adriana, but he was captured before he could get back to London. He was sent to a concentration camp. No one knows where he is now.'

My heart plunged. Surely that wasn't possible? I couldn't lose Roger twice.

'No,' I said, clenching my hands.

André brought his face close to the grille. 'You love him, don't you, Simone?'

I nodded, pushing away my tears with the heel of my palm. 'He wanted to come back for me after the war.'

'Simone, don't cry,' André said, 'As soon as I am out of here, I will help you any way I can.'

⚬⚬⚬

On my way to the prison exit, the guard accompanying me asked if I could wait in the corridor for a moment. He disappeared into an office and I leaned against the wall. There were some men sitting on benches, their faces bloodied and bruised. I strolled to the window and looked out. A group of women were in the exercise yard. I was only one floor up and could see their faces clearly. None of them were in prison uniforms; they wore civilian clothes and looked ruffled and dirty. But they were not working-class women; they had the tailored dresses and high heels of *Tout-Paris*. Some had shaved heads.

My eye fell to a blonde woman standing in the corner of the yard, smoking. Her hard blue eyes were remote from the fear and chaos around her. I inched closer to the window. Without make-up Camille's face looked haggard and old. I remembered her gliding onto the stage at the Casino de Paris and eyeing the audience, majestic in her skin-tight dress, her cape slipping to the floor. I had once been mesmerised by her beauty but the rot on the inside was starting to show through now. I remembered the cool mockery in Camille's eyes when she looked out at an audience and realised why she had never suffered stage fright — every toss of her head and flutter of her eyelashes had been practised to military precision. Camille never gave anything of herself, just as any friendship she had shown me had no substance or truth to it. She had done the worst thing she could have to hurt me. But I was at fault too. There was a saying in Provence: 'Those foolish enough to keep a snake as a companion will get bitten sooner or later.'

Camille looked up and our eyes met. She watched me without a trace of hesitation or fear. I understood then that she knew that I had found out what she had done, and she didn't care.

'Who are you looking at?' the guard asked, coming out of the office. He glanced over my shoulder and gave a scoff. 'Camille Casal? Your old rival? She doesn't look so glamorous now, does she?'

'She was never my rival,' I said, remembering what Monsieur Etienne had always told me. 'I was the better singer and dancer.'

'And prettier too,' the guard said, guiding me away from the window and down the corridor. 'Camille Casal is a cold bitch. I was there for her interrogation. Did you know that she once had a baby? She left it in a convent and never went back.'

I stopped and looked at the guard. He had rosy cheeks and a rotund stomach, the signs of a happily married man. 'Where is the girl now?' I asked him. 'She is a young woman.'

He shook his head. 'She never grew up. The girl died of a fever when she was five years old. Camille Casal was already a star then but she wouldn't give a centime towards medicine for the child. She is buried in a pauper's grave.'

The guard let me out of the prison gate and into the sunshine. I stood on the pavement for a long time, trying to take in all that I had learnt that morning. I ran over in my mind the things Camille had said to me over the years about supporting her child. None of it had been true. The image of Camille's face staring at me from the exercise yard burned into my mind. She had been shameless until the end. She had used me to get back on the Paris stage with '*Les Femmes*', knowing that she had destroyed my happiness with André. No wonder she never bothered to mention him.

A lump formed in my throat and I began to choke. I slipped down to sit on the cobblestones and covered my eyes. I wanted to go back and spit in Camille's face, to tear at her arrogant flesh with my nails. For minutes, I could not imagine standing up again for fear that I might kill her, but something tingled in my heart and the rage passed. If I confronted Camille now, what would change? She had ruined my past but I wouldn't let her touch my future.

Slowly my head cleared and my heartbeat returned to normal. I stood up and straightened my coat. I would cover Camille over as a dog covers over its dirt. I was done with her. I had no intention of attending her trial; there was nothing I could do to condemn Camille any more than her actions had already done. What I had to think about now was the future, and that future was Roger and my family at the farm.

THIRTY-FIVE

I wrote to General de Gaulle to see if anything could be done through his office to trace Roger. I gave Madame Goux instructions to make enquiries through the Red Cross on my behalf about him, as well as Monsieur Etienne and Joseph, while I tried to find out everything I could through network contacts. Von Loringhoven had refused to give confirmation that Odette and Petite Simone had actually left the country, and the best I could hope for was that Odette would write to me. Monsieur Dargent came to my apartment each day to help with my search. The underground newspapers were now openly published and it was in one of these that I first saw a grainy picture of skeletal bodies being bulldozed into mass graves in what were now being termed 'death camps'.

'Have faith, Simone,' Monsieur Dargent told me. 'No matter what it takes, we will find them.'

Besides searching for information about Roger and my friends, I yearned to see my family. I had not had any contact with them since I had last left them for Paris, and after all the hardships we had lived through, my family, Madame Ibert and the Meyers were the people with whom I most wanted to celebrate the end of the war. In order to hinder the Germans and assist the Allied invasion, the *maquis* had blown up bridges, dug out railway tracks and cut telephone lines. As a result, it was almost impossible to make contact with people in the south. But as soon as the barest train service was re-established, I was on it. I held out hope that maybe Roger had returned to France via the south and gone straight to the farm.

I reached Carpentras in three days and from there took a motor truck. The driver, who was from Sault, told me that the Milice and the retreating German army had been vicious in the last days of the war. Nearly fifty Resistants from Sault alone had been sent to concentration camps. I thought of Roger again and shivered.

The driver let me off a mile from the farm. It was early autumn and the countryside was peaceful after the chaos of Paris. I remembered how happy my family had been when Roger and I announced our intention to marry, and how it had lifted our spirits in the darkest of times. I tried to recreate that feeling of hope as I walked by fields of wheat and lavender that should have been cut months ago. I imagined how life would be at the farm once Roger and I were married. I saw myself tending a beautiful garden of roses and wildflowers in pots; little children running around the feet of my mother and Aunt Yvette while they cooked lunch in the kitchen; and Bernard and Roger standing side by side, surveying lush fields of purple.

In the last half kilometre before the farm, I became so elated at the thought of seeing my family again that I broke into a run. I caught a glimpse of my aunt's house through the trees. There was no one in the yard or the fields. No drift of smoke from the chimney. I turned the bend in the road and the house came into full view. I stopped in my tracks, my legs almost giving way beneath me.

'No!'

The lower part of the house was intact but the top floor was a desolate shell. Black burn marks scarred the holes where the windows had been. I turned to the empty space next to it, where my father's house should have stood. There was nothing left except a mountain of blackened stones.

'*Maman!*' I screamed. '*Maman! Aunt Yvette! Bernard!*'

My voice rang off the trees, echoing like a gunshot in the air. But there was no answer.

I bolted towards the ruins of the house, my heart thumping in my chest. 'Minot! Madame Ibert!' I called. I struggled to think over the ringing in my ears. That the Germans or the Milice had done the damage I had no doubt. But where was everybody? I tried not to believe the worst. It was possible they had fled before this had happened.

I tried the door of the house. It was stuck. I shouldered and kicked it until it gave way and creaked open. The kitchen was undamaged and stood like a surrealist painting against the ruin of the rest of the building. The table was set for six people. Would they have set the table if they were preparing to flee? I pushed open the door to the storeroom. It was stocked with preserved food, cans and bags of grain. If the Germans had been here, wouldn't they have ransacked it? Possible scenarios jumbled together in my mind. I opened the shutters and stared outside. Could a fire have started in my father's house and somehow spread to the top floor of Aunt Yvette's? Would that explain the damage? I turned the problem over in my mind. Something moved in the grass. There was a flash of fur. I stared at the green blades, trying to discern what it was. A rabbit? Two eyes blinked at me. No, not a rabbit. A cat.

I rushed outside and scooped Kira into my arms. I could feel her breast bone protruding through her matted fur and she was covered in thorns. She meowed feebly, revealing broken incisor teeth. I nursed her against my chest and carried her into the house. I recalled that I had seen bottles of anchovies in the storeroom, so I lowered her onto the table and mashed up the contents of one jar on a plate. I would get her water as soon as I had checked that the well had not been poisoned.

'What happened to you?' I asked, stroking her head gently with my finger.

An unsettling thought rose in my mind. If my family had been given enough warning to flee the Germans, why had they left Kira behind? Perhaps she had been hiding and they couldn't find her? But I could not believe that. She was a house cat and barely left my mother's side. I stood in the doorway and called out the names of the dogs and Chérie. But, as I had thought, Kira was alone.

I sank into a chair. It would take me an hour to walk to the village, but there was nothing else to be done. Perhaps my family was there. I watched Kira lapping up the anchovies, crouched on her bowed legs. She was eighteen, ancient for a cat. I wondered how she had survived with no one to feed her.

'Hello!' a man's voice shouted. I ran to the window to see the grizzled figure of Jean Grimaud coming up the road. Another idea flashed into my mind. Maybe everyone had fled to join the *maquis*. But what had they done with Madame Meyer?

'Jean!' I called out, running into the yard.

'I was in Carpentras,' he said, grimacing. 'I heard that you were making your way here.'

'Where are they?' I asked.

Jean swallowed and looked at his hands. And then I knew. The truth was all around me, yet I had refused to see it. I felt as though somebody had struck me in the heart with a pickaxe. I crouched on the ground. I wanted to sink into that chalky earth, to slip under it like a corpse, so I wouldn't have to face the terrible thing that Jean was going to tell me.

Jean squatted down next to me. 'I'm sorry,' he said, tears welling in his eyes.

Poor Jean Grimaud. Twice in his life he'd had to bring me bad news.

'What happened?'

Jean put his arm around my shoulders. 'They found the grenades Bernard was keeping for us from an Allied drop,' he said. 'There were three of us heading for the farm when we saw that the Germans were here. We hid in the trees. There was nothing we could do to save them. We were outnumbered.'

I choked on my tears. 'Where were they taken?'

'They were killed here.'

I pressed my face against his arm. 'All of them?'

Jean squeezed me tighter. I looked up at him and he nodded.

'You should be proud of them, Simone,' he said. 'They died like saints. They knelt down and held each other's hands. Then the Germans shot them.'

Maman! The blood rushed to my ears. I clutched my fists against my head. Despite the danger I had put them in, I never once thought that harm would come to my family or friends. While the battle for Paris raged, I had been comforted by the fact that they lived in a remote part of the country. I barely heard Jean when he told me that the first German soldier ordered to perform the execution couldn't bring himself to shoot Madame Meyer, so his commander shot him and performed the execution himself. I was too shocked to take in anything else.

'I will walk with you to the village,' said Jean. 'You can stay with

Odile. She has your dogs and one of your cats. We couldn't find the other one.'

'No,' I said, wiping at my dusty, tear-streaked face. 'She waited for me here.'

❦

I did not return with Jean to the village. I told him I wanted to spend the night in my aunt's kitchen. He didn't argue, he only said that he would return the following day. Before Jean left, I asked him to show me where they had shot my family, Minot and his mother, and Madame Ibert. He pointed to a spot near the distillery door. In the dappled afternoon light I couldn't see any marks in the wood, the way people said there were holes in the trees of the Bois de Boulogne.

'They shot them from behind,' Jean explained. 'In the back of the neck.'

He left me with kisses on both cheeks but I barely felt them. I sat down on a stone looking at the spot where my family and friends had died. Kira rubbed against my legs before settling down next to me. It was hard to imagine any violence had taken place here. When the sun began to disappear, a breeze rustled the trees and everything was peaceful. I remembered the first lavender harvest. I heard my father singing, saw my mother wipe the sweat from her face with the back of her hand, Aunt Yvette pulling down her sleeves against the harsh sun.

Someone laughed and I turned around before I realised that the sound was in my head. Minot was clinking his champagne glass against mine after my first performance at the Adriana. *'Congratulations on a superb show.'* I thought of his mother, patting Kira while she waited for her train from Paris to depart. Then Madame Ibert loomed up before me, shovelling sand in the attic.

I couldn't believe that it was all over, that I would never see those beloved faces again. When the sun finally disappeared and night fell, the numbness gave way to the full brunt of grief. 'Can you ever forgive me?' I wept into the silent blackness.

❦

Jean had told me that the villagers had buried my family and friends in the churchyard, but when dawn rose the next day I realised that it would be a while before I could bring myself to visit their graves. I was stuck in a dream, sandwiched between a reality I did not want to face and the happy memories of life at the farm. I had no intention of returning to Paris.

There were vegetables in the garden and the water in the well was good. I cleaned out the kitchen and set up a bedroo'm in the front room, even though there was a gaping hole in the roof. I scrubbed the floors and the walls with lavender water, struggling to eradicate the stink of smoke. I busied myself tending to Kira and I fed her eggs, anchovies, sardines and tinned meat, hoping to fatten her up again. But one day she stopped eating. When I awoke the following morning, she wasn't asleep next to me. I searched the house and the yard. It was not like her to wander further than that, but I could not find her anywhere. I ran out into the fields, terrified that an eagle had taken her as easy prey. I walked to the lavender fields and saw her lying on her side. She was panting. When I looked into her eyes, I knew she would not last the morning.

'Thank you, my friend,' I whispered, lying down next to her and stroking her fur. 'You waited for me, didn't you? You did not want me to have to discover what had happened here all alone.'

Kira stretched out her paw and touched my chin, as she had liked to do every morning.

❦

I buried Kira near the graves of Olly, Chocolat and Bonbon. All my life people had laughed at me for my attachment to my pets, but having lived through a war, I had come to prefer animals to people.

In the afternoon, I walked to the village. Jean was talking with Odile and Jules Fournier near the fountain. Odile saw me coming first and ran towards me. My throat was so thick with tears I couldn't bring myself to say anything. She wrapped her arms around my shoulders. Odile was a small woman, much shorter than me, and yet I felt the strength in her grasp. She was holding me up; grief had drained me.

'I have your animals here,' she said. 'Would you like to see them?'

Bruno, Princesse, Charlot and Chérie were sunning themselves in the courtyard of the bar like movie stars on the Riviera. They jumped up as soon as they saw me and vied for my attention. I patted, rubbed and stroked them all, although I couldn't stop thinking of Kira.

'I have grown attached to them,' said Odile. 'They are good company.'

'Can you mind them just a bit longer?' I asked her, picking up Chérie. I felt barely capable of looking after myself let alone the animals.

Odile patted Chérie and stroked my cheek. 'Come and get them whenever you are ready.'

She told me to sit at a table and she brought me a glass of *pastis*, although in my village it wasn't a woman's drink. It was strong and took the edge off the throb in my heart. Jean came in with Jules. I was grateful that no one expected me to talk. I listened to them chat about the change in season and the new crops. None of us wanted to discuss the war, but it was impossible to avoid it. It had changed everything. I wasn't the only person to have suffered. Ten families in our tiny village had lost a father, a son or a daughter.

'At least there were no collaborators here as there are in other villages,' said Jean with pride. 'We all fought as one.'

'The collaborators are being let off easily,' scoffed Jules. 'Even Pétain has had his death sentence commuted to life.'

'It depends how much money you have,' said Odile, rubbing her fingers together. 'If you are rich and famous or are needed in some way, you will be pardoned. Watch out if you are poor though. You will be shot as "an example to others".'

'No,' said Monsieur Poulet from the bar. 'De Gaulle has turned the whole of France into a nation of Resistants. It is the image he gives to the world so he can hold his head high when he stands with the other Allied leaders.'

De Gaulle, I thought bitterly, remembering the way I had idolised him. No hero is ever perfect.

That first afternoon broke my isolation. After that, I walked to the village each morning to send telegrams from the post office to Paris and Marseilles and letters to London. I was trying every link I could to find out what had happened to Roger. Each day I ate lunch with Odile before heading home. It was through her that I learned that the fashion designer Coco Chanel had not been charged with collaboration, even though she and her German lover had tried to influence Churchill to make a peace deal with Hitler. Perhaps if my family had not been killed, I would not have felt so bitter towards people like her. Her collaboration had not made her a happier woman, just a richer one. But why should my family have died trying to save the country when so many self-seekers were left unpunished?

The following day I returned to the post office to send more letters. 'There is something for you,' said the postmistress. 'It looks official.'

Official, I thought, alarm bells ringing in my head. That was not good. What I was hoping for was a handwritten letter from Roger telling me that he was all right. I opened the envelope and saw it was an article that Madame Goux had cut out from *Le Figaro*. Camille Casal had been found guilty of collaboration. Her punishment was to be banned from performing in France for five years. I remembered her hard face staring back at me the day I went to Fresnes prison. She was not going to suffer for her collaboration the way I had for my resistance.

'Is it good news?' the postmistress asked.

I shook my head. 'It is no news,' I said. 'No news at all.'

A few weeks later I received another letter from Madame Goux, informing me that the Red Cross had not been able to locate Roger. But she had heard from Odette. She and Petite Simone had reached South America and were waiting for passage to Australia, where they had been accepted as refugees. There was no word yet of Monsieur Etienne or Joseph. Madame Goux asked after my family and Madame Ibert, and I realised that she didn't know. I had not told anybody in Paris.

I walked through the autumn fields, relieved to have heard news about Odette and Petite Simone but still worried about the others. Australia? The irony was not lost on me.

'*A lavender farm? Like those in France?*'

'*Very much so.*'

I tried to imagine Roger's country as he had described it. I saw a rugged coastline and centuries-old wilderness, a place untouched by the bitterness of war. With no news from Roger, and more revelations of atrocities appearing in the newspapers every day, the grim possibility that he, Monsieur Etienne and Joseph were dead gripped my heart. I had lost my family, why not them too?

By the time I reached the farmhouse, a mistral was blowing. I built a fire in the kitchen but it wasn't enough to keep me warm. What would I do here during the winter? I thought of all the people around the world who were trying to trace their loved ones. If I returned to Paris, I could help the Red Cross with their searches. Maybe André and I could put together whatever was left of our fortunes to help war orphans?

Then another possibility came to me: maybe I should go to Australia. With my family dead, and the hope of Roger being found alive growing dimmer every day, what was there to keep me in France? I could not imagine myself singing or acting in films again, unless to entertain wounded soldiers or people in refugee camps. Perhaps I could make a new life in a new country with Odette and Petite Simone. But no sooner had my heart lifted with the idea than it crashed again. Trying to begin a new life was too painful. It was easier to stay here, in my cocoon.

The mistral howled louder. I emptied the contents of my travel bag on the floor, searching for another sweater. Something rattled on the flagstones. I saw the pouch my mother had given me with the rabbit bone inside. *You will need it. I can't watch over you for ever.*

You should have kept it for yourself, Maman, I thought.

I picked up the pouch and opened the drawstring. The bone was light in my hand. My mother hadn't told me what part of the animal it came from but I guessed from the shape that it was the leg. Something caught my eye. I moved to the lamp and held the bone up to it. Etched along the side were words written in a shaky, unformed hand. I squinted to read them: *A ma fille bien aimée pour qu'enfin brille sa lumière.* For my beloved daughter who shines her light at last.

I stared at the words, knowing that my mother had written them. But how? When had my mother learned to write? Or had she known how to all along?

Tears pricked my eyes at the memory of the woman who had always been a mystery to me, and now would be for ever so. The dead took their secrets with them. *For my beloved daughter who shines her light at last.* At least I could be sure of one thing: how much my mother had loved me.

After the fire went out, I huddled under my blankets, gazing at the moonlit sky through the hole in the ceiling. Sometime in the early hours of the morning the wind died down. I woke up, the moon shining on my face. I lifted myself out of bed, drawn to the light, and wrapped my blankets around my shoulders.

I shuffled into the kitchen and saw that the outside door had come loose on its hinges. It yawned open into the yard. The trees were magical in the silvery light. An owl sounded in the woods. I walked out into the courtyard with the floating lightness of a dreamer. The air was fresh and sparked with electricity against my skin. A shadow dropped like a curtain as a cloud passed over the face of the moon.

I turned towards the road and started. There were shapes moving in the spot where I had seen the gypsies dance so many years before. At first I couldn't make out what they were and squinted like a near blind woman into the blackness. Then the cloud passed over and the moon shone again and I saw them: the silhouettes of two men and four women, the eldest of whom leaned on a stick. One of the women stood in front of the others, her scarlet dress billowing around her and her hair flying over her shoulders like a flag on the mast of a ship. She raised her hand towards me.

I wasn't frightened but my breathing quickened. Tears blurred my eyes. Maman?

My feet pressed the ground with longing and desire. I wanted to run to her, to be enfolded in her arms. I wanted to be where she was, not alone in the moonlight. But gravity held onto my body and my feet would not move. Another cloud passed over the moon and I sensed something shift in the atmosphere. The others inched forward, their faces stars shining in the darkness. I looked at each of them in turn. Aunt Yvette and Bernard with their angelic blondeness; Minot's smile; Madame Ibert's graceful eyes; Madame Meyer's plump cheeks. I understood why they had come as clearly as if they had told me. They wanted to say goodbye.

I turned to my mother. She spoke to me without moving her lips: *Nothing is wasted, Simone. The love we give never dies. It only changes form.*

I caught a glimpse of Kira gazing at me with her vivid eyes and felt myself slipping back into the unconsciousness of sleep. Before I plunged into the darkness I heard my mother whisper: *Never be afraid to keep giving love.* The words landed on my aching heart as softly as a kiss.

'Simone, the lavender is waiting for you!'

I opened my eyes. The sun was streaming through the hole in the roof, filling the room with light. I stared at the blue sky, waiting for the dull pain that was always in my heart to seize me. But it did not come. Instead, a different sensation flooded me. I wondered how it was that I could feel these flickers of joy lighting up my soul when there was nothing worth living for.

The wind had dissipated and the air felt cool and fresh. I breathed in; there was a smell of damp and pine, the smell of autumn in Provence. I listened to a bird singing in a nearby tree, trying to work out what it was. Then another sound, like a murmur, started up. I sat bolt upright, straining my ears. The faint hum of a motorcar echoed in the air. Was it the motor truck bound for Sault? The sound became louder. I glanced around the room, looking for my dress. There were clothes hanging out of the dresser I had salvaged from one of the bedrooms, but nothing I could wear. Where was my dress? I spotted it hanging on the back of the door, where I had put it the night before. I tugged it on over my head and slipped on my shoes before running out of the house.

I still couldn't see the car, but I was certain it was heading for the farm. Then it appeared through the grove of trees. A dusty Citroën with the grille missing. Who is it? I wondered. Most of the cars in the village used charcoal gas for fuel, but this one was running on petrol. The car pulled to a stop in the yard. I couldn't see the driver through the glare of the glass. The door opened and André stepped out.

'André!' My heart melted at the sight of him. He has heard, I thought. He has heard and my dear friend has come to comfort me. André called my name back in greeting but said nothing more. He stepped around the front of the car and opened the passenger door. One leg stretched out, then another. A walking stick followed. Everything slowed down. André reached forward to help a man in an RAF uniform out of the car.

'Roger?' I whispered.

They both turned to me. I stared at the man in the RAF uniform, trying to find traces of my lover in the gaunt-looking figure. His head was shaved and there was a jagged scar above his left ear. No, it wasn't Roger. It was another Allied serviceman, a friend of Roger's perhaps, who had come to deliver bad news to me personally.

The man placed his stick in his right hand and limped up the rise. André stayed by the car. I could tell by the set of the airman's jaw that walking caused him pain. I should have moved forward to make it easier for him, but I was frozen to the spot. I feared I would not be able to bear the news he was bringing me.

The messenger looked up at me. 'Where are all the animals?' he asked. 'I was expecting you to have set up your own zoo by now.'

His face broke into a smile and then I saw beyond the ravages of war. The flickers of joy I had felt in my soul that morning burst into flame.

'Roger!'

I ran towards him, my feet barely touching the earth, and threw my arms around his waist. Roger pressed me to his chest and leaned down to kiss me. His lips were tender, warm, *alive*. I kissed him and kissed him as if he were the last breath of oxygen on earth. Tears ran down my cheeks and mingled with our kisses. The tears tasted of possibilities, and the return of love and laughter.

We parted for a moment, our gazes locking in an embrace of their own. I should have asked what had happened to him, how he had escaped from the camp, but I could not find the words. All I knew was that he had died, and that I had died, and now we were back among the living. We had been given another chance.

A motor started and I turned in time to see André wave at me through the window of the Citroën. His smile was gentle and his eyes bid me farewell. I thought my heart was going to burst. I watched him turn the car around and disappear down the road.

'André is the one who gave us this chance,' I said. 'He brought you back for me.'

'He's as tenacious as you,' Roger said. 'He searched every hospital until he found me.'

I closed my eyes, overcome by the sensation of flying. Green hills and forests loomed up ahead of me. Waves broke on the pristine white sands of wilderness beaches. I felt like an explorer coming upon a mystical land. It was beautiful, as if my soul had been set free from earthly restraints and I could see the past, present and future. There was pain and sadness and terror, but most of all there was goodness and love.

'I think I am hallucinating,' I said, opening my eyes. 'I am seeing Tasmania.'

Roger laughed and slipped his arm around my waist.

I gazed into his smiling face and found myself smiling too. We walked together towards the remains of the farmhouse. Whatever else I had to face, I would not face it alone. My Australian had returned. Just as he had promised.

ACKNOWLEDGMENTS

While Simone Fleurier was making her journey from Pays de Sault to become France's most famous music hall singer and a Resistant, I was making a journey of my own. Writing *Wild Lavender* has been a wonderful, enriching experience, due mainly to the people I met while researching and writing it.

Firstly, I would like to thank four men in France, without whose generous help and efforts this book would not have been possible: Xavier Jean-François, who generously gave of his time to translate research questions for me, contact organisations and academics in France on my behalf, and lend support to the project in any way he could; Michel Brès and José Campos who were wonderful researchers for me in Pays de Sault and Marseilles; and Graham Skinner, whose knowledge of French transportation systems and the railways at the time of the story was invaluable.

Also assisting me with my French research were: Nicolas Durr and his father, Gilbert Durr; Pascale Jones; Chris and Vanessa Mack; Antoine Carlier; Selena Hanet-Hutchins and her mother, Kari Hanet; and Robbi Zeck and Jim Llewellyn of Aroma Tours, who introduced me to the delights and history of lavender cultivation in Provence.

I am also grateful to the people who generously helped with research in the area of their expertise: Gary Skerritt and Adam Workman for information on vintage cars; Fiona Workman for medical questions;

Christine Denniston and Sophia and Pedro Alvarez for their information on tango dancing in Paris in the 1920s; Jeff Haddleton and Fiona Watson for information on ballroom dances; Barry Tate, aviation historian, whose excellent information on aircraft I didn't get to use in this novel but am saving for a future one; Steven Richards of Hewlett Packard for saving me from computer purgatory; Andrea Lammel for checking my German phrases; Dr Larissa Korolev for proofing my Russian phrases; Damian Seltzer for his irate Argentine tango dancer's curses, Alvaro Covarrubias for putting me in touch with Damian, and Rosalind Bassett for putting me in touch with Alvaro; and of course, thank you to my dashing dance partner, Mauro Crosilla, for taking up the challenge of learning the tango with me so I could experience the dance for myself.

Special thanks should also go to the staff at the State Library Information Service and Ku-ring-gai Library for always going the extra mile in finding information for me.

I would like to express my gratitude to my wonderful agent, Selwa Anthony, for all her enthusiastic support and for being a source of inspiration and balance for me during the writing and editing process. I am also grateful to her right-hand man, Brian Dennis, for giving wise advice on the practical matters of being a writer.

The journey of writing *Wild Lavender* was made all the more enjoyable by my 'pit crew' at HarperCollins*Publishers* who so skilfully changed my tyres, adjusted my suspension, checked my brakes and refuelled my engine before sending me off for another round of editing. In particular I would like to thank Linda Funnell, Shona Martyn, Catherine Day, Karen-Maree Griffiths and Kylie Mason. I would also like to say that getting to work again with my editors, Julia Stiles and Nicola O'Shea, on this book was one of the things that made it worthwhile writing a novel almost as big as *War and Peace* – the pleasure lasted longer that way! Their inspired insight was very much appreciated.

Finally, I would like to thank my family and my friends for being the constant support that they are during the writing process. Life would not be the same without them.

Thank you, all!

Author's Note

During World War II there was no unified organisation known as 'the Resistance' in France. In the post-war period the term is generally used to describe isolated groups such as communists, socialists, farmers, students and networks of everyday citizens who undertook a wide range of activities to 'resist' the Nazi occupation of their country. These individuals and groups did everything from producing underground newspapers, concealing Allied servicemen and forming escape lines for Jewish people, to performing acts of sabotage and taking part in combat. However, for the purposes of simplification, I have used the term 'the Resistance' to describe the cause with which Simone Fleurier aligns herself when she joins an escape network.

Part of the delight of writing *Wild Lavender* was to put my fictional characters in amongst the real characters of Paris and Berlin at the time such as Jean Renoir and Count Harry Kessler. I hope that readers familiar with the various artistic and social movements in Europe from the 1920s to World War II will take gratification in spotting the real personalities amongst the fictional. The Folies Bergère and the Casino de Paris were, of course, famous music halls of the day. The Adriana and its impresario, Regis Lebaron, and artistic director, Martin Meyer, are creations of my imagination.

As far as possible, I tried to be true to the timing of historical events but there is one place where I changed the year. The Folies Bergère production of '*La Folie Du Jour*', starring Joséphine Baker, and the lawsuit between Mistinguett and the Dolly Sisters, actually took place in 1926 but I brought these events a year forward to 1925 to fit the story.

It was certainly an eye-opening and pleasurable journey to write *Wild Lavender*, and I hope that reading it has brought you much enjoyment too.

Another Life

Sara MacDonald

A moving story of family history uncovered and present love realised.

Marine historian Mark Hannah finds a hauntingly beautiful figurehead in Newfoundland. He traces her ship, The Lady Isabella, back to a small port in Cornwall where he meets Gabrielle Ellis, the woman who is going to restore her to her former glory. Together they begin to trace jigsaw pieces of the lives of the carver, Tom Welland and the real Lady Isabella.

Gabrielle becomes increasingly haunted by Isabella's lost life. As Gabrielle's own life becomes inextricably involved with Mark's, her story runs parallel with the lives of Isabella, her husband Richard and Tom Welland, the carver.

Two women, living more than a hundreds years apart yet against the same wild backdrop of sea and landscape, make a rash bid for freedom to live another life. But for both of them, that choice means a loss which will greatly affect the next generation.

ISBN 0-00-717577-9

Always and Forever

Cathy Kelly

Fairy godmothers do exist, even in the
tranquil hills of Ireland

Once upon a time, in the beautiful town of Carrickwell,
lived three women whose lives were mapped out: ambitious Mel would have her career and her family; caring
Daisy a child with the boyfriend who is everything to her;
and hot-headed Cleo would finish her degree and step into
the family hotel business.

Until the landscape shifted and it all came tumbling down.

But Carrickwell, nestled in the shadows of Mount Carraig,
is an ancient, magical place. And when Leah, a woman
with her own secret turmoil, opens the Clouds Hill spa,
Mel, Daisy and Cleo are thrown together – and find the
courage to discover what really matters to them, always
and forever …

'Bursting with emotion, heartache and unreachable
dreams.'   *Ireland on Sunday*

'An upbeat and diverting tale skilfully told … Kelly knows
what her readers want and consistently delivers.'
                                          Sunday Independent

'A soap opera of tears and laughter.'   *Daily Mirror*

ISBN 0 00 715406 2

Unexpected Blessings

Barbara Taylor Bradford

A great dynasty began with one exceptional woman ...

A stranger just a year ago, Evan Hughes is now at the centre of the Harte family – in love with Gideon Harte and part of the powerful empire. But joining the dynasty that Emma Harte – the original Woman of Substance – created so many years ago re-opens old wounds. As determined as she is, can Evan make her mark on this extraordinary clan?

As Evan reads the letters Emma wrote to her grandmother in the 1950s, and Emma comes vividly back to life, she realizes that the Harte women have always had to match adversity with bravery and what she must do.

Emma's other great-granddaughters are strong, passionate women too. There's Tessa Longden, battling for her daughter's – and her own – future; Linnet O'Neill, a brilliant but envied businesswoman; and India Standish, who surprises everyone with a shock decision.

With a much anticipated family wedding approaching, it seems their collective strength will be needed more than ever. Because a deadly enemy has vowed to destroy everything that these remarkable women hold dear...

'A sweeping saga full of passion and intrigue...a gripping read' *Hello*

ISBN 0 00 651442 1